MORTHENSTAR

THE THIRD NOVEL IN
THE MORTHENSTAR TRILOGY

B. K. CAIN

To request permissions, please email the author at morthenstartrilogy@gmail.com

Library of Congress Control Number: 2025913403

Hardcover: 979-8-9993353-6-4
Paperback: 979-8-9993353-5-7
Ebook: 979-8-9993353-7-1

Second paperback edition September 2025

Portland, Oregon

Cover and book design by Rosie Struve and Bailey Cain
Illustrations by Katrina Zarate
Map created with Inkarnate

www.morthenstartrilogy.com

FOR SIENA AND THEO
AND ALL THE WORLDS YOU WILL IMAGINE

&

FOR MY SUDDEN DITCHES

TABLE OF CONTENTS

ASHAN FOREST

THE MEADOWS

TWO FALLS

ALBASTER

THE WEST COUNTRY

IN

THE NEW AGE OF THE STRIKERS

RIDDLETON

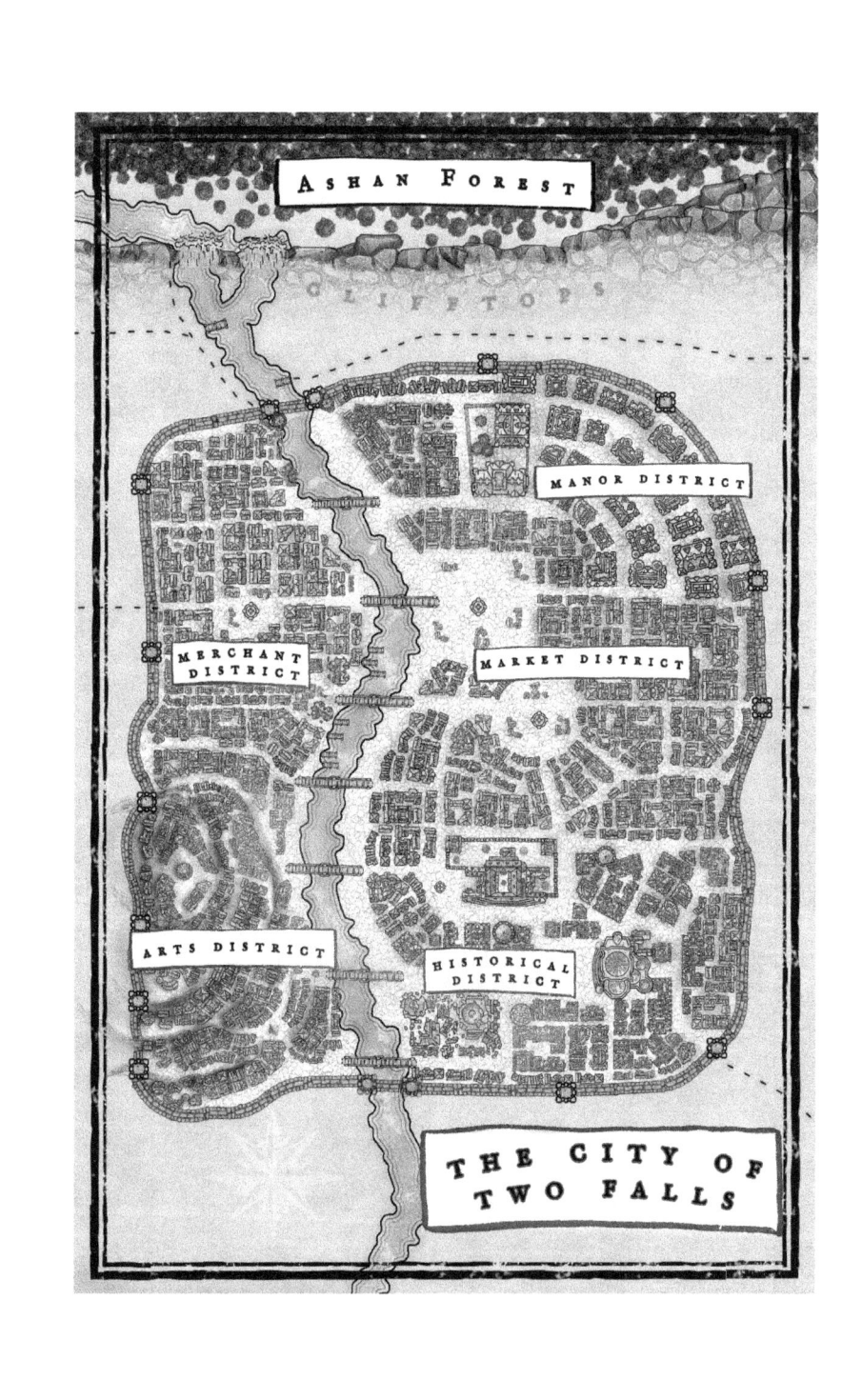

ASHAN FOREST

CLIFFTOPS

MANOR DISTRICT

MERCHANT
DISTRICT

MARKET DISTRICT

ARTS DISTRICT

HISTORICAL
DISTRICT

THE CITY OF
TWO FALLS

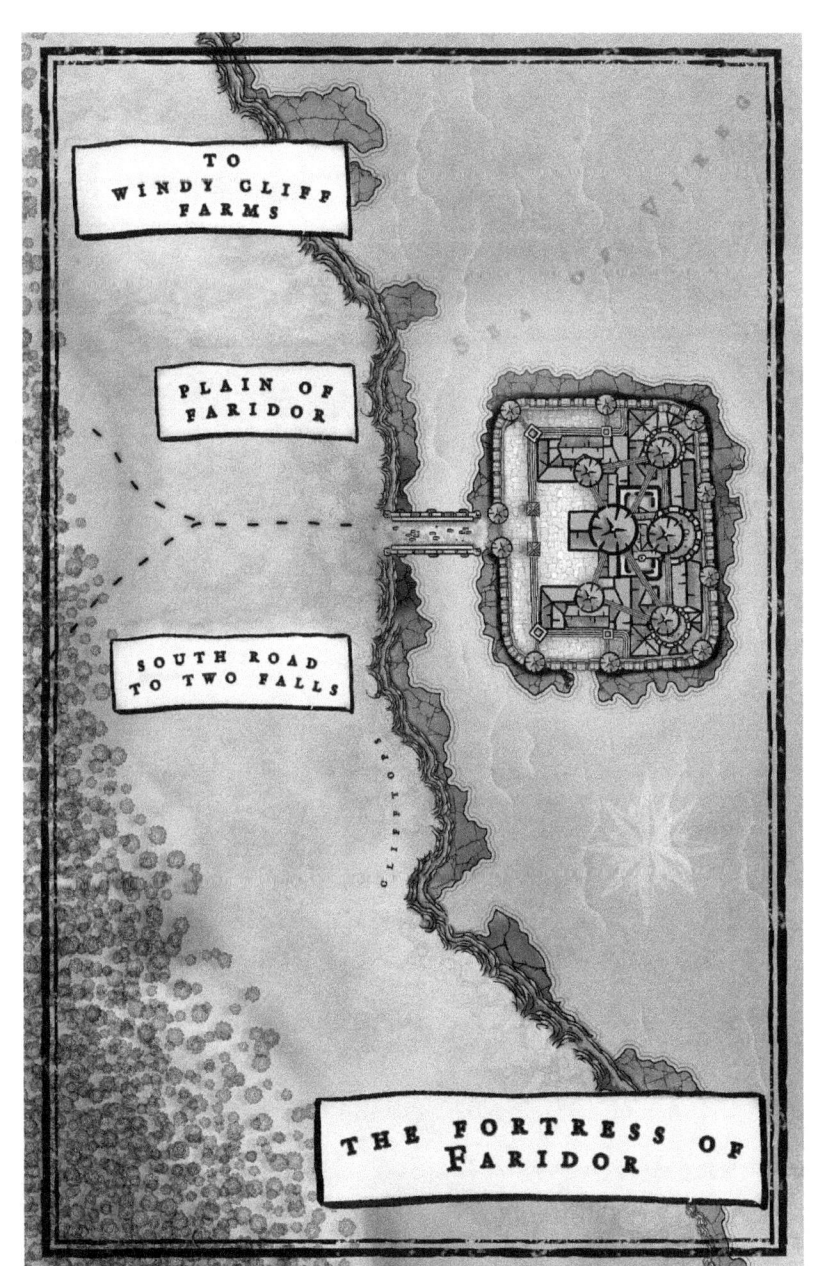

TO
WINDY CLIFF
FARMS

PLAIN OF
FARIDOR

SOUTH ROAD
TO TWO FALLS

THE FORTRESS OF
FARIDOR

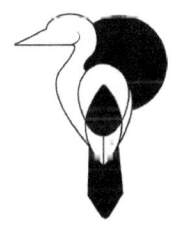

PROLOGUE

When she was a child of ten, a small political faction in the city of Joymaril hatched a conspiracy to assassinate Princess Cira.

"I tell you it's got to be done tomorrow night," hissed a woman, bending low over the table so that her voice would be lost in the chatter and clatter of the tavern around her. "*Tomorrow night.*"

"She's only a child," her companion muttered uncomfortably. He glanced surreptitiously over his shoulder to see if anyone was listening.

"Children grow up," the woman said flatly. "This may be our only chance. I've bribed one of the kitchen staff."

"But look," said her companion in what he hoped was a reasonable tone of voice. He was a nervous sort of man, and even when he wasn't plotting the assassination of one of the members of the royal family, his eyes had a habit of darting from side to side as though he were constantly looking for an exit. "There's no evidence that she *is* Kagai's heir; anyway, we can't be sure that any of it is true, it's all written in those old books..." He sounded as though he had an innate suspicion of old books in general.

"The others are with me," the woman said tersely, narrowing her eyes. Her blond hair was streaked in gray and was cut short in a severe line beside her sharp chin. "You can decide on which side of history you wish to stand."

The man clapped his clammy palms together under the tavern table and glanced around desperately for one of the bartenders, hoping that another flagon of ale would arrive and prolong his decision-making. He wasn't sure about this business, about the Hand, about any of it.

He'd been approached by the Hand only a few weeks before and, at first, had been interested in what they had to say. They were led by a self-proclaimed soothsayer who claimed to be a disciple of the ancient order of the Serpens (whatever that was) and was able to read the signs in the stars and the planets. The soothsayer insisted that these signs allowed her to predict the future. And all the signs, she claimed, pointed to one fact: that the heir of Kagai had been born and that she was poised to someday take the Jelani throne. Some had tried to argue with her. Princess Athela, who was the elder, was by law the first in line to rule, but the soothsayer had been proven right when, shortly before Cira's tenth birthday, the King and Queen had removed Athela from her place in line and deemed that Cira would be queen instead. This meant that when Cira came of age and took the throne, she would have access to nearly unlimited wealth and one of the best cavalries in known civilization. Not everyone believed such a wild prediction. But, the soothsayer argued, was it a risk worth taking? The life of one child versus potentially thousands of innocent others? They had not all agreed, but the plan was voted on, and it was decided. Cira must die.

"Fine," he said grudgingly. "I'm in."

Triumph flashed like a spark in the woman's eyes. She glanced around, but the tavern was dark and noisy and no one seemed to be paying them any heed. She reached into the leather bag at her leg and withdrew a small envelope.

"Here is your invitation to the coronation anniversary celebration," she whispered. "You'll get your instructions tomorrow morning. You must follow them to the letter."

With a scrape of her chair, she pushed back from the table and vanished into the night, leaving the man to stare morosely into his empty tankard.

The Jelani Queen's coronation anniversary celebration began at sundown the next day and was in full swing by the time the full moon had climbed into the sky. There was the usual pageantry: parades and singing, a round of sport dueling (the Queen's favorite had unsurprisingly won), dancing, and then the entire court had gone to the palace's great hall to be seated for dinner. Garlands of flowers hung in streamers from the vaulted ceiling, and long silk banners with the Jelani egret crest embroidered in gold and silver threads cascaded down to the floor.

The royal family was seated at the head table, elevated slightly above the rest of the attendees. The Queen herself was in a pale blue gown that set off her light hair, which had been swept dramatically over one shoulder. Her face was set in its usual expression of vague disapproval. To her right sat the King, who was staring vacantly off into the distance, humming tunelessly beneath his breath. And to her left sat her daughter Cira, almost an exact miniature copy of the Queen, with wide-set green eyes that gave her the look of a tiny, beautiful porcelain cat.

And at one of the far tables, far past those occupied by the King and Queen's favorite courtiers, was the group of conspirators who had met to plot Cira's death in a tavern the night before.

It was time for the coronation toast. Servants bearing large engraved silver pitchers came around to each of the tables, filling the crystal goblets with blood-red wine. It was customary for the underage princes and princesses to drink honey wine, and it was on this that the Hand hedged their bets. Prince Argolaith was still serving his ten years with the Army in the Meadows; his younger brother Cade, as usual, was ill and taken to his bed, and Cira's sister Athela, perennially out of favor with her parents—even more so since she'd been removed from the line of succession—was nowhere to be seen. Which left Cira.

The members of the Hand watched with bated breath as a different servant, bearing a small white porcelain pitcher, emerged from the door to the kitchens and strode up behind Princess Cira. The girl barely acknowledged the servant's presence as the golden liquid poured into her glass.

Seconds later, the entire room rose to its feet like a single wave, glasses held high and glinting in the light of the tapers on the wall; an eerie hush descended over the room. The members of the Hand studiously avoided meeting each others' eyes, but their leader could feel a lump tightening in her throat. It was traditionally the head of the Queen's council who gave the toast, and the council leader, a wizened old woman with waist-length white hair, intoned in a croaky voice:

"Long live her gracious Majesty, and long may she reign."

The words echoed around the room, and the glasses tipped back.

At that moment—unbeknownst to anyone in the palace of Joymaril or the surrounding city—across the lake, through the forests, and down an alley in the western corner of the city of Two Falls, a baby, newly emerged into the world, opened his eyes curiously to the room around him. A tuft of red hair swept over his forehead. He didn't cry. He didn't make a sound.

Back in the palace hall, the woman could hardly breathe as she stared across the room at the young princess at the head table. Cira sipped the honey wine, swallowed, and waited. *We've done it*, the woman thought grimly. *There's no going back.*

As one, the room took to their seats. The woman could barely breathe. She felt her eyes boring holes into Cira as she waited for a sign, any sign that something was happening. *Would it be quick?* She wondered. *Will it take a few minutes for the poison to take hold? Will they hold us here afterward?*

But the minutes ticked by, and nothing seemed to happen. The woman felt herself growing anxious. She glanced down the table at one of her confederates and furrowed her brow, but he shot back a shrug and a confused expression. They both looked over at Cira. She was sitting and behaving quite normally, picking at her food with her fork.

The woman glanced again at her confederate and jerked her head, indicating that he should come over. He smiled at the two people seated behind him, scooted back his seat, and came over to crouch by her table.

"What is going on?" the woman hissed, all of her built-up tension escaping through her clenched teeth.

"I put it in," he insisted under his breath. "I put it in!"

"Well, it isn't working," she snapped, then caught herself and forced a smile onto her face so that it would look as though they were speaking quite naturally about nothing in particular.

"Do you think the royal family has been inured to poisons?" he wondered. "As a safety precaution?"

It was possible, yet unlikely. No one in the ruling family had been assassinated in hundreds of years. The Queen was an effective and popular ruler, and protections against poisons were not high on the list of their priorities.

"There's nothing for it," the woman said grimly. "If we didn't get her this way, we've got to resort to other measures. We'll find a way to her bedchamber tonight and dispatch her there."

The man squirmed in discomfort. "That's a different matter, now, look, it's one thing to—"

"It's got to be done," the woman insisted, her mouth set in a determined line.

It was surprisingly easy, all things considered, to bribe one of the housemaids to let them up the back staircase. Three of them, trying not to look too conspicuous in dark traveling robes, stole up one of the marbled passageways in the dead of night.

Cira's chamber had been left unguarded (*unlikely that that would be the case after tonight*, thought the woman), and it was no great effort to slip in.

Once inside, they closed and latched the door, making as little sound as possible. The man lit a small match and held it up, casting just enough light around for them to see. The chamber was large and ornate, befitting the crown princess of a royal family. There was a small dressing table carved like a garland of flowers from a single piece of solid wood. Beside it, the gown that Cira had worn to the coronation celebration had been cast casually over a chair; clearly, she had sent her ladies-in-waiting to bed before she'd undressed. A large oval mirror rimmed in carved ivory leaned against a wall, and up a dais was the canopied bed. A small figure was barely visible beneath the blankets.

The woman felt beneath her cloak for the handle of the dagger she had in her belt. She tried to block the horror of what she was about to do from her mind. *It's for the good of us all,* she reminded herself. *If the soothsayer is right, think of the lives that will be saved, the destruction that will be prevented.*

They reached the side of the bed, and by this time, their eyes had adjusted enough to the dim light that they could make out the swath of Cira's distinctive pale hair on the pillow, her shoulder peeking out above the sheets, clad in a sleeping shift. The light of the full moon outside the window beside her bed spilled in a blue pool on the floor of her room, casting thick black shadows into all the corners of the furniture around them. Her back was to them. Now was their chance.

The woman slowly drew out the dagger with nothing more than a soft rustle from her cloak. She looked over at her two confederates, and one of the shadowy figures gave her a curt nod.

She raised the dagger over her head and stabbed downward.

The woman barely had time to register what happened, so confusing were the next few seconds. The dagger, razor-sharp, actually *bent* as it touched Cira's skin, as if it were made out of pliant wood. The woman felt the blade glance harmlessly off of Cira's shoulder.

The princess woke immediately and whirled around to face them, her green eyes wide with shock and fear. The three confederates were so stunned that they stood stock still for a full five seconds before galvanizing into action. The woman actually held the blade up to the moonlight to see what had happened: nothing. No blood, nothing strange about it. An instant later, Cira reached for a bell pull beside the bed and began tugging it with all her might, raising her voice in a loud, piercing scream that was filled with less fear than rage, the sound of which pursued her attackers from her room like an avenging fury. They had only gone about ten paces or so from her room before the night guards closed in on them, and there was no other way out.

They were held for a week in separate cells in the dungeons of Joymaril before the trial was scheduled to begin. Each cell measured only a few feet square, with a tiny rectangular shaft of light illuminating each room. The window, if one could call it that, was only big enough for them to slide their hands through; there would be no escaping that way. There was nothing to do but wait. So wait they did.

On the fourth day of her imprisonment, the member of the Hand was surprised to hear a creak at the heavy iron door, the turn of a key, and the lock slipping out of place. The door croaked open, and a moment later Princess Cira herself appeared. She wore a dress of dark purple velvet, with a black cloak pinned to each shoulder by a carved ivory egret brooch. Her white-blond hair fell loose down her back.

The leader of the Hand slowly drew to her feet and regarded the princess suspiciously. She could see the outline of two armed guards behind her. Was this it? Had the princess come to enact her revenge without even the due process of a trial? *Not that a trial will do much good, anyway*, she reminded herself wryly. *Having been caught red-handed fleeing the princess's chamber with a bare dagger the way I was.*

"Leave us," Cira said curtly to the guards behind her, and the men vanished. The door closed almost all the way shut, and the two of them were left alone. Cira regarded the woman coolly, with an expression that seemed far more mature than her ten years of age. Her wide-set eyes were off-putting; it made her face seem even more feline up close. The intensity of it forced the woman to drop her gaze down to her feet, and she felt embarrassed that she had to do so.

"Why did you try to kill me?" Cira asked in a low voice.

The woman looked up and stared at her, astonished. This wasn't what she expected. The girl sounded quite calm, as though she were inquiring after the weather.

"Tell me now," Cira pressed. "You'll be dead in a few days anyway. You have nothing to lose. Tell me."

The woman grappled inwardly but couldn't help feeling an inner compulsion to lash out, to taunt Cira with her knowledge. She felt her lips curl into a sneer. "Because of what you will become. Who you are destined to be."

"And who is that?" Cira asked.

"Kagai's heir," the woman snapped.

Cira's brow furrowed. She knew the name, but only as a character from legends and storybooks. "How do you know this?"

The woman found herself spilling out everything: the soothsayer, the signs they had read in the stars, the evil that Cira was destined to commit, why the Hand had felt compelled to take matters into their own hands. It was incredibly satisfying to tell her everything, to flaunt the knowledge that only she knew. But Cira listened impassively; the woman couldn't tell whether her words were making any impact on her whatsoever. Finally, the woman stopped speaking, feeling foolish.

"Your knife," Cira said after a short silence. "Why didn't it work?"

The woman glared at her. "I don't know. The blow glanced off." *But it shouldn't have, she thought to herself. My aim was straight. I could see her in the moonlight. It should have killed her, but it didn't.*

The girl regarded her thoughtfully, as if she could hear what the woman was thinking. "This soothsayer," Cira said in a quiet voice. "Where can I find her?"

This time, the woman bit her tongue and looked at the floor.

"You can tell me now, or I can have the guards torture the name out of you," Cira said in an almost bored-sounding voice. "It's your decision."

The woman didn't want to admit it, but for all her convictions and her willingness to assassinate Cira to prevent a full-scale war, she was a bit of a coward when it came to pain. And there wasn't any part of her that doubted Cira's willingness to torture her until she got the answers she wanted. Ashamed and refusing to meet the princess's steely gaze, she found herself mumbling the name. Guilt washed over her like a wave as soon as she had spoken the words.

She looked up, and this time there was definitely a look of triumph on Cira's face. The girl let the woman wriggle in her own discomfort, in the knowledge of her own cowardice, and without another word, turned and slipped out the door.

It was then and only then that the woman began to wonder whether she had made an enormous mistake.

A week later, a trial was held for the would-be assassins. It was of no surprise to anyone that they were immediately and perfunctorily found guilty of the attempted assassination of the crown princess Cira. The soothsayer and all the other members of the Hand were brought out together in an open plaza where the King and Queen typically held their public addresses.

The King and Queen and Princess Cira took their thrones and looked down on the ten hooded, cowering figures before them. And, to the shock of some of the onlookers, it was not the Queen who gave the order for their executions, but Cira. When the conspirators were beheaded, she didn't so much as bat an eye.

CHAPTER ONE

THREE MONTHS AFTER THE BATTLE OF TWO FALLS

Rane stood, her spine resting lightly on the corner of the wall. In her hand she held a large, smooth red apple, its ruby gleam burnished in the dim lamplight of the hallway. She glanced once again over her shoulder and, at the sight of a long stretch of emptiness that lasted almost all the way back to the dining hall, she folded her arms tighter over her chest and took a crisp, noisy bite of the fruit. Its tang burst in her mouth like an autumn-scented firework. She afforded herself a happy sigh, and her shoulders relaxed almost imperceptibly.

She remembered suddenly that an apple tree had grown outside her window when she was a young girl, and that for years she had marked the changing of the seasons by its blossoming, its green, heavily laden arms stretching out to her with offerings of fruit in late summer and autumn, and its cold, dark silhouette at the coming of winter. She thought she remembered being lifted up into its branches by a pair of strong hands. Whether those hands belonged to her parents or perhaps to a teacher at the Academy, she couldn't really be sure. It hardly mattered now.

"What're you doing in here?" a voice hissed, forcibly shaking her from her reverie. It was one of the senior kitchen staff, a woman whose voice, whether it was ordering cream puffs for Queen Cira's dessert or asking the weather, held the same urgently scolding tone.

"This is no time to be dilly-dallying!" she chided her, bustling forward towards Rane as if scolding a naughty child. She was tall and slender, her hair pulled back in a disapproving knot at the base of her neck, and wore a set of elegantly modest green robes that fastened tightly up her neck, befitting her position as a senior member of Cira's staff. "Shoo! Get to your station!"

Rane gave a roll of her eyes and pushed herself off the wall as if it were the hardest thing she had ever been asked to do. She had long ago realized that the best way to blend in with the rest of the house staff was to act as bored and supercilious as possible.

She slipped like a specter past the towering pillars lining the great hall at Faridor, where countless guests in rich, embroidered fabrics whirled and twirled like flowers spinning open and closed, colors sliding smoothly across the polished black obsidian floor, music from the small chamber orchestra on the dais soaring up into the curving dome of the ceiling.

Whether through fear or in the hopes of gaining influence with Queen Cira, it seemed that visitors from near and far had come to celebrate the Queen's birthday. Languages that Rane had never heard before, and at whose origins she could only guess, wafted through the air around her head like clouds. She glanced casually through the sea of whirling greens, reds, and purples. Far to the head of the room, on a slightly raised platform, was Cira's empty throne. Without really intending to do so, Rane found herself ducking her head down and out of sight.

Rane had been curious to see whether or not Cira would actually show up; the rumor was that no one in the fortress had actually seen her face-to-face in months. As the hours ticked by and the party continued on without her, the throne conspicuously empty at the head of the room, the more it looked as though she was going to be a no-show. Here and there, consternated looks were exchanged, and glances were cast at the empty throne. It was almost like attending a party for a ghost.

Rane stopped by one of the long tables set up around the room, this one piled high with food: breads and cheeses, a roast bird with its magnificent tail feathers set in a splendid array, exotic fruits piled high on a plate (here, Rane had swiped the apple—she assumed that one of the local visitors must have brought them as a gift, for it was too hot for them in the desert countries across the sea.)

She tugged her green sleeves down a little farther over her wrists and unconsciously raised a hand to her throat, where the high neck of her gown covered the nasty scar that had been left during her fight with Lord Seth in Two Falls; a grim echo of the wound he'd given Marc years before. She had altered all of her uniforms to have high necks, and she was sure to wear the traditional servant's hood and circlet that covered her distinctive auburn hair. In a flash, her mind flew to Lord Seth, to those cold, blank eyes, and her stomach twisted into a knot. She forced him from her mind as she had done countless times before, hating herself for the fear that crashed over her like a wave anytime she thought of him. She had work to do.

One of the guests came forward and stared down his nose at her while he loaded a plate with a slice of meat from the bird and some of the bread and cheese. Rane kept her eyes modestly lowered and bobbed a meek curtsy; once she could tell he was gone, she raised her eyes and continued scanning the swirling, teeming colors of the room. Finally— there. Cicada, dressed up in her official servant's uniform, standing on alert just across the room.

She met Cicada's eyes and gave the slightest of nods, which her friend knew better than to return. Cicada was tall and very thin, with the look of someone who had grown up without access to very much food. She had sharp features that gave her a rather vulpine face and dark brown hair gathered into a twisted plait at the back of her head. Only her eyes betrayed the fact that Cicada was not like many other young women. One immediately got the sense from her intense, watchful gaze that not a single insignificant detail could pass by her unnoticed.

Rane automatically ducked another curtsy as one of the party's guests brushed roughly and heedlessly past her. And then, as if the entire room had collectively exhaled, the music drew to a crescendo and stopped, and the pivoting figures on the dance floor drew to a halt. Rane straightened up slightly taller and glanced over at Cicada. She wanted to be sure that her friend was on the alert, which, of course, she already was. Cicada took a few steps, edging closer to Rane.

The sylphlike figure of a woman dressed all in white drew up from the crowd and cautiously picked her way up the steps of the orchestra's dais to stand in front of the musicians. Her reflection glowed back at her from the polished black floor of the hall. All the buzz from the crowd died down, and countless pairs of eyes turned to look at the woman. Even from across the Great Hall, Rane could tell how nervous she was. The woman in white glanced sidelong at the empty throne as if expecting Cira to materialize out of thin air.

"May it please Her Majesty," the woman stammered. "I've come here tonight to perform a song in honor of Her Majesty's feast day. Long live the Queen."

"Long live the Queen," the room echoed, and again the hall fell into silence. The air around the throne seemed to reverberate at the words.

The woman took a deep breath, opened her mouth, and began to sing. It was a high voice, clear and pure as a cold stream in autumn, achingly sweet to hear. Rane was so overcome that for a moment or two, she forgot that she was supposed to be paying close attention.

The woman sang:

Long is the road that my love and I walked
When my love and I walked alone
Deep was the night that my love and I shared
When my love he was all my own
Now that my love he has gone away
The summer sun has grown dim
For the road that I walked and the night that I knew
My love he has taken with him

A prickle of excitement thrilled up Rane's spine and neck. She straightened and glanced over to Cicada, who was watching her closely. Rane gave an infinitesimal nod, and Cicada turned and vanished into the sea of partygoers. Rane inclined her head to the left and, from beneath the nearby table, silently pulled out an empty silver platter. Holding the platter flat across her hands, she stole around the back of the room, back out past the pillars, and towards one of the guards at the door. The guard held up a hand as she approached, and Rane raised the platter by way of explanation. The silvery song of the woman in white echoed through the hallway behind her.

"I've orders to fetch more bread from the kitchens," she explained.

The guard grunted and stood aside for Rane to be allowed through. *Charming idea for a party*, she thought sarcastically. *Lock all the guests inside with no way to escape.*

Round one corner she went, then another, then, glancing quickly to either side, she ducked through a door and down a twisted flight of steps until she was in the maids' quarters. It was a long row of small rooms all sharing the same narrow corridor. It was deserted, as she knew it would be; all of the kitchen staff were at their posts, and all of the house staff had been ordered to stay in the Great Hall to tend to the guests' needs. Rane ducked into the twelfth room on the right, which was the small sleeping space she shared with Cicada.

She was rustling around her small trunk for paper and ink when there was the slightest footstep behind her, and Cicada swept into the room, barely closing the door before she began to sign.

"What song was it?" she asked eagerly.

"'Long is the Road,'" Rane replied. "Do you have the book?"

Before Rane even finished the latter half of her question, Cicada was already off and rummaging through the small trunk of belongings stashed beneath her bed. A moment later, she stood back up, a slender leather-bound volume clutched in her thin hands. She strode around the bed and up to Rane, furiously flipping through the pages, sharp eyes scanning to and fro. "Here," she signed finally, turning the book around and placing it before Rane.

The book was entitled *Folk Songs of the West Country*, a popular collection of lyrics and music from Two Falls and the surrounding areas. It was a commonplace book; Rane had even remembered seeing it on the shelves at Pieter's nephew's house years ago. It was the kind of book that would raise no suspicions if the Kagaian guards were to search through Rane and Cicada's belongings (which they had multiple times; such inspections were a routine occurrence.) Unbeknownst to the Kagaians and with the help of the ordinary little book, Rane and

Cicada had been effectively sending coded messages back and forth with Tarr for months.

"Hurry up!" Cicada chided her.

Rane hid a grin. It was a defining factor of their relationship that whatever Rane was doing, it wasn't fast enough for Cicada. When Cicada was "on the hunt," as Rane liked to think of it—working undercover out in the fortress—she was all calm, quiet, focused intensity, and alert watchfulness. But behind the scenes, without an immediate quarry to pursue, she was nervous energy and fast talking, her agile brain leaping forward in bounds rather than steps. Cicada's equilibrium seemed to settle only in situations where success and failure hung upon a razor's edge.

Rane reached into her trunk and withdrew a long, very thin knife, almost like a needle. She took the right sleeve of her garment and, with the needle, made a very small incision in the cuff and began to roll the fabric back to reveal a small hidden space in the seam. Carefully from the hidden compartment, she withdrew a piece of fabric only two or three inches in length, folded softly into a square. She laid it out on the bed beside the book, and Cicada peered over her shoulder, her agile fingers flipping up her pen. The message on the piece of fabric looked like a series of gibberish letters, with a series of five letters at the very top. A moment later, Cicada knelt down and began to decode the message onto a piece of parchment. Rane followed suit, but didn't bother trying to outpace Cicada. There was no one faster.

The system was both simple and brilliant. Using a copy of the same songbook, Tarr had pre-selected and numbered a series of words from the lyrics, which were then transposed and coded into letters of a message to Rane and Cicada. The two spies had only to identify the correct song for their cipher.

Cicada threw down her pen a full thirty seconds before Rane, who silently and good-naturedly swore under her breath. The two held up their papers to compare, and they were pleased to see that the transposition was exactly the same:

WEAPO NPLAN SAREB EINGH ELDIN NORTH
TOWER THIRD FLOOR SAFEU NDERG UARDP
ASSCO DEISNIN ENI NEEIG HTTHR EEXXX

"Weapon plans are being held in the North Tower, third floor, safe under guard. Passcode is nine nine eight three," Rane signed thoughtfully, a wave of excitement building in her chest. Cicada was already reaching for flint and tinder, setting fire to the message to eliminate any evidence that it had ever existed.

"Give me the platter," Cicada extended her hand. "I'll go down to the kitchens before we're missed."

"I told the guards we needed to fetch bread," Rane informed her, handing over the empty tray.

Cicada nodded curtly, her dark eyes flashing. "Be careful," she warned.

"I will."

The hunt was on; the trail was scented. Rane felt a thrill deep within her chest. *Perhaps tonight we find the plans,* she thought, trying not to be overeager. They'd searched so long for the plans, plans for some sort of weapon Cira was going to use against the Strikers, something deadly, something unusual. They'd first gotten wind of the weapon late the year before when Cicada had managed to intercept a missive from Vireg on its way to Cira's private desk. The actual plans for the weapon, whatever it was, had evaded their grasp so far, but tonight would be different. Rane tried to temper her excitement. Tonight, the plans would be theirs.

Minutes later, the two women went their separate ways. Cicada vanished with a gleam of green fabric into the crowd of the party, which was once again in full swing. Rane walked with a quick, light step to the other end of the room, ducking past the swinging arms of a dancing couple.

Four more footfalls, and she was up and spinning around one of the fortress's many twisting stairwells like a light shadow. She paused at the next landing above, listening for the breath of a guard or a passing handmaiden, but the household's focus was almost uniformly directed toward the party.

Once she was certain that the way was clear, she stepped out and did a quick lap around the entirety of the circular floor. The enclosed stairwell thrust through the center of the floor like a thick tree trunk. As she had suspected, the area was completely deserted except for a single guard standing conspicuously in front of a door. He gave her a bored glance as she passed by.

Once she had traveled halfway around the circular floor again, Rane paused and assessed her options. A distraction would clearly be best. She glanced around and noted the locations of a window, a dusty bust of a crotchety-looking old man sitting on a wooden pedestal nearby, and a decorative spear displayed further down the hallway. A split second later, Rane strode to the spear, took it, and thrust it forcefully into the statue's pedestal so that it stuck fast, then turned and went quickly up to the window and threw it open to the cold night air. She took a step back, took a short inhale of breath, and toppled over the bust so that the statue and its wooden pedestal went to the floor in a splintering, satisfying crash, the spear jutting threateningly aloft as if someone had thrown it through the open window.

She'd calculated which direction the guard was likely to go, and just like a squirrel playing hide-and-seek around a tree, she went the other way from him. When she reached the formerly guarded door, it was now refreshingly unprotected, but she only had a matter of seconds before the guard came back around.

Above the handle of the door was what looked like a small lock with numbers engraved around the round edges. With her thumbs, she deftly spun the numbers *nine nine eight three* into place, and the door opened with a satisfying little *click*.

She pulled open the door. Inside, it wasn't much more than a closet, with shelves at intervals from top to bottom. It was empty except for a small sheaf of papers bound in a leather folder resting on the center shelf. This went swiftly into her hand, and the door was shut and bolted an instant later—not a moment too soon, as the guard's heavy footsteps were clomping into earshot around the curve of the hallway. Rane darted in the opposite direction back around the bend, coming to a halt just out of sight of the guard's post. The guard came back around and, seeing that nothing was out of place, went tromping down the stairs, presumably to notify someone about the window.

No one noticed the maid coming down the stairwell, brushing by a group of five guards as they went rushing back up the stairs past her to investigate the disturbance on the third floor. No one noticed the leather-bound sheaf of papers in her hand as she threaded her way through the party, or saw her stow it under a tray full of food as she went around to serve the party's guests so that the papers were never out of her hand. And no one noticed her when, in the wee hours of the morning, she made her way back down to the room she shared in the maids' quarters with Cicada to finally have a look at what they'd discovered.

Poring over the papers, Cicada and Rane soon ascertained that the plans for the weapon were not in the packet they had stolen, and with that realization, Rane nearly had to stifle a loud shriek of frustration. There were other things that could potentially be of use, but they were written in a code Rane had never seen before and whose cipher they didn't have. Though she'd been up all night tending to the party, Rane lay awake in bed well after daybreak, silently fuming until it was time to get back up and begin her daily chores.

She knew, too, that the instant she slept, she would be gripped by the same nightmare: Lord Seth's black eyes burning into her until she felt herself being swallowed up by them.

Cira had never shown up for her own party. As the carriages of the party's guests gathered and slowly rolled back out over the bridge, rumors began to circulate that she had, in fact, gone completely mad.

Others began to whisper that she was dead.

CHAPTER TWO

"I tell you he ought to be hanged!" Minister Burlage insisted, scarlet rising in his pudding-like cheeks.

Tarr took a deep breath and exhaled slowly through his nose, clenching and unclenching his hands beneath the table. He felt Laith stir ever so slightly in the high-backed chair beside him, and he tempered his voice before replying.

"As I have told you before," he said slowly, trying to sound diplomatic, "Archer has fought alongside us since the beginning of this war. He has fought, and he has suffered, and he has saved countless lives by doing so. He was responsible for smuggling out over two dozen Ashan families during the occupation of Two Falls. I should think that that would be enough for clemency."

"It's too little, too late. The new government has no room for scoundrels and murderers," Burlage shouted. Tarr stared back, unflinching, keeping his exterior unflappable while his insides seethed and roiled with anger.

Tarr looked entreatingly to his right, where Pieter sat. Tarr could see that the old man was greatly perturbed, as well he might be in such a situation. His hands were steepled at the fingers, resting atop the dully gleaming council table. It was late afternoon, and Tarr felt as though they had been in the meeting for years.

Pieter shook his head. "The council is, of course, grateful for every-thing that the Strikers have done during the occupation of this city and the efforts you made in freeing it. That goes for Archer as well. But before this war began, he was one of the most highly sought-after criminals in this country. He was chased out of Two Falls for a reason. I believe that it would send the wrong message if he were completely pardoned after the war was over."

"So let me understand you," Tarr said, the heat building beneath his voice, "You'll let Archer go on risking his life night after night to protect this city, and then when or if Cira falls, you'll arrest him on the spot?"

Pieter looked uncomfortable and went back to staring at his finger-tips. Tarr glanced around at the eight other council members. All of them were older, and all of them were frowning at him with discon-certed expressions. Tarr felt as if he were shouting at the top of his voice into a blank void.

"What you're saying," Laith spoke quietly, his deep voice falling like music on the stale air, "is that our friend, who has saved all of our lives more than once, is better off with Cira in power than with you."

"That is treason!" exclaimed a councilwoman from across the table, her dark eyebrows knitting together in horror.

"It's the truth," Tarr cut in. He looked once again to Pieter, the man they had helped escape Cira's clutches, whom they had kept safe during the occupation of the city. But Pieter avoided his eyes.

Buoyed by the seeming support of the other council members, Minister Burlage once again leaped into full cry. "And for that matter, while we're talking about cleaning house, it is your duty to this council to turn over the full list of all of your spies, aliases, present locations, and operating codes. It is absolutely *intolerable* that this council not be made aware of every facet of the intelligence operation in Faridor and in this city. We must be able to advise your course of action."

Tarr's brown and green eyes narrowed, and he rose slowly to his feet, his eleven long fingers splayed out atop the table, the missing finger on his left hand just a nub hovering over the tabletop. His stare pierced straight through Minister Burlage's portly countenance, and when he spoke, his own voice sounded almost unfamiliar to him, filled with sarcasm and loathing as it was. "I have, at the request of this council, made weekly reports to keep everyone apprised of the initiatives we have going on at the moment."

Minister Burlage was apparently not placated by this answer. His lower lip jutted out, and for a moment, he reminded Tarr of an overgrown toddler. "You assumed sole control over a multifaceted spy ring with absolutely no experience whatsoever."

"I *created* a multifaceted spy ring out of sheer necessity," Tarr retorted. "We needed it in order to survive. We needed it in order to keep our citizens," here he paused and glanced pointedly at Pieter, who still avoided his gaze, "safe. By now, I have years of experience."

"Two, perhaps? Three? Need I remind you that it is this council, *not* the Strikers, who are now in control of this city. You serve this council, and you have been given direct orders to turn over the information requested of you."

"You hid," Tarr said through gritted teeth. "You *hid* the past three and a half years while we fought and bled and watched our friends die in the hopes of saving this city and the people in it."

"*You* never fought," Burlage sneered. "Never even lifted a sword."

Tarr felt as if he'd been stung. The words had found their mark. "I have fought the only way I know how," he replied, trying to keep his voice as measured as possible, the pressure in his chest almost unbearable. "I have saved lives."

"And cost them too."

"This city," Tarr growled, "is free because of our actions. Because of the decisions *we* made."

"And we're grateful. But you are children. Children who have been playing at war. That time is over, and *we* are now in charge." The minister swept his hand the length of the long gleaming table, then turned to face Tarr with a renewed vigor and antagonism. "*Turn over your agents,*" Burlage snarled. "Or we'll have you arrested alongside Archer."

The last vestige of Tarr's diplomacy sailed out into the afternoon sun. He pushed himself back from the table and felt Laith softly stand up beside him. "Fine," Tarr snapped. "Arrest me. Only you will find no written evidence of any of the information you so desperately want. It is here," he pointed to his temple. "Nowhere else. So go ahead, arrest me, try to torture it out of me. Hang Archer in the town square. Then try to explain to the people of this city your reasoning for doing so and why they shouldn't just march east to seek shelter behind the walls of Faridor."

Tarr stormed to the door of the council chamber, adrenaline prickling along his fingers and arms, Laith close on his heels.

"The council meeting is not adjourned!" one of the other ministers barked. Tarr and Laith paused and faced the room.

"With the gracious permission of the council, we would like to excuse ourselves from the proceedings," Laith said quietly, in such a neutral tone that the council couldn't tell whether or not he was mocking them.

"Do not tempt the anger of this council!" Burlage shouted biliously, incensed that Tarr had had the last word.

Tarr studied him silently for a moment, contempt in every fiber of his being. "The war isn't over yet," he said, and wasn't sure whether it was a warning or a promise. The two Strikers left the room without another word.

Tarr marched furiously down the hallway towards the Strikers' private chambers, swinging by the guard on duty without his usual polite hello. Laith strode in behind him, catching the door in one hand as Tarr attempted to dramatically fling it shut. The prince quietly stepped inside and held the door open for his dog, Breaker, then softly closed it. Tarr stood against the window with his back to his friend, leaning his head against the cool glass. He heard Laith draw back a chair behind him and seat himself, Breaker settling at his feet like a shadow. They lingered together in a gradually de-escalating silence. Tarr felt the rage and the anger draining out of him like water. His friend's presence was soothing; it was a comfort to know that Laith would remain there until Tarr was able to speak coherently once again.

Laith, for his part, rarely spoke anymore. In the few months since the Battle of Two Falls, silence had drifted over him like mist over the hills, so gradually that his friends had barely noticed it seeping in and taking hold. Occasionally, Tarr would look at him and remember in a flash the young golden prince he had first met, possessed of a brightness, an optimism, an unstoppable life force that seemed to emanate from every movement of his body. Laith had settled like a fallen leaf on winter earth. He existed in such stillness that sometimes it seemed perfectly reasonable to believe that when he sat or stood in a doorway, he would gradually freeze in place and remain so forever, like a living statue. All of the youthful flesh had vanished from his face, casting the planes of his bones—his sloping forehead, his cheekbones, his jaw—into startling relief. His face, though still unequivocally handsome, was now striking mostly for its haunting beauty. His chestnut eyes were hooded, cast under the shadows of his brow, and his motionless stare went as deep as the soul. Tarr had noticed that in conversation, many individuals studiously avoided meeting Laith's eyes. When the other Strikers— Marc or Athela or those who had known him long ago—spoke with him, Tarr could almost see them searching for some flicker, some sign of recognition that they could grab hold of, a branch in the midst of a rushing river.

"Sometimes I wish," Tarr said through gritted teeth, "that somehow Archer would have managed to not be *quite* so effective a criminal back in his heyday."

Laith shrugged a shoulder, then gazed out of the window, one of his hands absently scratching Breaker between his pointed black ears. "I can see their point. Archer committed many crimes, yes, but he has, in my estimation, atoned for them many times over by now. But atonement is reckoned differently by different people. It's different for us, being his friends, than for those who lived here before the war. I know Ari feels the same as many of the councilors." He paused and looked back over to Tarr. "I doubt you'll be invited back to the council meetings again."

"If they do, it'll just be for another dressing-down," Tarr ran his fingers distractedly through his short bark-colored hair. "I don't think I can stand to see Minister Burlage's face again without vomiting all over the table." He stopped and considered. The more he thought about it, the more that seemed like a preferable alternative to the usual agendas of the council meetings.

"I'll continue to go," Laith offered. "We need to have someone's eyes and ears in there."

"Thanks," Tarr said gratefully, and meant it.

Laith was silent for a few moments. "You know, he did have one point. Or rather, you did. About all of the network's information being only in your head."

Tarr stared at him, genuinely astonished. "You think I should turn over that information to them? For all we know, Cira's bought half of them already."

Laith smiled gently. "That may be listing slightly towards the realm of paranoia, Tarr."

"I'm a spymaster," Tarr grinned sardonically. "It's sort of my job."

"Fair enough," Laith agreed. "But what if something happens to you?"

"What do you mean?" Tarr asked evasively, picking at a spot on the corner of the table with his fingernail. He was fairly certain he knew exactly what Laith meant.

"If you're killed," Laith said bluntly, "all the information—the identities and code names of our spies, the codes themselves, the ciphers, all of that...we've lost."

"Well," said Tarr, trying to keep his tone light, "who on earth would want to kill me when there are lots more interesting targets running around?"

"Cira's no fool," Laith cautioned him. "She knows you're out there. And she knows she lost Two Falls in large part because of you."

"I didn't fight the battle," Tarr pointed out moodily, feeling the same raw twinge as when Minister Burlage had pointed the fact out earlier at the council meeting.

Laith fixed him with a level stare that clearly indicated that he didn't buy into any sort of false modesty on Tarr's part.

Tarr leaned forward, suddenly intent. "Laith, you know as well as I that pieces of paper—any piece of paper, regardless of the lock and key that guards it, can be stolen. Cipher keys can be broken. Identities can be discovered. Do you have any idea..." he swallowed, his throat suddenly feeling uncomfortably dry, "what would happen if Cira realized that Rane was in Faridor? That one of the Strikers was pouring her morning tea?"

"Rane can take care of herself," Laith replied calmly, and although Tarr knew he was right, he still couldn't quiet the frantic thud of his heartbeat as he thought of her walking through the fortress, one lost slip of code away from being discovered.

"Anyway, if they do catch me, I doubt they'd kill me right off," Tarr said, adopting the same mock-jovial air of bravado as before. He had discovered long ago that when talking about one's demise, it was best to keep the tone as light as possible. "They'd try to get something out of me first, and you'd have enough time to organize some sort of impressive rescue."

"We've never got anyone out of Faridor's dungeons, Tarr," Laith reminded him. "Are you sure," he paused and chose his next words delicately, "if they tried to...get something out of you...that you wouldn't give it up?"

Tarr stared at his hands, opening and closing them in his lap. It was the question that dogged his every thought, every time he sent a scrap of code or sent an order. "I don't know," he said honestly. He looked up and met Laith's calm, dark eyes. "I don't know. I'd like to think I wouldn't. But I've made...provisions." His mind went immediately to the small packet he kept with him at all times in his pocket, and the two small poison capsules contained within. He didn't know whether he'd be able to withstand Cira's tortures and didn't want to take the chance.

Laith gave a thoughtful, silent nod and patted Breaker's shoulder. Neither of them liked the thought of Tarr's "insurance policy." The dog laid his head down on the floor and gave a jerky wag of his tail. "How's the weapon tracking coming?" Laith asked.

Tarr shook his head. Cira's weapon, whatever it was, was the single biggest source of frustration for him. "I've had Rane on it since we found out that Cira was developing it last year. No luck yet. What's more, they've developed a new code we haven't yet been able to crack, and we think they've been passing information about the weapon with that code." He rubbed his eyes tiredly. "I really thought we had it with that safe box at Faridor, but I've just heard from Rane that it's a dead end unless we get the newest cipher."

Laith nodded and stood silently from his seat, Breaker instantly rising to sit at his heel. Inwardly, Tarr shook his head. He couldn't understand how Laith had managed to train Breaker so well; he'd never had the same luck trying to get Wolver to obey commands. Tarr had once suggested that Breaker "sit," and he could have sworn that the dog had slowly turned and fixed him with a baleful stare clearly intended to indicate that Tarr was unqualified to give him orders. Tarr hadn't tried a second time.

"I'm on duty soon, early shift," Laith informed Tarr. "We're still having issues with Kagaian loyalists in some of the Western districts of town."

There was a beat between them. Tarr had opposed the release of Kagaian fighters back into the city after Two Falls was retaken, and though at the time he'd been overruled by others who believed that clemency and mercy were the best avenues to take, over time he'd been proven right. Many of the fighters they'd released had since banded together to create their own underground resistance against the Strikers, an ironic reversal of the situation they'd found themselves in only months before. There were many occasions in which Tarr could have gloated or said, "I told you so," but such things seemed pointless and petty, especially when the Kagaian resistance was a very real threat.

Laith shook his head. "I'm going to try to get some sleep before I go."

Both of them knew that Laith barely slept anymore; when it was time to rest, Laith would sit quietly, motionless, in the chair in his small room. But Tarr said nothing.

"Do that," Tarr murmured, smiling at his friend as the prince moved to leave. When Laith closed the door behind him, Tarr didn't even hear it. Already, his brain had focused back on the new code, the few snippets of communication that Rane had managed to steal for him. It wasn't a basic substitution...they had given that nonsense up long ago. It wasn't even a poem code—like the one he'd given Rane at Cira's birthday. He'd had a few hours of rest. Perhaps if he went back to look at the codes with fresh eyes...

It was going to be another sleepless night.

The sun set, and the lights were lit in gentle whispering lines up one hall and down another over every floor of their Two Falls headquarters. A gentle knock sounded at the door, and Athela's eyes snapped open. She had been on night patrol steadily for the past two weeks.

"It's Kali, m'lady," came the quiet voice from outside.

"Yes," Athela replied, resting her forearm briefly over her closed eyes before pushing herself up to sit at the edge of the bed and gathering her thick, dark waves of hair into a messy knot piled on top of her head.

"Can I get you anything?" Kali enquired.

"No, thank you," Athela replied. "Who's with me on patrol tonight?"

There was a brief pause. "I believe it's Archer," came the soft reply.

Athela's eyes narrowed suspiciously, and her stomach gave a thrilling little lurch. *This has one of Tarr's character-building exercises all over it*, she thought grimly to herself. *Well, I simply won't cooperate.*

"Should I go wake him, too, m'lady?" Kali asked.

"No," Athela answered gruffly. "I'll do it. He's probably not wearing pants." *Exhibitionist that he is.* Kali was on the younger side and had stayed with them for much of the war. And, like most of the girls her age, she had a hopelessly big crush on Archer. Athela, of course, couldn't understand what all the fuss was about.

She lit the lamp beside her bed, casting dim shadows around her small, closet-like sleeping quarters. All of the Strikers slept in rooms on the same floor of the newly converted Striker headquarters (which had, until a few months before, been *Kagai's* headquarters.) All the Strikers' rooms were modest in size and heavily guarded. The turquoise light of dusk filtered in through a slit in her curtains, comingling with the golden light of the candle. An overturned saddle lay in one corner of the room with a rag and an open jar of leather soap beside it. Cleaning her tack had always been Athela's preferred form of relaxation, and over the course of the past month or two, her saddle had been gleaming as it never had before. She stared longingly at it for a moment, then screwed the top of the soap closed, pulled on her worn boots, and gave a cursory glance in the mirror. The same face: thick, dark brows, strong features, square lips, tendrils of hair falling loose around her shoulders. She grimaced, baring her teeth to make sure nothing was stuck to them, gave a shrug, and headed out the door.

Kali was already gone when she entered the hallway. Archer's room was four doors down from hers, and she found herself tiptoeing up. She knocked softly just above the doorknob, wondering why on earth her heart was thudding so heavily in her chest. She thought she heard a rustling sound from inside the room and pushed open the door just a bit to peek inside.

Archer was sound asleep; his face turned away from her towards the opposite side of the room. Enough light fell through the partially open curtains to cast a soft blue haze over him. He slept on his back with one pale arm trailing off the side of the bed, his white body curving away from her like a crescent moon. A haphazard curl of bedsheet barely covered his hips and twisted around his legs; her eyes followed the peaceful rise and fall of his chest, sloping down gently beneath the sheet. Even in the dim light, she could make out the delicate lines of the new tattoo on his left ribcage: beautiful scrollwork of thin loops and whorls that intertwined their way down his side, diving beneath the line of the sheet covering his hips and twisting to a stop just visible at the top of his left thigh. She knew that if she went to him and placed her hand on his chest, it would be as smooth, hard, and cool as polished stone.

Damn and blast it all, Athela thought fiercely.

She realized she'd been holding her breath. She backed out, not bothering to gently or quietly shut the door behind her, and strode down the hallway looking for all intents and purposes like a corporeal stormcloud. She stopped by her room and leaned her shoulder against the doorframe, gritting her teeth, willing the flurries in her stomach and chest to quiet. She would have to go down and have words with Tarr. It would do no good at all if his perverse sense of humor continued to manifest itself in these petty little pranks. Then she would need to get some food, for clearly she was weak from hunger, judging by her stomach and her wobbly knees. But first, she thought with a small mischievous grin, she'd go down to the cadets' quarters and ask Kali and the others to go and wake Archer. They could thank her later.

Many miles to the west of Two Falls, just on the outskirts of the Meadows, there lay the tiny market town of Albaster. It stood on the base of a large hill, close to the edge of an expansive wood that swept to the east, where it met the Ashan forest. There was a small river that wove past the town and up into the Meadows, providing clear drinking water for the people and the animals and leaving in its wake rich, dark soil ripe for tilling and cultivation.

Albaster was largely a place for farmers and craftspeople in the outlying lands to gather and sell their wares (for it was much too far from Two Falls to make that city a viable point of sale. The town itself was no more than a cobbled square surrounded by a few streets of solid stone structures that, over many years, had been overrun with ivy and moss. The houses had been built by farmers with little imagination or thought for comfort or architectural beauty; each house had two windows on the top or bottom floor and a door set between them. The effect of looking at a row of these houses (to the more whimsical viewer, at least) was that of a line of very disgruntled elderly faces sitting squat and stubborn upon the muddy earth, with the odd cascade of unruly ivy here and there spilling over like mops of hair.

There had traditionally been only a few dozen year-round inhabitants of the town, though this had increased dramatically with the tide of people attempting to flee from Two Falls after Cira asserted her rule over the city, and another wave after its liberation by the Strikers. The rest were scattered in tiny farmhouses and homesteads over the hills and up into the flat Meadows, where the land was better for growing crops and raising livestock. Every seventh day, the farmers would gather what they had to sell, traipsing across the hills and glades to the town where they would barter, exchange, or sell to each other and to the odd merchant who would then transport their goods to Two Falls.

There was a lesser-known side of Albaster that had to do with its unusual placement at the confluence of the Meadows and the hill country while still being relatively close in proximity to Two Falls and the Ashan forest, both of which were about a week's ride away. For while Albaster was a very nice, respectful, rather quaint place during the day, after the sun set it took on quite a different tone. Exiled Ashans, those who had fled from Two Falls during the war, deserters from the Jelani patrols in the Meadows, escapees from Riddleton—all seemed to make their way towards the town as if drawn by an unseen force. Those with families generally only stayed a short time in Albaster before packing up and seeking a better life further out into the Meadows. Those without families—or any particular prospects or optimism—remained. As usually happened when people found themselves isolated and turned from their homes and their accustomed way of life, some moved on to less savory pursuits as a way to pass the time and eke out a living. Many of these "new folk," as the local farmers distrustingly referred to them, scraped by in rickety shacks around the outskirts of the town, and while no official accord had been struck by the longtime townspeople and these newcomers, it was generally understood that during the day the town would be given over to the requirements of the farmers and tradespeople; after dark the town was given over to the recreation of the "others."

It was the night after a particularly successful market day, and a large bonfire had been struck in the center of the square. All of the farmers and their wares had vanished hurriedly into the dusk. Off to the side of the bonfire was a large ring of people from all races and seemingly from all corners of the land. The talk was loud and raucous; money exchanged hands freely, and a few jugs of hard liquor were being passed across the line. Every once in a while, the voices of all present would come together in a loud roar like the crash of a wave; gold coins chinked onto the ground like pellets of rain before being scooped up into nimble, greedy fingers. Albaster was an after-hours gambling town, and one of the most popular sports in the area was bareknuckle boxing. And the consensus was that tonight was going to be a good fight.

Two men stepped forward into the center of the ring. It was a balmy night; both were shirtless and barefoot. One of them was tall and about thirty years old with a hard leer and a nose that had been clearly broken in a few places. The other was short and stocky with broad shoulders and strong arms. He had ice-blue eyes and a large curved nose, a kind countenance that was marred by an ugly scar that split his face from his jaw up to his left ear. Even those who had known Marc well would have had to look twice, for he had shaved off his highly recognizable head of silky straw-colored hair. Only half an inch adorned his head; it somehow made his scar more prominent, his bearing more intimidating. Coins and eager muttering around the circle greeted the fighters while debates about their relative size and ability blazed as hot as the nearby bonfire.

The fight's organizer stepped forward. "On this side, we have Targis Rathborn, defending champion." The taller fighter raised his hand, which, like Marc's, was wrapped in white cloth up to his knuckles. "And on this side, we have the challenger, Marcus." Marc raised his fist in acknowledgment and was greeted by a few good-natured boos and some interested murmuring.

"Try not to kill each other," the organizer shouted by way of encouragement, and stepped out of the way.

As soon as the fight started there was no doubt around the circle as to who would win. Targis Rathborn was taller, but Marc had a low center of gravity, which made it nearly impossible for him to be knocked over. He was able to nimbly duck out of the way, as gracefully as a swordsman. Those who knew a thing or two about boxing could see that Marc was forcing his opponent to expend an undue amount of energy trying to land jabs and punches, glancing blows that Marc shook away almost uncaringly. Targis began to grow frustrated, and, egged on by the jeers from the crowd, he became careless. He darted forward in an attempt to throw Marc off his feet, but Marc ducked and spun round so that Targis's back was exposed and his balance was thrown off-kilter. Marc dealt him a playful cuff on the back of the head that sent him toppling through the astonished crowd and into the wall of a nearby building. The crowd cheered gleefully as Targis stumbled to his feet, growling audibly like a wounded bear as he swung around to face Marc again. But Marc was ready for him. Targis barreled forward, but Marc squared his stance and crouched down, landing two explosive blows to Targis's side that stopped the fighter in his tracks. Marc dodged back one step and aimed a blow to his opponent's temple. Targis went down like a ton of bricks, and the crowd converged on them. Marc was barely out of breath.

Someone nearby tossed him his shirt, and Marc pulled it over his head with a nod of thanks. He silently collected his winnings from the fight organizer, who clapped him on the back, called him "good lad," and invited him to return and fight anytime. As he was about to make his way through the crowd and out of the village, he heard his name called by a chorus of voices behind him. He turned to find five eager faces, perhaps a bit younger than him, with the distinct, elated air of people who'd just won a bet. Marc inclined his head to them courteously.

"We made a lot of gold on you tonight, mate," a young woman said. "Let us buy you a pint, eh?"

This was just what Marc had been planning on.

A few minutes later, they were ensconced in a teeming, deafening pub, the only official drinking establishment in the town, and Marc was being offered a foaming tankard at the bar, which he accepted gratefully. The five young people watched him drink, gathered around him like an overeager crescent moon.

"Really well done, mate," said the young woman who had spoken before. Marc couldn't quite pinpoint her accent. She could easily have been half-Ashan. "Where are you from?"

"Two Falls," he replied.

The others glanced at each other. "It's true, then," said one of the young men, "that the Strikers have taken it back? That the gates are open?"

"I left before they took it back, but that's what I've heard," Marc shrugged nonchalantly.

"What brings you to this forsaken hole of a town?" asked the other young man.

Marc took a deep swig and eyed them levelly. "I'm looking for my younger brother," he said, trying to keep the hopeful tremor out of his voice as he spoke. "He was kidnapped during the occupation, just before the Strikers took it back."

"Sorry to hear that, mate," said the young woman, taking a sip of her own ale.

"We think he was taken by a group of strange-looking people, cloaks and such. Would have stuck out. My brother's short, about fourteen, has a face full of freckles and red hair, though they may have dyed it to disguise him. Gray eyes."

Marc's heart pounded faster, and he gripped the handle of his tankard as the five looked at one another. Then he felt his heart sinking as each of them frowned in turn and began to shake their heads. The familiar sick feeling of disappointment washed over him like a wave.

"Not seen anything like that around these parts, sorry, mate," said the young woman. "And we'd have heard about it. Nothing happens around here without someone bragging about it."

Marc stared down at the foam in his mug, watching the tiny bubbles burst and dissolve into darkness.

"We could go back to Two Falls, now, though," piped up the youngest woman, who looked no older than Si herself.

"They say Cira's gone mad," one of the young men said darkly, shaking his head forebodingly. "Stark mad. She'll burn that city to the ground, you mark my words, and string the Strikers up along the gates like ornaments. Best to steer clear of all that nonsense until it's all over."

Marc sighed. "I couldn't agree with you more." He polished off the last of the ale and pushed himself away from the bar.

"You staying around here, then?" the young woman asked hopefully. She clearly intended to make some more money off of Marc if at all possible.

"I'd best be moving along. I've got to try and find word of my brother. Do you know the next town where there might be a boxing match or two?" he asked. "I'm trying to stay on the circuit. Make a bit of money as I go." *Not to mention the type of people to frequent an illegal boxing match are exactly the kind who may have word of Si.*

The youngest woman piped up, "If you ride northwest, there's another town called Uxley. But it's right on the border of the Meadows, and all of that land belongs to the Jelani. You can't go on there unless you pay them a tax. They patrol it, too."

"Rich, greedy bastards!" grumbled one of the young men.

"I hear they sacrifice children," said the other.

"And that they have forty-two gods with multiple heads," chimed in the young woman.

"Forty-eight," Marc corrected her. "More bang for your religious buck."

The others stared at him, wide-eyed, unsure if he was joking. Marc hid a smile and clapped the young woman on the shoulder. "Thanks for the drink. I'll look you up if I ever come back this way."

And Marc headed out of Albaster into the dark night alone.

CHAPTER THREE

Whitsun Forge was impossible to find for those who did not know to look for it. The forge was set deep within a nest of rocks at the edge of a mountain, with gaps and cracks in the black-blasted stone providing natural ventilation for the inferno that raged within. Long ago, the patriarch of the Whitsun dynasty had selected the location to ensure that their only clientele would be those who were willing to travel a long and hard road to reach them—before paying handsomely for the right to own a Whitsun blade. The family made only one weapon per season. If at any point the sword failed to meet their strict requirements, the weapon was cast aside, and the unlucky client was told to return at the beginning of the next season so that they could try again. There were only a few hundred Whitsun blades still in existence; such were their value that many owners had ferreted them away in the safest, out-of-the-way hiding places imaginable, only for them to be lost over time when their guardians passed without divulging the secrets of their locations. Alder Morthenstar was said to have been buried with hers; after three attempts were made to steal it from her tomb, the monument was moved to a more secret location, and rumors circulated that the sword had gone missing in the shuffle.

The Whitsuns of the present day consisted of three related families, about twenty individuals in total, all of whom had devoted themselves to one aspect or another of the bladesmithing process. Some carved ivory, others were skilled in engraving or leatherwork, others in inlaying jewels. All of them bore the same pale, owl-eyed, unsmiling expressions; they lived a monastic life up in the mountains and had the appearance of those who did not get out and see the sunlight very often. What set them truly apart, though, were their hands and arms: the men and women who worked the steel itself had forearms that resembled bands of thick leather cords, scored on all sides by burns and scars, blanketed by a thin layer of ash that gave them an even more ghostly pallor.

Their current client didn't stare at them, didn't seem to mind their unsmiling faces or long stretches of silence. He himself sat outside the forge most days, in the rain or in the shine, staring unblinkingly out at the horizon with black, deadened eyes. Looking at him, one couldn't tell what he was thinking or if he took any particular joy in the landscape he surveyed; those eyes simply stared into nothingness, as deep as a moonless night. Every now and again, a wind would rise up through the cracks in the rocks and blow through his pale hair, but he never stirred. For days on end, the only sound was the distant river that tumbled down through the cave to turn the grist, and the endless hammering from within the cave as the Whitsuns bent the living metal to their wills.

Finally, a month after he had arrived, the head of the family came out and gestured to their client to enter. The man with the black eyes stood and followed them into the gloom of the cave, where the members of the Whitsun family stood waiting in a row, clad in matching soot-colored aprons, all looking uniformly pale and gray and blinking at him like strange underground creatures.

"Lord Seth," said the family's patriarch. He was a small man with massive forearms that seemed twice the appropriate size for the rest of his spindly frame. His hair was as white and wispy as cobwebs and gave the impression that it could blow completely off his head at any second. Like the others, he had a pair of enormous gray eyes that caught the dim light like strange glassy orbs. "We have finished your sword." He motioned to one of his offspring, a girl with a large burn on the side of her neck that bloomed puckery pink against her gray skin. She carried a sword sheathed in an ornately engraved scabbard, and she extended it out to Lord Seth, who carefully took it in one long, delicate hand and examined it.

The Whitsuns had outdone themselves. The scabbard itself was a priceless work of art. It was made of polished jade with a long white-gold snake winding its way up the length of the sword and wrapping around the hilt, which itself was hewn from ivory, beautifully and meticulously carved into what looked like a nest of snakes rising up from the heart of the sword. Seth carefully pulled the blade loose of the sheath and held it up in one hand. The balance was absolutely perfect; the polished steel gleamed, almost wet-looking in the firelight. He tilted the blade to the left and to the right. When it caught the light, he could make out words engraved on the blade and the intricate filigree that continued the pattern of the writhing nest of snakes curving down along the length of the metal.

As Seth moved the blade to point toward the line of Whitsuns, one or two of them almost subconsciously took a step back. The elder Whitsun cleared his throat and glanced back at the rest of his family. "We have crafted the sword to your...specifications," he said. "The inside of the scabbard is coated with the serpent venom you requested." He coughed lightly. "It added considerable expense, of course." Seth made no answer, just continued to lovingly gaze up and down the length of the blade, taking in every inch of it. "The poison is deadly," Whitsun continued. "Even a small graze could be fatal. Be careful when handling it."

Seth silently looked down the row of Whitsuns. Finally, he gave a short nod as if to indicate that he was pleased with the work.

At this, the elder Whitsun seemed to relax just a bit. "Good," he said. For some reason, he felt the strangest urge to be rid of their silent client, and quickly. "Follow me, and we'll take care of the final accounts..."

Seth sheathed the sword at last and followed the family patriarch past the row of Whitsuns (all of whom silently followed him with their bulbous, pale eyes) and into a small antechamber where the business of fees was conducted.

The accounts completed and the agreed-upon payment delivered, Seth set out down the rocky slope, sword held carefully in one hand.

He came to a small cave where his horse had been tethered and cared for by younger members of the family for the duration of his stay in the mountains. A light mist had begun to fall around them as the low-hanging clouds dissolved in midair.

He had ridden only a little ways down the mountain path when the wheels in his mind began to turn. Something about the whole thing was unsatisfactory, and it rankled in the back of his mind like an itch in the dead center of his shoulder blades. It wasn't the sword. The sword was perfect. The sword was *too perfect*. It was the next in a long lineage of fine, elite craftsmanship, some of the most coveted in the world. And this sword had an important job to do: it was to be used to kill every last one of the Strikers, every one that he could get his hands on. It wasn't enough, he thought, for it to be the *next* in a long line of fine craftsmanship. It would do much better if this sword were the last. That the last sword ever crafted by the Whitsun forge would be the weapon used to kill the Strikers. How much more fitting, how much more pleasing a legacy that would be.

He contemplated this idea for a few more minutes without a sliver of change or emotion on his dead-eyed face. Then, as matter-of-factly as if he had forgotten his riding gloves back up at the forge, he turned his horse and began to ride up the hill. When the children saw him coming, they instinctively began to run.

CHAPTER FOUR

The moon rose like a lidless eye over the hills, casting its light down onto the gently rushing river that split the town of Two Falls. At the center of a small convergence of alleyways on the north side of town, Laith paused and turned, the half-crescent of his face framed against his dark hood.

"Now remember," he said, his voice low, "I want arrests only. No killing."

There was a murmur of assent from the half-dozen cloaked figures standing around him. A few of them shifted restlessly from side to side.

Laith slowly turned again, the gleam of his face disappearing in the night's gloom.

Two of the newest recruits eyed each other warily, then stared at Laith's immobile figure. How can he be so still? He frightened them. One of them, a young woman with dark skin and short-cropped black hair, was gripping the hilt of her dagger so tightly that her knuckles ached.

Suddenly, Laith took a step forward, and the rest of them followed as if pulled by some sort of unseen magnetic force. They strode silently across the clearing, down the street, and around another corner, walking straight up a dead-end alleyway to the back door of a narrow building.

Two of the six windows glowed from within with a dim, flickering light.

In a fluid motion, Laith reached one hand up and over to the hilt of the sword strapped to his back, drawing it with a dull metallic shing, and lowering it to his hip. He hesitated only one moment, and then rocked back on his heels and threw his weight into the door. It splintered immediately, and Laith vanished inside as a cry of warning went up among the inhabitants within.

The team ran heedlessly behind him into a state of complete pandemonium. They had been told to prepare for five Kagaian sympathizers, but once they were within the building, it seemed as though there must have been more. Shapes—figures—almost indistinguishable, darted between hallways around them.

The girl with black hair was jogging, not knowing the layout of the house, every sense tingling, her heart in her throat. Suddenly, someone darted across her path, heading straight towards a window in the adjacent room. Temporarily shocked to a standstill, all at once the girl's instincts galvanized into motion. She darted after the figure and made it to the window just as he was about to disappear out of sight. She clutched at the air and managed to grab a handful of the young man's shirt. His weight threw her forward against the windowsill, and she gritted her teeth, struggling to hang on to her wriggling quarry on the other side of the sill. The window banged awkwardly against her forehead as it waved in the wind. There were the sounds of footsteps behind her, and all at once, a black-clad hand snaked out, threw open the window, and pulled the young man sprawling onto the floor before them.

It was Laith. He easily wrestled the young man's flailing arms behind his back, pinning him to the ground with a knee between the shoulder blades. The girl didn't know what to do with her hands. She had never been in such close proximity to Laith before, and she was afraid to go any closer; he was strangely untouchable.

The captive young man's protestations subsided as he became resigned to his fate. Laith looked up at the girl, a streak of sweat and dirt across his brow. "Good work," he said. He wasn't even out of breath. The girl swallowed. "Can you keep him here?" he asked.

She nodded mutely and moved forward immediately to take Laith's place, holding down the young man's arms and leaning the weight of her knee into his back.

Like a dark ghost, Laith drew up and vanished from the room, his sword flashing in the dim light.

For a few moments they remained still, listening to the sound of footsteps pounding on the floorboards above them, muffled cries and yells.

"What will happen to me?" came a small voice beneath her.

She gave a start and realized her focus had drifted. She leaned more heavily on her prisoner's back. "We're going to take you back to the Striker headquarters," she told him in what she hoped was a firm, authoritative voice (but sounded slightly tremulous when it came out.) "You'll be given the opportunity to cooperate."

The young man was silent for a moment. "That sounds like a threat."

The girl's brow furrowed. "Why do you still support Kagai?"

He grunted. "What's your name?"

"Zee," she replied. "For Zamara."

"My father was killed in the Battle of Two Falls."

"So was my brother," she snapped back.

An uneasy silence returned and reigned over both of them. "I think you went to the same school as me," he said a few moments later, shifting uncomfortably beneath her knee.

The thought had already occurred to her minutes ago. "I don't think so," she said coldly.

"Look, you won't find anything in here," he said, his reasonable voice muffled against the floor. "We had a tip-off that there would be a raid; we cleaned house before you got here. There's nothing."

"Then I suppose we'll just have to take you in," she replied. *He's lying*, she thought to herself, glancing around the room. *He sounds like he's lying. There must be something in here, some clue as to where the other Kagaian loyalist meetings are being held.*

A few moments later, there were sounds at the door and Laith returned, flanked by two of the other Strikers. "Take him," Laith ordered in his quiet voice.

As they stood, Zee said loudly, watching the young Kagaian soldier's face all the while, "There's nothing in this room, sir. They wiped it clean."

Laith gave her an odd look, but Zee ignored it. She saw the flicker of a satisfied smile on the Kagaian soldier's face and saw his eyes glance unconsciously toward a small desk in the back of the room.

A moment later, the boy was escorted out and Laith turned to leave. "Wait, sir," Zee said urgently, and Laith swiveled back, surprised. Zee, feeling the heat of excitement rising in her chest, jogged across the room to the desk and began rummaging around in it, pulling out drawers and sifting through the contents within. There were books and old papers that she rifled through, but nothing seemed quite right (though she had to admit to herself that she really had no idea what she was looking for.) Then, a moment later, her hand closed on a scrap of fabric, and she withdrew it. On it was a little hand-drawn sketch of what looked like a waning crescent moon, and above the moon was a figure with a sword in one hand and a rose in the other, tilted slightly to the left. Zee had no idea what the figures meant, but it was cryptic enough that she was sure she had found the right thing.

Breathlessly, she passed the scrap to Laith, who surveyed it. Something—almost a smile—played around his lips as he looked back up at her and gave her a satisfied nod. "I'm sure this is it," he said quietly. "You've done very well. Thank you."

If a bell had rung or a choir had burst into song, Zee would not have felt more pleased with herself. She felt her chest puff and her height draw up a full two inches. "But sir," she said after a moment. "What does it mean?"

Laith furrowed his brow and stared down at the fabric for a moment or two, giving Zee ample time to take in his handsome face and the fine lines of his head and neck. "The moon indicates what time of the month they are to meet—waning crescent, so tomorrow—and the figure is positioned for the time, as it would be on a clock, so ten o'clock. As to where..."

In a flash of utter brilliance, Zee had an idea. "There's a pub in the north called Sword and Rose," she exclaimed. "Might that be it?"

This time, Laith did, in fact, smile. "I think it just might."

Zee felt herself float up into the air like a bubble about to burst.

The next night was rough and angry, a slowly gathering windstorm that gave the impression that winter was trying to get a last few dying roars in before spring made its way fully over the hills. Solidly built as it was out of stone and strong timber, Tarr's third-story office at the Two Falls headquarters nevertheless gave a few anxiety-inducing lurches back and forth, the panes of the windows creaking with some complaint against the pounding of the wind outside.

Tarr tried again to focus on the matter at hand. Or, rather, the *matters*. Two great questions loomed in front of him: the weapon (whatever it was) that Cira was somehow developing and the location of the Kagaian loyalist meetings in Two Falls. For the loyalist meetings, at least, they had a lead (albeit a small one), just the fabric scrap Laith had discovered during his raid. As for Cira's weapon—what it was, what it did—he was completely and infuriatingly flummoxed.

He was down to only a handful of spies at Faridor after Cira had purged most of her household a few months before. Though Rane and Cicada were undoubtedly his best spies, even *they* were having trouble deciphering the latest round of codes that were making their way through the fortress. Tarr was frustratedly certain that the recent spate of messages had to do with Cira's weapon, whatever it was, and he was powerless to know what they said.

In the past, a message intercepted within the confines of Faridor would be passed through safe channels to either Tarr or to Rane or Cicada, and they would do their best to decode it. Cira had learned that the safest way to communicate—even within the walls of her own fortress—was through coded messages, and Tarr was suspicious that she had an entire team of code writers at her disposal. A plainly written letter was far too easy to be seen; a chambermaid had only to casually linger by a desk or take too long pouring wine to give her a chance to see it and memorize its contents. This tactic had worked for him in times past.

Like Tarr, Cira's code writers had taken to using traditional poems and songs as keys—numbering letters and so forth, and using them to translate a message into code. But Tarr had become quite good at deciphering them, and it was clear that Cira's team had come up with something else, something much more difficult. Rane and Cicada had gathered a number of recent messages and kept them, hoping that the code patterns from one message to another would remain the same, but they were so far out of luck. It was infuriating.

The part of Tarr's brain that keenly loved puzzles was bright and alert, ticking away at such a rate and through so many hours of the night that Tarr spent many of his days walking around in a dazed state of semi-exhaustion. But another part of him was fed up. *Just screw up*, he thought. *Screw up once so that we can end this.*

As if in response to his thoughts, a window shutter clattered behind him, pushed by a strong gust of wind. Tarr jumped visibly in his seat. Disturbed and annoyed, he cast down his pen and decided that that was enough work for one night.

He jogged down the stairs towards the kitchens, immediately feeling lighter now that he had given himself the night off. A few people gawked at him as they passed him in the stairwell, and he nodded politely without breaking his stride. Now that they worked out in the open, he still wasn't quite used to people recognizing him. Laith and Archer were accustomed to that sort of attention. Tarr had always felt more comfortable under a blanket of anonymity.

The bottom floor of their headquarters had a large dining hall (which was usually occupied by a large group of Strikers relaxing after a shift or taking their meal), an infirmary, a weapons room, and the kitchens, which were tucked away back behind the dining hall, connected by a short passageway.

The kitchens were warm and cozy, as they always were. The room was a large square shape, dominated by an enormous wood-burning oven, stove, and hearth framing an ever-turning spit. Large pale flagstones had been laid across the floor to make them easy to clean, and because of the warmth of the fire, they were always pleasant to walk upon, even in socks (which Tarr had done on a few occasions when he'd been unable to sleep.) A long, broad table stood in the center of the room, which acted as an area to prepare food or to share a good gossip. There was always a fire burning day and night, and the flickering light and tempting smells made it one of the homiest rooms in the entire building.

Tarr ducked beneath the doorframe and entered, nodding a shy smile to two young people, a brother and sister, who were peeling carrots at the table. They blinked in surprise a few times at him and ducked their heads in small, modest bows.

"Can we get you anything, m'lord?" the girl said.

"It's Tarr," he said automatically, feeling awkward at the deference they showed him. "Just Tarr. And...er..." he glanced around the room, coming to terms with the fact that his walk hadn't been purely recreational. "You don't think there's a plate of those..."

"Over on the counter, there, sir," grinned the boy, pointing.

Tarr followed his gaze and walked (hopefully not too quickly) over to where he indicated. Sitting and looking very innocent on the countertop was a plate of small, perfectly golden-yellow cakes. Tarr grabbed one and, considering, grabbed another and was guiltily run-walking out of the room when a sharp voice barked out, "*Tarr!*"

Shortly after Two Falls had been reclaimed by the Strikers, a husband and wife showed up at the headquarters, offering their services as cooks. They had kept a modest tavern on the outskirts of the Meadows, but the war had hit them hard. After their son was arrested in Two Falls and executed for harboring Ashans in his home, they decided to pack up, sell the tavern, and move to the city to help where they could. It had been something of a surprise to them to find that the city had already fallen and been taken back by the Strikers. But Tarr and the others had gladly welcomed their help, and they had not regretted it.

The couple were in their late sixties and had raised many children together, all of whom had gone off to far distant lands. The wife was the sharper of the two. She took a no-nonsense attitude towards her job, carefully portioned everything out, and didn't spend a penny more than she had to. Tarr had heard it on good authority that she had gone to three different vegetable vendors at the market and had worked them all into a bartering frenzy just to get the best price off a pound of leeks for soup. Her husband was softer and would save treats or morsels if he knew that a certain member of the staff had grown fond of them. On occasion, the wife would find him out, and there would be a terrific row.

But for all of her fussiness, there was no denying that she was a talented cook and that her husband was a master of all things baked—breads, biscuits, and crackers, all in a variety of shapes, sizes, and flavors.

And what a change it had made!

For all of his life, Tarr had been only dimly aware of food as something to keep one alive: a necessity like washing or tending to one's teeth. He had seen a whole host of culinary marvels during the time that he'd spent in the Jelani palace, but he'd felt so awkward and so out-of-place that he'd been reluctant to eat anything beyond a bit of bread and cheese since he never touched meat (except for fish on rare occasions). During the years that they'd spent in hiding, both in the mountains and back in Two Falls, money had been so tight and food so scarce that they'd often gone hungry. The previous winter, Cira had nearly succeeded in starving them out.

But the victory at Two Falls had been a turning point. There were many old families, wealthy and powerful, who resented that Cira had taken over and demanded both their fealty and financial contributions to her crown. Some of them had fled the city to far-off estates at the first hint of trouble and had hunkered there like birds on a nest, waiting for the rainstorm to pass. And when word came that the Strikers had prevailed, that there might be a chance that Cira's reign could end, there had been a sudden and steady influx of money that had come pouring in to support the Strikers' claim. Laith, Ari, and the fledgling governing council had set about putting their financial affairs in place, making sure that their staff was paid and fed and that they were able to render help to those in the city who needed it.

When their new housekeepers had taken up residence in the kitchen, they brought with them a singularly precious commodity: honey. They had kept bees in the Meadows near their old tavern and had jars and jars of it with them, more valuable than gold. What's more, they'd made an arrangement with the people who had taken over the tavern that they would still get a share of the honey after it was harvested. This they brought with them to Two Falls and subsequently transformed into mind-bending concoctions of spices and rich, unctuous sweetness. Tarr had barely eaten sweets in his life, other than spots of honey in his tea. In his old life in the forest, there were berries and the like, which, when they could be found and foraged, were just as likely to be sour as not. So when he was first handed a golden honey cake, Tarr hadn't known what to expect. After taking a single bite, he had to sit down. He felt as though his head was ringing. It was that good.

Nor was Tarr alone in his estimation. The other Strikers, though they never actually spoke of it between themselves, were all guiltily addicted to the precious, expensive little cakes. Once, Tarr had passed Marc in the stairwell and exchanged solemn nods as though they were both off to do something very important—until Tarr had noticed a trail of golden crumbs littering the front of Marc's tunic.

The cook marched on Tarr now like a tiny five-foot tiger, a severe silver braid snaking down her back, dark eyes flashing as she brandished a ladle at him. Whatever hero-worshipping attitude was held towards the Strikers by their staff and followers, it did not extend to her. She chided all of them like a mother duck and frequently hinted that if they'd had good parents, they would have stayed home and learned manners instead of going off to fight a war. The only one of them to whom she deferred was Laith, who, with his preternaturally regal bearing and quietly spectral presence, was awe-inspiring enough to avoid her censure.

There were lines around her mouth, evidence of many years of pursing her lips in displeasure. Out of the corner of his eye, Tarr could see the siblings hiding grins over their peeling. Tarr straightened and tried to look responsible and commanding as he deftly tucked one of the cakes away in his pocket.

"A night like tonight, when you've got those poor lads and lasses up at all hours in all this wind and wet, and you're off stealing their cakes," she snapped.

"Ari's the one who sets the staff schedule," Tarr replied with some dignity, starting to edge a retreat towards the door.

She opened her mouth and furrowed her brow, her black beetle-like eyes flashing, but Tarr gave a hasty salute, turned, and withdrew out the door without another word. Undignified, yes, but he thought of the cakes in his pocket and chuckled to himself.

He went down the narrow passage and sat at one of the long tables set up in the dining hall. It had once been the entrance hall of the massive headquarters, crowned by a huge gold-domed ceiling that seemed to stretch up to the heavens and which inspired awe and wonder among all those who had looked upon it in days gone past. Tarr remembered marveling at the vast room when he and Laith and the others had first set foot in the building years before, hoping to ask the Two Falls government for support against Cira. But when the Strikers took the headquarters over after the Battle of Two Falls, Tarr, Ari, and Athela took one look at it and decided that it was too much space to be wasted on mere aesthetics. They'd converted it into a much more pedestrian, functional area. Those who came and went through the room for their meals or to catch up were, by this point, so used to its grandeur that they barely looked upwards anymore.

Tarr was halfway through his cake, enjoying the murmured sounds of conversation from the clusters of people scattered throughout the room, when he heard his name called out again. There was a note of irritation to it, similar to the cook's. Instinctively, he gulped down his bite and turned. Archer and Athela were advancing towards him. Athela was looking predatorial, dressed all in black with her ebony curls cascading over her shoulder, and Archer was sidling along behind her, looking rather bemused. He caught sight of Tarr's rather guilty expression and at the half-eaten cake in his hand.

"Nice," he grinned.

"Tarr," Athela broke in, as though continuing a conversation they'd already been having. She slid onto the bench across from Tarr, folding her hands and looking very serious. "It looks as though you and Ari have scheduled me and Archer to follow up a lead together tonight." She looked as though she were barely able to keep her fury under control. "This is *intolerable.*"

"I'm *right here,*" Archer exclaimed, mostly to himself.

Tarr rolled his eyes and took another bite of cake. *This again.*

He wished, more than anything else, that Athela had stuck to her usual self-discipline and hadn't slept with Archer the night of the Two Falls battle. If they had consciously planned it, the two of them couldn't have designed a more difficult and unpleasant situation than the one they found themselves in.

The problem was, in Tarr's opinion, that when it came down to it, both Archer and Athela were utterly besotted with each other, and their night together had only served to crystallize those feelings into something tangible. Tarr had known for years that Archer was in love with her, and while Athela tended to play her feelings closer to the chest, he knew in the way that she looked at Archer when his back was turned that she loved him, too. The war complicated matters. Athela, obviously afraid of her strong feelings for Archer, felt that it was irresponsible for them to be in a relationship when there was a great chance that one of them could die any day. She was terrified of having Archer only to lose him again. Archer was of the exact opposite mind: he reasoned that since there was a good chance they could die any day, they might as well make the most of it and pursue happiness where they found it. But Athela was immovable on the subject, and Archer, frustrated but respectful of the lines she had drawn, had taken to goading her and taunting her at every opportunity. Tarr had seen seven-year-olds act out their feelings with more depth and maturity.

While Tarr was inclined to agree with Archer about the whole love affair-during-wartime debate (he was, after all, ostensibly in a relationship with Rane, though they had parted on tense terms after she'd insisted on relocating to Faridor against his wishes, hadn't seen each other for months, and communicated solely through extremely dry coded messages about floorplans), he could understand where Athela was coming from perhaps a bit better than Archer could. Tarr knew that Athela's whole childhood was a series of personal disappointments; with few exceptions, she would be shown something she desperately wanted, only to have it snatched away again and held out of reach. If Athela desired Archer as much as he suspected she did, her greatest fear would be to lose him.

The consequence of all this was that interactions involving the two of them were almost unbearable. Every gesture and word was so fraught with conflict and barbed with feigned dislike—yet laced with an uncomfortably palpable undercurrent of sexual tension—that the other Strikers, who were much more sensitive to it than those who weren't as familiar with Archer and Athela, could often only put up with it for five minutes before having to desperately excuse themselves from the room. After a considerably heated evening at Ari's birthday party, Marc had half-jokingly suggested that they lock Archer and Athela in a basement together for three days to see if that put an end to it. "Either they'll kill each other, or there'll be a couple half-Ashan babies on the way, I guarantee it," he'd said, to which Ari (still wearing the paper birthday crown he had reluctantly donned at the beginning of the meal) had grimly replied that he'd prefer the sound of a hundred screaming babies to having to listen to another snippy conversation between the two. Having never known Ari to actually tell a joke before, Tarr was inclined to take him at his word.

Athela's refusal to take the plunge, however, didn't in any way lessen the petty feelings of jealousy that tended to arise whenever Archer paid attention to someone else. At one of their strategy meetings months ago, Archer had sat next to a nervous young woman who had just joined up and didn't know anyone in the group yet. Seeing that she was feeling left out, he had kindly talked to her throughout the meeting, and by the end of the evening, it was apparent that she was smitten with him. This had not been lost on Athela.

"He's such a flirt!" she had snapped under her breath to Tarr from where they sat at the other end of the table. "He'll go after anything with a pair of eyelashes."

To this, Tarr had mildly pointed out that both Laith and Marc had eyelashes but had so far escaped unscathed, to which Athela had made a very unbecoming huffing noise under her breath, folded her arms, and responded in monosyllabic grunts for the rest of the meeting.

It wasn't entirely true, either, Tarr reasoned. He had always enjoyed watching and observing those around him and pleased himself by conducting little sociological experiments in his head. He had long been curious about Archer's storied history as a lothario and had tried to figure out exactly what made him so attractive to people, particularly the opposite sex. He wasn't traditionally handsome, as Laith was; in fact, he was objectively very strange-looking, with his alabaster skin, yellow eyes, and spiky black-tipped hair—more like a humanoid hawk than anything else. He was intelligent and charming, certainly, lithe and tall and well-built. But the answer, Tarr had eventually realized, was much simpler than all of that: Archer simply liked women. He liked to be near them, liked to talk to them, was attentive but never aggressive, didn't create distance by emphasizing his gender or theirs. Tarr could see that women relaxed around him and felt safe. It wasn't that hard to understand if one looked properly—and Tarr, for his part, thought that Archer's reputation was actually somewhat unfair to him. To hear anyone else tell it, Archer was a rogue who used lovers and heartlessly cast them aside, but on any occasion when Archer had happened to mention someone he'd been involved with to Tarr; he'd always spoken of them with affection and respect. In his retelling, many of his breakups had been mutual, were the decision of the other person, or had been understood by both parties to be casual affairs.

Not that Athela would have heard any of this, though, if Tarr had tried to explain it. What they really needed was someone to knock some sense into the both of them. In the meantime, Tarr found small moments of amusement where he could by assigning them to carry out missions together.

"You are aware that yesterday Laith led a raid and discovered intelligence about the location of the next Kagaian loyalist meeting?" Tarr asked, mustering all of his outward dignity as he doggedly brushed the last few crumbs of cake from the edge of the table into his cupped hand and tipped them back down his throat. Archer gave him a revolted look.

"Yes," Athela scowled.

"Were you raised by *wolves?*" Archer demanded. "Who taught you table manners?"

"Probably the same person who taught you how to dress," Athela snapped back immediately.

"Both of you *shut up*," Tarr barked, his patience already frayed. "So help me, I am going to *force* you to work together until you can be pleasant enough to be tolerated in the same room."

"Don't hold your breath," Archer muttered audibly.

"Don't worry, I'm not," Tarr retorted, then sighed. "You are two of our best. If I can't assign you to work together, it will affect our abilities as a team." He let the reasonable tone of his words hang in the air for a few seconds, then lowered it into a more threatening register. "Either this or I'm assigning both of you to work double shifts with Ari."

That sobered them up quickly. "We'll be very good," Archer promised in a mock-childlike tone. "I swear."

"I'm surprised you'd do that to Ari," Athela said wryly. "Double shifts with Archer?"

This wasn't necessarily intended as a pointed jab. It was common knowledge that if there was anyone who could stand Archer less than Athela, it was Ari. He was just far less dramatic about it than she.

At least there's no sexual tension where Ari is concerned, Tarr thought, reminding himself to be grateful for the small blessings in life.

"You heard me," Tarr said grimly. "Now go. They have your orders at the door."

With a bit of creaking and scraping, the two stood up. Archer gave Tarr a cheeky wink, to which Tarr rolled his eyes. He watched the two affectionately as they went, Archer trailing a step or two behind Athela.

Not wanting to go back to his office and spend another handful of fruitless hours poring over code, Tarr shifted in his seat, brushing crumbs off the seat of his pants—and was delighted to come upon the second cake he had stowed away in his pocket. Perhaps it would be a good night after all.

Archer and Athela, followed by two guards, set out together on foot, a mutually disgruntled mood hanging over them like a dark cloak. The Sword and Rose tavern was in the north of the city, and they made their way silently under cover of darkness, holding their hoods down over their heads against the roaring wind. Spring still felt as though it was a long way off.

As they walked through the inky blue gloom, the shutters of the houses rattled overhead, and the signs hanging above shop doors swung haphazardly back and forth like a huge hand had given them an enormous push and then vanished around the corner. Even if the pair had wanted to continue sniping at one another, they wouldn't have been able to; the noise of the wind was so immense that any words were swallowed up into the air. At least some good had come of the weather: the streets were largely deserted, and there was almost no chance that they would draw any attention to themselves as they made their way through the city.

Finally, when they were a few blocks away from the tavern, Athela grabbed Archer's forearm and gestured him into the shelter of a small alcove next to a hardware shop. Their two flanking guards huddled in beside them, both keeping keen eyes peeled towards the street outside. Archer shook back his hood, his spiky black and white hair tossed every which way, looking more than ever like a rumpled humanoid osprey.

"Filthy weather," he said grumpily, casting a narrowed golden eye out at the night as if searching for someone to blame.

"Okay, the plan," prompted Athela.

"Good, you have one, then?" Archer said chipperly.

"Tarr's instructions said that this was to be a scouting mission, nothing more. The four of us scope out different corners of the building, looking for anyone coming in or out."

"There may be a tunnel from another building," Archer pointed out.

"True, so keep half an eye on the street as well; the entrance may be somewhere further down the block." She glanced back out at the windswept street beyond. "We're lucky, actually, that almost everyone is inside tonight. It'll make it easier to spot people entering or exiting."

"Got it," Archer agreed.

"If we see signs that the meeting has started, we alert headquarters, and they send over a troop of Strikers to come and make arrests while the loyalists are inside. Tarr will have them at the ready, poised to move out the minute we give them a signal."

"Sounds good, though I was sort of looking forward to barreling in and attempting to arrest them all single-handedly."

"I'm sure you were," Athela rolled her eyes.

The four of them fanned out, and each positioned themselves strategically in a ring around the Sword and Rose tavern, whose brightly painted sign rocked angrily on its hinges as the wind batted it back and forth, a moat of water leftover from a recent rain pooling around the front step.

Archer was crouched in the dark shadow of a doorway opposite the pub, his golden eyes looking for any sign of movement on the street around them. There was nothing. He could see Athela's shadowy figure perched on the balcony of an apartment above the street (clever, she must have scaled the trellis on the side of the building; why hadn't he thought of that?)

The minutes ticked by, and the agreed-upon time for the meeting eased past them. Archer felt himself beginning to grow frustrated.

A lone figure suddenly appeared on the street, and Archer instinctively hunkered down even further, pulling the side of his hood to cover his face, as his pale skin had a tendency to glow milky blue in the moon-light. They were heavily cloaked, and after sloshing through the puddle up to the front door of the Sword and Rose, the figure paused for a moment and then disappeared inside. From the glimpse that Archer got, there was no sign of light from the building within, no indication that a meeting was taking place behind the curtained windows.

Archer resisted the instinct to immediately leap up and warn the others. Whatever this individual was doing, it was clear that they weren't the entire Kagaian loyalist force, so perhaps something else, some other plot, was afoot. He wished that there weren't heavy curtains drawn over the windows so he could see inside.

The person, whoever they were, remained inside the building for about twenty minutes. Archer knew that Athela, at least, had seen the person from her perch and had made the same decision not to sound the alarm, at least not quite yet. When at last the door opened (the building within still pitch-black) and the figure slipped out, Archer again thought briefly about leaping up and seizing whoever it was. But then he thought better of it. He was much more keen to know what—or who—was inside the Sword and Rose. It would be easy enough to clear out the building and set an ambush for a later time.

Once the cloaked figure was well out of sight, Archer ventured into the street, motioning Athela down from her perch. The other two guards joined them a moment later, and they clustered together against a wall opposite the tavern.

Archer told them briefly what he'd seen. "So there's *something* in there," he concluded. "Somewhere."

"Well," Athela cast her eyes about, her hands on her hips in a businesslike attitude. "We could go back to headquarters and report to Tarr..."

"Or...?" Archer asked, catching her drift and grinning wolfishly.

She gave him a sidelong look and smiled in spite of herself. "Come on."

The small group of four darted across the street, and Athela stepped back to allow Archer to inspect the lock. After years of breaking into homes much more fortified than the pub, it was simple for him to pick it open. The door creaked ajar, and they piled inside.

The interior of the pub was scruffy and somewhat beaten down by age and wear but was nevertheless clean and had been freshly swept. The chairs had been turned upside down and placed atop the few round tables spaced throughout the room; each scratched and weathered table bore an oil lantern atop it. Glancing around, Athela could just make out a large painting hanging over the soot-blackened fireplace: a man in armor offering a rose to a buxom, blushing maiden.

In the gloom, Archer raised a single slim finger to his lips and slowly crouched down to the floor. To Athela's surprise, he removed his cloak, boots, and socks and laid them to the side of the entryway in a small pile. Like a slinking cat, he slowly tested one of the floorboards to see if it would creak, then put his full weight on it and went silently to one of the tables, where he struck a match and illuminated the oil lamp, adjusting it so that there was only a thin ember of light, just enough to see by. The orange glow cast eerie shadows along Archer's angular face and neck as he turned around to look at them, motioning them to follow.

Silently, Athela and the others took off their boots and socks and crept out onto the floor, testing one board at a time as they went, their progress painstakingly slow. Athela tiptoed across the room to the bar at the opposite side, and her eyes traveled from the rows and rows of burnished glassware down to the floor, where a door to the wine cellar had been cut out, a heavy iron handle resting on top.

She waved her hand a few times to get Archer's attention and pointed down at the cellar door. *Here?* she mouthed.

Archer's brow furrowed, and he tilted his head to the side. She could tell he didn't like it. It seemed too simple, too obvious.

At that moment, one of their guards over by the fireplace gave a tiny gasp as he nearly slipped and fell. He caught himself in time to prevent an out-and-out crash down to the floor, but there had been an audible thump; no one listening could fail to have heard it. The guard, a young man with tightly curled black hair, looked up at them, mortified.

Archer straightened up to his full height, looking furious, but then his expression changed, and he urgently beckoned Athela forward, looking triumphant. Athela went as fast as she could (there seemed to be little reason for further subterfuge; whoever was there would have heard them anyway), and a moment later, Archer pointed at the floor by the fireplace where the young guard had fallen. On the ground there were small puddles of water, clearly tracked in on someone else's boot.

Archer and Athela helped the young man up and clapped him silently on the back, assuring him that there was no harm done. They immediately began examining the fireplace, looking for any secret entryway.

"It has to be simple," Athela whispered to them. "There wouldn't have been time to add an elaborate triggering mechanism to a building like this."

Finally, after a few fruitless moments of searching, Archer ducked into the fireplace, covering his long white feet in dark soot, and threw his shoulder against the rear wall. Nothing. He crouched for a moment and glanced back at the others. Athela made a sliding motion with her hand. He gave her the tiniest nod, turned, and ran his fingertips along the edge of the fireplace wall. His sensitive fingers could just make out the tiniest groove running vertically down the wall. Readjusting his crouching position slightly, he fit his fingers into it and gave an almighty heave. The heavy stone back of the fireplace slid smoothly to the side, revealing a small opening behind.

Archer stuck his head in the opening and peered around for a moment, then turned to face the others. "Stairs," he mouthed and opened his hand. "Knife," he gestured to one of the guards, who immediately unbuckled the weapon from his belt and tossed it, hilt-first, into Archer's ready hands.

"Have a light ready," Athela whispered to the other guard, who nodded and crept back over to the lantern on the table. *This was a bad idea*, she thought to herself. *We should have gone back and gotten help. We have no idea what is down there. There's only room on those stairs for one of us at a time. Archer could be killed.* She glanced away.

When she looked back up, Archer had already begun advancing down the stairs to the hidden compartment beneath. Athela motioned to the other two guards and trailed close behind him.

The floor was cool under Archer's bare feet, and he kept his knife at the ready, holding his other hand against the wall to guide himself down the dim stairwell. His eyes slowly began adjusting to the creeping darkness; the staircase looked to be only about ten steps or so down to the floor below, and there was a small landing that, from what he could see, looked empty.

He had gone far enough down the stairs that the other three behind him had also managed to cram in the hidden passage; one of the two guards held up the lantern, casting sharp orange light on the floor. To the right of the landing below was a small open door leading into a room beyond. Archer reached the bottom floor and steeled himself instinctively for whatever was waiting behind the corner; he bent his knees a tiny bit and loosened his hold on his knife so that he'd have the flexibility to move if he had to. He slowed his breathing and edged to the corner of the doorway. There was nothing for it.

A moment later, he spun around the opening of the doorway into the inky darkness of the room beyond and was knocked off his feet by some sort of wild, unseen force. As soon as his mind registered the shock of the impact, he sorted out that whoever his attacker was, it was human, and there seemed to be only one of them.

It was chaotic at best, grappling for those first few moments in the utter darkness of the room, but he gritted his teeth and grabbed what seemed to be a forearm, pressing down against his throat, slowly blocking off his air supply. The arm that held him down was thin but wiry, and as he tried to lift up his knife, another hand clamped down and slammed his wrist against the cold flagstones of the floor.

Archer twisted his body from under the person and landed a solid blow with his knee to what he assumed to be the person's ribs. There was a soft "hunh" sound at the impact, and then a moment later, the lantern swung into the room, along with Athela and the guards, and Archer was temporarily blinded by the disorientingly bright light. His attacker was summarily hauled off of him (not without kicking a few blows at him first) and restrained, and Archer was able, still blinking painfully, to rise up to a seated position. He rubbed his eyes with one hand and gazed around blearily.

"All right?" Athela asked, her terse voice unable to fully mask the look of concern on her face as Archer checked to make sure that all his limbs were still intact.

"Mostly," he assented. "Who've we got here, then?"

His attacker, recognizing that they had been subdued, had largely stopped any attempts to struggle out of the current situation. Their two Striker guards were not taking any chances, though, and were essentially sitting on top of the suspect, jaws set in identically resolute expressions.

"Let them up," Archer beckoned. The suspect's hands were bound; there was no chance of escape. The guards obeyed and backed away, and the suspect clambered upright.

Athela was shocked to see that it was a woman with a mane of curly hair not unlike her own, which was braided along the back of her head. She had tan skin, dark brown eyes, and looked to be about four or five years older than Archer. Her features were delicate, with a neat, full mouth and sharply defined lips, a broad forehead, piercingly intelligent eyes, and a wide nose that gave her face great character. At the moment, those dark eyes were glaring furiously in Archer's direction. He, to Athela's shock, broke into a smile and began to laugh.

"Of course," Archer folded his arms. "It would be you, wouldn't it?"

"I should have taken your knife and finished you off," the woman spat.

At once, realization dawned on Athela with a disquieting wave of understanding, jealousy, and irritation. "Let me guess," she said sarcastically. "You two know each other." She put a heavy, dripping emphasis on the word know.

"We go way back," Archer said lightly, not giving her an inch. "Athela, may I introduce Persefea, who was a dear friend of mine until she decided to turn her back on all of her Ashan friends and become... what was it..." he looked towards Persefea, who met his mock-jaunty tone with a glare that could freeze stone, "a lieutenant in Cira's army?"

"I needed a job," she snapped. "I needed money."

"You should have found one that didn't involve killing Ashans," Archer growled back.

"Easy for you to say," Persefea hissed. "You don't know what it was like; you've never known what it's like to be hungry. And you? How many people have you killed under their flag?" she spat, jerking her head towards Athela.

"Enough, both of you," Athela snapped, and Persefea turned her glare in Athela's direction. Athela was unmoved; she could stare daggers with the best of them. "We're taking you in for questioning," she told Persefea firmly. "I hope you agree to come quietly."

Persefea made no reply, but her mouth tightened ever so slightly as the two Striker guards checked her bonds and took her firmly by the elbows, then began marching her towards the stairs. As they went, Athela folded her arms and looked expectantly at Archer, her black eyebrows raised. Archer, who had been watching the departing backs of the guards, took one look at her face and let out a bark of a laugh.

"Save it," he said. "I can assure you that this particular love affair was nothing to get hot under the collar about."

"I am *not* hot under the collar," Athela snapped, her color rising. "I'm just disappointed by how *predictable* you are."

Archer's ironic smile never wavered. He threw up his hands in resignation and left her to jog after the others.

Athela stood alone for a few moments, the tiny windowless room around her suddenly suffocating. "Balls," she muttered finally and walked up the stairs.

CHAPTER FIVE

Persefea was presented to Tarr for questioning as soon as she arrived at headquarters. Striker guards surrounded the returning group in the entrance to the great hall, crowding and eyeing the captive with suspicion and, in some cases, outright loathing. Tarr ambled downstairs in his usual unassuming way and looked her up and down with apparent interest.

"I've heard of you," he said pleasantly.

Persefea had been looking elsewhere and jumped when he spoke to her, clearly not expecting him to address her so directly. She narrowly took in his tall, thin frame, his melancholy-looking green and brown eyes, his tousled bark-colored hair. "*You're* in charge here?" she asked. The apparent surprise in her voice was unflattering.

"Sort of," Tarr said easily, letting the jibe slide past him. "We'd like to ask you a few questions. Is that all right?" He sounded as though he was asking permission to visit her for tea.

"No," snapped Persefea.

"Sorry, then," Tarr said lightly and gestured to the guards to take her downstairs to one of the holding cells.

As they watched her go, Athela stepped in closer to Tarr and lowered her voice so as not to be heard by Archer or the other Striker guards, who were still clustering around the entrance hall, watching Persefea and talking amongst themselves in low murmurs. Archer seemed to be retelling the story of her capture to a small group of rapt listeners.

"Archer *knows* her," Athela told Tarr as he leaned in beside her, his thin arms crossed across his bony chest. "From back in Two Falls."

Tarr's eyes flicked towards her with a look of comprehension. "Ah. I see," was all he said.

"From a few years ago," Athela prodded a bit further.

Tarr rolled his eyes to the ceiling. "For heaven's sake, Athela, either sleep with him or don't, but don't get angry about the people who *did* choose to sleep with him five years ago."

"I'm not angry!" Athela growled, wondering how many times she was going to have to say it that day and noting the irony that with each protestation, her irritation and volume swelled even more.

"Fine," said Tarr.

"I thought it could be helpful information," Athela continued, grasping at dignity.

"It is," Tarr agreed. "Thank you for telling me."

Athela stood there stewing for a few minutes, looking between Persefea's retreating back and Archer's gaggle of hangers-on. "I'm going to go soap my bridle," she announced to Tarr and the world in general.

"Good idea," Tarr said comfortingly, knowing that whatever mood she was in, it would be worked out in an hour or two. "I'll let you know if we get anything out of her. I'm hoping she'll be able to give us the location of the real loyalist meeting, since it seems to be so evasive."

Athela went off grumpily, twisting her black hair up into a knot on the back of her head. Tarr wasn't too worried. Cleaning her tack had a sort of therapeutic effect on her temper, and she would be just fine by morning.

Tarr spent the better part of the first hour trying to get any snippet of information out of Persefea, but she just sat with her arms folded and a sullen look on her face, staring rigidly into the corner past Tarr's right shoulder. Tarr wasn't one to use "extreme methods" during interrogation; it was mostly a gentle exploration: a poke here, a prod there, to see how difficult it was going to be. This was going to be difficult.

Tarr stood and smiled courteously, then excused himself from the room. Laith and Ari were waiting outside for him; Ari's bland good looks somehow dimmed in his close proximity to Laith.

"Nothing," Tarr shrugged. "And I don't think intimidation or threats are going to work very well here either. She's got nothing to lose, no pressure points we can identify. Not much to go on." A sudden flash of illumination occurred to him. "You know what? Go get Archer."

"Archer?" Ari blinked, then realization dawned. "Don't tell me, they..."

"*Knew* each other? Apparently," Tarr shrugged. "We can use it to our advantage in this case."

Ari was enough of a professional not to betray his innermost thoughts, but Tarr saw that he was fighting a desperate urge to roll his eyes. *You're as bad as Athela,* Tarr thought to himself. Ari went, however, without another word, and a few minutes later, Archer joined them. He was bleary-eyed and had clearly just been awakened after catching a few minutes of much-needed sleep, but he smiled gamely when he saw Tarr.

"How can I help the cause?" he asked, stifling a yawn.

"Would you mind just going in and talking to her?" Tarr asked, indicating with his head towards the closed door of Persefea's room. "We haven't gotten much out of her."

"No surprise there," Archer shrugged and rubbed a hand over the tattoo on the back of his neck. "Not sure what help I can be, but I'll try. What do you want me to try and find out?"

"Nothing in particular," Tarr shrugged. "Go in there without an agenda. Just talk to her. See what happens."

"Sure thing, boss," Archer smiled and extended one long hand to the doorknob. He paused and turned back to the others. "She's restrained in there, correct? Not going to go flying at me as soon as I walk in?"

Tarr laughed. "You're safe, don't worry."

"That's a comfort, anyway," Archer squared his shoulders and walked into the cramped interrogation room.

Persefea's eyes narrowed as he entered, but she didn't seem too surprised to see him. Her folded arms tightened a little more.

"So they sent you," she said sarcastically, her dark eyes flashing. "Sent their best to try and coax information out of me."

"Not really," Archer shrugged, taking the seat opposite her. "Just thought I'd come myself. See how you've been. You look well."

"I look like shit, don't try that with me," she snapped curtly. "You try living in a cellar for months on end and see how *you* look."

"I did," Archer said evenly. "Well, first it was a cave, and then we were in a safehouse, but not a lot of light either way. Hasn't helped my tan very much," he extended his two arms, milky and pale in the flickering lamplight. Persefea's face remained immobile. "Not even a laugh?" Archer ventured.

"I'll laugh if something's funny," she retorted.

I do seem to have a type, he thought to himself with an inward sigh. "I haven't seen you for some time."

Persefea swiveled her gaze to bear down directly on him. "*This* is why you came here? To make small talk? To chit-chat about the old days?"

Archer shrugged equably. "Just curious. One old friend inquiring after another. We can talk, or I can leave, and my brother Tarr can come back in and keep interrogating you."

"*That* was an interrogation?" she scoffed.

Archer spread his hands. "Either way, you'll have to put up with one irritatingly inquisitive Ashan man today."

Persefea sighed, and for the first time, Archer saw her armor loosen. She looked at him again, sideways, out of the corner of one eye. "You got a new tattoo, I see," she said, jerking her jaw in the direction of his neck.

"Oh, yeah, this," Archer's hand flew up and touched the whirling black lines just below his hairline. "Got a couple of new ones since I saw you last. Some of them not for public consumption, though." He grinned cheekily.

Persefea was beginning to thaw. "They look good," she conceded. "What's that one mean, then?"

"Tarr out there, he and I performed a traditional Ashan ceremony to become brothers. Ashans tell the stories of their families in these tattoos. Some Elders' tattoos stretch all the way down their spines. Tarr has one, too," Archer told her. "Our tattoos are a bit shorter, of course. Just us."

"Him?" Persefea wrinkled her nose. "Your brother? He doesn't look like much."

Archer let out a barking laugh. "Looks, in this case, can be very deceiving."

"Have you heard from Kai and Rowan?" Persefea said more eagerly, her arms loosening slightly. She leaned forward. "No one's seen anything of them since...since the beginning of the war."

Archer nodded slowly. "Rowan was taken and held in Faridor. I saw Kai. She was working for Cira, too," he glanced down at the green tunic that Persefea wore even now. "She was doing it to save Rowan, though, so I suppose if you have to have a reason, that's a good one."

Persefea looked down at her hands. "Where are they now?" she asked, somewhat hesitantly.

"I let Kai go under the promise she would go to Faridor to kill Cira. I don't think she made it. She hasn't come back, and neither has Rowan," Archer shook his head. "But Kai was always a fighter; she knew what the price would be, and I respected her for it. Rowan... we don't know. I hope she got out. She may have left. I hope she did. Maybe they both did, and just left this place. I wouldn't blame them."

"I hope so, too," Persefea said softly, and there was a moment of silence. "Hard to imagine this is where we'd be, isn't it? All these years later?"

"It is," Archer smiled ruefully, fiddling with the edge of his sleeve. Tarr had sent him in with ulterior motives, but he couldn't help but feel a wave of genuine remorse washing over him and building up like a rock inside his chest. "I'm sorry," he said quietly. "I'm sorry for what I said earlier. I know that you wouldn't have chosen this path without your reasons. Even if I don't agree with them."

Persefea blinked, looking surprised. "Thank you."

Archer straightened slightly, releasing his sleeve and looking her directly in the face. "That's not to say that I don't wish you'd chosen differently."

She heaved a sigh and glanced away from him to the wall. To his surprise, he thought he could see the glint of a tear in her eye. "You know Archer," she said, "there's days when I wish I'd chosen a different way, too."

Archer could see that she meant it. "So that's all right, then," he said gently.

"It's far from all right," she retorted, looking squarely at him again, her eyes glassy.

"As far as I'm concerned, I mean." he continued.

Persefea looked at her hands, then blinked, and suddenly a large smile bloomed across her delicately-featured face.

"What is it?" Archer asked, smiling himself at the sudden transformation.

"Nothing, I was just remembering," she laughed to herself. "I was just remembering the last time that we were all together, here in Two Falls, and it was after you and I had broken up but before you'd taken up for the third time with Kai..."

"Don't remind me," Archer groaned.

"And we were all waiting at the Shore Inn for Rowan to get there, and she keeps not showing up, and keeps not showing up..."

Archer laughed, remembering the story and picking it up, "...And then *you* suggest that the brilliant thing to do would be to go searching for her at every single pub in town instead of just *waiting* for her at the agreed-upon location..."

"I'd had a few!" Persefea interjected, laughing. "It's not my fault that your pours are lethal."

"And so off we go, to the bloody Sword and Rose, to the Fox Den, to the Silver Crown—"

For a split second, Persefea's face blanched. The smile vanished from her face, and her eyes grew wide. It was as if he had stumbled around the corner to find her ferreting something away in a secret drawer. Archer noted this, but before he had time to wonder what had made her react that way, he instinctively continued as if he had noticed nothing at all. "—the Four Corners, and then after all of that..." he continued on with the story, and watched as Persefea quickly tried to mask her sudden reaction with a flickering smile that didn't quite reach her eyes. But as Archer continued prattling on, he could almost see the thoughts in her head: *Maybe he didn't notice. Maybe everything is fine.* By the end of the story (in which Rowan had been found asleep in Archer's room, completely unaware that anyone was looking for her), Persefea had joined back in, and Archer was confident that she believed that he had noticed nothing.

"I'm sorry about Rowan," she said finally, after their laughter had died down. "I always liked her."

"Me too," Archer said quietly.

"Do you honestly think they're still alive?"

"I don't know," he said.

"I wish none of this had ever happened," she said suddenly, and it looked as if she'd almost caught herself by surprise. Then, emboldened, she continued. "I wish I'd never joined the bloody war. I wish I'd left. I would leave today if I could, erase everything."

Archer considered. "Maybe I agree with you. Though I'd have never met *them*," he inclined his head towards the door, "if there hadn't been a war."

"You had friends before," she pointed out.

"It was different. They're different." He struggled to find something to express himself without sounding trite. "I think I've changed. For the better, I hope."

"Oh yes?" she sounded dubious.

He considered. "Perhaps. Still a bit impulsive. And a quick shot with a bow and arrow."

She studied him seriously, taking in the angular lines of his face, the familiar half-smile. "So maybe you haven't changed *that* much."

Archer let her words fall between them like a feather dropping slowly to the ground. "So," he prompted finally. "You're really not going to tell me anything?"

Persefea's guard was up again, but softer, more gentler this time. "No, I don't think so. Other lives may be lost if I say anything, you know."

"Interestingly, our policy is *not* to execute our prisoners," Archer said conversationally.

"Tell that to General Grey," Persefea shot back.

Archer opened his mouth to protest. General Grey's execution had been one of the first indications that governing Two Falls alongside the council was going to be a bumpy road. Tarr, Laith, and Athela had fought tooth and nail to oppose his execution, arguing that much could be gained from the potential knowledge he kept. But the council, newly appointed after a long Kagaian occupation, only wanted blood. Tarr had been more furious on Grey's execution day than Archer had ever seen him before. All of this was pointless to say to Persefea; from her perspective, every part of the Strikers' resistance, the council included, was as culpable as the other. He could see that their conversation had come to its logical end.

He tilted his head to the side a bit and gave her a last, lingering smile. "It was good to see you again," he stood, turning to the door and feeling her hard stare boring once again into his back.

Tarr and Ari were waiting outside the door, seated on the floor with their shoulders resting against the wall opposite. They had the air of people who had been sitting for a long time without saying much to one another.

Tarr shot gratefully to his feet and raised his eyebrows expectantly. "Well? We heard laughing."

"Reminiscing about old times," Archer assured him.

"Did you get anything?" Ari asked, looking dubious.

Archer tilted his head from side to side, indicating a "maybe." He motioned for them to follow him down the corridor, away from Persefea's room. She wasn't the type to stand against the door with her ear pressed to the wood, but he wasn't about to take any chances.

"There was one thing," Archer said in a low voice as the other two huddled around him. "Something happened when I mentioned the name The Silver Crown. You know it?"

Tarr shook his head, but Ari nodded. "A tavern in the east of the city, yes, I know it."

"When I mentioned it, she stopped dead still. I pretended like I saw nothing, but something definitely triggered a reaction in her."

"Do you think it's something to do with the loyalist meetings?" Tarr asked, feeling slightly breathless.

"Can't say. Got nothing else—no times, no possible dates, but I think it's definitely something to go on."

Tarr turned to Ari, a growing look of triumph in his eyes. "I want that tavern under surveillance. Put our very best on it. We don't want the loyalists getting the wind up that we may be on to them."

Ari nodded and turned without another word. Archer watched

him go, and once he was out of sight, Archer called, "How about a 'good job'?"

"If you're waiting to get validation from Ari," Tarr shook his head, "you're in for a long wait."

"Don't I know it," Archer muttered.

"Good job, then," Tarr clapped his brother on the back. "Go get some sleep."

"I will," Archer agreed, his golden eyes suddenly looking tired. "And Tarr..." he turned towards the direction of Persefea's room. "Go easy on her. For me. She's had a tough life. She did what she had to do to survive."

Tarr studied him for a few moments. The usual easygoing jocularity was gone, and Archer looked uncharacteristically serious. It took him by surprise, but then again, Archer tended to be particularly sentimental towards the friends from his former life. "She'll be fine," he promised.

"Good," Archer smiled, looking relieved. "Get some sleep yourself. You look like hell."

"Thanks," Tarr replied.

CHAPTER SIX

The next morning, some miles north of the city of Two Falls, a young woman awoke on the simple cot she slept on in the farmhouse kitchen. At first, she rose with a start, as if expecting to find herself somewhere else, somewhere dangerous, but as her eyes adjusted to her surroundings, her body visibly relaxed, and she rubbed her face with the back of one hand. For a few moments, she stared up at the ceiling above her head. Dark wooden beams stumped their heavy weight in a long row; here and there, the pale yellow plaster was cracking and chipping. It was a far cry from a palace, but every morning she took solace in staring up at that aging roof. Anything would have been better than opening her eyes to see the ceiling of her cell in Faridor.

It had taken months, but the color had gradually begun to seep back into her skin and cheeks like a blush spreading across a rose. Her naturally dark tan skin still looked a bit washed out and sallow after her months of imprisonment, but she no longer carried around the deathly pale gray pallor that made people look at her sideways out of the corners of their eyes when they thought she wasn't looking. Her hair was growing back, too. It would be some time before it was back to its full length—years, perhaps. She sighed and rubbed her hand over a birthmark, spreading like a violet stain over the right side of her neck.

It was warm and comfortable in the little farmhouse kitchen, there next to the stove. When she'd first been found and brought up to the house by the couple who'd discovered her, they'd kept her there beside the ever-burning fire, wrapped up in blankets as though she were a half-drowned kitten. When at last she'd regained consciousness and was able to speak, she said almost nothing about who she was or where she'd come from and had refused to move into the smaller guest room that the couple offered. The compact cot beside the stove had become a permanent fixture in the farmhouse kitchen. So adamant was she not to reveal any detail about herself, no matter how insignificant, that gradually the couple had stopped asking, assuming, perhaps, that she'd suffered a loss of memory.

The truth, of course, was that Rowan had forgotten nothing. She remembered every excruciating second of her imprisonment in the dungeons of Faridor, every line in the ceiling, the number of stones on the floor, the cold feeling of it under her bare feet. And she remembered the night of her rescue, so strange and disorienting as to be a dream, when her sister had appeared suddenly at the door in the middle of the night, pulled her out, and told her to run as fast as she could. How they'd come to an open window, the freezing winter air roiling like the sea beneath them, and she remembered standing at the precipice, looking down at the water, thinking to herself *I can't go back. Death is preferable to life in this prison.* And she jumped.

The wind had whistled past her as she hurtled through the air, the freezing cold bringing a stinging clarity to her cheeks. She had only time to brace herself for impact before she plunged into the water, limbs tugged in every direction by the force of the waves. Any relief she felt at not being dashed to bits on the jagged rocks surrounding the island had quickly evaporated as she was battered to and fro by a seemingly ceaseless torrent of water bent on crushing her down to the sea bottom. And the cold—the cold like a thousand jagged, painful needles pricking every inch of her skin, burrowing under, breaking into fractals of ice within her chest.

For a moment she'd foundered, almost allowing the water to suck her under, but something, some deep stirring of a will to live, galvanized her into action. As the dark night roared ahead and the sea swept her from side to side, she'd oriented her body in the direction of the crashing waves. *Land*, she thought. *I'm not far. The shore's not far. The waves will carry me to shore.*

She was too weak and emaciated to swim properly, but she let her body go limp and slowly felt herself being picked up by the swell of a wave as if she were coasting on the back of an enormous hand. Slowly, too slowly, she inched her way towards the shore, taking gasping breaths where she could and fluttering her arms and feet in an almost comical approximation of swimming.

At last, she'd felt a great surge beneath her that seemed to pick her up by her toes and carry her head over heels, toppling like a pin through the water. And a moment later, she felt her feet rippling as the wake of the enormous wave caught them and sucked her under, then plunged her headfirst onto the sandy shore.

Her mouth and nose filled with water and sand, but something in her registered that it was land, and with all her might, she scrambled from the grip of the sea as it tried to pull her back into the breaking surf. Her thin fingers clawed at handfuls of rounded, polished rock, scattering them behind her as she desperately made her way as far away from the waves as she could. For a moment or two, she had lain there, starting to shiver as she gulped down mouthfuls of freezing air, exhausted but alive.

They'll come after me, she thought suddenly, and again, that throbbing, inescapable will to live had sparked in the back of her mind, forcing her frail arms and legs to move. She grappled her way to her hands and knees, the waves shushing around her ankles, and, as unsteady as a newborn colt, rose to her shaking legs and looked down the shore. Except for a few flickering lights just above her on the bridge, it didn't seem as though the alarm had been raised yet. She turned and stared through the inky black night down to the south. *They'll expect me to return to Two Falls*, she'd thought to herself. *I'm not going to outrun soldiers on horseback.*

But the Strikers are in Two Falls, another part of her reasoned. *They can help. Archer can help.*

They have done nothing for me. No one has come, she thought, and a steely resolve closed about her heart. *I have to save myself.*

One shaking hand reached up to brush a piece of sand from her eye, and she could feel small, spiky bits of hair around her forehead that had frozen solid. Either way, she didn't have much time. She turned north, away from Two Falls, and began to hobble as fast as she could.

She skirted beneath the dark, looming shadow of the bridge that connected Faridor to the mainland. Still no shouts, no voices. She still had time. She felt as though she had never before exerted herself as hard as this, but at the same time, she was all too aware that her progress was dangerously slow. As she went, stumbling every few feet over a rock or a trailing piece of slippery, icy seaweed, she chanced a look over her shoulder and could see torches flashing atop the bridge. The alarm was sounded. She hoped that the sea would wash away any remaining scent she had left on shore so that the dogs couldn't pick up her trace. She changed her course slightly to run near the surf, where the waves would wash away her footprints.

She rounded a point, and the fortress disappeared from sight, but even then, she didn't stop running. With every scrabbling footfall, she anticipated the sound of yells right behind her, the sound of horse hooves, of dogs. Her breath was coming in heaving, haggard gasps, but the one positive of her flight was that the exertion kept her warm; it kept her from falling asleep and slipping senselessly into the cold night.

At last, she felt she could go no further, and she stumbled to a halt, her hands resting on her bony knees and her head hanging down between her shoulders. A short ways up ahead, the shore began to taper up and up into a steep cliff face, but just at the base of where the cliff began to rise, she could see a few dark oblong shapes, almost like large animals beached on the sand. She forced herself forward, and as they slowly grew bigger, she could see that they were boats—fishing boats, moored up out of the reach of the waves. She drew up to the first one. For a moment, she glanced around. Where there were boats, there must be people, and perhaps those people would have pity and take her in. Perhaps, though, they were Kagaian loyalists and would turn her over to Cira. She didn't want to take that chance.

She peered into the bottom of the first boat. It was deep and broad, with a flat bottom arrayed with carefully folded nets and rope. It all looked tidy and well-kept. *I'll just sleep here for the night*, she thought desperately. *I'll leave as soon as the sun rises, before anyone comes out here and finds me.* Weak from her exertion and shivering from the cold, she crawled into the base of the boat. The sides of the small vessel shielded her from the wind, and she fashioned a makeshift blanket by draping all the netting and rope over her body and tucking her head in and out of the weather. And there, curled in the bottom of the boat, she fell asleep.

But she did not wake up at sunrise. She was so exhausted that she slept right through mid-morning.

Near midday, a farmer came down from his cottage to check on the state of things after the rough night before, and to his everlasting shock, he found her. Her skin and lips were as blue and gray as the sea itself, and she was curled like a child in the bottom of the boat. He was even more astonished to find that somehow she was still alive.

For the following weeks, she lay wrapped in blankets, huddled up next to the stove in the homey kitchen, safely out of the way of the cold wind outside. At first, she could only eat broth, which was painstakingly spooned down her throat, one drop at a time. Gradually, her strength returned, and the house around her swam ever more clearly into focus. For the first time in a long time, Rowan felt as though she might actually survive.

The only disruption to her recovery came a few days after she'd first been found. She'd been fast asleep, then found herself being swaddled and carried upstairs to the guest room. There, she was laid in the bottom of a trunk next to a bed, told to stay very quiet, and felt objects being piled on top of her before the trunk closed with a loud thump. Through the wood in the floor, Rowan could hear the sounds of footsteps and voices. The clanking of heavy boots echoed throughout the cottage for over an hour (she could hear them come up next to the trunk in which she lay hidden and even felt the creak of the trunk door opening a crack) before they left. She was still slightly delirious, and perhaps it was this that kept her from panicking about being found. But after the soldiers left, she was brought down, and they were troubled no more. The soldiers had given no reason for their search, but it was easy to guess what they were looking for.

Rowan found herself wondering in the weeks that followed why the farmer and his wife had gone to such lengths to protect her, seemingly at such risk to themselves. It would have been plainly obvious to them that she was a captive escaped from Faridor, and there could have been very little benefit to them to harbor her. But as Rowan got to know the couple better, she could understand perhaps a bit more why they had made the choice to keep her.

The farmer and his wife were named Mr. and Mrs. Ulster. Their farm was small, but they were able to produce a good amount of crops from their fields and milk from their herd of hardy little windblown cows. After the war had broken out, they'd been ordered to supply produce solely to Faridor rather than selling it in Two Falls, as they had done for years. These orders effectively set them against Kagai, as they lost considerable profit selling only to the fortress. Furthermore, they had no love for the intolerances that Kagai preached, so though it was a great risk for them and their livelihoods, there had been barely any discussion between them as to what they would do with Rowan after she'd been found.

For the first few days after Rowan's arrival, the couple had waited on tenterhooks for word of an escaped prisoner to circulate around the clifftop community. But to their surprise, no such notice was sent. Eventually, they reasoned that, rather than risk Faridor's reputation as an impregnable fortress from which there was no escape, the Kagaians had inadvertently aided Rowan by suppressing any public word of her flight. Once the immediate danger had passed and the Kagaians had made their search, Mrs. Ulster found it easy to explain away Rowan's sudden appearance on the farm. To any visitors, she simply said that the girl was her niece, the daughter of her sister, who had lived near the Meadows and had fallen on hard times and been sent there to straighten herself out. No one who chanced to look at the girl in those first few weeks after her rescue could fail to notice the haunted look in her eyes and her haggard, unnaturally thin frame, so the story had been accepted without question by all the neighbors and tradespeople who came to visit.

Once Rowan was strong enough, she'd followed Mrs. Ulster out to the garden and had begun helping her tend to the plants. It was very different than any work Rowan had done before in her life, and she found that she took to it rather well. She enjoyed being out in the open air, the wind through her short hair, tending to the winter crops, and looking down along the rolling, lush hills to the sea below. Off in the distance she could see Faridor, but she liked having it there, liked having the reminder that she should never get too complacent, never forget that the enemy was close at hand.

As a rule, Rowan rarely spoke to her rescuers, but this didn't seem to bother the couple very much. They could tell that she had much on her mind and a good many things that she still seemed to be grappling with. Sometimes, Mrs. Ulster would stand at the kitchen window and watch Rowan as she crouched down among the plants in the field, wrapped in a thick woolen shawl, her dark birthmark peeking over the top of her scarf, short black hair sticking wispily out over her forehead, nimble fingers plucking out any weeds that might be crowding the potatoes or the large clusters of winter greens that were growing so plentifully there. She wondered what the girl must be thinking about, and more often than not, she found herself wondering how a weakened slip of a thing like that could possibly have made it out of the fortress alive. She was the only one to do so successfully, as far as Mrs. Ulster knew.

In reality, Rowan's mind often wandered away to where she would go next. The couple was kind to her, and she had made a comfortable home there, but it was only temporary. Faridor was not far off, and sooner than later, the neighbors would start asking more questions—prying questions—about where she'd come from. She thought vaguely that she would try to return to the forest to seek out her Ashan mother's tribe, though she was unsure of how well she would be welcomed amongst them. While the levels of tolerance and acceptance varied from tribe to tribe, half-Ashans weren't always afforded the same rights and privileges as full-blooded Ashans. Her sister Kai had had more interactions with the tribe than she. She swallowed, trying to put Kai from her mind.

Sometimes, she wondered about the Strikers and why they had left her for dead. She and Archer had loved each other once; surely, he would have at least *tried* to get her out. But perhaps he didn't even know she was there. Perhaps no one did. This thought, coupled with her uncertainty about trying to make a new life among the Ashans in the forest, left her feeling considerably alone, and she was given to falling into long bouts of melancholy, staring out over the pastures at the horizon.

Once a week, the farmer would drive the ready crops and dairy products to Faridor and would return over the bumpy hillside path, large cart rattling over the stones, the green grass rippling back and forth like a piece of fabric being shaken in the breeze. Rowan would watch with some trepidation, imagining that soon she would see a few specks in the distance slowly crystallizing into the forms of soldiers on horseback, but the days passed, and none ever came. Against her better judgment, Rowan felt herself beginning to relax ever so slightly. The scant handful of neighbors, when they visited, gawked at her, so she kept as out of the way as she could without appearing too suspicious. There must be talk among them, but such was the impugnable reputation of her hosts that much of the gossip died down before long, and whether the Ulsters were actively dissuading them or not, the visits grew less frequent. Even as she grew to appreciate her new life on the farm, it was only a matter of time before she'd have to leave. Whispers, however small, still had a chance of making it back to Faridor.

It was on this thought Rowan dwelled as she stood on the edge of the cliff overlooking the ocean, the wind bitingly cold through the wrap she had drawn around her shoulders. She dropped a stone into the water and imagined the ripples spreading all the way south until they reached the rocks of the distant island, standing like a black smudge against the pearly sky.

CHAPTER SEVEN

A Striker lookout waited in the small empty flat opposite the Silver Crown tavern. He stretched and rolled his neck from side to side and settled down farther into his seat on the floor. He didn't hear someone come stealing up behind him, and nearly jumped out of his skin when there was a light touch on his shoulder.

"Sorry," Laith apologized, setting down a small satchel and pulling back the black hood from his golden head. "Didn't mean to startle you."

"Quite all right," the sentry replied, trying to sound nonchalant instead of audibly panting with fear. "Shift's up already?"

Laith gave a quiet nod and knelt next to him, peering out through the small slit in the curtains that afforded them a view of the pub opposite.

"Nothing yet," the sentry volunteered without being asked. He had to try hard not to stare at Laith as the prince peered through the window, a slant of the dimming sunset light throwing his aristocratic profile into sharp relief. Being next to someone so famous was an unusual thrill, and he hoped Laith could see that he was taking his role very seriously.

"Not to worry," Laith said finally, after his dark eyes had finished scanning the street outside. "Well done, I'll take over. Get some rest."

"Thank you," the sentry said gratefully, and got in one final sidelong gawk before he clambered to his feet and left the room.

Laith settled in, leaning his shoulder against the wall and keeping an eye on the street below. He didn't mind keeping watch. Ostensibly, someone of his standing in the Striker forces would have "better things" that they could be doing with their time, but he liked the peace and solitude that the hours on watch afforded him. He was grateful to Tarr, too, for allowing him to stand one shift at watch every day. Though they hadn't spoken about it, he got the feeling that Tarr understood why he liked to be alone, in that all-seeing, all-knowing Tarr way of his.

Laith sat quietly at the window as the hours wore on, the light turning from brilliantly burning hues of pink and gold to grays, blues, and lilac, spilling from the windows and down onto the streets. The days of surveillance that the Strikers had conducted over the tavern had so far yielded very little, but it was early days yet, and there was always a chance that if they were patient, they could hit upon a goldmine. Tarr and Archer had seemed reasonably certain that the Silver Crown had something to do with the Kagaian loyalist meetings, though Tarr, tight-lipped as ever, hadn't provided too many additional details about how he'd come by the information.

Below him, Laith watched the townspeople scurry by, heading home after work to their hearths and families after work for a meal and to tuck in for the night. Years ago, he might have entertained himself by studying them and wondering who they were and where they were going, perhaps even inventing backstories for them, but no more. He watched them come and go dispassionately, as if they were members of a completely different species whose cares and habits had nothing to do with him.

As he sat, he watched people enter and leave the Silver Crown. It was the normal stream of after-work customers, who laughed and chatted together as they approached the door and certainly didn't seem as though they were up to any furtive or illicit dealings.

But then, at last, his interest was piqued, and he sat up straighter. Below on the street, he thought he saw someone he recognized: a woman in her fifties with curly brown hair that fell to a bob on her shoulders. Unless Laith was very much mistaken, he was sure that she had been one of a handful of people accused of smuggling arms to Kagaian loyalists just after the Strikers had taken back the city. She had vehemently denied her involvement and had subsequently been let off due to lack of evidence, but Tarr had instructed the others to keep an eye on her. And here she was. It could easily be a coincidence, Laith thought.

Or perhaps not.

For a few moments, he debated the best course of action. He could easily leave his post and head back to the headquarters to summon backup. Or he could simply walk across and do some investigation himself. The pub was crowded at this time of day; it would be easy for him to slip in and out without being noticed. If all seemed well, he'd resume his surveillance.

His mind made up, he sat up and buckled his sword around his hips and strapped the sheath against his leg so that it would lie flat beneath his cloak. There was no reason to bring more attention to himself than was necessary.

A few moments later, he was on the stoop below, the black hood drawn up over his head and a scarf tucked over his nose and mouth. He crossed the street in a few broad strides and sidled up to the door, pressing against it with one shoulder as he entered.

The light was dim inside, and it took him a moment to adjust. A warm, cozy glow emanated from the large fireplace at the head of the room, an oversized silver crown placed in the center of the mantle. Laith stood to one side and scanned the room, trying to look as though he were searching out a person he was there to meet. He only attracted one or two glances from the occupants of the nearest table as the door swung shut behind him.

The pub was bustling, to be sure, but there was something strangely *off* about the surroundings. Laith couldn't quite put his finger on it. The longer he stood there, the more he began to feel as though he'd made a terrible mistake by coming in.

The entrance to the pub was framed by a half-wall that formed a short passageway into the large main room. There was very little space for Laith to hide, and he realized that he would have to sit down soon, or he would start to attract attention. He picked the wall nearest him, where a long bench ran behind a few tables and, with a nod, squeezed in beside a table full of men, who had been steadily conversing in low voices. As he sat, the men all sent him sidelong glares and then met each others' eyes as if they had all tacitly agreed to pause the conversation until the intruder left.

Laith's keen, dark gaze continued to press for some explanation, some reason for his feeling of unease. Aware that the men beside him were staring at him, he leaned over and pretended to fiddle with the buckle of his boot while he covertly glanced up and studied the room more closely.

Outwardly, nothing was amiss. There were people at the bar, people at tables, people talking. But something was absent. The usual jovial, letting-off-steam atmosphere of the pubs he had been to before was missing. The room was suffused with a heavy, pressing *intensity*—there was no other word for it. There were a few tables clearly patronized with oblivious townsfolk, telling jokes and draining tankards, but the vast majority of tables were filled with people hunched over their drinks and talking in low voices.

Laith's eyes narrowed even more, intrigued—even though he was aware that the group at the table next to him was beginning to eye him with greater and greater suspicion. He hadn't yet pulled back his hood or pulled down the scarf half-covering his face.

Then, at last, he saw. A grim-looking barmaid was delivering drinks, and with every drink, she set down a simple round paper coaster. Occasionally, the drink would be lifted, and the coaster would be slowly, casually, flipped over in the recipient's fingers as if there was something written beneath. Then the barmaid would be summoned to a different table, and in her willing hand, the paper coasters would silently travel from table to table.

With a lurch, Laith realized that he hadn't just found a single Kagaian loyalist, or indeed a table of them. What he had stumbled into was the *entire* Kagaian loyalist meeting being played out in full view, a covert network of communication humming before him. And he suddenly realized what a fool he had been to walk into such a dangerous nest with absolutely no protection or backup. As confident as he was in his own ability to handle himself in an even fight, the current odds were stacked against him at least sixty to one. He had to get out.

He leaned up from fiddling with his boot and made an exaggerated show of placing his hands over his chest and at his hip as if looking for a money bag that he had forgotten elsewhere. He heaved a sigh (feeling very much like an amateur actor putting on a show for the tables beside him) and rose to his feet, muttering under his breath as he stood. He gave a curt nod to the table watching him and strode out of the pub, trying not to walk too fast.

It was remarkable, he thought, how much the night had seemed to dim, even during the few short minutes that he was inside the Silver Crown. He turned right outside the door and began to walk, trying to look unruffled and unhurried as he went, keeping his ears keenly attuned behind him to try and pick up on whether or not anyone had decided to try and follow him.

For a moment, he thought he had gotten away with it and almost let himself relax, thinking how fortunate it was that the desperate individuals gathering in the pub would overlook a stranger who entered, hooded and veiled, and left only a few minutes later after an almost comical pantomime performance. Lucky it was, too, that they had missed seeing the sword at his hip.

And then he heard the footsteps behind him. Sharp, insistent, and slowly growing closer to him.

A few yards ahead of him, a window swung open, and a woman shook some dust out of a dishrag into the air of the street. In the reflection of the glass, Laith could see that behind him was a group of at least ten individuals bearing down on him—the loyalists at the table beside him had clearly been suspicious enough to call in reinforcements. Laith again cursed himself for his stupidity, for the sheer hubris of blithely walking straight into the enemy's nest as he had just done. It was something a headstrong green recruit would do to show off, not someone with as much experience as he.

As Laith contemplated his options, he saw a new group turn a corner up ahead and walk straight for him. A high alert must have gone out around the Silver Crown the moment that he set foot outside. This new group would have had to run to get up, around, and ahead of him as they just had.

Laith considered, and his hand slid down under his cloak to his sword. Engaging in an open brawl in the middle of the street was one option, but he was still not terribly delighted with his odds, especially with this new oncoming group in play. Laith wagered that they would try to subdue and take him away, possibly even all the way to Faridor as a prize for Cira, if they could manage it without killing him. He didn't much like that option, either.

The safety of the Striker headquarters lay to his left, but all roads in that direction were blocked by the advancing mob of loyalists. There was nothing for it. He'd have to run and try to lose them as best he could before doubling back to the headquarters.

Without warning, he dodged to his right down a narrow passage that led between the two buildings beside him. He heard a shout go up from one of the groups and knew without looking that they had given chase. The street was barely wide enough for him to squeeze down, but he still managed to unbuckle the sword from his leg and swing it up to lay across his back, re-fastening the hilt across his chest. Once his leg had been freed from its cumbersome burden, his pace increased dramatically.

He guessed that some of the loyalists would try to catch him again at the end of the alley, so he flew like a black streak up to a heavily laden wooden trellis framing the wall of an upcoming building. Like a cat, he scaled it and grimly held on as he felt a hand swipe at his foot from down below. He kicked out and heaved himself up onto a red tiled roof, slipping a bit before clambering up to his feet at the peak.

He barely had time to gather himself as he stood on the ridgepole of the apartment building. Behind him and below, the loyalists were beginning to scale the trellis after him, shouting to each other as they drew closer. He dropped to a crouch and slid semi-gracefully down the opposite side of the slanting roof. With a small hop, he cleared the edge, then caught himself with both hands on the stone gutter just beneath the eaves. He heard a startled scream below him as his feet struck against the side of the stone building, but it sounded more like an onlooker than one of the loyalists pursuing him.

He clambered sideways like a large black spider, using the gutter as his handhold, balancing his toes against the side of the wall below to keep himself steady. At last, he reached a vertical drainpipe that ran down the corner where two of the walls of the building joined and, with some trepidation, switched over his handhold and slid down.

His touchdown was light enough to only attract a few small gasps from those closest to him; by this point, the light had dimmed almost completely into night, and, cloaked in black as he was, he was able to blend into the shadows of the street. He glanced this way and that, then up to the roof, where he could see a few of the loyalists making their way trepidatiously down the same way he had come.

Laith took to his feet again and ran along the larger main street that lay ahead. The torches were being lit along the length of the road; as he went, he saw a flame above flicker and then catch, casting sudden light onto a group of five figures bearing towards him with unmistakable intensity. Laith cursed and dove to his left, heading down another long, narrow street that, after about thirty seconds, ended in a T shape, one path to his left, one path to his right. As he stopped, he could hear the footsteps drawing closer behind him.

Desperately, Laith cast about himself for some way out. He had gone further west than he'd intended and was being driven farther and farther from the safety of the Strikers' headquarters. He'd have to find somewhere to hide, and fast.

To his left, at the end of another long, dark alleyway, there glowed a single orange window, and in the night air he could hear the clink of glasses and the chatter of voices. There were no other options. He bolted towards it and slipped into the back of the building.

The pub within was noisy and crowded, and a thick haze of smoke hung low in the room. A few of the patrons glanced at him curiously as he came in, but Laith ducked his head and moved quickly. His pursuers couldn't be far behind.

As he went, he realized that he may have made another error in choosing this route of escape—the pub was much larger than he had anticipated and seemed to take up the floor of the entire building; it had likely been a private residence before being converted into a bar. The interconnecting rooms were like a maze, less a single large gathering place than a web of small hubs. He walked quickly, trying not to look suspicious as he pushed gently past patrons sitting and standing in clusters throughout the rooms, conscious all the while of the precious seconds he was losing as he tried to find a way out.

A pretty, curvy barmaid was polishing a glass at the bar and shot him a curious look as he glanced over his shoulder and tugged down the scarf that had so far covered his nose and mouth. It seemed in the rooms behind him that there were sudden flurries of erratic motion and the sounds of scuffling, which meant that he hadn't long before the loyalists caught up. And this was no place to start a fight. He was bound to be taken. *Where was the exit?*

He swung back around and started right, only to realize that he had already been through that room. Suddenly, he felt a warm hand slip into his palm, and there was a gentle tug at his arm. He started and turned. It was the barmaid.

"Come this way," she said urgently and pulled him to the left. They wove between chattering patrons, ducking a cloud of smoke as a woman blew it out the side of her mouth. The barmaid led him to a small alcove near where two men were talking in deep conversation; their heads bent low over their pints of ale.

Slightly bewildered, Laith glanced around for an exit and realized there wasn't any. He opened his mouth to speak, but the barmaid cut him off.

"Sit," she ordered and pushed him into a seat back in the corner of the alcove. She tugged back his hood and pulled his cloak over his shoulder so that it masked his sword more fully from view. She glanced behind her, and she must have seen something, for she whipped back around, and, much to Laith's surprise, she nudged his shoulders back against the wall and climbed softly into his lap. Laith barely had time to register this before her cheek was against his. "Put your hands on my waist," she said in a low voice in his ear.

Mind racing in a number of different bewildering directions, Laith raised his arms from his side and did as she ordered, his fingers feeling curiously numb and stiff as he finally understood the ruse she was attempting to pull on his pursuers. He ducked his head beneath her shoulder, and a strand of her brown hair fell against his ear. With one eye, he peeked up and glanced into the room. A pack of five loyalists, the ones who had been closest upon him, charged into the room. They pushed some of the patrons roughly to the side, which aroused some expletives and protestations, but all quickly subsided, and one of the riders turned in their direction. Laith ducked his head again and raised one hand to the young woman's head, threading his hands through her hair to give the full effect. A few moments later, he raised his head again, and the loyalists were gone.

He breathed a long sigh of relief, and then, as if in slow motion, he suddenly became aware of the young woman sitting in his lap, her smooth hair between his fingers, her breath against his cheek, the warmth of her body so near his. All at once, he felt as though he had been sitting in the cold for a long, long time. A curious feeling washed over him, an uncontrollable need to weep. He wasn't sure he could fight it, so he gently pushed her back and tried to avoid making eye contact. She made no motion to get up, though. It seemed rude for him to eject her from his lap, so after a moment or two, he was forced to meet her gaze, really looking at her for the first time.

She had a rectangular face and square jaw that were attractively offset by round, feminine features, dark olive skin, and a smattering of freckles across her nose. She had long chestnut hair that she wore tumbling down over one shoulder. Her eyes were hazel and framed by long lashes, but there was a look in them—Laith couldn't quite place it. She had a preternaturally solemn expression, an innate gravity that told him that she had seen the face of war and that it had not been kind to her. But even as she regarded him, perched still on his lap without even a trace of coy flirtation on her face, he became uncomfortably aware again of her nearness, of her weight, the gentle, soft curves of her body against him. He realized his hand was still resting instinctively against the small of her waist, and he gave a start, flexed his hand, and lowered it to rest tentatively on her knee.

"Quick thinking," he managed to say, his eyes darting from her face to the floor. He wished she would look away. "Thank you."

In response, she tilted her head slightly to the side and fixed him with a quizzical expression. Unwillingly, he met her eyes again. Slowly, she leaned in and kissed him softly on the lips, warm and sweet. At the instant that they touched, Laith again felt a tightening up in his chest and his throat, almost like a sob that was afraid to escape him. She pulled back and fixed him again with that same curious expression, but this time, Laith couldn't look up at her face. He kept his gaze squarely on the toe of her boot, protruding slightly from beneath her dress.

"Why'd you do that?" he asked, fighting to keep the cry from coming out.

"You looked like you needed it," she said. She wasn't making fun of him; he could hear it in her voice.

It seemed as though an eternity had elapsed in the time that they'd sat there, but it couldn't have been longer than thirty seconds or so. Regardless, the coast was bound to be clear, and if he was able to exercise at least some modicum of caution, he shouldn't have any trouble returning to the headquarters.

"You have to go," she said, as if she'd read his thoughts. "Is it safe now?"

"Yes," he nodded, feeling as winded and disoriented as if she'd clubbed him in the head. The weight in his lap shifted, and she rose to her feet. Her warmth departed, leaving him in the cold.

CHAPTER EIGHT

Since the night of Cira's celebration, Rane and Cicada had made infuriatingly little progress in uncovering any information that would lead them to discover what her secret weapon was. No new codes were broken, no new guards were bribed; the fortress, with its maze of hallways and nooks and secret passageways, remained as impenetrable as ever. Rane was not what anyone would call a hotheaded person, but even she was feeling the strain of their mounting frustration. Each day ticked past, bringing with it hours and hours of seemingly interminable chores: mopping out the kitchens, cleaning antechambers, scrubbing, waiting, watching. Without the excitement of new information or a new objective, their hours of drudgery had begun to feel like just that.

So Rane was not expecting it when Cicada came excitedly into their shared dormitory room while she was eating her late lunch one afternoon. Rane had spent the morning wiping down the frames of portraits in one of the long gallery halls. Other than the fact that she'd discovered the entrance to a hidden linen closet (behind the portrait of a woman waving the severed head of a conquered foe), the morning had been largely uneventful. Even the hidden closet wasn't anything too interesting. Lord Kagai, when he'd constructed the fortress, clearly had been in the late stages of some sort of mania or madness and had tucked away hidden rooms left and right. The passageways of the towers and dungeons twisted into themselves like the spiralings of an unhinged mind.

Rane was tucked up on her cot with her legs folded beneath her, chomping away at a piece of bread and hunk of cheese, when Cicada hurriedly came in and shut the door behind her. The woman's thin, vulpine face was bright, and her eyes had that sharp, triumphant look that told Rane she had important news to share. Rane dropped the bread onto her plate and brushed her hands against each other to clear off any crumbs so that she'd be ready to sign back to her friend.

"I think I may have found something," Cicada said excitedly, perching at the end of the bed, her hands flying.

"Yes? Go on!" Rane urged.

"Since the coronation anniversary, I've been systematically going through each and every hallway and making note of the guard assignments. I figured that if there was something that Cira truly wanted to protect, she would want to keep it secret and safe while still not drawing too much attention to it."

Rane had to appreciate her friend's dedication. The fortress was vast enough that going systematically through it one hallway at a time would take weeks if not months, and the mere thought of it made her ill.

"And I may have found something," Cicada said. "I figured that there has to be some sort of code room, someplace where Cira has her codewriters and codebreakers working. I've already ruled out the dungeons."

Rane nodded. Cicada often worked shifts down in the dungeons, cleaning and maintaining the processing room where new prisoners were brought after their capture. Because she was deaf, Cicada was frequently assigned to care for parts of the fortress where security was at a high level, as it was assumed that she wouldn't overhear anything of value or note. The sheer level of stupidity that went into this underestimation and how dearly it had cost Cira and her troops never failed to make Rane smile to herself. Twice a week, Cicada would be down in the dungeons, where her quick thinking and nimble fingers had given them invaluable information about the location of Striker prisoners and new campaigns Cira was about to undertake. But as far as their current mission of uncovering the location and description of Cira's weapon, the dungeons had been sadly fruitless.

Cicada took a deep breath to clear her thoughts, and then her hands began moving again.

"Well, there's one hallway in particular that I've had my eye on. It's the only one that I've seen where there are always at least two guards patrolling, but they're set up so as not to draw attention to themselves. One guard is at each end of the hall, and there's always at least one of them in view at all times."

Rane nodded, feeling the familiar sensation of a growing intensity and excitement in her stomach. *There's a target*, she thought. *We have a target.*

Cicada continued: "So I was in that hallway cleaning the floors around lunchtime today." (This didn't surprise Rane in the slightest; Cicada was so overlooked that she was able to pretty much go and set up her cleaning anywhere she liked without being questioned about it.) "One of the maids came around the corner with a tray of food. The minute she saw me, she stopped and acted as though she'd turned down the wrong hallway, but I'm sure she hadn't. A minute later, one of the guards from that end came up to me and directed me to work somewhere else. And so I packed up and left, and as I'm leaving, back around comes the maid carrying the lunch tray, with her nose in the air and avoiding looking at me."

"Did you see which room she went into?" Rane signed eagerly.

Cicada shook her head. "No. The guard was watching me too closely. I had to leave for the time being. But there's something going on in that hall, I'm sure of it. I was hanging around later on the upper stairwell and saw the same maid come back down the hallway carrying an empty tray."

Rane processed this for a few moments. Cicada's agile hands twisted together a few times as she stared expectantly at Rane. "If it is the code room, the cipher we need could just be waiting there for us," she said. "Just waiting."

Rane grinned at her friend, and Cicada couldn't help but grin back. It was one of the things that Rane had grown to love most about Cicada: the two of them shared an unabashed love of the chase. Give them a quarry to pursue, and the two of them would hunt it down like bloodhounds.

"There's a delegation from Vireg arriving next week," Cicada reminded her. "The kitchens will be short-staffed. In that kind of confusion and shuffle, it might be just the right opportunity for us."

"You're right," Rane replied, her mind already whirring to put the pieces of a plan into place. "What time was the lunch delivered?"

"One o'clock."

"What did the maid look like? Which one was she?"

"Short girl, with shoulder-length hair, usually in a pink bow."

"I know the one." Rane frowned, considering.

"If I can get into that code room, I can get us the cipher," Cicada said. She wasn't boasting. Cicada's skills at sleight of hand were formidable.

"It's getting you in that's the problem," Rane pointed out. "There could be some sort of code or password. We have to be careful. We're going to have to be utterly above suspicion. If we are in a room, it's going to be because we were ordered to be there. If we're carrying a tray, it's because someone told us to do so. Any suspicions will need to be immediately explained away, and we'll need to have witnesses to corroborate."

Cicada was silent for a moment and nodded. "They'll never assign me," she said grudgingly. "The cook and the housekeeper know who I am. They know there would be no reason for me to be down in the kitchens for service. I'm cleaning staff only."

"But the guards in that hallway wouldn't know that," Rane mused. "And the cook and housekeeper don't know me as well by sight. I'm all but invisible."

"What are you thinking? We trade places?" Cicada suggested.

Rane pondered their options for a moment. It was highly risky, even by their elevated standards. "I don't like not knowing what's inside the door of that room," she said.

"Just get me inside," Cicada told her flatly. "I can handle it."

"It's likely that we'll have only this one chance to get our hands on those ciphers if they're in there," Rane reminded her. "And it's sure to be execution for us both if we're caught."

This was another thing that Rane loved about Cicada: the young woman digested what Rane had said, considered the warning she had made, then flicked a small crumb off of her knee and shrugged as if the prospect of torture and certain death was not much of a concern.

"We'd better start planning, then."

The delegation from Vireg arrived the next week with a great deal of ado. There were three delegates, and with them, they each brought servants and traveling staff and mountains of luggage, which were unloaded from a long, sleek boat that docked at the base of Faridor's rocky island. The guests were ferried immediately to the mainland, back across the bridge, and up to their rooms (which had been prepared the day before by Rane and Cicada, who had then been told unequivocally that they were not to be seen by a single soul during the guests' stay.)

Still, for the sake of collecting relevant information, Rane had managed to steal a glimpse of the newcomers as they were conducted through Faridor's twisting hallways up to the guests' quarters. They were so heavily wrapped up against the cold in layers of heavy blankets and furs that Rane could really only see a nose or a strip of cheek here and there. The resplendent way in which the heavily-swathed entourage had swept through the palace (even though they were only there for a day or two of meetings) and the high degree of stress under which the entire household staff was operating all combined into a dizzying air of over-the-top theatricality that had Rane constantly on the verge of laughter. She had to duck her head and bite her lip every time she was issued an order or told to leave a room; the housekeeper, the butler, and all the heads of staff, usually so impassive and stern, seemed to be afflicted by a condition that raised the octaves of their speaking voices by about three levels.

But she and Cicada had a mission that was anything but a laughing matter. The entire thing was highly dangerous, and in her written reports back to Tarr, Rane had tactfully omitted some of the details of what they were going to attempt, as she wasn't sure Tarr would entirely approve of the risks they were taking, especially since he wasn't there to directly oversee and exert some control over the operation himself.

The first day of meetings commenced in the morning, and while the envoys were out, Rane and Cicada filled the time making beds, collecting dirty linens, and stoking the fires to make sure that the rooms were warm when their occupants returned. They were watched at all times by servants who had accompanied the visitors from Vireg. In each room, a servant would stand silently in a corner of the room while Rane or Cicada worked their way across. It was slightly off-putting to have to go about one's duties under the narrowed eye of a stranger standing like a rock with their arms folded imposingly across their chest. Rane surmised that the servants had been given explicit orders to make sure that none of Faridor's waitstaff made off with any goods or valuables. It was a shame, really; Rane would have liked to talk to the other servants, to see if they understood the Common language, and to learn more about their desert city, but she got the sense that any attempt at fraternization would be met with suspicion and alarm.

Finally, Rane and Cicada finished their chores and closed the door of the last guest apartment. They met one another's eyes only briefly, and Cicada gave Rane the tiniest of nods and a flicker of a smile. Rane's arms were filled with a basket of laundry; she tossed back a lock of auburn hair that had fallen out from beneath her hood and gave Cicada a wink. She turned and headed down to the laundry rooms, which were located on a lower level of the fortress next to the kitchens.

The laundry room smelled of heat and fabric, static and soap, and was always oppressively humid. Rane deposited her bundle next to a steaming cauldron of water, which was manned by a large woman with an unsmiling face and massively developed forearms. Rane bobbed a curtsy and headed over to the kitchens.

The kitchens, day or night, were almost always a hum of activity, and today it was especially so. The room was enormous, wide and open and low-ceilinged, with a long row of narrow windows over the sink that allowed in enough light to illuminate most of the room. A cool storage cellar had been built into the south end; at the opposite side were a row of hearths, each of which had a cauldron bubbling away or a hunk of meat roasting on a spit. The cook and her staff seemed to have skipped their own lunch and were in the middle of preparing the meal for the delegates; their heads were down, and a nervous buzz of energy hung over them. Rane relaxed as she walked in. They'd timed it well so far; it was time for the daytime household staff to take their meal before returning to work, and the long tables in the kitchen were crammed with servants bent over trays, chatting and eating quickly, as though someone were standing over their shoulders with an hourglass in one hand.

Rane took her time and let the sounds of the kitchen waft around her as she collected a hunk of bread and her bowl of stew from a cauldron bubbling away over one of the kitchen fires. Behind her, two of the kitchen maids—who were clearly not focusing on their tasks as much as they should be—were pounding loaves of dough on a countertop, sending puffs of flour up into the air. From what Rane was quickly able to glean, they were gossiping about a young woman who had shown up at one of the nearby farms.

"I heard she came from the city and that she had a *troubled past*," said one of the girls, clearly operating under the belief that having a "troubled past" was one of the most romantic attributes anyone could possess.

"I heard she barely speaks to anyone, but that she's got dark hair and that she's very pretty," said the other resentfully.

"Do you think it was a *man*? Do you think she got in trouble with a *man*?" whispered the first eagerly, clearly still hung up on the "troubled past" aspect of the mysterious young woman's arrival.

"Shut up and get to work!" barked one of the kitchen staff, and the girls fell silent, kneading the knobs of dough with a renewed vigor.

Trained as she was to keep her ears peeled for any information that may be useful, this exchange caught Rane's interest. The kitchen, which was the hub of the servants' activities, was the optimal place to absorb the local news and gossip, and many of Rane's best pieces of intelligence had come just from dawdling in the kitchen for an hour or so on a busy night.

A few months ago, the main gossip had been that there may have been an attempt on Cira's life, and then there were further whispers that a prisoner had escaped the same night—though who the prisoner was and whether any of it was actually true remained unconfirmed. The rumor had been effectively tamped down almost as soon as it had begun. In any case, it was rare for a new face to show up at one of the clifftop farms; their proximity to Faridor meant that anyone with a checkered history who wanted to hide from Kagai's forces tended to drift west in the opposite direction of the island. But the timing was certainly interesting. And notable, too, that the new farm worker was a young woman. After a moment or two of pondering, Rane shrugged it off and filed it away at the back of her mind. It could very easily be nothing. She had to focus on the matter at hand.

She scoped out the tables. In the far corner, she could make out the pink bow of the maid Cicada had described. There was a seat open to the girl's left, and Rane squeezed in, jostling with her elbows a bit as she tucked into her lunch.

As Rane wasn't scheduled to serve during the delegates' lunch, she ate with less urgency than the others. She kept a sideways eye on the girl to her right, watching the pink bow bobbing up and down as the maid chatted merrily with her friend. Rane ate in silence, carefully monitoring the level of water in the girl's cup, trying to match her speed. Finally, the girl finished the last sip and set her glass down on the table. Rane could see her considering the cup out of the corner of her eye, clearly debating whether it was worth it to stand up and get more.

With one motion, Rane drained the rest of her cup and set it down on the table, letting out a small "aah!" so that the girl looked over at her. Rane pushed herself back from the table, leaving her half-eaten plate at her place, and stood, reaching for the empty cup.

"Would you mind filling mine, too, while you're at it?" the girl asked, holding out her cup. She had a high-pitched voice and an eager expression, clearly relieved that Rane could take care of this one small errand for her.

Rane shrugged carelessly, took the girl's cup, and walked it over to the pitcher of water set on the kitchen counter. With one elbow, she knocked an apple off the counter onto the floor beside her shoe (prompting a chiding "Watch it!" from one of the cook's assistants.) As she bent down, she undid the stopper on a small vial of clear liquid from inside her sleeve, then replaced the apple on the counter and began to pour. The clear liquid ran from the vial into the girl's cup, mixing together with the water as it splashed and filled. It was odorless and colorless; the girl would notice nothing.

Nonchalantly, Rane pushed the small vial back up within her sleeve and walked back across the crowded kitchen to her seat, where she set down the girl's cup and gave only a silent nod to the girl's perky "Thank you!" She finished eating in silence, watching with satisfaction as, over the course of the next five minutes, the girl drained her glass of water, having noticed nothing amiss.

"Right, you lot!" bellowed the cook after ten minutes or so. "Get up; it's time to get in your places before the lunch is served."

There was a flurry of commotion as the last of the lunch was gulped down, chairs were pushed back, and trays were deposited unceremoniously in the vast washing tub, currently manned by two glum-looking teenage boys who had clearly thought that joining Kagai's household would have led to a life of greater adventure than this. Plates of delicacies were carried out of the kitchens and up to wait in the holding area beside the great hall above them; servants brushed the crumbs off of their vests and combed back their hair so as not to invite any censure from the heads of household. And then, almost as suddenly as the flurry of motion had begun, it had stopped. The room was eerily quiet. There was only Rane, the girl with the pink bow, and a few other servants scattered here and there who had been on duty in the rooms or in the stables.

Rane leisurely finished off the last hunk of her bread and was satisfied to see that the girl had a rather preoccupied look on her face as she pushed around the last of her stew in its bowl. The girl rose and dropped off her tray to the two boys at the trough, then went to wait by the long counter in the kitchen.

"It's almost ready," said the cook distractedly. She was a weedy-looking woman who wore her hair tightly pulled back under a kerchief; she resembled Hopkins, the head of household staff, so greatly that Rane suspected that they were somehow related. For all the food she prepared, the cook usually looked immaculate, but today had clearly been a strain on her nerves; her face was red, and some strands of grey hair had fallen out in front of her face.

"I don't feel very good," the girl with the pink bow mumbled under her breath.

"What's that?" the cook demanded.

"I don't feel so good," the girl repeated meekly, the look of distraction on her face growing more intense by the second. Rane took this opportunity to stand and amble unconcernedly over to the trough with her tray, then headed towards the door.

"Oh, no, you don't," the cook was saying to the girl. "You don't get to skive off your duties just because we have a special event happening. You'll stay right where you are and—"

But she was cut off by the sound of the girl dry heaving. The girl clasped a hand to her mouth, turned a deathly shade of puce, and looked around, searching for a place to vomit.

"Oh, no!" the cook cried and pushed the girl towards the trough. The girl broke into a run and, to Rane's amusement (and the horror of the two teenage boys, who obviously hadn't imagined their workday taking such a dramatic turn), began to vomit freely over the mountains of dirty dishes. The boys yelped and dove out of the way, then whirled around to stare entreatingly at the cook, as if to suggest that *surely* this wasn't about to be their problem.

"Get to washing!" the cook snapped. Any patience she had maintained after the rush of the lunch had vanished out the window. She muttered a few things under her breath, which Rane could hear as she approached the door to the kitchen.

"You!" came the call, as if on cue.

Rane paused at the door and turned around to face the cook. "Me?" she asked.

"I need you to deliver this lunch," the cook ordered, her face beet-red and murderous.

"I'm on my break," Rane called back, then turned to go out the door again. The momentary silence was punctuated by another loud round of vomiting from the trough.

"Don't you take another step!" the cook barked. "You set foot out of that door, and I'll see to it that you get no more breaks ever. Come here and fetch the tray."

Rane heaved a dramatic sigh and rolled her eyes. She slouched up to the counter, where the cook pushed across a large silver tray with handles at each end, bearing a load of stew, bread, fruit and cheese, and a pitcher of water.

"Where's it going?" Rane asked, trying to sound as ill-tempered and grumpy as she could.

"Hallway on the north end. You know where the portrait of the dogs is? There. Fifth door on your right. Knock three times like this," she demonstrated by rapping rhythmically on the countertop. "Then you go inside and drop off the tray, you don't talk to anyone, you leave immediately. Then go back in half an hour and pick up their things and bring them back here."

Rane heaved a sigh as if this was the biggest favor she'd ever deigned to grant anyone in her entire life. She took up the tray while the unfortunate girl had another bout over the trough, her pink bow drooping sadly down her back.

Once outside the kitchen, tray firmly in her hands, Rane felt her mind sharpen. Her footsteps fell quickly on the floor as she wove her way out of the maze of passageways surrounding the kitchens and up the staircase to the floor above.

As they'd planned, Cicada was waiting for her near the landing, sweeping the corridor with her back to the wall so that she could keep an eye out for Rane's approach. As soon as she saw Rane, she straightened up, and her eyes flicked around to make sure that they were alone.

Rane drew close, quietly handed Cicada the tray, and took the broom Cicada held out to her. "Fifth door on the right," she signed. "And you knock like this to enter." Cicada watched her as Rane knocked on the wall and nodded her confirmation. Rane could see the glow of the chase burning in her friend's eye.

"Be careful," Rane told her and took the pitcher of water off of the lunch tray.

Cicada nodded curtly and turned, striding towards the hallway and the suspected code room. As soon as she was out of sight, Rane sidled up to a nearby recess in the wall and stashed the pitcher of water behind a decorative vase. Then she began to sweep the floor slowly, deliberately, her ears trained for any sounds of alarm off in the distance.

It was a short walk from the stairwell to their target. As Cicada had observed before, the hallway in question was guarded by two sentries, one at either end. Cicada kept her eyes modestly lowered as she walked by the guard, then counted—*one, two, three, four, five* doors down on the right. The door itself was perfectly nondescript. She rapped three times on the door in the rhythm Rane had demonstrated. As she turned the handle, she could feel the sentries' eyes on the back of her head. The door wasn't locked, and she went inside.

Her heart leapt as she took her first step inside the room, for without a shadow of a doubt that they had hit on it. There had always been the nagging possibility in the back of her mind that her educated guess could have been wrong and that she could have walked in to find a team of seamstresses working on a new gown for Cira. Instead, she had come into a surprisingly long, narrow room that had the appearance and atmosphere of a claustrophobic, stuffy office. Four people, two men and two women, were hunched over a lengthy table covered with papers. Even from her first cursory glance, Cicada could see that they were working on deciphering various codes. And to her amusement and shock, she saw half a paper sticking out from beneath a sheaf that was written in her own handwriting. *I'd better figure out how that managed to get there*, she thought to herself, half-irritated and half-impressed that Cira had a spy good enough to intercept one of her letters.

Cicada was unsure how the lunch routine was usually carried out, but she spotted a squat buffet set against a far wall that seemed a likely candidate for service. Unlike the other surfaces in the room, it was completely devoid of paperwork and clutter. She walked towards it and, glancing to the side, noticed with a lurch that Cira's coders were watching her narrowly. They had expectant expressions, as if a question had been asked and they were waiting for an answer. Cicada swallowed and bobbed a curtsy. Keeping her eyes downcast, she gestured to her ear and shook her head.

She watched as the coders' guards visibly lowered before her. Two of them spoke to one another in an undertone. The one nearest her drew forth a piece of paper and scribbled something on it. He pushed it towards the corner of the table and motioned Cicada forward to read it. She did as he indicated, taking the opportunity to quickly scan the table for the cipher they were looking for. She hadn't expected the space to be so cluttered. Perhaps it would be impossible to find the right paper.

She pulled the note towards her and read:

You aren't the usual maid who serves us.

She shook her head and gestured for the pen. She wrote back:

Yes. She was taken ill. I was asked to step in.

The coder scanned her note and shrugged carelessly. Cicada was relieved to see that two of the others in the room were now talking freely, completely ignoring her. She wasn't a threat. The last coder, however, the one farthest down the table, was still watching her carefully. He was an older man with a pair of round spectacles perched on the tip of his nose. There was a quiet air of authority all about him. If there was a leader between the four of them, he was it, Cicada was certain. And if any one of them was in charge of using Cira's most top-secret cipher, it would be him.

Her thoughts were interrupted as the coder nearest her tapped her arm and gestured towards the lunch tray. He motioned to each of their places, seemingly telling Cicada that she should serve them. Cicada nodded and went to the tray. If she had been serving them with no ulterior motive, it would be more efficient, she thought, if she doled the food out onto the plates and then brought it to them. However, since she was trying to buy herself some time, she decided to dawdle a bit. She collected the cups, plates, and silverware and quietly passed behind each of the coders, setting down the utensils in front of them. The first three were completely ignoring her by now and were having some sort of conversation, their body language relaxed and informal, clearly mentally on their lunch break. They didn't even bother trying to hide their work from her as she went by. *Stupid,* she thought with grim satisfaction. But none of the ciphers or paperwork in front of them stood out to her as what she was searching for. She wasn't entirely sure whether the cipher in question would have any distinguishing features, but she trusted that her gut would tell her when she found it.

The last man, the one she suspected to be their leader, wasn't talking with the others and seemed more aware of her presence as she quietly set the plate and cup down before him. Cicada's sharp, dark eyes scanned his comparatively neat work area as she slowly placed the knife and fork beside his plate.

A little to the right of the place setting was a small yellow card. Something about it—perhaps its strange colored paper—captured Cicada's attention. She leaned slightly to the side, daring to stare at it for a split second longer. It was easily recognizable as a cipher, much like many of the others strewn haphazardly across the table, but in the corner of this one was Cira Kagai's own seal. Cicada recognized it immediately. She had seen Cira press her ring into the green wax many times before as she worked in her private chambers. There was no reason Cira herself would have stamped a cipher unless it was of the utmost importance.

Cicada felt her heart physically lurch within her chest, and a spark of excitement shivered its way through her all the way down to her toes. *This is it*, she thought to herself. *This has to be it.*

The momentary euphoria of this discovery almost instantly gave way to the very real question of how to spirit the cipher out of the room without being caught. Cicada turned away and walked back to the serving tray with the food, brain ticking through her options with every step. She picked up her tray and walked to the first coder, ladling some stew onto his plate and placing some bread, cheese, and fruit beside it. The coder chatted away with his companion, paying her no attention. She repeated this process with the next two.

As she approached the lead coder at the end of the table, it grew increasingly clear to her that if she was going to get her hands on it, he was going to have to move the cipher somewhere farther away from himself, somewhere she could easily grab it without it being noticed.

As soon as she decided on her course of action, she moved fluidly and assuredly. She ladled the stew onto the lead coder's plate, then jolted her arm ever so slightly so that a fat glob of stew plopped atop a nearby paper.

The coder immediately pushed his chair back from the table and threw his arms up in the air, yelling something incomprehensible at her. She ducked her head meekly and tried to look contrite. The coder turned back to his workstation and snatched the yellow cipher up and out of the way, tucking it safely out of sight underneath a pile of papers across the table from him. Cicada nearly purred with satisfaction. She could see the cipher's yellow corner jutting out, just barely visible.

She scurried around the table and set down the food tray beside the cipher. She then made a great show of bustling back around and trying to help the coder clean off the soiled paper with the edge of her apron. He brushed her efforts away brusquely. Finally, she curtsied and went around to retrieve her tray from the other side. The lead coder shot her one last glare and then glowered grumpily down at his meal and began pushing the stew around with his hunk of bread. The other three were conversing. Now was her chance. Her mind whirred, and for a few protracted seconds, it was almost as if the world around her was moving in slow motion.

She angled the food tray forward ever so slightly as she lifted it so that it shielded her hands from the coders' view. And then, deftly and confidently, one hand darted to the cipher. Her agile fingers gave a quick tug to its corner, and it slipped out of the pile of papers. She pressed the precious document flat against the bottom of the tray as she straightened. She swallowed, trying her best to slow her heart, and purposefully kept her eyes lowered as she walked back around the coding table to where she'd set up her service station. As she set down the tray, she pretended to adjust her skirts slightly and slipped the cipher into her apron pocket. She set about replacing the serving utensils on the now-empty platters of food.

Mere moments later, something touched her arm and she gave a startled jump. It was one of the coders. Immediately, she took a respectful step back and dipped her gaze. The woman lifted up her drinking cup expectantly, her expression exasperated.

Cicada tried to make a show of looking panicked. Her eyes darted from the woman's empty cup to the tray, and gestured helplessly. There was no pitcher of water. The woman rolled her eyes and motioned her urgently towards the door. *Fetch some water. Hurry up.* Cicada curtsied and scurried off.

As the door closed behind her, she managed to breathe a small sigh of relief, though the danger was far from over. At any moment, the coders might notice that the cipher was missing and come running after her. But her best bet was while the coders were distracted by their lunch. *Just get it to Rane*, she thought grimly. *Get the cipher to Rane. I don't care what happens to me.* She hunched slightly lower as she passed by the guard at the end of the hallway, felt his gaze on the back of her neck as she went.

Rane was still sweeping the floor at the head of the stairs and snapped to attention as soon as she saw Cicada approaching. As soon as she knew no one could see her, she quickened her step and half-jogged up to Rane.

"Did you get it?" Rane demanded eagerly.

Cicada nodded and gestured to her apron pocket. Rane jerked her head towards a nearby corridor, farthest from the windows and conveniently cast in darkness. They rounded the corner just as a guard mounted the stairs on the floor below. They waited with bated breath as his steps rose and slowly passed them. Cicada was uncomfortably conscious of every second that ticked by.

"I'll copy it," Rane signed, holding out her hand. "You keep watch."

Cicada nodded and handed her the yellow cipher, Cira's green seal emblazoned on the corner. Rane smiled faintly at the sight of it, then vanished into a nearby broom cupboard, where she'd earlier stashed a pen and paper.

The cipher was relatively small and would not take long to copy, but every moment of waiting and watching felt agonizingly painful. Cicada returned to the landing and swept the floor quietly in long, lingering circles near the entrance of the corridor, wondering whether they were taking too long, whether it was a believable amount of time to have elapsed before she returned with the water. It wasn't any good worrying about that now.

After what seemed like an eternity, she happened to glance over her shoulder and saw the door to the cupboard open and close. Rane re-emerged and gave her a triumphant nod. Glancing around to make sure they were alone, she extended the cipher back to Cicada, who took it.

"Please be careful," she said. "How are you going to get it back in?"

"Hopefully, they haven't noticed it's gone," Cicada replied, returning the cipher to her apron pocket. "And I can just slip it back."

Rane walked over to the nearby decorative recess on the landing and retrieved the pitcher of water she had hidden there earlier.

"Good luck," she said.

"We have it," Cicada allowed herself the faintest edge of a smile. "Rane, we have it. Whatever happens now, we have the code."

"You did it," Rane agreed. "But please don't get arrested."

"I'll try."

Cicada gripped the pitcher in her hands, its smooth sides startlingly cold against her hands. She swallowed and squared her thin shoulders. This was, if anything, the trickiest part of the whole operation. *They won't have noticed*, she assured herself. *They'll just be finishing their lunch.*

Time seemed to be operating in fits and starts. An eternity had elapsed while Rane was copying the cipher in the cupboard, while it took barely any time at all for Cicada to make the short walk past the guards and back to the code room. She gripped the pitcher tightly in one hand, braced herself, and gave the rhythmic knock on the door.

The instant she stepped inside, she knew that something had gone very, very wrong. The four coders barely acknowledged her appearance, as they were all in the middle of a deep, intense conversation. Two of the four coders were standing at their places, their empty lunch plates shoved to one side. They were rifling through the piles of papers on the table as if they were searching for something. The old man she had identified as the lead coder had an expression of agitated consternation on his face.

Cicada felt her stomach tighten. Her hands reflexively began to grip the pitcher of water so hard she had to force herself to loosen them for fear of breaking the handle. She ducked her head, bobbed a curtsy, and walked over to the first coder. She began pouring a slow, steady stream of water into his cup while her mind raced, looking for a way, *any* way that she could plant the cipher back in the pile of papers without being caught. Her dark eyes flicked up, and she saw that the lead coder was snapping something at his colleague. He gestured towards the pile of documents he was inspecting, his expression knit in frustration.

Cicada slowly, deliberately made her way to the next cup and began to pour. She could try to get out of the room and simply take the cipher with her, but once the coders had realized it was truly gone, it would take almost no time for them to identify her as the culprit. She could attempt to knock a pile of papers over and drop the cipher among them in the confusion. But she had already caused a stir when she'd dripped some of the stew on the lead coder's papers, and two such incidents were bound to arouse suspicion.

She poured water into the third glass, avoiding being hit as the nearest coder motioned wildly with her arms in the direction of her superior. The coder pointed at the papers before her and glanced down at the floor, obviously trying to see if the cipher had fallen. Cicada cursed inwardly. She couldn't simply drop the cipher on the floor now that the coder had looked there. She finished pouring and lowered her pitcher down to her hip. Using the pitcher as cover, one of her hands snaked into her pocket and withdrew the cipher. She cupped it in her hand against the bottom of the pitcher. Now all she had to do was find an opening, to get the coders to look away from her for just one second...

She approached the fourth cup, the lead coder's. He was on the opposite side of the table from her but was close enough that she couldn't see a good opportunity to sneak the cipher past him. She was just about to start pouring and was trying to see if there was some way she could use the pitcher to mask her hands again when something out of the corner of her eye stopped her.

One of them had waved at her to catch her attention. All four were now staring at her. Cicada felt a cool rush wipe through her mind like a wave, and she immediately began calculating ways to get out of the room, to fight her way out if need be. She was in the corner farthest from the door now. Not ideal. She could perhaps throw the pitcher, buy herself some time. She knew Faridor's corridors well enough to lose them. She could hide out until she and Rane could come up with a way to smuggle her out. She could...

The lead coder was pointing at her now and saying something to her. Cicada shook her head demurely, keeping her head lowered and her eyes downcast. The female coder to her left said something, too, but Cicada again shook her head. She had an inkling of what they were talking about; she suspected that they might want to search her, to turn out her pockets. She took a preemptive step back and tried to look anxious and confused. It wasn't too much of a stretch.

The lead coder approached her, his expression narrow and suspicious. He pointed at the pitcher in her hands. Cicada blinked blankly and reflexively pulled the pitcher in closer to her chest, her palm pressing the cipher against the bottom of the jug. The coder reached for the pitcher in her hands and gave it a tug. Cicada again tried to feign confusion and wrestled with him for a moment or two, then relented. She intentionally ceded control of the jug one grip at a time, sweeping the cipher neatly behind her back and taking another distressed step towards the corner, both hands clasped at her tailbone. The lead coder set the pitcher down on the table and turned to her once more. It was clearly his intention to search her for the cipher. And with that realization, Cicada could see a narrow, risky opening.

Time once again seemed to slow as the coder came towards her. He was elderly but still vigorous and clearly felt as though he could overpower her with little trouble. Feigning confusion as to what was happening or what the coder wanted from her, Cicada reflexively raised her empty hand in front of her. The coder grabbed her thin wrist, and once his grip had tightened sufficiently, she pretended to try and wrestle her arm away. She pushed him, then pulled her arm back so that he was forced to take a step towards her, so close he nearly stumbled right into her. And as he did, she slipped the cipher into his pocket.

It wasn't a moment too soon, for once the female coder to her left saw that she was going to put up a struggle, she stepped forward to assist her colleague. The female coder held her arms as her supervisor checked Cicada's apron pocket and the pockets of her skirts, and ran his hands up and down Cicada's sleeves and back to see if there was anything hidden on her person. After a first few moments of struggle, Cicada had relented and kept her eyes downcast as the search took place. She gritted her teeth in discomfort as the female coder felt around her legs but made no more attempts to back away. After about thirty seconds of close examination, they stopped and stood away from her. They had found nothing, but their expressions were still heavily laden with suspicion. Finally, the lead coder pointed to the empty plates on the table and waved his hand towards the door.

Rane had told her that the protocol was to come back and collect their lunch things in half an hour, but Cicada was willing to bend those rules if it meant that she would be able to get out of the room a bit faster and not have to come back. She began moving down the table, collecting the coders' plates and utensils and piling them. Every few seconds, she allowed her eyes to dart up to take in what was happening in the room.

The coders were no longer searching the table, but were talking amongst themselves in what seemed to be rational, measured tones of voice. As Cicada brought the plates back to the serving table to organize them on the tray, she looked over her shoulder and saw the coder nearest her wave his hand and give a shrug, indicating some sort of question or suggestion. The lead coder's hands went to his chest and patted a few times, then dove down into his pockets. Cicada's breath caught for an instant. The coder froze. A moment later, he withdrew the yellow cipher from his jacket pocket.

The others in the room threw up their hands in relief, and one or two of them seemed to roll their eyes at the fuss that had just been made. Cicada angled herself so that she had a better view of the proceedings, tidying as slowly as she dared. The coder shook his head in consternation and stared at the cipher in his hand as if he couldn't quite believe what he was seeing. He shook his head and gestured towards the pile of papers on the table and seemed to make some sort of protest to his coworkers. But the others had already moved on and were settling themselves back into their work. One of them gave a last little shrug and said something dismissive, waving her hand and shaking her head.

It was as long as Cicada dared stay. She lifted the tray with the empty lunch things piled atop it and walked steadily towards the door. She chanced one last glance at the lead coder and found that he was watching her, his wariness now tinged with doubt. That sliver of doubt was all she needed to see. It would grow and grow, and she was confident that soon it would replace any lingering suspicion. After all, people misplaced things all the time.

She closed the door to the code room behind her, basking in the sensation of the heavy, satisfying snap of the lock as it shut fast. Balancing the tray in her hands as she walked past the guard, it was all she could do not to run.

CHAPTER NINE

After nearly three months away Marc returned late one evening, blown in by a gust of nighttime wind. Tarr had been sleeping, and was roused from his slumber by a soft knock on his door, followed by Athela's dark, curly head poking in to tell him that Marc had come back.

"Is he alone?" Tarr asked sleepily, rubbing his eyes with the back of one hand. It had been Marc's idea in the first place to set out to try and find Si, wherever he was, and it was mostly out of pity and an unwillingness to oppose Marc's stubborn, single-minded focus that he had let him go at all. It wasn't as though their ranks were so full of talented fighters that they could afford to spare him. But Marc was bullheadedly convinced that Si was still alive, and nothing could talk him out of finding him.

The boy's sudden disappearance on the eve of the new year had hung like a cloud over them. It had happened so suddenly; Si's last cryptic farewell to Marc did little to assuage their worries about his safety. Tarr and the others had grilled Marc over and over again on the last few moments he remembered before Si had disappeared, and nothing that he said seemed to make sense. Tarr himself had spent long sleepless nights thinking of all the strange powers that had started to emanate from Si; how the boy seemed completely unable to control them, and what kind of trouble they would wreak if Si wasn't well-guarded, if some sort of solution wasn't discovered.

After some time had passed and it seemed apparent that Si was not going to return (at least not immediately), Tarr had quietly talked to the others about what they thought they should do. The others believed him to be alive, too, but their opinions as to the meaning and reasoning of his disappearance varied. Laith assumed that Si had been unable to face the pressures of the war, had run away in a moment of panic, and was now reluctant to come back to face them. Athela, ever suspicious, thought that Si had been kidnapped by some faction or other, though couldn't supply any reason why they hadn't been sent a ransom note or heard anything from Cira's camp about him being in their custody. Tarr personally was of the baseless opinion that for whatever reason Si did not want to be found by them, and that he would return when he was ready, if he ever did.

But none of this mattered to Marc. Tarr hadn't ever seen him so wracked by grief and guilt, not even when Si had briefly been kidnapped the year before. He viewed the disappearance as his personal failure to protect the boy. During their meeting, Marc had calmly listened to all sides, all of their reasoning, but none of them really seemed to matter to him. His objective was simple: to find Si and bring him back home where he would be safe and cared for. There was nothing Tarr could do. Marc's unwavering loyalty and boundless capacity to love were two of his greatest qualities, and there was a particular hurt in his eyes that Tarr thought he could understand. If Si had chosen voluntarily to leave, then he had also chosen to leave Marc behind. In a strange way, Tarr could see that it was easier for Marc to mentally and emotionally wrap his head around the situation if Si indeed had been kidnapped, rather than if he'd left on his own accord.

Tarr rolled over and sat up. "Is he alone?" he asked again.

"Yes," Athela replied quietly. "Get dressed. We'll be waiting downstairs in the hall."

Tarr heaved a sigh. He had harbored hope, of course, that Marc would be successful in his quest to find Si, but the news came as little surprise to him.

As Athela had suggested, he quickly dressed, pulling on his boots and a thin sweater against the drafty air of the hallways. He stepped out to find Athela leaning against the wall, waiting for him, and the two fell into step through the dimly lit corridors.

Though he was interested in learning what, if anything, Marc had found during his sojourn, Tarr was struck by his own sheer happiness at the prospect of seeing Marc again. He had missed Marc's gentle good nature, his willingness to undertake any task, his reliable competence in all things. With Archer and Athela constantly at one another's throats, Rane far away in Faridor, and Laith a ghostly slip of his former self, Tarr had truly missed his steadying presence.

Marc was surrounded by a small group of well-wishers in the great hall, his back to them as they approached. Tarr almost did a double-take; he knew Marc immediately from his build; the way he stood, the broadness of his shoulders, but he had apparently shorn off almost all of his straw colored hair so that it was close-cropped to his skull. On hearing them approach, Marc swiveled around and greeted them with his familiar smile, spreading from one side of his face to the other, his white, ice-blue eyes twinkling as he clasped Tarr in a hug so strong that the wind was temporarily knocked out of him. They were disparate enough in height that the nexus of the hug was located somewhere in the vicinity of Tarr's diaphragm.

"It's good to have you back," Tarr told him weakly, feeling his bones creak.

Marc released him, and the two looked each other up and down. Overall, Marc seemed none the worse for wear; Tarr could see a few fading bruises slowly turning to ash high up on his cheekbone. The old scar that split his face diagonally from his temple down to his jaw was white in the dim light. He was thinner than he was before he'd left; still broad as a bull, but leaner.

"You've eaten?" Tarr prompted.

"Not yet," Marc replied.

"Let's get you something and find someplace to talk," Tarr suggested, glancing meaningfully at the knot of onlookers. Marc was friendly and popular among all the Strikers' supporters, and many of them had awakened to greet him, but what Marc had to say was appropriate only for the innermost group.

A short while later the core group of Strikers and Ari had arrayed themselves in Laith's bedroom, sitting alternately on the floor, the bed or the single chair Laith had in the corner. The door was safely shut and a guard posted outside, and Tarr settled down onto the floor opposite Marc, who was tucking into a steaming bowl of stew.

"So," Tarr raised his eyes. "What did you find?"

"A lot of rumors and not much else," Marc shook his head, his blue eyes dark and sad. "I didn't want anyone to know who I was or who I was looking for, so I had to keep things fairly vague. There were a few runaways, some missing kids that I wound up finding, whose descriptions had been somewhat like Si's. But none of them were him."

They sat in silence for a moment, absorbing what Marc had told them. Tarr leaned back, looping his long arms around his knees. "Any chance he could have gone south?"

Marc shook his head, scratching at his cheek with his thumb, just below the white line of his scar. "I passed through all the wayposts where he would have had to stop. Went to Riddleton," (here, Tarr reflexively grimaced in sympathy) "and Eldrest to the south. There was nothing, no signs. Went and surveyed down around the forest, even up north past Faridor. When he left, he would have gone without taking many supplies. He would have had to stop, or at least get help from somewhere, an inn, a farm. But there was nothing. No one had seen him or given him shelter."

Tarr glanced around at the others. Ari's brow was furrowed slightly, Laith had his arms crossed, his beautiful face as impassive as a statue. Archer and Athela, who were sitting an awkward eight inches apart from one another on the bed, exchanged glances but said nothing.

"There was something rather strange," Marc continued, scraping at the bottom of his bowl. "I passed briefly by Joymaril. Just, you know, to see if I could see anything, if there was some sign that he had gone past that way. I couldn't get too close, obviously, because if anyone was going to recognize me, even with my hair gone, it would have been there. But there were no guards at the lake, at least as far as I could see. And when I got closer, I tried to look up into the city. And there was no one."

"No one?" Athela echoed, her nose wrinkling.

Marc shook his head. "It was morning, and you know, usually, even from across the lake, you can see people walking the streets or going to the market. And there was no one. I couldn't see anyone walking in the palace. Something had happened."

Tarr was stunned. The city and palace of Joymaril had, since the moment of Cira's takeover, been a dark, looming shadow just to the southeast of them. The majority of Cira's armed forces had been moved north to Faridor, but there were still enough fighters and cavalry in Joymaril to be unpleasant if Cira decided to plan a coordinated siege on Two Falls.

"Did you find anything else? Were you able to get any closer?" he pressed eagerly.

Marc again shook his head, laying down the bowl on the floor beside him. "No, unfortunately. No such luck. Couldn't risk it. They could have been lying in wait for me, for all I know. But it was definitely strange. You got the sense that there was something amiss."

Tarr's mind whirred. *How am I going to get a spy into Joymaril?* His two best, Rane and Cicada, were already assigned to Faridor and he couldn't risk moving either one of them now.

"We're glad you're home," he said aloud. "We'll leave you to get some rest."

Marc nodded gratefully and stood. The others filed past him, clapping him on the back and squeezing his arms as they trooped out to head back to their beds. Tarr lingered a bit, waiting so that he and Marc were the last to leave. They walked down the dark corridor to Marc's room, pausing on the threshold and regarding one another.

"He's alive," Marc said preemptively, a challenge in his eyes as though he were daring Tarr to contradict him.

"I know," Tarr agreed quickly. "I know he is."

"I've thought a lot about it," Marc said quietly, and Tarr suddenly had a glimpse of the many hours that Marc had spent alone on horseback, wandering through the woods and over valleys, "and I think you may be right. That if he left, he had to leave. And that he'll come back when he's ready."

"That's what I believe," Tarr affirmed.

Marc regarded him, his eyes tired. "I wish he had trusted me."

"He trusts you," Tarr reassured him. "He trusted you to know that he could take care of himself. That he would be all right. That you had given him what he needs to survive."

Marc heaved a contemplative sigh and a sad smile played at the corner of his mouth. "I hope you're right. Goodnight, Tarr."

"Goodnight."

The next night, much to his own astonishment, Laith found himself standing at a strange door at the top of a rickety flight of stairs, his dog sitting obediently at his heel. Breaker's ears pricked, wondering what his master would do next; Laith realized that he had raised and lowered his hand to knock almost three times and done nothing. It would have been funny, if anyone else had been watching. Laith looked down at his dog and shrugged, as if to say, *I'm not terribly sure what we're doing here, either.*

Finally, with the feeling of someone stepping heedlessly off the edge of a precipice, Laith raised his hand and knocked. Breaker's long black ears twitched at the sound and he cocked his head to one side with a searching, inquisitive stare. Laith met his gaze and jerked his head slightly to the side.

"Come back in fifteen minutes," he ordered.

Breaker obeyed, standing and tip-tapping back down the staircase to stand watch in the blue shadows of the street below. Laith watched until the dog vanished, then a tiny creak drew his attention.

The door opened a crack and Laith took a preemptive, uncertain step back. The door opened wider and he found himself face to face with the young barmaid who had saved his life a few nights before. She was as he had remembered: tall, taller than Athela, with a strong, healthy curving body and the air of someone who had spent a good portion of her youth running barefoot through the outdoors. A long tumble of rich, dark brown hair fell over one of her shoulders and Laith found himself met with a pair of level hazel eyes that regarded him with a startling lack of surprise.

"It's you, then," she said, as if he was late for a previously made appointment. She tilted her head to rest on the edge of the door. "My name is Tess. You'd better come in." She stood back and held the door open, as he ducked under the doorframe and walked inside, more than a little unsure of himself. He wondered if he had done the right thing in seeking her out, if it was something that she would have wanted him to do; if his mere presence there made her uncomfortable. He hoped not. He just wanted to thank her and, if he was being honest with himself, perhaps to take another look at her.

Laith glanced around and swiftly took in his surroundings. The apartment was small, shaped like a U. In the curve of the U was the front door where they now stood; at one end, the one closest to them, was a small kitchen with a table tucked in opposite the large wood stove. At the other end of the U was a tidy cot beside what looked like a baby's crib and a door that Laith assumed led to a toilet and bath. Small pieces of furniture stood in the cup of the U beside them; a large bookshelf cluttered with tomes and loose papers, and what looked like a work table with a lantern burning brightly over small bits of carved wood, delicate tools, and a large pot of ink bristling with pens. What was unusual about the room was that everything—the floor and the walls and even the furniture—were almost completely cleared from the floor to a height of about two feet. Laith took another step inside the room and by craning his neck slightly saw that there was what looked like a small human form sleeping on the cot in the crib; he could dimly see a curly head of black hair and a tiny balled-up fist peeking out from beneath the blanket. The sight of the child startled him and also plucked at a strange chord within his chest, a pang as sharp and painful as if he'd been struck there. He began to wonder anew if he hadn't made a mistake in coming there and disturbing their peace.

Tess was pouring tea from an old, battered copper kettle in the kitchen across from him, but she saw the beat of surprise in his eyes as he looked at her son. How odd and out of place he seemed, standing there in her warm, comfortable den like a tall black shadow, his cloak falling to brush the floor, the shadows from the fire in the grate casting the bones of his eerily beautiful face into sharp relief. His eyes were strangely hooded; he looked untouchable, as though he'd vanish if she all but brushed his arm with her finger. Silently she handed him a cup of tea and walked over to the couch, tucking her feet underneath her as she sat. She regarded him closely over the top of her cup.

Laith stepped over to the worktable and reached out a hand to gently brush some of the objects that rested there. There was an intricately carved column that had been fastened with great care and skill to some sort of pedestal. Laith held the delicate thing, turning it with his fingers and examining it with growing wonder before placing it back down on the table. In one corner there was a piece of parchment that had rolled in upon itself. He gently pressed it open. There, in meticulously drawn lines, was a sketch of the front edifice of a building, something every bit as grand as the palaces in which he had grown up.

"Are you hungry?" Tess's voice came gently, snapping him out of his reverie.

"No, thank you," he replied.

"Good," she said, blowing over the top of her tea to cool it. "All I have is applesauce and cheese. The little one is rather picky these days." She looked affectionately over in the direction of the sleeping lump in the cot.

Laith followed her gaze. "Boy or girl?"

She smiled faintly, with a visible swell of motherly affection. "A boy. His name is Julian."

"How old?" Laith asked, mostly to be polite.

"One and a bit."

Laith wished he could provide some sort of wise and meaningful anecdote about one-year-olds and their proclivities, but found himself at a loss. He stared deep into his cup of tea and it was about a minute later that he glanced up and found Tess watching him with a mixture of curiosity and bemusement.

"So, Argolaith, exiled prince of the Jelani, did I get your tea hot enough?" This query was accompanied by a cheeky raise of an eyebrow and a long, deliberate sip from her cup.

Laith couldn't help but smile. Against his will he felt his shoulders relax as he realized that this young woman, whoever she was, had a very subtle, ironic sense of humor and oddly enough it made him feel at home. Her tendency, he began to understand, was to hold her face in a very solemn expression until it bloomed with mirth. The effect was utterly beguiling.

"It's hot enough," he replied slowly. The smile that had played around his lips a moment ago had vanished, but the tiniest hint of it remained in his dark eyes. Tess felt she wasn't sure yet whether his level, unblinking gaze was a challenge, a flirtation or some sort of intimidation tactic. She tossed her head back. She had tended bar for many years and knew well enough how to deal with any one of those three scenarios. She was both a good listener and a good storyteller.

"D'you know, I had to give up tea when I was pregnant with Julian? Someone's mother told me it was bad for the baby and I was so afraid of mucking it up that I gave it up for the full nine months. Hardest thing I've ever had to do." She shot a mock-irritated glance over towards the sleeping child. "All I can say is he'd better grow up to be a world-renowned mathematician or inventor, or *else*."

Laith followed her gaze, and as he watched as the miniature hand beneath the blankets bunched and released, tiny fingers curling like leaves. "Where's his father?" Laith asked quietly, though he felt he already knew the answer. The apartment, small and comfortable though it was, was completely devoid of any male presence. He could tell from Tess's momentary silence that he was right.

"I grew up in the Meadows," she said finally. "Did you know we've met before?"

"What?" Laith asked, astonished.

She grinned broadly, her freckled nose wrinkling. "I lived on a farm. That's where I grew up. And one day my brother came running up the path to the barn where I was playing saying, 'Tess! There's a bunch of men on horses! Kings and Princes with swords and armor!' It was the most excited I've ever seen him. He was a few years older than me and he always tried to be blasé, a bit cool, you know? But not that day. And so he and I ran down from the barn and this long train of riders and horses and wagons—it seemed to go on forever, like a big black snake over the hill." Her hand traced the line through the air. "And you stopped by our well to water your horses. By that time my father and mother had come down to watch, too. They spoke to the head—the general, I think you call him? A big, huge man with a face like carved wood."

Laith couldn't help but smile at the retroactively childlike description of General Calchas. He racked his brain, trying to remember the well, or stopping by a farm somewhere in the Meadows, but they had been gone for so long and there had been so many farms.

"At the end of it," she continued, "my mother walked back over and picked me up so that I could watch the soldiers go by. And I remember her pointing at you...she said, 'That one there is a prince.' And you rode by on your horse with a blue tunic embroidered with ivy across the front. It was funny because I had always thought that princes were older, but you were my age. You sat up so straight in the saddle."

"Did I look down at all?" Laith asked.

"Not once." She considered. "Well, I imagined you did. Just a glance. But I probably invented the whole thing." She leaned down to take another sip of tea and paused, her lips poised on the brim. Rather cheekily, she said, "You were handsome back then, too."

Laith tilted his head to one side, bemused. "I can't remember."

She laughed gaily, unruffled. "It's all right. I only remember because it became one of my favorite stories. My mother had to retell the story of the day with the big men and the prince on the horse over and over. She probably hated you by the end of it."

"How'd you get here, then?" he asked curiously.

"I was sent here for school," she said. "We had a village school; it wasn't really anything special. But I was good at math. I was *very* good at math. And drawing things. So my parents scraped up the money and sent me here to Two Falls. I started university when I was fifteen and began to study architecture and engineering. Years later I was part of a research team that was going to work on restoring the foundation of the library when the war..." A dark cloud passed over her eyes and she looked down at her hands as if they were suddenly very interesting. "When the war came."

The war. Laith regarded her, watched her composedly tuck a fallen strand of hair behind her ear. Her hand was not shaking. She looked back up and her eyes were dry. "I'd met Julian's father at university. He was an artist. An Ashan. He was killed a few months after Cira closed off Two Falls and started rounding up the first wave of Ashans. I found out later I was pregnant. A man who ran a bar gave me a job and helped me find this flat. His son had been a classmate of mine at school. He felt sorry for me."

"Why did you not go back to the Meadows?"

"They wouldn't let any single mothers out. On suspicion of the children being half-Ashan. They'd have been right, in my case. I didn't have the money for forged papers. No one I knew in this part of town knew how to contact the Strikers or the underground. So I hid Julian as best I could. Took the job at the bar." She took a breath and shrugged lightly. "And that's that. We've made do." She forced a smile. "And what of you?"

"You know the stories they tell," Laith said softly. His face betrayed nothing.

She knew the stories. His family was gone, too. She nodded, and it was as if some unspoken understanding had passed between them. Like hers, Laith's eyes were dry. His hands were steady.

"Why'd you kiss me?" he asked suddenly. "The other night?"

Tess opened her mouth, surprised at his directness. She was unsure of what to say. His eyes never left hers. It was both unsettling and strangely exciting. The men Tess had known—even the most forward of them—would always look away from her at some point; at her foot, her hand, the wall opposite. But Laith met her eyes so openly that she almost felt words were superfluous.

Numerous replies, ranging from saucy to witty to honest, flitted through her mind. She decided to go with honest. "Like I said. You looked like you needed it," she shrugged with an apologetic smile.

Laith nodded, but Tess couldn't tell what he thought of her answer. His face was sphinxlike, impassive. As a barmaid accustomed to knowing and anticipating the thoughts of other people, it frustrated her not to know what was going on inside his head. It was maddening. She realized how much she wanted to kiss him again, so she stood up abruptly, walked over to her son's cot, and slid the tip of her index finger into the center of his soft, chubby palm. The little fist closed reflexively around her finger as he slept.

Laith must have stood up silently and come up behind her, for she felt his light touch on her arm before she heard a footstep. She jumped, startled, and looked up at him. His face was so beautiful, even up close where miniscule flaws in his skin or bones would be most visible. A thin white scar ran like a thread over his ear. His dark eyelashes were so long that when he blinked (which he rarely did), the tips of them grazed his cheek. She felt her breath catch ever so slightly.

"I have a small favor to ask," he said.

Tess felt herself unconsciously leaning back against the hand on her arm. "What?"

For the first time that night, he seemed to struggle for words. Finally, he said, "Can I come back here? Once in a while? You don't have to make a fuss, don't have to do anything, don't even have to talk to me if you don't want to. If I could just...be here. It might...help." The last words looked as though they took him a great effort to say, and immediately she understood. He was lonely. Profoundly lonely. And she knew something herself about loneliness.

"Anytime. Of course. I sleep in the afternoons, while Julian is away. I sometimes work early. Sometimes work late."

"It's all right."

"Nothing more," she added carefully, remembering that this was still a man she barely knew, even if he had a good reputation. "There won't be...anything more."

"Nothing," he agreed. "I promise. You ask me to go at any time, and I'll go."

She believed him, even though in her mind she could hear every maternal figure she had ever known yelling at her about allowing strange, good-looking men undue liberties. "All right, then," she replied, feeling surprised even as the words left her mouth.

A strand of her hair had tumbled down over her elbow, and softly he caught it between his thumb and forefinger. She could feel the slight motion against her back as he rubbed the lock of her hair gently between his fingers. Tess felt lightheaded and a bit wobbly in the legs, but she tried to keep her face as closed as his, even as she was taken by the nearness of him. The expression in his eyes was so curious. She wished she knew him better so that she could decipher what it meant.

"You'd better go," she said. She was nervous; not because of anything he had done but because she was clearly incapable of keeping her head straight around him. *How long has it been?* she thought wistfully. Her life had been so full of raising and protecting Julian, scraping together enough to keep them both alive, dodging swipes at the bar where she worked, that part of her had pushed aside the sheer, elemental pleasure of being held against a warm, strong chest.

He took a step away, and all of a sudden the wave of cold air swept back over her, unpleasant and unbidden. Already, Laith's presence, his touch, felt like a mirage.

He opened the door, revealing a large black dog with pointed ears waiting patiently on the stoop. The dog rose to his feet at the sight of his master. Tess was surprised.

"He could have come in," she said. "I don't mind dogs."

"He's standing guard," Laith told her, leaning down and patting him between the ears.

"Against what?" Tess asked curiously. The night was so still and Laith's presence so reassuring that it was hard to imagine any sort of threat lurking in the darkness.

Laith shrugged evasively. "There's always someone. Go on, give him a pet. He fancies himself a ladies' man."

Tess walked up and stroked the dog's soft fur, which the animal accepted with a noble, self-important expression on his face. He panted a few times at her and thumped his large tail against the floor of the landing. She straightened up and faced Laith. Though she'd been the one to ask him to go, she hadn't truly wanted it, not in her heart of hearts. She thought fleetingly of changing her mind, but forced her hand to grip the doorknob.

"Thank you," Laith said. "Tess."

"Laith," she said, and he was gone.

CHAPTER TEN

The next morning, Tarr was working at his desk and trying not to think about the council meeting that was taking place in the room down the hallway. Since his shouting match with Minister Burlage about Archer, Laith had generously offered to take his place, as there was precious little any of the councilors could say or do to ruffle him (and, Tarr suspected, they were all frightened of him anyway.) Tarr trusted that Laith wouldn't give an inch on the important issues and would represent them well in any questions of governance that came up. In one of his more mischievous moments he had toyed with the idea of sending Athela to the meeting in his stead, just to see what would happen when she met Minister Burlage face to face, but even Tarr wasn't brave enough to actually try it.

He was sitting far back in his chair, tapping a pencil against his teeth and thinking alternately of Cira's weapon and of the loyalist meeting that Laith had stumbled into. The prince had been somewhat vague on the details of his infiltration, but Tarr knew him well enough to read through the rather bland lines of his report and realize that something must have happened, for Laith had shown up back at headquarters that night very late indeed, looking more rumpled than his usual composed self. He'd also advised Tarr that their undercover presence at the meeting had been compromised, which Tarr interpreted as a dry way of stating that he'd been found out and the loyalists were going to find a different way to meet. This was all well and good, as far as Tarr was concerned. Even if they hadn't been able to spring a trap and make arrests, it had bought them some time until the loyalists were able to regroup.

There hadn't been any word from Rane or Cicada at Faridor, which meant either that the wind was up and they'd had to lie low, or that they were up to something. Tarr fervently hoped that it was the latter; it wasn't very easy to sit around and wait for some unnamed, unknowable weapon to come up to the Two Falls gate and demand entrance. He trusted that Rane would alert him if and when they found anything at all.

He snapped to as there was a soft knock on the door, and a moment later Laith admitted himself, Breaker tip-tapping in behind him and settling immediately on the floor. Laith sat in the chair opposite Tarr.

"Hullo," he said.

"Hi," Tarr replied, then eyed him narrowly. "You're looking more..."

"What?" Laith asked.

Tarr groped for words. He had almost concluded his sentence with "more alive than usual," but even as close as they were, he couldn't quite figure out how to say that without being offensive. "Chipper," he decided finally. "Chipper than usual."

Laith raised his eyebrows, as if "chipper" was one of the last adjectives he'd have used to describe himself. However, he shrugged and continued. "Council meeting's just let out. There's some issues with the water system in the northwest corner of the city, and they're going to send out repair patrols tomorrow to see if it can be mended. Some of the old streets by the market are in need of upgrades and we've had petitions."

"Fine, fine," Tarr muttered, scribbling it down on his papers and hoping he would remember what "sewer roads" meant when he tried to reread his notes later in the week.

"They want to try and send another envoy to the Ashans to ask them for aid," Laith continued, "but I told them we'd gone down that road by sending you and Athela out there last year and that we'd had no luck with it."

"Too true," Tarr muttered. "A months-long waste of time, more like."

"So that issue was tabled. And *someone*," Laith said sarcastically, "just happened to let it slip to Minister Burlage that Archer and Athela captured a Kagaian officer and that she'd been interrogated and was still being held under guard."

Tarr groaned and rolled his eyes. "Let me guess, he's calling for blood."

"He wants public executions to come back into vogue," Laith confirmed.

"It's one way to curry favor with the people," Tarr muttered darkly. "We'll have to move her and double the guard. He's not getting anywhere near her."

"The council also *requests*," Laith continued, with a similar sarcastic emphasis, "that you report any intelligence that you have gleaned in the course of your interrogations to them immediately."

"Ah," Tarr tapped his pencil against his chin, grinning slyly and adopting a mock-apologetic tone. "Unfortunately, she's a tough nut to crack and I haven't been able to uncover anything from her yet. But I'll keep at it!"

"I told them as much," Laith agreed. "They seemed slightly suspicious, though, *almost* as if they believe you to be good at these sorts of things."

"How flattering," Tarr smiled.

If pressed, Tarr wouldn't have been able to articulate exactly *why* he was so reluctant to take the governing council into his confidence, other than his general mantra of treating everyone and everything with a certain degree of suspicion. One obvious reason was that there were many of them and he couldn't be absolutely certain of their loyalties, not really. He certainly didn't trust someone like Burlage, who was obviously no Kagaian loyalist but was ambitious and unscrupulous and too conscious of his own public image. Tarr held them all at arm's length, and he comforted himself with the thought that this tactic had been largely successful for them in the war thus far, if somewhat isolating for him personally.

And, of course, there was the rather immature satisfaction he couldn't help but feel as the bearer of privileged information and knowledge that he could dispense or dispose of as he wished. There was some fiendish delight he derived from calmly folding his arms and smiling while others like Burlage grew red in the face throwing tantrums and demanding that he divulge his sources. He wondered if this meant that someday he would be a bad parent.

He and Laith had fallen into amiable silence for a few moments before the prince stirred and glanced down at Breaker, whose dark head was resting on his paws a few inches from Laith's feet. Laith smiled fondly down at him, and ruffled the fur between his up-pricked ears.

"Tarr, I—"

But he was cut off; there were footsteps heavy in the hallway outside, and something about their cadence conveyed an urgency that had Tarr start back from his desk and Laith's hand reflexively go to the knife at his belt. The two whipped just around as there was an insistent knock at the door. Tarr thought wildly for a moment that there had been some sort of invasion and the headquarters was being taken, but then he remembered that marauding invaders would be unlikely to knock. He swallowed and called out in what he hoped was a steady, authoritative voice, "Yes?"

The door opened and there stood a very ruffled-looking Striker guard, who had clearly run a long way to get there. His pale cheeks were flushed and clammy. "Sir," he said hastily, "Horses—there are horses—a convoy of some sort, outside the city."

"What?" Tarr asked, confused. He glanced at Laith, who looked similarly puzzled.

"Soldiers," the guard panted.

"Kagai?" Laith asked sharply.

The guard shook his head, trying to recover his breath.

"Speak up!" Tarr yelled, more sharply than he wanted to. "Take a breath, pull yourself together, and tell us what's going on."

He never got the chance to, for a moment later there was a light footstep in the hall and Athela whirled around the doorjamb, fairly elbowing the panting guard out of the way without any semblance of apology, her black curls tumbling haphazardly around her face. If anything, the guard looked grateful to be let off the hook.

"Laith, Tarr—" she said.

"What is it?" Tarr yelled, his blood rising in even greater alarm at the sight of Athela.

"It's Cade," she said, and the name fell like a stone into the space between them.

"What?" Laith said faintly.

"Cade," Athela repeated. "*Your* brother, *my* cousin, has just ridden up to the eastern gate at the head of a battalion and is requesting entry."

Tarr and Laith met one another's eyes, but neither of them quite knew what to say. A million questions raced through Tarr's mind.

"A battalion?" he repeated. "Are they armed? Are they hostile?"

"There are soldiers on horseback, but they don't appear to be hostile. What do you want me to do?" Athela backed away and stood beside the door expectantly.

Laith and Tarr rose steadily to their feet, again exchanging a long, meaningful glance. "Cade's no supporter of Cira, I'm sure of it," he said, as if he were reading Tarr's thoughts. "Here, come on. Get your things."

"But where has he been the last three-odd years?" Tarr demanded. "Why now? And if he's the head of a battalion from Joymaril, who's to say that Cira didn't place him in charge?"

"She wouldn't," Laith countered evenly. "He's too smart. She wouldn't be able to control him, and she'd know it. If anything, she'd lock him away."

Tarr suddenly flashed back to his very first meeting with Cade in the palace of Joymaril: the young man's shock of blond hair, the cool detachment, the feeling, even then, that he was being sized up by a crafty, careful intellect. He looked from Laith to Athela, who slowly nodded in agreement.

Feeling as though he were taking a step off a precipice, Tarr looked to the out-of-breath messenger, still hovering nervously around the door. "Let them in. Direct them to the headquarters."

The guard nodded and vanished, and Tarr could hear him puffing down the hallway as he ran.

"Come on," Laith urged him again. "We should go out to meet them."

Tarr brushed his hands down his front. He wished he was wearing something more imposing and authoritative than a simple gray sweater with a few small holes around the neckline, but reasoned he could just stand a step or two behind Laith and let the prince act as the figurehead as he usually did.

The three Strikers wound their way quickly through the residence quarters and down to the main hall. Though no one said anything to them (and perhaps Tarr was just being overly alert), there seemed to be a palpable buzz in the air. Even more than usual, those who passed by them stared at them openly and opened their mouths as if to question the Strikers about the impending arrivals. *I don't know!* Tarr wanted to yell. *I'm just as surprised as all of you.*

They paused just before the front door of the headquarters and gathered themselves. Athela looked guarded and wary, Laith's face was studiedly blank. "Where are the others?" he asked.

As if on cue, Archer, Marc, and Ari jogged towards them. "Here," Marc called out. "We've only just been told."

"Didn't know you guys were planning a family reunion," Archer tilted his head sarcastically at Laith. "You didn't give me time to roll out my bunting."

"Laith goes out first," Tarr told them swiftly.

"Troops have all been alerted," Marc added. "Ready to attack if need be."

Tarr sincerely hoped that there wouldn't be any reason to start a bloodbath on the front steps of the Striker headquarters, but he nodded gratefully, glad that Marc had had the presence of mind to organize support.

The heavy doors swung open and admitted them out into the glaring sunlight. Tarr squinted a few times and peered around. Cade's battalion wasn't in sight yet; the plaza outside of the headquarters was conspicuously empty, almost as if all the townspeople had scurried off to gawk at the newcomers. Here and there stood small clusters of off-duty Striker guards, talking to one another in low voices. Tarr saw them peering up at him as he strode up behind Laith and stood, waiting for whatever was coming their way.

They couldn't see the troops but after a few seconds Tarr's brain put things in order and he realized he could hear them quite well; there was the unmistakable sound of bodies, of horses clopping on the stone streets, the clink of metal drawing ever closer to them, echoing over the rooftops to the north. *If Cade is coming and he doesn't mean to do harm, he wouldn't have everyone in full armor, would he?* Tarr wondered again, hoping (not for the first time) that he hadn't just made a decision that would doom them all. He stole a few glances at those around him. Marc, Athela and Laith, all of whom were more accustomed than he to being in the public eye and facing this sort of scrutiny, kept their expressions carefully neutral; Tarr could see that Marc's hand was resting lightly on the hilt of his sword, strapped to his hip. Ari hadn't grown up amidst the palace intrigue that the others had, but as usual he fit right in. When Tarr's gaze slid to Archer, his brother met it with his yellow eyes and raised his eyebrows. Tarr was glad to be beside him.

There was movement at the far end of the square; Tarr's throat tightened as the first horse in the column rounded the corner and began to come towards them. With a lurch, Tarr caught a glimpse of white-blond hair.

The procession drew closer, and at last Tarr was able to make out the riders. The first group of about ten or so were the only outfitted in full Jelani battle armor (whether this was actually for protection or just a way to look more impressive, Tarr couldn't be sure.) Tarr had only seen Laith once in his full regalia during the battle of Two Falls, and it had been truly frightening to behold. Cade was naturally smaller and lighter than his brother, so the effect wasn't quite as impressive, but the gleaming shine and bulky shoulders made him look more royal and less like a little brother than Tarr had remembered him.

Tarr did not recognize the young man riding on Cade's right hand. He was strapping and broad, and he looked to be about the same age as Cade, if not slightly older. His hair was a mottled gray and tawny brown, almost like the pelt of an animal; in his armor he fairly towered over Cade beside him, even though their horses were about the same in height. There was a strange look in his eyes that Tarr began to perceive as the riders drew near. It was some sort of barely restrained wildness, almost like a madness was there, contained behind a plane of glass and pressing, fairly bursting to break out. It unsettled Tarr to his core.

At last, the riders stopped, and silence descended. The trail of riders stretched out of the square and out around the corner; Tarr was relieved to see that they wore the livery of the Jelani royal houses, twisting silver ivy and white egrets flying across their breastplates, rather than the snakes of Kagai. (Though, he reflected, this too could be a ruse.)

A silence stretched out between them as the two groups sized one another up. Townspeople had begun to file into the edges of the square to watch them and to see what would happen; the interaction had begun to take on the atmosphere of a public sporting event. Tarr could see out of the corner of his eye that some of the younger Striker guards were looking back and forth like a ball was being tossed between the two groups; it would have been funny in almost any other situation. The horse belonging to Cade's riding companion tossed its head and pawed nervously at the cobbles with the tip of its hoof, clearly attuned to the tense atmosphere. Beside Laith's heel, Breaker gave out a high-pitched whine.

Finally, Laith broke the silence. "Cade," he said, as matter-of-factly as if his long-lost brother had just shown up somewhat overdue to a family dinner. "What brings you here?"

The tension dissipated, at least a bit. Cade's face actually cracked into a smile and Tarr saw the young man's shoulders loosen ever so slightly within their shell of polished armor. "Heard you were fighting a war," he replied, matching Laith's easygoing tone. "Thought we would drop in."

Laith took a step forward and went down the stairs, the others following cautiously behind him. Laith took Cade's horse's bit in his hand and held it steady as the young man dismounted. The two brothers regarded one another searchingly. Cade stood much shorter than Laith, but their shared genealogy was more pronounced than Tarr remembered. Cade no longer was a young boy; he was a man of twenty, and the childlike roundness of his face had vanished.

Standing before him, Laith could see instantly that whatever had happened over the last years in Joymaril, Cade had had a rough time of it. The difference in age and maturity was obviously apparent, but he was thin and had an oddly stunted look, as if nature had intended him to be taller and sturdier than he had turned out to be. There was a look in his eye, too, that Laith couldn't quite place. The boyish insouciance was gone and in its place was something hard and wary. It filled

Laith's chest with a heavy sadness that washed through him from his head down to his feet.

"I'm so sorry," he said quietly, so that only Cade could hear him. "Whatever has happened to you, I'm so sorry."

The young man looked momentarily disarmed and blinked in surprise. "We'll talk about it, I'll tell you everything," he assured Laith in the same low tone. "Hug me, quick, they're all watching."

The two brothers embraced quickly, pressing each other in a tight squeeze. Cade was the first to release the hug and stepped back. Raising his voice a bit so that everyone in the plaza could hear him, he announced, "We've taken back Joymaril from Cira's control." (At this, an audible buzzing of whispers rose up from the onlookers surrounding the plaza.) "I am now the King of Joymaril, and I've come to offer up our support in the fight against our cousin."

Laith took a step back, visibly shocked, but Cade maintained the same level expression as if to say, *well, what did you expect? Not bad for a little brother.*

"We're grateful," Laith replied, recovering himself. "We thank you for your support. Come inside. We'll find room for your soldiers and your horses in our stables, please have them follow Ari."

Ari stepped forward and beckoned, and began to lead the mounted column leaders around to the stables adjoining the building headquarters. The strange rider with the tawny hair and wild look dismounted and moved forward to stand beside Cade.

"My bodyguard, Wolf," Cade gestured to him, and Wolf nodded. "He's unable to speak."

"You are both most welcome," Laith said courteously, extending an open arm to Wolf, as if to sweep him through the front doors of the headquarters. Wolf inclined his head ever so slightly. He stood in near-perfect stillness, but there was something about his immobility that buzzed and hummed as though any moment he would explode into a thousand pieces. It was unsettling to be beside him, and Tarr felt himself take an inadvertent step back. He glanced over to Archer and saw that his brother's watchful yellow eyes were trained on Wolf's face, searching him and trying to figure him out.

Cade began to walk beside Laith up the steps of the headquarters, stopping and greeting each of the Strikers in turn. Marc welcomed him warmly, with genuine unadulterated affection; he must have considered Cade a surrogate younger brother after their years in the palace. Cade seemed to be gratified and surprised by the reception and smiled the first genuine smile Tarr had seen yet.

"Grown up, then, have you? Staged your first coup?" Marc said fondly, clapping him on the shoulder. Even Marc, shorter than all the rest, stood at about an even eye level with Cade.

Cade laughed and turned away to greet Athela, who was somewhat less effusive in her demeanor. She eyed him warily and gave him a sort of light diagonal hug (which even for her was chillier than usual) then stepped back to continue eyeballing him, glancing alternatingly between him and his phalanx of armed troops. Cade was introduced next to Archer, who nodded and smiled, flashing his sharp rows of white teeth. Finally, Cade turned to Tarr. Cade took a moment and faced him full-on before slowly extending a rigidly formal handshake. Tarr took his slim, cold hand in his six fingers and regarded the young man with unabashed interest. How strange it was to see so many family lines—Laith, Cira, even Marc, who was a distant cousin—converging in one face.

"Where's Rane?" Cade wheeled and asked Athela suddenly, snapping Tarr out of his wandering thoughts. Cade asked it casually, and really it was a perfectly reasonable question to ask—but there was an underlying shrewdness in his tone that immediately put Tarr back on his guard.

"She's been sent on an errand to the Meadows," Tarr lied smoothly, giving Rane's standard cover story. "She's been away for some time."

Cade nodded his comprehension and stared thoughtfully up at Tarr, and the Ashan again had the sensation that he was being sized up and analyzed for weaknesses. Whatever had happened to Cade during the long years of the war, and whether he had really come to Two Falls for the reasons he'd given, it was clear that Cade had his own private agenda. Tarr thought that he detected the faint sweet smell of blatant ambition hanging about Cade like a perfume. *Fine, then,* Tarr thought to himself. *As long as your interests align with ours and you don't get in my way, this should work out just fine. But I'm not going to trust you.*

As if he had read Tarr's thoughts, Cade smiled more broadly and turned away, clapping Laith collegially on the arm and starting towards the door of the Strikers' headquarters.

It was a short while later that the Strikers, Cade, Wolf, and a young woman—vaguely familiar, but whose name escaped Tarr's memory— gathered together in a small meeting chamber in the Two Falls head- quarters. Tarr was fairly bursting to pepper them with questions but maintained at least a façade of collected calm while their comforts and needs were seen to by the household staff. Once the drinks were set and food had been offered (and politely refused), Tarr posted guards outside the room and shut the door, then settled himself down into the chair to the right hand of Laith, at the opposite end of the long table from their guests.

Laith was acting very strangely indeed. Whoever the young woman was, Laith kept looking at her in a very obvious way, as if he wanted to say something to her but couldn't quite work out what it was. When he wasn't eyeballing the young woman, he would lapse into long periods of staring at his younger brother, as if he couldn't quite believe what he was seeing. This behavior was so odd that Tarr felt himself growing genuinely concerned for the Laith's well-being; he had clearly been badly shaken up by Cade's unexpected arrival. Tarr wasn't the only one who seemed to have noticed; he saw Marc stealing perturbed sideways glances at Laith every few seconds.

"Well," Cade said, looking around the table. "I think we should begin." He glanced from side to side at the two individuals seated beside him. "You've met Wolf already. This is Nadia, who was a former hand- maiden to Lady Ilaina. Nadia helped facilitate my escape from the dungeons of Joymaril."

So that's it, Tarr thought. *I thought I recognized her. No wonder Laith looks strange.* She had been the handmaiden to Laith's wife Ilaina. Tarr was sure that Laith wanted to ask her about his wife, a painful ellipsis in his life, but this was neither the time nor the place. Tarr looked at the young woman Nadia with fresh eyes. She was maybe a year or two younger than the rest of them, with dark blond hair and a watchful expression that suggested many years of waiting and listen- ing and being overlooked by those who considered themselves more important than she. Tarr wondered whether she had ever considered work as a spy. She met his gaze for a few seconds and stared at him, unafraid and challenging.

"The dungeons?" Athela blurted out. "You were in the dungeons?"

Cade regarded her levelly. "The dungeons. After you left Joymaril, Cira seized control and imprisoned many individuals. Myself and Wolf included."

There was a brief silence. "You were imprisoned for this entire time?" Laith echoed, his skin draining of color beneath its light tan. The hollows around his eyes seemed somehow even more pronounced and skeletal.

"Yes," Cade replied, and though his answer was simple, it was fraught with meaning. *Yes*, he seemed to say. *Yes, while you were galavanting around the countryside with your newfound friends, I was rotting away in a dungeon. And you left me there.*

Guiltily, Tarr realized that after they'd left and the whole adventure had started that he'd given very little thought to what had happened to the young man—or indeed, to any of the Jelani of Joymaril (with the exception of Ilaina, Laith's wife) after Cira's takeover. He'd been so preoccupied with the situation at Two Falls and their attempts to infiltrate Faridor that in the back of his mind he'd assumed that all the Jelani had sworn fealty to Cira, and that had been it. But, of course, there must have been some who resisted and he had been foolish not to see it.

"How many others were imprisoned?" Marc asked suddenly, eyes wide and intent. There was an undercurrent in his tone that implied an unspoken question.

"Many," Cade told him. "I don't know how many."

"Oren—" Marc began haltingly, as if afraid to let his boyfriend's name escape his lips.

"He was imprisoned," Cade confirmed shortly. "I don't know if he survived. My guards were just beginning to release the rest of Cira's political prisoners when we left for Two Falls."

Marc's face lost any vestige of color, but he tightened his jaw resolutely and absorbed the unwelcome news with the barest hint of a nod.

"Cade, I—" Athela began, but Cade raised a hand and waved it away.

"Whatever you have to say, save it for later. There's really only one person to blame in this instance, and it's Cira." He leaned forward, intensely, eagerly. "Our sole objective is to find a way to defeat her, once and for all."

Not your sole *objective*, Tarr thought cynically. *Seizing her throne for yourself—maybe control of Two Falls while you're at it—wouldn't be such a bad prize at the end of all this either, would it?*

"Can you tell us the whole story?" Tarr asked quietly, speaking up for the first time. "Everything that happened at the palace? After we left."

Cade shifted in his seat. "It started with an inquisition. Nearly everyone in the court was forced to come up and answer questions about their loyalties. Ostensibly it was the Queen holding the sessions, but everyone knew that Cira was behind it. Cira started to gather power, started trying to wrest it away from our aunt and uncle. Finally, she gave them an ultimatum. Give her the throne, or suffer the consequences. Wolf overheard it. They refused to cede control to her, so she killed them. And declared herself Queen." All this was relayed without the slightest hint of emotion.

"Were you condemned by the tribunal?" Laith asked in a hushed voice.

"No," Cade shook his head and picked at something invisible on the surface of the table. "I lied through my teeth and made it out all right. So did Wolf. But he and I were working together to try and figure out some way to resist. Then someone, probably one of Cira's allies, planted a letter that indicated I was in touch with you," Cade inclined his head towards Laith. "Which was enough for Cira to throw us in the dungeons. And to cut out Wolf's tongue."

Silence greeted the end of this speech. Tarr tried to wrap his head around it, the enormity of that length of time spent alone. He had endured one night in the dungeons—with Athela and Si for company— and still it had almost been too much for him to bear. He tried to think back over every day that had passed since they left Joymaril, tried to imagine those days spent in the same small sunless room, with no one to talk to, nothing to do. Tarr was fairly surprised that Cade hadn't completely lost his mind during his captivity. Something must have kept him going, kept him focused. Revenge seemed to be as good a driving force as any.

Laith turned slightly towards Nadia. "And you?" he asked, his voice hoarse. "Was it the same for you? Were you imprisoned?"

Nadia met his gaze squarely. "No," she replied. "After...you left..." she trailed off, and Tarr could see that what she really meant was *after your wife died*, "Afterwards...After Cira came to power, she put Lady Vera in control, and she went off to Faridor."

"Vera?" Athela snorted. "*That* moron?"

"The very same," Nadia nodded wryly. "I was assigned to be her handmaiden, and so I tended to her for those three and a half years, waiting for an opportunity to try and get Cade and Wolf released. Over time she grew frustrated with the limitations that Cira had put on her power, so I convinced her that she would garner support by pardoning political dissenters that Cira had imprisoned. And she agreed. She let him out shortly after the new year."

Tarr was impressed, not only with Nadia's patience and cunning, but also with the enormous stupidity of Lady Vera, who really sounded like a piece of work. *I have to see if I can recruit Nadia,* he thought to himself. Toppling a ruler and freeing another to enact a coup was no small accomplishment.

"So we were released," Cade continued chiming in. "And we took back control from Vera. I've declared myself King."

Laith cleared his throat reflexively and glanced sidelong at the others. This did not go unnoticed by Cade.

"A King?" Marc asked dubiously. "In Joymaril?" His face was puzzled—Jelani were traditionally ruled by Queens.

"And why should I not?" he asked, sitting up taller in his chair, a challenge rising in his voice. He seemed to interpret Marc's skepticism as a personal affront. "As a member of the royal family, isn't it my right?"

"No, by all means," Laith said quickly, assuaging Cade's defensive tone.

"I established a network of supporters to stay in Joymaril and ease the transition. I gave orders to release the other political prisoners, as I said, and to see that they were cared for and nursed back to health, if at all possible. And then I took our reserves and marched here. I put your old compatriot Dominic," he nodded towards Laith, "in charge of leading the transition. With the Third to enforce it." He spread his hands. "And here we are. Now," he continued, leaning forward, a keen look on his face and a glint in his gray eyes, "Where do we stand?"

At this, Laith turned and looked inquisitively at Tarr, silently searching for some indication of just how much information he should convey to Cade about their plans and their means of attack. Tarr grappled for a moment, then realized that it wouldn't get them off on the best foot if he kept Cade obviously in the dark. He gave a small shrug of his shoulder and a nod.

The prince turned. "The last bastion of Cira's power is the fortress of Faridor, which, as you know, is nearly impenetrable. It sits on its own island, removed from the mainland, and is connected by a single bridge. Crossing that bridge is impossible with an army. Laying siege from the water is impossible; the walls are too high and sheer. And we have no navy."

"So surround it," Cade shrugged. "Surround the fortress and starve her out. Block supplies."

"Cira has established relations with the country of Vireg across the ocean. We don't know to what extent they're willing to support her, but *they* have an almost unstoppable navy, endless supplies and wealth at their disposal, and technological capabilities we're only dimly aware of," Laith informed him. Tarr watched as Cade's expression of interest grew keener. He liked the sound of Vireg, Tarr could tell. "They're a sword precariously dangling above our heads. If we surround her by the sea, then she calls to Vireg and they wipe us out."

"Why aren't they here already?" Cade asked. "Lending troops and supporting her?"

Tarr cleared his throat and decided to reply directly. "Vireg's alliance with Cira is, primarily, one of convenience rather than conviction," he said. "I can't be sure, but I get the sense that King Tarik is waiting to see how the war shakes out. From his perspective, this is nothing more than a family squabble over an inconsequential spot of land. He'll send aid to Cira if needed, but won't risk the lives of his troops otherwise. For her part, she'd have to call in a favor. A big one. And so far she's been saving her favors. She doesn't want to be beholden to him. We can only hope she continues to isolate herself. We've also," he brushed his pant leg judiciously, "had reports that Cira hasn't been actually *seen* at the fortress since the new year."

Cade blinked. "What do you mean?"

"She's withdrawn even from her servants within Faridor," Tarr replied. "So we can't know what she's up to. Not for certain."

Cade looked perplexed. "An extra security precaution?"

Tarr shrugged. "Perhaps."

Cade nodded thoughtfully. "All right. What else do we have?"

"We know a few things," Tarr replied. "We have our old Faridor blueprints from years ago, but so far they haven't yielded results. We haven't been able to pinpoint how to exploit Faridor's construction to allow us a way in. It's too solidly built." *Not to mention Kagai was in an unfit state of mind when he built it, so the layout makes no logical sense.*

"In the meantime," Laith chimed in, "our spies have discovered word of some sort of weapon that Cira is collaborating on with the help of Vireg's scientists. But so far we haven't had luck in establishing what that weapon is or what it does."

"Not to mention the fact that half of our work here is dealing with Kagaian loyalists who are trying to raise an insurrection from within the city walls," Athela added, her arms folded across her chest.

Cade waved a hand. "We needn't worry about that. With my troops here, I think we can quash any rumblings of rebellion for the time being."

Tarr blinked. *That was easy.* Perhaps having Cade around wouldn't be so bad after all. "Thank you."

"Now we just need Faridor," Athela said with a wan smile.

"Have you sent envoys to Vireg?" Cade asked. "To try and get Tarik to turn his allegiance? It seems that without their support, Cira is backed into a corner."

Tarr shook his head. He had never met Tarik, but he had done extensive research, and the ruler was, by all accounts, highly cautious and shrewd. "Like I said, my sense is that he's going to watch and wait as long as he can without getting involved," Tarr shook his head. "And Cira is still technically the declared ruler of this entire country."

"For the time being," Archer cut in.

"For the time being," Tarr echoed. "He's not going to place his support behind an upstart rebellion like ours."

"Even with the weight of Joymaril behind it?" Cade pressed.

"Even so," Tarr coughed lightly. "My research has indicated that the people of Vireg have a...somewhat...dim opinion on the fighting prowess of the Joymarillian people. Even its cavalry."

Cade smiled rather serenely and looked around the table at each and every one of them in turn. "I'm assuming that efforts are underway to find out more information about Cira's weapon, whatever it might be?"

"You're correct," Tarr said guardedly.

"Well, it seems like until we have some more information about that, the best plan of action is to establish more law and order here in Two Falls, fortify the defenses, and see what might be done about setting our sights on Faridor. Call some sort of planning meeting. With *all* of our allies. Everyone who may have something to contribute."

"Once we have something to go on," Tarr added.

"Sounds very reasonable," Laith agreed, in a tone that sounded like he was unsure whether to be amused or annoyed by his little brother's show of authority.

"I think it would be a good idea if you were made part of the Two Falls governing council as well," Athela suggested, leaning over and catching Tarr's eye with a twinkle in her own. She knew how much Tarr despised the council.

"That's a great idea, Athela, thank you," Tarr agreed with a straight face. There was something quite pleasing about the thought of loosing Cade on the council. He wondered what the councilors, all seasoned politicians themselves, would make of this young upstart King.

"I'd be honored," Cade looked pleased.

There was a general sense that the meeting was coming to a close, and Tarr felt as though they'd been reasonably successful. Whatever his motivations might be, and however naturally suspicious Tarr might feel of him, there was no doubt that the additional power of Joymaril would be a boon to them in their fight against Cira. He began to push himself away from the table to stand and bid their guests farewell for the day when Cade caught him by surprise.

"One last thing," Cade said rather slyly, as if he'd caught Tarr trying to sneak something past him. "Where is Si Morthenstar?"

Tarr slowly pulled himself back to the table, feeling the other Strikers' eyes resting on him as they waited for him to make the next move.

"Why do you ask?" Tarr asked.

Cade spread his hands. "Ostensibly, Morthenstar is the banner everyone is rallying behind. But I'm told that he also hasn't been seen for months. Not since before the new year."

Tarr didn't have time to wonder about the logistics of Cade somehow picking up this piece of intelligence between his arrival at the front door of the headquarters and their meeting on the second floor. "He's been sent into hiding. For his own safekeeping. We can't afford to risk him being found or captured, not while the Kagaian loyalists still have a presence in the city."

"His security is my responsibility," added Marc, joining seamlessly into Tarr's lie, and such was the gravity of his tone that even Tarr almost found himself believing him. "There were a number of kidnapping and assassination plots and we simply couldn't afford to risk him being out in the open."

"I'd like to meet with him," Cade said, though it sounded less like a request and more like an order.

"You'll see him when we deem that it's safe for him to do so," Marc said sharply, then softened his tone somewhat. "Sorry, Cade. But that's the way it has to be."

Tarr could see that Cade didn't like this answer, but he moved past it. "In that case, my team and I will excuse ourselves for the time being. Thank you for taking the time to meet with us. It's been...illuminating." He rested his gray eyes for a beat on Tarr, then pushed back from the table and stood. Laith offered to walk them out. Tarr watched the three file out of the room, followed by the rest of the Strikers. Archer hung back. After the room was empty and the door shut, his brother swiveled his head around on his long neck, raised his eyebrows and whistled shrilly through his teeth.

"Well, there you go," he said. "The King of Joymaril."

"Apparently so," Tarr agreed, his arms folded across his chest, mulling over the events of the meeting.

"I have to tell you, I don't know who I trust the least out of all of them," Archer continued. "It's a close playing field."

Tarr couldn't help but agree.

CHAPTER ELEVEN

A thick fog had rolled in overnight and blanketed the coast in a white coverlet, hanging so low that it was almost impossible to see farther than twenty feet or so. Rane spent most of the night lying awake, refusing to let herself slip into a sleep that would inevitably bring with it images of Lord Seth, of his black stare, the waxy white skin of his face pulled tight over his skull, the edge of his sword against her throat. She swallowed and closed her eyes, hating him for what he had done and what he had taken from her, the fear he had managed to instill in the core of her being.

Stop, she told herself firmly. *Do not engage with the things that don't serve you.*

Pushing all thoughts of Seth aside, she instead focused all her energy on willing the sky to clear, imagining the fog rolling back out over the sea as the sun peeked over the horizon. And that's exactly what it did.

It was shortly past dawn that Rane slipped out of the front gate of Faridor. She came to the head of the bridge that connected the island to the mainland and waited patiently as the guards checked her letter of instruction (anyone leaving the fortress had to have a signed letter from the head cook or housekeeper authorizing them to leave; Cicada was particularly adept at forging these), and searched through her basket to make sure she wasn't smuggling out any contraband. Rane kept her expression neutral and her gaze lowered, and after they finished their inspection, the guards waved her past, looking bored.

"Which farmhouse are you visiting?" one of the guards asked. Rane supposed this was intended as more casual conversation rather than interrogation. It was probably a fairly tedious job, standing there and watching over the bridge early in the morning.

"Windy Cliff farm," she replied in a dull monotone.

"Cart driver says there's a new girl working up at the vegetable farm on the clifftop, been there a few months," said the guard. He looked off in the farm's direction. "Said she's pretty." He winked at Rane. "Give her my regards, will you?"

Rane rolled her eyes as the other guard snorted and finished reading over the papers and handed them back to her. "I'll bet she's bad luck, though," he scrunched up his face. "Birthmarks like hers mean bad luck."

Rane's eyes flew to him and it took all her self-control not to let her mouth fall open in shock. The person they'd just described could be someone she knew, a person she thought was dead. *Rowan.* Was it possible? *Could* it be possible? There was always the chance that there were two young women who fit that description, but from what Rane could see it was unlikely. Was Rowan alive after all this time? How on earth had she escaped from Faridor? Was she really living in a farmhouse only a little ways away? She remembered all at once the rumors of an escaped prisoner, and the conversation she'd overheard in the kitchens about the mysterious young woman who'd turned up overnight at one of the cliffside farms. How even then it had piqued Rane's interest for reasons she couldn't quite put a finger on. She made a mental note to tell Cicada, ask her to follow up if she could, and to tell Tarr. *If it is her,* she wondered, *what is she doing here? Why hasn't she returned to Two Falls?*

But there was no time for that now. She had to keep her mind sharp. There were even more pressing matters at hand, and as she walked on and the walls of Faridor fell behind her, she pushed the possible discovery of Rowan's identity to the side, focusing all her attention on her objective: the weapons test would be happening that very morning.

Once on the mainland, Rane kept to the path that led up to most of the farms dotted along the edge of the coastline. But once she was certain that she was out of sight of the guards at Faridor bridge (really, she was fairly sure that they hadn't given her a second thought once they'd waved her past), she turned to her left and dove into the edge of the wood that rolled over the hills and gradually down into the Ashan Forest. The woods were dark and filled with a silvery, misty dampness and Rane was acutely aware of the strange quiet that had fallen. It was that liminal time between night and just after dawn, when the night's creatures were retreating and the morning birds hadn't quite found their full voice.

The messages she and Cicada had decrypted using the cypher they'd stolen had been quite simple. They'd been able to crack a series of missives that were essentially direct back-and-forth correspondence between Cira's highest-level agents and their contacts in Vireg, arranging for the shipment of the weapon to Faridor's shores. Rane was alternately frustrated and impressed that Cira's agents had been able to keep the delivery of the weapon a secret; there hadn't even been whispers of it down in the kitchens, where nearly every piece of household gossip was aired and distributed to one and all.

Rane remembered the sweet, heady feeling of victory as Cicada had looked up from her last round of codebreaking, holding the message in her hand, clear as day and impossible to misconstrue: the weapons test would take place that morning, in a secluded valley just off the coast near the foothills of the mountain. Rane and Cicada had been able to collect a map of the surrounding area from the Faridor library records (some careless person had conveniently spilled something sticky across the floor in the records room, giving them an entire morning to work undisturbed) and had identified the only possible location for the test as described in the coded message. It was a clever place: safely removed from any of the coastal settlements and in a rather difficult area to reach, so it was unlikely that any passers-by would happen upon it. The walk was about an hour and a half from Faridor itself; an hour if one hurried, which Rane certainly did.

As she walked, she felt rising excitement growing in her chest. With every step she felt herself drawing closer to the answers that had eluded them for so long. But she also cautioned herself to not be careless. If Cira and her agents had been this careful in transporting the weapon under extreme secrecy to Faridor, it was absolutely likely that there would be sentries posted at various locations in the forest to catch anyone who might happen across the spot, remote though it was. She was on her guard.

Gradually, Rane became dimly aware of a strange noise starting to echo through the forest. It seemed to be coming from the direction in which she was heading, but the sound was unlike anything she'd heard before. The closest thing she could liken it to was thunder, but it was shorter, more controlled. It puzzled her, and she felt her already rapid footsteps picking up the pace.

About an hour into her journey, she determined that she would soon be within range of any sentries that Cira had posted, so she veered off the wooded path and out into the brush. She tucked the end of her cloak up into her belt to allow herself more freedom of movement, and to ensure that it wouldn't catch on any branches as she picked her way through the wood.

It was a good thing, too, for about five minutes later she caught a flash of green fabric up ahead on the path off of which she had turned. Immediately, she crouched down lower and began to creep through the undergrowth. Her cloak was dark and she had purposefully chosen a drab brown dress with trousers underneath it; she blended in seamlessly to the forest, and especially in the dim light of the morning it was easy for her to slide through the trees unseen. Much of her training in the Jelani Academy had had to do with stealth; she passed between the trunks like a ghost, one foot deliberately placed in front of the other on the open patches of soft earth, avoiding any twigs, dry leaves, or branches that would have betrayed her presence.

The guard was patrolling lazily back and forth, like a leaf in a slow-moving stream. Rane waited until his back was turned and then she whispered past him, no further than ten feet away. He didn't notice a thing.

About twenty feet past the guard the wood suddenly ended and opened onto the sloping edge of a hill that dove down into a small valley. On the other side of the valley, the hills grew and grew and massed onto one another, rising into foothills that, even further beyond, led up into the mountains that crowned the northernmost tip of the country.

Rane peered down into the basin of the valley and could see a group of about twenty Kagaian guards in green cloaks clustered around a strange object that she could not quite make out. She glanced over her shoulder. She didn't much like having to move out of the cover of the wood and into the open air, but she was protected by the fact that the guards were likely only to be watching for intruders coming from the outside, not behind them from the valley.

Keeping low, she slithered her way across a short expanse of open grass and took shelter behind a large knoll of earth. Waiting a moment to make sure that she was in the clear, she crept her way down until she found a knot of rocks jutting out from the side of the hill, which provided her with ample coverage both from the eyes of any sentries up in the forest and from the guards down below. Carefully tucking her earth-colored cloak about her hair and hunkering down amongst the rocks to blend in as closely as possible, she looked through a crack in the cover down to the valley floor.

At first, she couldn't quite understand what she was seeing. There were twenty Kagaian guards, as she had estimated before, but to her surprise Cira was not amongst them. From their insignia, though, they were all high-ranking officials who reported directly to the queen. All were clustered around a gray metallic object the size of a large dog or small pony. It seemed to consist of a large round body mounted on a heavy base fitted with wheels, and the cylinder could be adjusted to have its end pointed up or down. At that moment, the end of the cylinder was being cranked up so that it pointed higher into the air.

As Rane watched, one of the Kagaian guards drew a long pole, twice as tall as he was, and fed it into the end of the cylinder, as though he were trying to clean it. Next, another guard reached into a large crate about ten feet behind the object and withdrew something that looked like a large round wadded package, and fed it into the mouth of the cylinder, now pointing away from the group and down the valley. The package was followed by bits of paper and then something that looked like a perfectly round spherical ball. Rane watched the whole process with dumbfounded amazement. She had never seen any such thing before in her life.

Then again came the man with the pole—this time Rane could see that there was something tied to the end of it, something soft, and the man rammed the whole end of the pole into the end of the metal cylinder, as though he were tamping it down. He stood back and trotted around to the back of the strange apparatus.

There was a lot of fiddling now—the operators of the strange device were huddled together around the back of it, so that it was hard to make out what they were doing. But then they backed away and though Rane had no idea what was about to happen, she began to grow uneasy just from the sight of them—the guards were leaning away from the device, and bracing themselves as if something was about to happen. She could see a thin trickle of smoke emanating from the back of it and wondered whether it was about to catch fire.

Suddenly there was a small flash of orange light at the back. A huge sound, full and bellowing and so loud that it sent Rane nearly toppling over, blew out of the end of the cylinder, accompanied by an enormous cloud of gray smoke. Rane instinctively covered her head and tried to hunker down further, but out of the corner of her eye a split second later she saw something explode: a peaceful patch of earth many, many yards from the object suddenly blew up as if pushed from below, clumps of earth wrending horribly and spewing in arcs through the sky, the thick cloud of smoke from the machine covering the land in an awful, nightmarish haze.

Rane could scarcely believe what she saw. She looked from the object to the cleft now smoking sullenly in the earth. For the first time, her excitement at having discovered the identity of Cira's new weapon evaporated, and was replaced by a cold feeling of abject dread. *Did that... thing...somehow make the ground explode? How could it have done that?* She suddenly realized that her arms were shaking beneath her as they braced against the rock, and she forced herself to slowly take a deep breath to try and calm herself.

Down below there was some moderate activity; a group of six people came forward and, with great difficulty, began to roll the weapon on its cumbersome wheels back about twenty feet from where it had first stood. Rane could see from their efforts that the weapon was quite heavy and hard to move.

The group reset and after another short conference the process began again—the man with the long pole, the packing of the wad and the ball into the mouth of the cylinder. And then (Rane found herself bracing now for the awful, ear-splitting blast) the thin trickle of smoke emanated once more from the back of the object, there was a flash of fire, and the thing kicked back with a gut-pummeling roar.

Again, the earth split apart as if it had been violently kicked by some unseen giant; rocks flew this way and that, and a small tree which had been growing innocently beside a small cluster of bushes was obliterated so completely that it was impossible to tell that anything had ever been living there.

Rane was conscious now that hot tears of fear and shock and amazement were streaming down her cheeks. She brushed haphazardly at her face with the edge of her sleeve, but kept her head low and her eyes trained on the scene below. Never before had she seen any weapon that could do that. An arrow looked like a child's plaything in comparison. How on earth could their armies ever defeat this thing? Even as they ran toward it, it would fire once or perhaps twice, and ten or twenty of their fighters would be dead, without a Kagaian guard having to do much more than light a match. Rane's stomach turned, and she felt a swell of revulsion at the people who had even had the imagination to invent such a thing.

Focus, she thought. *Remember everything you see here, everything. If Tarr is going to find some way to beat this thing, he's going to have to know every detail of it. Every possible place that there is a weakness.*

So Rane watched, keenly as a hawk, as the weapon was moved and reloaded three, four more times in succession. From what she could glean, the team was mostly trying to work on the accuracy of the weapon's targeting. She noted everything she could: how many people it took to move the thing, how quickly it rolled, the mechanisms used for raising and lowering it. She wished she had brought a piece of paper and a pencil so that she could make a sketch of it, but knew better than anyone that papers could be misplaced or stolen. Worse, if she was found with such a sketch on her person, she would be immediately denounced as a spy. So she focused and memorized every line, every curve of the hateful thing and burned them into her mind so that she could effectively recreate them later.

After another hour or so, the test was clearly over and Rane was presented with the problem of how best to escape without being seen by any of the Kagaian guards. If she waited too long, she might be missed back at the fortress before the morning cleaning shifts had ended. But if she moved now, she may be seen by some of the sentries up on the hill. Weighing the two options, she determined that it was best to wait, and wait she did. She remained quietly hidden among the cluster of rocks, huddled beneath her dirt-colored cloak, contemplating the end of the world as she knew it. *If the people of Vireg have a weapon like that, which they're so willing and ready to share with a kingdom across the sea,* she thought to herself, *what else must they have? What are the weapons they still want to keep secret?*

She didn't much like the thought of it.

After another hour, the mist over the grass had dissipated and the sun had climbed high into the morning. The valley was once again still and quiet; the only evidence that the soldiers had been there at all were the huge, unnatural tears in the earth where living things had once grown. Rane sat motionless for some time. When she was sure that the way was clear, she began to pick her way back up the hill and through the wood, hurrying to make sure that she would return to the fortress before the test party arrived. As she went, she thought of the report she would have to write Tarr. She wasn't sure what she was going to say.

"What is it?" Tarr asked distractedly as the door to his office opened. He was rummaging around in his desk for his favorite pen, which he was sure had somehow dropped down behind one of the pull-out drawers. Cursing under his breath, he jiggled the drawer up and down and back and forth, the clamor filling the otherwise monastic silence of the grand room. He glanced over the top of his desk and was somewhat relieved to see that it was only Ari.

Ari cleared his throat and shifted his weight to one leg. Tarr gave a sigh. Clearly something more was afoot than simply a routine check-in. Tarr abandoned his efforts with the drawer, straightened up and raised his eyebrows expectantly.

"We've had a report that there's been a sighting in the mountains," Ari said. "Of Lord Seth."

Tarr felt the blood drain from his head. *The mountains?* he wondered faintly. *What was Seth doing there?* He knew that Seth had not been at Faridor, at least not according to Rane's reports, in which he had detected an undercurrent of relief in her oblique coded language.

"And?" Tarr prompted, trying to look more unconcerned than he felt.

"He's heading back to Faridor. Our agents up at the mountain headquarters followed him for as long as they could before they lost him, but his direction was unmistakable. He's returning to the fortress. He should be there very shortly, only a matter of days."

Rane, Tarr thought urgently. *I have to warn her.*

"Rane should be warned immediately," Ari continued, in the same unaffected monotone that belied the urgency of his words.

"The thought had occurred to me," Tarr said tersely.

"As soon as possible," Ari continued. "We must send someone."

Tarr frowned and tapped his knuckles on his desk. The situation was indeed urgent. Seth was the only one who could potentially identify Rane and blow her cover, having attacked her and nearly killed her before the battle in Two Falls. She would need to be put on her guard. There were two options available: send an envoy immediately to somehow get word to her, as Ari suggested, or send a coded message to her himself by the usual route. The coded route was safer but slower; it was complicated by design. There were multiple stops and handoffs, so that the thread of the message's passage would be difficult to follow.

"Tarr, we must send someone," Ari pressed again. "A letter will be too slow."

Who do I trust to do this? Tarr thought to himself, flipping through his mental catalog of the myriad faces in the Strikers' forces. The short answer was: nobody. There was no one he trusted to be smart enough and capable enough to get themselves safely into Faridor, to find a way to contact Rane or Cicada and let them know about Seth's impending return. No one, for that matter, who he trusted with the information regarding Rane and Cicada's true identities. There was no way around it.

"I'll write to her," he told Ari, turning swiftly to his desk and sitting down, only to remember that his pen was wedged somewhere in the back recesses of the drawer. He jiggled the handle loudly again, the racket undermining the authority he had just put on display. *Who the hell designed this thing?* he thought angrily.

Finally giving up, he fished a stick of charcoal out of the recesses of his pocket and set about dashing off a quick coded message. Glancing out of the corner of his eye, he could see by the tightening at the edges of Ari's mouth that he disapproved of Tarr's decision, but out of respect was refraining from voicing further concerns. Tarr was grateful for that, at least. He was late for a walk with Archer, and he anticipated that his brother was going to bring up his former friend Persefea's capture and imprisonment, which would be a whole complicated conversation in itself. The less time he wasted arguing with Ari, the better.

The message written, Tarr stood up hurriedly and strode to the door, passing the letter off into Ari's capable hands. "It will get there in time," Tarr assured him, trying to let the confidence of his own words seep in a bit. "This is the safest way."

Ari gave a short nod and tucked the message into his cloak as Tarr brushed past him into the hallway. Tarr squared his shoulders, aware of Ari's eyes watching him as he left, and tried to keep his walk looking upbeat and confident. For about the thousandth time, however, he felt himself wondering whether he had just made a critical mistake, and for a moment he considered stopping and turning back. But as he rounded a corner and vanished from Ari's view, he felt the urgency physically ebb away. *It will be fine*, he assured himself. And with that, he shook his head and forced the doubts from his mind.

"It's not looking good," Tarr said grimly, as he and Archer strode out together into the late morning air, cool and deliciously tart against their faces. Tarr stretched his arms in appreciation and closed his eyes for a moment, basking in the warmth.

"Persefea's not a threat, I promise," Archer insisted. "You release her now, she'll leave. She won't bother us again."

Tarr sighed and opened one eye, looking over at his brother, who looked earnestly upset. "I suppose you have her word for that?"

"I trust her," Archer maintained stubbornly.

"Archer," Tarr said tiredly, "I don't know her as well as you, but look—she's been fighting for Kagai all these past years, it's not exactly a glowing personal reference. And you do tend to be *slightly* softhearted about your past relationships." He didn't feel the need to mention the time that Archer had spared the life of his ex-girlfriend Kai, who had summarily turned around and very nearly succeeded in assassinating Laith.

Archer said something snotty to him in Ashan, which Tarr didn't bother to dignify with a response.

"So, what, we go with the alternative and let Burlage drag her out in the middle of the town square for a public lynching?" Archer snapped testily.

"Of course not," Tarr retorted wearily. "That's not what I mean."

"Burlage is calling for Persefea to be handed over to him and the rest of the council immediately," Archer reminded him.

"Which I don't intend to do," Tarr shot back. Though the two of them had set out to take a pleasant mid-morning walk together through town, they hadn't yet gotten further than fifteen feet from the headquarters doors. Tarr didn't much like the idea of having this kind of confidential conversation in public, either. He took a deep breath and steadied himself, and then put his hand under Archer's elbow to steer him forward and away from the building, and with a concentrated effort lowered his voice so that it could only be heard by the two of them. "I don't intend to hand her over to anyone," Tarr repeated.

"Tarr," Archer's voice was still tense, but at least he had lowered it to match the level of Tarr's. "You're not the king, here. You are not acting with immunity, as much as you may think you are. You do have to answer to others. Eventually Burlage and the others will force you to comply."

"I do not think that!" Tarr snapped, his voice level rising again before he could catch it. But something in the back of his mind stung.

Archer could see that his aim had struck its mark and he regarded Tarr with his level golden eyes. "Sooner or later, the council can put enough pressure on you to give up *something*. And you're going to have to compromise. If it's not the identities of your agents—"

"I would never," Tarr cut in.

"I know," Archer said patiently. "If it's not the names of your agents, it's going to have to be something else. Something else that will placate them and keep them happy. Like, for example, a high-ranking Kagaian officer that we've captured."

Tarr didn't like it. He certainly didn't appreciate what Archer had said about acting like he operated with complete impunity—but the truth of it was that Tarr *didn't* feel that he was somehow beholden to the governing rules of the council. He never had. *They haven't been where I've been or seen the things that I've seen*, he thought to himself. *They didn't fight in the battle, they didn't take back the city. They hid.* But Archer had a point. Technically, they were in charge, and they had been at loggerheads with him for months. Sooner or later, something would have to give.

"Since when have you decided to become so sensible?" Tarr asked Archer in mock irritation.

"Since I decided to go legitimate," Archer grinned back at him. "Believe me, it's taken much of the fun out of many aspects of my life. Back in the day, I would have just made a night of it and taken the entire council out and plunged this whole city into the anarchy in which it belongs."

"That's not funny," Tarr grumbled, though he couldn't quite hide his smile. Archer smiled serenely and shaded his eyes with one long hand against the cool sunlight. They passed the next few minutes in companionable silence, attracting a few stares along the way that Tarr was mostly able to ignore.

"So let us say that you decide to go rogue and spring a certain former Kagaian officer from jail," Tarr said cautiously in Ashan, seeing Archer's gaze come swinging sharply around at him. "What sort of guarantees do we have that she will leave for good? And not fight for Kagai any more?" He looked over and saw Archer blinking in apparent surprise at this turnaround. "We know how well setting Cira's old troops free worked last time around."

Archer was silent. He, too, had been opposed to showing the Kagaian riders clemency after the Battle of Two Falls.

Tarr sighed. "Look, Archer, I hate the idea of setting her free.

I think it is a bad decision. But I really enjoy provoking Minister Burlage, too, so..."

"I'll guarantee it," Archer said quickly. "Personally. I'll pack her off across the border, and if there's even a hint that she's returned, I'll hunt her down and kill her myself."

Tarr knew Archer well enough to recognize that this wasn't hyperbole; but again Tarr remembered Kai and how close that situation had come to outright catastrophe. Tarr gave another sigh (which he seemed to be doing a lot lately in the course of his responsibilities.) The Kagaian loyalists in the town were likely to know of Persefea's capture, and would suspect that she had given away their meeting place to the Strikers in exchange for her freedom. They would be unlikely to welcome her back into the fold.

"I want to know nothing about it," Tarr said finally in Ashan, and felt Archer relax beside him.

"Nothing," his brother echoed, looking victorious.

"And be careful," Tarr cautioned him.

"Always," Archer assured him.

Tarr could hear the wheels already turning in Archer's mind as he began to work out how best to spirit Persefea out from under the council's noses. He glanced over at Archer walking beside him and felt a wave of affection rise in him. The white Ashan's skin was gleaming in the sunlight, his spiky black-tipped hair sticking out at odd angles. How fortunate it was, Tarr thought to himself, that they'd found each other. Silently, Tarr raised one hand and clasped his hand over the tattoo on the nape of Archer's neck, a sign of affection that the two shared.

Archer smiled down at him. "What is it?"

"Nothing," Tarr shook his head. "Just glad to be out of the office."

"I know what you mean," Archer stretched out his arms. "I think they're having an art-makers fair over near the falls entrance. Shall we go that way?"

So the brothers ambled north, enjoying the sunshine and their stolen moments of freedom.

Archer wasted no time in effecting his liberation of Persefea; she was gone that very night. It was all done very neatly. Archer realized quickly that the easiest way to extract her would be during a transfer of housing, so he gave conflicting orders about moving the prisoner to multiple groups of Striker troops. At sundown she was brought out of her heavily guarded cell and marched across the headquarters to one of the receiving rooms, where her party was met by Archer and a handful of other guards, who said that they were there to take her the rest of the way. They were then met by a third party, who had been given orders to take Persefea the rest of the way, and then report to Marc for a reconnaissance mission in the Old Quarter that night. In the utter confusion, the guards dispersed one way and the other, with no one certain of who exactly had given orders to whom. Archer and Persefea were left to their own devices, and slipped out of the headquarters without being seen by anyone.

From the moment Persefea realized that Archer was making good her escape, the two of them went almost without speaking a word. When they reached the eastern gate of Two Falls Archer spoke quietly to the sentries (who had not yet been alerted to the prisoner's disappearance) and they were admitted out of the gates and into the freedom beyond.

They walked along the path out of the city, side by side, not saying much. Eventually, Archer turned off the road and led Persefea into a wooded glen. He pressed a small coin purse into her hand and the two faced each other. His unearthly skin glowed blue in the moonlight. He was different than she remembered him—older, obviously, and still possessed of that strange, alien attraction—but where he'd once been flippant and unendingly ironic, he now seemed to have a streak of genuine sincerity running beneath it all. It suited him.

"How much trouble are you going to get in for breaking me out?" Persefea asked finally. Archer waved away her words with one long hand.

"Negligible, I assure you," he grinned. "What are they going to do? Throw tantrums at me?"

"They may imprison you, too," she cautioned him.

Archer laughed outright. "I'd like to see them try. It probably wouldn't sit well with the entire city that we liberated. And Tarr wouldn't let them."

She tilted her head. "Be careful," she warned him.

"Now, look," Archer said, his voice growing grave. "The only reason I even bothered trying to get you out of there was because the governing council was calling for your head on a platter, as a warning to the other Kagaian loyalists. Everyone else—all the other Strikers— think that I'm nuts for believing you when you say that you want out."

"You *might* be nuts," Persefea agreed. "They have a point."

"I've felt guilty," Archer said after a moment. "All these years. For the things I did back then. I've tried to make a difference. But I think…" his voice drifted, wistful, "I haven't been able to shake the feeling, all this while, that it may be too late. Too late to really make up for it." He looked down at his boots, then swiftly up at Persefea. "And then there were the people we couldn't help. Kai, Rowan. You."

"It wasn't your responsibility," Persefea said sharply. "I knew what I was doing. As did the others. We did what we needed to survive."

Archer looked around helplessly. "What I need from you is your word—your solemn word, swearing on whatever it is you still hold sacred, that you will not join in this fight again. That you're done. That you'll leave, find somewhere else to live and that this is the last time I'll ever see you."

Persefea shook her head. "You're too soft a touch, Archer. Kai betrayed you before. I could, too."

"Promise," he insisted, not batting an eye.

"I promise," Persefea agreed. "On the souls of my family, living and dead, I promise. I'm done fighting. I hope you will be too, some-day soon."

Archer seemed to accept this. "Where will you go?" he asked.

Persefea glanced over her shoulder. "North, I think," she said finally. "Far north. I've never been there. I'll take the easternmost road around the forest until I'm safely past Faridor and then I'll turn up and travel north. I've always wondered what's up there."

"Snow, probably," Archer volunteered. "And lots of it. I suggest not having much to do with the Birch tribe. Not a very friendly bunch."

"You seem to be the exception."

"Yeah, well, that's why they kicked me out," Archer grinned.

"I'll keep to the coast," she told him. "And then if I run out of coast, I'll take a boat to wherever else there is to see." She paused for a moment and then tilted her head to one side, regarding him thoughtfully. "By the way," she said, almost casually, "I'm almost certain that there are a fresh set of plans—fully detailed drawings of every inch of Faridor, more thorough than any that have been made before—that are being kept in a blacksmith's shop called the Arrowhead. I think they're hidden somewhere in the eaves of the house."

Archer regarded her with frank, amused astonishment. "You *think*?"

She shrugged casually with one shoulder. "I have a hunch."

"Well, we'll just have to check that out, won't we?" Archer asked.

"Might be worth a look," she agreed coyly.

The moment waned, and the two of them looked around rather awkwardly at the night. It was apparent that the time had come for her to go; it wouldn't be long before her presence would be missed at the Two Falls headquarters and the guards would be alerted to what had happened. Tarr would, of course, still feign ignorance that he had been in on the whole plan, and would send off a group to look for them as he usually would have.

"Good luck, then," Archer reached out and squeezed her arm.

"Maybe I'll see you someday," she said. "On the other side of the world."

"Maybe," Archer agreed, and there was something wistful in his voice that to Persefea felt a little bit like an opening, a gentle invitation. She took a step forward and reached up to him, closing her eyes.

"I know the moonlight makes me irresistible," Archer said with a gentle humor in his tone that was calculated to softly dissolve any tension between them. "But I can't. Lovely though you are."

Persefea caught herself and her eyes snapped open. "I'm sorry. Living a life of celibacy, are you?" Her voice was more sarcastic than she intended; she'd been caught off-guard by Archer's unexpected refusal of her kiss and she felt a bit embarrassed.

"Worse," Archer said morosely. "I'm in love."

Persefea burst out laughing. "Oh, I might have known. You poor thing."

"It's not funny," Archer said grumpily. "I'm living in torment."

"I bet," Persefea shook her head, still laughing. "You always did have a type."

"What, sadistic?" Archer said sarcastically.

"Smart and uncompromising," Persefea replied. "Whoever they are, I can tell you're in good hands."

Archer let out a small, pathetic whimper, and she laughed again.

She left him shortly thereafter. Archer watched her vanish into the night, and as she faded away it was almost as if a door was shutting, softly and quietly and without anger. He felt a strange wave of sadness; perhaps longing for a past time or for a future that would never quite come to pass. He thought again of Kai, of Rowan, and all the people from the old days in Two Falls who by now had died or been scattered, one way or another, to the winds. He thought of the blithe happy ignorance with which he and his friends had faced the world back then; how careless they had been with each other, with their minds and bodies and hearts, and how selfishly they had taken advantage of the lives and livelihoods of others. And yet he still wasn't sure that he could have changed the young boy he had been. Or that he even wanted to.

After a time, he sighed, stretched and brushed a moth from the sleeve of his coat where it had been gently pulsing its wings like a heart-beat. It wasn't much fun, he thought, this growing up business.

He turned and headed home.

By the time that Archer and Laith had made their way back to the headquarters at sunup the next morning, news had spread like wildfire that the Kagaian officer the Strikers had captured had somehow escaped in the middle of the night. It didn't take much investigation to reveal that Archer had somehow been involved with it, and once this news had arisen, it was passed along like a burning torch to the members of the council, who at once called a special meeting to discuss the escape. They "requested" that Tarr and Archer be present.

"Didn't waste any time, did you?" Tarr muttered to Archer, as the two of them met in a hallway on the way to the council chambers. Archer looked bleary from lack of sleep but gave him a half-smile and a thumbs-up.

"Model of efficiency," he quipped.

They were admitted into the council chambers, and saw that Athela and Laith were already seated at the long council table, with two open chairs next to them. Both of them had strange looks on their faces, and stared silently at Tarr and Archer as they entered the room. Tarr tried to read their expressions, but found that he could not. He looked around at the rest of the faces at the table, and they ranged from quite grave to demonstrably angry to, in one particular case, on the verge of volcanic eruption. Tarr regarded Minister Burlage's scarlet face with an ever-increasing sense of content serenity, watching as he saw the man's inward fury build and build like a stoked furnace.

The meeting was called to order, and pleased as he was at having once again provoked Burlage, Tarr began to feel a sense of unease, as if he really had done something wrong. He didn't like the way they were staring at him, as if he were just a stupid child. He tried to keep his expression neutral, but felt anxiety clawing at his throat.

"I'll cut right to the chase," Pieter began, with a sharp tone that Tarr hadn't heard before. "We have reason to believe that the Kagaian officer who had been held in custody by the Strikers—but whose intelligence had *not* been handed over to this council—has escaped. We also have reason to believe that you," here, he looked pointedly at Archer, "were somehow involved in this escape. The prisoner was a known former associate of yours."

All eyes swiveled around again to stare directly at Tarr and Archer, even, to Tarr's discomfort, Athela and Laith. The scrutiny was so intense that Tarr couldn't help but squirm in his chair. Archer, to his right, looked as cool as ever and lied easily without breaking a stride.

"We'd been made aware of some threats on the prisoner's life and naturally wanted to ensure her safety," Archer said smoothly. "I gave the order that she should be moved, but worried that the transfer would need to be overseen. I went down, and found that there was some disagreement among the transporting officers and that the orders had somehow been mixed up. In this confusion during the transfer, I found myself alone with the prisoner at which point she successfully made her escape."

This was all said without a moment of hesitation or the slightest blush of shame, and was so utterly convincing that Tarr inwardly found himself making a note to never trust Archer's word on whether or not his hair looked all right or whether he had anything stuck in his teeth. He looked around at the faces staring at them, and now saw some thoughtful frowns rather than a chorus of suspicious scowls. Pieter, however, still looked stern and Burlage looked positively bilious.

"We have reason to believe that you gave two groups of guards conflicting orders with the intent to create confusion and provide an opportune moment for your prisoner to escape," Pieter pressed.

"I gave one order," Archer said shortly. "Whether that order was conflated or mistakenly passed along, I don't know."

"What of reports that you were seen after midnight at the east gate of the city with another individual?" Pieter continued.

Tarr wasn't sure how Archer would lie his way out of this one. It wasn't as though there were other tall, pale, yellow-eyed Ashans walking around.

"They were mistaken," Archer said calmly, drawing a line in the sand. Pieter had stated his argument, and there was nowhere to go. It was going to be Archer's word against the word of the guards who had been on duty; he had been effective enough in creating a sense of confusion that Tarr got the sense their testimony would be jumbled at best.

"And you, Tarr," Pieter continued, rounding on Tarr, whose attention immediately reverted back to the proceedings. "Did you know of this?"

"There was no plot, so there was nothing *to* know," Tarr said, trying not to make his words sound too hasty. "I did know of the intention to move the prisoner."

"But you did not give the order."

"No, Archer did."

"Why is that?"

"He was concerned for her safety, as he said," Tarr shrugged.

Pieter seemed to sense that he was at an impasse. He shook his white-haired head and laced his fingertips in front of him on the table. "Fine. I can see we are going to get nowhere with either of you. But this is very serious indeed. A political prisoner with key knowledge that could have benefitted us in our fight against Kagai has escaped or been given an unauthorized release. There's no telling whether or not she will rejoin Kagai's forces. Not to mention how weak and disorganized this kind of blunder makes us look."

Tarr once again squirmed uncomfortably in his chair. He was starting to seriously second-guess the decision he had made, and felt resentful of Archer for even asking him in the first place (and perhaps for looking so calm and unruffled as he sat there beside him.) Archer was truly reckless, he realized with a sudden dash of horror. Reckless in a way that wasn't as charming or endearing as it had always appeared to him, blinded as he had been by his love for his brother. Archer went through life with the blithe carelessness of someone who believes that his doom is just around the corner and cares little for the consequences. Tarr could not afford to do the same.

He won't change, Tarr remembered Ari saying, and with a twist of guilt, he looked at Laith's face, remembering how close the prince had come to death the last time Archer had allowed this to happen. *And I helped him.* He wished the floor would swallow him up.

"I trust," Pieter continued, "That every effort will be made to recover the prisoner? That perhaps she can be found and returned?"

"Of course," Tarr said, in what he hoped was a smooth voice. "Every effort."

"This is intolerable!" burst out Minister Burlage, who had clearly been exercising a very serious effort to not break into the proceedings sooner. "These two should be arrested immediately and tried for treason!"

Immediately, Tarr felt his hackles rise, and he looked at Burlage's florid countenance with a dripping disdain. "You want to arrest *us?*" he repeated. "For *treason?*"

"That's what I said!" Burlage snapped back. "And that is what you have committed. Treason! By allowing an enemy of the state to escape and evade punishment for her crimes, you have aided and abetted the forces of Cira Kagai herself."

"Look," Tarr said through clenched teeth, leaning forward onto the table. He could feel Laith's steadying hand reach out and touch his knee, but he was so incensed that he ignored it. "You are upset because the prisoner's escape has thrown a wrench into your making a public spectacle of her execution, which you hoped would win you elected office. You care nothing for the lives of the people in this town, for *anyone* who has fought in this war—on either side. You care only for yourself."

Burlage sputtered, and glared at Tarr and Archer with deep loathing. Though Tarr didn't glance over to look at his brother's face, out of the corner of his eye he could see that Archer had his arms folded across his chest, as if he were thoroughly enjoying the whole thing. Thumbing his nose directly at authority came naturally to Archer; it did not so to Tarr, who felt as rushed through with adrenaline at this confrontation as if he were running away from a pursuing group of Kagaian soldiers.

"You are children," Burlage snapped. "Children who have no business making decisions that shape the lives of others."

"Perhaps," Tarr retorted, "But who closed their eyes and ears when Cira was taking power? Who refused to listen? Who put us in this position in the first place?" He leaned back, fuming. "At least we didn't spend the duration of the war hiding in our cellars and paying out a fortune in bribes so that Cira's soldiers would look the other way." He saw with satisfaction that this jab hit home; as well it should, since it was common knowledge that this was how Burlage survived the occupation of Two Falls after the city's former government had toppled.

"I formally propose that the Strikers be removed from this council, and that Tarr and Archer be arrested and tried for treason," Burlage announced, his eyes boring holes into Tarr's as he said it.

Tarr expected the rest of the council to meet this with the swift dismissal that they usually did, but to his growing horror, he saw a few of the council members move uncomfortably in their seats and glance at each other, as though they didn't want to throw their lot in with Burlage (who was clearly out of control), but that they didn't totally disagree with him, either. Tarr desperately wanted to look over to Laith and Athela to gauge what they were making of this whole debacle, but forced himself to sit up straight, square his shoulders, and look as blameless and noble as possible.

"The council will take it under advisement," Pieter said slowly. "No such steps shall be taken today." At this, Burlage began to sputter in fury, but Pieter swiftly cut him off. "*But,* the Strikers shall be advised that while they were undeniably responsible for the liberation of this city, and that this council recognizes their contributions, there is no King or Queen in Two Falls. Not now." Here, he looked directly at

Tarr. "No single individual may make decisions affecting the fate of this city with immunity. There must be a governing body, and a consensus reached. I think that even if the process is difficult or contentious," he concluded diplomatically, "that the Strikers would do well to remember that."

Tarr felt as though he were a child being scolded by a disappointed parent. His chief desire was to look down at his hands and make himself as small as possible—*anything* so that the council members would stop staring at him.

"Thank you for your words," Laith broke in, his smooth, deep voice like a balm on the fraught atmosphere of the room. "We thank the council for their time in considering this matter, and will take steps to recover the prisoner before she is able to get too far."

The tension in the room relaxed infinitesimally. Laith had that sort of placating effect. Pieter adjourned the council meeting moments later; Burlage stalked from the room, seething, refusing to even look at any of them as he went. Tarr and Archer exchanged glances. Archer raised his eyebrows, a subtly gleeful expression that said *we got away with it!* but Tarr couldn't quite share his sense of triumph. Tarr pushed his chair away from the table and began to get up.

"Tarr, wait," Laith said quietly, and there was a serious note in his voice that told Tarr he wasn't quite out of the fire yet. They waited until the room cleared completely and the door shut behind the last council member, then Tarr forced himself to look at his friend. The room, with its filtered sunlight and dark wooden appointments, seemed even more cavernous and intimidating than when it had been filled with people.

If Tarr had felt uncomfortable when the council had been staring at him, it was nothing compared to how he felt looking at Athela and Laith.

"Is it true?" Athela asked quietly. Somehow this was much worse than her usual bulldog-like approach to any sort of confrontation.

Tarr glanced towards the closed door, just to be certain that no one outside could hear them where they sat. Silently, he nodded, and watched as Laith's face grew graver and Athela's shifted visibly into a state of barely repressed exasperation.

"Why did you two do such a thing?" Laith asked, looking from

Archer to Tarr. "Without talking to any of us?"

"If we'd known it'd be the end of the world, we *would* have," Archer cut in, more flippantly than Tarr would have liked. "Look, they were going to kill her, *publicly*, to set an example and score political points for that—" he jerked his head towards Burlage's vacated chair, searching for an appropriate euphemism, "—piece of work."

"Archer, we're at war. Former friends of yours don't just get a free pass. As you *know* they shouldn't," Laith added quietly, letting his point fall so squarely and gravely that even Archer had to look at his hands for a moment. "She was fighting for the enemy."

"She gave us valuable information," Archer insisted earnestly, looking back up. "And she gave me intelligence about where to find the latest Faridor blueprints. She—"

Tarr quickly reached out and grabbed his brother's wrist to silence him. They had indeed recovered incredibly detailed blueprints of Faridor right where Persefea had told them to look, but there were too many eyes and ears in the Two Falls headquarters for Tarr to feel safe discussing them openly.

"You're not seriously saying that you want to give Burlage the satisfaction, do you?" Archer asked sharply, and Tarr could hear that the flippancy was gone and that they were brewing towards an all-out fight. He squeezed Archer's arm again to try and steady him, but to no avail. "Getting to reduce a person who I have known and loved to some cheap point on a political scoreboard?"

"Of course not," Laith said levelly, not rising to it. "But you have to see beyond those feelings, Archer. You have to see their potential consequences. We could have kept her safe."

"We would have needed a bone to throw at the council, and she would have been it," Archer said, echoing what he'd told Tarr earlier. "You know it, and I know it. It's not like we can give them Tarr, or any information about his operatives. We'd have to give something. So I took her out of the equation."

"Leaving us in a worse position with the council than when we started," Athela cut in. "Now we *don't* have any other cards to play. Not even any goodwill. You've provoked them into outright antagonism. It's going to be us versus them, rather than everyone working together.

Unless Laith can go in and salvage it with some of them."

Throughout all this, Tarr kept quiet. He wasn't sure what to say, and couldn't remember the last time they had argued like this together. What was even worse was that he could clearly understand both sides. Archer's loyalty to his friends ran deep, but with the benefit of hindsight he knew that Laith and Athela were right. He and Archer had made a reckless decision without consulting the others, and it had placed them in a precarious political and strategic position.

And yet something niggled at the back of his mind, that small voice that piped up again: *where was the council during the war? They didn't fight. They have no right to tell us what we can or can't do.*

"I'm sorry that we didn't tell you," Tarr said finally. "We should have. But I'm not sorry we did it, or that we did it without the council's permission. The Strikers are not in the business of making examples of political prisoners. I still haven't forgotten what happened to General Grey."

Laith looked long and thoughtfully at him. "You know, Tarr, I don't completely disagree with you. We all regret what happened. But what bothers me," (here, Tarr was surprised to hear that even the prince's normally unflappable calm was rising in temperature) "was that *he*—" he pointed his finger at Archer, "came to ask permission from *you* and you alone, and that *you* moved forward with it." He lowered his hand, his voice returning to its usual deep, honeyed tone. "Pieter was right, Tarr. You're not the king of Two Falls. And I think you'd do well to remember it."

Tarr was shocked, and felt as though he'd been stabbed in the gut with a red-hot poker. "That's ridiculous. I don't think I'm the king of *anything*. How could you—how could you even…"

Laith raised his hands peacefully and leaned back. "I've said my piece, disagree with it if you want. But keep it in mind. That's all."

"We survived the war so far together," Athela agreed softly. Her gray eyes were solemn and she leaned in towards them, looking from Archer to Tarr and back again. "*Together*."

"I *get* it," Tarr said sharply, irritated, suddenly wanting to get as far away from all of them as possible, as quickly as possible. He stood roughly up from the table. Unsure of whether or not he should say anything to them before he left, he hovered for a moment, then nodded silently and went out, closing the door behind him.

At least no one had been listening at the door, not as far as he could see. He had the sneaking suspicion that some of the council members—Pieter especially—knew exactly what had happened between them and exactly the sort of dressing-down Tarr and Archer had gotten from their friends as soon as the council had left the room. Tarr mentally tried to shake it all off, to turn his attention to the rest of the tasks he had to do that day. But as he walked, his mind kept turning over the conversation, and a fear and doubt began to grow in his stomach that maybe, somehow, all of them were right about him.

CHAPTER TWELVE

It was morning, too early even for Rane and Cicada to come to the kitchens for their breakfast before beginning their morning chores. But both were awake; Cicada was seated at her desk, contemplatively braiding her hair into a long dark plait, her sharp eyes occasionally glancing over to Rane, who was seated partially out of sight, writing on the floor beside her cot. There was a loose stone in the wall near her bed that she had been able to pry out, using the space behind to store her papers and other communications with Tarr.

Like the other maids' chambers, there was no window in the little room. It was but one in a long corridor of servants' quarters located near the belly of the fortress by the kitchens. It was outfitted sparsely, with two beds, a small desk, a washstand and a short chest of drawers where Rane and Cicada stored their few clothes. They kept it neat, as inspections were frequent.

As if she could feel Cicada watching her, Rane, without glancing up, signed, "Almost done," and returned to her writing. She was working on the weapons report, detailing every minute observation she had made during the morning in the valley. From what Cicada had seen, it was already a few pages long. Rane would finish writing the report in longhand, and Cicada would code it later that afternoon to send to Tarr.

Rane paused for a moment, and as she did something perked her attention—a noise out in the hallway. She glanced towards the door, then at Cicada, who could see from Rane's face that something was amiss. Rane gave her a short nod and Cicada rose immediately, flipping her braid back over her shoulder and striding to the door. She opened it and peeked outside.

Down the corridor was a troop of green-cloaked Kagaian guards, banging on the maids' doors and shouting something. Their expressions were stern.

Immediately Cicada withdrew and turned to Rane. "Guards down the hall for an inspection, move fast," she said.

Quick as lightning, Rane folded the paper she was working on and tucked it into the empty hole in the wall near the floor. She quickly replaced the stone that covered it and stood, brushing herself off and returning the pen, ink, and remaining paper to the desk. Cicada moved to the bed and rumpled it a bit. Rane strode to the washbasin and poured some cold water into the bowl, then splashed her face, grateful for the shock of it on her skin. She could hear the racket of the guards getting closer, the sounds of doors opening and slamming. *It's probably just a routine inspection*, she thought to herself. *Just routine.* And yet something nagged at her.

Though they'd been expecting it, the harsh knock on the door made Rane jump. Cicada, who watched her reaction, turned around reflexively. The door flew open and a guard leaned inside.

"All servants assemble in the Great Hall," the guard ordered. "Now."

"We just had an inspection!" Rane protested, trying to sound whiny and immature.

"Don't make me open this door again. I want you both out of here in ten seconds," the guard growled. He pointed to Cicada, who was watching him cooly from her seat on the bed. "YOU!" he said loudly, with emphatic gesticulation, as though Cicada couldn't understand him. "OUT."

Watching him narrowly, Cicada rose from the bed and glanced at Rane, who met her gaze for only a moment. Rane twisted her auburn hair back into a low roll and tied it in place, then reached for her green hood and pulled it over her head and hair. There was something curiously comforting about the anonymity it gave. She wondered why she felt so jittery. It was just an inspection. They'd already had three that month.

The corridor was chaos. Maids and household servants were scurrying about, pulling on robes and looking frazzled. Some of them had slippers or socks, even more were barefoot and looked decidedly uncomfortable about having to walk on the cold stone. There was something in the air; a pitch of urgency that Rane didn't like.

"Was there any news from Tarr this morning?" she asked Cicada, keeping her hands low and unobtrusive.

Her friend shook her head. "Nothing. I checked."

Rane nodded and forced herself to swallow. *It's just a routine inspection,* she told herself again. *Tarr would have warned us if there was anything important.*

They all made their way in a disorganized pack to the great hall, where the morning sun was filtering bleakly down in patches on the shining, reflective black floor. A shaft of sun from the large window at the end of the hall fell in a diagonal slant down the stairs that led to Cira's throne.

The fifty or so servants arranged themselves into a long snaking line that ran down the center of the hall. All of the faces around them were a strange juxtaposition of sleep and wild alarm. Rane faked a yawn, while her eyes darted this way and that, around at the other servants and to the green-cloaked guards who now waited at attention. Cicada had been shuffled around in the crowd and was a few places down the line from her.

And then, almost like a premonition, Rane felt a wave of cold fear wash up her back and along her neck, which began to prickle as though electricity were running through her skin. She felt her head whip around and there, at the other end of the hall and flanked by another four guards, she recognized Lord Seth, the man who had scarred Marc for life, killed Laith's wife and had very nearly killed her too. His face and hair were a crescent of white, and even from where she stood she could feel the cold emptiness of his lifeless black eyes.

A lifetime of honing her own capabilities and developing a capacity to trust herself even in dangerous situations had rendered Rane fearful of very little. Cautious, yes, when the time was appropriate, but it was very seldom that she felt the clench of hysteria in her chest or felt her blood begin to race, felt herself seized by the sudden urge to run as fast as she could, as far away as she could go. Rane had never experienced physical terror like this. As Seth drew closer to the line of servants, she had to choke back the urge to turn and flee, feeling every inch as if one of her nightmares of him had come to life. *Perhaps I could get out*, she thought to herself.

No, she countered firmly. *You are invisible. You have a face that no one remembers. There is no way he will be able to recognize you.*

She forced herself to keep her face perfectly immobile, her eyes staring straight ahead and concentrating all her energy on slowing her heartbeat and stabilizing her breathing. She wouldn't put it past Seth to be able to smell her fear, to pick the salty, acrid scent of terror out of the air like a hungry wolf.

He was close enough now that she could see those eyes, which she remembered them all too well—as dark and flat and endless as a well, with no light or reflection or sign of life behind them. And there was his immobile half-smile, still frozen in place as if it had been painted on with a single sharp, thin crimson brushstroke.

He stopped at one end of the line. The guard beside him spoke. Rane shivered.

"Queen Cira suspects that there may be a traitor amongst you," the guard said quietly. "She has asked us to find out who."

The smile on Lord Seth's face grew ever so slightly, and he tucked his hands behind his back and began to walk slowly along the line, searching each servant's face with his cold, empty stare.

Rane's legs were shaking, but she fixed her gaze forward and repeated to herself: *You are invisible. You are invisible. You are invisible. He will not know you. You are invisible.*

Ten servants away.

You are invisible.

Five.

You are invisible.

Two.

You are invisible.

Rane's gaze bored ahead into nothingness as Seth's black shape drew up in front of her. She held her breath, refusing to look up into his face. The shape moved ever so slightly. Slowly, one of his long pale hands extended from beneath his robe, and she felt her breathing halt as he tipped one finger up under her chin, tilting her head into the light, gently, like a lover might. His skin was cold as ice.

Rane felt the grip of fear clench around her heart.

Then his other hand came up and gently pulled down the hood that framed her face, revealing the long red scar across her throat. Rane felt as though she were about to black out, and her eyes traveled up unbidden to meet his. His smile split, his mouth wet and red, revealing a row of small, sharp white teeth. His eyes were like two hollow, endless pits. After a moment, he gave a tiny nod and tipped his long finger beneath her chin one last time. Rane could feel the eyes of all the other servants boring into her.

Caught you, his smile seemed to say.

He snapped his fingers and stepped back to allow the guards to come forward.

A few places down the row, Cicada was trying to repress the urge to leap forward. *What is going on?* she thought, bewildered. *How on earth did Lord Seth recognize her?* She kept her face purposefully impassive, reflexively flinching as she saw Rane falter ever so slightly as she stepped forward from the line of servants into the knot of guards to be led away. Rane did not look back over her shoulder as she went, and Cicada could do nothing but watch her slowly disappear down the distant hall. She dug her fingernails into the palm of her hand.

Cicada's mind churned furiously as she considered what to do next. She was no fighter; any attempt to pursue the guards and Seth to rescue Rane would surely be suicide for them both. Besides, there was a chance—ever so slight—that they would keep Rane alive as a tool or a bargaining chip, or at least a source of information. Cicada swallowed hoarsely.

What would the guards do next? Search Rane's room. Then it occurred to her: *the weapons report.* She had to find some way to get the weapons report out of Faridor, and fast. Now that Rane had been uncovered, the fortress would be completely locked down; she, as Rane's roommate, would be under near-constant surveillance and there would be no other chance to smuggle it out. *Get it out, and then figure out a way to help Rane.*

All of these thoughts occupied the space of only a few seconds. Rane wasn't even out of the room before the other guards turned around and barked something that Cicada assumed to be a dismissal. The movement of the other servants changed; they turned to one another and began to whisper and gossip. She saw how their eyes shifted nervously, mouths barely moving as they kept up a near-constant stream of chatter. She had only a few minutes to come up with a plan, and was conscious of every second that ticked past.

She walked as fast as she dared back through the Great Hall, down the winding passageways into the belly of the fortress, back to the maids' quarters and her room. She threw the door closed, knowing that she was taking a great risk; since she wasn't able to keep an eye on the hall-way she would have no idea when the guards would come bursting in. She only knew that they were coming. They were already on their way.

She stood for a moment, grasping for stillness, for a wave of clarity. *I can't grab the plans and run*, she thought. There was no way that she would not be intercepted and brought back for interrogation. It was similarly impossible to find someone to help her; there must have been other Striker spies in Faridor, but she had no idea who they were. Tarr had kept them all purposefully separate to protect their safety; they transmitted messages through a complex system of pickups and dropoffs throughout the fortress. She had no way to reach them in time. Then an idea—only the scrap of one—blossomed in her head.

It was a very long shot, but it would have to do. On the day that she'd returned from the weapons test, Rane had told Cicada that—though she couldn't be sure—there was a chance that a girl at one of the farms was someone with connections to the Strikers from the early days back in Two Falls. Rane believed that she had escaped from Faridor and was hiding out at the farm. It was all unconfirmed, of course, and Cicada had no idea whether the girl was even still there. But from where she sat, it was her only chance. She was just going to have to gamble. There was no other way.

She had to rely on the fact that they would underestimate her because of her deafness, as everyone always did.

Immediately, the necessary actions fell into place and Cicada moved quickly and smoothly. She felt suddenly calm, the frantic thoughts of a moment ago falling away from her like a discarded cloak. The guards could only be a minute or so away. She removed the rock from Rane's hiding place in the wall and pulled out the weapons plans. She hesitated for a moment, looking at the stack of codes and precious ciphers piled in the back of the hideaway. Then she steeled herself and replaced the stone without pushing it in fully so that the guards would have little trouble finding it. There would be far less suspicion cast upon her if the guards were able to find some evidence of Rane's work.

She flew across the room and seated herself at her desk, grabbing a blank sheet of paper and putting it atop Rane's report. She took the pen and ink and forced herself to inhale and exhale deeply, then dipped the pen into the ink and began to write as quickly as she could without compromising her penmanship. It could not look rushed.

Her fear that the guards would enter before she could get any convincing writing on the paper ebbed with every passing second. She wrote:

and although the other girls say that it isn't so, I do think that one of the cooks is having a love affair with one of the archers who keeps the late watch. I have seen them a few times exchanging glances, and even saw them talking together at one of Queen Cira's events. Mark my words, mother, she sighs whenever someone mentions his name, and it is the most ridiculous thing. Back home she would be covered in tar and feathers for such shameless behavior.

She went back over what she'd written, her heart racing, and made slight glancing pen marks under the words *archer, mark, sigh, tar—* anyone casually reading it would think they were only scribbles, but there was the slightest chance that someone reading it and looking for a hidden message would notice them.

Breathing evenly, she began the next paragraph, which she tried to make sound as trivial as the first. And then, just as she suspected, she felt the slight *whuff* of air from the door opening and looked up as three guards entered the room. She forced herself to look surprised and slowly stood, the papers clasped in her hand.

The head guard said something and gestured around the room, making it clear that they were there to perform a search. He said something to her directly, but she shook her head. One of his compatriots leaned in and whispered something to him. The lead guard nodded and snapped his fingers at one of the blank pieces of parchment on Cicada's desk. Silently, she proffered the paper and her pen.

YOUR ROOMMATE IS ARRESTED FOR TREASON. WE ARE SEARCHING YOUR ROOM.

Cicada shrugged casually, as if this was (not entirely exciting) news to her. She gestured around the room in an unspoken invitation, and the two other guards began to comb through Rane's belongings. She swallowed dryly as they flipped Rane's mattress over and overturned her trunk, scattering her friend's possessions across the stone floor.

She felt a nudge on her arm, and saw that the lead guard had written something else on the piece of parchment:

DID YOU EVER SEE HER WRITING ANYTHING? HIDING ANYTHING?

Cicada shrugged again, trying to look disinterested in the mess being made of her room. *Make them overlook you*, she thought to herself. *Be as boring as you can.*

She took the pen in her own hand:

She wrote letters sometimes. We work opposite shifts. I don't see her much.

The lead guard eyed her narrowly, but seemed to accept it. It was a lie, and if the guards really wanted to do their due diligence, it would not be hard to disprove. But Cicada counted on the fact that they wouldn't care enough to dig deeper. They had their Striker spy. Perhaps that would be enough.

On the opposite side of the room, the other two guards had discovered Rane's hiding place, just as Cicada had intended. She tried not to boil with fury at the sight of smug victory blooming over the guards' faces. They motioned to their leader, pulling out the small stack of ciphers and codes, flourishing them like trophies. The leader said something to them, then turned back again to survey Cicada's reaction. She arranged her features into an expression she hoped was something between puzzlement and detached surprise.

The lead guard gestured inquiringly to the stack of papers in her hand. Cicada's pulse beat quickly for a moment or two. She wrote to the guard:

It's a letter to my mother.

The guard snapped his fingers, ordering her to turn them over to him. Slowly, Cicada extended them. She watched with bated breath as he took them and scanned the first line of the page. He snorted derisively and flipped the stack over for a moment. He muttered something beneath his breath, something clearly sarcastic and dismissive. He carelessly thrust the papers back to her, and she tried to keep herself from snatching them from him.

He pointed at her and jabbed a finger at the door, ordering her to leave.

Cicada screwed up her face petulantly and held up the sheaf of papers, then pointed back at her desk with her pen. *I want to finish my letter*, she indicated angrily.

In response, the guard took her roughly by her thin shoulder and fairly threw her out of her own room into the hallway. He fixed her with one last glare and closed the door solidly behind him.

Cicada gathered her papers together and folded them quickly. She capped the pen and tucked it into her pocket. She felt another sudden urge to run back into their room, to try and save some of their treasured codes, but physically forced herself to take a deep inhale. *They're gone*, she told herself firmly. *Let them go.*

She began to walk, keeping close to the wall, her head ducked down low. As she passed through the maids' quarters she could see thickets of servants still bustling around the subterranean halls, whispering and chattering about what had happened. She slipped past them like an invisible shadow.

She went down into the kitchens where preparations were already in full swing for the household breakfast. The cooks looked harried as usual, and the servants were running to and fro, fetching water and peeling vegetables.

Cicada sidled up to Hopkins, the head of the household staff, and tapped her on the shoulder. Hopkins whirled around, about to snap at whoever was interrupting her, but upon recognizing Cicada as one of the lead chambermaids, her expression changed.

Hopkins creased her brow and jerked her chin up in an unspoken question: *What do you want?*

Cicada pointed to a nearby vase of weedy, wilting flowers, and then jerked a finger upwards in the direction of Cira's tower. *More flowers for the Queen's room.*

Hopkins looked, if anything, even more exasperated. She rolled her eyes and withdrew a gold coin from her apron and handed it to Cicada. She then pointed in the direction of the fortress courtyard and urgently shooed Cicada away. The meaning was clear: *Hurry, the wagons are about to leave.*

Cicada nodded and whipped around, her mind clear and her step purposeful. She speed-walked as fast as she could up the passage, along the great hall and out to the open air of the cobbled courtyard. The courtyard lay within the inner keep of the fortress, surrounded on all sides by the sweeping dark outline of the walls. There, the morning shipment was about to go out. There were about five different wagons; some headed for the outlying farms along the northern cliffs, some heading south past Two Falls. Bigger ones were even headed for the Ashan forest paths and the Meadows beyond. She was relieved to see that none of them had left quite yet. Some of the drivers were still talking and a few were making their way to their wagons.

One of the drivers, whom she recognized as the one who drove to the clifftop farms, hopped up into the seat and shook his reins; his horses stirred and shook their heads and the wagon began to roll forward. Cicada streaked up to him like a dark shadow and tapped him on the ankle.

The man jumped and looked down at her, pulling the horses back to a halt. He said something to her, some sort of disgruntled question. Cicada shook her head and took out her pen, leaning against the side of the wagon. She scribbled a few words on the folded papers and held the note out for the man to read:

Need flowers for Queen from first farm on the cliff.

As he read, she eyed the baskets in his wagon. The farmers were usually paid with coin, fish to use for food or for fertilizing crops, and seaweed, which grew plentifully along the coast and was harvested and brought into Faridor. *Which basket was it?*

The driver finished reading and shook his head violently, raising his arms in a shrug. *It's impossible*, he seemed to gesture. He waved his arms through the chill air around them. *It's winter.* He pressed the papers back at her.

Cicada raised her eyebrows insistently and stared at him wide-eyed, raising the note again. It was clear that she would not take no for an answer.

Perhaps it was the unspoken threat of Cira's displeasure, but eventually the driver heaved a dramatic sigh and said nothing more. Cicada rooted around in her apron pocket and withdrew a gold coin. She gestured around to the baskets, her expression questioning. The driver ungraciously jerked a thumb towards one of the baskets in the far back of his cart.

Cicada went round the back of the wagon and climbed up on the wheel, tipping forward over and sorting through the piles to find the basket that had been indicated. The driver had turned back around and was adjusting something with the reins. Cicada saw her chance and whipped the packet of papers out of her apron and tucked them into the very bottom of the basket. Quickly, she reached forward with her pen and wrote the word *Rowan* beneath her note to the driver. Then she covered the papers with the seaweed and fish and tucked the coin into a leather payment purse nestled in the side of the basket.

She glanced over to the driver and saw that he was waiting

expectantly, his eyebrows raised exaggeratedly.

She nodded and hopped back off of the wheel. There was a flap of the reins and the horses pulled away, out of the courtyard and onto the long bridge that connected Faridor to the mainland. The wagon grew smaller and a latent torrent of adrenaline coursed through her system. After a minute or so it began to ebb away, leaving only a hollow echo and dull, increasingly persistent thoughts of Rane being led down to the dungeons. Finally, she turned away, adjusting her apron. It was time to get back to work.

CHAPTER THIRTEEN

In the height of the late afternoon, Rowan stood with her back against the sun, shading her eyes and looking down the rows of winter lettuces, growing happily in a long line down the garden path. She surveyed them with an appreciative eye, pleased with the work she had done. As she habitually did, she rubbed the birthmark on her neck, then tilted her head from side to side, satisfied to hear the weary crack in her spine. The cool sea air nipped at her cheek, and she brushed a smudged, dirty hand beside her eye, lowering the small trowel she carried in her other hand. It was satisfying, she thought, tending to a garden. To be able to see the evidence of one's hard work, to reap the benefits of it. *Wherever I go next,* she thought, *I would like to have a garden.*

It had been a long day of work; the Ulsters were out, and she was ready to head to the well at the back of the house, wash up, and eat some food. There was a cold bottle of milk in the cellar. She wiped her hand again, this time over her mouth.

Almost unconsciously, she turned to look over her shoulder. There, on the path leading out of the forest, was a lone rider on a horse. She felt her heart drop to her feet. The figure was cloaked, and she couldn't discern whether the livery it wore was Kagai's, but she took an unconscious step back, all too aware of how alone and vulnerable she was with the Ulsters away and the whole place to herself. There was no doubt that the rider had seen her, whoever they were, and to her great surprise the rider pulled to a halt, as if they were studying her from afar. Rowan felt her heart beating faster and turned away to try and walk as slowly as she could back into the safety of the house. *Weapon*, she thought. *I need a weapon.*

She had taken three swift steps towards the house and was nearly on its threshold when the rider shouted something. The wind carried the words away, but it was a woman's voice and Rowan felt herself turn and look back. The wind blew past her.

"Rowan?" the voice called.

Rowan's brow furrowed and she stared back at the rider, unsure of whether to continue into the house to protect herself or to stay and see who it was. But after a few moments, her curiosity won her over and she took a hesitant step back into the front yard of the small farmhouse.

By this point the rider was moving again, and the horse had turned off the path that led out of the distant forest and onto the walk that went to the front door. The rider was still too far away for Rowan to identify, but there was something in the way that the figure had said her name—questioning, unsure, that made Rowan feel as though there was no threat. She took another hesitant step.

The rider raised a hand and threw back the hood of her cloak, and with shock Rowan took in the deep brown skin, broad nose and forehead, the delicate mouth. Two piercing brown eyes gazed down at her.

"Persefea," Rowan whispered.

"Rowan," Persefea echoed, equally as stunned. "I thought you were dead. We all did."

"I am dead," Rowan replied, with a grim attempt at a smile.

"What on earth are you doing here?" Persefea asked incredulously, looking from Rowan to their surroundings: the farmyard with the gardens, the cliffs stretching down to the sea, the rolling windblown grass stretching north as far as the eye could see. "Of all the places..."

Rowan didn't know how to respond. She had no idea what she was feeling at that moment. She wasn't even sure that she was glad to see her friend, to be reminded so jarringly of the old days and the life that had once been hers. Finally, she summoned a few words. "Tie up your horse and come inside."

Persefea stared at her for another long moment, as if her eyes couldn't quite believe what they were taking in, then she shook her head, kicked her foot out of her stirrup, and landed on the ground with a gentle thump.

Minutes later they were seated across from one another at the farmhouse table, tumblers of milk standing cold and undrunk before them. Neither seemed sure of quite what to say. Persefea peered around at the room, the cot in the corner by the fireplace, the modest yet comfortable appointments. It was all so incongruous, sitting across from Rowan like this, as if they were casually out to breakfast. After a minute or so Persefea began to laugh.

"What is it?" Rowan asked curiously. She wasn't smiling.

"I'm sorry," Persefea shook her head. "This is all so strange, finding you here like this. Never in a thousand years..."

"What are you doing here?" Rowan cut her off. She was still grappling with her feelings at seeing Persefea again, and found herself in no mood for small talk of any kind. She found herself wanting to know only whether Persefea was indeed a threat, and to send her on her way as soon as possible. It was as if a rupture had been roughly torn in the neat little life in which she'd hidden herself.

"I'm riding north," Persefea said evasively, raising the glass of milk to her lips and giving it a short, searching sip. "Mmm, this is good."

"Why are you riding north?" Rowan asked shortly. To the north was nothing but snow and ice and desolation. Persefea wouldn't be going in that direction unless she had no other choice.

Persefea again looked evasive and Rowan was at once on her guard. When they had been friends before, what seemed like three lifetimes ago, she had always known Persefea to be forthright and to the point, no matter what. This kind of behavior was uncharacteristic. Rowan narrowed her violet eyes and stared Persefea down, not giving an inch. Persefea avoided her for as long as she could, then finally heaved a sigh.

"Fine," she said. "Fine. Tell me where you've been, and I'll tell you where I've been."

Rowan, too, took a moment to steady herself and reached for her cup, but suddenly found that she wasn't very thirsty anymore. She tried to think of how best to describe her imprisonment without sounding overdramatic. "I was taken shortly after Cira's coup in Two Falls," she said finally. "I was held there as a bartering tool. At first because of my connections in Two Falls, and then because Cira found out that Archer...that Archer and I..." she trailed off. "She thought that he would come for me and she would trap him. But he never did." She took a drink, and the milk felt cool and soothing against the back of her throat. "In the end it was Kai. Kai returned from Vireg and bartered with Cira for my life. She said that she would give Cira the Strikers in return for my freedom."

Persefea's brow furrowed. Clearly, Rowan had been freed, but Cira had not been given the Strikers so something, somewhere, must not have gone according to the plan.

"Kai failed," Rowan said shortly. "She failed, but she broke me out. Just in time. She's dead. I escaped and I came here."

Persefea hung her head. So it was true. She remembered her conversation with Archer, how they had hoped that Kai and Rowan had both somehow escaped. She remembered Kai so well: her vigor, her humor, her seemingly unstoppable life force, her single-minded focus. There was no situation so dire that Kai couldn't have found a way out of it; it seemed absolutely incomprehensible that she was gone for good. Kai was a few years older than most of the other girls in their gang, and perhaps Persefea had been jealous for some time of Kai's seeming maturity, her coolness, her aloofness, of the self-assurance that somehow felt so foreign to the rest of them as they struggled to find themselves. How stupid it all seemed now, all that insecurity, the concern with appearances. At that moment, Persefea would give anything to see Kai come sauntering through the door, rolling her eyes at the solemnity of the conversation they were having.

Persefea shook her head. "Rowan, I'm so sorry. For everything. Kai was..."

"Don't," Rowan snapped, her eyes flashing. "I don't want to hear it. I know what she was. She made her choices and she knew the consequences. I'm grateful to her."

"But she..." Persefea didn't want to let it go. She wanted to say something, anything.

"The person you want to eulogize is long gone, and I don't want to hear it," Rowan said, softening her voice slightly, and with a flicker of her old humor. "Besides, you stole her hairstyle ten years ago, so in a way I suppose she lives on."

Persefea allowed herself a halfhearted snort, and dramatically twirled one of her braids and tossed it over one shoulder. "So what, you'll just live here now? So close to Faridor? *Farming*?" The last word was said with not a small sneer.

Rowan tossed her head restlessly. "I don't know, maybe."

"Come with me." Persefea blurted it so suddenly that Rowan could tell that she hadn't planned on saying it at all. Rowan raised her eyebrows and stared at her, giving her a few moments to think about what she'd proposed. But Persefea tightened her delicate mouth and raised her jaw, as if in defiance. "I mean it. Come with me now, leave this place behind. We'll ride north, and if there's nothing there—"

"There's not," Rowan cut in with a wry smile.

"—if there's nothing there we book passage across the sea," Persefea continued, leaning forward. Rowan could tell that she was beginning to really embrace the idea. "There's a northen port. Come on. You basically said it yourself. There's nothing for you here."

The surprise of the suggestion wore off and Rowan began to seriously consider it. She took another long, thoughtful sip from the tumbler. Beneath all the teenage dramatics of their former days, she had genuinely always liked Persefea, always admired her. They'd both been romantically linked to Archer at one time or another, but who in their friend group hadn't? None of that really mattered. Certainly not now.

"I don't know," Rowan shifted uncomfortably in her seat, trying to put off making a decision. "You didn't tell me why you're leaving in the first place."

Again, Persefea took a long drink from her tumbler and Rowan got the sense that she was evading the question. "I was...trapped...for a long time. I got out." She looked up and met Rowan's violet eyes with her own. "Archer helped me get out."

"Archer," Rowan blinked in surprise. "I didn't realize he was still alive."

"The Strikers have taken back Two Falls," Persefea said, and Rowan nearly dropped her cup.

"What?" she gasped. The Ulsters had never told her.

"Yes!" Persefea blinked in surprise. "You didn't—"

"I was imprisoned, remember?" Rowan cut in, and at once Persefea looked embarrassed.

"Of course, I—"

"Tell me." Rowan didn't want to bother with Persefea's discomfiture.

"They've taken back Two Falls and are setting their sights on attacking Faridor." Almost unconsciously, the two of them looked out of the nearby window where the island fortress sat low, the sea pulled taut along the horizon.

"They thought you were dead, Rowan," Persefea said quietly. "I talked to Archer. We all thought you were dead. He knew Kai had gone to rescue you, but when you didn't come back and neither did she he thought..." she swallowed. "He *hoped* that she had gotten you out, that you both had left. That you were free."

"Well, he was wrong," Rowan snapped, her bitterness like an open wound.

Persefea could hear the tone of her voice and raised one eyebrow, cocking her head thoughtfully to the side. "What does that mean?" she asked.

"I sat there rotting," Rowan said through gritted teeth. Somehow it helped to be able to say it aloud. "I sat there rotting in a cell for years, and none of them—none of *you* did anything. Nothing to help me."

"Your sister did," Persefea countered quietly. "Kai did. She gave her life for you."

Rowan said nothing, but stared at her hands. The well of anger and frustration and hurt boiled at the back of her throat like a glowing yellow ball.

"It took me a long time, too," Persefea continued. "Everyone did what they needed to do to survive. Archer did, you did, and I did. And you were saved, in the end, weren't you? Kai came for you."

"I just..." Rowan searched the room desperately, her eyes growing hot. "I wish it didn't have to be her. That my freedom had to be at the cost of her life. I wish that we could both have gotten out. That there had been someone, some way...some way she could have lived, too."

"I know," Persefea said quietly. "I know."

Rowan could see now, as a hot tear flowed down her cheek and onto the dirt-smudged lap of her dress, how foolish she had been to have harbored the resentments she did. Of course none of this was Archer's fault; it was no one's fault except Cira's. Kai had loved her; she had made her choice. As Rowan sat there, she felt a curious sensation, like a cauldron of boiling water within her had been spilled out, leaving behind it an emptiness and a sorrow that she didn't want to have to face. She raised one hand to her throat, feeling the hard line of her collarbone jutting out against her skin, wishing she could wash all the feeling away. She placed the fingers of her other hand on her temples, willing herself to regain control, to stop crying. And after a moment she succeeded, facing Persefea with moist but steady eyes.

"Yes," she said finally. "I'll come with you. I'll go north."

Persefea blinked in surprise, as if she hadn't expected Rowan to actually take her up on the offer. But she recovered quickly, and managed a smile.

"Good," she said. "Good. Do you need to gather anything? Prepare anything?"

Rowan looked around the farmhouse kitchen. There was to be a delivery from Faridor later that day, but the Ulsters had promised to be back before then and would manage it without her. In terms of material posessions, she had almost nothing, just a few sets of clothes. It was almost comical to think of how little she now had in the world, how oddly freeing it was to be ready to go, to move on in a matter of seconds.

"Not really." She stood and went to her cot and stuffed her things into a small rucksack hanging by the door. She cast about for a parchment or pen, but there was none. She didn't want to leave without leaving the Ulsters some indication that she was safe and had gone of her own accord, and hadn't been taken by force. After a moment or two she stepped out the front door and took a smooth stone from beside the stoop, and plucked a wavering green sprig with small enclosed buds, the first sign of approaching spring. She placed the sprig beneath the stone in the center of the table, hoping that they would see it and understand that she was safe.

She shut the door, feeling the slightest pang of regret as she did so, and followed Persefea out the front door and towards the horse, who pricked its ears up and looked at them with benevolent interest.

"I swiped the horse from the border patrol at the forest edge," Persefea laughed, looking from her mount back to Rowan. "We'll get another when we hit the next northern town." She quickened her pace slightly and began checking the horse's girth. She turned around and held out her hand for Rowan's rucksack, looking at her with an expectant smile.

But something held Rowan back: a small question tickling at the back of her mind, growing louder and louder with every second that passed. She slowly held up the bag, then lowered it slightly and fixed Persefea with a quizzical expression.

"Persefea," she said slowly. "You didn't say where you were during the years of the war. What you'd been doing. What were you doing?"

Persefea's face fell and at once Rowan knew. Persefea opened her mouth as if to speak, but no words came out. To her credit, she never once broke eye contact; her gaze seemed to say everything: *I'm so sorry, I regret what I've done, I'm sorry.* Rowan felt her insides contract with revulsion and felt herself take an unbidden step backwards, as if Persefea were some sort of contagious disease.

"Rowan," Persefea began. "Rowan, I..."

"Go," Rowan said abruptly, and turned on her heel. She clutched the bag of her belongings to her chest, hugging it close. She refused to look back over her shoulder; she never wanted to set eyes on Persefea again. How long Persefea stood there and watched her before mounting up and riding away, Rowan didn't know or even care.

She walked up the steps of the farmhouse and found herself once again in the dim, comforting light of the interior. She set down her rucksack on the cot by the stove, then looked down at the table where she'd placed her goodbye to the Ulsters. After a moment she took the rock and the stalk of unopened buds and placed the rock on the windowsill above the farmhouse sink and arranged the sprig in a small cup of water. There she sat, staring at it, her eyes vacant and far away.

It was here, some time later, that the Ulsters found her; when they spoke to her she started and stared at them as if they were old friends from long ago that she hadn't expected to see ever again.

The fallout from Tarr and Archer's disastrous meeting with the Two Falls governing council had stretched out across the days following. Laith had called private meetings with members of the council and done his best to charm them into patching things up; he had even brought Cade along with him on a few of them so that they would be dazzled by a visit from real Jelani royalty ("two princes for the price of one," Archer had observed wryly, before it was pointed out to him that technically Cade was now a king.) From what Tarr had heard through Marc and some of the others, the meetings had been relatively successful, and that now the anti-Striker sentiment burbling in the council was concentrated more towards himself and Archer, rather than at all of them. Tarr knew that technically he should look at this as an accomplishment, but somehow it didn't make him feel better.

Everywhere Tarr went he felt (though he realized he was being more than a little paranoid) like a pariah, and even found himself going out of his way to avoid the other Strikers, Laith and Athela especially. He didn't even really want to talk to Archer, which was a strange and rather unpleasant feeling.

That afternoon, Tarr found himself in his office, staring disconsolately out the window at the city beyond. There was a strange hum in the air, electric, as if lightning was about to strike not too far away. He told himself that he was being stupid, that all he needed was a good night's sleep, but he couldn't quite shake the feeling that something was amiss.

He remembered that there was a balcony just off of one of the empty rooms beside his office, and, feeling uncharacteristically caged in by his own quarters, he strode out, passing through the darkened vacant room and walking out to the sun-drenched balcony. He closed his eyes for a moment and bathed in the light. He opened his eyes and gazed out over the tiled roofs of Two Falls; once so foreign and now an oddly comforting, familiar sight. A few spirals of blue smoke from distant chimneys curled and dissipated into the cold air.

At once his heart was hit by an odd pang and he realized that now, more than ever, he wished that Rane was there with him. He needed her to listen to him, to give him advice, to simply *be* beside him. There, where he could touch her face and feel her arm against his. Most of the time, out of sheer necessity, he was forced to compartmentalize his feelings for her, and the relationship that they (someday) hoped to have. He had to think about her impersonally: a source of information, a piece on the game board that could be moved and angled to his advantage. If he actually thought for a moment about the person he loved and pictured her in Faridor, in some windowless room, risking her life day and night, slipping through doorways and around corners just in the nick of time...if he tried to reckon with the number of times per day that her life was in danger and the chance that he would never see her again...it was hard for him to stand.

He had never been in love before; there had, of course, been mild crushes back in the forest but it was all childish infatuation and hadn't really led anywhere. Besides his friend Juniper, most of the others his age had always thought him to be a bit weird. He remembered that Rowan had lightly flirted with him when they'd first met, but that had been more flattering (and terrifying) than anything. With Rane, it had always been different. After those first few delicate, tentative days with her when it felt as if every moment could shatter into a million pieces, he found that he kept staring at her when she wasn't looking, as if he couldn't quite believe or understand why this miraculous creature had deigned to return his affections.

He thought how strange it was that their relationship had come to this. The ardent nights they had spent together had given way to dry coded letters back and forth a few times a week. He wondered vaguely if he was doing this whole "love" thing right, and if he should have put up more of a fight about her leaving (not that it would have done much good, for her mind had been made up.) He hadn't had a lot of experience with love, all things told, nor many examples of what a healthy, loving relationship between young people looked like. There was Laith, of course, who was all but completely consumed by his ghosts, and then there was whatever Archer and Athela were doing, which Tarr wanted absolutely no part of.

He sighed and flicked a speck of something he hoped was not dried bird poop off of the balustrade. He knew what Rane would do if she were there. She would look at him levelly with her clear lake-blue eyes and tell him to be smart. The fate of the city, of the country, of its people, rested on fewer shoulders than one might think. He had to recover from the Persefea debacle and move on.

Feeling slightly cheered, he turned and headed back inside. He whistled tunelessly between his teeth, shut the door behind him, turned into the hall, and stopped dead in his tracks.

There, standing in the middle of the hallway, smiling easily back at him, was Si.

Tarr felt his jaw fall open and a surge of goosebumps rolled down the skin of his arms, as if he had come face to face with a ghost. He glanced back over his shoulder and saw that the rest of the hall was deserted. They were completely alone.

"Hello," Si said in his light, soft voice, smiling wider.

Tarr narrowed his eyes. There was something *off* about the boy; he had changed, but Tarr couldn't quite put his finger on just how. He looked none the worse for wear, wherever he had been, and was much the same as Tarr had remembered four months before, but there was something in his expression that was almost as if someone completely unknown were looking back at Tarr through Si's familiar gray eyes.

Without another word, Tarr walked quickly up to Si and put his hand on the boy's shoulder, almost dragging him down the hall and through the doorway of his office. He shut it quickly behind him, terrified of the thought of them being seen. Something told him he had to hide Si away, and fast.

The door shut, Tarr took a breath and tried to calm his pounding heart. He indicated for Si to sit in the chair opposite his desk, which the boy did, tucking a strand of his copper hair behind his ear, and tilting his head up to gaze at something on the ceiling. He had an odd, faraway look about him. Tarr was at once taken aback. Si had always been one to daydream, but he seemed so...*vague*. He began to worry that Si had been drugged, or that he'd been given something to permanently alter his state of mind. Tarr's heart continued frantically racing.

"So," Si said smoothly, coming back to earth so suddenly and so lucidly it made Tarr jump. "I'm back. What do you want to know?"

CHAPTER FOURTEEN

"What do you want to know?" Si said again with an easy smile, leaning back in his chair and folding his hands on his narrow stomach as if inquiring about the weather.

Tarr swallowed as thousands of questions washed through his head like a wave. He took another deep breath and decided to start with something general.

"Are you...are you all right?" he asked lamely.

"Oh, yes," Si said pleasantly.

"Are you..." Tarr groped for words, realizing how stupid his question was about to sound, "Are you still Si?" he asked. He half expected Si to laugh, but he did not.

He tilted his head contemplatively. "In a way."

The hair on the back of Tarr's neck prickled. "What happened to you while you were away?"

"I learned."

"Learned what?"

"What I am. What I'm meant to do."

"And what are you meant to do?" Tarr asked, his voice now so hoarse that it was barely a whisper.

Instead of responding, Si gave him an enigmatic smile and raised his eyebrows, as if the answer were a delightful secret he didn't dare give away. "Meet Cira," was all he said. This wasn't much help.

Tarr paused and tried again. "Who took you?"

"They didn't take me. I went. It was my choice."

"Who were they?"

"The Serpens."

Tarr remembered vaguely that the Serpens were a group of scholars devoted to Morthenstar's legacy, and who seemed to have tapped into some sort of ancient magic that Tarr couldn't pretend to understand. Tarr had dismissed much of the talk of magic as hooey, and had been reluctant to believe in it even after Si had started showing signs of having mystical powers. He was shocked to hear that Si had chosen to go with them of his own accord without telling the others.

"What...what did they teach you? Exactly?"

Again, Si didn't answer. A strange, dreamy look came over his face and it was as though he were far, far away—somewhere spinning among the stars. Tarr briefly debated saying something, hoping to snap him out of it. Finally, Si spoke again.

"I had never seen them before," he said.

"Seen what?" Tarr glanced up in the direction of Si's gaze, but saw nothing but an insect crawling along the ceiling.

"They're all so beautiful," Si murmured, mostly to himself, as if Tarr were no longer there.

Tarr was beginning to feel a strange combination of terrified and annoyed. Why couldn't Si just come out with it? What was he talking about? Had he...had whatever the Serpens done to him driven him completely mad? What on earth had happened to this morning, to the life he'd had two minutes ago, when the most he had to worry about was the outcome of a war and a few disgruntled council members? That life seemed very far away.

"Si," Tarr whispered, leaning forward, and at the sound of his name, Si turned. Tarr nearly leapt back in shock. The boy's eyes were glowing with a sort of strange, unearthly light. Tarr blinked, sure he was imagining it. "Si," he said, trying to keep his voice from shaking. "You've got to tell me. Explain to me so I can understand."

"I see it all, Tarr," the edges of an excited smile began to creep around the corners of Si's mouth. "I see *everything*. It's as if everything is joined by these beams of light, everything...that bug up there, your desk, I see the wood it was made out of, I know the tree it came from, I see where it grew, I know where it stood in the forest, I know the man who cut it down, I know when he was born and when he will die. I can *see* it. I can follow each strand as it moves and converges and changes. And it's so beautiful...so beautiful, Tarr, you couldn't possibly imagine."

His gaze had drifted off again and Tarr pushed himself back from his desk a little bit. *He's mad*, he thought. *They drove him mad. Whatever has been done to him.* He felt a surge of anger inside him as he thought of what he'd like to do to the people who had taken Si away and returned this husk back to him. *What on earth am I going to tell Marc?* he wondered. *He'll search high and low until he finds the people who did this.*

"You don't believe me," Si said with a coy grin, as if he and Tarr were sharing some sort of delightfully naughty secret.

"I believe that you believe it, Si," Tarr said carefully.

"Put your hands on your desk," Si told him, with the same conspiratorial smile.

With some trepidation Tarr stretched out his eleven fingers and laid his palms flat on the desk before him. He was unsure of exactly what Si was trying to prove, or whether he should fake some sort of reaction to make Si happy. Si sat with his arms crossed, a calm smile on his face.

And then slowly, so gradually that at first Tarr thought he was imagining it, he felt the cool wood of his desk begin to get warmer, and warmer, until it was so scorching hot that he gave out a yelp and snatched his hands back from the table, stumbling out of his seat and knocking over his chair. The desk was glowing, vibrating with energy and heat, until all at once—with an almost audible *whoosh*—it went back to normal.

Tarr took a tentative step forward and reached out the tips of his fingers to the wood. It was smooth and cool. Tarr felt suddenly faint, and groped for his overturned chair, flipping it over and easing tenderly down into it, his legs tingling with so much adrenalin he felt as though his limbs and head had been overrun by a swarm of bees.

All the while Si hadn't moved a muscle.

A thousand thoughts exploded inside his head like fireworks and Tarr felt himself on the verge of bursting into awestruck tears. Regardless of how many times he'd been told that the war and the rise of Kagai had been pre-ordained, or that it had tapped into some sort of ancient mysticism, he'd always managed to shrug it off as a half-truth, had reasoned that Cira would always have been power-hungry and would have made a bid for the throne whether she'd been born that day or twenty years before, Kagai's supposed heir or not. Even when they had had their shared vision in Morthenstar's cave, even when they had discovered the medallion and Si had begun to have visions, to have his bursts of strength, Tarr had always believed in the back of his mind that it could all be chalked up to momentary lapses, seizures, or nightmares, or some combination of afflictions.

But here—in that single moment—Si had offered him irrefutable proof that he'd always been wrong. There had been magic, in one form or another, hovering just over his head, just out of reach. He suddenly felt very, very small. The enormity and depth of all that he didn't know, that he could *never* know, was overwhelming; he could barely grasp at the worlds and mysteries contained within the small figure of the boy sitting opposite him.

All at once, his head reeling as if from a second blow, Tarr felt a paralyzing fear wash over him from head to foot—a fear of what would happen if Si fell into the wrong hands. He felt an overwhelming urge to leap up, grab Si, and shut him away in the nearest closet, to lock the door and throw away the key forever, anything to prevent him from being found.

"What—what did you do?" Tarr asked him faintly, surprised at how hoarse his voice sounded. "To the desk?"

"It's life, Tarr," Si uncrossed his arms and leaned forward. "I can see it. I'm all a part of it. And I can move it, bend, be with it as I please."

"You can make things hot and cold?"

Si laughed out loud. "Much more than that. I could break it, put it back together, if I wanted. It doesn't matter."

"And you...you can see the future?"

"I can follow the beams of light where lives began and go with them where they will end. I can see where they intersect. All the lights, all those threads, how they twine together and come apart."

"You can see people?" Tarr said curiously, not quite believing. "Living and dead?"

Si nodded. "Everything. Plants, animals, too."

"Wolver?" Tarr asked suddenly. "What happened to Wolver? Where did he go?"

"His task was complete," Si said cryptically.

That's not very helpful, Tarr thought, frustrated. "Are Silva and her brothers alive?" he asked tentatively.

Immediately, Si shook his head. "Killed the day we escaped. They never made it out of their house."

The enormity of it hit Tarr like an anvil, and he placed his head in his hands for a moment. More lives to be weighed on the scale, more people they had left behind in their wake. In a flash, he had a memory of Silva, her bright green eyes and heart-shaped face, and the way she gazed at Laith whenever he entered the room. So bright, so hopeful. Tarr shook his head, and looked back up, feeling as though he were walking on the edge of a precipice, unable to resist teetering closer and closer to the edge. "You know what's going to happen with all of us?" Tarr asked, his throat dry.

"When you were born, when you'll die."

"Archer?" Tarr blurted out, barely thinking as he said the words.

The response was immediate. "He won't live very long," Si told him quietly.

Like a falling stone, Tarr's stomach dropped and his body froze.

"What does that mean? Like, he won't live to be eighty or he's going to die next week?" he demanded.

Si shook his head and opened his mouth to reply, but Tarr raised a hand frantically and stopped him. "No!" he said sharply. "No, don't say anything else." He wanted to shout at Si, wanted to take back the last five seconds of his life, wished he had never ever said anything or mentioned Archer's name. *He's going to die. Archer is going to die.* A weight, heavier than he could have ever imagined possible, settled on his thin shoulders and bowed him over until his head was in his hands. He felt, in that awful moment, as if his friend were already gone.

"Don't!" he cried, leaping to his feet, unsure of whether he was talking to himself or to Si.

"Do you want to know how it will happen?" Si asked calmly. "I can tell you."

"Yes—no!" Tarr yelled, pulling back and facing Si as if defending himself from an attacker. "No! I don't want to know anything about it. I want to forget that anything was ever said." He paced around in a circle and faced Si once again. "Can it be prevented somehow?"

Si tilted his head back and forth noncommittally. "Things shift all the time, Tarr, with the choices people make. Sometimes an empire topples and it only alters the makeup of the universe a tiny bit. Sometimes a small change is cataclysmic."

"If outcomes are always shifting and changing, then does that mean Archer could live?" Tarr asked tentatively, almost afraid to hear the answer. "Does he just need to...I don't know...forget to brush his teeth one morning and that will be the difference he needs?" *A person could lose their mind thinking of all the ways, all the choices that might lead to one fate or another,* he realized. It was too much for him to wrap his head around.

"You can always *try* to change the path of a life. But it gets complicated very fast. And sometimes things just tend to follow a course, despite our best efforts," Si told him patiently.

"Why did you tell me all of this?" Tarr felt as though he were about to weep.

"You asked," Si said simply.

"Well...don't. Next time, ask me if I'm sure before you tell me."

"All right," Si smiled easily, looking totally unconcerned.

Tarr stared at him, overcome by fear and anguish and wonder. Si's expression was strangely blank. Whereas the old Si would have been mortified at the thought of causing him pain, this Si seemed to take it all in stride, curiously detached. He had given his answer so freely—never stopping to ask whether Tarr really wanted to hear the answer, not bothering to tell him that some information was only for a privileged and enlightened few. What Tarr had asked he had told him, unequivocally and without hesitation.

And then Tarr stopped to consider. If all of this were true, and Si knew all the things he said he did, then he could see the way his friends would live and die. The pain that Tarr now felt with a mere sliver of knowledge, Si must feel a hundredfold. And yet he just sat there, his gaze occasionally drifting up towards the light on the ceiling where the bug had been a few minutes before.

"How do you stand it?" Tarr whispered.

Si's eyes flickered, and it was almost as if the boy he had once known peeked out from behind a curtain. "Each strand of light I see is beautiful," he said finally, "no matter how long or short it is. And a life may end, but the light doesn't completely fade. Not ever. It's all so vast," his hand sketched an arc over their heads.

Slowly, Tarr felt his way back to his chair, never taking his eyes off Si. Then a thought occurred to him.

"What about people who are dead?" Tarr asked cautiously.

"What do you mean?" Si asked.

"I mean, can you bring them back to life?"

"What do you mean?" Si asked again.

Tarr made an exasperated wave with one hand. The more he was asked to clarify, the sillier he sounded to himself. "You know. Walk and talk." *What do you think I mean by 'bring back to life?'* he wondered irritably.

"Oh, *that*," Si said, sounding almost disappointed in Tarr's lack of imagination. His eyes narrowed shrewdly. "You really think that when people die, they're just gone? Just like that?"

Tarr's thoughts traveled back almost unbidden to that awful night all those years ago, Laith dumbly trying to process the news of his wife's death, his gaze blank and unseeing. Of Silva's now-vacant house near the cliffs, the darkened windows like shuttered eyes.

"In my experience, yes," Tarr replied flatly.

Si shook his head. "There are echoes of light everywhere."

Tarr stared at him, bewildered.

"An echo needs something concrete to continue on, to keep it from fading. Something tangible to reflect it back out. A name spoken aloud. A memory," Si concluded with a hint of amusement, as if at a private joke. Suddenly, his gray eyes fastened with startling clarity on an area just over Tarr's left shoulder. The hairs on the back of Tarr's neck prickled, and he felt himself give an involuntary start. Feeling foolish, he swiveled around and looked behind him. There was nothing there.

He turned back around, glaring narrowly at Si, trying to suss out whether the serene smile of familiarity playing vacantly around the boy's lips was some sort of put-on.

"I can't see what you see," Tarr said slowly, opting for the most neutral observation he could muster.

"No," replied Si pleasantly. "Not now at least."

"What?" Tarr asked sharply.

"You could someday. Not like me, exactly. I'm a bit special."

You don't say, Tarr thought wryly.

"But it's not impossible. You've just got to look the right way and you'll see that the lines aren't cut at all." With sudden unexpected intensity, he leaned forward and lifted his hand, setting it on Tarr's desk. His small fingers were clenched into a fist. "You hold on so tightly to the things you can see, you can hear, you can touch." His gray eyes bored into Tarr as though he were trying to make some sort of point. And then slowly, he eased his hand open, like the petals of a flower slowly unclasping. Words hung between them, unsaid.

Tarr stared at the open hand, turning this over in his mind. *The things I can see, can smell, can touch. So...reality.* From where he sat, watching Si's eyes once again begin ambling back on their curve towards the ceiling, there were some benefits to staying tethered to reality. He cleared his throat, which didn't seem to do much to attract Si's meandering attention.

"What about Cira?" Tarr asked, his voice hoarse.

"What about her?" Si asked.

"Is she..." *First things first,* Tarr thought. "Is she alive?"

"Oh, yes," Si said easily.

Well, there goes that rumor. "Does she know? Can she do what you do?"

"Yes and no," Si said, suddenly focused and sharp. "She's tapped into it, the same as me. The key that unlocked it for me, she has done the same—opened the door and looked inside. That same wash of energy, she's in it, too. But she doesn't know it yet. She can't control it. It's pulling her down like a current in the water."

"Good!" Tarr said, feeling relief for the first time since Si had started speaking. "Then we've got the upper hand."

But Si's face was grave. "Do you remember, Tarr, when we first found the medallion and I unlocked it? How I couldn't control things anymore? That any strong emotion I felt just sort of *flew* out?"

Tarr was certainly not about to forget. As a reflex, he felt the rush of dread and confusion that had accompanied those days. He nodded silently.

"Well, that's how it is for Cira," Si said. "She has it...but she doesn't know what it is. She doesn't know how to harness it. Anyone she comes in contact with is in danger. Even someone fifty miles away may be in danger. She has no control—she's being pulled further into it without being able to come out. And so she's very, very dangerous at the moment."

He suddenly began to put the pieces together...the rumors of Cira's reclusiveness, her paranoia. After Joris's execution, the stories had started to take shape. Cira's servants had suddenly, inexplicably been executed; nearly every new staff member in Faridor was gone in the blink of an eye.

"Why hasn't she blown us all to bits yet, then?" Tarr asked, not sure he wanted to hear the answer.

"I don't think she knows that she can," Si replied. "She doesn't know what she's capable of."

Tarr's stomach dropped. "Let's hope she doesn't find out," he muttered. "But she's *aware* that things are happening to her, right? These powers?"

"Yes," Si affirmed. "But she doesn't know *why* it happens or *how* it happens. And the visions, the dreams that I had—remember? She'll have them too, only they'll grow and grow and pull her in further and further until they consume her waking life as well."

"She's shut herself away for months," Tarr said slowly. "Has she lost her mind?"

"Certainly not," Si said matter-of-factly. "How would *you* feel if you suddenly discovered that you were able to shoot energy out of yourself? If you'd suddenly been pulled headlong out into the void of all existence, been able to *really see* it for the first time but not truly understand? Not to be able to turn it off and go back to the way things once were?"

Fair point, Tarr conceded.

"I would imagine that is why she's pulled away. She has access to powers beyond her comprehension."

Against his best instincts, Tarr felt a twinge of pity for Cira, alone and isolated in her tower.

"She's not completely evil, is she?" Tarr said slowly.

"No one is *completely* evil, Tarr," Si said patiently. "Not really."

"She's coming awfully close," Tarr muttered.

Si tilted his head thoughtfully. "Do you think she was selected to be Kagai's heir because she was a person inherently bent towards destruction and power, or do you think she moved down the path of destruction and power *because* she found that she was Kagai's heir?"

Tarr resisted the urge to hurl Si, chair and all, off the nearby balustrade. "But you and she were marked as the heirs," he reasoned. "It's not like you had a choice in the matter."

"Ah," Si seemed pleased Tarr had brought it up. He held up a conspiratorial finger. "You see, that's where you're wrong. She and I were identified as the vessels for this power, to be sure. But we were both given choices. I could have chosen to turn away from my calling, to live the rest of my life as I once was. I could have chosen not to learn how to wield my powers. But to follow this path, to learn the full extent of the magic with which we're surrounded...Cira had these choices, too."

"What would have happened..." Tarr began hesitantly, "if you hadn't followed the Serpens? When they asked you to go?"

"Cira would have won," Si said simply. "We would have all fought and died. And eventually, centuries from now, another Morthenstar would rise up and the cycle of conflict would begin again."

Tarr stared at him, dumbstruck. Part of him wished to protest, to maintain that they would have found a way, *some way*, and still kept Si the way he was. But Si was so certain, so flat in his response that it left little room for misinterpretation. He would have to take more time to wrap his head around it.

Changing the subject onto more solid footing, he began again. "So...if Cira *does* learn how to use her powers..." he trailed off.

"How do *you* think she'd use them?" Si asked rhetorically. Tarr

MORTHENSTAR

imagined it for a moment. It would be a matter of expediency: the Strikers would be gone, instantly. The resistance, gone. In the blink of an eye, with no resistance, and no fuss. Any threat to Cira's rule would be brushed away, neat and tidy and without a second thought. The thought chilled him.

"Does Cira have a group of teachers...someone trying to help her, like the Serpens did for you?"

"They tried to make contact in Vireg, I imagine," Si mused. "And afterwards. But as I said, the choice to learn is a choice she had to make, too. She and I chose differently. For better or worse, she is completely alone."

"Which still leaves her out of control of these powers, sinking into a waking dream life, and highly dangerous," Tarr pointed out.

"Exactly."

"She'll be able to see us, then," Tarr said, feeling the hope draining out of him. "She'll be able to see when we're planning to attack, if we wind up attacking Faridor."

"I don't think so," Si shook his head. "She's opened a book in a language she can't read. The signs may be there, the lines may swirl and converge, but she won't always know what they mean. Not the way I do. She'll feel me, though. She'll feel me coming. Ours is the strongest connection of all."

"And you...you can beat her?" he asked. Tarr gave Si a sideways look, not wanting to sound as though he were doubting the boy's powers.

"I don't know," Si said honestly.

"You can't see it?" Tarr asked curiously.

"I know we'll meet," Si mused, the faraway look back in his eyes. "But something strange happens. I don't know how to interpret the lights yet. I guess I'm going to find out what it means. I'll know when I'm there."

"But you can kill her?" Tarr asked, not bothering to worry about seeming crass. "From here, maybe?" he added, trying not to sound too hopeful.

"Tarr," Si leaned forward, his young eyes alight. "It's not that simple. Killing her is not a simple thing. Killing itself is never a simple thing." He looked pointedly at Tarr. "You'll understand that before long."

194

What on earth is he on about? Tarr wondered.

"It has to do with how this all started," Si said.

"How what all started?" Tarr asked, regretting the words almost as soon as they'd left his mouth.

Si's eyes glazed over sightlessly as he began. "Back during the first battle between Morthenstar and Kagai, they were just humans. Powerful, but human nonetheless. People knew something of magic then—it wasn't as dismissed and forgotten as it is today. Kagai found a group of mystics who had devised ways to tap into the connected energy of all things—a deep magic, deeper than any others had ever known. He began to bring them over to his side, hoping that they would begin to do his bidding, that they'd give him power enough and knowledge enough to conquer the world. And, eventually, to destroy Morthenstar.

"A faction of these scholars knew better than to go with Kagai. They knew that he meant to do harm, that he would bend the knowledge towards evil. So they formed a separate group, the Serpens, in order to combat the work that was being done by those that served Kagai. They respected one thing—the one thing that Kagai and his followers did not, the single rule of all life."

"What was that?" Tarr whispered.

Si smiled gently. "Balance, Tarr. All life exists in balance, with each part having its weight and counterweight. Kagai, with the help of his servants, tapped deeper and deeper into this magic with the intention of using it to destroy, to take life away. They began their work, creating fissures and cracks in the fabric of the universe. They splintered the fundamental elements of life apart. And they've been fractured ever since. The Serpens, on the other hand, have worked to restore the natural order. The natural balance. This power wasn't meant to be concentrated and channeled through only two people as it has been; it was supposed to be spread across all life, all existence, in equal measure. Until that happens, the cycle cannot end.'"

"What do you mean, 'the cycle?' Why didn't it end before? When Kagai and Morthenstar were killed?" Tarr asked.

"Those forces, those elemental forces were still divided. Still separated. Still unbalanced. It *couldn't* stop," Si shook his head. "It has to continue on until something is done to right it. To entwine the two together. And that hasn't happened yet."

"So there's no end to it?" Tarr said, reeling, his voice very small and thin. How futile it all felt. How useless everything—all that they had done over the last four years—seemed just then. "It never stops," he said again. "Ten years from now, a hundred years from now. These wars, this conflict, will never stop. There will always be two people, two sides of a coin, with access to magic and powers beyond comprehension, with the power to wipe out thousands of people with a blink of an eye."

Si nodded silently. "Unless we find a way to balance it once again. To close the door once and for all."

Tarr felt himself letting go—of all of his responsibilities, of all his cares. He thought of taking Rane far away, living with her on some remote mountaintop and letting the world burn down around them. Of growing old and dying without wondering what sort of world he'd be leaving behind. Did it really matter now, he wondered, whether he turned and walked away from it all? What difference would it make?

"Si," he said, as measuredly as he could, "what can we do?"

"We can't kill her," Si said. "Not while I'm alive."

His words fell like a stone on the empty silence of the room.

"Ever?" Tarr asked, and Si shook his head. "But Kagai and Morthenstar were able to be killed. They were, during the battle. Why are you and Cira any different?"

"We're not like Morthenstar or Kagai—regular people who were pulled into this current of...magic, if that's what you want to call it. Cira and I were selected before we were even born. We were created to act as conduits. We've drawn up alongside each other, Tarr. We run together—those strands of light I was telling you about? Ours are side by side, and have been for centuries, the power concentrating down, becoming more potent, getting stronger. We were always running in that current. We just needed to be awakened to it, that's all; we needed the key to turn. Like a river underground, when suddenly it comes pouring out into the daylight. That's what the medallions did."

A thought occurred to Tarr. "If you *unlocked* your power with the medallion, can't you...*lock* it again? Go back to..." he nearly said the word *normal*, but caught himself.

Si shook his head. "Not while Cira and I exist."

"Exist? But you just said," Tarr protested, "that she couldn't be killed!"

"Not the way you mean it," Si said cryptically.

"Oh for heaven's sake," Tarr exclaimed, thoroughly exasperated. He stood and paced the length of the room before returning to Si, trying to calm the churn of his mind. He was surprised at his own sense of disappointment. A few months ago, they were all waiting and hoping for signs that Si would develop some sort of power. Now, Tarr would have given almost anything to have him back the way he was.

Si eyed him levelly as he returned to the desk. "Tarr, the thing is... neither one of us—Cira nor I—can be killed while the other one lives. You could stab me through the heart right now, it wouldn't make any difference. She sustains me, and I sustain her."

Tarr was taken aback. "You almost make it sound like love."

Si spread his hands. "Isn't it, though? My being—everything I am—is more connected to her than any other being on earth. She and I are the reason the other exists. I can't read minds, I can't control other people's thoughts, but she's *there*, Tarr, everywhere around me. I feel her always."

Tarr felt disturbed by this, but his brain was so exhausted by this point that he let it go. "So what, Si?" he asked tiredly. "Do you have a plan or not?"

"I do," Si nodded.

Tarr was a little surprised. He had half expected Si to say something philosophical and nihilistic about the existential futility of planning. "Oh? And what is it?"

"She and I have to meet," Si said simply. "Take me to her, Tarr, and I think I might be able to end this."

Tarr was puzzled by this and pressed Si to expand further, but he refused and the faraway look began to creep back into his eyes. Tarr sat back and regarded him for a long while. It was so strange speaking with someone who looked exactly like the Si he had known and loved but who was for all intents and purposes a complete stranger.

"Right," Tarr said, feeling more tired than he ever had before. "I've got to come up with some sort of story. Some explanation for where you've been."

"You'll do a great job," Si assured him kindly. "I'm sure the story will be great."

Tarr felt like rolling his eyes. He could tell that Si was going to be absolutely no help whatsoever on this front. "We've got to tell the other Strikers. Marc is going to lose it. You're going to have to tell him where you were," he added, sending Si a sidelong look. Si's expression was nonplussed.

"Sure," he agreed.

Tarr began to run through the scenario of Si telling Marc about his sojourn in alternate astral planes, and it was so absurd that it was all he could do to keep himself from laughing aloud. Then he sobered immediately. What on earth was Marc going to make of this new entity sitting before him? Si was so changed that there was seemingly only a shadow of the boy they had known before. This new person, this *being*, would break his heart. There had been no signs so far that Si would ever go back to the way he was, if there was any way of breaking this spell.

"Come on," Tarr told him, "We've got to find you somewhere safe to hide." He stood and peeked out of the window, half-expecting someone to be hanging onto the wall and listening outside. He cast about the room, wishing there was a curtain or blanket or something he could use to smuggle Si to a safe space (though he imagined that walking next to a blanket-covered humanoid shape would attract more attention than if he and Si just went strolling together down a hallway.) "You can't turn invisible, can you?" he asked, only half-joking. *Why not? Weirder things have happened in the last five minutes,* he thought to himself.

Si appeared to seriously consider this. "I'm not sure," he mused. "I could try."

Tarr waited for a moment but nothing seemed to happen. He wasn't sure whether Si was actually trying to make himself become invisible or if he had been distracted by the play of light on the windowsill.

After a few moments, Si blinked dreamily and smiled back at Tarr. "No, I don't think so. I have to practice. I can make myself be dead, though, want to see?" A wash of ashen gray began to spread across his face.

"No, no," Tarr said quickly, holding up a hand, and at once the lively flush spread back across Si's forehead.

Tarr felt sick. This Si, whoever he was, was an immediate danger to himself and to others—he had immense power, so immense that Tarr couldn't begin to wrap his head around the extent of it. And in a rather deadly combination, he wasn't certain that Si had any sense of self-preservation, or that he'd somehow be immune from coercion if captured. And while that doubt remained, he would have to be fanatically careful.

"Come on then," he said, rousing Si from his chair where the boy had once again lapsed into a sort of waking daydream. "We're going to find Marc. And we're going to find some way to keep you safe."

"Good idea," Si agreed, and stood.

CHAPTER FIFTEEN

Rowan sat motionless at the end of her cot beside the farmhouse stove, staring at the sheaf of papers in her lap. A candle beside her bed had burned down almost to its end, the wax dripping like a puddle of frozen white tears onto the floor. She wasn't sure how long she had sat there. She still didn't know what she was going to do.

The supply wagon from Faridor had rolled up to the cottage only an hour or so after Persefea left her to ride north. The Ulsters had returned home to find Rowan sitting at the kitchen table and staring out into nothingness. As it was late winter and they were not flower growers, they were utterly unprepared when the wagon driver had demanded fresh blooms for Queen Cira's rooms. The Ulsters had only a few early sprigs growing at the farm, it being still too cold for most of them to have emerged yet, but they scrambled around the edges of the house, scavenging a few stems of hellebore and clipping as best they could. The wagon driver had grunted and passed them their basket, which contained a coin and some seaweed and fish from the coast that they could use to feed their plants.

The wagon was already out of sight when Mrs. Ulster had walked back into the cottage and set the basket on the table in front of Rowan. "I hope they got what they wanted," she fretted. "Imagine trying to find flowers now at the tail end of winter. Be a dear, won't you, and put those things away, I have to help the mister with the horses." With that, she bustled out the door.

Rowan rose like a spectre and went to unpack the basket. The coin was generous; more generous than she would have expected for a few weedy flowers. She wondered whether there had been some mistake. Still, she put the coin into the can that Mrs. Ulster kept on the shelf above the linens, and reminded herself to tell her hosts of their good fortune. The few fish were fresh but small; there weren't enough to feed all three of them. Rowan thought with a pang how much it must be costing the Ulsters to house and feed her for so long. Her basic chores of weeding and puttering in the garden seemed an inadequate way to repay them.

Still, she could use some of the fish for dinner if she made a sort of stew to stretch it out, and the others she would save to use for the garden. Some of the longer seaweed they dried and used for broths, so she took up the basket and carried it down into the cellar to set about storing it until it could be smoked. She shivered as she groped in the darkness of the cellar for the oil lamp hanging above. Finally, she grasped it and lit it, and the warm light filled the space.

She bent down and began to take up the seaweed in large hunks to hang from the ceiling hooks, then she stopped still and stared down at the bottom of the basket. There was something white at the bottom, something that looked like paper. There was nothing else that should have been in there. Perhaps the wagon driver had made another mistake?

She finished hanging the last hank of seaweed and wiped her hands on her skirt. She bent down and withdrew the papers, her brow furrowing with confusion. There was a strange note written on it: *Need flowers for Queen from first farm on the cliff.* And then, below it, her name. *Rowan.*

Her heart began to beat quicker and she glanced around herself, suddenly feeling like she was being watched. *Someone knows my name,* she thought. *Someone knows I'm here.* But if they knew where she was and meant her harm, then where were the soldiers to take her away?

There was a paragraph on the first page that made little to no sense, and for a moment Rowan thought again that the paper must have made its way into her basket by mistake (*but why was her name written on it?*) She read it and then reread it again, trying to make sense of it. It sounded like the journal entry of a teenage girl, something about a romance between a cook and an archer. Rowan furrowed her brow. An archer.

All at once Rowan's eyes widened and it clicked into place. There were tiny lines beneath some of the words in the paragraph: *archer, sigh, mark, tar.* Archer she knew, and she remembered the boy Si from when the Strikers had been with her in Two Falls. Slowly she rearranged the papers in her hand. The next pages she found were entirely different, written in a small, neat script rather than the scrawl of the first paragraph. It seemed to be a description of some sort of bizarre weapon; something that could shoot projectiles and destroy things from great distances. As she read, Rowan felt her heart beating harder in alarm.

It began to dawn on her what had happened, and how the papers must have found their way to her. It was clear that the letter had come from a Striker agent in Faridor, but the whole thing reeked of desperation. There was so much that could have gone wrong: the basket could have been handed off to the Ulsters instead of her, the papers could have been glanced at and then immediately disposed of. Something drastic must have happened to warrant the papers being smuggled out in such a fashion. They must be vitally important.

Rowan slowly turned them over again and read them through, trying to make sense of the whole thing. The parts of the document that described the projectile weapon, whatever it was, were written in such a distinct handwriting from the cover page that Rowan could only imagine that the first page had been meant to disguise the contents of the rest of it, to convey some message to her in the event that the papers actually made it into her hands. And the description of the weapon was bizarre and terrifying in the extreme.

Slowly, as though she were lowering a sleeping child, Rowan placed the pages carefully back down at the bottom of her basket and turned her back on them to continue arranging seaweed on the drying hooks. As she worked her mind churned; she could feel all of the questions and the existential crises she had faced since her arrival at this farmhouse boiling up into the air around her. She realized that she was faced with a single, starkly simple decision: she could either take the plans to Two

Falls and deliver them into the hands of the Strikers, or she could run away. Either way, staying at the farmhouse was no longer an option. If the Strikers' spies at Faridor had discovered that she was alive and living with the Ulsters, it would not be a stretch of the imagination to assume that Cira's spies would soon learn of it, too. And Rowan couldn't bear the thought of the Ulsters being found out and being arrested or executed as traitors harboring an escaped prisoner. She had already stayed too long. She had put them all in danger, and every second she stayed in the refuge of their kindness was a second toward ensuring their deaths.

Her work finished, she lowered her hands by her side and stared off into the wall before her. Listlessly, she turned and picked up the basket and carried it upstairs, setting it by the front door and taking the papers out of it. She folded the papers in three and slid them into the lining of her pillowcase.

She carried out the rest of the day's chores in a sort of daze. She could feel the eyes of the couple on her as she worked. They could sense that something was wrong and wished to ask her about it, but knew better than to expect an answer. Dinner was carried out in an uncharacteristically heavy silence; when the bowls were cleared from the table, Rowan lit another lantern in the corner of the room and came to sit down across from the couple, who regarded her with a kind of expectant resignation, as though they knew what was coming.

Rowan arranged her skirt over her legs, and looked at them levelly with her dark violet eyes. "I have to leave," she said finally.

No expressions of surprise crossed either of their weatherbeaten faces.

"Where will you go?" asked Mrs. Ulster.

Rowan's mind shot over to the folded papers hidden in her pillowcase, of the choice that confronted her. "I don't know yet," she said truthfully. "But I have to go."

"Are you in danger?" Mr. Ulster asked. Rowan could hear the unspoken question beneath it: *Are we in danger?*

"Not yet," she said. "But soon, if I stay any longer. You should be safe as long as I leave by the morning."

"I'll pack a bag for you," said Mrs. Ulster. "With food, and a blanket to keep you warm."

Rowan shook her head. "You have already been too kind to me...I..." she groped around in the air for words to articulate the gratitude she felt towards them for their inexplicable kindness, felt it growing in her chest like a warm bubble about to burst. "I would have died without you...how can I ever..."

Mr. Ulster raised a hand. "We did what we could. I hope it was enough."

Enough? Rowan shook her head. They still didn't understand the enormity. She opened her mouth again, but Mrs. Ulster smiled at her, reached out and clasped her hand over Rowan's.

"Don't say anything more. Take care of yourself as best you can. I think you'll be all right now."

Rowan swallowed and stared into the woman's kind, crinkled eyes. She wished she could be as sure.

And so she found herself hours later, perched on the edge of her bed, staring at her dying candle, with the papers spread over her lap. To return to Two Falls was to embroil herself once again in a conflict that had very nearly been the end of her life. To flee, to get as far away from it as she possibly could, also meant leaving behind everything she'd ever known for strange lands and unknown dangers. She realized that she would never be able to make a decision just sitting there. She had to get up and go, and just trust that her feet would lead her in the direction they were supposed to.

It was in the first gray moments of dawn when she quietly closed the front door, rucksack thrown over her back. The Ulsters had given her a pair of walking shoes; Rowan had big feet, and so she had fit into Mr. Ulster's old pair without too much issue. Rowan was glad of them. They were sturdy enough to see her through rougher terrain, if that was where her path led.

Silver mist rose eerily off of the grass as she walked steadfastly past her beloved garden; she found herself attuned even more than usual to the sights and smells around her. She felt herself saying goodbye to it all, to the barn behind the house, to the wooly little cows that peered out at her from the byre, from the sounds of the sea down at the foot of the cliffs. She was grateful, she realized. Grateful that she had been there, even for a short while, and that she would be able to carry the farmhouse away with her.

She reached the end of the long path that led up to the road. With no hesitation, she turned right, heading north, away from Two Falls, from Faridor and the rest. It was like the crest of a wave; as soon as she set her feet on the path, she felt a pulse of anxiety rise and fall and she resolved herself to the road she was on. She steeled herself, gripping the straps of her rucksack a bit tighter, forcing away any nagging thoughts that whispered at her.

She had gone about two hundred yards from the house when another voice, louder, piped up in her mind. Slowly, her gait slackened until finally she stopped and felt herself, almost unbidden, turn around and look back down at the sloping cliff.

There was the farmhouse, now small and boxy, peeking out of the creeping mist. In the distance, perched in the water like a malevolent bird on a rock, was Faridor, black amid the soft gray of the morning. She was suddenly struck with the awful realization that no matter how far she went, no matter how many miles she put between herself and those cliffs, that Faridor would always be there, a blot on the horizon, like a festering pinprick in the back of her mind. She swallowed, her throat dry. She could never be sure. Never stop feeling hunted.

Almost unbidden, she heard Mr. Ulster's words float back to her, as clearly as if he were speaking them in her ear: "We did what we could. I hope it was enough."

Rowan stared out at the land spreading before her. How small the farmhouse looked, how vulnerable. She thought of the sheaf of papers in her rucksack. She had no idea of their actual value. She wondered whether someone had given their life to get the papers to her. If they had, and if she just turned and walked away into the mountains, that life would have been wasted. The thought of it turned her stomach.

Slowly, and with great effort, she took a step, back towards Faridor, back towards Two Falls and the Strikers. She swallowed, feeling as though she were descending into some sort of icy black pit from which there was no return. *I'll give them the papers. I'll give them the papers and then leave. They can't ask for more than that. That's all I'll do, and then*

I'll be free, she told herself. But there would likely be no turning back.

She took a step towards Two Falls. She hoped that it would be enough.

Tarr soon realized that there really wasn't a good way to reveal to the others that Si was alive. Every possible configuration of events resulted in either an overly dramatic flourish, as if Tarr were a magician making their friend reappear out of nowhere, or a revelation so comically understated (Tarr opening the door of a room to reveal Si sitting there nonchalantly, as if nothing had happened) that either way it was sure to result in heart attacks across the board.

He had squirreled Si away in his own chambers for much of the day. At first he'd felt guilty about hiding him there alone with nothing to do while he went and rounded up the other Strikers, but realized quickly that this new iteration of Si needed very little to entertain himself; just a few beams of light coming in through the window and maybe an insect or two.

Standing outside in the hall with the others, Tarr watched anxiously as he placed a hand on the door to open it. He was especially concerned about Marc.

"Don't freak out," he cautioned them.

The others stared at him, their eyes wide and growing looks of concern on their faces.

Wishing he had kept his mouth shut, Tarr opened the door to admit them. Athela was first inside and stopped dead, so abruptly that the others crashed into her back, and there was momentary confusion on all sides before they sorted themselves out and realized what was happening.

"Hello," Si said. He was perched ike a little red-headed bird on the edge of a chair by Tarr's writing desk.

The others gaped at him in amazement, and then one by one each of them swiveled their gazes around to stare at Tarr.

"Ta da!" Tarr said weakly.

"Did you have him hidden here all this time?" Athela said sharply, her gray eyes full of a frank suspicion that cut through to Tarr's core.

"Of course not," he shot back defensively. "Si only just turned up and I came and got all of you immediately."

Marc had already crossed the room in three strides and had folded Si into a big hug. Si's face, Tarr was glad to see, looked genuinely happy to be reunited with his surrogate big brother. Marc released Si and held him at arm's length, and Tarr could almost feel the beginnings of a stern parental where-on-earth-have-you-been tirade brewing from somewhere deep in Marc's core.

Before Marc could speak, Tarr cut in. "I've talked to Si already about where he's been." He filled the rest of them in on the Serpens, and the training that Si said he had undergone, the powers he now said he had. Even as the words were coming out of Tarr's mouth, he could hear how ridiculous and far-fetched they sounded. Even though he'd witnessed Si's abilities firsthand, it was hard to say the phrases out loud, here in the room with the skeptical expressions of all of his friends facing him.

Throughout Tarr's explanation, Marc's eyes never left Si's face. By the time Tarr finished, he looked completely stricken. Marc struggled for a moment and then squared his shoulders.

"You're all right?" he asked Si, as if he wanted to assure himself just as much as the boy. "You're sure you're all right?"

"Quite," Si said pleasantly.

"You...ah...believe all this?" Laith asked Tarr in an undertone. Of all of them, he was looking the most grave and Archer and Athela the most skeptical. Ari, characteristically, could have been sitting in the middle of a presentation on potato fertilizer, for all the interest his expression betrayed.

"He showed me," Tarr replied. "He showed me what he can do. And it's true, Laith."

Laith's expression grew even darker. Behind him, Athela and Archer's faces were unwitting mirror images of one another; a single eyebrow on each face slowly raising higher and higher the more their incredulity grew.

"All right, then, what do we do? Do we try to keep him hidden somehow? Or do we let people know that he's returned and just keep security as tight as we can?" Laith folded his arms.

Out of the corner of his eye, Tarr could see that Marc was still staring searchingly into Si's face, as if he were trying to find some vestige of what had been there before. "I don't fully trust anyone outside this room," Tarr said slowly, "but I think that if Si stays here, Cade will find out in no time, and is going to wonder why we're trying to keep him hidden. He's already suspicious."

"Too true," Athela nodded. "And it might do the troops well to have him here in the open, as a source of morale. Someone to rally behind."

"But if what you're saying is true and Si suddenly has all of these dangerous powers..." Archer trailed off.

Tarr glanced to the side at Si, who was blinking serenely and seemed not at all upset that the others were standing around discussing what to do with him, as if he was a stray dog who had wandered into headquarters. "I'm very worried about him falling into the wrong hands," Tarr said cautiously. "Or of anyone else learning about what he's capable of."

"So we let it be known that he has returned, but keep a close eye on him at all times, and keep him at a distance from everyone who is not in this room. No conversations with anyone else," Laith said.

"Agreed," Tarr nodded.

"Agreed," chimed the others.

Athela rose and bounced once or twice on the tips of her toes. Tarr could see that her deeply pragmatic mind had already moved forward to the obvious next question, and that she was struggling with whether or not enough time had elapsed before it was socially acceptable to ask. "So," she half-blurted after a few brief moments of internal grappling, "Does he have a plan?"

"He says he has to meet her face to face," Tarr replied.

Athela's face fell and immediately became skeptical again. "Oh. Is that all?"

"There are rumors that she's dead," Archer pointed out. "Some of the townspeople are saying that she died long ago and that her captains are just saying that she's still alive so that there will be a reason to fight a war."

"Oh, she's alive," Si said pleasantly, and the others jumped and looked over at him as if they'd momentarily forgotten that he was sitting there.

"She is?" Athela asked sharply. "How do you know?"

"I know. She's sort of a blue color right now. Blue and dark red," Si's eyes grew even more vacant, and a small smile played around the corner of his mouth.

"Is she now?" Athela asked slowly, her gray gaze boring into Tarr's as if to say *you better be really, really certain that he hasn't just gone nuts.*

"Come on," Tarr gave a sigh and beckoned them forward to follow him. "We'd better tell Cade. We can say that we called him back out of hiding so that we can begin to formulate a final plan."

"You go on ahead," Marc said to them over his shoulder. "I'll be right there behind you."

Tarr gave a sad little nod and ushered the rest out of the room. The door closed quietly, and Marc and Si were alone. Marc turned to face Si again, searching every inch of his now strangely unfamiliar visage.

"You're disappointed," Si said slowly. "You're disappointed that I've changed, that I'm not the way I was before."

Marc considered this for a beat, and tilted his head slightly. "You say you can hear what people are thinking? That you can tap into every living thing?"

Si smiled mildly. "I can *feel* what they're thinking. It's different."

"All right then," Marc squared his shoulders and looked Si dead in the eyes. "Feel what I'm thinking. I'm not disappointed in you. I could never be disappointed in you."

The room was silent for a moment, and then the hairs on the back of Marc's neck rose as a strange electric crackle filled the air around them. He felt a strange energy running from his temple through his arms and out the tips of his fingers. It was almost indescribable, as though a current ran through him and straight into the boy sitting opposite.

Si smiled faintly. "No," he said softly. "No, you aren't."

"Good," Marc nodded firmly, as if he were glad that he had put an end to that line of worry. "Besides, if I understand it correctly, this is who you are. Who you always were. Right?"

"That's right," Si agreed.

"Good, then," Marc opened his mouth, then shut it and gave Si a sidelong look. "You had to leave, didn't you? I couldn't have come with you."

"No," Si confirmed.

Marc swallowed and forced down all the worry and anxiety and guilt he had felt for the past months. "You were with the Serpens?"

"Yes," Si replied. His attention was drifting away, like mist dissipating into the air, and his voice had become dreamy and vacant.

"Are the Serpens planning on coming back and...erm...helping us out?"

"They're gone," Si said softly, his eyes blank. "Once they saw I was ready, they knew their role was complete. They're gone. Forever. It's just us now. Just me."

Marc wanted to pry further, but decided to take Si at his word. He sat back away from the boy and rested on his heels while he assessed the situation.

"Right," Marc said, suddenly businesslike. "We're going to lay down some ground rules. You don't talk to anyone who wasn't in this room. We're going to have lodging prepared for you. Do not go anywhere with anyone who wasn't in this room. Come to think of it, don't go anywhere with anyone who isn't me or maybe Tarr."

"All right," Si said vaguely, staring off at the ceiling. Marc wasn't sure whether any of this was actually registering with him, but he plunged forward nonetheless.

"If someone who is not one of the Strikers tries to come and take you away, you need to try and fight."

"Fight?" Si asked. "Why?" The question was pure in its innocence.

"Because you need to stay with us. If you want to come face to face with Cira, you need to stay with us."

"Someone else could bring me to her," Si pointed out reasonably.

"Yes, or they might kill you," Marc retorted.

Si shrugged, as if this was of no importance. His gaze trailed off to the left, as if he were following something crawling along the walls with his eyes. Marc glanced over his shoulder and saw nothing. He took a deep breath. He wished there was some way to verify that Si was absorbing this information in a way that made sense to him.

"If anyone comes to take you away or tries to hurt you, I want you to...tell me. You can connect with people, right? Connect to their energy and their feelings like we just did a moment ago?"

"Oh, yes," Si said pleasantly. "Easy."

"Great," Marc said, relieved. "I want you to send me a sharp ping, so that I'll know something is wrong, and I can come and find you."

"Yes, all right," Si agreed.

Marc considered for a moment and then his curiosity got the better of him. "Do you know how this all ends? The war? All of us, everything?" he asked finally.

"I can see the picture," Si said evasively, meeting Marc's eyes with him. "I can see where lifelines end and where they begin and where they interconnect. I told Tarr and he got upset."

Marc's knee-jerk reaction was to ask, *what did you tell Tarr?* but he caught himself. He shook his head. That type of knowledge was an abyss from which there was no return.

"No, don't tell me. I don't want to know. I won't ever ask again, I promise," he assured the boy, then clasped Si's thin shoulder in his large hand.

"All right," Si agreed.

"I'm glad you're back," Marc said softly.

"I was far away," Si said dreamily.

"Yes," Marc agreed with a rueful smile, "you were."

CHAPTER SIXTEEN

Two days later, Athela found herself on horseback patrol with a handful of the newer training recruits from the Two Falls headquarters. It was in the early hours of the morning, one of Athela's favorite times of day. The city was just beginning to rouse itself awake, the lamp lighters flitting about the streets like shadows, putting out the flames in the lanterns slung across the tops of the streets. A frosty mist hung low above the slow-moving water in the river cutting through the center of the city, and a pink haze was just beginning to bloom on the easternmost edge of the sky.

"Hold steady," she said in a reassuring voice to two of the recruits riding behind her. For some of them (mostly those who had come from the city), this was only their third or fourth time on horseback, and even in the dim light of the morning Athela could see the whites of their eyes as they clung to the reins and rested their hands on the pommels of their saddles. Anyone looking at the riders would have thought that their mounts were wild and out of control, rather than the tame, rather lazy beasts they really were; ambling along the riverside and punctuating the cool air every now and again with a silvery yawn.

Athela's duties as the training officer to the new recruits were first imposed out of necessity. Marc had been the training lead before he'd left the headquarters to search for Si, and Athela had subsequently been assigned to take over in his absence. The appointment at its outset bore all the earmarks of one of Tarr's character-building exercises, so Athela had regarded it with extreme suspicion and trepidation. She'd occasionally had to teach lessons in the Academy back home and had always faced them with a certain degree of self-consciousness and insecurity. But though it pained her to admit it, she found that after the first few awkward weeks she actually truly enjoyed it. She had a knack for communicating with the recruits. She had been made to feel stupid and uncomfortable in so many social situations growing up that she was extremely careful never to make the recruits feel the same when asking questions or needing her to repeat an instruction. She liked the feeling of teaching them something new, something no one had ever told them before, liked the feeling that she was empowering them, and liked the way in which they regarded her with frank, unabashed admiration. She found that she felt very protective of them, and it amused her to observe the ways in which the feeling appeared to be mutual. Some of the trainees would shyly say hello to her if they happened to see her in the hallways of the Striker headquarters, and when she stopped to talk to any of them, they would blush beet red to the tips of their ears. She also liked it when she could tell that one of her young recruits had a question they wanted to ask and was working up the courage to say it aloud. She always waited patiently, listened attentively, and answered as thoroughly and respectfully as she could, regardless of how simple or ostensibly silly the question might be.

The recruits trained for three months at a time; their duties included patrolling the city, helping with the day-to-day running of the headquarters (helping in the kitchens or with the building maintenance), and, as they grew in experience, they were gradually given lessons in combat and assigned to accompany the Strikers on raids and other missions around the city. Laith occasionally taught some of the upper-level combat classes, which was the high point of the whole program for the new recruits. Athela had heard her students whispering about Laith's supposed exploits in dramatically hushed and reverent tones, to the point where Athela had to excuse herself from the room to keep herself from laughing.

She swiveled around once again in her saddle to survey the recruits riding behind her. "You all right?" she asked one of them, a young woman with long black hair and a petrified expression. She was sitting atop her horse as rigidly as a statue.

"I think so," the girl squeaked. She was from an upper-class family in the north of the city, and had joined the Strikers after her parents were imprisoned in Faridor for harboring and aiding Ashans.

"You're doing great," Athela assured her. "Take your arms and shake them out and roll your shoulders a bit. Horses are telepathic; if you're tense, your horse can feel it and may start to worry that something's wrong."

The girl's face blanched and she shook herself with a sideways jitter, giving her horse a reassuring pat on the neck. Athela hid a smile. The horse she had chosen for the girl was one of the slowest and most idiot-proof animals in the stables; a small explosion could happen a few feet away from it and all the horse was likely to do was shift his weight from one hind leg to the other. A nervous recruit was nothing.

"Great," Athela gave the girl another smile and turned back around. Athela's horse, Aria, was being uncharacteristically well-behaved that morning. Usually, Aria was only satisfied if he was at an all-out run, but for the moment he was doing well at a slow jog that only occasionally devolved into a few frustrated crowhops. Most of the students were completely terrified of Aria, and their awe of Athela for being able to control him had only increased over the weeks of their training.

The group crossed one of the bridges and headed towards the southwest corner of town, just past the arts district. Athela generally liked to bring them on a loop around the main parts of the city so that those who had grown up outside of Two Falls would get used to its twists and turns and alleyways and gradually be able to orient themselves.

"Athela," piped up a boy from behind her. His voice held the hesitant note with which she had become quite familiar, the sound of someone unsure of whether or not their question was appropriate to ask.

"Yes," she replied, swiveling around once more.

The boy was one of the newest recruits, and she didn't know him very well yet. He was in his early teens, with thoughtful eyes, dark skin, and a puff of black hair that hung on his head like a cloud. "Are we going to have to fight in the final battle?" he asked. "Will we be ready by then?"

Athela considered. The thought of any of these students—children, really—going into battle made her stomach turn. With few exceptions they had joined the fight for moral reasons, or to avenge a lost loved one, rather than to experience the thrill of fighting. "I don't know," she said finally. "I suppose that depends on when the final battle is going to take place. And where."

"It'll be Faridor, right?" another boy piped in.

"I don't know," Athela answered truthfully.

"You don't have a plan?" came a girl's voice, sounding skeptical and slightly disappointed.

"Of *course* they have a *plan*," the second boy retorted.

"I can't tell you much," Athela replied, deciding that at this point being evasive would probably be the most impressive tactic. It implied that the Strikers were working behind the scenes on elaborate battle plans using well-plotted maps instead of scrambling around trying not to get themselves arrested by the city council and hiding their recently returned and possibly unhinged friends in various closets.

"We'll be ready," chimed in the girl who was scared of her horse. "We'll do everything you say, and we'll be ready."

Athela again tried to hide her smile, and marveled at the swell of emotion rising in her chest. It didn't matter to the recruits that she had grown up unwanted and unloved and cast out by her family and community. They didn't know, and they didn't care. They liked and admired her simply for who she was now. It touched Athela more than she could express.

"Thank you," she said, trying to convey the sincerity that she felt. "Truly. Regardless of where the battle takes place, we'll need each and every one of you."

"We'll be ready," the first boy nodded, his round jaw clenched in determination.

"Good," Athela said softly. "Heels down, eyes up. Pretend there's a rope pulling from your chest all the way to the sky."

As her charges resettled themselves, chests puffing and shoulders squaring like a flock of preening birds, Athela turned back to face front. Their patrol was almost over; denizens of the city were now starting to open windows and scrub their front steps. A few wagons heavily laden with vegetables creaked by on their way to a marketplace in the center of town. One wagon's wheel caught in a rut between two of the cobblestones and gave a loud *thump* as it went in; Aria snorted and darted up on his delicate hind legs, taking the opportunity to give his head a ferocious shake and aim a bite at the horse nearest him. The horse calmly moved its head out of the way, completely ignoring Aria's antic display. They were all used to him by now.

Athela worked Aria's head down so that he was chomping the bit close to his chest, and was about to turn him in a small circle when one of the voices behind her piped up again.

"Isn't that Lord Argolaith?"

Athela wheeled Aria around and stared in the direction that her student was pointing. Barely visible at the far end of a little street, Athela could see a figure very much like her cousin, clad in a black cloak, coming down the stairs of a second floor apartment. Athela was doubtful as to whether or not the person was, in fact, Laith—until a moment later when he was joined by an unmistakable black dog. It was Breaker, who had been lying amongst the shadows of a bush at the bottom of the flight of steps. Laith hadn't seen them, and began walking in the other direction towards Two Falls headquarters.

"Whose house is that?" one of the girls behind her asked keenly.

Athela opened her mouth, mind racing. She was, by nature, a blunt and honest person, and lying didn't come quite as easily to her as it did to Archer or Tarr. But she could see that it wouldn't do to be mysterious and to have her students starting a lot of gossip in the barracks.

"Laith's been running missions with Marc," she informed them. "To try and find possible safehouses in case of a Kagaian attack."

"Oh," said the girl, disappointed. "So that's one of them? A safehouse?"

"Probably not," Athela shrugged, trying to sound as though the topic wasn't of much interest to her. "Most of those leads don't pan out."

"It's early for a meeting," said the boy with the intelligent eyes, looking thoughtfully at the porch at the top of the staircase.

Athela adopted her best "teacher" voice. "The fight against Kagai doesn't keep regular business hours," she chided them. "If he was there, it's because he had to be. Now come on. We've fallen behind schedule. Let's try a trot."

The terror of a faster gait had the instant effect she'd counted on, as her students' attentions were immediately diverted from Laith to the more pressing issue of staying aboard their mounts. After a few tense seconds, the group was slowly-clip clopping along, each student bouncing up and down looking like a rubber ball, hands gripping white-knuckled to their horses' manes to try and steady themselves.

"Grip harder with your knees and thighs, and you'll be able to sit. I don't want to see any air between those bottoms and that saddle!" Athela called out, sitting Aria's gliding trot with the ease of a feather. Before they turned the corner, she stole one last curious look at the shuttered apartment, sitting quiet and unobtrusive at the end of the street.

Hours later, after the sore-bottomed students had wobbled their way into the hall for breakfast, Athela returned to the apartment, her distinctive curly black mane of hair covered by a dark cloak, keen on finding out who lived there. It was an hour or so before there was any stirring within. Athela saw the flick of a window being cracked open, and the twitch of a curtain, but couldn't make out the face of anyone inside. Another half hour passed before the door opened and the apartment's tenant emerged into the morning sun.

Athela wasn't sure what (or who) she had been expecting, but it wasn't this. A strong-looking, curvy young woman with lovely chestnut hair came out with a baby perched on her hip. She turned to lock the door behind them. She was talking animatedly to the little one as she went; he looked sleepy and had his head against her shoulder. One fat fist was jammed in his mouth, and he was absentmindedly twisting his stubby fingers through her hair with the other, gazing out at the world with the sort of serene benevolence of someone who knows that they are well cared for. The young woman carefully made her way down the staircase, still talking quietly to the little boy, punctuating their one-sided conversation every now and again by planting a kiss on his curly dark forehead.

A thousand thoughts raced through Athela's mind as she stepped out into the street to silently follow the young woman through the city to her unknown destination. Laith had clearly spent the night (or a good portion of it) at this young woman's house. Who was she? How had they met? She thought with a pang of Laith's wife, her best friend, then swallowed and mentally took a step back. She looked at herself, assessing the churn of emotions roiling in her chest. Was she angry at Laith? Had he betrayed his wife's memory by moving on with someone new?

No, she thought to herself, and her heart lightened at the realization. Years ago, perhaps, when she was younger and quicker to judgment, she would have snapped at the thought of Laith having feelings for anyone other than Ilaina. But today, staring at the back of the pretty stranger's head, she realized she was glad for him, whatever their relationship might be. Glad that he had found someone, and overwhelmed with curiosity as to who the young woman was, and how long this had been going on. She felt a twinge of hurt that Laith had kept such a thing to himself, but she thought that she could understand why. Perhaps he thought that she and Marc—those who had known and loved his wife, too—would be angry at him for moving on. Perhaps he wanted to protect the young woman. Perhaps he just wanted something for himself.

The young woman made her first stop at a house only a block or two from the apartment. She was greeted at the door by a kindly old woman who smiled at her and took the boy from her arms with a solid kiss on his curly head; they disappeared inside for a few moments, and then the young woman reappeared alone and continued on her way.

Athela continued to follow her, and as she went, she felt a growing rise of alarm creeping up beside her curiosity. Whoever the young woman was, she hadn't been trained in fighting or espionage, that much was certain. She never turned to check behind her, and seemed to be completely unaware that she was being followed, to the point where Athela relaxed some of her more overt precautions. She found that as they walked she felt a rising sense of affection for the young woman, a strange intimacy borne of studying someone so closely without their knowledge. The young woman had a fast, swinging gait, and a light yet purposeful step; she seemed confident and friendly and open to the world in a way that Athela admired. Occasionally, she paused along her way to peer in a shop window or inspect a display of produce on one of the open wagons lining the street. Athela watched as she carefully inspected a tray of apples. The young woman's fingernails were cut short (practical, Athela thought to herself with approval) and Athela could almost see the wheels in her brain turning as the young woman thought to herself before returning the fruit to the display and flashing a winning smile at the vendor.

A short while later, they drew up to a nondescript pub and Athela hung to the side of the door, out of the young woman's line of vision. The young woman went inside. Athela was surprised that she had gone in for a drink at such an early hour, but a few minutes later the door opened and she saw that the young woman had settled in and was scrubbing down the bar with a towel. Clearly, she worked there and would be there for the rest of the day.

Athela squinted up at the sign above the pub door and said a small "Hm!" to herself, then drew her cloak about her and started making her way back to the Strikers headquarters.

As she went, Athela felt a rush of protectiveness both towards the young woman and her son. Undoubtedly, Laith had thought to keep them safe by visiting the apartment in secret, but the truth was that he had been careless. If Athela herself could have so casually stumbled upon the young woman's identity and location, an agent of Kagai could do so as well with very little effort. And Athela knew all too well that her sister Cira would be keenly interested in the identity of any person that she could use as leverage or damage against Laith or any of the other Strikers, for that matter. The young woman would have to be protected.

Her mind set on a course of action, Athela slipped anonymously through the crowds, tracing the path that led back to headquarters and up to Marc's rooms. She would talk to him; would respect Laith's wishes by keeping the girl's identity vague, the reasons for her protection obscured. Marc would take care of it without asking, and would see to it that the right individuals were sent to watch over her. The young woman would be safe. Athela would see to it that she was.

Perhaps because of the surge of excitement after Cade's unexpected arrival in Two Falls, or perhaps due to a general need to blow off some steam, that night an impromptu celebration began in the Great Hall of the Strikers' headquarters in Two Falls. The recruits and soldiers, as if drawn together by some subliminal beacon, began to flood into the hall shortly after sundown. Someone produced a drum, and some flutes, and a few stringed instruments. And once the music started, it had broken out into a full-out party.

Tarr had been briefly alarmed when he heard the sound of distant pounding emanating through the hallways below his office. At first it sounded a bit like the sounds of battle (which didn't speak much to the soldiers' musicianship.) There was a pile of papers on his desk, including a long-overdue coded update from Rane about the state of operations in Faridor, and he was obligated to go through them as quickly as possible and destroy them before any of the council members' spies got a hold of them.

But he felt himself pulled downstairs towards the party. It had been so long since they'd had the chance to cut loose or celebrate. Since Si's disappearance, it had seemed somewhat callous to observe birthdays and holidays and the like. Tarr heaved a sigh and promised himself ten more minutes of work before going down to see what was going on.

He sat again at his desk and focused again on the task at hand. There was something about Rane's latest message to him that felt a bit off, though it was hard to pinpoint exactly why. A few of the letters in the message had been miscoded here and there, but it could just have been that she had done it in a hurry. It wasn't the first time. None of his agents, even Rane, were completely infallible. Any small mistakes were entirely reasonable. And the message itself didn't contain anything particularly of note, just a check-in with a few small details about visiting envoys. Nothing new. Nothing that warranted a second look.

And yet something was niggling Tarr in the back of his mind, something that told him it wasn't quite right. He knew to trust his instincts by this point. If the voice was saying the letter needed a second look, then it did. And so instead of burning the letter immediately as he usually did, he glanced about the room looking for a hiding place. A swell of music and clapping rose distantly from downstairs as he picked up a stack of papers (a riveting pile of vending permit drafts for the Sunday market), and tucked Rane's letter inside.

A few minutes later, he was down in the Great Hall, the worry of Rane's letter already evaporating. The music was raucous and seemed to rise and fall in a way that made Tarr want to dance. He loved human music and couldn't possibly hope to understand it or how it was made, but adored the way it made him feel. He let himself break into a little awkward half-step shuffle as he walked towards the crowd of Striker soldiers, whose backs were turned to him as they faced the musicians and dancers.

"Nice," came a drawling voice behind him, and Tarr turned around and saw Archer regarding him with a cocked eyebrow and sly grin, his arms crossed over his chest. Far from being embarrassed, Tarr increased the exuberance of his awkward step until it was a full-on uncoordinated jig, which he executed with a perfectly straight face, eyes boring unblinkingly into Archer's. Finally, after a few seconds of this one-sided standoff, Archer broke and laughed out loud, raising his hands in a gesture of surrender. Tarr gave a slight self-conscious bow and grinned.

They joined the fringes of the crowd (as soon as those around them saw them they scrambled to make room and move out of the way) and stood in companionable silence, watching a few of the newer recruits whirling and twirling with careless abandon. They were far removed from the usual shy, deferential young soldiers Tarr was used to encountering in the hallways. The crowd began clapping in time with the music; Tarr tried to join in but couldn't quite find the beat, and after a few seconds realized that Archer was laughing not at the music and dancers, but at him.

"Oh, shut up," Tarr growled good-naturedly, stopping his efforts.

"Look, it's not your fault that you spent the first two decades of your life without exposure to a recognizable time signature," Archer said comfortingly.

"Look at them," Tarr said under his breath, surveying the swath of laughing faces. "Did you ever think that all these people would come to fight alongside us?"

"To be honest, no," Archer folded his arms, scanning the crowd as well. "They're all so young. So many of them I don't recognize."

The dancing and music carried on, with couples trading out and occasionally pulling others into the mix. Across the way, Athela was talking under her breath with Marc; from their expressions, the conversation was serious. Tarr wondered briefly what it was about. He also wondered where Si was, and who was watching him if Marc was down at the party.

At the thought of Si, Tarr suddenly remembered what the boy had said about Archer not living very long and he looked sharply over at his brother, taking in the familiar profile: his long, aquiline nose, sharp cheekbones, yellow eyes, the familiar smile playing about his lips as he watched the dancing (with a periodic sideways glance over in Athela's direction), the way his skin glowed faintly blue and orange in the lamplight. Tarr imagined what it would be like if this were the last time he saw Archer. He imagined never turning around and seeing that easy, sardonic smile or the comfort of knowing that Archer was standing at his shoulder. The thought of it clutched around Tarr's throat like cold fingers.

"What on earth is wrong with you?" Archer asked suddenly, and Tarr was jolted back to the present. Archer was staring straight at him, bewildered.

"What?" Tarr asked innocently.

"You were looking at me like I was some sort of..." Archer groped for an appropriate simile, "...orphaned baby duck."

Tarr stifled a laugh and blinked a few times. "You mean you're not?"

"All right," Archer shook his head and looked away. "Keep your secrets, then, spymaster. I won't take the bait."

Tarr smiled serenely, but still felt a pang in his heart. "I wish Rane were here," he said suddenly, so out of the blue that he surprised himself. Archer looked over at him and blinked. Tarr shrugged deflectively. "I just hope she's all right."

"She's fine," Archer assured him. "She could fight her way out of that fortress with only a cooking pot. Or a broom."

Out of the corner of his eye, Tarr noticed a sudden flurry of activity, and saw Ari push through some of the crowd to try to reach Marc and Athela. His face was dark and focused, and Tarr was instantly on the alert, nudging Archer with one elbow and tilting his head in their direction. Archer followed his gaze and furrowed his brow. Across the room, Ari whispered a few words in Athela's ears that seemed to galvanize her into action. She scanned the crowd, made eye contact with Tarr, and motioned for him to come around and meet her.

Tarr and Archer broke away from the crowd of spectators just as another wave of applause broke out. They fell into a swift lockstep together as they made their way around the hall to meet up with the others.

As soon as he caught sight of Athela, Ari and Marc, he jogged a few feet to catch them. "What is it?" he asked breathlessly.

"Someone's here," Ari said shortly.

"Again?" Archer asked sarcastically. "Who is it this time? Laith's old housekeeper?"

"It's Rowan," Athela chimed in shortly, with a pointed look at him.

Archer's jaw dropped and his mirth instantly evaporated. "She's alive?" he asked hoarsely.

"Apparently so," Athela nodded.

"Where's Laith?" Tarr asked sharply.

"Laith's on patrol," Ari told him. "I'll get someone to fetch him here. I had them take Rowan to the North office to wait." He stopped. "Should I tell Cade as well?"

The other Strikers halted in their tracks and looked at one another. Tarr's initial knee-jerk reaction was to say no, and Athela could read it in his face.

"At some point we have to at least *pretend* like we're fighting on the same side as him," she pointed out reasonably. "It will engender absolutely no goodwill whatsoever if he finds out that an escaped prisoner from Faridor showed up and no one bothered to tell him."

"She's right," Marc agreed levelly.

Tarr didn't like it, but looked over at Ari and gave a short nod. Ari peeled off from the rest of them and disappeared down a hallway.

"How did Rowan escape?" Archer asked, as they picked up the pace of their half-run down the hall towards the North office. "How on earth did she get out of Faridor?"

"I don't *know*, Archer, we haven't *talked* to her yet," Athela replied through what sounded like gritted teeth.

"Or was she released?" Tarr mused. He wouldn't put it past Cira to somehow send Rowan to them as a double agent.

The North office, while rather unimaginatively named, was a beautifully appointed room with large windows facing northward. It had been used in the past as a waiting room to receive visiting dignitaries, and sported expensive, intricately carved wood furnishings, dark blue and gold wallpaper, and a domed ceiling decorated with gilt flourishes. It was here that they found Rowan, seated quietly in a small chair, looking incongruously small and gray compared to the ornate beauty of the surroundings.

She stood up when they entered, and though Tarr wasn't sure what to expect from someone who had spent years as a prisoner in Faridor, he stopped in utter shock. She was thin and gaunt, her once-shining black hair cropped close to her head, all the beauty and life burned from the flesh of her face and body. She was only a shadow of the vivacious young woman who he'd seen in Two Falls all those years ago; Tarr would not have recognized her at all if he'd passed her on the street. But as those first seconds ticked interminably by, he could see vestiges of hope—a flush of color in her cheeks and a fire in her eye that told him that her spirit was undimmed. The rest would take time, care, and proper nutrition, but that spark remained, and that was what mattered.

"That good, huh?" Rowan wisecracked at the unflattering looks of shock greeting her appearance.

Silently, Archer walked up to her, and, as much to Rowan's surprise as everyone else's, took her in a close embrace, his hand cupping the back of her shorn head, pressing her against her shoulder. Tarr saw her blink in surprise and almost alarm for a few moments, then she closed her arms around his back. Archer was murmuring something in her ear that the rest of them could not hear; whatever it was, Rowan's eyes were darting back and forth as she listened, then she silently nodded and closed them, embracing him fully. It was an intimate moment, and it made Tarr feel uncomfortable being there to witness it. He looked down at his boot and poked the toe of it at an invisible speck of dust on the floor.

A few seconds later, Archer released her and stepped back, and Tarr was surprised to see that there were tears in Archer's eyes. His brother was usually so unflappable; Tarr couldn't remember having seen him cry before. Tarr purposefully avoided looking over at Athela.

Rowan faced them and raised her head up proudly, almost challenging in her expression. Tarr opened his mouth to speak, but suddenly there were footsteps behind them. Cade appeared, his blond head emerging out of the darkness, his presence blissfully breaking the tension that permeated the room. Cade surveyed them all, from Archer's ruffled demeanor to what was sure to be barely suppressed fury from Athela (Tarr still hadn't dared to look), to Rowan, standing almost defiantly before them. Finally, Cade looked to Tarr, silently prompting an introduction.

"Rowan, this is Cade, the new King of Joymaril," Tarr said, extending an arm. Rowan mimed something resembling a curtsy and the two regarded one another. Tarr thought he could see something pass between them. "Cade, this is Rowan. She's an old friend of Archer's and helped us when we first arrived in Two Falls. She was arrested by Cira shortly thereafter and has remained in Faridor ever since."

"I don't want to stay long," Rowan said. "I only came here because I have something to deliver to you. After that, I'm leaving." She sat, and the others followed suit, pulling up chairs to form a semicircle around her. Cade's bodyguard Wolf slipped in and remained stationed at the door.

Rowan drew up a knapsack that she had slung on the floor next to her chair. She withdrew a small sheaf of papers and handed them to Tarr, who had sat down beside her. "These, I believe, were smuggled out of Faridor with the intention that they be given to you." She told them.

Tarr frowned and began to sift through the papers. The top page made no sense, but as soon as he began to read the rest, a light began to dawn on him. He felt the blood drain from his face.

"What is it?" Athela asked urgently.

"The weapon," Tarr replied, and even he was surprised to hear how faint his voice sounded. "It's the weapon. She did it." He caught himself and looked over at Cade, who looked smugly satisfied. He had likely guessed who *she* was, and knew now that Rane was at Faridor, not running reconnaissance in the Meadows as Tarr had originally told him.

The other Strikers leapt to their feet and gathered around him, looking over his shoulder. It was all in Rane's familiar neat handwriting, and contained diagrams and a detailed description of every part of the thing.

"How bad is it?" Archer asked, craning his long neck. He was at the back and couldn't make out what the papers said.

"Not great," Tarr admitted, his eyes tearing through the lines. His initial rush at finally having answers had given way to a sinking dread at realizing what the thing actually was. Even with the description and the rough sketches Rane had drawn, it was difficult to imagine such an object: something that could fire at great distances and rend destruction with deadly accuracy and little to no effort on the part of the attacker. Tarr swallowed, his throat dry, mind racing to think of ways they could get past it.

Faridor was already difficult—if not impossible—to overcome. The only access to it was the bridge to the mainland, which was heavily guarded and created a bottleneck for any army that tried to rush it. And now, with these weapons mounted on the walls, Cira could fire endless rounds into their ranks as they stacked up at the entrance of the bridge. It would be over in a matter of minutes, and the death and destruction it would wreak was devastating to contemplate. Attack by sea was out of the question. They had no boats, no navy, and the walls of the fortress were all but sheer from the sea side.

Tarr silently passed the papers over to Athela, who held them up for Archer as he looked over her shoulder, each of them forgetting about their interpersonal war for a few blissful seconds. If Tarr hadn't been so mentally agitated, he would have taken time to enjoy the moment.

"Balls," Archer observed after a long, protracted silence.

There was a soft knock at the door and Laith was admitted, followed by Ari. Laith looked rather out of breath, and cast down the black hood of his cloak from his head as he entered. Marc rose to meet him and filled him in with a few quiet words. Laith flashed a reserved smile of greeting in Rowan's direction and took the papers as Athela handed them to him.

"I think it's time," Tarr said.

"We need to call a council and formulate a plan of attack," Cade agreed with a firm nod. He met Tarr's gaze with his steely gray eyes and Tarr could see conviction and not a small bit of ruthlessness in them.

"Where is General Calchas?" Tarr asked Laith, whose aristocratic brow was furrowed as he read what Rane had written.

"Close by," he said. "A few days' ride away in the Meadows. He's been recruiting help there for the past few months since we took back Two Falls."

"Send for him at once," Cade said, in a tone that sounded very much like an order. Tarr, who had opened his mouth to more diplomatically suggest the same thing, closed it with a twinge of annoyance.

Laith responded to this by slowly raising his eyes and eyebrows up to regard his little brother. "Happy to," he replied, and Tarr thought he detected a certain delicate strain of fraternal sarcasm in his tone.

"We'll need a secure location," Cade said, swiveling around now to Tarr.

"I'll handle it," Tarr said quickly. He didn't think he could take much more of Cade's authoritative manner.

"Good," Cade said, satisfied.

"How did you get these?" Tarr asked, suddenly turning back to Rowan. It occurred to him that it was strange for the papers to have gone somehow to Rowan, instead of through one of their usual routes.

"And how did you get out?" Archer chimed in.

Rowan looked from one of them to the other, took a breath of resignation, and told them how Kai had bargained for her rescue, and killed in the process. How Rowan had barely survived, and had wound up at the Ulster's farm. She mentioned seeing Persefea, and if she noticed the sudden tension that pervaded the room at the sound of the name, she didn't mention it aloud. Finally, she told them of the day she'd discovered the letters hidden in the bottom of her basket, had deciphered their meaning, and had decided to bring them to Two Falls.

Tarr wondered again why the papers had made it out that way rather than through one of their typical channels of communication, but things happened so quickly at Faridor that Rane must have done the best she could. He could only imagine what a struggle it had been for Rowan to decide to return the papers to them after her escape, and felt sincerely grateful to her for doing so. "You've saved hundreds, if not thousands of lives by bringing us these," he told her. "Thank you."

Rowan shrugged one shoulder, as if those lives mattered very little to her. "Good. But I won't be staying long. I want to leave as soon as possible."

"To go where?" Archer asked quietly.

"North. Anywhere but here. Away from all of this." She gestured around at them and their opulent room with a sense of distaste.

"I was imprisoned too," Cade said quietly. He had listened silently as she told her story and seemed to be regarding her anew. "In Joymaril. For nearly four years, almost as soon as they'd left."

Rowan assessed him thoughtfully, as though she'd only given him passing notice before. "You're Laith's brother?"

"Yes," he replied, "Cade."

Tarr thought it interesting that he didn't bother to add "King" before his first name. Rowan had had a sort of softening effect on him; some of the pompous, grandiose façade melted away and Tarr could see, almost for the first time since he arrived, the young man beneath. A young man who had been through more pain and suffering than he himself could possibly imagine, and who had come through the other side. Tarr felt a sudden begrudging respect for him.

"You look like her," Rowan said after a few moments. "Like Cira."

Cade, Tarr could see, was thrown off-guard. He wasn't quite sure what to say; whether to apologize or simply smile and acknowledge the unfortunate family resemblance. Finally, he spread his hands in a gesture of surrender. "We can't choose our relatives, I'm afraid. Or our hair color," he said. "But I assure you, I'm not her."

"Good," Rowan said, sounding unconvinced. "I hope not."

Well, this is interesting, Tarr thought, rather enjoying himself. It was like watching two cats circling each other, warily sizing each other up, unsure of whether to attack or purr.

"You should stay," Archer cut in, and Cade and Rowan looked over to him as if startled that there was someone else in the room. "At least for a few days."

"I can't," Rowan shook her head, but her voice held less conviction than it did before.

"There may be a group heading north who you could ride with," Marc pointed out. "It would be safer."

Rowan considered, finally giving a sigh and nodding. They broke up the meeting shortly afterwards, the precious plans clutched in Tarr's hands. As everyone stood and bade each other goodnight, he noticed that Cade's watchful gray eyes never strayed far from Rowan.

The next night, across the city of Two Falls in the top floor of her flat, Tess laid another kindling log and stoked it a few times until the sparks flew up in a crackling cloud up the chimney. She closed the door of her squat iron stove and flipped her hair over her shoulder in one smooth motion, standing and stretching as she crossed the kitchen to her workbench by the front door. She perched on her stool, peering over a particularly stubborn joint in an archway she was carving. Almost unconsciously she glanced over her shoulder.

Laith lay asleep on her sofa, an arm tucked behind his head, one knee bent, the other long leg trailing down towards the floor. His head was turned slightly away from her, the line of his jaw running unbroken into the graceful curve of his neck. She turned back and fiddled with the piece of wood between her fingers.

He came to visit her often, every two or three days. On rare occasions he showed up on concurrent nights. She'd find herself glancing at the door in the hour before he came, always in the dead of night, appearing on her doorstep like some sort of dark shadow. She couldn't deny how much she had come to crave his visits, though they talked very little. True to his word, he made no demands when he visited, and she often found herself wondering what he got out of his time there. He rarely spoke. If Julian was awake or fussing, he'd play with the boy, pulling faces or lying on the couch and lifting him up into the air while her son cackled with glee.

Oftentimes, if Julian was asleep, Tess would sit late into the night at her workbench while Laith lay on the couch and quietly watched her. Sometimes he stared at the ceiling, his hands folded across his chest. Frequently he'd fall asleep—like a child, so deeply and still that Tess was afraid to wake him. But every morning, before the sun rose, there'd be a scratch at the door and Laith would awaken immediately, without so much as a start. His dog would be waiting on the stoop, and with a smile and a nod, Laith would be gone. Like a gust of wind, fleeting as a memory. There'd been a small scare a few nights before when his dog hadn't summoned him, and he'd overslept and left shortly after sunup, later than he usually did. Tess had found herself wondering what it would be like for them to wake up together, to make breakfast, to go about the motions of cohabitated domestic life that she only dimly remembered. It would be easy, she thought, to fall into that life once again.

She wondered what he thought of her. She knew full well what the rest of the male population of Two Falls thought of her. She had been a barmaid long enough to know that after a few glasses of liquor any inhibitions fell away and that if one was possessed of a pretty smile and a curvy frame, it mattered very little what sort of academic degrees one had received in time gone by. But Laith had made no untoward advances towards her at all; except for the moment when he'd stroked her hair during their first meeting, they'd never touched. In the conversations they'd had—if one could call them conversations, with Tess herself doing most of the talking—he'd seemed content to just sit and listen, a curious half-smile on his face.

She laughed a bit to herself, imagining herself trying to explain her relationship with Laith to an outside party. There wasn't really any "relationship," per se. She didn't try to embroider it. She couldn't say for him, but she was well aware that much of her attraction to him was purely superficial. He was one of the most beautiful creatures she'd ever seen; she felt her eyes lingering a little on the lines of the broad shoulders beneath his shirt, the planes of his well-shaped head, his graceful neck and his large hands, and felt like giggling every time she caught herself.

Still, though, she thought she knew him. She knew him better than she reckoned anyone else did. All the unspoken pain and loneliness that radiated with his every gesture was something she had felt, something she had forced herself to hide under a cheery smile and a faux-flirtatious manner as she poured drink after drink and watched them disappear down a long line of hoarse, scratchy throats. And there was the fact of the strange intimacy that came with sleeping next to another person. They'd somehow bypassed the hellos and getting-to-know-yous, even the physical intimacy, and gone straight to spending hours and hours in close proximity at the time when they were at their most human, their most vulnerable. She didn't know the names of Laith's parents, what he had studied in school, what kind of foods he liked, but she knew that he preferred to sleep on his back with his head turned to the side and his arms crossed over his chest; he didn't snore but sometimes muttered beneath his breath, and that when he was dreaming his eyelids fluttered like a butterfly drying out its wings.

She knew how hollow she felt, especially at night. She still reached out sometimes to the empty side of her bed. She wondered whether he did the same. She wondered what he would make of it if she invited him to lie beside her.

Enough, she thought.

She pushed herself back from the desk and stood for a moment, her arms folded in front of her chest. Laith slept on, oblivious, his breathing steady. It was always as if he hadn't slept in weeks. She crossed over to him in three strides and knelt down by the couch.

Almost instinctively, the prince turned towards her in his sleep as if sensing her warmth. His dark lashes rested like a crescent atop his cheekbones. The thin white scar over his ear was barely visible, tracing an uneven line through his short sandy hair. She reached out her hand, and was surprised to find that it wasn't shaking, even though her heart was pounding. She'd always had the strange fancy that Laith would disappear the instant she tried to touch him; that he would vanish like a sweep of dust. She felt a jolt as her fingertips touched the skin of his temple. She stroked the scar gently, lightly, following its length towards the back of his head. The short-cropped hair over his ear tickled the tips of her fingers.

Suddenly, his eyes flickered, and the dark lashes parted. Without a sound, he was awake. She hesitated and withdrew her hand ever so slightly, searching his face for any sign of discomfort. She expected him to say something, to sit up suddenly, to push her away and tell her she had the wrong idea, but he lay there quietly, watching her with his enormous dark eyes.

Once, when she was a little girl, her father had trapped a fox behind the barn. He fed it medicine to make it sleep, then called her over and let her pet it. She remembered the feeling of fear and excitement as she'd run her small hands along the soft red fur—the thrill of coming in contact with something wild and unreachable.

That same tiny shiver went up the back of her neck as she again lowered her fingers and ran them along Laith's white scar, then went gently down to trace the curve of his jaw. He was quite still, his expression blank, but she could see the bob of his neck as he swallowed. She ran her hand slowly down the slope of his neck and over the dip at his throat, then traced the arch of his dark eyebrows, his cheekbones. She hesitated ever so slightly and ran her thumb slowly over the curve of his lower lip. His eyes flickered open and shut and his whole body suddenly seemed to shudder and relax.

Tess withdrew her hand and sat back on her heels. His face was still unreadable, but she could see his breath coming quicker and the pounding of blood in his neck. He wanted her too, she could see it. His eyes had never left hers. She felt as though every one of her senses was heightened; she was aware of every sensation from her fingers to her toes. Every passing second felt like an eternity.

Slowly, he unfolded his arm from beneath his head and pushed himself to sit upright. They faced each other squarely, Tess kneeling before him on the floor. Tentatively, she placed her hands on his legs. Never breaking his gaze, he reached for her. His warm hand slid slowly up her arm from her wrist to her forearm, and she felt his grip tighten. He was so strong, she realized, and felt a flutter deep in her core. He pulled her arm towards him so that her face was mere inches away. He hesitated only slightly, his lips brushing hers for the span of a single breath. Then he pressed her to him.

It was as if the entire world had been suspended and then came crashing down the moment their lips touched. Their kiss sparked in the cold air, and in another instant, his hands were in her hair, reaching for her waist. They almost grappled back and forth for a moment, fighting to see who could pull the other closer. But then her tongue brushed against his and he let out a low moan and slid an arm beneath her, scooping her up onto his lap astride him. He slid her skirt up her leg, fingers gripping the soft flesh of her thigh. Then in one fluid motion he flipped her beneath him on the couch, urgently pressing against her with the length of his lean body. Even Tess was surprised at how hungrily, ravenously she kissed him, how impatient she was now, wrapping her legs around his hips and frantically pulling at his shirt.

And then—*scratch scratch*. Breaker was at the door. Laith froze and broke away, his dark gaze darting towards the door and back to her. The two of them remained there, motionless, their hearts racing in time, longing burning through every inch of their bodies. Tess searched his face.

"Stay," she whispered. "Please stay."

He closed his eyes and took a deep breath in, and when he let it out she saw that his mind was already made up. He kissed her one last lingering time, then moved his lips to the dip at the base of her throat, his warm breath on her skin, one hand still curved over her breast. Tess let out a long sigh of desire, pleasure, and frustration all wrapped in one, and for an instant she thought he'd give in. She knew she could keep him there if she tried even a little.

But he gave the slightest shake of his head and she saw the muscles in his temple pulse as he gritted his teeth in visible frustration. There was something else there, too—guilt, perhaps. His head slumped forward, and he rested his forehead on her chest. Then with a heavy sigh, he allowed his whole body to relax and he lay atop her fully. From above him, she could see his eyes close. She stroked his hair, holding him, trying to fight back a sudden spring of tears welling up in her eyes. After a few more seconds he pushed himself off of her to sit on the edge of the couch, his head in his hands.

"I can stop coming here," he murmured after a moment. "If you want."

"I don't want that," she said shortly, her hair splayed out on the couch beneath her, one bare shoulder exposed.

"It's all..." he trailed off helplessly, shaking his head in frustration. His eyes lingered hungrily on her shoulder, the slope of her neck.

"I know," she said quickly.

He put his head again in his hand and rubbed his fingers through his short hair. She sat up beside him, pulling her dress up to cover herself. "This is the only place I can go," he said, so quietly she could barely hear him. He turned to look at her, his dark brown eyes searching her face. "I don't forget. I never do, and there's this weight on me that is constantly..." his hand tugged at his chest as he groped for words. "But here, it seems like the war could end. And that there could be something on the other side."

"I know," she said softly. "I understand."

He smiled ever so gently and nodded. "You do."

The air between them crackled. It would be so easy, Tess thought, to pull him back. But she let him go.

When Laith stood to fetch his cloak Tess followed behind him, their bodies moving unconsciously in unison. He opened the door and stopped on the doorstep. Breaker was on the other side, and gave a good-natured thud of his tail at the sight of them—impatiently, Tess thought. Laith turned back to her.

"I realize this is a bit of an odd time to ask," he said, "but a group of us are going to get together soon, and we could use someone who knows about buildings and things."

"Are you planning something?" she asked incredulously, trying not to laugh at the term "buildings and things," which was a funny way to describe her profession.

He smiled evasively. "We have a couple drawings, and we could use someone like you."

Tess was taken aback. "I know about buildings. And things," she conceded with a smile.

"Would you come? It'd just be this, no need to do anything more. And I'll understand if you'd rather not."

Tess considered for a moment, glancing back towards the interior of her house. *It's just a meeting*, she thought. It was odd...Laith was a fighter, but the thought of him actually in combat or in danger made her stomach turn. And though she didn't completely want to acknowledge it, part of her wanted to impress him. She wanted to prove to him that her knowledge extended beyond beer and filling glasses with wine. She wanted to see him somewhere outside of their insular little world. And her heart gave a longing thud at the thought of working with buildings or architecture again. She had spent so long fiddling with her models and drawing imaginary edifices in the quiet of her room in the dead of night. She wanted a tactile problem; a riddle to solve. Any reservations about meeting with the Strikers were pushed to the side.

"If it's in the evening, I'll need to bring Julian," she said.

"Bring him," Laith told her, and for some reason he looked amused. "Believe me, there'll be plenty of people to look after him. I'll send word soon."

She nodded quickly and stepped back. She knew better than to think that Laith would give her a kiss goodnight; if they touched again he would not be able to leave.

For one more moment he smiled at her, then with a turn of his cloak he was gone. Tess shut the door.

CHAPTER SEVENTEEN

Tarr organized the strategy meeting as carefully and meticulously as he could, wondering snarkily whether his arrangements would meet with Cade's high standards. Only the Strikers and their most trusted allies were invited to attend; it was to be held in an underground cellar that had formerly been a storehouse for a beer brewery in town. It was secure and private and also (quite helpfully) had been outfitted with a secret escape tunnel hidden behind a seemingly immovable rack of casks on the far side of the room, just in case they needed to make a swift exit. Tarr knew much better than to lock the entire organizational power behind the Strikers in an enclosed room.

Still, he was relatively certain that security would not be an issue that night. He had spent a week with a team of his best forgers concocting an interconnecting web of conflicting messages and false information that he sent out with some satisfaction to contacts at various parts of the city. He took some pleasure in imagining all of Cira's spies scurrying around Two Falls trying to find them like a disoriented group of ducks.

It would be a good meeting, Tarr reckoned. There were the Strikers, of course. Ari was bringing some of his trusted lieutenants, Khan, Ella, and Itzhal. Rowan had agreed to come, and there were Cade and Wolf, some of their high-ranking warriors, including Nadia, the young woman who had traveled with Cade from Joymaril after his takeover. General Calchas would be there with his newly appointed right-hand lieutenant, a short, stocky and utterly intimidating woman named Teague, who had taken the place of Lady Burton after she'd fallen in the Battle of Two Falls. Between all of them, Tarr thought, they should be able to come up with *something*. He wished that Rane or Cicada could be there. They'd be invaluable.

"I hear Laith is bringing a date," Athela muttered to Tarr in a low voice as she helped him scoot a chair around the long table they'd set up in the middle of the cellar. Tarr was shuffling piles of papers, including Rane's report about the weapon, and the stolen layout of Faridor they'd taken after Persefea's tip-off.

"Really?" Tarr asked, surprised. Laith had barely spoken to *them* about anything other than work in months. He could hardly imagine Laith striking up a conversation with a stranger.

"He's bringing a *date*?" Archer asked incredulously, not bothering to keep his voice quiet. "To a *strategic planning meeting*? Boy, he *is* out of practice."

"We're allowed to bring dates?" Marc chimed in with mock irritation, Si standing starry-eyed and vague at his side. "Why didn't anyone bother to tell me?"

Tarr had fixed it so that the attendees would be escorted carefully into the building one at a time, with a good length between each arrival. It made for a very leisurely start to things, and the group began milling and talking in small groups together as newcomers showed up every ten minutes or so. Though they'd set up as many lamps as possible to light the table and the paperwork atop it, the room was still dark, filled with the imposing shadows of large racks of barrels, strong wooden beams looming across the low ceiling.

Tarr suddenly felt an elbow digging into his ribs and he looked up to see Athela waggle her dark eyebrows suggestively up and down, pointedly staring across the room. As casually as he could, Tarr swung around, doing his best to act as though he'd just remembered something important, trying to stifle a grin at what rubbish spies he and Athela would make. A tall young woman with a lovely, solemn face and a swath of chestnut hair entered the room, a small, sleepy-looking child perched on her hip. She looked uncertain, scanning the faces in the room for someone she recognized. She stared for a few moments at General Calchas but didn't approach him. She seemed to smile at the sight of him. Then her gaze slipped away and finally settled. A shy smile flickered across her mouth as Laith, newly arrived himself, strode over to greet her.

Tarr was immediately interested and tried his best to gauge what was going on. Though they made no physical contact, they stood in close proximity together and conversed in low, familiar tones. It all seemed fairly intimate. The woman, whoever she was, was facing him and from her expression it was immediately apparent that she was thoroughly smitten, which surprised Tarr not a whit.

It took Tarr a moment to realize that he, Marc, Athela and Archer were all standing in a straight row watching Laith and his guest with their heads cocked to the side and their arms folded, identical expressions of furrowed appraisal on their faces. Stifling a snort, Tarr very loudly and obviously cleared his throat. Immediately, Athela blinked, glanced around, and straightened. Archer grinned and he and Marc made a beeline for Laith and the stranger. A moment later, smiling introductions were made, and the sleepy child was transferred from the young woman to Marc, who busied himself pulling silly faces at the little boy as he cradled him in the crook of one strong arm. The boy seemed comfortable enough with Marc, but after a short time fastened his eyes on Si, and though Si was doing nothing overt to keep the boy's attention, the child didn't seem to want to look away, almost as if he could sense that Si was different than the others. The young woman with the chestnut hair smiled proudly at her son and stroked a lock of his dark hair, then laughed prettily at something Archer had said.

"She's got a nice smile," Tarr said in an undertone to Athela, who grunted noncommittally. "Are you going to be nice to her?"

"I," said Athela with some dignity, "am *always* nice." But to Tarr's surprise and relief, she indeed looked more interested than irritated at the presence of the newcomer.

Laith broke away from the young woman to help Athela greet a few of General Calchas's soldiers, who had just entered the meeting.

Marc and Archer, by this point, had the boy grinning coyly at them from behind a fat little fist, and the young woman was regarding them all with a fond, bemused expression. Tarr figured this was as good a time as any to introduce himself, so he sidled up to her.

"I'm Tarr," he extended his thin hand, and the girl immediately fixed him with a radiant, beguiling smile. She had hazel eyes and a smattering of freckles across her nose. There was something about her that Tarr couldn't quite pinpoint—a quiet confidence with which she held herself that gave her the air of someone being eminently capable. She would be the kind of person you'd call if the wheel broke on a carriage or if you didn't know how to arrange a seating chart at a party. She gave the air of being eminently levelheaded, logical, and reasonable. He wished he had met her at the beginning of the war.

She took his hand with a naturally strong grip. Her skin was rough and calloused across the palm. Tarr liked her immensely.

"Nice to meet you," she said. "I'm Tess."

The two of them watched as Archer tried to duck down behind Marc's shoulder and pop out to surprise the boy. Marc was easily a foot and a half shorter than Archer so this maneuver was achieved with a certain degree of difficulty. Tarr got the sense that the toddler was humoring them to some extent.

"How'd you meet Laith?" Tarr asked.

"I saved his life," she said casually. When Tarr looked at her in surprise, she reconsidered for a beat. "Well, sort of. I sat on him."

"Goodness," Tarr said mildly.

"I know," she agreed. "Unconventional. But it worked."

They continued to chat, and she filled him in with some general information about who she was and what her life before the war had consisted of. Tarr was interested in hearing about the university in Two Falls; he remembered that in the old days, Ma had rented out rooms in her house to students, but at the time Tarr was only dimly aware of what that meant. *Perhaps I could have gone to the university*, he thought wistfully, *if I hadn't been standing in the square with Wolver that day. If they hadn't mistaken me for the other Ashan, the one who was supposed to have been here all along.* He gave an inward sigh.

He shook his head and cleared his thoughts. "Well, we have some documents we'll want you to look at. You'll be a great help," Tarr said finally. He paused, desperately wanting to know more about her relationship with Laith. *How is he doing?* he wanted to ask, realizing how odd it would be to ask a complete stranger about the mental health of one of his best friends.

As if she'd read his thoughts, Tess looked over in the direction of Laith and asked suddenly, "What was he like before the war?"

Tarr took a deep breath. "Lighter," he mused, trying to remember. It seemed so long ago that his friend had been carefree and young and engaged with the world around him. "Quicker to smile, easy to be with. He's a good man."

Tess looked thoughtfully at the prince, who was now talking with his younger brother. "Yes, he certainly seems to be," she agreed, then looked directly up at Tarr. "We're not sleeping together, you know. Despite my best efforts."

Tarr blinked, taken slightly off-guard. "It...it's none of my business."

Tess shrugged a shoulder, as if it mattered very little to her. "I'm sure everyone else thinks we are."

Tarr chose his words carefully. "If you were," he said slowly. "I think we'd all be relieved."

Tess laughed at this, her freckled nose crinkling beguilingly. Her son let out a squawk behind her, and she turned to take him back from Marc and Archer, who seemed to have successfully riled him up.

"I think we should call this meeting to order," Cade announced. After a moment, the chatter died down and there was a small ripple of murmuring as everyone took their places around the table. Laith pulled out the chair for Tess, who sat beside him with her son on her lap, bouncing him up and down as he batted the palm of his chubby hand on the edge of the table.

"Right," Cade said, immediately taking charge of the meeting once the rest had sat down. He looked especially kingly that night, in a dark burgundy tunic embroidered with gold, his light hair swept back away from his face. Tarr wondered whether he was trying to impress Rowan, who was watching him with a wary interest from the opposite end of the table. Rowan, for her part, was already looking much improved in health; though she had initially been very resistant to remaining so long in Two Falls, Tarr had convinced her to prolong her stay so that she could attend the meeting. She was in a plum-colored dress the same color as her birthmark (Tarr remembered her penchant for the color purple from their earlier dealings with her in Two Falls) and had wrapped herself in a warm charcoal-colored shawl against the damp of the cellar.

"New information has come to light which may influence a plan of attack on Faridor. Faridor is our last objective in removing Cira from power and stamping out the Kagaian flame. As we all know, the fortress is almost impregnable." He drew forth a large map of the island from a stack of papers before him and set it at the center of the table. Some around the table craned their necks to see it closer. "There is a single bridge connecting the island to the mainland. The fortress's outer defenses are high sheer walls built atop uneven rocky terrain that rises out of the sea. All exits and entrances, save for the front entry across the bridge, have been sealed. And Cira, we have recently discovered, has secured a weapon from the country of Vireg, which she hopes to use as a defense against any potential assault. Tarr?"

Tarr rose and withdrew another large sheet of paper, which included an enlarged sketch of the weapon that Rane had described. He moved it into the center of the table alongside the map of Faridor island.

"This is the weapon, and from what we've discovered, Cira has at least two of these. It's called a 'gun' or also a 'cannon.' They are able to fire explosives accurately and from a great distance, and were engineered by top scientists in Vireg. An attack on Faridor's gate is already a difficult proposition, and with these weapons, it's now next to impossible. Our army would be destroyed in a matter of minutes."

A rather grim silence followed this speech. Tarr looked around at the faces at the table. Some looked as though they were trying to puzzle out some sort of solution, others had skeptical expressions, as if this entire enterprise was already looking hopeless.

"So we starve her out," Calchas spoke up. "It would be easy to block the supply trains going into Faridor." Beside him, Cade nodded in mute agreement. Tarr remembered that Cade had been in favor of such a plan at their earlier debriefing.

"From the land, yes," Tarr pointed out. "But Cira has an agreement with Lord Tarik across the sea in Vireg. If she calls upon him, he's agreed to supply the fortress with ships and food. If we push her too far, we risk having to fight Vireg, too. And we don't have a navy, nothing that could remotely compare to Vireg's. We can't beat them at sea."

Another thoughtful silence descended. "Say we could get across the bridge," said Teague, Calchas's second-in-command. "How do we breach the walls?"

"Great question," Tarr smiled grimly. "No one has ever been able to. When Morthenstar and Kagai's armies battled before, it was in the open plain on the mainland. Not at the fortress. The fortress was conceded once the army surrendered in the field."

"So just to recap," Athela broke in, "We can't attack from the sea, we can't attack from the land, and even if we *could* attack from the land or the sea, we couldn't get close to the walls without being blown up."

"May I see the floorplans of Faridor, please?" Tess said suddenly. Tarr looked around at her with surprise. As she was the newest and least experienced member of the group, he'd expected her to mostly remain silent throughout the meeting. Silently, he passed her the papers, and was impressed by the keenness in her eye. He wondered whether she'd be able to see anything in the floorplans that he hadn't.

Tess bounced Julian on one knee and kept the papers safely out of his reach as she pored through.

"Can we send an envoy to King Tarik?" Teague asked. "Try and get him to withdraw his support of Cira?"

Cade had asked the same question weeks earlier when he'd first been appraised of their situation. Tarr shook his head. His opinion hadn't changed. "My guess is he's going to wait and watch. Stay out of it as long as he can."

"But *if* Tarik decided to back us, then we could lay siege?" Teague pressed.

"*If*," Tarr conceded. "It's a big if. And it will take time."

"May I see the map of the island and the weapons diagram?" Tess asked suddenly.

Tarr glanced over at her, again surprised. *What is she thinking?* he wondered, silently laying the requested papers down in front of her, just as Julian let out a large stream of babbling sounds that made everyone around the table jump a little.

"Sorry," Tess said a bit absentmindedly, giving Julian a bigger bounce on one knee as the boy flailed his arms wildly in the air. She was peering closely at the Faridor floorplan and almost unconsciously took the weapons diagram and slid it into her field of vision. Tarr noted with amusement that some of the older members of the council, Calchas included, were staring at her as if they didn't quite know what to make of her. Tarr imagined that not many of their past strategic planning sessions had featured the input of toddlers.

"I still think a siege is the best idea," Calchas shook his head. "We have her backed into a corner. If this King Tarik is as clever and cautious as you say, Tarr, I can't see that it benefits him that much to send aid."

"No," Tarr agreed reasonably. "It wouldn't benefit him much. Unless he sends aid and then, after landing his troops on our shores with little to no resistance from anyone, including Cira, he displaces Cira and seizes power himself. And then," Tarr looked directly at Cade, "we have a much bigger, much more powerful enemy with wealth and technological advancement behind him. We would either be conquered or wiped out." He said this last sentence flatly, matter-of-factly. It was the truth.

The others stared at him. "Is there any evidence that this sort of plan is in place?" Calchas asked in a dark voice.

Tarr shrugged. "No, not really. But it doesn't take a great stretch of the imagination to see that this could be Tarik's play. We need to keep him at bay as long as possible. Cira, at least, is an enemy we know and can meet head-on. And who, as you say, we have cornered."

"A tall, fortified, armed, impossible-to-breach sort of corner," Archer said drily.

Tess cleared her throat, and all the heads snapped back around to her. She stood, handing Julian off to Marc, who took the boy wordlessly. Julian, though he seemed momentarily surprised to be displaced in such a way, was quiet and watched his mother with large round eyes as she leaned forward, pushing some of the plans further into the center of the table.

"There are two things I see that may be a benefit to us," she said, and pointed to the larger diagram of Faridor. "There's a way into the fortress here," she pointed a finger to the south side of the rocky island.

"What?" Tarr said with frank astonishment before he could stop himself. He craned his neck to see where she had indicated. He'd been over and over the plans a dozen times and hadn't seen anything of the sort. Tarr could tell from the puzzled looks on the faces around the room that they couldn't quite make out what Tess was talking about, either.

Tess caught the drift, for she turned the map around and faced it to the end of the table, then pulled the blueprint of the fortress and laid them side by side. "You don't see it if you look at one or the other. You have to look at both together," she explained. "There's a small passage-way here," she pointed to the drawing of the fortress, dozens of lines interconnecting to indicate walls and passageways. "But structurally, the passage has no entry or outlet. It's just a hallway that apparently ends at a wall for no reason. And here," she pushed the island map forward, "right in the same place, there is a natural inlet positioned just under the end of that dead-end hall. Which leads me to believe that it's an entrance into the fortress that can be accessed from the sea."

Tarr stared at her, thunderstruck. She blinked back, only a small smile betraying her triumph.

"Is it…" Cade cleared his throat. "How big is it?"

"If you're thinking of bringing an army in there, you're out of luck," Tess shook her head. "The inlet would only be able to accommodate a few boats. The rest would be pushed outside the shelter of the cove, where they'd be spotted by guards up on the wall. But a *small* group could absolutely get in that way, provided the space isn't guarded."

Tarr looked excitedly over to Athela and Laith, and he saw that they were both staring at Tess with looks of awed astonishment.

"And," Calchas leaned forward, looking at her with keen interest, "You said you had something else?"

"Yes," Tess replied, pulling up the sheet with the drawing of the weapon on it. "From what your source has said in their notes, it takes a crew of people to move this, and even then it is not able to move at high speed."

"Yes," Tarr agreed, his heart beginning to beat faster.

"So you must ensure the weapons are pointed away from land," Tess said simply. With one long finger she tapped on the eastern wall of Faridor, the one that pointed out to sea. "Trick her. Make her think that the attack is coming from the sea, and she'll move the guns to be ready to face them there."

"And then we attack from land," Cade breathed out.

"A land attack is still risky, but from what you've said, Tarr, it's the only way in," Tess pointed out. "And this way, if you can cross the bridge, breach the main gate, and take the wall, you'll have a fighting chance of getting an army in."

"What if she is able to move the guns back to a position facing the land?" Rowan asked.

"She may," Tess agreed. "You'd have to stop her."

"What if she only moved one gun?" Ella asked. "Left the other pointing towards land?"

Tarr and Laith glanced at one another. "It would still buy us time," Laith said. "More time than we would have otherwise. A chance to get across the bridge."

Silence fell and Tess looked up, surveying the blank, rather over-whelmed expressions around her. "Well, that's just what I saw," she said finally. "Hope it helps." And with that, she sat back down and Marc, ice-blue eyes wide as an owl's, re-deposited her son into her lap.

"Erm..." Tarr rooted around for something with which he could follow that up.

"We...um..." Cade also seemed at an uncharacteristic loss for words, and even met Tarr's eyes and grinned at him, relaxing his guard for just a moment.

"That certainly seems like the best chance we have," Calchas frowned, breaking the stunned silence. "It's going to take some planning yet, to figure out exactly how to bring an army in through the front..."

"But it gives us a fighting chance," Laith interjected, then smiled faintly at his own unintentional joke. "So to speak."

"We still need to find out how to trick her into turning the guns away from the land," Cade had finally recovered himself well enough to fall back into the conversation, and seemed to be gathering momentum. "I can lead a group to a heavily timbered area on the coast, a little ways to the south. Tarr, can you manage to find some way to leak our whereabouts to Cira's agents?"

"I think I might be able to," Tarr said, smiling slowly. His heart was racing.

"In that case," Cade continued, "we might have ourselves the first semblance of a plan of attack."

"We just might," Athela agreed, her gray eyes flashing.

"I'll start pulling a team together for the expedition to the coast," Cade said. "I'll leave as soon as we think we'll be able to execute the plan."

"We'll call a separate council to discuss the land attack," Laith added. "It's not impossible, but it's going to be difficult, especially breaking the wall. As Tarr said, a full-blooded Ashan could breach the wall, but many of the Ashans in Two Falls left after the battle, understandably. Many, many others are sick or injured or recovering from captivity and hiding. I don't think we'd have enough in fighting condition to take the wall or do anything more than run headlong to their deaths."

"I'd like to offer my advice on strategy," Calchas volunteered. "We'll come up with something." Laith nodded with a grateful smile.

Tarr looked around the table. Where moments before the faces had been glum and dour, there was now a palpable feeling of excitement. Tess jogged Julian up and down on one knee a few times, seemingly oblivious that it was she who had turned things around and given them the only ounce of hope they had.

"Good," Tarr said finally. "Meeting dismissed."

There was a loud screeching and scraping of chairs as they were pushed back from the table. Tarr let out a long, exhausted breath and motioned to Cade and Wolf, as they were the first scheduled to leave with an escort. The rest of the group broke away again into small groups, chatting easily now that the difficult work was done.

Tarr came to stand beside Athela, who was still seated at the table, staring down at her page of notes from the meeting. "Tarr," she said, businesslike, "do you think that Cade, when he goes, should…"

"Give it a rest," Tarr said tiredly, placing his hand on her shoulder and rubbing his eyes. "We can talk again in the morning."

Athela clearly wasn't in the least bit sleepy, but Tarr appreciated her humoring him. She shrugged and creaked her chair back. She happened to glance over Tarr's shoulder towards the basement's stairwell entrance, and something in her face flinched. It was such a strange expression that Tarr at once turned to see what she was looking at.

Laith was standing beside Tess and holding her little boy on his hip. The toddler, who had been dozing through the last ten minutes of the meeting, didn't seem to be bothered much by being awakened again. He was tapping the flat of his hand against Laith's mouth. Laith raised his eyebrows and pantomimed eating the tiny fingers as they batted at him. He laughed and turned to Tess to say something. For that split second it was suddenly as though all the years and the battles had fallen away from him. For a fleeting instant he was the good-humored, happy young man Tarr had met four years ago. And then an instant later, it dissolved into thin air, and the haunted look settled behind his eyes once again.

Tarr turned around to find Athela standing a few steps behind him, her arms folded, watching. Laith and Tess seemed completely unaware that anyone else was in the room at all, much less that they were being watched. Again, Tarr searched her face for signs of disapproval or jealousy, but found none.

"Did you see that?" Athela said finally. Her voice was soft.

Tarr turned to look at the couple again. "Yes."

"I'm worried for her, Tarr," Athela said in a low voice, stepping closer. "If anyone, *anyone* finds out who she is or that she is involved with us in any way or, heaven forbid, what she means to Laith, her life is in serious jeopardy."

"I know," Tarr agreed.

"He's being careless," Athela said sharply.

Tarr eyed her sidelong. "Would you rather Tess hadn't come?" he asked. "Without her we basically would be sitting here on our hands."

Athela frowned and shook her head. "No, not at all. But they're in their happy bubble and aren't aware enough of everything that could come up and destroy it."

Tarr, still watching them, said under his breath, "I want to find some way to recruit her."

"I want to find some way to make her my friend," said Athela with thoughtful determination, and she walked away.

CHAPTER EIGHTEEN

Days later, Tarr once again found himself at his desk, staring down the missives from Rane that just seemed to rub him the wrong way. And once again, he was infuriatingly unable to identify exactly what it was about them that didn't sit right.

The ciphers were all there, and correct, with Rane's verification symbol signaling that she was all right and not under duress. The messages themselves made sense, again aside from a few basic typos that could easily have been made in haste. The content of the messages was nothing special. There was some indication that a lower-ranking officer in Kagai's forces was undercover in Two Falls in a tinker shop, but there was nothing really of note. His other spies had gone quiet, too, but that wasn't anything out of the ordinary. He expected that security was just a bit tighter at the Fortress. Perhaps that's why Rane had had to smuggle the plans out through Rowan, why there had been a brief delay in Rane's reports. *If anything has gone wrong*, he told himself over and over again, *one of them is going to get word to me. Rane will find a way.*

But she's only human, said another voice, the one in him that doubted and worried and gnawed at every infinitesimal detail as it passed by. Tarr knew that if there was one certainty in the world, it was that mistakes could be made and no single person was above error. It was the mantra he lived by. It had kept them alive so far.

As he had done before, Tarr told himself that for the time being he would have to calm down, and that everything was probably fine. He had been working late every night that week, and he needed sleep and a hot meal, and needed to sit down at a table and eat it next to his friends like a civilized person instead of absentmindedly fishing bits of day-old bread into the corner of his mouth as he scattered crumbs across his desk and into his inkpot.

But still, as he had done with Rane's earlier messages, instead of burning the letter he flipped it over, scribbled a few notes on it to disguise it, and hid it in a stack of papers on his desk. If the little voice was there, he would trust it.

Tarr wandered down in the general direction of the kitchens, hoping that fortune would smile down upon him and that there would be some honey cakes set out and blissfully unattended. It was an uncharacteristically fine night: crisp and cold but not unpleasant, so on his way Tarr made a slight detour and crossed through an open courtyard set into the north wing of the headquarters. In the summer, he predicted, it would be one of his favorite places to sit and read or even do paperwork; there were vines and plants and an abundance of flowers just going to bud, and some benches set by a small fountain. They were now only barely on the cusp of spring; the frost still threatened and the air had a tendency to cut like a knife through any small green tendril that dared to peek its head out of the earth, but the trees in the garden looked comfortable in their slumber, and even the silent fountain held a promise of warm days to come.

After a moment strolling between two trees, Tarr caught a glimpse of movement out of the corner of his eye and nearly jumped clean out of his skin. He darted behind a trunk to avoid being seen. Was it an enemy? Had someone broken into their headquarters? But he relaxed when he heard a voice and recognized it as Cade's. He sighed with relief and was on the verge of stepping out to reveal himself when a female voice joined in and he realized that Cade wasn't alone. Rowan was with him. They hadn't seen him.

Tarr found himself wishing faintly that it *had* been an enemy interloper after all. It was going to be nearly impossible to extract himself from the situation without them seeing him, and from the gentle tones of their voices as they spoke to one another, it didn't sound like the kind of scene Tarr was interested in interrupting.

He peeked around the side of the tree to try and gauge how far away they were from him and whether or not he'd be able to make a convincing run for it. They were seated close together on one of the benches in the courtyard and their faces were turned upwards towards the hazy purple dome of sky arching above them. Their expressions were peaceful, and as Tarr watched, Cade glanced down and spent a few seconds unabashedly marveling at Rowan's face. From what Tarr had known of them as separate individuals, he would not in a million years have predicted that they'd have any kind of emotional connection or attraction, but the years spent alone in imprisonment under Cira's orders and must have brought them together. Tarr could imagine that there weren't a whole lot of people who could truly understand the physical and psychological toll that had been taken. He was happy for them.

He was *not* happy, however, that they had picked that particular location and time for their romantic stargazing, and as quietly as he could (reflecting with each exaggeratedly delicate step what an absolutely useless undercover agent he would make), he picked his way to the far corner of the courtyard and slipped through a door to the hallway inside. Whether or not Cade and Rowan had heard him or spotted him making his ungainly crab-footed exit from the courtyard, he didn't bother to find out.

Once safely inside, he let out a sigh of relief. It was nice, in a way, to see Cade having some demonstrably human interaction with another person. He was so intent and focused on his mission of defeating Cira that anything resembling a personality tended to be shunted to the side.

Tarr wandered down to the kitchens (no honey cakes, alas) and served himself a bowl of thin brothy soup dotted here and there with chopped up root vegetables, then trooped back up to the main hall to eat at one of the long tables in the great hall. Trying not to slosh hot soup over his lap, he glanced around to see if any of the other Strikers were about. Ari was there, in a far corner, reading a book by himself while two girls (and a hopeful-looking boy), who Tarr thought might be members of the newest wave of recruits, were staring longingly at him over a trio of long-empty soup bowls. Ari was always going to be an enigma, Tarr concluded to himself, regarding him thoughtfully while slurping down a leek. He was almost as single-minded as Cade was in his mission, but for one reason or another Tarr trusted him implicitly and barely trusted Cade at all. Perhaps it was Cade's ambition. If the war ended tomorrow, Tarr had no doubt that Ari would quietly go back to his old life and never pick up a sword again.

Without looking, Tarr felt the presence of Archer behind him, and a moment later something sailed into his field of vision. Tarr was just able to reach out and catch it before it hit the table.

"Dinner roll for you," Archer quipped, sliding in beside him at the table and rumpling his black-tipped hair with one long white hand. "Saw you were in need."

"Thanks," Tarr smiled at him, and watched as Archer took in the little scene with Ari with unabashed amusement.

"He knows he's not serving in a monastery, right?" Archer asked sarcastically.

"You're one to talk," Tarr shot back.

"Speaking of which, any news from your lady love?" Archer asked, ignoring Tarr's retort.

Tarr had been on the verge of blurting out the intimate interaction he had just witnessed taking place between Cade and Rowan, but decided not to. He was glad for the two of them, and wanted to respect their privacy, even if it meant missing out on what was sure to be a priceless reaction from Archer when he heard the news. Instead, he shrugged one shoulder and toyed with a lump of potato at the bottom of his soup bowl. For a moment, he also considered telling Archer about the strange feeling he had regarding Rane's latest spate of letters, but thought better of it. Archer would likely just tell him that he was being overly paranoid.

He was spared, however, from having to come up with something evasive by the unexpected arrival of Athela, who entered from across the hall, surveyed the room's occupants, and approached them tentatively. A bowl of stew was held in her hands.

"Mind if I sit?" she asked, sliding in across from them.

"Not at all," Tarr gestured expansively before them.

"Thanks," she said gratefully.

There was something soft and almost distracted about her manner; the usual combativeness wasn't there. She didn't seem to be interested in immediately striking up an argument with Archer, or saying something snarky about Cade. She pushed a leek around aimlessly in an ever-narrowing circle in the center of her soup bowl, her mind elsewhere.

Tarr and Archer glanced at one another. "Everything all right?" Tarr asked slowly.

"Oh, yes," Athela seemed almost startled by the question. "Just thinking."

Tarr and Archer again made eye contact, this time with an undercurrent of alarmed wariness. "I'm, er—going to go get more soup," Tarr announced loudly, and stood. It was utterly unconvincing, and Archer sent him a withering look as he shrugged helplessly and made his way to the exit of the hall.

Archer faced Athela directly and cocked his head. "What are you thinking about?" he inquired.

"One of my new recruits," Athela said. "He's having trouble getting his horse to take the right lead, and I'm wondering if there's some other issue going on. Like he has a tight tendon."

"Your recruit has a tight tendon?" Archer asked blankly.

"No, the horse," Athela replied, as if it were obvious.

"Ah, of course," Archer agreed. "Well, have you tried suggesting to your student that they should get *off* the horse and walk on the ground with their own two feet as nature intended?"

"I thought of it, but he's not a very fast runner," Athela said sarcastically.

"The horse?"

"No, the recruit."

Their volleying repartee complete, the two eyed each other with unspoken satisfaction.

"I've missed you," Archer said.

Athela ducked her gaze back down to her bowl. "I've missed you, too," she concurred begrudgingly. "I'm surprised you haven't..." her gaze swept the room, surveying the varied assortment of Striker soldiers.

"Moved on," she concluded lamely.

He studied her closely. "Is that what you want me to do?"

"No." It was said quietly; he could barely hear her.

"I thought not." He stretched and pretended to thoughtfully consider his options. "Well, under normal circumstances I'd set my sights on Laith, but I'm pretty sure he's clinically depressed. And besides, he's not my type. Too sweet. Too rich. I like a little tartness. Some heat."

Athela attempted to summon a scornful glare from deep within her core, but couldn't quite manage it. She laughed, despite herself.

"Ah, there it is," Archer smiled gently. "You're slipping, Athela."

"Clearly," she agreed regretfully.

"I think about you all the time," he said abruptly.

She met his eyes. He could see that certain memories were swirling in her mind, too. She moved her hand slightly, closer to his. Light as a feather, she drew her finger down the length of his forearm. The touch crackled. Archer wondered what the other Striker soldiers in the dining hall would make of it if he leaped across, took Athela to him and started doing unspeakable things to her on the dining table.

She must have seen the shift in his expression, for she caught herself and withdrew her hand, looking abashed.

"I'm sorry," she said, a little breathlessly. "I'm sorry."

"Don't," he said shortly. "Don't do that. Don't pull away. At least talk to me."

Athela looked angry and flustered. "Look, I'm confused, too."

"*I'm* not confused," Archer shot back. "It all seems like a pretty simple situation to me. Except for why you won't just—"

"It isn't. You wouldn't understand."

"So explain it to me."

Athela glowered at him, openmouthed, groping for words. Even beginning to try and make him understand would entail delving deep into past childhood trauma, fear of commitment—things which she'd barely acknowledged to herself, much less another person. "Never mind. I asked you to respect my decision."

Archer spread his hands. "That's what I *am* doing. But I *don't* understand it. And I don't have to like it."

"Fine."

They glared at one another in stony silence. Athela's throat felt hot, flushed, though whether from anger or something else, she wasn't certain. It would be so easy, she thought, to throw everything away, take him by the hand, and lead him up to her bedroom. To shut herself away with him and perhaps never come out again. She ached at the thought.

Stop it, she told herself sternly. *You have more self-discipline than that. You cannot get involved with him. Not while you can still lose him so easily.*

"I'll save you the trouble," Archer said harshly, as if he had heard her thoughts. He hadn't bothered to keep his voice down and a few soldiers glanced over at them curiously. He stood and gave her an ironic inclination of his head. "My lady."

He turned and walked away without a backwards glance, leaving Athela sitting disconcerted and desolate behind him.

If the Strikers were going to make any sort of show of building a fleet to trick Cira into turning the guns, they needed to move quickly. Though many of the details of their attack on Faridor were still being worked out, it was agreed that Cade would depart as soon as possible for the coast so that he could get the process underway. They had secured an area of forest just south of Faridor, which was flush with good timber. They had managed to contract with a local shipyard to loan them workers to begin the building process, and Tarr had arranged it so that the contract appeared to come from the palace of Joymaril rather than anyone working with the Strikers in Two Falls. He was acutely aware, however, that anyone who was even vaguely on the lookout would be able to trace the order back to Cade.

It was a relief to have Cade sent on his own mission away from the rest of them. He had the irritating habit of watching Tarr, oftentimes with a thoughtful frown on his face, as if Tarr were a puzzle he was always on the verge of solving. Tarr's feeling of unease was compounded by the fact that wherever Cade went, Wolf seemed to go too. The bodyguard seemed to regard everyone and everything with a cold, rather predatory look, as if he were sizing them up as fodder for his next meal. Tarr wasn't sure which one of them made him more uncomfortable.

"You two are birds of a feather," Archer would laugh anytime Tarr complained to him about Cade (which wasn't at all the kind of commiseration Tarr was hoping to hear.) "Too clever by half."

But the day soon came when Cade was to embark on his journey to the coast, and, after having stumbled upon them that night in the courtyard, Tarr was the only one not terribly surprised to hear that Rowan would be accompanying him on the journey. Reactions from his friends ranged from absolute disinterest (Ari) to amused incredulity (Archer) to suspicion (Athela.) Archer had the chance to briefly talk with Rowan; her version of the story was simply that she was interested in seeing part of the country which she had never before visited, and that Cade had invited her along.

"He's too short for her!" Archer had exclaimed in exasperation after he had relayed their conversation to Tarr. "And he's not at all her type."

Tarr shrugged, wiping a smudge of ink from his index finger before dipping his pen again and resuming writing. "There is no such thing as 'too short.' And people change. Tastes change."

Archer threw up his hands. "*Tastes change.* It's like going from... white asparagus to..."

"Yes?" Tarr asked, interested in seeing what sort of vegetable Archer would choose to equate to the king of Joymaril.

"A little winter radish," Archer said finally. "Tough and crunchy. And bitter."

Tarr laughed and shook his head. "I think they understand each other, that's all."

Archer made an unattractive noise in the back of his throat and turned away, slumping back in the chair in Tarr's office. The chair was the only bit of guest seating in the room, and was far too short for Archer, so anytime he found himself sitting there, his lanky legs and arms went comically sprawling every which way like a white spider. Archer had been spending more and more of his off-patrol time hanging around Tarr's office while he was working, and seemed to be in a bit of a funk. His humor had been more caustic and less warm lately, and he seemed in need of companionship. He had spent hours sitting silently lost in thought while Tarr wrote or leafed through paperwork, not bothering to explain his presence or discuss what was happening.

Tarr had never seen him so out of sorts, and he suspected that something had recently happened with Athela. Whereas before, the two of them had seemed to seek out opportunities to meet and argue, they now were avoiding one another at all costs. Part of Tarr was almost impressed that his friends had somehow managed to make an already strained situation even more intolerable, and another part of him wondered if it would be too cruel to ship one or the other of them off to the coast with Cade, too, just to dispel the bizarre atmosphere they'd managed to create over the past few days.

There was a brief knock at the door. "Come in," Tarr called, not looking up, scribbling furiously to get a few last words into the line he was writing.

It was Ari, blandly handsome as ever, dressed head to toe in black. "I'm just getting back, I was on duty," he reported, with a sideways glance at Archer, who had laced his fingers over his stomach. "Cade is set to depart in an hour or so." They had decided that Cade and his entourage were to depart under cover of night, to try and keep up the impression that this was a covert mission.

"Thanks for letting me know, Ari," Tarr dipped his pen and signed the letter. "Anything of note on your patrol?"

Ari closed the door behind him and took a few steps forward, lowering his voice so as not to be heard. "I watched the tinker's house, the one you said might be of interest. I didn't see anything, but it may warrant further surveillance."

"Thanks, I'll take that under advisement," Tarr nodded. Rane's last communication had pointed vaguely towards the tinker shop, and Tarr had hoped something more might come of it.

Ari cast a sidelong look in Archer's direction and straightened. "There are a few other things, but I'll report them later."

"Don't mind me," Archer said sarcastically.

Tarr could see a muscle working in Ari's jaw. He stiffened even more and ignored Archer's words. "As I said, I'll check in later."

"Thank you, Ari," Tarr said respectfully. Ari ducked his head and turned to go.

"Whatever you want to say, you can say it now," Archer gestured with one hand, his tone jocular, but his attitude decidedly confrontational.

Not now, Archer, Tarr nearly rolled his eyes. Normally, Archer wouldn't have bothered, but something about the mood he was in clearly made him want to scrap. Ari, for his part, was usually immune to Archer's provocations, but this time he stopped and looked Archer straight in the face.

"I have confidential information to share with Tarr, and I do not wish to speak in front of you," Ari said quietly. "I choose who to work alongside. People I respect. People I trust."

"In other words, people who are not me," Archer retorted.

"That is correct," Ari replied evenly.

"Brave of you to say so to my face," Archer maintained the same ironic jaunty tone, but Tarr could see that he could detect an undercurrent of surprise at Ari's unexpected directness. Though Ari and Archer had been rolling their eyes behind each other's backs for years by that point, only on a handful of occasions had one of them come right out and actually voiced their distaste; the last time there had been an outright confrontation it had nearly escalated into an actual fight. Whatever lighthearted humor Tarr had found in their tepid feud began to dissipate into thin air as he saw the temperature between them rising.

"Bravery, I'm afraid, is something you know very little about, Archer," Ari continued stolidly.

"Interesting take," Archer fired back. "There are few people on the Striker side who would agree with you."

"Ari, Archer, please," Tarr protested placatingly, standing between them and raising his hands.

"I said it before when you shot the Kagaian officer and it resulted in the killing of an innocent young boy. When you let your associate go free, and she nearly succeeded in poisoning Argolaith. When you spirited out a convicted Kagaian criminal against explicit orders. You have not changed. I was right then, and I am right now." He took a beat and the silence hung heavy and ugly around them. "You lack the fundamental courage to change. You are reckless and headstrong and careless. As long as you take the lives of others without regard for the consequences, as long as you still hold a weapon in your hands and manage to justify it to yourself as serving some sort of higher noble purpose, your path is set."

"Anything else?" Archer asked. The sardonic tone had worn away; his words were now nearly a snarl.

"I don't particularly like you very much, either," Ari said thoughtfully, then after a moment, clarified, "On a personal level."

"Ari, that's enough," Tarr interjected.

"Rest assured, it's mutual," Archer snapped.

"Yes, thank you," Tarr said again. It wouldn't do to have two of the Strikers coming to blows in his office. Ari swung around, his face impassive, and gave Tarr another curt nod before leaving the door.

Archer swiveled around, widening his golden eyes as if to say, *have you ever seen the likes of him before?*

"What he said was uncalled for. But you provoked him, too," Tarr shook his head. He wasn't going to let Archer off the hook for that one. He didn't like the fact that he'd found himself privately agreeing with some of what Ari had said.

"He acts like we're fighting on different sides," Archer spread his hands.

"If you could stop picking fights with our friends and allies *for one day*, I'd very much appreciate it," Tarr said exasperatedly. His latent frustration and guilt at the episode with Persefea, the latest bout of unpleasantness with Athela, and even his own worries about Rane's letters burbled over before he could stop it.

Archer blinked, and Tarr could see the hurt on his face. It stung. "You?" Archer asked slowly in Ashan. "You, too, believe what Ari has said about me?"

"No, that's not what...what else am I to do?" Tarr shot back in Common tongue. He felt out of sorts all of a sudden; nothing was right, nothing was lining up. Speaking Ashan had always been a gesture of intimacy between them, but for one reason or another that night he didn't want it, he felt fed up with everything. He needed some space.

As if reading his mind, Archer gathered his long limbs underneath him and stood. "I'll go," he said quietly. There was pain in his voice, not anger, and it made Tarr feel wretched. He put his head in his hand for just a moment and rubbed it distractedly through his hair and down to the nape of his neck. "Archer, I—"

But the door was already shut. Tarr swore aloud into the silence.

Shortly before midnight, Cade knocked once and let himself in to Laith's room. Laith looked up at him, his hands in his lap; Cade realized that before he'd entered, Laith had just been sitting alone in silence. Laith didn't seem surprised to see him. The two brothers surveyed one another for a few moments.

"We'll be leaving shortly," Cade said finally. "I came to say goodbye."

Laith nodded. "I wish you luck," he said simply, and left it at that, as though already inviting Cade to take his leave.

Cade nodded and glanced around himself. "May I sit?" he asked. It felt strange to act so formal around his brother, but so much time and experience had passed between them that by that point they were almost strangers. Laith gestured to a small chair in the corner of the room, and Cade drew it forward and dusted it off a few times before sitting lightly atop it.

"We haven't had much of a chance to catch up," Cade began awkwardly. "I know that we've both been busy since I arrived."

"I was glad to see you," Laith said, and his voice sounded genuine. "Glad to know that you were alive. It was a relief. After we left, we were cut off. I had no idea what happened...to anyone. Anyone that we left behind."

"I know," Cade looked up to the corners of the dark room where the ceilings joined the walls. "I wish..." he said suddenly, before he could catch himself, "I wish you had taken me with you. When you left." Even to him, the words sounded childish.

Laith blinked at him in surprise. "I do, too," he said quietly. "I wish we had known what a difference that day would make. I wish we'd have done things differently. I think about it all the time."

"But we can't take it back," Cade said quickly.

"No, we can't," Laith agreed. "This is the path we're on." He eyed him sidelong. "And look, now here you are. The king."

Cade straightened. "That's right."

"You think you're ready?" Laith asked.

Immediately, Cade felt himself bristle, the knee-jerk reaction of the younger brother. "I'm not the boy I was when you left, Laith," he said.

"I had to grow up. And I've been through things you haven't. Things you couldn't imagine."

Laith raised his hands to pacify him. "It was just a question. I didn't say you won't make a good king. You were always clever. And brave."

"I am ready," Cade said firmly, though he felt a nagging twinge of self-doubt in the back of his mind.

"Good, then," Laith said mildly. "I'm glad to hear it."

"I'm sure your friends don't agree," Cade said suddenly. "Tarr doesn't trust me."

"Tarr doesn't trust anyone," Laith shrugged.

"That's not true," Cade frowned. "You're his friends."

"Of course," Laith agreed. "But he won't give up control. To any of us. It's why he's so good at his job."

"I'm his king," Cade said stubbornly, before he could stop himself.

"Cade, the title is one thing," Laith said patiently. "The love and support that goes along with it will have to be earned, especially from people like Tarr, who have every reason to distrust the monarchy or anyone who wants to put themselves in a seat of power. And, if I may make a suggestion, utilizing phrases like 'I'm his king' as sole grounds for loyalty is a surefire way to find yourself at the receiving end of a coup."

Cade considered this. It had been an immature thing to say, but being around Laith brought out the petulant boy in him. Laith was right, but he didn't necessarily want to give him the satisfaction of admitting it.

"It's all right," Laith said mildly, as if he could read his thoughts. "You're still young. You're still learning. So am I. You won't always say the right thing. But I think that you could be a great king, a just and fair ruler. And because of that, I will always be honest with you. Whether or not you choose to listen or even like what I have to say is your own affair."

"Thank you," Cade said, touched.

Laith looked thoughtful and Cade could tell that he was deep in a memory. "You know," he said finally, "I said something similar to Cira. Long ago, before all this, back when we were at Joymaril. I told her she had the makings of a great Queen. You and she have so many of the same qualities. Ambition, cleverness, a way of *seeing* people, of knowing what they want. But she made her choices, and here we are, four years and countless lives later." He met Cade's eyes, and Cade could see him carefully considering. "I wonder what you'll choose to do. When the time comes."

Cade wasn't sure what to say to that.

The conversation lulled, and the two brothers looked around at the spartan contents of the room. There were no books, no artwork, no decorations, just a spare pair of riding boots in the corner, a pile of neatly folded clothes atop the dresser, and a black cloak hung on the back of the door. Cade could see that Laith was trying to find some way to draw their talk to a close, to usher him out the door. But Cade wasn't quite finished yet.

"Well," Laith began, and straightened up with the intonation of someone about to announce that he was retiring for the night.

"There was something else," Cade said quickly, cutting him off, and Laith eyed him sharply. "I should have talked to you about this the day I arrived, but it never seemed the right time."

Laith regarded him levelly, giving him the time to gather his thoughts. His large brown eyes were curious.

"The day you left, the day Ilaina was...killed," Cade began, then faltered. At the mention of his wife's name, a shadow dropped over Laith's face, and it immediately became a blank mask. "I was there," Cade said finally. "I was there. I saw it happen."

Laith's face blanched, and he stared unblinkingly into his brother's face. "You were there?" he repeated hoarsely. "You...saw?"

Cade nodded, and swallowed. He looked down at his hands. "And I wanted you to know that afterwards, I buried her. Nadia and I did. We took her and we buried her in the family mausoleum. She's at rest, Laith."

Laith's face had closed off to the point where his expression was completely unreadable. The two of them didn't speak for a long time.

"So she..." Laith said finally, his voice scratchy. "She really is dead, then?"

Cade stared at him, almost startled by the question. Surely, after all these years, Laith hadn't really thought that there was a chance she could still be alive? But then he realized how strange it must have been for his brother to go from one day knowing that his wife was alive and well and only a short ride away, to having to wrap his head around the fact that she was somehow gone forever, that no matter how hard or far he looked for her, he would never find her. Cade, at least, had been there and had witnessed it, had had a chance to say his goodbyes, as awful and as painful as they had been.

"Yes," Cade whispered. "She is. I'm sorry, Laith. I'm so sorry."

For an anxious moment, Cade wondered if Laith was going to break down weeping. Cade wasn't sure of what he should do if that happened. But the prince just sat there. Somehow his stone-faced silence was worse than if he lost control.

"It was Lord Seth?" Laith asked. "He really did it?"

"Yes," Cade answered. "On Cira's orders."

Laith looked away, his dark eyes staring vacantly into emptiness. Cade straightened up, trying to lean forward and catch his eye, but the prince saw nothing. "I buried her, Laith," he said again, not sure of why it was so important for him to convey that. "You can see her. When this is all over. You can say goodbye. And you'll see her again someday. In the next life."

Laith looked at him sharply, and Cade searchingly examined his brother's face. He could only imagine the thoughts that were going through his head.

"Doesn't that..." Cade faltered again, feeling ever more like the little boy searching for Laith's approval. "Doesn't that help? At least a bit?"

Laith's dark eyes bored holes into him, and Cade realized in one uncomfortable moment that while he had experienced loss and pain and imprisonment, there was still a great deal he had yet to learn about grief.

Cade suddenly stood, feeling more uncomfortable than he could ever remember. His arms felt as if they were in the wrong place; his stomach was tight and wracked with shame. He wished he had never told Laith, never said anything to him at all. He wished he had just let him alone.

"I'm sorry," he mumbled, turning for the door.

"Cade, wait," Laith said suddenly, and Cade halted in his tracks.

"I thought it would help," Cade said. "I thought it would help you to know."

"Thank you," Laith said quietly. "Thank you for telling me."

The silence hung heavy between them. Cade tried to force a smile, but it felt artificial on his mouth.

"I'll see you on the other side," Cade said, by way of farewell.

Laith smiled, an expression that did not reach his eyes. He nodded, but it wasn't convincing.

He doesn't think he'll see the other side of the war, Cade realized suddenly. *Or he doesn't want to.*

Sorrow fell on his shoulders like a dead weight. He wished that he could think of something else to say, something that would bring comfort to his brother or express in some small part how Cade loved and admired him. But the chasm between them was too great, and Cade couldn't help but feel that he had just contributed to even more of that distance. He felt like a stupid, awkward child who had gone blundering into a room filled with delicate glass, shattering everything he touched.

"Goodnight, Laith," he said finally.

"Goodnight, Cade," Laith replied.

CHAPTER NINETEEN

For the first week after Cade left, it was almost as if miniscule fracture lines had appeared overnight in the earth around them. Tarr felt completely out of sorts, almost disoriented. Since the beginning of the war, he had been able to count on the consistency of the friends around him. But now that foundation was cracked. Archer and Athela were completely avoiding each other, which was easy since Archer had barely been seen at all at the headquarters over the past week, having taken every possible patrol shift available and only returning to headquarters to change his clothes and bathe. Athela was likewise avoiding the headquarters as much as possible, ostensibly to avoid running into Archer. Marc was nowhere to be found, consumed as he was with keeping an eye on Si. Laith had withdrawn so deeply into himself that he was almost catatonic; Tarr assumed that this must have something to do with his brother's departure, but couldn't be sure as Laith barely said two words to anyone anymore. The only person around Tarr who still seemed to be fully functional was Ari, which was something of a letdown since a spirited conversation with Ari tended to lack any elements of wit, humor or joy. Tarr had never felt so alone. As the days wore on, it was as if all the color and excitement were slowly seeping from his life.

The weather had, for some days, been leaning into the possibility of spring, but then came a day when it made an abrupt turn back to winter. The winds changed and blew icy and uncompromising through the streets, banging shutters and billowing beneath capes with a great bit of to-do, as if to chide the people of Two Falls for even daring to hope that warmth was on its way. Tarr was sitting rather morosely at his desk, staring yet again at Rane's letters, wondering for the umpteenth time what was wrong with him, or with the messages, or both.

The first read:

> Report tuat all is sucured at Faridor. Wili send refort again next week.

The second:

> Kommander hidden an tinker shop north pact of town. Edvise investigate.

The third:

> No new inpormation ti give. Inder scrutidy. Will pause reports for two weeks. Will sent at next full moon.

That damn tinker shop. It was the only lead Rane had passed their way in weeks, but Ari had surveilled the shop without seeing anything notable. Tarr threw the letters down on his desk in frustration and stared out the door. He wished one of the others was there with him. He wished Athela would stop by. Naturally suspicious as she was of anything that walked, crawled, or breathed, he felt he could show the messages to her and be validated in his feelings that something wasn't quite right with them. He paced back and forth a few times under his window. He needed to do *something. Anything.* Anything except sit there inert in his office for another moment.

He crossed to the door and summoned an aide, who summarily fetched Ari. "Get a group together and I want you to raid the tinker shop tonight," he said. "See if you can find the Kagaian officer that is stashed there. We can bring them in for questioning, see if there's any new information we can uncover."

Ari blinked slowly. "We've been surveying the area, as I said, and we haven't seen anything of note. Are you sure?"

"I'm sure," Tarr said firmly, with more confidence than he felt. "Rane sent us the information, got it from Faridor. Go at sundown."

Ari gave a nod and was gone. That was one good thing about Ari. There was never much need for small talk.

Tarr waited for a moment after Ari had left, searching to see whether taking action had actually made him feel better. But the unsettled feeling in his stomach persisted and he threw himself down in his chair, disgruntled and frustrated. He stared out of the window of his room at the tiled rooftops stretching out across the city, watching the wind blow its way roughly against the shutters and batter against anyone foolish enough to step foot outside.

Across the city, Tess stood behind the bar, drying a few glasses and glancing up occasionally every time a large gust blew the door shut behind a customer. There was an unaccustomed chill in the air, and Tess shivered, glad to be inside on such a day. As her hands went through the automatic task of dunking the glasses in warm, steaming water and drying them with the soft towel, she let her mind wander, as it so often did, to the Strikers. She wondered what progress had been made on the plans they'd discussed at their strategy session. She hadn't seen Laith since that meeting, and he hadn't come to her house since the night that they'd nearly made love. She hoped that he was all right. She hoped that he'd come back. She'd tried hard not to spend hours every day replaying their kiss in her mind—his hand moving up her thigh, his breath against her neck, that delicious feeling of falling—but by that point she'd mostly given up.

She rubbed away at a stubborn smudge on one of the glasses and set it upside down to finish drying in the neat, orderly row that she had started down the end of the bar. It had been a slow day. It seemed as though most people in Two Falls were too afraid to venture out of their homes, so the bar was largely empty. This was fine by Tess; she was planning to leave a bit early that evening, anyway, and it would be easier to do so if business was slow. Nan, the older woman who took care of Julian during the day, had a daughter visiting and was going to bring Julian to the bar so that Tess could take him home before she and her daughter went out to do some shopping at the evening market. Tess had only met the daughter a few times over the years, as she lived outside the city and travel permits were hard to come by, but she remembered her as being a terribly loud gossip and not at all her cup of tea. Tess hoped that they'd be in a hurry to leave and get about their errands.

Tess glanced down the room to make sure that no one needed anything. There were a few people clustered around some of the tables along the back wall, and only one person sitting near her at the bar itself. Tess hadn't paid him much mind when he'd first come in a few minutes before, but this time she stopped to consider him more closely. He wasn't one of the regulars. She wished one of the other bartenders was on duty with her so she could ask them about him, but she was working alone. The man was fairly nondescript: middle-aged and lean, with wispy gray hair that fell out in untidy strands from beneath a knit cap and a downturned mouth with permanent creases on either side. He had a tankard of ale in front of him, from which he had been taking long, deliberate sips. And yet there was something about him that raised her suspicions. If he was just an old barfly, then he was taking too long between drinks, almost as if he were trying to prolong his stay at the bar. And he kept stealing glances at Tess when he thought she wasn't looking. Though this behavior in itself wasn't uncommon, his expression was shrewd and calculating, almost predatory. Long ago, Tess had learned to trust her gut instinct (which came in handy in her line of work), so even though she had no concrete evidence that the man was up to no good or intended her any harm at all, she was instantly on her guard. A wariness settled over her as she picked up a new tray of glasses and began methodically cleaning her way through them. She hoped that Nan and her daughter would arrive soon.

She hadn't long to wait. The door banged open with such suddenness that Tess jumped, her hands just able to keep the glass from falling and shattering on the floor. Nan, bearing a sleepy-eyed Julian on one hip, entered, followed by her daughter and a strong gust of cold wind.

"Close the door!" Tess called, rather unnecessarily, for Nan and her daughter were already fighting to shut it against the force of the wind outside. Finally, they managed it and the latch held, even as the door gave a few protesting rattles on its hinges.

"Sorry, love," Nan shook her head and patted a wrinkled hand against her hair to attempt to smooth it back into place. "Filthy weather today, isn't it?"

Nan's daughter, a stout, ruddy-cheeked young woman in her late twenties, bustled straight to the bar, looking bright eyed and breathing heavily, as though she'd just been for an invigorating run. Tess dimly remembered from the previous time they'd met that the daughter's indefatigable joie-de-vivre was one of the most exhausting things about her.

"Tess, you're looking *gorgeous*," she exhaled, settling onto a barstool directly opposite Tess. "How long has it been?"

"Er...a while," said Tess lamely. She had quite forgotten the daughter's name.

Nan came up and Tess swung around the bar to take Julian. Nan bent her hip, glad to be relieved of her burden. Tess gave her son a quick kiss on the forehead as he nestled in beneath her chin. "Hello, my darling," she whispered to him. "Did you have a good day?" Out of the corner of her eye she darted a look at the suspicious man down the side of the bar, who at that moment took a long, deliberate swig. She could tell that he was listening, though whether it was spying or sheer run-of-the-mill nosiness, she couldn't decide.

"Move along there, Rose," Nan urged her daughter, who leaned aside and helped her mother clamber up precariously onto one of the barstools.

Ah, Rose, that's right, Tess thought to herself, then surveyed the women now sitting before her. She had been glad to see them when they'd come in; they'd momentarily relieved the anxiety she'd felt about the strange man at the bar, but she was now a bit dismayed to see that they now seemed to be settling in and in no hurry to get about their business. The weather being what it was outside, she could hardly blame them.

"Plans tonight?" Tess prompted them gently, shifting Julian to one hip. She was quite adept at doing things one-handed by this point, and had no trouble whatsoever continuing her bartending duties with her son on her arm.

Nan and Rose glanced at one another with a fond smile, the kind shared by a mother and daughter who now had the luxury of enjoying one another's company as equal companions. "The night market in town center is tonight, I thought Rosie'd like to see it," Nan said. "Though with this wind, who knows? It may have blown over by now."

Tess poured them a couple of (pointedly small) tankards and pressed them on them, even as Nan tried to resist.

"Oh, go on," Rose urged, and Nan finally gave in.

"*Since* it's a special occasion," she said with a naughty twinkle, and clinked tankards with her daughter, her creased face cracking into a broad smile.

After they'd drunk a few sips and were starting to visibly relax, Rose leaned forward, a keen look in her eye. "*So*," she said, with the air of someone on the verge of gobbling a delicious morsel, "Tell me all about this *young man* you've been seeing."

Tess's stomach dropped. Again, her eyes darted down the bar to the shifty-looking man, then back to the women in front of her, who were both smiling and completely oblivious. Tess hiked Julian up higher on her hip and hugged him closer. "Man?" she asked, forcing what she hoped was a bewildered smile. "I don't know who you're talking about."

"Oh, mother's told me *all* about it," Rose gushed, waving aside Tess's words so that they seemingly dissipated into the air. "Some of her friends were over today, and it was all they wanted to talk about. So don't give me any of *that*. You're quite the dark horse, aren't you?"

Tess locked eyes with Nan, who smiled guiltily and gave a helpless, apologetic shrug. "They're all mighty curious," she agreed.

"They *said*," Rose said mischievously, "that he's been seen entering and leaving your apartment. *Late at night.*"

Tess again tried to force a smile, which must have appeared as ghastly as it felt, for Rose leaned back in her chair and laughed aloud. "Look, mother, I think we're embarrassing her. Her cheeks are getting red just thinking of him."

Nan, who knew Tess better than her daughter, gave Tess a strange sidelong look, as if she couldn't quite understand why Tess was acting so bashful. Tess, meanwhile, felt herself gripping her son so tightly that she was surprised he hadn't squawked in protest. She took a deep breath and tried to appear casual, forcing herself not to look down the bar to where the strange man was sitting. "I'm not sure what your friend thinks she saw, but I can assure you she's wrong."

"Are you sure?" Rose teased. "They said he's supposedly very handsome."

Tess felt like throttling her, an urge that she channeled into what she knew to be a very convincing eye roll. "It sounds like your mother's friend has a very active imagination," Tess shook her head. "I should ask her to come over and tell Julian some bedtime stories once in a while."

"Perhaps we'd best let it be," cut in Nan, who hadn't taken her eye from Tess and seemed to realize by this point that her daughter's line of questioning was unwelcome. "I'm sure that if Tess wanted to tell us about her gentleman caller, she would."

But Rose, who had inherited many things from her mother except a sense of tact, pressed on. She leaned forward on both elbows, winking conspiratorially, as if she were teetering on the edge of the juiciest piece of information yet. "You know what they *say*," she said in what she clearly believed to be a low voice, but which could nevertheless be heard by anyone within a ten-foot radius. "They say that he's one of the Strikers." She inched even closer, a gleeful grin across her mouth. "*Lord Argolaith.*"

For a moment, Tess forgot to breathe. She wished that she had launched herself across the bar and shut Rose up while she still had the chance. She lifted Julian up in her arms and took a deep inhale of his sweet curly hair, steadying herself. She forced an insouciant look across her face. "I'm sure," she said sarcastically, "that *Lord Argolaith*, the *Sun Prince* of *Joymaril Palace* is dating a *barmaid* from *Two Falls*." She hiked up Julian again for emphasis. "A single mother, to boot."

Rose looked slightly deflated, and leaned back in her chair, her eager expression waning as she considered it. "Well, it's what they *said*," she maintained defensively.

"And I'm sure that whatever 'they said' is gospel," Tess said sarcastically.

"So who *did* they see?" Rose needled, regaining some of her lost momentum.

This time, Tess didn't even bother to try to be polite. She stared outright at Rose, not quite believing her nerve. "Why on earth does it matter to you?" Tess demanded, her voice harsher than she wanted it to sound.

"Rose, darling, perhaps we should..." Nan began, but Rose cut her off.

"Don't get so touchy!" Rose exclaimed, with a girlish giggle. "I didn't remember you being so sensitive! Just wanting to dish the dirt, that's all! I've been aching for a good gossip."

Tess forced herself to relax her muscles, and tried to stop her jaw from visibly clenching and unclenching. "Of course," she said, trying to sound slightly more even-keeled. "Of course, I understand. I just like to keep those things private. That's all."

"Even from your friends?" Rose asked teasingly.

Tess made no response, merely blinked at her. Her gaze clearly conveyed her meaning. *You are not my friend.*

Rose, oblivious to any social cues as she appeared to be, apparently caught Tess's drift, and sat back, sipping her ale and looking rather put out. "Fine," she said, and thought for a few moments. For a blissful instant, Tess thought that Rose was finally going to let the subject alone and move on, but it was not to be.

"They say Lord Argolaith is one of the handsomest men in the world," Rose said innocently, eyeing Tess keenly over her mug of ale as she took a dainty sip. This time, even Nan looked over at her daughter in apparent shock.

"I wouldn't know," Tess said coldly. "As I haven't seen all the men in the world. Or Lord Argolaith, for that matter." *Leave,* she prayed inwardly. *Please leave.*

"They say he can make a girl swoon with just one look," she pressed on.

I will also settle for a meteor falling from the sky, Tess thought.

"They also say," Rose said, with the satisfied air of someone slipping a noose around a deserving neck, "that he has a black dog, who goes everywhere with him." She blinked with seeming innocence. "And isn't it interesting—my mother's friend said that *she* saw a black dog waiting outside your apartment. A few nights in a row. Fancy that!"

Tess was completely at a loss for words. Rose, sensing that she'd apparently won, settled back contentedly in her chair and drained her tankard. She slid it back across the bar and blinked up at her expectantly.

Tess silently took it from her and did not offer her another. Beside her, Nan looked absolutely mortified, and kept glancing back and forth between her daughter and Tess, as though she wasn't sure whether or not she should apologize or just try to beat a hasty retreat.

"I should try to get Julian home," Tess said quietly, looking desperately over her shoulder for any sign of one of the other bartenders. They were running late. Of course they were. She had never wanted to get out of there faster.

"Yes, and we should get along to the market," Nan smiled weakly, her eyes still searching Tess's face.

As they began stirring and rustling and screeching their chairs backwards, Tess chanced a look down the bar. The man was still there, immobile, over his tankard of beer. He couldn't have helped hearing everything that had been said, and Tess felt a clutch of fear tug at her chest. She placed a hand protectively over Julian's small head and hugged him to her tightly, taking comfort in the weight and warmth of him.

She trailed Nan and Rose to the pub door, ignoring the smug looks of triumph that Rose kept shooting her as they went. She smiled wanly at Nan, who squeezed her arm entreatingly and somewhat apologetically. "I'll see you and the little love tomorrow afternoon?"

Tess nodded mutely, and shut the door gratefully behind them, thankful for the burst of cold air, like water splashing across her face. She tilted her head and glanced down at Julian. She saw that his eyes were still barely open, dark lashes brushing the tops of his cheeks as he blinked.

She wondered again if Laith was going to visit her that night; for once, she hoped he'd stay away. Perhaps in the morning she'd go to the headquarters and ask to see Marc or Athela, to see if they could give her some advice about what to do. She had no evidence that she was in any danger at all, but she knew better than to ignore the gnawing voice inside her gut.

Slowly she turned from the door and looked back out over the room. The man at the bar was gone. The awful sinking feeling settled like a stone in her stomach.

Numbly, she took a few steps forward and groped her way to the bar, where she dropped down in one of the tall chairs, hugging Julian to her chest. She felt his little fist wrap itself in her sleeve.

"Tess?" came a voice behind her.

Tess spun around. Evie, one of the other barmaids, was standing in the hallway behind her at the other side of the room. Her pert, pretty face was drawn up in a curious smile. "Tess?" she asked again. "What are you doing?"

All at once, Tess realized she was shaking. "Nothing," she said, forcing her voice to be steady. "Just taking Julian home."

She kissed her son, his small hand still tightly clutching her shirt.

The blustery day had given way to a blustery night, with no sign of letting up. Tarr still felt uncomfortably boxed in, and had tried to walk off his anxieties about the tinker raid with little to no success.

He had left orders with the house guard that he was to be notified as soon as Archer, Laith, or Athela arrived back at headquarters, and even though he had been inwardly praying for their arrival for a number of hours, he still gave a jump when there was a tap on the door.

"Archer's returned," a young woman reported. "Shall I bring him here?"

"Please," Tarr nodded.

Archer arrived a short while later, looking like a windblown osprey. He still wore his coat, and appeared to have been brought up directly from the front door. His greeting lacked some of its usual warmth, and Tarr couldn't help but feel his heart constrict.

"Archer," he ventured, his tone tentative.

Archer's head snapped up, and his golden eyes searched Tarr's face. Then, as if he could sense what Tarr was about to say—the awkward apology he was attempting to conjure out of the air—he waved his hand to one side. "Do not worry."

"Are you certain?" Tarr asked anxiously.

"I am sorry too," Archer smiled, and Tarr felt infinitely better.

"Good, I—" Tarr began.

There was another tap at the door and the girl's head once again poked inside. "Ari wants to see you."

Tarr shot a quick look at Archer, who shrugged equably. There was no fight in him tonight. "Send him in," Tarr said.

A few moments later Ari appeared, looking decidedly un-Ari-like in his demeanor. His brow was knit together and his blue eyes were anxious; he looked as if he had run up to see them. As Tarr's eyes traveled over him, he saw that Ari's arm was cut and that blood was running down his sleeve.

"What happened?" Tarr asked sharply.

"The raid on the tinker—something was wrong, they knew we were coming. It was an ambush," Ari panted, his eyes wild. "We lost five."

Tarr reeled, as if a blow had been dealt directly to his stomach. "Five?" he whispered. It was the worst casualty they'd taken in a long while.

"What's the status now?" Archer asked sharply.

"Still getting the wounded out, but they captured two of the new recruits. We couldn't see where they'd gone. I tried to go after them, but they jumped me, too. We were scattered. It was chaos. I only just got away."

"Are there any still left behind?" Archer asked.

Ari shook his head desperately. "I don't know."

"See to your arm, I'll gather some of Cade's remaining troops and we'll go over to help secure the area," Archer said briskly.

A tap sounded at the door and this time all three of them jumped and spun around. The messenger girl apologetically popped around the corner. "Archer, Tarr, you've been summoned to the north wall. It's urgent. They need you to leave now."

Tarr threw up his hands in exasperation. "Of course they do. Did they say what it's about?"

The girl shook her head, looking anxious.

"Are you certain that Tarr has to go?" Archer asked.

"They asked for him specifically," the girl said fretfully.

"Fine," Tarr sighed. The girl's head vanished.

"I'll go with you," Archer said.

"Shall we summon horses?" Tarr asked.

Archer made a face. "It will take too long to get them fetched and saddled. We'll go on foot; it will be faster."

"We should send protection with you," Ari insisted.

"I'll go with him up to the north wall, and then go to the tinker's shop to see if any salvaging can be done. Will you be all right?" Archer asked Ari, his tone businesslike. Ari looked at him curiously, as if surprised that Archer would be showing him any concern after the rather harsh words they'd recently exchanged.

"It's not deep," Ari said finally. "Be careful."

Again, the persistent tap sounded on the door. "What *now*?" Archer demanded. The girl's head reappeared around the corner. "Athela is back at headquarters, shall I summon her up as well?"

"Tell her to wait downstairs, we'll see her," Tarr said, catching up a cloak that Archer threw to him from a peg by the door.

They met Athela downstairs and appraised her of the situation. "I'll come with you," she said immediately. "I just have to speak with Marc about something really quickly. Do you have time to wait?"

"Not much," Tarr shook his head. "Catch up with us. We'll go up the market pass."

"Right," Athela nodded, her gray eyes grave, and was gone a moment later.

Archer didn't give Athela a backwards glance as he and Tarr headed for the front door. As they walked, a few wounded troops made their way inside, ostensibly returning from the raid.

"We were set up," Tarr said gruffly, furious at himself for letting something like this happen, for his recklessness, for his impatience. *Five.* The number echoed in his head like a drum. One slip, one moment of impetuousness, and he had failed them. "Someone knew we would raid the tinker's shop, and they were ready for it."

"Who did you give the order to?" Archer asked.

"Ari," Tarr said slowly.

Archer let his name hang in the air, an unspoken question.

"I don't think so," Tarr shook his head. "I know you don't like him, Archer, but I just don't think he's a traitor. If he was, he's had plenty of opportunities over the years. Opportunities much better than this one."

As they passed out of the "safe zone" of the area immediately surrounding the Strikers' headquarters, Tarr sensed an almost unconscious shift in Archer. The wind was buffeting them from all sides, angry and insistent. Tarr didn't like it, and he could tell that Archer could sense it, too. Like a bird, Archer's head would twitch left and right, taking in everything around them, and Tarr felt himself being steered to one side of the alleyway, farther away from the flickering lights of the street. Archer's bow was held casually in one hand, quiver slung over his back.

They went north through the winding avenues of the city. The streets narrowed and widened and occasionally converged together in miniature circular plazas shaped like the sun, with streets like rays spreading out in all directions. They only passed a few other towns-people on their journey, and those who were out and about were being blown back and forth like toy boats in a hurricane.

They walked for about ten minutes, not speaking much. Dusk had passed and night was settling in above them. *Athela should catch up to us soon*, Tarr reminded himself, and was comforted by the thought. *Maybe she'll bring Marc, too.*

As they walked, the streets grew more and more deserted. It was almost as if they were the only two people in the entire city. Beside him, Archer's face glowed pale blue, like one of the veiled stars high above in the sky.

They turned right into a small plaza. Lanterns above them were swinging from side to side in the wind, casting eerie silhouettes along the walls of the buildings. Tarr found himself searching within every corner they passed, imagining that the shadows were taking corporeal form.

"*Tarr*," Archer said suddenly, and Tarr froze.

Archer had stopped stock still, and held out an arm. Tarr instantly felt the hair on the back of his neck prickle. His brother's body was as tense as a bowstring. Archer's golden eyes darted about in the flickering lamplight as a fresh gust of cold wind caught his cloak and lifted it up into the air. In one fluid motion, Archer shook back his cloak and drew an arrow taut to his bow. He leaned his head to one side, sighting up the shaft of his arrow to the rooftops above.

"What is it?" Tarr asked again, this time in Ashan. His heart was pounding.

"If they come you must climb," Archer told him through gritted teeth. "Climb for the roof if you can, and get away back to headquarters."

"What are you talking about?" Tarr hissed. "I do not see any—"

All at once, they were swarmed from every direction; black shapes from all corners of the plaza sped towards them. Immediately, Archer loosed an arrow with a screaming hiss and reached back for another. After a moment of protracted shock, Tarr's muscles galvanized into action. There was a low-hanging lamp that provided a stepping-stone up to the rooftops and he leaped for it, but there were too many attackers—just as he was about to swing his legs up and away he felt someone from the black-cloaked group below leap up and grab him about the waist. Startled, Tarr's hold on the lamp loosened and he crashed to earth, pinning his attacker beneath him.

"Archer!" he cried, using all his strength to roll away and scramble upright. The person who had grabbed him was again on his feet and advanced towards Tarr. Tarr instinctively aimed futile blows their way, but he was unarmed and untrained—he could feel his terror rising at how much he was outmatched.

People clad in black ran dizzyingly past; it seemed the empty city was now a flurry of activity. Tarr's attacker gave him a rough shove against the wall, momentarily stunning him—and then suddenly, out of nowhere, Archer launched himself like a cat, completely knocking Tarr's opponent off his feet. He straddled the cloaked figure and dealt a hefty blow, then leaped to his feet and caught Tarr's arm, dragging him around the corner of the street and down the alleyway.

Another black-clad figure darted out at them but Archer whipped out his knife and swiped it through the air, then bent and slammed his entire body weight against them, pinning them against the wall. Then the knife spun in his dextrous fingers and the figure went limp. Tarr didn't bother to look over his shoulder. The others were only a few seconds away.

We aren't going to make it, he thought, the fear flooding his brain like. *We won't make it.*

Is this where Archer dies?

Is this where I die, too? Did Si see this coming?

Archer caught Tarr under the elbow and darted around another corner. Archer stopped, looking up and then down, a plan forming lightning-fast in his mind. He saw an unlit lantern hanging a few floors up. A moment later the bow and the arrow were raised and he'd fired at the lantern—a glancing blow that sent it creaking and swinging above them.

Satisfied, Archer's hawklike eyes snapped down to their feet, where there was a double cellar door. He raised his foot and kicked the door open, then grabbed Tarr's arm, forcing him down.

"Hide!" he ordered, and Tarr's stomach fell.

"I—am—not—leaving—you," Tarr retorted through clenched teeth.

With more force this time, Archer took his brother's arm and fairly threw him down into the dark cellar.

"Tarr," he said, his voice deadly serious. "They cannot take you."

"Archer, no—"

The merest glint of a wolfish smile glimmered in the dark of the street. Without allowing another word of protestation, he pushed Tarr down, banging the cellar doors closed over his head. Darkness swallowed Tarr whole.

The audible sounds of Tarr's breath hissed in the cold room. *Archer will make it*, he told himself, panting. *Calm down. He's made it through tougher scrapes than this.*

He won't live to be very old, Si had said.

And then, like a scream rising inside his head: *How did they get the better of us?*

The cellar was dank and smelled of mildew and mold, but Tarr shrank to the side, sliding his hand along the slippery, damp wall. Footsteps like thunderclaps sounded above, stopping just outside the door of the cellar. There was a moment of silence.

"Archer's this way!" came a hoarse yell, and some of the footsteps took off. Tarr squeezed his eyes shut and prayed.

"The lamp's moving, he must have gone to the roofs, see if there's access." More footsteps. A yell, farther away, sounded.

"They got him?" asked another voice, a woman's, incredulous. "Forget the other! They got Archer?"

Tarr wanted to scream, but he forced himself to remember what Archer had told him to do. He knew logically that revealing his hiding place in an ill-fated attempt to save his brother would result in nothing but getting the both of them killed. The voices outside the door became more jumbled, more excited. In a moment, all of the footsteps and voices took off and faded away down the street.

Though every fiber in his body told Tarr to leave the safety of the cellar and go to help Archer, he made himself stay still. Again and again, he cursed himself for never learning to fight. Minutes—minutes that seemed like years—passed. And Tarr waited. He didn't know how much longer he should stay where he was.

He tried to take a deep breath and analyze the situation in which they found themselves. It was too convenient that the massive band of attackers had known the exact route and time he and Archer would be walking outside the guarded safe zone near the headquarters. It was a trap, that was easy to see.

Who knew they'd be coming? Who had given the order to summon them?

Tarr felt a swelling of burning hatred inside his chest for whoever had betrayed them.

Suddenly there was a lighter footstep above him, halting directly over his head. Tarr could picture whoever it was stopping and assessing the scene. Then, a slight rustling sound, a creaking rumble at the cellar door, and a thin beam of thin blue moonlight as the cellar doors creaked open. Tarr braced himself.

"Tarr?" came a familiar voice. Tarr's breath came in a sudden gasp. He had never been so glad to hear that voice in his life.

"Athela!" he cried and clambered shakily into the outside world, giving Athela the shadow of a relieved hug before breaking into a hurried run-walk in the direction he had heard the footsteps go after Archer.

"What on earth is going on?" she demanded, falling beside him. "I was tracking that group, and then they gave me the slip. I went around to meet with another bunch and *they* gave me the slip, and then there was this big kerfuffle and I tracked them here."

"They took Archer!" he panted.

Athela grabbed his arm, hard, right where Archer had taken it a few minutes before. He winced.

"What?" she demanded, and in the dim light of the street lamp Tarr could see the flash of genuine fear in her slate-colored eyes.

"They took him. I think they took him, Athela, and they're going to take him to Faridor, I know it. They're going to take him there and then Cira's going to kill him." He was babbling now. "And Si..."

"What about Si?" Athela demanded.

It would be so easy. Tarr felt himself teetering on the edge of the precipice, the awful knowledge that Si had imparted to him on the edge of his lips. *What if today is the day?* It took all the self-control he could muster not to tell her.

"Where's Aria, Athela?" he asked. "You can't let them take him."

"I left him back a few blocks away so they wouldn't hear me, there were sounds of fighting." Her pace was increasing now, and Tarr could feel the contagious panic rising between them. "Tarr, you've got to get back to headquarters. You've got to make it to safety yourself, can you do it?"

"I can do it, Athela, just get him back!" Tarr half-shrieked. He was almost lightheaded.

Athela flashed him a look, all steely determination, and nodded, then broke into a full run. She raised two fingers to her lips and whistled loudly.

She ran ahead as Tarr panted to a halt, letting her go on. He closed his eyes, his hands on his knees, chest heaving, and prayed to whatever spiritual life force was out there that she would be fast enough to save Archer.

Athela was running flat out, her long black mane of hair streaming behind her as she went. Her heart pounded in time with the rhythm of her footsteps on the cobblestones; somehow they sounded too slow, far too slow. She dug in deep and ran faster. She crossed another square, heading towards the center part of town, the river, where they would have taken Archer. *They'll use the northern gate*, she thought grimly. *That's the quickest way to get to Faridor.*

There was a distant familiar clatter behind her and a few moments later her gray horse, Aria, came cantering up beside her. They were next to the river now, the broad open thoroughfare that ran along its length through the center of the city. There were very few people out; those who were stopped and turned to stare at her as they went past.

Aria kept in time alongside Athela. Without slowing her pace, she reached up and grabbed hold of the horn of her saddle and pulled herself up so that her feet were skimming the cobbles as Aria bore her along.

Then, in one fluid motion, she gave a quick bounce on the ground and used the momentum to swing herself up and onto his back. A moment later her feet were in the stirrups, her reins were in her hands and it was as if she had suddenly grown a new set of limbs. She crouched low over Aria's withers, squeezing her heels sharply into his side, and her horse, taking the cue, took the bit in his teeth and lengthened his stride so that they were fairly flying alongside the river. His hooves sounded like thunderclaps through the stillness of the night, but Athela hardly cared if she woke up the whole city, as long as she could get Archer back.

Horse and rider soared along the river to the north gate, which was guarded, as usual, by a group of rather dazed-looking sentries. She sank down into her heels and wheeled Aria to a stop; the horse, always reluctant to slow, spun in frustrated circles on his haunches, tossing his head.

One of the sentries, an older woman, stared at the horse as if she couldn't quite be sure whether they were some sort of demonic apparition.

"Did riders go this way?" Athela barked.

"Yes—yes, but they had the livery of the Strikers, they just—" She pointed, but Athela and Aria were already through the gate and out onto the open road.

At the first pass, Athela banked a hard right, knowing that the coastal road was the easiest way to the fortress. And there—by the light of the half-moon, she could make them out. Dark shapes—two horses and three riders, fleeing as fast as they could down the road ahead.

Athela's blood was pumping in her ears as she leaned forward and hissed to her horse. His ears flicked back at her then pricked, and, as if he had sighted their quarry too, kicked into an even higher gear than before. They were gaining.

The cold night air bit into Athela's skin; her eyes were streaming, and her hands were numb from keeping their tight grip on the reins. A small hill rose in front of them, then another. They were getting closer—each time they rounded another hill, they were closer. Athela gritted her teeth even harder and bent as low as she could over her horse's neck. *They were not going to get away.* No one could outrun Aria.

A grove of trees loomed up, dark and black before them. Perhaps the other riders would try to lose her there? She wouldn't let them.

The path, milky in the moonlight, dove into the dark shadows of the forest and Athela was borne along with her horse, who was going almost too fast for her to stop. She prayed inwardly that the path would be clear—any fallen trees would be impossible to see, and if Aria so much as stumbled, they'd both break their necks.

Out of nowhere a branch came and whipped her hard across the face. Athela was swung back in the saddle, her foot coming loose from the stirrup, unbalancing her horse for a few strides. Frustrated, she dropped her other stirrup and gripped with her knees, urging Aria on. The horse took a few heartbeats to recover, to gather himself, and then he was off like a shot. The riders were still in front of her; she could see their outlines reflected every few moments in shafts of moonlight as it fell cool and blue between the gaps in the trees. And there—a brightness ahead. They were nearing the edge of the wood. She almost had them. If she could pull up alongside, close enough to grab their reins, trip their horses, get her sword out—nothing would keep her from getting Archer back.

All at once there was an enormous crashing sound and a horrific scream that was both human and animal and the shadows of the riders vanished. Athela barely had time to process before she saw it: an enormous tree trunk looming up before them like a wall. As fast as she could, she checked Aria's stride and gave him a quick squeeze with her legs, signaling him to jump. The horse obeyed out of instinct, taking an awkward half step before the trunk and hopping over it with an uncomfortable lurch that jarred them both so much that Aria's legs buckled and Athela came tumbling out of the saddle and onto the ground.

But he had gotten them across it, which was more than could be said for the other two riders. Athela, who had been anticipating her ungraceful landing, rolled into a neat, uninjured somersault and came out of it on her feet, her sword out and her hair tumbling wildly over her shoulders. There were three shapes. Three of them and one of them had to be Archer. The fury that someone had taken him, had harmed him, rose so high in her blood that she felt her eyes burning with it.

She ran to the first figure, still lying senseless on the ground and ripped back the cloak. A young man. Not Archer.

She bared her teeth and tossed him to the side as if he were a discarded piece of paper. She went to the second figure, who had rolled up on its hands and knees and was starting to try to crawl away. She ripped back the cloak. It was an older woman.

Starting to feel frantic, Athela shoved the woman back down, where she lay quietly. Athela stood, squinting about her in the dark. The third figure was lying prone back by the fallen trunk. Heart leaping, Athela ran forward and pulled back the hood.

It was not Archer.

Athela froze, wind tossing her hair into her eyes. She brushed it back and slowly stood, looking about her—the three riders. Two horses. No Archer.

She slowly swiveled on the spot, her mind frantically racing. Off to the side past the edge of the trees rose a hill facing the coast. Athela began to run again, forcing her legs and feet to move, feeling sick inside. She scrambled, half standing, half on all fours, to the top of the rise, her heart drumming so hard she could feel it in her fingertips.

The night sky was littered with stars and the land stretched out low and blue before her. A swath of cloud passed from the face of the moon and bathed the coastal plain in a soft misty light. Athela squinted her eyes, hoping desperately that she was wrong.

But there, on the path leading from the eastern gate of Two Falls was another small troop of riders, so far in the distance now that they looked like specks, moving smoothly and easily up the coast. It was the group of Kagaian riders bearing Archer to Faridor. They had tricked her by splitting up and mixing their tracks. And Athela knew there was no way she could catch them in time, even with Aria's considerable speed. Not even if she rode all night. She was too late. She was too late to save him.

And once Cira had him, there was no way she would let him live.

A little sob escaped unbidden from Athela's lips and she felt her legs give way. She fell to her knees and cried out as though her whole body was being torn in two. No one heard her except the cold, uncaring sky.

Tarr burst into the headquarters like a thunderclap, out of breath and near tears. His appearance was so astonishing that the guards on duty, many of whom were off to the side attending to wounded casualties of the botched raid, stopped in shock at the sight of him and tentatively reached out to try and help him. But Tarr brushed past them, half-blinded.

He stumbled back up to his office and slammed the door shut, heading straight to the pile of papers that contained Rane's messages. The raid on the tinker's house had been a setup, that much was obvious. The seed was first planted in one of Rane's messages. And either Rane had been purposefully fed false information, or someone else had written the message in Rane's hand knowing that Tarr would read it.

He pored over the papers anew, his heart thudding. The handwriting was hers, undeniably hers. He knew it as well as he knew his own. And in the corner was one of her verification symbols, written to signal that she was safe and not under duress. So it couldn't have been someone pretending to be Rane. They wouldn't have known the codes or symbols, anyway, not unless they'd found all of Rane's coding materials. So how could Rane have made a mistake this glaring? He squinted his eyes, forcing himself, willing himself to see something, anything.

And then he saw it.

How could he have been so stupid?

It had been there all along. The letters that he thought had been casual misspellings in the notes. When he took the misspelled letters and replaced them with the correct letters, together they formed a message that made his blood run cold:

HELP. CIRA. FOUND.

Tarr reeled back in his chair, his mind now an echoing blank space. Slowly, after a painful and prolonged few seconds, his mind began to turn again as he tried to grasp the awful enormity of the situation: Archer had been taken, Rane had been found out. *Somehow.*

His mind suddenly flashed back to the day Ari had come to tell him about Seth's return to Faridor. Had Tarr's letter of warning not reached her in time, just as Ari had thought? Had Seth found her out?

I've failed them all, he thought. *I've lost them.*

Rane was being held in the hands of his enemy. Cira knew. She had Rane. And she had used Rane to plant false information that had left five Strikers dead.

Rane's life hung by a thin, rapidly fraying thread. Perhaps Cira was only keeping her alive to use her to send false messages to Tarr. Perhaps now she had outlived her usefulness.

Archer, for all Tarr knew, might already be dead. *Please let Athela get him back.*

But, he realized suddenly, Cira's forces could not have known the day and time of the raid on the tinker. She had to have someone working on the inside, someone who had helped coordinate the planned attack on him and Archer. Someone inside the Strikers. He didn't believe it was Ari, he *still* didn't believe it could be him, though ostensibly all signs pointed in that direction.

It didn't sit right. Tarr went back out into the hallway and finally found the messenger girl who had popped in on them so many times earlier in the night. She was only fifteen or sixteen, and looked extremely nervous, as though she could sense that something had gone terribly wrong and that somehow she was involved. Her eyes kept darting from side to side, as if looking for a mode of escape, though whether this was due to general nerves or to actual guilt, Tarr couldn't be sure.

"How can I help you, sir?" she asked in a trembling voice.

Tarr didn't want to bother with niceties. "Who was it," he said slowly, "Who requested that Archer and I be sent to the north wall tonight?"

The girl's eyes raced as she stumbled over the answer. "It was a boy, sir. A boy who had returned from the raid at the tinker's."

"He was unhurt?" Tarr asked.

She bit her lip and nodded anxiously.

"Who is he?"

"He's a page, sir. I was surprised that he went out on the raid tonight, as he's usually assigned elsewhere, sir."

"Oh? Where?"

"Minister Burlage's house guard, sir. He's served there for years."

Her words dropped before him, and all at once, things fell into place, as if laid on a platter at his feet. "I see," he said, his voice cold.

"Is that all, sir?"

"Yes," Tarr replied, and turned away from her. He barely noticed her leaving the room.

So that was it. The Minister had decided to get rid of him and Archer in the most convenient way possible—by selling them off to Kagaian sympathizers. It fit together. It made sense. He had betrayed them. And Tarr hadn't seen it coming.

Tarr sank into his chair, his heart racing and his mind spinning. He thought back over the past few days, cursing himself again and again for not seeing, for not understanding, for not being fast enough, smart enough. It was his fault as much as it was Burlage's. The others had trusted him to keep them safe. And he had let them down.

As he sat there, he felt a huge wave of white-hot anger, such that he had never felt before, welling in his chest. It threatened to overpower him. He thought of Archer, of the certain torture and death that awaited him at Cira's hands, if Athela lost him. He thought of Rane, trapped in a dungeon of Faridor, desperately grasping for a way to warn Tarr, to beg for help, only for Tarr to be too stupid, too blind to see.

And finally, he thought of Burlage, of his self-satisfied smirk, of his jowly face, of the gleeful crow he'd probably let out the minute he learned that his plan had worked, that he'd done it, that he'd outwitted the Strikers, that he'd eliminated Archer. Tarr had never felt so much blind hate for one person before; it infused his blood and filled his ears, so that all he could hear was a strange, rushing sound.

And then something inside him snapped.

All he wanted, all he could see, all he could imagine, was Burlage dead. And he wanted it done now. He would not allow Burlage to live, to enjoy the satisfaction that his betrayal had wrought.

Tarr rose to his feet as if in a dream, and walked back to the door. He went through the hallways, immune to the faces of the people who passed in front of him, who stared at him, openmouthed, as they ran by. Everyone was running. Everyone knew that the raid had ended in disaster. They looked to Tarr for help, but he just glided past them like a specter.

Tarr walked until he came to the soldiers' barracks. He knocked hollowly at the main door and stood silently to the side as the Striker guards opened it. Surprised at the sight of him, they scurried to find the ranking officer to come and meet him.

There was a lieutenant in the barracks, a capable man whom Tarr had always liked. He was lean and soft-spoken, with dark hair and skin the color of burnt caramel. He saw immediately the gravity in Tarr's face. He stepped out into the small hallway beside the barracks and closed the door behind him, shutting out the chorus of curious faces peering out at them.

"What is it, sir?" Itzhal, the lieutenant, asked in a low voice.

"We have been betrayed," Tarr replied, a red haze still before his eyes as he spoke. He felt strangely light, as if he were outside of his own body looking down at himself moving and speaking. "I need you to take care of it."

"Who?" Itzhal asked.

"Minister Burlage," Tarr replied, his voice cold.

If Itzhal was surprised by this, he hid it. "Immediately?"

"Immediately," Tarr confirmed.

"It will be done," Itzhal nodded. He was a seasoned fighter, capable and honorable, and had been with them for nearly two years. He would keep his word.

Itzhal turned and vanished back inside the barracks for a moment, and then re-emerged carrying a helmet, a knife, and a thick cloak, which he threw around his shoulders. Tarr silently watched him prepare, watched the knife buckled around his waist, felt the pure welling of satisfaction at the sight of it, at the thought of Burlage's terror, his fear, his realization that he had *not* gotten the upper hand, that he should never have dared to oppose the Strikers.

And yet, as Itzhal gave him a curt nod and brushed past him toward the door of the headquarters, Tarr felt a sudden twinge, an urge to call him back. But he thought again of Archer, bruised and bloody, being dragged from the back of a horse, and he forced the feeling down. Now was the time to be strong, to be unwavering.

He realized that he had been standing alone, unmoving, in the empty hallway for a full minute, his hands clenched into fists at his sides. Slowly he forced his hands to relax and open, like brittle leaves uncurling.

CHAPTER TWENTY

The night stretched on. The half-obscured face of the moon circled overhead. Tess sat as usual in her small apartment, perched at her work-table, her legs crossed beneath her. Julian was asleep in his crib. Laith had not come to see her and while part of her was relieved, she longed for the comfort of his presence. She focused on the tools in her hands, and the little piece of wood that was gradually coming to life—a joint she felt could work well for a bridge, providing stable support without too much weight. She leaned back in her chair and swept her long chestnut hair over one shoulder. She turned the half-finished joint from side to side, brow furrowing as she studied it, deftly and absent-mindedly twirling the long, thin knife between her fingers. Finally, she set the joint down softly on the table, stretched her arms from side to side, and stood.

It must have been very late, for her candle was flickering low and uneven, a tall pile of milky wax at its base. She absentmindedly ran her fingers through her hair, and reflected with some amusement that her bed, where she had lain alone more or less contentedly for the better part of two years, was suddenly somehow distasteful to her. Her mind flickered again to the strange man she'd seen at the bar earlier that evening. He had seemed so unsettling in the moment, but here, in the safety of her own room and with a bit of time and distance between them, she decided she'd been paranoid. She had been planning to go and see the Strikers in the morning, to perhaps ask them for help and protection, but realized now that it was stupid. They had plenty of other things to worry about without having to provide a bodyguard for her.

There was a small noise outside the door and she turned slightly. It wasn't Laith. He always announced himself with a quiet, intimate knock, one only she could hear. A moment later, all was quiet, and she restlessly went to stand by Julian, her hand on his round stomach, rising and falling freely and without trouble.

An instant later the room burst into mayhem—the front door flew open with a crash that made Tess reflexively jump back. Tess whipped around to see three shadowy figures rush into the apartment, pausing on the threshold for only a moment before honing in on Tess, standing there with her son. Julian started awake at the first slam and gave voice to a full-throated wail of fear, and Tess felt her heart lock into place. She had no idea who these men were, but they were clearly there only for the purpose of harming her and her baby.

In three strides she went to her workbench and at once had hold of the sharp carving blade in one hand. She sized up the three intruders, and launched herself forward at them, slashing haphazardly through the air with her knife, her blood and fury and fear beating in her ears like a hot drum. Her frenzied motion caught them somewhat by surprise; one stumbled back into the other two, and she knew that she'd landed one of her frenzied blows when she heard a male voice cry out in sudden pain. They quickly recovered, though, and she felt a hand close around her wrist, which only enraged her further. She would not—she *could* not let them get anywhere close to Julian.

She had gone completely wild, a hurricane of violent, frenzied clawing, with her nails, her knife, her teeth, whatever she could aim at them. She kicked at them as hard as she could. She was tall and strong and, after stepping back and gathering herself, was able to bowl one of the intruders over onto the floor. She rolled on top of him and slashed with her knife. To her surprise, a fist shot up out of nowhere and hit her soundly on the side of the head. Stunned, she fell temporarily senseless onto the floor.

There was another noise, and in the mayhem and frenzy of the moment with her son's agonizing cries pitching through the small room, she found herself completely and utterly disoriented. Black splotches like ink bloomed and faded in front of her eyes and she lashed out desperately with her foot and connected with something hard, someone's leg. There was a yelp and the person pitched over with a crash. She heard a loud growl, not human, and then blinked up as a familiar black shape darted past her towards her son's crib. Shaking her head brought another shower of sparks before her eyes and as they cleared she recognized Breaker, Laith's huge black dog, who slid beside her son's crib as it began to teeter and topple over, and there was a fresh crescendo of screaming from Julian. Her stomach twisting in terror, Tess scrambled as fast as she could towards her son, but it was too late. The crib overturned and Julian pitched out of it—but Breaker dove beneath him and broke the boy's fall.

Tess reached out to him, but was grabbed again from behind by one of her unknown assailants. A fresh surge of fear and anger filled her and she clawed unseeingly behind her, hoping to connect with flesh. Breaker backed the screaming toddler into the corner and was on guard, hunkered down on his front legs, his hackles raised and his teeth bared in a terrifying grimace. One of the attackers came a step too close, and Breaker lunged forward, clamping his powerful jaws around the man's arm and wrenching to the side, the force of it flipping the man over onto his hip.

It was only then that Tess dimly became aware that Breaker had not come alone. There was another person, not one of the three intruders, who was there with her. She didn't have time to stop and look. The attacker behind her had her in a stranglehold, and she could feel the pressure on her trachea as she struggled for air. Gritting her teeth and using all of her weight, she managed to throw the man behind her against one of the walls, cracking through the thin, cheap coat of paint and sending a cascade of dust spilling out over everything. She fell forward forcibly, then rolled onto her back, hand groping in a wide swath for her knife, which must have fallen from her hand beneath her couch. Then her fingers closed around something that felt like her knife. And she brought it unhesitatingly down on her attacker, again and again, until he lay still.

There were two others, she knew it. But, strangely, the sounds of combat had died away, and the only sound was Julian's terrified screaming from the corner of the room. Three seconds thudded by, interminable, as she tried to clear her head and get her bearings—feet, hands, head, breath. She tried to move, but was pinned beneath the terrible heavy body of the man she'd killed. She shoved him off with all her might, then rolled over and scrambled across the floor towards her son, wanting nothing but to feel him warm, alive, whole in her arms.

Breaker was still crouched before the boy, blood spattered on the ground around him and over his muzzle. She forced herself not to look at the body of the man beside the dog. She brushed Breaker aside and reached for her son, a swell of love and sick relief as she clutched his howling form against her, kissing his curly head again and again, struggling unevenly and unsteadily to her feet, a hand groping against the wall to try and right herself.

She didn't see the third attacker, and she took a hesitant step forward, ready to do anything—launch herself, teeth bared if need be, at anyone who still meant to do her harm. But a second later a man stepped round the corner from her kitchen, red blotches at his temples and his arms. Instinctively she froze, but then her eyes and mind cleared as she recognized him.

"Marc?" she breathed, her voice hoarse.

He strode up to her, short and stocky, his pale cheeks flushed and red, ice-blue eyes serious and grave. If it weren't for the old scar that split his face, Tess would hardly have recognized him as the genial, sweet young man who had played with Julian at the Strikers' strategy session.

"Are you all right?" he asked. "Are you hurt?"

"I'm fine," Tess replied. "Bruised, but nothing worse." She was surprised to hear that her voice wasn't shaking. Just a bit croaky. Her knees felt weak and tingly and Julian's sobs were ebbing like waves into her shoulder. "How did you...why did you come here? How did you know?"

"We've been keeping an eye out, just in case Cira found out that you were involved with us. Athela sent me to check in on you tonight. There was another group of loyalists that nearly gave me the slip, but

I doubled back and got here in time."

"Where...I can't...do we stay here?"

"No," Marc said firmly, and Tess felt relieved, then immediately ashamed. Her little home, the sanctuary she had worked so hard to build, no longer felt safe. Every moment that passed, she realized she was glancing at the door, as if ready for it to burst open again.

She nodded mutely. "Where must I go?"

"We have places all around the city. I'll send someone tonight to fetch your things and we'll have the place cleaned up for you. But we have to go now." The emphasis on *now* was calm but firm.

She was about to take a step forward, but halted. "The third one..." she asked. "Did he get away?"

Marc shook his head grimly. "In the kitchen. Try not to look."

She nodded mutely, and hugged Julian even tighter.

They walked quickly through the night in the direction of the Strikers' headquarters in Two Falls. Tess felt as though her feet were barely touching the ground as she walked, and found herself turning every second or two to glance over her shoulder. She felt safer with Marc alongside her, but had to control herself from breaking into a flat run in the direction of shelter. She was gripping Julian so tightly she was surprised that he didn't protest.

They drew up to the noble edifice of the headquarters, where Marc nodded to two sentries on duty and immediately passed in through the front door.

At once, almost as soon as she had set foot across the threshold, Tess could sense that something was awry. There was a tense energy in the air—almost a buzzing, an indecipherable hum indicating that all was not well. She saw that Marc sensed it, too, as he swiveled on his heel and glanced up at her.

"Is he sleeping?" he asked, nodding to Julian.

"Almost," Tess replied hoarsely. "Marc—"

But she was cut off as another man appeared around a corner and strode toward them with a purposeful step. It was the blandly handsome one who could have passed for Laith's cousin. He took Marc wordlessly by the elbow and guided them into a small hallway off the main entrance hall.

"Ari," Marc said. "She—"

"Archer's been taken," Ari said immediately, with no discernible betrayal of emotion. "It happened about an hour ago. He and Tarr were ambushed, and they got Archer. Athela went after them, but they got away. He'll be taken to Faridor."

Marc reeled visibly. "Tarr and Athela?"

"Safe. Athela's inconsolable. Tarr believes that we've been betrayed. He's given the order for us all to go underground. The lead Strikers are to vacate the headquarters and go to safehouses for the night. Laith is with him. He's ordered me to remain here to act as liaison but no one else is to know where you all are."

A million thoughts and questions flashed through Tess's mind, and she nearly opened her mouth to voice them, but Marc squeezed her arm ever so slightly, signaling her to wait. She stayed silent, and bounced Julian up and down in her arms a few times.

"Tess was ambushed tonight by some of Cira's soldiers," Marc informed Ari in a low voice.

"Do you think it was a coordinated attack?"

"Quite possibly. Where are we to go? She'll have to stay with us and you'll need to have some of your people remove her things from her house and bring them here for safekeeping. There's a mess to clean up, too."

Ari said a few quick words in succession, that Tess assumed were part of some code, for they made no sense to her.

"Don't worry, it's close," Marc told her, with another quick squeeze to her arm. "You take care of yourself, Ari," he told the other Striker gravely.

Ari nodded mutely, and strode off across the hall with the same brisk, businesslike step.

"What if the loyalists capture him, too? Or torture him? To get your whereabouts?" Tess blurted out.

Despite the gravity of the situation, Marc guffawed. "Could you imagine? We once tried to get him to tell us whether he had any siblings and it was like trying to squeeze tears from a rock. I'd have more sympathy for the interrogators."

They slipped out again through the front doors, a little more surreptitiously this time, and did a few quick loops through some of the smaller alleyways, which Tess recognized was a tactic to shake any tail they might have picked up at the headquarters. A short while later, they came to a nondescript townhouse that had a short flight of steps leading down to a basement door set below the road's surface. Marc trotted down and gave a few quick raps on the door. It opened immediately.

An elderly pair of ladies waited for them on the other side, a small lantern on the wall casting a golden glow onto the dark floor. "Marc," said one of the women, tall, thin, with a pinched face and a blue scarf about her hair. "It's good to have you here again. It is our honor."

"How are you?" Marc asked warmly, embracing each of them and gesturing back to Tess, who entered quickly behind him and shut the door. "This is Tess and her son, Julian. She's one of us and needs shelter as well."

"What a dear," said the woman in the blue scarf. "Come, come, you're most welcome."

"We only got word tonight," said the other lady, who was slightly shorter and was clad in a heavy dressing robe. Her voice was anxious, her eyes worried. "Are things very bad, Marc?"

"We don't know yet," Marc said honestly. "The orders were recently given. I think we're to expect some visits tonight or during the day tomorrow, if you don't mind."

"Just like the old days," said the shorter woman, with a twinkle.

"I'll warm some sweet milk for the little one," chimed in the other. "You know the way down."

The two ladies headed up a small passageway, and Marc took the lantern from the wall and held it aloft, casting dancing shadows around the basement. Tess was surprised to see that it was not dank and cluttered, but clean and well-kept. There was a long hallway that led away from them, dotted with doors that Tess assumed must be for other rooms. It was a good deal larger than it had looked from the street above.

Marc led her down the passageway to one of the doors and held it open for her. Inside was a simple room, more concerned with utility than comfort. There was a bed and a small washstand, a lantern sat on a small table next to the bed. Marc immediately went to light the lantern, and Tess gently laid down her sleeping son on the bed. She turned back to Marc, suddenly feeling completely exhausted.

"I'll send word to Laith," he said, as if reading her thoughts. "And we'll get your clothes and things here by morning, if that's all right. They'll send down water and that milk for Julian in a moment."

Tess nodded mutely, too tired to say anything.

"I'm going to stay here all night. There may be people coming and going, but you'll be safe. Don't worry."

He smiled kindly, his white-blue eyes warm. He gave Julian an affectionate pat on the head, then quietly walked from the room, leaving Tess alone next to her sleeping son.

Even before he mounted the steps of the headquarters, Laith could sense that something was deeply, terribly wrong. Striker guards were running to and fro, their faces confused, their eyes anxious. A thicket of Cade's soldiers, who had been commanded to remain in the city, rode past in full battle dress, almost running Laith down as they went. He crossed through the front door, where Striker soldiers were either clustered together in agitated little knots, or were scurrying down the hall, looking scattered and disoriented. Laith looked from one group to the other, and broke into a slow run himself, searching for any one of the other Strikers who could tell him what was going on.

Finally, he saw Ari across the great hall, kneeling beside a young woman on a stretcher. He could see that she was speaking in a low, wincing voice and that Ari was listening intently and nodding thoughtfully. Laith dashed up to him and took him by the shoulder.

"What's going on?" he demanded.

Ari's face was grave as he slowly rose to his full height and told Laith about the catastrophic raid on the tinker shop.

"What else?" Laith asked.

"They took Archer," he said flatly. "Archer and Tarr were called to the wall and were attacked. Tarr got away, but they took Archer. Athela went after him, but they've taken him to Cira at Faridor."

Laith's stomach plummeted and he began to feel physically ill. "She'll kill him," he whispered, almost to himself. Ari made no response. He didn't need to. "Where is Tarr?" he asked.

Ari shook his head. "He's back safely, but can't be found. He's somewhere in the headquarters, though."

Laith knew the grief and anguish Tarr must be feeling. "And what else?"

"There was a separate attack you should know about. I've only just heard," Ari said slowly, and Laith looked at him sharply.

"Who?" he asked, though with a sense of foreboding he thought he already had an idea of who it could be.

"She's safe," Ari said preemptively. "I've gotten word from Marc. Tess and Julian were attacked in their apartment tonight. Athela had asked Marc to check on the apartment, and he brought Breaker with him. It sounds like Marc was able to intervene in time. They're in a safehouse, and Marc is staying with them."

Laith felt himself growing lightheaded, as overwhelming sensations of guilt and relief fought for dominance in his mind. "You're sure," he asked, feeling increasingly more numb, "you're sure they're all right?"

"Yes. And Marc is with them," Ari reiterated.

"How did...why did Athela..." Laith struggled to articulate the questions spinning in his mind. *Why had Athela known to assign Marc to protect Tess? How did she even know where Tess lived? I didn't tell her anything. I didn't tell any of them.*

Laith felt himself reach out unconsciously with one unseeing hand, and finally clasped Ari on the shoulder to steady himself. Ari moved forward to prop him up, his blue eyes filled with concern. A few of the other Striker guards had seen Laith waver and rushed forward to help, but Laith waved them away, recovering himself. He tried to wrap his mind around it, to make sense of it. Archer taken. Their troops killed. Tess attacked. He had to find Tarr, and quickly; had to find Athela, to see if there was any hope of recovering Archer before they made it back to the fortress. But even as he thought of it, he realized that Athela would never have let Archer go if there was even the slightest possibility of him being saved. Laith swallowed.

"I'm all right," he muttered and stood up fully. He opened his mouth to speak again, but saw a strange look of alarm wash over Ari's face, and whipped around to see what Ari was looking at.

On the opposite side of the great hall, framed by a dark doorway, was Si. He was dressed simply in white, looking like a sleeping child who had stumbled out of bed and gotten lost. His normally placid expression was deeply disturbed. Laith and Ari exchanged a single look and broke into an open run, matching each other stride for stride as they dodged around other Striker guards, tables and benches, to reach him on the other side of the hall.

Laith grabbed one of the boy's arms and Ari caught the other, and they fairly lifted him off his feet as they scooted him down the hallway and into the nearest room, which turned out to be a sort of windowless closet filled with buckets and cleaning supplies. Ari peered out of the door, checking to make sure that they had gone unseen, and shut the door closed behind them with a curt nod of affirmation to Laith.

"What is it, Si?" Laith asked urgently. Si's features were twisted in anguish, as though there were a deep-set pain in his stomach.

"It's Cira," he managed. "She's glad. Happy. It hurts."

Laith swallowed and locked eyes with Ari for a split second before turning back down to Si. "Can you see what she's going to do to Archer?"

Si shook his head, pain etched across his face. Whatever he was feeling, it was deeply physical. Laith was almost having to hold his bodyweight up completely to keep him from sinking to the floor. "I can see where the lights converge and diverge, and I can feel what she feels. Archer's light hasn't gone out. Not yet."

Laith wasn't entirely sure that he understood what Si was talking about but nodded confidently as if he did. He glanced up again at Ari for some kind of support or input as to what they ought to do, but Ari remained silent.

All of a sudden, Si let out a piercing, agonized cry that shook the room around them, and actually shocked Ari so much that he flew back against the door. Si convulsed and Laith caught him before he fell to the ground, cupping his head to avoid it striking the floor. Si's gray eyes were gaping open and he was staring up at the ceiling above them as though they weren't there, even though Laith tried to lean over him and force him to meet his eyes.

"She's happy...there's so much *hate* in it. So much..." he trailed off. "Fire."

"Fire?" Laith asked, his forehead wrinkling. He resisted the urge to look up at Ari again; Ari wasn't going to have any better idea of what was going on than Laith did.

"There's a fire," Si said, his voice faraway, his eyes still gazing vacantly above Laith.

"A fire?" Laith repeated for the second time, feeling stupid. "Like, an actual fire?"

"Houses. Just outside the city."

Laith stared at Si for a long moment. "Are you saying," he said slowly, "that Cira set houses on fire with just her mind?"

"Her hatred," Si corrected.

"Wait, her hatred set something on fire?" Ari asked dubiously. "Does that mean she can just set *us* on fire, too, whenever she wants?"

Si shook his head. "She doesn't even know it happened. Her energy had to escape, had to go somewhere. It shot out."

"Miles away from her?" Ari still sounded doubtful.

"I see," said Laith quickly, though he didn't at all. Ari could nitpick later, as far as he was concerned. "Are there people? In the houses?"

"Families," Si said quietly. The pain he had felt earlier seemed to have ebbed.

Laith gently set Si down so that he was lying flat on the ground. Si closed his eyes, and for all intents and purposes looked as though he was asleep.

"I'm going to go try and help," Laith told Ari. "Can you make sure things are stable here? Take Si back to his room, and make sure he's safe."

"How will you find the fire?" Ari asked.

"I imagine there'll be smoke," Laith said wryly. "Can you do it?"

"Yes, of course," Ari assured him. "Be careful. Where's Breaker?"

"I don't know, you said he was with Marc," Laith racked his brain, trying to think of where his dog had gotten to.

"Want me to call him?" Si said, his voice soft and dreamy again.

"Can you do that?" Laith asked curiously.

"Yes, I think so," Si said, and relaxed backwards.

Ari and Laith both stared at him for a second. "Right," Laith said, and turned the knob of the closet.

Directly outside, sitting with his ears pricked upright, was Breaker.

The dog looked, for all intents and purposes, as if he had been waiting there for some time. At the sight of his master, he broke into friendly panting and thumped his tail once or twice.

"Laith," came Si's sweet, drowsy voice from within. "There's a black spot circling the city. Going around and around its walls, looking for a way in."

Laith felt his brow furrow again as he tried to piece together Si's rather infuriating clues. "A black spot?"

"Just like a moth to a flame," Si echoed. "Around and around."

Laith looked with frank bewilderment at Ari, who gave a helpless shrug. "Be careful," Ari said again, as though he could think of nothing else to say.

"Come, Breaker," Laith ordered, and went out into the hallway, his dog at his heel.

Minutes later, Laith was speeding westward through the city atop his horse Arfolasth, Breaker keeping time at the horse's back hooves. A thick blanket of choking smoke had begun seeping over the city walls and was being gusted through the streets by the furiously whipping night wind. The smoke got worse and worse the closer he got to the west wall, and when he finally drew up to the gate, he could see the guards frantically darting to and fro, pointing at something in the distance to the west. An eerie, unnatural orange glow lit up the night sky, and Laith felt a deep swell of foreboding.

"Open the gate!" Laith ordered the sentries curtly, and they fairly tripped over themselves in their haste to obey him. "I've sent for help."

"No one can get near it!" one of the sentries called down frantically. "Sir, it's too dangerous!"

"It just burst into flames," cried another. "It just exploded! For no reason! Out of the blue!"

But Laith merely picked up the reins and urged Arfolasth forward and out of the gate, the wind blowing so hard in all directions that he was nearly knocked out of the saddle by its force the minute they left the shelter of the wall.

The fire had burst into being about a hundred yards from the walls of Two Falls, in a small cluster of houses just beyond the border of the city. Even before he got to the houses, Laith realized that it was too late to save anyone who may have been inside them. It wasn't just a fire, it was a billowing inferno, a column of solid flame that twisted up to the cold night sky. Buffeted this way and that by the wind, Laith could see that it was in danger of spreading, perhaps even reaching the city wall.

He sat there atop his horse, looking helplessly at the destruction before him. He had been too late. Too late to help, too late to save them. And even if Ari was able to put together a team of people to come and help control the flames, it would be too late. The Striker troops had already been stretched too thin that night; their forces weren't strong enough to contend with another disaster.

Laith thought of Si, lying motionless on the ground in the closet. He wondered whether Si could feel what he was feeling or sense what he was thinking. *Si, if you're there, you must do something,* he thought to himself, every fibre of his being aching as he tried to will Si to hear him. *I don't understand your powers, I don't know if you are able to do anything, but if you can hear me, you must help.* He concentrated all of his energy into that one word: *help.*

The seconds stretched on interminably as Laith watched, his breath bated. And then—so slowly that at first Laith thought he was imagining it—he saw small beads of water begin to form together, rising slowly from the blades of the grass around him, from the bare patches of earth, from the air beside his face. The tiny beads of water condensed together into larger and larger droplets, hanging like millions of glistening diamonds suspended in the air. Though the wind continued to roar and the fire burned, loud and frustrated before him, the droplets of water swelled and grew bigger, until Laith could see the reflection of the flames in the water itself. Slowly, unbelievingly, Laith raised a hand and touched one of the droplets, which had been swelling in size a foot or so from his face. It burst and a blissfully cool trickle of water ran down his finger.

The hair on Laith's arms and neck prickled, and he felt a wave of goosebumps roll down his side. His mind and heart tried to make sense of what he was seeing. *It's true*, he thought to himself. *Si has powers we can't even imagine.*

Which means Cira does, too.

The water droplets rose higher in the air, and then, in a sudden *whoosh*, rushed towards the blaze and pummeled it with a wild rush. The protesting hiss of smoke and flame was so enormous that Arfolasth snorted and half-reared; Laith immediately dismounted and laid a hand on the horse's neck to steady him. The flames sputtered and bowed, but weren't yet destroyed. They began to lick their way back up the charred skeleton of the buildings they'd consumed.

Like a moth to a flame, Laith thought all at once, seemingly out of nowhere. He gave a jolt. *What had Si said?* A dark spot, circling the city, like a moth.

Instinctively, he drew his sword and turned, surveying the dark swath of land behind him that sloped up to the city wall. Breaker, he could see, sensed his sudden alertness and rose, growling low and steady, ears pricked. It would be hard, Laith realized, for him to smell anything here; the smoke and flames were so overpowering.

Around him the mist began to rise again off of the grass and off the earth, forming the same glittering orbs. Laith was almost too distracted this time to notice them.

He was here. Laith knew he was here.

Lord Seth.

Sword up, he advanced through the rising droplets of water, peering unsteadily out into the blackness, his mind entering into a familiar place of cool humming wherein he ceased to think and every ounce of energy in his body was directed towards instinct: reaction and action He twisted his sword in his hand, Breaker stalking behind him almost in slow motion, black tail straight out like a ramrod.

There was a loud snap behind him as one of the buildings' timbers gave way, but he ignored it. The roar of the flames was gradually dying down; the strange suspended raindrops gently splashed against his face as he moved inch by inch through their veil. He felt the drops go running down the back of his neck and streak down his spine.

He scanned a blank expanse of land to his left and then turned slightly. Something made him swivel back. And where before there had been nothing at all, a shape suddenly loomed out of the shadows. Seth's black hood was cast back and his pale hair shone orange and red in the light of the fire. Even though they were well away from one another, Laith was close enough to see his eyes—those eyes, as black as pits, not even reflecting the light of the fire that burned beside him, face like a waxy skull.

Lord Seth grew closer, to the point where Laith could make out the sword that he wore at his belt. It was different than the one that Laith had known him to carry, and he immediately identified it as a sword made at the Whitsun forge, which put it amongst the rarest and most deadly of weapons ever made by human hands. Almost as if Seth could hear his appreciation, a smile began to creep around the edge of his cruel red gash of a mouth. *How on earth had he acquired that?* Laith felt himself wonder, momentarily breaking his concentration. *And moreover, for what purpose?* It was well known that Whitsun blades were usually only commissioned by those who wished to use the swords for a specific, often deadly reason.

He tightened his grip a bit more around the hilt of his own sword and raised it to an attack position, again letting his mind slip away into its meditative hum. Breaker kept close beside his leg, his ears pricked up now that the quarry was sighted, every muscle taut as he stalked through the grass, his unblinking amber eyes trained on the figure ahead.

At last, Seth drew the Whitsun sword and it caught in the gleam of the fire. The unblinking black eyes bored into Laith's as they advanced closer together. The closer they came, the more Laith could see that the blade itself was unusual. It seemed almost stained on the edges by something; a strange sort of discoloration that Laith had never seen on a weapon before.

In another instant Seth was on him, the blade flashing in the fire-light as he swung it fully at Laith's head. Laith had time to duck, his taut muscles galvanized into action as he dodged and whirled. He was out of practice, he realized instantly, as far as dueling was concerned. Gone were the days of leisure when he had spent hours honing his swordplay at the Academy or training with Marc or Athela. He had been too busy acting as a leader and trying to survive to have kept up on his footwork.

Still, decades of training were hard to shake and after the first few ungainly off-balance parries, Laith felt some of the rust starting to creak away and his old abilities pushing through to the fore. Seth was smiling openly now, his cold, cruel gaze still unblinking, his scarlet lips curled back over his row of small white teeth. Laith, his confidence recovered somewhat, went on the offensive. His blade whirled almost too fast for the eye to see as he beat Seth back down over the gentle slope of the hill, taking over the high ground, relishing in the advantage it brought him. Breaker was circling them, looking for an opening to attack, but the swords were flashing so fast that he couldn't quite get there in time. His ears were pricked, his eyes eagerly awaiting his chance to strike at Lord Seth.

Laith took a step down, and misjudged his placement, his foot striking a rock that had lain unseen in a clump of grass. It sent him off-balance, tumbling off to one side, where he rolled down the curve of the hill and struck his left ear on another stone. It stunned him for a second, but he shook it off as fast as he could, keenly aware of Seth swooping at him from above like a diving hawk. He heard Breaker give an enormous bark and saw his dog come flying at Seth from the side, managing to grab a hold of Seth's cloak in his jaws. Breaker wrenched him to one side so that Laith had time to scramble up to his feet, his sword again at the ready.

Seth's teeth were bared now in malice, and he aimed a few swipes at Breaker, who dropped the cloak and dodged out of the way, his canine face eager with the thrill of the chase. Laith, his balance regained, darted in while Seth was otherwise distracted and managed to land a small blow on his arm, though Seth was able to dodge out of the way before the full force of it landed. They skirmished back and forth, Laith's grace and assurance returning with each step. It began to feel easy, as it always had to him. Laith thought that he detected the bitter end of worry creeping into Seth's fathomless eyes.

Seemingly out of desperation, Seth dodged back and then darted forward again, his blade held straight out. Laith could see it coming and nimbly ducked out of the way, but the blow was sufficiently forceful to push him back a few critical feet. Breaker, seeing an opening, flew forward, his teeth bared, and clamped his jaws on Seth's arm.

Laith's opponent didn't even cry out as the dog's teeth sunk in, but he swung the sword around at Breaker, his black eyes drenched in fury. Breaker again was forced to release his arm to avoid the blow and scurried out of the way, much to Laith's relief—though he thought he heard the slightest hint of a yelp as the blade barely grazed the dog's shoulder.

And then, the strangest thing happened. Almost as soon as he had started, Seth stopped. The sword was lowered to his side. He looked from Breaker, teeth bared, hackles raised, back to Laith and smiled—that awful, sphinxlike smile that didn't reach his eyes. The fire beside them was dimming down to nothing; Si's magic had worked well and the water was being drawn steadily from the air and earth around them and being sucked into the flames, extinguishing them inch by inch. It began to grow quiet and dark, the smell of rich, thick smoke still choking the air.

Laith's sword was still up and at the ready. He could feel a trickle of hot blood running from his left ear down his neck where he had struck it on the rock. "Come on!" he shouted furiously. The heat of rage and bloodlust was pounding in his temple. "Come on!"

But Seth merely smiled and took a step back. Breaker, unsure, took a tentative step forward, then looked back to Laith, as if waiting for some sort of order to attack. And then, just as the fire died, Seth turned and vanished as quickly as he had appeared.

His disappearance caught Laith entirely by surprise. For a moment, he couldn't quite believe that Seth had just left him. Why hadn't he finished it? Did he know he was outmanned?

After a few seconds standing alone in the field, Laith slowly sheathed his sword. The wind was blowing less harshly now. The burnt husks of the farmhouses had died down to mere embers. There was nothing, and no one, that could be salvaged. The best thing for Laith to do would be to return to the wall and wait for help. He turned to walk back over to Arfolasth, who had removed himself to a safe distance.

"Come, Breaker," Laith ordered, as he walked towards the horse, wiping his sleeve along his ear to try and stem some of the bleeding. Behind him, there was silence.

"Breaker, *come*," Laith said, stopping and turning. He had never before had to call his dog twice.

The wind gusted around him, flipping back the edge of his cloak. Slowly he began to retrace his steps, peering around for any sign of his dog. Had Seth taken him somehow? Had Breaker left Laith to pursue their attacker into the night?

His slow footfall collided with something soft, and at once Laith's heart sank. He slowly knelt down to the ground and placed his hand on Breaker's neck. There was no movement. No pulse. His dog was dead.

Laith felt a wave of grief take him, and he hung his head for a few moments, trying to gather himself. He reached out and stroked Breaker between his ears. Breaker's eyes were still open, and there was a slight foaming at his mouth where his tongue lolled across the ground. It made no sense. Seth hadn't stabbed the dog; he'd landed a glancing blow, if anything. There was no way it could have killed him.

And then he remembered the dark stain on the edges of Seth's sword, the gleeful glint in his opponent's eyes after he had landed the tiny cut on Breaker's shoulder. *The blade itself was poisoned*, Laith realized.

"Good boy," Laith patted his dog for the last time, taking care to avoid the small nick in his shoulder. "You did well. Good boy."

He reached up and unbuckled his cloak, his hands moving automatically, his head numb. He wrapped Breaker's body in the cloak and carried the bundle over to Arfolasth, where he laid it across the front of the saddle before mounting up behind.

He rode back to the city gates. By this point there was a crowd of onlookers who had gathered to watch the fight out in the field; all of them stared at him with open-mouthed admiration as he passed. A few brave souls even called out his name or shouted encouragement as his horse parted through the crowd. But it was as if he saw and heard nothing. He went by them all as silently and lightly as the mist still rising from the earth.

Almost unaware of what he'd been doing or how he'd gotten there, Tarr found himself standing atop the roof of the Two Falls headquarters, looking out across the black night. For hours he sat and watched the fires burning in the west, like a lantern lit against the horizon. He wondered what they could be. He wondered whether this would be the end, whether in one night Cira had managed to snatch back from them what they'd taken. They'd been so disorganized, so unprepared. It had all been his fault. He'd been a fool to think that he could hold them all together. He'd been too cocky, too self-assured. One slip and everything he'd built had tumbled to the earth.

It had been a long time since he had stood out in the open in a place so high above the ground. There was nothing to keep him from teetering off the edge if a strong gust of wind blew him over. It was different than standing on a balcony or behind a window. But his natural Ashan affinity for heights put him at ease. There was nothing to fear up here, no one was dying or imprisoned because of mistakes he'd made. All was still and peaceful, except for the wind gusting around his ears, the flapping of his shirt. It felt simpler up here, easier.

It was one of the first things taught to young Ashans when they first learned to climb. There was nothing keeping you from tumbling out into the open air. Nothing but yourself. *You have to trust yourself not to fall.*

His heart ached at the memory. How he wished he could still believe that. For a moment he closed his eyes, and could almost see the filtering buttery-gold light spilling through the paper screens inside the old Ashan library. Then the wind buffeted him across the face, pulling him harshly back into reality.

The fire, which he'd been watching with a sort of detached curiosity, began dying down, almost as if it were being extinguished by an unseen hand. Tarr wondered what had caused it and what had put it out. It seemed quite far away from him now. He couldn't hear any voices from up on the roof; the shapes below seemed to belong to an entirely different world altogether.

He thought he'd been in control. He thought that he'd held all the strings together in his hand. But it was all an illusion. How fast it had all shattered.

He didn't know how long he stood up there. If Archer had still been there, he would have found him eventually. But no one came, no one knew where to search for him; the night felt like a hollow void. Eventually, he headed back down and made his way back to his office where he sat in a small chair facing the window.

After a time, there was a soft knock at the door, and Tarr inclined his head slightly to the left to indicate that he was listening. A voice came, the same young woman who had been the unfortunate messenger of all the rest of their ills that night. "I have a message from Itzhal, sir," she said wearily.

"What?" Tarr asked sharply. His heart quickened.

"He says it's done," the girl told him, and left him once more.

Tarr turned back around to stare out at the window. So that was it. Burlage was dead, on his orders. He waited for the swell of satisfaction that he expected his retribution would bring, but he didn't feel it. It wasn't as though Archer was going to turn around and walk back in through the door. Tarr sat back, looking at himself as though from a distance. What was he feeling at that very moment? Happiness? Anger?

One thing he knew for certain was that he wasn't sorry he had done it. He should have been ashamed, both of his actions and his lack of remorse, but he wasn't. And, as the seconds ticked by, he realized that that was the *only* thing he felt. An absence of shame. That was it. *How odd*, he thought to himself, still observing as if from afar. The feeling itself was cold and faceless, completely devoid of the rage he had felt earlier. He just felt empty.

The door opened without a knock and he heard slow, light footsteps behind him. It wasn't Ari, or Marc or Laith. With little effort he tipped his head to the side to see who it was.

It was Athela. She looked wretched; her normally wild hair was tangled and loose around her face and there were scratches along her cheek as if she'd fallen and scraped herself. Her eyes were red-rimmed and there were dark circles beneath. She was still dressed in her riding clothes, torn and dirty. Her hands hung limply at her sides. Tarr had never seen her in such a state before.

"I tried to get him back, Tarr," she said hollowly, her gray eyes pleading, as if begging him to shout at her, to chastise her for failing. She looked exactly the way Tarr felt inside.

But as Tarr looked at her, he realized quickly how utterly ineffectual their grief was, how pointless it was to stand around like this. He didn't blame Athela for what had happened. And his own guilt wouldn't help them get Archer and Rane back, even if it felt masochistically satisfying in the moment.

"They bested us tonight. That's all there is to it. I know you tried," Tarr said comfortingly. He reached out a hand and Athela took it, squeezing it tight in release. She knelt beside his chair, resting her curly head on his arm. He laid a long hand over the crown of her head and rested his chin against it for a moment. It felt good, to be there with her, knowing that they each felt the same exact way. She took a few deep breaths and then stared back up at him, her eyes questioning.

"We can't go down this road," Tarr warned her. "You have to forgive yourself and I have to forgive myself. Then we've got to get them back. That's all. We've got to think, and then we've got to find some way to get them back. They're not going to die. They're not."

Athela blinked and searched his face once more. Finally, she nodded, a hint of resolution showing around the set of her jaw. "What is it, Tarr?" she asked after a moment. "Your face...it looks..."

Tarr shook his head. He may not have felt sorry for what he'd done—not yet, anyway—but that didn't mean that he wanted to share it with the others. For a moment he thought of what Athela would say if he did tell her, wondered if she'd be glad or horrified. Tarr wasn't sure which would be worse.

"Are you going to try and get any sleep tonight?" Tarr asked, changing the subject.

Athela made a jerking motion with her hands. "As if I could."

"Pull up a chair, then," Tarr indicated with a motion of his head towards the wall, where a few empty seats rested.

Athela smiled faintly and did as he suggested, pulling up beside him and sinking down heavily, resting her head exhaustedly on the backrest of the chair. Silently, she reached out, her hand open in an unspoken invitation. Tarr took it, closing his eyes thankfully for the solace it offered. Together they sat and waited for the sun to come up.

For the rest of the night, Tess was caught in the terrible place between utter exhaustion and complete alertness. She endlessly replayed the fight in her mind, shuddering as she realized how close she and her son had come to death. There was only a squat oil lamp to light the little safehouse room, so she had no idea what time it was. The already surreal night slowly faded into a strange sort of waking dream as she listened to the sound of the blood pounding in her ears, her fingers threaded in her son's curly dark hair.

A few times during the night there was the sound of muffled voices outside her room, but she didn't venture out to see who it was. She trusted Marc's word when he said that he would not leave them, but she couldn't help but fight back rising swells of dread as she imagined her door crashing open again.

Is this what it's like? She wondered finally, tilting her head back against the wall. *To become involved with these people?*

How could I have been so stupid? How could I have put my son in so much danger?

Finally, she must have drifted asleep, for the next thing she was starting awake at the familiar sound of a soft, conspiratorial knock at the door. A moment later it opened, and Laith's unmistakable figure slipped inside, the light casting the sharp planes of his cheekbones and his slightly sunken eyes into startling relief. He had clearly come straight to her from some sort of fight, for his face was streaked with dirt and there was sweat shining around his hairline; a small trickle of blood ran from his left ear down the side of his jaw. His clothes were caked in mud and dust, and one sleeve had been torn. He stopped at the sight of them, a strange expression on his face. Tess tried to read it.

"I'm so sorry," he said, still at the door. His dark brown eyes traveled from Julian up to Tess's face. "I'm so sorry this happened."

"How did they find out?" Tess asked hoarsely. "How did Cira find us?"

"I don't know," Laith whispered. "It was my fault." He looked as tired as she felt. He ran a hand through his short sandy hair and walked over to the foot of the bed and sat. The mattress moved slightly with his weight. Tess tucked her knees up closer to her, almost afraid to be near him. There was a long silence.

"You were in a fight," Tess observed. He looked so tired.

"Yes," he replied.

"Are you all right?," she replied. He made no answer, so Tess changed the subject. "Laith, I..." She groped for words, feeling desperately frightened. "Why me? Why did they come after me?"

Laith's head sank on his shoulders. "I don't know for certain. We weren't careful enough. I wasn't careful enough. Someone may have seen me coming or going from your place and put two and two together.

I was stupid. And careless. With your life, and with Julian's." His voice was hoarse. He looked towards Julian, his dark eyes blacker than Tess had ever seen them. She smelled the scent of smoke, of fire emanating from him and thought she must be imagining things.

Tess's brow furrowed. "What could she care? Even if she thought we were together, what difference would it make? I'm no one to her. I'm a barmaid."

Laith seemed to be visibly struggling to find words, and his reluctance made Tess feel all the more frightened. "You know that Cira is my cousin?" he asked finally.

Tess had a vague recollection of this and nodded.

"With her, it's personal. It's not just a matter of winning the war. She wants to hurt us. She wants to find our vulnerable spots and exploit them so that they hurt the most."

Tess felt a surge of rage at him that quickly subsided into nauseating fear. "Oh," she said, rather coldly. "So you *knew* that if she found out, this would happen to me. To us." She clutched Julian even tighter.

Laith heard the tone in her voice and looked at her, his face plainly anguished. "Tess, I'm sorry. I should never have put you in this position." His eyes went back down to his hands. "I...I can't explain it but the only real peace I've known since the beginning of this terrible war has been on that shabby little couch of yours. I...couldn't *help* myself." He rubbed his hands through his hair again, and Tess felt her anger subside ever so slightly. She drew herself up.

"My couch is *not* shabby," she said tartly. "Take it back."

He half-laughed, rubbing the back of his head with one hand, and looked up at her searchingly, his face entreating. She was struck, perhaps for the thousandth time, by his beauty.

She was angry, she realized. Not only with Laith, but with herself. If he was guilty of endangering her life and that of her son, she was guilty too. She wasn't naive. She knew in her heart that any sort of association with the Strikers was dangerous. And yet she had invited Laith back to her house night after night. Why? Broad shoulders and a pair of beautiful brown eyes? She had to have known better. And why on earth had she attended their strategy session? It had been pure vanity on her part, a desire to relive a day of her life before the war, to feel herself fulfilled by something she had once loved and had devoted her life to. And she had enjoyed it. That was the worst part. She had replayed that meeting over and over in her head while she tended to her son and washed dishes and did the shopping and cooking; she found herself thinking back to the Faridor plans and wishing she'd had a longer time to look at them, to see if there was another way in they hadn't seen before. She found herself wishing for a different life. Forgetting her duty as a mother. And now here they were.

She shook her head ever so slightly, almost to herself.

"What does that mean?" he asked.

"It means that I'm exhausted," she said. "It means I want you to sleep here with us, and I want you to hold me all night." Laith blinked once, slowly, and she raised her head, facing him with unwavering resolve. "And then as soon as it's safe, I want Marc to take me back to my house, or wherever it is he thinks that I can protect my son, and I never want to see you or any of the other Strikers ever again. "

Laith looked at her steadily and Tess searched his face for any hint of protest, any sign that he wanted to convince her to let him stay with them. Her mind was made up. It had been made up the instant the door had opened and the Kagaian guards had rushed towards her baby. At last, Laith nodded mutely, his dark eyes heavy with sorrow.

He placed his hands on the bed and pushed himself up, then very formally unbuckled his belt and scabbard and hung them loosely over the small bedside table. He undid his black leather boots and slid them off, one by one, placing them carefully beside the door. Then he reached one hand behind his neck, tugged off his black shirt with one smooth motion, and tossed it to the floor. He turned and faced Tess, barefoot in his trousers, letting her see him for what he was. She didn't bother trying not to stare. His body was beautiful in the history that was written across it; spare and scarred, battle lines old and new crossing and crisscrossing down his torso.

She scooted over as far as she could to make room for him, pulling back the bedclothes as she did. The bed was quite small, and it was already a tight fit with just her and Julian. Laith walked over to her, leaned over the lantern and gave a short breath, and suddenly the room was pitch black. The bed creaked and gave in to his weight as he slid in beside her. She turned on her side to lay an arm protectively around Julian and felt Laith settle in easily behind her, molding his body against hers and laying his warm cheek against the nape of her neck. One strong hand took her hip and pulled her in a bit closer against him; she felt a sigh escape her, sure that he could feel her heart drumming through her back against his chest. As always when she was with him she felt her senses heightened; acutely aware of her pulse, every shift of his hard body against hers. But that soon gave way as the rhythm of their breathing joined and slowed, and within minutes all three were fast asleep.

CHAPTER TWENTY-ONE

The entire city was frozen in place like a frightened animal cornered, holding its breath until the danger was safely past. The wind, which had howled like a gutted beast throughout the entire previous day, slowly died as the sun crept unsteadily into the gloomy sky. Everything was still.

And as the light filtered into the gray corners of Tarr's room, he took stock of their situation. Archer had been taken. Rane was imprisoned, or worse. Their spy network inside Faridor was compromised. He had no idea whether Cicada had survived. Tess had been attacked. Laith had fought Seth, barely escaping with his life. And twenty—*twenty*—of their Striker guards around the city had been killed, both in the initial catastrophic raid on the tinker's shop, and in subsequent scuffles around the city, all of which had burst up as suddenly as wildfire.

And, of course, there was Burlage. He was dead, too. Tarr wasn't worried that he would be suspected. Burlage's death would be chalked up to just another one of the surprise attacks carried out by Cira's loyalists during the course of the night. But still, every few minutes in the endless churn of his mind, Tarr would return to Burlage, wondering why he didn't feel more remorseful, more guilty. There must be something wrong with him, seriously wrong.

One by one over the course of the morning, the remaining Strikers crept into Tarr's office, joining Tarr and Athela in their silent vigil. Tarr couldn't quite understand why the presence of the sun in the sky made him feel even more tired, but it did. Everything around him seemed to throb dully, exhaustion creeping at the edges of his vision. Finally, he stirred and turned, and when he looked around he saw Ari, Marc and Si sitting behind him. Si, out of all of them, was the only one who didn't look beaten down.

"Laith's coming," Marc told him. "I sent word. He went to make sure Tess was all right."

Tarr silently nodded and straightened, turning to face the others. He had a sudden urge to make some kind of apology, to beg their forgiveness for not being able to rout such a disaster from happening. He opened his mouth, then looked down at his hands.

The door opened slightly and Laith slipped in. He was still dirty and clad in his clothes from the night before—he must have gone straight to Tess from his battle with Seth, and then come straight to them from Tess's hideout.

Tarr had already been told what had happened to Breaker during Laith's duel, and his heart ached for his friend. Laith's face was dirty and there was a long line of dried blood down the left side of his neck. He seemed, if possible, even more detached than usual. His feet and hands seemed to move without him controlling them. He found a seat and faced Tarr. He didn't even make the pretense of trying to smile.

"How's Tess?" Tarr asked finally.

"Alive," Laith croaked, his voice scratchy and dry with sleep and smoke. "Like the rest of us." This last bit was said with the slightest hint of irony.

Tarr sighed and looked back at Athela, who regarded him with her red-rimmed gaze. Exhaustedly, Tarr turned away and reached across to his desk, where there was a little bell for him to use to call his aides when he needed them. He detested the bell, and preferred to walk to the door to fetch things himself. But right now, the door to his office seemed a very long way away.

He tinkled the bell, its light, cheery sound incongruous in the dim atmosphere. A moment later the door opened. A man with graying hair stood outside, his eyebrows raised.

"Could you please," Tarr requested tiredly, "ask Sian and Nora to send some food up? And some strong tea. Anything we have. Thank you."

"I'm not hungry," Athela said hollowly as the door closed.

"We need to eat," Tarr shook his head. "All of us. There's much to be done."

They didn't talk until the meal was brought. Once the platter arrived, they all moved to sit on the floor in a circle around it. Tarr hadn't much stomach for food, either, but forced the pieces of bread and cheese down his throat, and after a few minutes began to feel somewhat revived.

"All right," he said finally. "There's a lot of blame and guilt to be thrown around. I know I've spent a good portion of the night in it. I know you all have. But what happened has happened, and we have to think about what to do."

"Are they still alive?" Athela asked Si suddenly, her gray gaze intense. "Archer and Rane?" Tarr was glad to see that she was at least managing to sip some tea.

"Yes," Si said, with an air of infuriating triviality. "They're both still alive. Want me to tell you if or when one of them dies?"

The other Strikers looked sharply at one another, shocked by the callousness of his words. Tarr could feel Athela make a starting motion, as if she were going to shout at Si, but Tarr touched her arm. Marc sent her a frown and turned to face the boy.

"Not unless we ask you, Si, please," Marc said in a patient, calm voice. "If we're not ready to hear it, I think it would make us upset."

"Oh," Si said remotely, as if the very notion of this kind of reaction was intriguing and somewhat puzzling to him. "All right."

The group collectively relaxed again. Laith stirred beside them and looked up. There was a deadened expression in his eyes; Tarr couldn't tell whether it was sheer exhaustion or whether something else was seriously wrong with him.

"So Archer is alive," Laith began slowly. "But not for long, at this rate. Cira will keep him alive for a few days. She'll want to toy with him, like a cat. She won't kill him outright. That would ruin it for her."

"Laith's right," Athela agreed. "So we have two options. We break into Faridor and try to get Archer and Rane out, or we move up the day of our siege. We attack Faridor and end this, one way or the other."

"We're not ready for that," Tarr said automatically, almost a gut reflex.

"So what?" Athela asked. "There's no time. They're going to die."

"We can't risk the lives of hundreds of our soldiers on a shoddy plan of attack," Tarr pointed out. "Just to get back Archer and Rane. No matter how hard it is. The soldiers would die, we would fail, Rane and Archer would die too."

Athela shifted, frustrated. She wasn't a patient person by nature, and Tarr could see her struggling to tamp back her impulse just to leap to her feet and go barreling out the door and ride out to Faridor alone. "No one has ever been able to break out of the dungeons of Faridor, and you know it," she said. "Not even Rowan; she was rescued from one of the towers. What option do we have other than an outright attack?"

"What about your spies in the fortress?" Marc asked Tarr.

"I might have one left, though I can't know for sure," Tarr replied. "But I have no way of contacting her with a new cipher. Anything I send her will be intercepted and will be decoded. They've got Rane. They've cracked it. They've dismantled the network."

"Why aren't we ready?" Athela protested. "Calchas has gathered all the available troops from the Meadows. He should be back soon. We'll have all the strength we're going to get right here."

"But we have no plan," Laith pointed out reasonably. Athela made a frustrated *tsking* noise in the back of her throat at the insignificance of this detail.

"Besides, there's the small matter of the wall," Tarr pointed out patiently. "And how to get over it."

This seemed to slow Athela's momentum for a moment. "There *has* to be another way in," she said finally, almost pleadingly.

"You heard Tess at the strategy meeting," Tarr shook his head. "The fortress is impenetrable, except for that small hidden cove at the base of the island. But that's no place for us to land an army or stage any sort of attack. We'd be seen there immediately."

"*And* we have no navy," Laith pointed out.

"We could sneak a small party through the cove and try and get to the gate from the inside?" Marc suggested.

"Too risky," Tarr shook his head. "There's almost no chance they'd make it through Faridor without being found out. And there are two gates to open. They open one and they're dead before they open the other."

"What about Si?" Ari asked suddenly. Everyone stopped and swiveled up to look at him. He very rarely talked during their discussions; he generally seemed more content to keep to the sidelines and to listen. Ari raised his eyebrows at all of them. "With his powers, it seems as though we could end this today, if we wanted."

"What, kill everyone at Faridor?" Athela asked sarcastically.

"Yes," Ari said quietly. The others stared at him. Ari spread his hands. "I mean, that's what we'd be proposing anyway by attacking with a full army, isn't it? Only now, we'd be able to ensure that no one on our side gets killed, too."

Tarr could see where he was coming from, yet the idea deeply bothered him. From the looks on the others' faces, it seemed that they were thinking along the same lines.

"I mean, you can do that, can't you, Si?" Ari asked Si directly. The boy looked up, as if surprised to be addressed in such a way.

"What, kill everyone?" Si asked.

"Yes," Ari said.

"Oh, yes," said Si unconcernedly, and went back to staring at the way the light was refracting off of the window behind Tarr's head.

"He's a human being," Marc said, bristling. "He may have these abilities, but that doesn't mean we should *use* him like some sort of... mindless weapon. Taking those lives would do something to him. It would take something *from* him. It means something different to him than to us."

"As I understand it," Ari pushed back gently, "he has the extent of time and space and the entire universe wrapped up in his head. I imagine that makes him more qualified to understand the weight and significance of such a thing than any of us."

This rang true, but Tarr still didn't like it. Si was still too suggestible, too pliant, strange in his seeming innocence. They were wading rapidly into a morally gray morass. "Si," Tarr asked slowly, as Marc glared at him, "You could help us in that way, couldn't you?"

"I could," Si agreed softly.

"*Would* you?" Tarr asked. The others watched Si, tension static in the air between them.

"It's not how we get inside," Si said with a tinge of coyness.

Tarr goggled at him. "Then how do—"

"He doesn't want to," Marc interjected flatly. "Drop it."

"I agree with Marc," said Laith diplomatically. "It may be old fashioned of me, but in our training we're taught that everyone on a battlefield stands there because they are *willing* to risk their lives for the chance to carry something they believe in. And the battlefield, as awful and as cruel as it is, still gives them a chance to fight for their cause and perhaps even to survive. We'd be robbing everyone in Faridor of that chance."

"I don't see," Ari said, a bit coolly, "why they should deserve it."

Tarr looked at Ari curiously, the blandly handsome mask facing him hiding a seemingly impenetrable morass behind it. He was used to Ari's uncompromising attitude when it came to Archer and his past sins, but this was the first time that he had really heard Ari hold forth about those who had turned to fight for Cira. It struck Tarr that Ari's attitude towards both was consistent: no forgiveness, no redemption, no quarter given. And it made sense. Ari's entire family had been killed by Cira's troops. Tarr couldn't imagine what that was like. If the pain he felt at Rane and Archer's mere *abduction* was any indication, Ari's grief must be overwhelming. However, it was still surprising to hear him being so cold-blooded.

"What if Si just put everyone to sleep?" Athela asked suddenly, interrupting Tarr's train of thought. "Everyone at Faridor. And then we just walked in and plucked them out of the dungeon?"

It wasn't a bad idea, Tarr thought, but almost as soon as the words were out of Athela's mouth, Marc had bristled and leaned forward, his ice-blue eyes blazing with intensity. "I don't care if it's putting a whole castle to sleep or lacing up your riding boot, *Si is a human being, not a tool to be used*. And you're not going to use him like that while I'm here. He gets to choose when to use his abilities and when not to. You're not going to try and convince him to do something he doesn't want to do.

If he wanted to end the war that way, he would have."

Eyes still burning, Marc sat back down alongside Si, who looked at him with a pleasant interest. "There is something I want to do," Si remarked matter-of-factly.

Please let it be that you want to put the whole castle to sleep, Tarr prayed inwardly.

"I want to see Cira," Si told them. He looked around at the group, his young face bright and suddenly alert. "I need to see her, face to face." As with other times that he had discussed Cira and the connection that existed between them, Si suddenly seemed more lucid than usual.

"Then we'll find a way," Marc assured him.

"That cove Tess found at the foot of the fortress might not be big enough for an army, but it might be big enough for a small group to make their way into Faridor," Athela said thoughtfully. "Si and one or two others."

"Then there's just the matter of actually getting *through* the entire fortress and up to her tower, or wherever she is," Tarr pointed out wryly.

"She's in the tower," Si piped up, and his eyes suddenly looked faraway, as though he were watching something on a distant horizon. "She's pacing back and forth."

Again, silence fell as the others regarded him, then looked around at one another, as if searching for some kind of cue. Seemingly oblivious, Si stared intently at a spot in the distance which, Tarr realized with a chill, was precisely in the direction of Faridor island from where they were sitting.

"Si could see whoever's coming, couldn't he?" Athela said again, breaking the tension. "Since he wants to get to Cira. If he and a couple of others made it into the fortress through the cove, they could avoid the Kagaian guards and get up to her undetected. Right?"

All eyes wheeled back around from Athela to Si, who snapped out of his reverie and blinked up at them.

"Yes, I could do that," Si confirmed, folding his hands lightly in his lap.

"Well, that's at least how to get Si into the castle," Tarr gave a little sigh. "Now, we just have to figure out how to get an army in." He peered sidelong at Si, wondering if he could ask the boy for some sort of hint as to a solution without Marc erupting at him again. "Si, how do we—"

"Don't worry," Si piped up suddenly, as though he had only just started listening to what the others were talking about. "It will all be the way it needs to be. The circle is closing. A way is coming." Again, the chorus of heads turned towards him.

"Wait, what?" Tarr said quickly. "Do you mean that in a sort of existential, encouraging 'you're going to find a way' sort of way, or do you mean that there is something physically coming towards us that is going to help us figure out how to get through the wall?"

"Yes," Si replied.

"A way through the wall," Tarr clarified disbelievingly.

"No," Si countered evenly.

"But you just said—" Athela protested.

"But someone *is* coming?" Tarr said hurriedly, trying to backtrack and pick up the trail of thought where they'd lost it. "And we find a way?"

"Yes," Si answered.

"Which one?" Tarr asked.

"Both," Si said. Then his eyes traveled up to the ceiling and there they rested.

Tarr threw up his hands in frustration and looked around at the others, who shrugged helplessly. Athela looked on the verge of erupting. It didn't seem as though they were going to get much more information out of him. *Someone else is coming?* Tarr wondered. With a pang, he thought of Archer's joke about everyone, including Laith's old housekeeper, deciding to show up at Two Falls. He missed Archer more than ever.

"Be patient," said Marc soothingly. "I'll talk to him later and see if I can get him to explain more."

"That would be helpful," said Athela sarcastically. "The sooner the better, if he wouldn't mind."

Marc spread his hands. "He doesn't reckon time or space or world events the same way we do. For all we know, he's watching planets forming up in that funny head of his; most of what we're dealing with down here on earth must seem pretty trivial."

"Black hole, actually," Si murmured, his eyes not moving from the spot on the ceiling. "Watching it spin."

"Whatever that is," Athela grumbled beneath her breath.

"Right," Tarr sighed, not sure if he was more frustrated with Marc, Si, or the cosmos as a whole. "The best thing we can do is try to get some sleep. We need to rest, and we need to regroup, and we need to find a way through that gate. And we need to find it fast. We need to think." Though he was ostensibly instructing the others, he was mostly telling himself. Gone was the lethargy that depression and guilt had brought on the previous night. It was time for them to galvanize into action.

The others gathered their things and stood. "By the way," Laith said, looking Tarr straight in the eyes. "You heard that Minister Burlage was killed last night as well?"

Tarr shifted uncomfortably under Laith's probing stare. "I did." Abandoning any pretense of trying to look upset by the loss, he straightened and faced Laith head-on. "He won't be mourned by many, least of all me."

"Interesting that out of all the council members, he was the only one killed," Laith frowned thoughtfully. Tarr couldn't tell whether Laith was genuinely puzzled, or whether he knew exactly what Tarr had done and was leading him on.

"Very," Tarr murmured, not giving an inch.

Laith lingered beside him for a moment. Up close, in the full light of morning, Tarr realized that he had never seen Laith look quite so ill. His skin was an ashy gray, and the skin beneath his eyes was so dark as to almost have been bruised. His eyes themselves had lost something. Concerned, Tarr reached out and touched his shoulder.

"You look awful," Tarr said in a low voice, as the others began filing out of the room.

Laith shook his head. "It was a long night. I lost Breaker."

Tarr nodded, squeezing Laith's shoulder. "I heard. I'm so sorry."

"Seth is determined to kill me," Laith said, his voice hollow. He didn't sound afraid or emotional. It was a flat statement of fact, without any affect. Tarr searched his face, trying to discern exactly what Laith was feeling. He felt a sudden twist in his gut as a thought dawned: *Laith might actually welcome it. Laith might actually be* looking *for it.* But he couldn't think of the right words to say, anything that could possibly help. He felt stupid and deeply inarticulate.

As he opened his mouth, Laith blinked once at him, the shadow passing from his face like a bird lifting its wing. "You're right. Rest is the thing. I'll see you tonight. We'll try and put the pieces back together again." And without another word, he was gone, leaving Tarr standing alone in his dark wake.

In the forests to the east of Two Falls, just down the coast from Faridor and set only a short way away from the sea, Cade had established what he thought to be a fairly impressive camp, considering it had only been a handful of days since they'd settled themselves there. Every day their soldiers and hired shipbuilders toiled away, felling trees and slicing timber and going about the motions of building a fleet of sleek, mid-sized boats; large enough to transport horses but built for speed and agility rather than sheer strength.

The true plan, of course, was only known to Cade, Rowan, and a few of Cade's closest advisors. A copy of the contract between Cade and the shipbuilders in Eldrest had "accidentally" fallen into the hands of a known Kagaian sympathizer en route to Tarr in Two Falls. The clue was oblique enough that it wouldn't obviously look like a trap, but would be easy enough for Kagai's agents to trace back to its source, and hopefully to their build site. Every day as the sun set behind the trees, Cade would survey the work that they had done, his back aching and sweat pouring down his neck, almost freezing in the cold air, hoping that the effort wasn't ultimately in vain.

Cade heard footsteps behind him and swung around. Rowan was approaching, wrapped in a large fur, the cold wind rifling through her short-cropped hair. She gave him a wary, watchful smile. He thought he had made some headway in establishing a sense of trust with her, but was keenly aware that she still held him at arm's length. He tried to imagine, not for the first time, what she had been like before her imprisonment, then remembered that it didn't matter. Like him, whoever she had been before was gone. There was no point in wondering.

Still, he had asked her to go with him, and she had agreed. That was something.

"Food is being served," she told him, indicating over her shoulder to one of the large royal purple tents that had been pitched amidst the trees. The troops' sleeping quarters encircled the work area; Cade had abandoned his royal right to his own tent and had made do with sharing a space with Wolf, Nadia, Rowan, and a few trusted others. Glowing lamplight emanated out of the soldiers' dining tent, and Cade could hear the clinking sounds of plates and knives. It was comforting to him: hearing those sounds, being on the outside and listening in.

"I'll be there in a minute or two," he told her, folding his arms across his chest and staring out at the large clearing they had made. Before them in the open field, upturned boats loomed above like giant carcasses, the broad curves of their pale wooden skeletons eerie in the low light. Without the hubbub of construction and activity, the field bore the otherworldly atmosphere of a graveyard populated entirely by enormous mythical beasts.

"Do you think they'll find this?" Rowan asked, gesturing out at the clearing, the piles of shavings and sawdust rising like drifts of snow on the ground.

"I trust Tarr that they'll find it if he wants them to find it," Cade replied with a smile. "Tarr seems adept at getting what he wants."

Rowan shot him a curious sideways look but said nothing. She took another step to stand shoulder to shoulder with him, the fur from her wrap brushing softly against his hand. Now that she was closer, Cade took the opportunity to steal a glance, admiring her dark curl of lashes and elegant profile.

"What will you do with the boats?" she asked suddenly.

Cade was taken aback. "You mean, afterwards? I don't know."

"Seems a shame," Rowan mused.

"Why?" Cade asked curiously.

"To build something so completely intended for a single purpose, and then to deny it that purpose," she said thoughtfully, still gazing out at the clearing.

Cade stared at her. "I'll use one in my bathtub," he joked after a moment. "Will that help?"

"It might," Rowan smiled. "You really live in a palace, then?"

"Currently, I live on a hard flat cot sandwiched between two body-guards," Cade replied wryly. "But yes. I suppose after all of this, I will live there again. Someday."

"Are there gardens?" she asked suddenly.

He looked at her curiously. "Yes, many. Beautiful ones."

"Oh," Rowan smiled faintly. "That's nice. And once this is over you'll govern Two Falls as well?"

"Perhaps." He was surprised. His intention to unite Joymaril, the Meadows, Two Falls and the Ashan forest into a single country was an ambition he had harbored deep within; one he hadn't shared with another soul. And yet Rowan had seen through him almost instantly.

"They won't go for it," Rowan told him flatly, with a little grin.

Cade blinked at her in surprise. "What makes you think so?"

She laughed. "I mean, where have you been the past four years?"

"In prison," Cade said drily.

"Well, *I* know that," she said with a wave of her hand. "But to them you're someone who not only is Cira's cousin but bears a startling resemblance to her, who waltzed in at the last minute and now intends to declare himself king over all of them, just as she declared herself Queen. Why should they follow you? You don't know them, you don't know the city, or the people."

"But *you* do," Cade suggested.

"Yes, I do," she looked at him sidelong. "But if you think that's me putting in a job application, you're quite wrong."

"Weren't you?" Cade smiled craftily.

"No," she said firmly. "Just stating the obvious in case no one else had pointed it out to you yet."

"They hadn't," Cade said truthfully.

Rowan shrugged. "You'd better get yourself better advisors, then."

"Who would you suggest?" Cade probed. "Tarr?"

Rowan made a noise in the back of her throat. "Tarr serves no one."

"Still, better to have him on our side than not," Cade mused, almost to himself.

"Undoubtedly," Rowan concurred.

In the distance amongst the gloom of the trees, an owl let out a long, eerie call. For a moment, Cade thought he glimpsed some movement there, but dismissed it. "The...er...job you were not applying for earlier," he said tentatively. "What job did you think it was?"

She looked at him in surprise. "I was only joking, but I don't know...some sort of advisory...something? If that was presumptuous of me, I'm sorry."

"What about something more than that?" Cade asked quietly. He continued to look out at the gathering night over the tops of the trees, but could feel her turn around to look at him with an expression of amazement and alarm.

"You'd better not be asking what I think you are," she said guardedly.

"Why?" Cade asked innocently.

"We barely know each other." She laughed suddenly, overcome with the absurdity. "You've never so much as kissed my hand."

"We could start with the hand," Cade agreed. "And depending on how that goes, we could progress from there."

She laughed again, mostly with astonishment, as if she had never quite seen the likes of him before. "Goodness, when you want something, you certainly go for it."

"Does it put you off?"

"I don't know yet," she tilted her head, regarding him thoughtfully as if assessing him under a different light. "I've always been distrustful of ambition."

"Why?"

"Look where Cira's got me." Rowan wrapped herself closer in her coat, pulling away from him a bit. He could sense her reserve had settled back into place.

"Look," he said finally, waving his hand around at the space surrounding them. "I think that this land, this...country...could be something good. If it's brought together. Not the way Cira did, by sowing seeds of hatred and discord, but by creating a unified identity. A single voice."

"You're talking about assimilation," Rowan countered, looking suspicious.

"I'm not. Let the Ashans be Ashans, let them keep their traditions and live in their forest for the rest of time. But let them also be citizens of a unified country, and let the triumphs and struggles be shared. If that had been the case when Cira had first tried to seize power, it would have been much easier to throw her out."

"And you think you're the one to do it," Rowan pressed.

"I think I could help," Cade said simply. "I'd like to try."

Rowan digested this for a moment, and then a few moments later, almost under her breath, she muttered again, "You're going to need better advisors."

Cade laughed. "Probably."

All at once, Rowan's violet eyes darted to one side and Cade could feel her tense up beside him. "There's someone in the trees," she said in a low voice, her lips barely moving.

"Yes," Cade assented calmly.

"One of ours?" she asked nervously.

"I don't know," he replied. "We should try and look natural."

Rowan forced herself to relax and turned to face him directly. They were about the same height, though at the moment she was standing on slightly lower ground than him. "I want to believe you," she said finally. "About your intentions."

"With you or the country as a whole?"

"Both."

"You can," he assured her.

"We'll see," she said, and laid a hand on his arm. The touch was warm, surprisingly tender.

She turned and began walking back to the dining tent. "You should hurry up," she called over her shoulder. "It's all going to be gone by the time you get there."

"I'll be there in a minute," he replied. When he was sure that her back was turned away from him, he stared after her. His gaze slid from her to the tent, and then off to the side where he could see Wolf and Nadia standing and watching. He wondered how long they had been there. They certainly would have seen him talking to Rowan.

He ambled over to them, trying to look unruffled and unconcerned and certainly unaware of anyone who could be spying on them from the trees. He drew close to them and as soon as he was in earshot, Nadia hissed under her breath, "Our guards say there's someone out there."

"Looks like our plan may be working," Cade replied in a low, matter-of-fact voice. "It seems that Cira's spies may have stumbled onto our camp."

Wolf's eyes glittered as he gazed out over the clearing, his teeth baring ever so slightly into a cold, animal grimace.

Cade gave him a wary look. "We should, of course, give no indication that we are aware someone may be watching. We should continue on very much as usual."

Wolf's eyes flicked in his direction, to at least indicate that he had heard, but his entire body was tensed, rather like a horse about to bolt. Wolf's single-minded focus on his vow to kill Cira lent him a certain drive, a forward momentum that Cade could latch onto and use to his advantage. He wasn't ashamed of it; he and Wolf had an understanding. But there were times when he looked at the creature who used to be his friend, and wondered how in control he really was.

To settle him, Cade reached out a hand and touched his shoulder, and Wolf snapped to, his eyes darting coldly from the hand up to Cade's face.

"Relax," Cade murmured.

"What did Rowan want?" Nadia asked, her voice strained in its seeming nonchalance.

"She was calling me in to dinner," Cade said. "Have you eaten yet?"

"We were waiting for you," Nadia replied. Her eyes were sad.

"I didn't realize, I'm sorry," Cade apologized, distracted. He was looking past her into the gloom. After a moment he stirred. "Come on, let's go."

The three of them ducked into the dining tent, Cade keenly aware of the figure still moving among the trees.

The same evening, Tarr walked through the gaping hallways of the Two Falls headquarters, feeling newly hollow. The previous night's wounded were being tended to; guards had been stationed in larger numbers around the city, the walls were fortified, General Calchas and the troops he had taken were called back from the Meadows and their recruitment tour. They were on their way. He should feel comforted. He didn't.

Now that he had fully surveyed the damage, his thoughts—of Burlage, the lives that had been lost, the friends who had been taken— were coupled with a sneaking, shameful, desperate relief of having come through the night alive when he had been surrounded by so much death. He had met with those who had been injured in the raids, and they hadn't blamed him for any of it, which almost made him feel worse. No one knew that it had all been his fault.

As the day wore on, he faced the uncomfortable realization that he felt more pain for Archer's capture than Rane's. Logically, it was easy to understand: he was already so used to Rane's absence from his everyday life that coming to terms with the fact that she was now imprisoned in Faridor and on the brink of death was for him only a small (albeit unsettling) mental leap. But with Archer, the reality of his disappearance was painfully acute. All day, Tarr would come around a corner expecting to see his brother's black-tipped head poking up over a crowd of Striker guards, or imagining his voice echoing through one of the corridors behind him. Every time he entered his office he found it empty, Archer's long frame no longer slung across the vacant chair beside his desk, feet propped up on the corner of the windowsill, waiting for him.

He kept replaying those wild, confusing seconds in the moments before Archer was taken. He wished he had fought harder, refused to let Archer push him to safety in the cellar, stayed by his side as he should have. He found his mind falling into an endless loop, and over and over again had to shock himself out of it. He was wasting time. Instead, he tried to coalesce the thrum of his mind into a single purpose: getting Archer and Rane out of Faridor.

Marc found Tarr in his office some time after dinner. Ascertaining correctly that Tarr had been staring furiously and unproductively at the ceiling for a few hours, Marc declared that a change of scenery was in order and ushered him up and out of the office. They walked downstairs to sit at one of the empty tables in the great hall.

"Did you get any further with Si?" Tarr said wearily, leaning forward onto the table.

"Sort of," Marc shrugged. "Si kept saying that they were on their way, that they were nearly here. But I couldn't really get *who* he was talking about."

"Maybe it's a comet," Tarr said gloomily. "And tomorrow morning

Two Falls will just be a crater."

Marc smiled faintly. "Si would like that. He likes comets and things. He did tell me, though, before he went to sleep, that Archer and Rane are still alive. That they survived the day."

"I wish there was some way we could communicate with them," Tarr said abruptly. "Si can't *talk* to them, can he?"

Marc shook his head. "Not words, anyway."

"And yet he said he *called* whatever is coming towards us," Tarr rolled his eyes. "I'm never going to understand those powers of his."

"I don't think we're supposed to," Marc said gently. "Maybe it was hyperbole."

Tarr sighed and laid his head down on his folded arms. "Do you think we'll get them back?" he asked, his voice muffled.

"Yes," said Marc quietly. "But we need you here, Tarr. We need that mind of yours sharp."

"I feel like we've all unraveled," Tarr set his head against the heel of his hand and gazed thoughtfully at Marc. Marc's straw-colored hair was mussed, eyes calm and watchful, face split corner to corner by his white scar. "I can't think my way out of a hat box right now, Athela's blaming herself for losing Archer, Si's on another astral plane altogether, and Laith..." he trailed off, trying to find a way to articulate the dark dread he felt whenever he thought of the prince. "Marc, I'm afraid that Laith is going to..."

Marc's brow furrowed and then unclenched as Ari suddenly appeared beside them. He was breathless, and looked uncharacteristically ruffled. Tarr shot straight up, alarmed.

"What is it?" he demanded. "Another attack?"

Marc's hand automatically went to his belt, his broad shoulders tensing as though preparing for some sort of onslaught.

"No," Ari shook his head, and Tarr was shocked to see that he was nearly smiling. Nothing in their current situation merited any semblance of joy. "Everything is all right. Come with me."

Tarr and Marc exchanged bewildered looks, and both slowly stood, their speed picking up as they trailed in Ari's wake towards the front entrance of their headquarters. Tarr slowed as they approached, trying to puzzle out the scene that stood before him.

There was a group of twenty or so strange people standing before him in a group, looking around themselves as if impressed and a little overwhelmed by their surroundings. Many of them had their necks craned up and were peering at the domed ceiling above them. Tarr had expected to see someone he knew, so it confused him at first that they should all be unknown to him. And then after a few seconds—taking in their simple, earth-colored clothing, their tall, thin frames and draped traveling cloaks—it dawned on him.

He looked down beside him and saw that Marc was regarding them too with an interested, puzzled expression.

"Who are they?" Marc asked in a low voice. "Do you recognize them?"

Tarr smiled, feeling his heart growing lighter. "They're Ashans."

"What?" Marc said curiously.

"Ashans from the forest," Tarr's eyes felt hot.

Marc's ice-colored eyes widened, and Tarr could nearly see the dots connecting in his head. "You and Athela went to the Forest to try and recruit help..."

"Almost a year ago," Tarr nodded. "We didn't think any of them would actually come to help us." He straightened, looking at the group of Ashans before them. "But apparently we were wrong."

Tarr's heart was leaping for joy, not because of the added support—twenty or so fighters would realistically do very little to change the outcome of a battle—but because of the solid, inextricable link that they provided between Tarr and his home. He had been away for so long. He hadn't realized how much he missed it, how much he missed his own people, especially now that he felt so unmoored by his current situation. He felt like rushing up and embracing each one of them.

He took a step forward, and all of the heads turned towards him like a flock of birds, eyeing him up and down with a mixture of interest and reserve. "Welcome," he said in Ashan. "The Strikers welcome you to Two Falls."

Now that he was closer, his giddy brain leaped about trying to find anyone he recognized, trying to sort them into their respective tribes. Was there anyone from his home tribe of Aspen? His eyes scanned over each of the faces, and as he did he realized something: there was not one of them who could have been over thirty years of age. They were all so young.

"I am Mickela. The Ashans have come to fight alongside you," replied an Ashan towards the front, whom Tarr assumed to be their de facto leader. Tarr's ears perked with interest. They used a third form of the word *I* to indicate that they were neither male nor female. Furthermore, they must have been from one of the western tribes, for their accent sounded strange to him, more clipped and less lilting than Archer's now-familiar northern one. They had dark olive skin, and a face that was devoid of beauty but full of character. Their hair was close-cropped to their head, and they bore an air of natural authority. They glanced back at the relatively small group. "We are sorry, for we know the day is late and we are few."

"We are glad to have you here, I thank you," Tarr said, speaking slowly and carefully. He was using a very formal version of Ashan, the type used on ceremonial occasions or when greeting dignitaries from another tribe. He was quite rusty, as he never used this kind of address when he was chatting with Archer in their native tongue. It furthermore didn't help that over the years he and Archer had devolved into tossing Common words and phrases in to mix with the Ashan when they suited, a sort of hybridized bastardization that would have absolutely horrified Tarr's Ashan grammar teachers.

Squaring his shoulders and hoping he wasn't making too many obvious semantic errors, Tarr faced them anew. "Please, come with me and tell me how you came to be here."

As he spoke, he all at once saw a face in the back of a group that was so like Archer's that the shock nearly knocked him over. For a fleeting second, he thought it *must* be Archer, and that his brother had somehow escaped and returned to Two Falls, hiding himself in the group of Ashans as a joke. But as he stared, he realized that it wasn't Archer, but some sort of mirror image. A nearly identical face, golden eyes like an eagle's, and with hair the exact opposite of Archer's: black, with white tips at the ends, spiky and sticking out at all angles. Whoever this Ashan was, he and Archer had to be brothers, if not twins. *Archer never told me he had a twin*, Tarr realized with a sudden pang. Behind Archer's double was a woman who must also be from the northern

Birch tribe, strange and alien with skin almost pure white, long black hair that fell down her shoulder like the wing of a raven, and glittering eyes the color of emeralds.

Realizing that he'd been gawking at the northern Ashans for an uncomfortable amount of time, Tarr recovered himself and faced the group's leader again. "Please, come with me." He gestured with one arm. "Do all of you speak the Common tongue?" he asked politely, realizing that it would be easier for Marc and Ari if they were all communicating in the same language. All of the Strikers had a smattering of Ashan, which they used as code, but most of the others couldn't keep up with rapid conversation, and certainly not a formal version of Ashan.

"Our Northern siblings do not, but we can translate for them," replied Mickela, taking a step forward and motioning to the others.

"Come this way, please," Tarr gestured again, and the group trailed behind him as he led them to the same receiving room where they'd brought Rowan upon her arrival. By this point, word had apparently spread, and Striker guards were appearing out of hallways left and right to gawk at the group of Ashans.

Once gathered in the room, Tarr sent for water and invited them to sit, and dispatched guards to fetch Athela and Laith at once. The Ashans sat down awkwardly on the chairs (those from the far-away tribes after a great deal of curious inspection—chairs were a more foreign commodity the farther one got from Two Falls.)

"What is your tribe?" Tarr asked, as soon as they were settled. Athela and Laith had joined them silently, their eyes brimming with wonderment.

"Yew," the leader replied. This made sense. Tarr remembered vaguely that the "ck" sound was very popular over in Western tribes like the Yew.

"It's very nice to meet you," Tarr said courteously, and introduced the other Strikers. "Now," he said, leaning forward, "how did you come to be there?"

Tarr's guess had been right. The previous year, when they had still been living in the mountains, he and Athela had gone as emissaries to various Ashan tribes, asking for their help in fighting the war against Cira. They had met with the elder council members, who, one after another, had refused to help them. But all the while, apparently, the younger members of the tribe had been watching and listening. After a time, some of them began to talk amongst themselves and came to question the elders' decisions. As Mickela recounted it, they were all staunchly forbidden from leaving to participate in the war, which had put a stopper on more widespread efforts. But Mickela and others like them had refused to sit back. They and one other member of the Yew tribe had set out to see if there were any others who felt the same. It took a long time, and they were not always welcome. But enough young Ashans believed in the fight to risk being exiled. They formed a small group and made their way to Two Falls to see if they could be of service.

As Mickela unfolded their story, Tarr found his eyes searching hungrily over every inch of the Ashans before him, realizing how far away from them he had truly felt. There were some Ashans in Two Falls, of course, though many fewer since the war had broken out and many had been killed or fled. There were half-Ashans fighting for them, but even then it wasn't quite the same. There was an air about the Ashans from the forest, a sense of belonging, an air of being so specifically from another place, another time in Tarr's life. The collective memories that he shared with them were not of the war or who he had become over the intervening years, but rather who he had been before. There was something about the very particular lines of their faces and noses; even though they all came from different regions and different tribes, they shared a sort of deep-set commonality. Even small things struck him anew, like the familiar front drapes of their traveling cloaks, that particular gray-green color of the fabric achieved by using walnut hulls and blackberries. He suddenly remembered it all, watching groups of adults dyeing cloth by the river, helping to mash the berries with a rock, the stain lingering on his fingers for days afterwards. He glanced surreptitiously down at his own clothes, keenly aware of how different he must look to them, how like a citizen of Two Falls he was now in his black trousers and boots, his loose black shirt with silver embroidery at the collar.

He suddenly realized that one of the young female Ashans was staring at him, and after a few moments of puzzling, he realized with a jolt that he knew her. It was none other than his friend Juniper from his home tribe, the Aspen, with whom he'd used to climb trees and stalk birds. As he looked at her with fresh eyes, he wondered why he hadn't recognized her before. She didn't look quite so different; just taller, more mature, more grown-up. She met his stare and smiled, a familiar sort of silent greeting, private between just the two of them. The exchange did not go unnoticed by Athela, who arched one dark eyebrow in an unspoken question. Tarr gave her a quick, dismissive smile.

By this point, Mickela had finished speaking. "We're grateful you are here," Athela told them. "More grateful than I think we can say."

"I know there aren't many of us," Mickela said again. "But we are here to help."

Laith thanked them, too, and Athela began to ask questions about the journey and the route they had taken. Tarr's mind was drifting again, back to his days in the forest with Juniper. They had raced together, up one tree and down the other, swift and sure as two small squirrels, darting from one branch to the next. He could remember those days, remember how sure he'd felt up there in the trees. He hadn't climbed anything in a long time, he thought ruefully. Everyone outside the forest—humans, half-Ashans, everyone—kept their feet solidly, infuriatingly, on the ground. *I've been a fool,* he chided himself. *I'm an Ashan. I'm meant to climb.*

The world seemed to pause as Tarr inhaled sharply. He'd been so distracted by the shock of the Ashans' arrival that he hadn't put the pieces together.

Help is coming, Si had said.

To get us through the wall? Tarr had asked him.

No.

To climb over it.

A broad, calculating smile spread across his face, a devilish glint winking in his green eye. His heart began to beat faster and he leaned forward in his chair, feeling his face come alight. The others looked at him curiously, and then some of them began to smile, too, almost as if in reaction to Tarr's infectious smile.

"As it happens," Tarr said slowly, "we have ourselves a small problem."

Mickela was smiling warily at him, as if wondering what was about to come around the corner at them. "Oh, yes? And what is that?"

"We have a wall that needs to be climbed," Tarr told them, now grinning outright.

Mickela studied him for a few moments, thinking. "The wall at Faridor?"

"Yes. Stone. Almost no holds. Quite high, quite slippery. Guards at the top."

Now, Mickela smiled too. "Sounds like fun."

"Wait a minute," Laith cut in, raising one hand. "I agree that this may be the best chance we've got, but this would mean placing the twenty-odd of you at the direct head of an army. In the first line of fire."

Mickela swiveled a cool gaze onto Laith. "We did not come all this way to hide in the back," they said. "If this is what needs to be done, then this is what we will do."

"We can't take the wall with twenty," Marc shook his head. "Can't be done."

"Where twenty go, they can make a path for others to follow," said Laith, frowning. Tarr could tell that the idea was growing on him. It felt good to see Laith engaging with them once again. "Can you get me up the wall with you?" he asked Mickela.

They studied him thoughtfully. "Yes. If we move fast."

"If you can get me onto that wall, we'll take it. We'll hold it," Laith said simply, and looked over to Tarr. "And we'll open the gate for the rest."

Mickela studied him thoughtfully, and Tarr could see that they were trying to decide whether to take him seriously or not. To anyone else it may have sounded like profound, possibly catastrophic hubris. He wondered whether stories of the prince's fighting prowess had reached the western Ashan tribes. He highly doubted it. He managed to catch Mickela's eye and give them a tiny nod. Laith was right: if they could somehow manage to get him up onto the wall with the other Ashans, they stood a much greater chance of being able to hold the wall and open the gate before Cira's troops were able to rally together. There was no one who could match Laith.

"It would all need to be very fast," Athela pointed out. "The only chance we've got is if we catch them unawares. If they can't see us coming."

"But how do we spring the trap?" Laith pressed. "Even trying to get twenty Ashans across the open field and across the bridge would be impossible. We need some sort of cover."

Tarr racked his brain. *Cover*. It snapped into place. "We use the bridge," Tarr said suddenly. "We use the bridge as cover. Creep our first wave in a bit at a time and have them take shelter *underneath* the bridge, in the support beams. They can gather under cover of darkness, cross beneath the bridge, and wait to strike when we're ready."

The Ashans, who had barely had time to take off their traveling cloaks, much less be briefed on the layout of Faridor island or on battle tactics, were now watching this quick, back-and-forth exchange as though it were a fencing match.

"You can't hide our whole army under the bridge," Athela maintained.

"But you *can* hide twenty fighters. And if they take the wall and get the gate open, we have a chance to get the rest in."

"The rest...who will have been *where*, exactly, in this scenario?" Marc asked.

"The trees," Laith interjected, cutting Tarr off. They were on the same page, he could tell, and their momentum was growing. "Take the army out of Two Falls and hide them just beyond the border of the trees. Then, when the gate is open, we make a run for it across the open plain and across the bridge."

"Going to have to be a pretty fast run," Marc muttered, mostly to himself.

"Athela," Tarr said, turning to her. "You're good at going fast. Think you can do it?"

"We need a foot to catch the door and wedge it open," Laith chimed in.

Athela looked between the two of them and nodded. "We can do it. Fast as we can. We'll catch the gate open before they can close it again. I promise."

Ari, who had been silent this entire time, cleared his throat. "Won't Cira and her troops be alerted once you move the army out of Two Falls?"

This stopped the momentum for a moment. Tarr thought to himself. "We'll have to make it look like it's part of our plan to attack from the sea. Remember, if we've played our cards right she thinks we're attacking by boat. If we can reinforce that idea, we can hopefully reinforce her decision to turn the guns out to sea. We'll take the army out of Two Falls' east gate and then under cover of darkness we go north and get them in place."

"Not to put a damper on everything," Ari continued, and Tarr couldn't help but sigh inwardly, "But we likely won't even know whether the guns *have* been turned out until the last minute."

"Probably not," Tarr agreed reluctantly.

"Post a spy," Laith said. "Near Faridor. Tell them to let us know the instant the guns are turned."

"And if they still aren't turned?" Ari pressed. "If Cira doesn't fall for it?"

Silence fell. No one had an answer for that. Still, it was the makings of a plan, a plan that they desperately needed—time was ticking inexorably past; Tarr was acutely aware of each lost instant.

"When does Calchas get back to Two Falls with his army?" he asked Laith.

"Tomorrow," Laith replied.

"Then we'll give it three days," he said. "Three days. And then we set out for Faridor. We attack. And we end this."

The room was silent. *Three days.* Even to Tarr, who had said the words confidently, almost with braggadocio, was shocked at how soon it sounded.

"Erm...*three* days?" Athela asked tentatively.

"We're not ready," Ari shook his head.

"It's not enough time," Athela protested.

"Do we want to gamble for more?" Tarr asked, with a pointed look reminding her that she'd been the impatient one only a short while ago. Athela studied him for a moment and then silently shook her head.

"If I may..." Mickela spoke up for the first time in a long while, "We didn't follow all of that. Please, can you explain?"

Tarr laughed and waved his hand. "Of course. We're being terrible hosts. You all are tired. We'll show you to your rooms and let you get some rest, and then we will talk about all of these things in more detail."

"Come with me," Ari said gallantly.

They all rose, and Tarr could see Juniper starting towards him with a smile on her face, but she was pulled to the side by Mickela, who began speaking to her in rapid, authoritative Ashan, relaying orders about who was to bunk with whom. Juniper listened, nodding occasionally, still watching Tarr out of the corner of her eye.

Tarr swiveled his attention from her to the Ashan with black hair, the one who could almost have been a carbon copy of Archer. He was hanging back and, under the guise of stuffing something in his cloth knapsack, was stealing furtive glances at Tarr. He looked so like Archer that Tarr had to keep holding himself back from rushing over and embracing him in relief.

Tarr came up beside him and said in Ashan, "You are from the Birch tribe?"

Archer's copy straightened. "Yes," he said, in a voice uncannily the same as Archer's. "My name is Jet."

"You look..." Tarr swallowed. "You resemble my brother Archer." *An understatement if ever there was one,* he thought.

Jet regarded him. "Many years ago, I was his brother. Before his exile. We are twins."

The words that he used for *brother* and *twin* had a much more nuanced meaning in Ashan, with no real translation to the common tongue. Because of the way in which Ashans chose their family units, there were two words for "brother": one that literally translated to "brother of the bone," someone with a physical and genetic relation, and another that meant "brother of the spirit," or the one an Ashan *chose* to be their brother. In Archer's case, Jet was the former and Tarr the latter. Tarr also smiled a bit to himself at the word for "twin," which in its literal translation was "brother of the shared darkness," which he'd always thought was a rather poetic way of putting it.

In any case, this amount of information Tarr already had put together on his own; Jet could not have been anyone other than Archer's twin. It was funny, though, to hear such a familiar voice—the same timbre, the same lilting accent—come out of such a familiar face, and yet at the same time he *wasn't* Archer. The playful ironic glint wasn't there, the easygoing warmth. His twin was much more reserved.

Jet looked at Tarr with fresh interest. "You are his brother-of-the-spirit?" he asked.

"Yes," said Tarr proudly. Jet's yellow eyes flicked down to the back of Tarr's collar, where the tattoo he shared with his brother peeked out around the nape of his neck. The two of them sat there for a moment, unsure of what to say. Technically, their shared relationships with Archer—especially since Archer had been exiled from his tribe and struck from all ties to them—were nonexistent. Jet shouldn't even technically have referred to Archer as his brother. And yet, Tarr could feel something there between them.

"Why did you come?" Tarr asked. "If Archer was exiled? Surely you did not come for him. He left the tribe many years ago."

"I am different," Jet shrugged. By now, they were lagging behind the others and began to walk slowly to catch up, lest they be left behind. "I do not believe that exile is a good thing. I do not agree with the decision to cast out members of a tribe."

This, Tarr knew, was tantamount to high treason in a tribe as remote and conservative as the Birch. "You have said this to the elder council?"

Jet shrugged. "I have said so, and the elder council has punished me for it. They do not agree with my sister's" (here, he used the word for "sister-of-the-spirit", and gave a nod towards the retreating back of the young Ashan Birch woman about ten feet in front of them) "and my decision to come here and fight. But I am not alone in the way that I think. And someday they will be gone, and *we* will be the elders." He shrugged again. "It will not be so forever. If it should change, if it is the right thing, it will change."

Tarr smiled softly, mostly to himself. "Yes, I think so," he agreed quietly. Jet's unflappable stoicism reminded him in some ways of Ari. He might not be Archer, but Tarr still found that he liked him.

The Strikers ushered their guests to a suite of rooms on one of the upper south floors and bade them goodnight. By this time, it was quite late. Tarr and his friends found themselves alone at the top of a large stairwell that wound down to the entrance hall, and stood there for some time, not moving and not speaking. There was the dim buzz of conversation from a couple of Striker guards down in the hall, and a lower rumble of voices from below them in the barracks. Otherwise, everything was still.

In unison, Marc and Athela turned to Tarr. "Does Archer have a twin?" they chorused.

"Apparently so," Tarr shrugged.

Athela shook her head in frank astonishment. "I thought I was dreaming for a minute," she said in a low voice, and Tarr could hear the wistfulness in it. For a split second, she had also believed that Archer had somehow returned to them.

Tarr gave a brief summary of his exchange with Jet. Then, preemptively, he explained how Mickela had identified themself and the way they should be properly addressed. "Ashans like Mickela usually serve important leadership roles when they come of age," he told them, feeling rather like he was giving an introductory seminar on Ashan culture. "It would have been a great loss to the tribe for them to leave and come here."

His friends had listened to all this with interest. "We have something similar back home," Laith said thoughtfully. "There's a special division of the Jelani cavalry called the Third. Very elite."

"Speaking of which..." Athela segued doggedly, widening her eyes in Tarr's direction. "Three days, huh?"

Tarr chuckled and shrugged. "Now or never," he said.

"It'll be a full moon," Laith pointed out. "Harder for us."

"Can't be helped," Tarr said grimly. "We don't have time to wait."

Athela tucked a runaway curl of black hair behind her ear and tilted her head to one side. "We've got a lot to do. Do you really think it will work?"

In a chorus, all heads turned back to Tarr. He felt the tension in his chest build, the pressure of everything to come. He shrugged.

"It has to," he said.

CHAPTER TWENTY-TWO

The next days passed in a blur. Tarr barely had time to blink, much less breathe. Calchas and his troops arrived, the Ashans were looped into the planning they had done, everything was abuzz. Tarr didn't have time to worry about whether or not any spies from Faridor would see their preparations and go report them to Cira. He assumed that they already had. They wouldn't have the advantage of complete surprise, but he hoped against hope that they had done enough to convince her they were headed east for the coast and could trick her into facing the guns out towards the ocean. For good measure, he had sent out a new contract to a shipbuilder in Eldrest, requesting to buy a few larger transports in the interest of moving their horses a short way up the coast. Tarr prayed that it would be intercepted.

Any time he even considered the possibility of rest, he was galvanized forward by the thought of Rane and Archer. By Si's account, the two of them were still alive, though Tarr could not be sure of what state they were in. He was surprised that Archer had been kept alive as long as he had, but was little comforted by the knowledge that the only reason Cira would have kept him alive so long was to either torture him for her own amusement or to try and extract information out of him. Tarr knew better than to think that Archer would give up any sort of critical information; he was too bullheaded for that. Tarr found himself torn between gratitude for Archer still being alive and worry about the state they'd find him in if they managed to storm the castle and break him out.

Rane was a different matter. Her success as a spy was deeply entrenched in the fact that everyone who met her (Tarr excepted, of course) seemed to overlook her. She was constantly underestimated. So Tarr hoped with every fiber of his being that that would continue to be the case. He prayed that Cira would take her and forget about her, or be so distracted by the capture of Archer that Rane would cease to be of interest. If they could just hold on a while longer, if only they knew that the others were coming for them...

And then, before he knew it, the three days were up and it was time to move out. They planned to leave after nightfall, with enough troops remaining in the city to quell any skirmishes, should Cira's loyalists seize the opportunity to try and start trouble while most of the Strikers were gone. They were to leave Two Falls and ride east for a few hours to meet with Cade and the company he had taken to build their imaginary fleet of boats in the forests just off the coast.

From there, they would divide up and move under cover of the night to take their places for the battle to come. Athela and Marc would lead the cavalry and footsoldiers to hide in the woods across the open plain from Faridor; Laith and the Ashans would creep down the coast to take their places under Faridor's bridge until it was time to strike. And it had been decided that Si, Tarr, and Ari would split off from Laith and the Ashans and swim for the cove at the base of Faridor, and through there attempt to reach Cira in her tower.

Marc had protested mightily, strongly petitioning to be the one to accompany Tarr and Si into Faridor, but the truth was they needed him on the front lines since he'd had active military experience. And as Laith had gently pointed out, Marc was not a terribly strong swimmer. So Ari had been chosen to go instead.

Tarr hoped with everything in him that the plan would work. He hoped that the guns would be turned in time.

The afternoon before they moved out, the entire headquarters was a flurry of activity. The council, with Pieter at their head, had fully taken all responsibilities for governing the city (*and good luck with it*, Tarr thought snarkily). Athela was out in one of the training arenas in the stable complex, choosing riders to go alongside her in the first charge to try to reach Faridor's gate. Ari, Laith, and Marc were with General Calchas going over drills and formations with the footsoldiers. Swords were sharpened and passed out, and there was constant clanging from the blacksmiths over in the stables and at the armory. Striker guards were being outfitted with armor; every tailor and seamstress in the city was dyeing fabric and sewing cloaks. Tarr tried not to look at the brave young faces of the new recruits, tried not to imagine how many of them would fall in the battle. He smiled at them when they passed, watching as they tried on their helmets, staring out at the world for the first time from within the shell of cold, dark metal.

For a time, he pored over Faridor's blueprints, trying to map out the best route to get up to Cira's tower, where he was sure she would have barricaded herself. It was mostly an exercise to take his mind off everything that was happening around him; the inextricable link between Si and Cira was sure to pull them in the right way. So he let his mind turn over the plan they had concocted: the hidden Ashans beneath the bridge, the army rushing the fortress from the cover of the trees. He was by no means a tactical expert, and there was so much that could go wrong.

Laith had relayed their plans to General Calchas, who had by far the most combat experience amongst them, but the General had for the most part merely listened and nodded. For the past forty years, Calchas had had the advantage of leading a command in a time of relative peace; their campaigns in the Meadows were mostly training missions and exploratory campaigns, with the odd skirmish here and there, small battles that were put down in a day or two: the perfect way to train young soldiers. There had not been anything of this scale, no outright siege on a fortress of Faridor's magnitude—not in his lifetime, at least. He had made some helpful suggestions as to the formation of the army, and the avenues that they should take when (and if) they were able to get their forces through the main gate and into the fortress. Tarr had been half-wishing for, half-dreading a scenario in which Calchas would take a single look at the plans laid before him and laugh, telling them that they were going about it all wrong and that the plan was sure to fail, that they had to do things a different way. But he hadn't. So there they were: the plan was set and all there was left to do was hope.

Their Ashan visitors had been welcomed with curious, reserved courtesy by the rest of the Striker guards, who regarded them with interest and a little distance. It was rare to encounter Ashans in Two Falls who had not, in one way or another, been cast out from their tribes like Archer, left on their own accord and assimilated, or been temporarily sent out as Tarr had. Most of those currently serving in the Striker guards were half-Ashans who had been raised in the city and had managed to avoid capture during the first raids after Cira had seized control. Tribal Ashans straight from the forest were a rarity, and Tarr could see the others watching them with interest, taking in their mannerisms, the food they ate, the clothes and weapons they bore.

For the first day or two they'd been so consumed with the first flurries of preparation that Tarr hadn't had a chance to talk with Juniper. He got the sense that she'd been trying to hang about and seize a moment with him, but the timing didn't match up until the afternoon of the second day. Tarr was walking back from an impromptu meeting across town with the remaining members of the Two Falls council, informing them of the Strikers' current plans to move out to the coast and meet up with the shipbuilding contingent—though after Burlage's betrayal Tarr was too careful and too paranoid to tell any of them the real plan. It had been a strange experience, meeting with them, conscious all the while of Minister Burlage's absence, the empty chair at the table. He found himself wrestling still with the fact that he felt more guilty for his lack of guilt than for the actual actions he'd taken. None of the others (Laith excepted) suspected him, he knew that much. He guessed that the other council members didn't believe that he'd have it in him to do such a thing. *Well, they're wrong*, Tarr thought to himself hollowly. He hunched his shoulders with his hands in his pockets, walking a few feet ahead of the two bodyguards who had been assigned to accompany him through the streets from the council's temporary meeting place. *I had it in me all along. I'd told Archer I never wanted to kill anyone. I thought I could be different. But here I am, and I'm just the same as all the others.*

When they approached the Two Falls headquarters, he again could hear the ringing of the hammers in the forge, and the neighing of horses from the stables. A small group of Striker trainees ran by in formation, led by Marc, who gave Tarr a small wink as they passed. And then, as Tarr approached the front steps of the headquarters, he saw Juniper, sitting with an air of nervous excitement near the front door. She jumped to her feet as he came near. He wondered how long she'd been there.

"Hello," she greeted him in Common as he approached. Her accent was broad and southern, the same as his.

Tarr smiled in greeting and waved his bodyguards off. As soon as they had gone, he turned back to Juniper and motioned her to join him. For a moment, she raised her hand, and Tarr could see that she was about to give him the traditional Ashan greeting; she clasped her hand over the tattoo on his neck. But then she faltered, and Tarr could almost read the reason on her face: she must have heard that his family tattoo bore the emblem of Archer, an Ashan exile. By law, she was therefore forbidden to touch it in greeting. For all her tribal disobedience in leaving the Aspen to fight alongside the Strikers, the laws against exiles were so ingrained that even she couldn't shake them off. Tarr suddenly felt a surge of distaste and straightened, turning away before she could make any further movement towards him. "Let's walk, shall we?" he suggested, hoping his voice sounded kinder than he felt.

And walk they did. They went around the side of the headquarters, to the back area where the blacksmiths were working. They wandered too close, and the incessant clanging became too loud, so they found themselves turning away towards the stables where they began strolling up and down the rows of stalls. Many of the stalls were empty but here and there an inquisitive equine head popped out, ears pricked. Tarr could sense from the way that Juniper dodged the heads when they came out for inspection that she was rather leery of the animals. It made sense; Ashans had little use for horses, living in the forest the way they did. He had once felt the same.

All this while they had said almost nothing to one another. Objectively, Tarr found himself marveling at how unnecessarily awkward the whole thing felt. Here was a person with whom he'd spent more time in his life than even Archer or Rane, but he could barely think of what to say to her or how to say it.

"How are things back…" he nearly said the word 'home,' but it didn't quite feel right in his mouth. Luckily, he didn't have to try and grope for a simile, for Juniper relaxed, as if relieved to have some sort of conversational strand to grasp onto.

"Things are good," she said. "Much the same as before you left. Some of the elders have passed and been replaced."

"Tell me," Tarr encouraged her.

Juniper began to tell him stories of home. The river near the tribe's main camp had flooded over the winter, and they'd had to move a few of the lower-set village buildings to higher ground. Juniper had adapted to life with her chosen family well; she showed Tarr the tattoo on the nape of her neck with a rather bashful smile. Tarr could see that she wanted to bring up the fact of his being sent away, but he demurred, instead prodding her for more information about the other tribe members: what they were doing, marriages, births, deaths. The Speaker, the village elder who had made the decision for Tarr to be sent away, had died. Tarr digested that news and felt curiously empty. The person who had irrevocably altered the course of his life was gone, as quickly and without fanfare as a leaf blowing away in the wind. Any anger or resentment or hurt Tarr may have felt towards him was gone, too, the object of its focus dissolved.

As she talked, he felt himself being transported back to the quiet of the woods, the waving boughs overhead, long summers spent climbing trees and chasing each other up one bending branch and sliding down another. The dew glittered on every leaf and bough in the spring mornings, so brilliant and dazzling it hurt his eyes. Frost spread across the fallen trunks in winter, delicate and fragile, shattering with a single touch. Again, he could hear the sounds of the sliding doors shutting, the golden filter of light filling the rooms of his house. He was an adult now with responsibilities if he returned, and he would be expected to pull his weight in the tribe rather than running around the treetops all day. But as Juniper spoke, his former life bloomed more vividly before him than it had in years.

It was some moments before Tarr realized that Juniper had stopped talking. He regarded her thoughtfully, as he had the night the Ashans had all arrived, trying to match the young woman before him to his memory of the girl with whom he had grown up. It was the same face as before, the same merry pair of gray-green eyes, dark bark-colored hair just like his, brown skin like his. His eyes traveled down to her hands, each with six fingers, casually hanging by her sides. He unconsciously flexed his left hand and thrust it deep into his pocket.

"Many of the others asked me about coming to see you," Juniper said. "Our friends. They wondered if you'd be much changed. We were all so surprised when you didn't return after the year was up."

"I had a lot to do," Tarr said a bit tiredly.

"We thought you'd come home," Juniper pressed him.

Tarr shrugged. He didn't know what to say. Juniper had the innate confident glow of someone who had been accepted since the day they were born, who never had to question herself or her place in the world or the part she was intended to play. She had never felt as though she'd lost agency over the course of her own life, had never had to fight to take back that control one desperate handhold at a time. She trusted others implicitly, Tarr could see, and why would she not? How on earth could Tarr make her understand, standing there awkwardly beside a puddle in the middle of the stableyard?

"Did you really become *brothers-of-the-spirit* with the Birch exile?" she asked curiously, her eyes flicking to the nape of his neck. "The *bone-brother* of the one who came with us?" Tarr began to wonder whether Juniper's true intention in coming to aid the Strikers was motivated by belief in their cause, or whether she had come out of sheer curiosity to investigate him and the apparent legends that had grown around him.

By way of reply, Tarr reached up and pulled down the nape of his collar, fully revealing the tattoo of the two leaves joined together, birch and aspen. Juniper's eyes grew larger as she studied it, and she rubbed the heel of her hand against her cheekbone, a dark smattering of freckles beneath. "There are stories, you know, that have made their way back to the forest. About you."

"Oh?" The notion was profoundly uninteresting to him. Juniper seemed to sense it and backed off her line of questioning.

"Why didn't you come back?" she asked outright. Her tone had changed. The light, conversational, friendly-gossiping chitchat was gone. Her gray-green eyes were flinty, trained on his face. *There we have it*, Tarr thought to himself. *I'll try to cobble together some sort of response that will have made this voyage worth your while, though I don't guarantee anything.* "Why didn't you?" she asked again into his silence. "You weren't exiled like your brother was. Many members of the tribe have been sent out and come back to be great leaders. You could have done the same. Why?"

Tarr tried to think of some way to explain it. Her face was so sweet, so disarming in its earnestness, that he didn't want to say anything that would disillusion her. "I had to stay," he faltered. "And help. They needed help."

Juniper looked even more puzzled. "You were chosen to fight?"

Tarr's mind flashed suddenly back to that day, standing there with Wolver at his side, Laith on his black horse like an apparition, and felt the same echoed surge of apprehension as he remembered it. *It wasn't supposed to be me, they got the wrong person.* Trying to explain the mistake to Laith and the others, the way they waved him aside and took him with them anyway. How he'd again tried to leave, how Archer had convinced him to stay. "No," he said finally. " I wasn't chosen. I was never chosen. I'm not a fighter. But I've done the best I can." *And failed*, he thought dully. *But I'm trying to redeem myself.*

"But once this war is over," she persisted, still not quite understanding him, "you will return to the forest? Your role here will be done."

Tarr turned away from her. It was almost as though they were speaking different languages. "What about you?" he said suddenly, swinging back around to her. "Aren't all of you risking exile by coming to help? What about the Ashan laws of fighting and killing, aren't you disobeying those?"

Juniper blinked her eyes, as if surprised to find herself suddenly on the opposite end of the interrogation. "I believe that it is the right thing to do," she said stubbornly, and Tarr saw in a flash that she still had a habit of almost childishly jutting her lower lip out when she was trying to argue her point. He tried not to smile at the sight of such a familiar mannerism. "I wanted to come here. I made my case to my family. They understood. I spoke, too, with the council elders before I left and if I return—" the 'if' hung between them for a breath, "—then

I will argue my right to them." She looked a tad guilty for a moment, and Tarr knew he'd been correct, that much of her motivation in coming to Two Falls had been to find him again. He let it pass.

"And you think you are willing to fight? To kill?" he asked. "Those laws are forbidden to the Ashans."

"'The Ashans'?" Juniper mimicked. "Who do you think *you* are, Tarr?"

Tarr remained silent and looked down at the toe of his boot.

"We are permitted to fight, to kill if need be, to protect ourselves, our families and our tribe," she said sternly, quoting word-for-word the Aspen law. "So that is what I am doing. I believe that our people are under attack, and I am trying to protect them. It is the natural thing to do, the *right* thing to do. I am obeying Ashan law."

Tarr's mind immediately flew to Burlage, the order he'd given, the life he'd taken. He hadn't even had the courage to do it with his own two hands, as Juniper was prepared to do. He stared at Juniper for a long time, that jutting lower lip, the fire in her eyes, how *certain* she was that everything she was doing, every choice she had made and was prepared to make was the right thing to do. She seemed as though she were from a completely separate planet. *I must have been like her at some point*, Tarr thought to himself, but couldn't remember when that would have been. They were the same age; she made him feel ancient.

Juniper was looking at him thoughtfully now, as if trying to read what was going on inside his head. "If you have killed," she said slowly, and Tarr's head snapped up, "I am sure that it was for these things as well," she said. "To protect your family."

No, Tarr thought coldly. *It was revenge. It was boiling, furious revenge, completely devoid of any sense of honor. And it felt wonderful.*

She reached out and touched his arm, and the touch of her hand made him flinch so badly that she immediately drew back. Her eyes fastened on his left hand, at the nub where his sixth finger used to be. Tarr could see the shock and knee-jerk revulsion flit across her face, then immediately, a wave of pity and concern spread across her as she looked back up to him. He couldn't stand it.

She tilted her head to one side, care and sympathy emanating from her, misreading him more and more by the second. "The elders would understand what you've been through. What you've done," she said, and he could hear the raw emotion in her voice.

Want to bet? he thought wryly.

"You would be welcomed back, I am sure of it. There are many who would speak for you. You have acted with honor and nobility, and you do credit to your people."

Tarr could see that she honestly believed it, believed that he was a good and noble person, that her words could forge some sort of bridge between them and enable him to come home. He could see the way he looked through her eyes—young, intelligent, unjustly cast out from his tribe, someone who picked himself up and became a hero in the most unlikely of circumstances. He suddenly wished that neither she nor the other Ashans had ever come to Two Falls. It was all he could do not to turn and walk away from her without another word.

You do credit to your people. It almost made him laugh.

"It's good to see you again," he lied, forcing a smile, trying to think of some mundane way to fill the awkward chasm between them. He turned away again and began twiddling the nose of a nearby horse with the tips of his fingers. The horse gave a few halfhearted attempts at lipping his hand, then snorted with boredom and retreated to the dim, musty warmth of its stall. Juniper eyed the horse with a healthy dose of suspicion and took a tentative step closer.

All of a sudden, Tarr wanted to get as far away from her as possible. He wasn't much of an actor, and he wasn't sure how convincing he'd be, but he straightened and widened his eyes, as if he'd remembered something.

"What is it?" Juniper asked.

"I just remembered I was supposed to have a briefing session right now with Ari and some of the others," he lied swiftly. "I'm late as it is."

"You'd better go," Juniper looked disappointed, but tried to mask it.

"Thanks," Tarr gave her what he hoped looked like a grateful smile and began to speed-walk away. He chanced only a small glance back at her over his retreating shoulder and saw her standing alone, her arms folded across her chest, looking warily at the row of horses. He continued walking, his speed increasing by the second until he was half-running away with absolutely no destination in mind.

Athela was standing in her stirrups, balancing over Aria's withers as the horse ran in place beneath her. His neck was pulled tight into a curving arc, and he tossed his head when he could and tried to bolt at every opportunity. The horse's black mane fell over Athela's hands, knotted in the reins and resting on his neck. Athela stood cool and collected, still as a bird resting on a swaying branch. Her gray eyes followed the riders circling her around the ring of the little warmup arena behind the stables. It was a group of ten or so, all new recruits, each vying for a place to ride beside her in the charge towards Faridor.

The night before, all the recruits she'd taught had found her in one of the headquarters' offices. She'd watched in astonishment as they filed in, shoulder to shoulder as they jostled for space. Then, one of her oldest students—clearly designated as the spokesperson of the group—had asked that they all be given the chance to ride alongside her into battle. She had stared around at them, her eyes wide, not sure whether to laugh or start weeping. Their faces, down to the last one, had been set, determined. They would not take the answer "no" lightly.

Athela had suddenly become fully aware of how the world around her had shifted. This group wanted to follow *her*. Not Marc, not Ari, not even Laith. For the first time, she saw herself as if through their eyes: not some cast-aside, unwanted daughter, not a sharp-tongued, abrasive misanthrope, but a teacher. A mentor. Someone worthy of leading them into battle. Someone they trusted with their lives.

Moved though she was, Athela wasn't about to sign the death warrants of so many young recruits. She'd informed them calmly that they were welcome to try for a place in the first wave, but would have to demonstrate their riding prowess to do so. And so she found herself in the training arena the next day, watching as wave after wave of recruits came through on their horses, focusing hard on keeping their heels down and their hands quiet, their seats steady. Athela was filled with pride as she watched them.

Sensing that her horse Aria would soon spontaneously combust, she loosed the reins a bit and gave him room enough to take off at a jittery canter, fighting her each step of the way. They fell alongside the pack of recruits; the student nearest Athela shot her a nervous smile before returning her concentration fully on keeping her seat. Aria pinned back his ears and sneered at the other horses, clearly calculating the best angle to land a bite; Athela twitched his head away and loosed the rein some more, speeding up ever so slightly and inviting the others to join her at the faster pace. Her mass of dark curls had been pinned up into a haphazard mass at the top of her head; a few strands began to tumble down her back and over her ears. For a brief second, as the group of horses sped around the arena, Athela felt just as she had when she was a little girl and had fled the aggression and cruelty of the palace to lose herself racing across an open field. For a moment, she forgot about Archer sitting in the Faridor dungeons, the upcoming battle, the lives and the country's future on the line. She enjoyed the speed, enjoyed the way Aria kept fighting, pushing against her grip on the bit, wanting to be allowed to break free and run as fast as he possibly could.

A quick glance to her right, though, showed her that some of her students were starting to look anxious at the speed they were going, so she reined Aria in and signaled for the others to slow. Her horse shook his head violently in protest as he reluctantly slowed the pace, and out of pure spite snapped at the neck of the horse beside him, who squealed a bit at and rammed his hindquarters into Aria's.

"Hold him steady," Athela instructed calmly; the girl on the neighboring horse looked absolutely petrified and had taken a huge hunk of mane in her hands, her face white. "He's all right," Athela said soothingly. "Aria's a bully, I've got him."

The girl attempted a smile, which somehow made her look even worse, but after another uneventful ten seconds, the group had slowed to a walk (all except Aria, who was performing a dramatic series of half-rears almost in place.)

"I'm sorry," said the girl who'd been riding beside Athela. She looked a bit dejected, as if she'd already failed.

"Don't be, you did great," Athela assured her. "You held on, you held your horse steady even when there was a distraction. That was well done."

The girl brightened and beamed. The other recruits pulled their horses into a line at the center of the arena, and Athela dismounted, keeping Aria's head at arm's length as the horse danced around her, trying to edge away.

"*Cool* it," she told him, elbowing him none too gently in the shoulder. He finally came to an irritated standstill with a sour look on his face and occasionally pinned back his ears to leer at the other horses. Athela gave his glossy, sweaty gray neck an affectionate pat and looked around at the recruits, all of whom were eyeing Aria with looks of fear and distrust.

"You all did very well," she told them. "You have made great improvements since you began. You three," she pointed to two at the left end of the line, and one in the middle. "You will ride with me in the battle." The three she'd selected were natural riders, calm and collected, and hadn't been ruffled even when Aria had joined them.

The chosen recruits smiled and nodded, looking satisfied, while the others looked crestfallen. Athela felt for them; she'd been in their position more times than she could count. She tried to think of the words she'd have wanted to hear when she was dealt a disappointment like this.

"Look," she said, clearing her throat and digging the scuffed, worn toe of her leather boot in the dirt of the arena, "It means more to me than I can...er...say, that you all want to ride with me. All of you should know that. Just because you weren't selected to be a part of the advance guard doesn't mean you don't have an important role. We need each and every one of you. And even if you don't ride in the charge, I'll want you to come find me and fight alongside me during the battle itself. Does that sound good?"

The recruits' faces brightened at this, and they nodded, looking slightly less downhearted.

"Good," Athela said finally. "Walk your horses around and cool them off, then I want them bathed, cleaned and ready to move out by sundown."

The recruits dismounted, and Athela began to lead Aria behind her towards the gate of the arena. She could see (but pretended not to notice) that a few other Striker guards and recruits had gathered by the arena walls and had been watching.

"Is Aria the fastest horse in the country?" a young man asked her curiously as she passed. He was perched on the side of the gate, lightly, rather like a bird.

Athela glanced up at Aria, who was looking at the young man with a bright-eyed interest that indicated he was trying to calculate whether he'd be able to land a bite before Athela pulled him back. "He'd certainly like to think so," she said.

"I think he is," the young man said thoughtfully, and at once she recognized him as part of the group that had been riding with her the morning they'd spotted Laith leaving Tess's apartment. He had dark skin and black hair that puffed up above his head like a cloud, and his eyes saw everything that passed before them. He reminded Athela of Tarr in that way.

He hopped off the gate and opened it for her as she passed. "Can I pet him?" he asked.

Athela turned to stare at him. Aria's "charms," such as they were, were generally lost on anyone who wasn't her; people liked to keep at least a ten foot distance from him. No one in Aria's entire natural life had ever expressed a desire to "pet" him. "You can try," she said dubiously, liking the young man instantly.

The boy sized Aria up and bravely stepped forward, placing a hand on Aria's dappled gray shoulder. Aria's ears went up and he looked around, as if wondering who this person was who dared to touch him. For a split second he was still.

"He's quite soft," the young man observed, stepping back with relief on his face, clearly pleased that he'd survived the encounter.

"Good oats," Athela agreed. "And oil."

The youth, who had to have been around fourteen, fell into a natural step alongside her as they headed back to the stable. Athela didn't mind; anyone who was willing to talk about equine nutrition was all right in her book.

"You and Aria are not just *in* the advance guard. You will be the first to lead the charge, won't you?" the young man said in an undertone. "Towards Faridor gate?"

"How did you know that?" Athela asked, astonished. She had kept the Strikers' order of attack a secret, even from the recruits.

"I'm Ari's secretary," the young man straightened. "*Personal* secretary," he added, with a proud bit of emphasis.

"Ah," Athela hid a smile. "He trusts you with a lot, then?"

"He knew me before the war," said the young man, as if he could sense the hidden meaning behind Athela's seemingly innocuous question. "Our families were friends."

"What's your name?" Athela asked.

"Gael," the young man said.

"Gael. You know, though, that those plans are confidential and not to be shared with *anyone*?"

"Oh, yes," the young man assented, and his face was quite serious.

Athela looked at him sidelong. If Ari trusted him, she would too. "Yes," she agreed. "We're going to try."

"There won't be much time," Gael pointed out. "You'll have to go fast."

"Luckily, that's what Aria tends to enjoy," Athela smiled.

"I hope you make it," Gael said seriously.

"Me too," Athela said.

Gael hung around for a few minutes, watching as she tied Aria to a post, removed her saddle, and pumped water into a bucket. She then sloshed the bucket over beside the horse and began sponging water over Aria's sweaty back. It was still chilly, and the steam rose off of him in a misty cloud. Gradually, Gael faded away towards a cluster of other recruits, and Athela was once again alone. She registered the sounds of the rest of the trainees filing in with their horses, listened to the creak of water being pumped, the occasional whinny as one of the stabled animals recognized a returning companion out in the courtyard.

She leaned down and checked Aria's legs; the horse, as he always did was whenever it was bathtime, stood uncharacteristically still and quiet. His gray head was raised, and his ears continually flicked back and forth, his black nostrils flaring as he tested the wind. She ran her hand down and around his foreleg; his tendons were sound, sturdy, and strong. He was in as good a shape as he'd ever be; now was their best chance if they were going to try and attempt the possibly suicidal charge at the Faridor gate. She patted his shoulder and stood, scratching him contemplatively on the withers. She took a deep breath, aware that the young recruits were still watching her from afar.

Tarr wandered around aimlessly for much of the afternoon. He didn't want to go back to the headquarters for fear of running into the group of Ashan visitors again, and yet there was so much for him to do there that he didn't want to stray too far. He found himself at dusk lurking around the kitchen entrance where all of the tradespeople came in to make deliveries. A few of the kitchen staff caught sight of him as they came out to dump water or take in a sack of potatoes; they looked at him a bit curiously but said nothing.

After a time, sitting there and stewing in what seemed like an endless morass of thoughts and indecision, Tarr straightened up and recognized a familiar figure walking past him through the near-dark, following the path that led around to the front of the headquarters.

"Laith!" Tarr called and leapt to his feet. The figure halted and turned and waited for him to catch up.

Tarr was glad for Laith's company but wasn't sure what to say and didn't much feel like making small talk. They hadn't spoken alone together since the catastrophic night where everything had gone wrong. Laith pushed back his black hood, his head tilted forward and down on his long neck, his dark eyes cast towards the ground. Suddenly, the prince looked up at Tarr.

"By the way," he said conversationally, as though they'd been talking for some time. "Does Archer have a twin?"

Tarr smiled and shrugged. "Apparently so," he said again, same as he had to Marc and Athela. Laith nodded thoughtfully and digested this information in silence.

"What did Lord Seth want, do you think?" Tarr asked suddenly. "When he fought you by the wall?"

"What does he ever want?" Laith shrugged tiredly. "You could ask the same of a bolt of lightning. Or a plague. Or a hurricane. You'd probably get a more satisfying answer."

"Did Cira send him?" Tarr asked.

Laith's brow furrowed, and he looked up and studied Tarr thoughtfully. "I don't know. I don't think she sent him to the fire. When I spoke to Si before I went to go investigate, he said something about Seth circling the walls, like a moth around a flame. I have a feeling that he was just prowling around Two Falls when the fire started, and went to it, just as I did."

"And you put the fire out?" Tarr asked. "How?"

Laith shook his head. "I didn't. Si did."

Tarr blinked. "How? How did he do it?"

Laith seemed to grope for words. "I could see that it was nothing I could take care of myself. So I asked Si, begged him inside my mind to do something. And then a moment later it was like he called all the water out of the sky and the earth and sent it towards the building."

"Hang on," Tarr said quickly. "Si said he can't speak telepathically." This was one of the few rules Tarr had been able to cling to as he tried to sort out the myriad strands of Si's strange new powers, and it felt important to him that that rule be validated. And yet, he cast his mind back to when Si had predicted the coming of the Ashans, and even before that to when he had sensed General Calchas's first arrival at Two Falls. Tarr had thought that it had been hyperbole when Si said that he called them. But had he?

"Well, he didn't say anything back to me," Laith agreed. "So maybe he just felt it? Felt what I wanted? Knew in some funny, non-verbal way? I don't know." His face cleared. "He also *called* Breaker somehow. Summoned him, I mean. I couldn't find him, and then a second later I opened the door and he was sitting there."

"If Si can do that with you, maybe he can do that with Rane or Archer," Tarr said excitedly, feeling suddenly bright and full of energy for the first time that day. "Maybe he can...I don't know, communicate something to them."

"Maybe," Laith sounded dubious. "What could he communicate to them without words? What would be of help?"

"I don't know..." Tarr scrambled, trying to put his thoughts in order. "You wished for Si to help, right? Maybe he can send some comfort to them. Tell them in some way that we're coming. Maybe..." his mind skipped a few steps. "Who's to say that either of them even *know* they're both in the same dungeon? Or that they're both even in the fortress? What if we can connect them together? What if it can help them in some way?"

Laith still looked less sure than Tarr felt, but he raised his dark eyebrows. "It couldn't hurt. It's worth a try. If Marc allows it, at least."

They picked up their speed and circled back into the headquarters, which was right in the middle of the soldiers' dinner service. Tarr no longer cared whether he met any of the other Ashans along the way; in fact, now that he had something else to focus his mind on, the problems of earlier that day were easily pushed aside.

They found Si in his room, accompanied by Marc, who was ensuring that the boy ate dinner (something which Si routinely forgot to do if left to his own devices). Si blinked pleasantly up at them as they entered.

"Hullo," he said, around a mouthful of roast potato. "Want any potato?"

"That is *your* potato, Si," Marc said sternly, and Tarr could tell that the meal had been something of an uphill battle. "*You* need to eat it."

"All right," said Si placidly, and poked absentmindedly at another potato piece on the plate in his lap.

"Sorry to interrupt," Tarr said hurriedly, and the tone of his voice snapped Marc to attention.

"Is something wrong?" he asked immediately, his hand already reaching toward his sword, sheathed and leaning against the wall. Si missed the potato and the fork dinged against the tin plate.

"No, we just...we just thought of something that could maybe help Archer and Rane," he said.

"You're not using him are you?" Marc asked, his eyes narrowed, instantly on guard.

"Not to harm anyone," Tarr said hurriedly. "Not to manipulate. Just to communicate. To talk."

"I like talking," Si said, brightening, as if glad that he had found a human activity in which he could still participate.

"Si," Marc said slowly, easing his gaze from Tarr to Si. "Would you like to communicate with Archer and Rane?"

"Sounds nice," said Si absently and Tarr relaxed.

"Si, you're able to...talk to people, even if they're far away, right?" Tarr continued, kneeling on the floor before Si. He heard Laith settle into the corner behind him.

"Not talk," Si corrected. "Not with words. Their energy, yes."

"So the other day," Laith spoke up from behind Tarr's shoulder. "When there was the fire and I asked you for help..."

"I could feel it. I could feel that you were afraid and that you needed help. I could feel the heat from the fire. So I sent water," Si said simply.

"Right," Tarr said slowly. "Is there any way you can connect with Rane and Archer? Send them...I don't know...love? Try and make them feel as though we're coming for them?"

"Are they in the same dungeon?" Laith asked.

Si nodded. "Right next to each other, actually. Archer is moved every day, in and out," he traced an invisible line with one finger in the air, as if he was following the path of a tiny speck of dust, "but Rane has stayed in the same place all this time." He lowered his hand and stared at Tarr, his gray eyes level and calm.

Tarr was torn with relief for Rane and horror for Archer. There was only one reason Archer would be brought out of his cell, and that would be to be tortured for information. He swallowed, his throat suddenly dry and scratchy.

"Is there any way to...connect them?" Tarr asked. "Let them know that the other one is there? That they're close? If they are, if they know, maybe they can do something."

"I can try," Si said, and his gray eyes, which had been intensely trained on Tarr's face, suddenly became faraway and vague. The whole room suddenly felt warmer, as if the temperature had turned up and the walls were slowly bending inwards.

Far away, in the bowels of the Faridor fortress, a small figure was sitting curled up in the corner of the dungeon, knees drawn up to her forehead, head resting on folded arms. Rane raised her head suddenly, hearing the faint echoes of noise coming from far away down the head of the cell block. It was dinner time. Not that it mattered much at this point.

The days since her arrest had slowly begun to bleed together as they passed by the walls of her windowless cell. The only thing she had to go on was her sleeping cycle, and even that in itself had gone slightly awry with no visible sun or moon to help govern it. At first they had taken her from her cell and forced her into a small room. She'd been terrified that she would be met there by Lord Seth, the mere thought of whom sent her body into near-uncontrollable paroxysms of fear.

But no, she was only instructed to write letters to Tarr using her code and her verification symbols. Her captors had confiscated her precious collection of private ciphers so it was no use sending him a distress symbol; the Kagaians would have caught it immediately. Instead, she had tried to alert him to her capture by purposefully making spelling errors in the letters she wrote. But it was dangerous—her captors were highly paranoid that she would try to pull a fast one on them. Rane guessed that this was why they kept her messages largely simple and devoid of information; anything too detailed, and they (rightly) believed that she would try and hide a warning in her code. They'd made her send one letter about a tinker shop, but that seemed relatively innocuous, and she fervently hoped that it wouldn't lead to any unpleasantness for Tarr or the others. Eventually, she determined that it was too risky to continue trying to reach out to Tarr even in the oblique way she had been, so after a few messages, she stopped trying. And then quite recently they had stopped taking her out of her cell altogether.

Moreover, what could Tarr do? Other than an all-out assault on the fortress, which was ludicrous, their options for rescue were severely limited. No one had ever broken out of a cell in Faridor's dungeon. Tunneling was impossible; the prison was technically underwater. The cell blocks were a maze, just like the rest of Faridor's hallways, with watchposts located at the end of each hall. For someone on the outside to come down and rescue her, they'd have to bluff their way past twenty or so guards.

Even getting out of her cell was going to be difficult, though Rane had given it considerable thought during her incarceration. Essentially, she was being kept in a stone box, with no windows. There were a few small ventilation slits between the stones in the top of her door, wide enough only for her to stick a finger or two through. There was a sliding metal opening at the bottom of the door, which was used to put food in and out, and she figured—in looking at it and measuring with her body—that she could maybe fit her head or a single arm and a shoulder through the opening, but it wasn't remotely big enough for her to wriggle out. And even if it *had* been wide enough, the sliding metal door could only be opened from the outside.

She had seen the entire door from the hallway each time she had been brought in and out of her cell to do her coding. The door was locked by a heavy wooden beam, two hands' breadths wide, which slid across the cell door in and out of a metal bracket on the outer doorframe. She had seen a similar mechanism on many stall doors in the stables at Two Falls and Joymaril. There was a large round circular metal handle fastened to the sliding wood beam. The whole setup made it relatively easy to access from the outside, but nearly impossible to escape from within.

Rane knew, almost as soon as she had been arrested, that the most critical thing to do was not to lose hope or give in to any despair. Her situation was so dire, the chance of rescue so slim, that it would have been almost too easy to give herself up for lost, to tell herself that everyone she cared about was either completely unaware of her predicament, or was powerless to help her. The thought that she might die there in the dungeon was something that flitted through her head once or twice, but she batted the thought away as though it were a fly buzzing around her head. Deep down, she had the conviction that wherever he was, or whatever else was going on, Tarr would not rest until he had found a way to get her out. That thought in itself was comforting.

The hardest thing to counteract, after the first few adrenaline and shock-filled days of finding herself thrown into a tiny cell in the bowels of the dungeon, was the sheer boredom and loneliness of being trapped in that same hateful room for hour after hour, day after day. She spent a great deal of time meditating, as she had been trained to do during her time the Academy, allowing her mind to come to a place of calm and stillness. She stretched and exercised for a few hours each day, knowing that she would need to be nimble and ready should the slightest opportunity for escape present itself. For at least an hour every morning, she probed every corner of the cell, looking for any weakness or chance of a way out. There was a small hole in the corner which was used as a toilet, but upon investigation Rane couldn't be sure that it led anywhere that would help her get out—at least not without getting hit in the face by tons and tons of ocean water or filth from the waste system.

She wondered if Cicada had managed to be in touch with Tarr during this time. Cicada was another potential lifeline, but Rane trusted Cicada to be cautious above all else, and not throw herself into any potentially suicidal feats of heroics on Rane's behalf. Rane suspected that after her arrest, Cicada would have ceased all communications with the outside. It was more useful to have one functional spy still within Faridor's walls than to risk both of them being arrested and killed. Cicada, furthermore, was no fighter; she hadn't been trained as Rane had. It would be impossible for her to try to force her way down into the dungeon, if she could even manage to locate where Rane was being kept. No more would it be possible for her to try to sneak down into the dungeons in disguise or under the ruse of some errand. The house staff and the prison staff were kept separate; there was no reason for a servant from the fortress to be called down to the dungeons. The prison staff were thoroughly vetted; no stranger would be admitted without the highest possible clearance. She trusted Cicada to stay alive and to stay vigilant. But she couldn't rely on her as a mode of escape.

Her best opportunity, she decided, would be if her captors removed her once again from her cell and brought her out to do some code-writing. But for some reason, for the past week or so (she couldn't quite tell, the days ran together so much) she had been completely ignored. Rane wondered vaguely whether they'd simply tired of her, or if she'd seemingly outlived her purpose for them (in which case, why hadn't they yet had her executed?) The other possibility, one that made her feel a mixture of trepidation and hope, was that they'd found something else, some sort of distraction that had diverted their attention from her. This seemed to be supported by the few clues she had managed to glean during her imprisonment—she could hear the cell door next to her being opened every morning around breakfast and she had discerned the sounds of someone being dragged back in and locked up every afternoon. She wondered who it could be.

She stood and went to the door of her cell and pressed her ear against the small sliding metal sheet at the base of her cell door, through which her food (such as it was) was presented in the mornings and the evenings. The metal was thin, which made it easy for her to hear the activity that was going on in the hall outside. She could hear the continuous sounds of the little food slots being opened and closed as plates and forks were thrust through to the occupants inside. She had toyed briefly with stealing one of the forks, but one evening she had heard a rumpus outside the door after dinnertime and realized that the sounds were from a prisoner who'd had a similar idea and was being soundly beaten until the stolen implement was recovered. She'd since decided against it. Barring the possibility of being removed from her cell (which was beginning to look increasingly less probable as the days wore on), finding some way out during the mealtime routine was beginning to look like her best bet. But she wasn't certain yet how she could possibly do it, and find her way out of the labyrinthine dungeons. *Just get out,* she told herself calmly. *Just get out, and you'll be able to improvise the rest.*

If she could escape her stone prison, then at least she would be able to fight. Weapon or no, if she were able to fight, she would stand a good chance of being able to claw her way out of the dungeon, one way or another.

She, as she had dozens of times, tried to pry the metal food door open with her fingertips, but it was impossible. There was a handle on the outside that allowed her captors to slide it open from the hallway, but it was impossible to budge from the inside of the cell. Eyeing it narrowly, Rane moved away from the door and sat with her back against the wall, waiting for the now-familiar moment when the slot would fly open and her plate would be thrown inside. She realized, with a bit of a sinking feeling, how much she had been looking forward to this moment all day; the brief glimpse of the outside world, of a hand, an arm, even for a second. She caught herself and sternly gave herself a mental shake. *You are biding your time, that's all. You have to stay sharp.* She would meditate again after she ate. She had to eat. The food was almost nothing and she barely had an appetite, but it wouldn't do to be weak and malnourished in the event that she needed to fight her way out. She had to stay prepared.

Suddenly, she was struck by a strange sensation. At first she thought she was imagining things, but then she became acutely aware that some outside force was taking a hold of her mind and her body. For one wild moment she wondered if she'd somehow been poisoned or drugged—but that was impossible, as she hadn't even eaten her food yet. She forced herself to take a deep breath, resisting the instinct to bolt upright and start to scream.

Commanding herself to breathe slowly and calmly, she objectively analyzed what seemed to be happening to her: the feeling was strange and warm, starting in her stomach and spreading up through her chest and out along her arms and legs. There was a low hum almost audible in her ears and a pulsing feeling like a drum or a heartbeat; she seemed suddenly acutely aware of her blood and how the air circled inside and out of her lungs. *Am I dying?* she thought wildly. *Is this what dying feels like?* And even in her moment of panic, her mind was shifting backwards, trying to work out what possibly could have caused this, grasping for an answer in the few seconds before she was certain the world would go black around her forever.

And then, all at once, she stopped being afraid. The feeling, indescribable and alien as it was, suddenly vibrated with a new wave of sensation that shook her throughout her core. It felt...she tried to understand...it felt like an embrace from a loved one. Not the *physical* sensation of it—of arms encircling her and holding her—instead, it was the *feeling,* the emotion, the mental space—one of comfort, of empathy, of protection. Rane had no idea what could be happening to her, but she suddenly realized that it was nothing to fear. If this was dying, it wasn't so bad.

Slowly, still forcing herself to rhythmically breathe so as to stave off any rising hysteria, she slid up the wall to stand on her own two feet. She was pleased to note that she still seemed to have control of her limbs and her body. The curious sensation, soft and comforting, persisted, enveloping her like perfectly warm water.

Then, almost as if someone had whispered something behind her, she became acutely aware of a presence at her back. She whipped around, but there was only the stone wall of her cell. She stared at it, wishing that her eyes were powerful enough to bore through it. *Someone was there.* Someone, as sure as if they'd been standing behind her. She reached out a hand and touched the stone wall, closing her eyes. She focused all the energy her swirling mind could muster on reaching out to whoever was beyond that wall.

Again, another wave seemed to break against her and her eyes snapped open. *Archer.* Somehow, some way, Archer was the person she could feel on the other side of her cell wall.

Logically, she could not hope to explain how she knew this, but she was as certain of his presence as if he'd been in front of her in the broad light of day. If she had been standing with her eyes closed and a loved one had slipped their hand into hers, she would have been able to instantly differentiate between Tarr's hand and Athela's, Marc's and Si's. It was the same now. Whatever the energy was, beyond a shadow of a doubt it belonged to Archer.

She raised her hand again and pressed it against the cold stone, and was surprised after a few seconds to feel it begin to grow warm, almost hot under her hand, as if a beam of energy was connecting her to the other side. She drew closer and laid her cheek against the stone.

Archer, she thought, *is that you?*

There was no reply, no voice in her head verbally confirming it. But the air around her crackled anew with a fresh pulse of warmth and electricity, and she was sure that she was right. It was almost as if she could see him, a glowing outline mirrored on the other side of the wall. They were separated by only a few feet.

Then, almost as suddenly as it had begun, the strange sensation began to ebb, like a tide slowly rolling back from the shore. The air seemed to grow dimmer and colder; the stone was once again damp beneath her hands. Rane pulled her cheek back from the wall and took a step back, staring at it, trying to make sense of what had just happened.

She couldn't understand where the energy had come from, or what weird, inexplicable magic had surrounded her for those few fleeting minutes, but she was certain of one thing: Archer had somehow been captured and was in the cell directly adjacent to hers. The past week now made complete sense to her. It would be absolutely typical of Cira to forget about her and cast her aside in the interest of toying with a new plaything. She was grateful that Archer was somehow still alive, and had managed to survive the tortures she was sure Cira had visited upon him.

She also knew that whatever the strange connection had been or wherever it had come from, he had felt it, too. He could sense she was there. It had given her hope. She prayed it would sustain him, too.

There wasn't enough time to tunnel through to reach one another—whatever she was up to, Cira wouldn't let Archer live long enough for that. But perhaps now that Archer knew she was there, he could do something, find some way to help her when he was dragged out the next morning. She would have to be ready.

The sliding metal sheet at the base of her door suddenly snapped open and her food was deposited sloppily within. As always, there was a bowl filled with a hunk of stale bread floating drearily atop some indiscriminate, lukewarm brown liquid. A moment later, a wooden spoon was tossed inside, clattering to the ground beside the bowl. The metal door snapped shut.

Rane stood there for a few moments, staring at the bowl and the spoon, her eyes moving from them to the little door and back again. There was a chance, a small chance, and it all depended on a two-person plan (here, she almost had to laugh at the sheer absurdity of it) involving a person she had no way of communicating with. She would have to be fast, and she would have to be ready. She felt convinced in her heart that somehow Archer would do whatever it took to help her get out. She trusted him. She trusted that he would think quickly.

And she hoped that afterwards he would stay alive long enough for her to come and get him out, too.

That night, as the full moon slowly slid into the dome of the sky, the Striker army moved out of Two Falls to meet Cade and his troops, who were waiting in the trees by the coast nearly three hours away. The army kept together in a narrow column, riders on horseback leading the way, followed by those on foot. Tarr rode behind Marc and Si, cloaked unassumingly in black. There was something comforting in watching Marc's back: straight and square, broad shoulders relaxed, hips swaying with the rhythm of his horse's walk as the clatter of hooves and armor and swords swelled beneath them. For as nervous as Marc looked, they might have well been riding out to the Saturday market, rather than heading off to a battle and an unknown fate.

Tarr twisted around in his saddle as they approached the east gate. He could see the faint orbs of people's faces peering curiously out of their windows in the surrounding houses, gaping at the sight of the army going past. No one cheered, no one made a sound. The cold bit at Tarr's eyes and ears, and the wet damp of winter still hung mutely in the air. A short breeze gusted through the eastern gate and (though he may have imagined it) Tarr thought he could smell a whiff of the sea, a scent that was dark green and salt-crusted.

The gate loomed up above his head and passed behind. Tarr turned around and faced forward. He didn't look back at the city again.

The army came to the edge of the forest and continued riding east, snaking through the trees towards the coast.

CHAPTER TWENTY-THREE

Three hours later, one of the advance scouts, sent out before the head of the army to ensure their safety, came back with the report that Cade and his troops were waiting for them at the base of a small wooded hill. In the darkness of the woods, Tarr could barely make out how far the army stretched back into the trees. Now that they were all together, it certainly seemed like a lot of people with them, but Tarr had the uneasy feeling that in the harsh light of day under the shadow of Faridor's wall, their army would look quite small and insignificant by comparison.

Cade was waiting for them; Wolf, Nadia, Rowan, and a few others Tarr recognized were beside him. Cade's blond hair glowed in the filtered moonlight as he moved his horse forward to stand beside the others.

"The guns haven't turned," he said immediately, as though he could read the thoughts rattling around in Tarr's head. "I've just had one of my scouts come back. They're still pointed towards the land."

Tarr cursed beneath his breath and turned around to look over his shoulder at Laith and Athela. Laith was hooded and sat like a shadow on his black horse, Athela's face looked blue and eerie.

"We'll have to put on a show, then," Athela suggested. "Make camp here. Hope that word is brought up to the fortress that we're moving east towards the coast. She has to believe we're attacking by sea."

"Good idea," Tarr agreed. "We'll rest for two hours. Get everyone organized. Light a few fires. Give them time to get the word back to Faridor."

"And if the guns don't turn?" Cade asked quietly.

Silence fell around them. Tarr looked back at all of the soldiers waiting behind him, standing expectantly, trusting. "I don't know," he said honestly. "I don't know."

"I'll send a few of my troops out to where we have the boats hidden in the cove, and have them act as though they're readying things for the army," Cade suggested.

"Can we spare them?" Athela asked.

"Honestly, no," Tarr said truthfully, with a shrug. "It's a gamble."

"If it raises the odds that this ruse will work," Laith spoke up, invisible and dark beneath the folds of his black hood, "We should try it. We're outnumbered anyway. We know for certain that if those guns don't turn, we're all dead."

"I'll do it, then," said Cade crisply. He took one step, then paused and turned. "By the way," he said. "I was just passing by a group of Ashans. Does Archer have a twin?"

"Apparently so," Athela and Tarr said together.

"Hm," Cade frowned thoughtfully.

"Tell the troops to set a few campfires," Tarr reminded him. "Two hours until we march north, one way or the other."

The orders passed through the army behind them like a whispering breeze; soon, the column had dissipated and the soldiers had spread out and made little camps here and there throughout the forest. Fires lit and took hold, scattered amongst the patches of open ground among the trees. Suddenly the forest seemed less of a dark, forbidding place. Temporary tents were pitched, offering the troops a chance to catch a last snippet of sleep (if they were able to) before the battle the next morning.

Laith was alone on the outskirts of the makeshift camp, readying himself for the battle. His usual full battle armor would be too cumbersome, and he needed to be able to move and climb with almost complete freedom, so he had opted for leather. It offered much less protection against arrows and swords than his regular armor, but it was just one more thing that would have to be risked if they were to have any hope of victory.

Arfolasth was tied to a nearby tree, his back leg relaxed and his eyelashes drooping. Laith watched him fondly, then scratched him behind his ears, straightening his forelock and patting his neck. He sat down on a nearby tree stump and began lacing up his left vambrace. Cade and his troops had brought Laith's leather armor and Whitsun sword from Joymaril; it was rather like being reunited with old friends again. The Whitsun was a ceremonial gift, bestowed on the occasion when the Queen had presented him with his own sigil. It was too fine a weapon for practicing or teaching at the Academy, so Laith rarely used it and hadn't even thought to take it with him when he and the others fled Joymaril. It seemed fitting, however, to carry it into this final battle; a more perfectly balanced, expertly crafted weapon would have been hard to find. The hilt was designed to emulate the rising sun, with a gigantic yellow diamond as its center stone and a shower of perfectly inset topaz radiating out along its handles. Minute strands of golden filigree shone delicately down the blade, where the metal had even somehow been tempered to fade from a dark black tip to almost pure silvery white beside the diamond.

The lightweight leather armor had been made specially for Laith, and was intricately embossed with his house sun, intertwined with the crests of the royal houses of Joymaril—the egret of Athela's family, and the ivy of his own. It was awkward, as it always was, trying to tighten and tie the laces one-handed. Laith was just about to lean forward and use his teeth when a calm, deep voice cut through the darkness.

"Let me help you," said the voice, and a dark figure rounded a tree, bearing a lantern in one hand. It was General Calchas, resplendent in his full Joymarillian battle dress, his armor increasing his already considerable height and breadth to truly intimidating proportions. The general stepped forward and kneeled before Laith, setting down the lantern beside the stump on which Laith was seated. The lighting threw the craggy angles of General Calchas's visage into sharp relief and Laith remembered suddenly how Tess had described him as having a face carved out of wood. The thought of her made him smile.

Calchas tightened the laces expertly with his thick, roughened fingers, cocking an eyebrow up at Laith. Seeing the expression on his face, Calchas chuckled.

"Something funny?" he asked.

Laith shook his head. "Never mind. Sorry you have to do this. Usually it's Marc's job. Can't think of where he's got to."

"I don't mind, Calchas said gruffly. "Here, hand me your greaves."

Laith did as he was told, and as Calchas shook the folded pieces of supple leather loose and straightened out the laces, he began thinking (as he was certain Calchas did too), of the many nights that the general had helped him on with his armor as a young boy, when he was too small even to manage the buckles himself.

Calchas worked in silence, and Laith, who had wanted to be alone in the short time before they moved out to take their places for the battle, was suddenly glad for his company. The lamplight flickered beside them; the only sound was the cracking of flame and the low murmur of talking over at the camp.

His task done, Calchas stared down at the ground for a moment, and Laith could see that the general wanted to say something to him. He waited patiently until Calchas looked back up, and Laith was surprised to see that his face looked grieved.

"Do you remember what I said to you all those years ago, the day you left the Meadows to return to Joymaril?"

Laith did, but stayed silent.

"I said I believed you to be a good man. I said that the world isn't kind to good men or women, but that it needs them desperately. In this case, I'm sorry that I was right. It's been a hard time for you, I can see it in your eyes." he said finally.

Laith made a dismissive hand gesture. "I've not had a harder time than anyone else," he said finally. "And a good deal easier time of it than many. I just..." the words formed almost before he could stop them from tumbling out. Perhaps it was General Calchas, the years between them, the way Laith had always looked up to him. "I just can't seem...to stay afloat anymore. I don't know why. Everyone else seems to be able to. But I can't." He shrugged. There it was. He had finally said aloud what he had held inside for years.

Calchas regarded him with concern, and Laith was forced to look away. "That's not weakness, Argolaith," Calchas said.

"I know," Laith said quickly, and he groped for the right words. "I know. But something is cracked. There is this black place inside." His hand fluttered at his chest. "It pulls me down. Every day. Pulling. I don't know how to mend it. I don't even know if it *can* be mended."

Calchas sighed and raised his eyes up to the sky above for a moment, then lowered them back down to earth. "Do you *want* to mend it? That, I think, is the first question to ask."

Laith was silent.

"To do so would not be," Calchas said slowly, and Laith could hear that he was choosing his words very carefully, "a disservice to her. Or to her memory."

Laith looked down at his hands, knowing immediately to whom Calchas was referring. And the General had hit closer to home than Laith had expected him to. "I know," he said. "But this...thing...this broken piece...it's bigger than her. Bigger even than my grief for her. It grows and grows. Even on *good* days, it grows. I don't know. I can't describe it."

Calchas looked very grave, and, still kneeling, raised one of his enormous hands and placed it on Laith's shoulder. "Do you remember what we taught you about death, Laith?"

Laith looked up at him with a pained little smile. "Are we going to go through all our old lessons tonight?"

"I'm serious," Calchas said sharply.

"Yes, I remember." Laith swallowed, feeling rather like a chided schoolboy. "We are either death's king or we are its subject."

Calchas stared at him pointedly, resting his elbow on his knee. "Which of those are you planning to be tomorrow, Argolaith?"

Laith flinched. In an instant, he had recovered himself again, but Calchas had already seen the truth of his intentions on his face and in his eyes. Sadly, Calchas shook his head and rose to his full height, looking down now upon the prince, who found himself feeling very small.

"I can ask you, Argolaith, not to do this thing," he said. "But that is not my choice to make. That is your right. Your right alone." He touched Laith's shoulder again, more gently this time, and shook his head, turning to go.

"I wish..." Laith said suddenly, and Calchas stopped, turning.

"What?" he asked. He could see from Laith's face that the prince had not expected to speak the words aloud.

"We were children," Laith said finally, his dark eyes black as he stared up at the General, and there was the hint of accusation in his voice. "We were *children*, when all of this began. Where were you? All of you? How did you let this happen?"

Laith looked slightly abashed at his outburst, and Calchas studied him thoughtfully. "We couldn't see," he said. "You will understand someday. As you get older...somehow you spend more and more time looking behind you, thinking of how things were, how things have always been, and that is where you come to live. Sometimes you lose sight of what's to come, of the role you are to play in it. And how best to protect those who must live in it." He raised his hands helplessly.

Laith's expression was inscrutable as he studied Calchas for a long time. Finally, he looked down and inspected the buckles around his legs and boot. "Good luck tomorrow, sir," he said finally, not looking back up.

"You as well, my prince," said Calchas, and left him.

Tarr tried to force himself to relax, but he didn't have the discipline of a soldier. He found himself peering out at the trees, trying to see whether any of Cira's spies were out there watching them, whether they'd see the army massed so close to the coast and send word back that they were making their move. He wondered whether the efforts they had gone to—building the boats, the whole elaborate deception of it all—was for naught. Every shadow, every branch that bent in the slightest gusting breeze, seemed to him to be a figure slipping away into the darkness. He wandered around the camp until he found Athela, who was contemplatively soaping an unidentifiable piece of leather beside a small fire.

"You brought saddle soap?" he asked, with mock incredulity, "to a *battlefield?*"

She squinted up at him. "Little-known fact, Tarr, it's cleanliness, not physical prowess, that wins battles. This right here is going to spell the difference between defeat and victory." She considered. "Somehow."

"If you say so," Tarr laughed. "How's Aria?" So much of their success tomorrow depended on Athela and whether she would be able to lead the run to the gate in time. He wondered how she could possibly manage to look so unruffled.

Athela glanced backwards over her shoulder to the distant trees, where he assumed Aria was either tied up or was trying to take a bite out of some poor unassuming groom charged with minding him. "Oh, he's nuts," she said with a fond smile. "Ready to run. As always. Everyone else is going to have a job keeping up, I can tell you." She faced him again. "When do you, Si, and Ari split off?"

"As soon as the army moves north," Tarr told her. It struck him suddenly how different she looked, half-illuminated by the campfire. Her face, always strong and full of character, was open and confident; gone was the suspicion and reserve that had been her calling card for so long. The change suited her.

"Here," she said abruptly, giving him the opposite end of the inde-terminate equine accoutrement she was working on, and pressing a oily-feeling scrap of cloth into his hand. "Soap something. I promise it will help."

Tarr laughed, and did as he was told, more to please her than anything. But after a few moments, he realized that she was right.

Si was sitting alone beside a small campfire at the entrance of his makeshift tent. Marc was about fifty feet away from him, deep in conversation with a few of the recruits, who had gathered around him in a reverential semicircle, their eyes shining as he spoke to them. Every now and again he turned around to glance back at Si, but there was nothing much to worry about. Si was, as usual, gazing up at the stars, a peaceful look of wonderment across his face as his eyes traced their paths back and forth. Though most of the camp had split off into groups of twos or threes, talking and some even laughing, Si was distinctly alone. The others gave him a wide berth, and as they passed they glanced at him sidelong. As his eyes swept across the sky, he whispered words under his breath, calling the stars by their names. Suddenly, there was a small sound, and the gray eyes focused, drifting back to earth. The boy turned around to look at the person who was now behind him.

It was Ari, standing awkwardly, his hands dangling at his sides. He looked uncharacteristically unsure of himself, and took a hesitant step forward. He had the air of someone steeling himself up for something.

"Hello," said Si pleasantly, and Ari realized that Si was completely unsurprised to see him. He must have known he was coming. "Have a seat."

Ari did so, and as he did the logs in the campfire shifted a bit, snapping and sparking and sending up a fresh cloud of smoke that went winding up into the swaying treetops above them. A cool air blew past them, intermingling pleasantly with the warmth of the fire. Ari sat in silence for a moment. The boy's eyes were studying him thoughtfully, his gaze direct, not drifting and vague as it usually was.

"I've come to ask you something," Ari began. "I need to know."

Si nodded, prompting him to continue. Ari's hands were clasped between his knees; he relaxed them momentarily and stared down into the depths of his palms.

"Will I die?" he asked finally. He looked suddenly up at Si, an unspoken pleading in his expression. "Will I die at Faridor tomorrow?"

Si waited for a moment, regarding him solemnly with large gray eyes. Again, it struck Ari how completely unsurprised he seemed to be by any of these questions. "Are you sure you want to know?" Si asked finally. "Tarr and the others seem to get upset whenever I try to tell them things."

"I want to know," Ari said quietly. "I'm sure."

"Yes, you'll die in the battle," Si said.

Ari's hands relaxed again and he re-folded them between his knees, looser this time, the knuckles slack. He straightened his back and gazed out into the dark cobalt blue of the trees and the night beyond. The campfire light cast dark hollows into the planes of his face. His eyes seemed to see nothing. "How?" he asked. "How does it happen?"

Si told him, and Ari listened quietly. After Si was done speaking, Ari was still staring out through the trees, but there was a rueful sort of smile playing about his lips. "So that is it," he said. "And you're sure? There's no way out?"

Si shrugged. "You always have a choice. You could turn around now and leave the camp tonight and not fight in the battle."

"And if I do that?" Ari ventured.

"There will be a great impact. On the lives of a great many people."

"But one life," Ari protested. "All you're talking about is one life ."

Si shook his head. "There's no such thing. Lives do not exist in isolation. There are always ripples, roots, a constellation. You can't possibly know the full extent."

Ari's brow furrowed. "I suppose," he said guardedly, "I suppose I should also ask you about the others. About whether or not they make it. Whether we even win. Whether any of it matters." He looked sharply again in Si's direction, as if looking for some sort of clue in Si's reaction. But the boy was still studying him, and gave nothing away. It was strange to see his attention focused in one place for so long when by this point they were all used to him drifting like a branch on the water. "Would you tell me if I asked?"

"Of course," Si assured him. "If you asked I could tell you what will happen to us all." He cocked his head shrewdly. "*Are* you asking?"

Ari thought for a long time. "No," he said finally. "No. This is enough, I think. Enough for me to know now."

He stirred. He rose heavily to his feet and for a moment looked as though he were about to leave. But at the last moment he hesitated, literally teetering back and forth on the balls of his toes before setting his foot firmly down and swiveling back around to Si. The boy was still watching him, the light of the campfire beside them dancing over his smattering of freckles.

"Si, I want to trust what you say. I want to believe that you are right. I am almost ashamed to ask any more of you, for it's a very self-ish thing to wonder," Ari said. It took a great deal of effort for him to say the words and they came out haltingly, as though his entire body was still trying to keep them inside. "But if I go tomorrow, I must ask again...I must know that my life will have meant something. That I will have made a difference."

"Oh, yes," said Si, leaning forward eagerly. "It will make a tremendous difference. Like a single dewdrop on a blade of grass that grows into a swelling river. Hundreds of lives, their children, their children's children, all will exist, will come into being, because of you. I can see them, you know," here, his eyes started to drift into their familiar dreamlike state and it seemed to Ari that he had ceased to be there beside the fire, even though his body remained. "I can see them," he said quietly. "All of the crackles and the sparks when life forms. Like fireworks, like a glittering spiderweb written across the whole arc of the sky." He raised one hand and painted it over the night curving above them. "The most beautiful thing. Thousands of colors, Ari, that go on for hundreds of years, exploding and exploding one after another like a chain reaction." As if to punctuate his words, the campfire let off a fresh hiss and a pop and a little cloud of sparks flew up, so suddenly that Ari, who had stood stock-still and wide-eyed through Si's entire speech, jumped.

The sound of it seemed to draw Si back to earth, too, and he blinked up at Ari, a broad, genuine smile of peace and happiness spreading across his face. He gave an encouraging nod. "That is what you'll leave behind. That is your legacy."

Ari stood there for another long while, thinking to himself, wrapping his head around Si's words. Finally, he nodded, and the familiar stoicism dropped back into place, settling over him with a calm finality.

"All right," he said. "I believe you. I believe what you say."

His voice betrayed nothing. His eyes were dry. He gave Si a curt nod and walked into the forest to stand alone beneath the stars. He rested his back against the spreading trunk of a tree, and for hours he stared up at the stretching arc that swept blue and eternal above his head.

In the blink of an eye, it seemed, the two hours were up and it was time for the army to move north. There had been no word from any of their advance spies. For all any of them knew, the guns were still facing towards the land. *There's still time*, Tarr kept chanting to himself. What would they do if the guns were not turned? They would have to use Si, Tarr realized, and resort to one of the last-ditch plans that Ari had suggested, of putting all of the troops in Faridor to sleep or something. Tarr didn't like it one bit, and he knew they would basically have to physically restrain Marc to keep him from stopping them. He thought about what Marc had said, that every time they used Si's powers, it took a little piece of Si's humanity away from him. He could feel in his core that Marc was right. He realized, with a wrench, that unlike

Marc, he was still willing to use Si as a tool if it meant defeating Cira. *There's still time*, he reminded himself. *There's still time. They have to turn. They have to turn.*

All around them lanterns were being snuffed and campfires doused, casting the forest once more into eerie, inky shades of gray and dark blue. The shadows of soldiers surrounded him at all sides, moving quickly. No one was talking. A horse near him, seeming to sense the tension, pawed anxiously at the ground and cracked a twig beneath his hoof. The snap made Tarr jump.

There was a group of five or ten advance scouts, the best they had (Itzhal, who Tarr had sent after Burlage, was one of them), whose job it was to move ahead of the column and track down and eliminate any of Cira's sentries who might be stationed in the forest, waiting for sign of their attack. Once they'd had their head start, it was time for the army to move. Laith and the other Strikers were leading the first column, Cade farther back leading the second.

Tarr, Ari, Marc, and Si hung a little ways off to the side. It was almost time for them to split off, to try and infiltrate Faridor through the grotto entrance that Tess had discovered in the blueprints and make their way up to Cira's tower to try and defeat her. Marc was going to escort them to the coast, and then ride north to rejoin the rest of the army.

For a moment, the Strikers stood together in silence. In the dim light, Tarr could just make out their outlines—Laith, dark as a shadow beneath his hood, Athela with her horse dancing beneath her. None of them were sure what to say; everyone was keenly aware that it could very well be the last time they would all see one another alive.

Silently, Tarr felt a small hand slip into his. It was Si's. Tarr glanced down at the pale orb of the boy's face, and thought he understood. He reached out and took Laith's gloved hand as he sat, cold and stately, atop his black horse. He could see the shadow of Laith's arm reach out to Athela's beside him. Soon, they all stood together, a quiet, intimate circle, an army waiting behind them.

Tarr's hand began to glow with warmth, and after a moment he felt a beam of energy, light and so full of feeling it made him catch his breath, rising in his chest. It shot through his arms, and though none of them outwardly looked any different, he could practically see the beam careening around the circle, passed through their joined hands. Then, almost with a gust of wind, it vanished. Tarr released the hands to either side of him, the glowing energy still throbbing in his palms and feet. There was nothing they could say. In his inimitable way, Si had said everything for them.

"It's time," Si said softly and raised his face up to the sky.

Out of habit, Tarr followed his eyes upwards, not expecting to see anything but the pale circle of moon and the spreading stars above. But then he stopped still.

A black, perfectly round shape had edged its way over the rim of the moon, blotting it out completely.

"What is that?" Athela asked urgently. She and the others had looked up as well. There was a hint of fear in her tone.

"Are you doing that, Si?" Laith asked.

"No," Si said dreamily. "The wheel is turning."

Tarr knew he must be imagining it, but it seemed almost as if the shadow was creeping farther and farther over the face of the moon as he watched.

Around them, Tarr could hear whispers rising through the trees as the troops noticed what was happening, too.

There was the sound of hoofbeats and Tarr caught a glimpse of white-blond hair as Cade rode up from the head of the second column. "Do you see the moon?" he asked breathlessly without preamble, dropping his usual cool, aloof façade. "What does it mean? Should we turn back?"

"Si says it's all right," Marc told him calmly. "It's all right, Cade."

Even in the growing darkness Tarr could sense that Cade was dubious. "These things happen," Tarr offered. "I've seen it before. We kept a record of them back home."

"I know, it's just..." Cade trailed off, and Tarr got the sense he felt a bit abashed for losing his head and rushing up to them like a frightened child. Tarr could understand Cade's reaction, however. For such a phenomenon to occur on the night before a momentous battle felt like more than just mere coincidence. It felt like the universe was trying to convey some sort of message in a language that he and the others (with the exception of Si) could not hope to understand.

"Keep the troops calm," Laith told them. "We can use this to our advantage. It will be easier for the Ashans and me to get beneath the bridge under cover of darkness. We should move out now."

Cade nodded resolutely, the mask firmly back in place and the frightened boy gone. He rode away back towards the head of the second column. Through the trees, Tarr could see the soldiers still watching the blackening moon with awe and more than a little trepidation.

"It's a good omen," Laith announced, loudly enough for the nearby troops to hear him and pass back the message. "We move out."

Tarr, Ari, Si, and Marc stepped to the side and watched as Laith and Athela turned their horses, facing them north through the woods. Then, with a slight nod, Laith moved forward, and the entire snaking column began to weave its way quietly through the trees past them.

Tarr's group watched for a few minutes. After a time, Tarr felt a nudge in the small of his back. Marc had mounted up and was waiting atop his horse; there was one other horse he held at his side. It was important for no one—not even their own troops—to know of Si's plan to reach Cira, so they planned on riding double atop the horses so that when Marc caught up with the army, he would have only one extra horse to lead. One extra horse would catch less attention than three.

Ari swung aboard his horse, and Tarr awkwardly scrambled up behind him, looping an arm loosely around Ari's sturdy waist for balance. Si perched behind Marc, and the four of them slipped unseen into the depth of the forest, riding east for the coast.

It was a short ride to the edge of the water. Above them, inky blackness continued to seep over the face of the moon. Tarr could hear the sea before he could make it out in the darkness, but soon they rounded the crest of the last rise, where the forest gave way and the hill cascaded down from the forest to a slope of rocks, and still further into a dune of sand. At the edge of the sand, Tarr could see long, thin slivers of white as the waves broke unevenly along the coastline. He looked to his left, and could see the black rocks of Faridor, not too far away, dozens and dozens of tiny pinpricks of light peeking out through the windows and reflecting hazily on the black water below.

Tarr swallowed. "It's not so far," he said, mostly to himself.

"No," agreed Marc from atop his horse. "You'll be able to walk down the coast just a short ways but you'll have to start swimming before long. And Tarr..." he could see Marc turn and glance at Si.

"I know," Tarr said quickly, leaving Marc's request for him to take care of Si, to keep him safe, hanging in the night air between them. "I will."

The three of them dismounted and Ari handed the reins over to Marc. Marc pulled Ari's horse a bit closer, so that its head was at his horse's flank. He wasn't so far behind the Striker army. He could catch up with little effort.

"Goodbye," came Si's light, effervescent voice from somewhere beside Tarr.

"Goodbye," replied Marc, and he turned. Tarr could see that it was taking every ounce of effort Marc had not to find some excuse to stay and go with them. But he was needed elsewhere and he knew it.

The three of them waited until Marc had been enveloped by the dark blue of the forest. They then began picking their way down the hill, sliding over some of the more slippery rocks that had been beaten smooth and sheer by the wind and the waves. Finally, they found themselves down at the water's edge and, keeping low, began to walk north towards Faridor. Tarr prayed that if they were seen, even in the darkness and at such great a distance, no one would think much of it, or decide to raise the alarm. They could be fishermen, for all any of the sentries knew. Three individuals didn't pose much of a threat to the fortress.

They had walked for perhaps ten minutes (Tarr keeping a close eye on Si to make sure that he didn't wander off) when suddenly Ari stopped stock still. It was getting close to the point where they would have to slip into the water and begin swimming. At first Tarr glanced around at their surroundings to see if anything was amiss, or if something had indicated to Ari that it was time.

"What is it?" he asked in a whisper. He didn't really need to lower his voice; they were quite alone and the roar of the waves so close to them was enough to mask any sounds.

Ari pointed with one finger in the direction of Faridor and Tarr's stomach dropped. *We've been seen*, he thought immediately. But no, it wasn't that. Tarr narrowed his eyes, seeing motion barely visible along the top wall, way off in the distance. There was a cluster of five or so soldiers, as small as beads, moving along the top edge of the fortress, bearing torches in their hands. The extra light made it possible to see just a little better. They looked as though they were dragging something, something heavy and hard to move.

"Tarr," Ari said, and even with the sound of the waves crashing in his ears, Tarr could hear the excitement in his voice. "Tarr, they're turning the guns. They're turning the guns out to sea."

CHAPTER TWENTY-FOUR

Tarr, Ari, and Si slipped into the black water, bracing themselves against the first few crashing waves before they could dive below. It was shockingly cold and Tarr couldn't help but let out an audible "Ah!" as the daggerlike chill cut into him. Tarr was a fair swimmer, having spent many long summer days during his childhood in the forest paddling around some of the quieter pools in the river near his home. Swimming in the ocean was quite a different prospect; the black expanse gaped before him, seemingly unending. He did not relish the thought of all of the small, inquisitive fish or eels that might be lurking beneath the surface of the sea ready to bite at his toes. His boots were tied together and slung around his neck, and he kept his head as low as possible so that just his nose popped above the surface of the water. The moon was growing ever darker, but they still could not risk the possibility of a sentry spotting them on Faridor's wall.

He had swum only about twenty feet or so before he realized that Si was no longer with them. As quietly as possible, he nudged Ari and flipped over onto his back. Si was treading water, staring at the surface with a delighted expression as the water began to glow from deep within, the waves lifting and cradling him gently.

"Look, Tarr!" he said excitedly. "Look at them glow!" As Si's arms and legs moved rhythmically in the water, Tarr could make out little animals or insects like tiny fireflies swirling and whirling with the currents of the water. As if in response to Si's words, the miniscule creatures seemed to brighten even more until Si's entire face was illuminated by an eerie blue light.

So much for subterfuge, Tarr thought exasperatedly. "Si," he said aloud with as much patience as he could muster, "could you calm those things down a bit? Remember, we don't want to be seen."

"I'm sorry," Si said, though Tarr could see that he was still smiling. Like the dimming of an oil lamp, the light from the tiny creatures faded away and they were once again swimming through the inky blackness.

Faridor hadn't looked very far away from the spot where they had begun to swim, but Tarr quickly realized that the distance had been some sort of optical illusion. Still, the sea was remarkably calm, and unless Tarr was much mistaken, it seemed to grow a touch warmer. While not exactly balmy, it wasn't intolerable. Moreover, it was as though there was some sort of following current that bore them right up to the fortress, which he imagined was Si's doing. They picked their way carefully through the quiet waves for nearly half an hour before they began to draw up to the looming black shadow of Faridor's wall. The fortress was jutting up from the impressively large rocks at the base of the island. As he craned his neck to look up, it seemed to Tarr as though the wall went on forever into the vault of the sky. A few tiny lights flickered high up in a tower above them.

After what seemed like an eternity, Tarr reached out one long arm and made contact with a rock on the southern side of the fortress. He began to tread water, bobbing up and down with the gentle push of the waves, until Si dogpaddled up beside him and rested a hand on one of the slippery black rocks to steady himself. The young man was panting, but gave Tarr the tiniest flash of a grin. Ari drew up with a stately, unhurried breaststroke and Tarr had an inkling that Ari could have left them both behind had he chosen to swim at his fullest speed. Far from dashing them against the rocks, the sea seemed content merely to pleasantly bob them up and down, like a mother rocking her children. Tarr was infinitely grateful that Si was with them.

"Stay low in the water. It'll be harder for them to see us if they happen to look down. The entrance Tess told us about should be just a bit farther around the island," Tarr whispered to them. They faced the rocks and, using them as handholds, began to push their way around with only mild difficulty against the incoming current of the ocean. Just as Tarr managed to find a foothold in one of the slippery rocks, the sea picked him up and pulled him off to the side, away from the rocks, as easily as if he had been a rag doll.

Spitting salt and shaking his head to clear the water from his ear, he felt a wiry hand grab his arm and pull him forward against the current.

"Sorry," he heard Si's soft voice say, "I got distracted for a minute. The sea will behave now, I promise."

"The entrance is here," Ari called from around the corner of the nearest rock, as another wave took hold of Tarr and tried to pull him away. "Come on, kick."

Tarr blinked the stinging water from his eyes. A semicircular hole in the otherwise impenetrable wall—just large enough to admit a rowboat or two—loomed up before them like a gaping black maw. Tarr kicked his tired legs a few times and slid into the opening.

It was pitch black in the entrance, and Tarr fervently hoped that Tess had been right and they weren't going to be stranded all night in a dark cavern, feeling the cold eating away at their fingers and toes. *I wish we could see*, he thought frustratedly. Then a thought dawned on him.

"Si," he said in a low conversational tone. "Any of your friends still floating in the water?"

"Sure!" Si said chipperly. A moment later, the creatures began to glow bright and blue at the surface of the water and around the dark waving shadows that were Si's arms and legs. The light spread out, unearthly and pale, to either side of them until Tarr could make out the extent of the space above them, and about a foot or so of the water below them.

As Tess had shown them, it was a small room in the shape of a crescent bordering the curve of the circular island. The stone ceiling was low, resting only a few feet above them as they treaded water. There was the open passageway behind them that led back out to the sea, but he could see no door before them that could admit them into the fortress. It was just a long, blank wall. His throat constricted.

"Look, Tarr," Ari pointed. The ocean swelled and heaved beneath them, and Tarr swiveled to look. His heart sank. There were a series of metal rings affixed to the blank walls, and roped to one of them was a boat, rising and falling with the gentle pulse of the water.

"There may be no entrance here," Tarr agreed. "This could just be where she keeps some of her boats to protect them from the rain and weather." His mind was already racing to try and find another way for them to gain entrance. But they had searched through all the plans and there was only the front gate—all the other exits, even those from the kitchens, had been sealed up over the years.

To give himself a moment to think, Tarr began a desultory swim towards the lone boat. The phosphorescent creatures lighting the room were oddly comforting as they blinked and swirled alongside him, and he placed a hand up on the side of the boat. It was about fifteen feet long and made of wood. He tipped it over enough that he could climb halfway up the side of the boat, his torso hanging out of the water. He didn't want Si and Ari to see the anxiety on his face. *Think,* he ordered himself sternly. *Think.*

His eyes scanned up and down the inside of the small boat. Even knowing very little about them, he could see that this particular vessel was meant for speed. Perhaps it was used for Cira's mail? But if she was sending mail to anyone across the sea or down the coast, she'd need a method more reliable than a rowboat. Something began to click in the back of his mind.

Amid the coiled ropes and nautical accoutrements stored in the small belly of the boat, he saw a long wooden pole. And at the front of the boat (here, he pulled himself hand over hand towards the bow) there was a strange circular opening with a fastening ring and screw around it.

"Removable," he muttered to himself, his face brightening as he turned around to face the others. "Ari! The mast on this boat is removable!"

Ari looked at him quizzically. Tarr pushed himself away from the boat and splashed over to him, his heart light. "The boat has a removable mast. It needs to be able to get *under* something. And when Tess looked at the plans for the fortress, she said she thought there was something funny about this wall." As he spoke, realization began to dawn on Ari's face. Tarr felt elated, lightheaded. "There *has* to be an entrance. Under the water. The wall doesn't go down all the way. They bring the boats in here, wait for the tide to go down, take down the masts, and take the boats in under the wall."

Ari turned to Si, who was treading in place and scooping handfuls of water in an attempt to investigate the glowing creatures. "Si, go hold on to the rope on that boat and save your strength. Tarr and I are going to dive down and find the entrance. Stay here."

Si nodded, paddled his way over to the boat, and held on to the rope, affixing it to the wall.

"You start over there," Tarr pointed to the opposite end of the room, and Ari gracefully stroked away. Tarr took a deep breath and pushed himself beneath the waves, running his hands and feet along the wall in front of him, searching for an opening. Nothing. Blank, cold wall. He kicked up to the surface, was greeted with a splash of brisk, bracing salt water to the face, and then took another gulp of air and slid below. Stone, stone—and then, his long fingers hit a corner. He slung his foot forward and it hit nothing but water. There was a rippling tug at his ankle, as if the current were pulling him forward. He'd found an opening. He kicked up to the top.

"Ari, Si, I think I found it," he gasped, and immediately Ari swam back to him.

"I'm the stronger swimmer, I'll test it," Ari said and pushed himself beneath the waves. The silence seemed to stretch on forever as Tarr and Si bobbed along with the swell of the sea. After about a minute, Ari's blond head broke the surface.

"There's a room," Ari panted. "Just a short dive. Take a deep breath, Si, and keep close to me."

The three of them plunged back beneath the surface and kicked forward. Tarr fought back a moment of claustrophobic anxiety as they entered the underwater passageway, but after about ten seconds, Tarr felt Ari rise beside him and Tarr followed, tugging on the back of Si's shirt.

The three of them broke the surface on the other side of the wall, and without another word, the water around them began to glow with the light of the little sea creatures. Tarr couldn't help but gasp.

This room was enormous; much bigger than the antechamber from which they had just come. The ceiling was beautifully domed and carved from sculpted rock, and the dark oblong shadows of dozens of boats surrounded them, black and intimidating against the glowing water.

Though the room was clearly empty of any guards or other human life, there was something so eerie about its enormity and the shapes of the boats around them that the friends were reluctant to communicate anything out loud. Tarr nudged Ari under the water and inclined his head towards a staircase at the opposite end of the room, which rose out of the water and led up to a small landing and door.

Tarr frog-kicked his way in that direction, keeping his head low and checking every few seconds to make sure that Si was still with them and that he was both aware of his surroundings and not about to test out the acoustics of the domed ceiling.

Tarr's feet hit the underwater stairwell and he stumbled forward on his hands and feet, more glad than ever to be out of the water after spending nearly an hour in the ocean. He dropped his sodden shoes heavily onto the landing. His clothes clung to his skinny arms and legs and he shook the salt water from his head, helping Si not to slip as the boy clambered up behind him. The three of them stood on the landing, surveying the room, blue-lipped and starting to shiver.

"We wait here until sunrise," Tarr told them, though the authority in his voice was undermined slightly by the audible chill rising in his throat. "Once the attack begins and the household guards are called away, we can enter Faridor. And then we find Cira."

Si's freckles were nearly white and the boy gave an uncontrollable shake. "I've got an idea," he said suddenly, and took Tarr's thin hand in his, Ari's hand in his other. He closed his gray eyes and took a quick intake of breath, and suddenly Tarr felt a wave of bright golden heat sweep through his hand and shake through his entire being, like an irresistible current. He felt a jolt and looked down at his torso, where steam was literally rising off of his body.

"That's better!" Si said cheerily, and sat down on the cold flagstone. Tarr blinked in surprise and passed a hand down the shirt on his arm. His clothes were completely dry.

"Thanks, Si," Tarr said appreciatively. Ari was staring at Si with uncharacteristic wonder, steam still rising off of his shoulders so that he looked rather like a human bowl of soup. Without saying a word, Ari carefully scooted down alongside Si.

"Can you leave the lights on?" Tarr asked quietly. There was something comforting about the cheery blue lights blinking and winking in the water below. It somehow made the enormous room slightly less intimidating.

"They're nice, aren't they?" Si asked. "I'm tired now. Will you tell me when it's tomorrow?"

Tarr nodded, and Si rested his small head on Tarr's shoulder.

CHAPTER TWENTY-FIVE

The Striker army snaked through the forest paralleling the coast. The moon had all but disappeared, yet the clouds seemed illuminated from within by a strange unearthly glow. Starlight filtered down through the trees onto the long column of horses and soldiers below.

At a crucial bend, as close as they could get to Faridor under cover of the treeline (still somewhat south of the fortress), the column halted. The troops took the opportunity to rest, to drink water, to make nervous last-minute adjustments to their equipment. There would be only one more push north to the trees directly facing the fortress, and there they would wait until dawn for the battle to commence.

Laith, swathed in shadow, turned on the back of his horse and faced the others. "It's time, I think," he said calmly. He dismounted, followed by Athela and Marc, who had managed to catch up with them with little issue. Their goodbyes were short; Athela gave her cousin a swift kiss on the cheek and a squeeze of the hand; Marc clapped him in a hug. Whatever they should have said to one another in that moment—wishes for luck, or for safety, or assurances that they would see one another at the end of it all—somehow seemed unnecessary.

All at once there was a tiny sound off to their left, and the Strikers (and all of their soldiers within hearing distance) tensed, and their hands flew to weapons. A moment later there was another rustling sound, and a figure took shape in the darkness.

"Lord Argolaith," the figure panted. Laith relaxed a hair's breadth, peering forward.

"Identify yourself," he ordered in a hoarse whisper.

"Itzhal, my Lord," the figure replied, and Laith straightened, loosening the hand that had flown to the hilt of his sword. "Sir," Itzhal continued, and it sounded as though he had been running flat-out for some considerable time, "Sir, the guns. The guns have been moved to face the sea. They've turned the guns. Both of them."

Laith's head whipped around to the others and though he could barely make out their faces in the gloom of the wood he thought he could see Athela's shoulders square slightly in what looked like exaltation.

"Good," Laith clapped Itzhal on the arm, shaking it slightly with emphasis. "Good. Pass the word back to the others."

Laith handed over the reins of his horse to Marc, and gave Arfolasth a final pat on the neck. He undid his cloak and draped it over his saddle, re-buckling his sheathed sword across his back. By now, the group of Ashans from the forest had moved forward and were standing like expectant shadows just off to the side.

Without a word or another backward glance, Laith strode away from the column and fell into step alongside the group of Ashans. Silently, they began to travel eastward and soon struck the edge of the trees.

In order to get to Faridor's bridge and take their places in the structures supporting it, they would have to make a very dangerous and risky traversal of the open plain that led to the fortress. They would have to painstakingly pick their way across the field, keeping low and out of sight, never rushing, never getting impatient, never losing their nerve. If one of them went too early, or moved at the wrong time, or was spotted by the sentries atop the wall, the entire operation was for naught.

Hugging the ground, the Ashans and Laith spread out slightly and when the way was clear they advanced forward. Laith could hear the rustling of the grass as the Ashans moved behind him, slowly, deliberately. Cold blue starlight glittered dazzlingly above them. The eclipsed moon was fully overcast in shadow now, but rather than disappearing completely it had started to glow dark and blood-red. Laith stared at it and swallowed, his throat dry.

Mickela, the Ashan closest to Laith, let out a low whistle through their teeth and immediately all of the Ashans dropped to the ground. The grass was about knee-height, and would help to shield them from the eyes of the sentries (or so Laith hoped.) Even so, he kept his cheek close to the damp earth, the smell of rich soil slightly muted by the cold. His ears strained while the seconds ticked by at an interminable pace, as they waited for the sound of an alarm to be raised from the battlements looming up in the distance.

The low whistle sounded again, and slowly Laith drew his head back up and pushed himself up off the ground, landing in a low crouch. All was quiet. The night was cast in that strange red darkness, and together they scrambled forward as quickly as they could. As the faintest edge of a sentry's lantern began to glimmer distantly into view, the whistle sounded and down they went.

They continued in this stop-start way until they reached the opposite side of the plain. The land rose into a last rocky outcrop beside the head of the bridge before descending sharply down a vertical cliffside to the sand and sea below. At the earliest opportunity, the group scuttled out among the clifftop rocks, which would give them ample coverage from the eyes of the sentries on the wall. It would be a delicate matter, however, crossing down the cliffs and clambering up under the bridge. There were sentries and patrols on the bridge itself; their proximity made the venture extremely dangerous.

Mickela was to go first. Laith peered around the edge of his rock, dark eyes flicking from the guards moving above them on the bridge back down to Mickela as they picked their way partially down the cliff. Then, with the nimbleness that only an Ashan could possess, they fairly skipped along the side of the rocky cliff until they vanished beneath the edge of the bridge. They made it look easy.

Laith was quite sure that he wouldn't be nearly as graceful or as fast as they were. He watched carefully as the next Ashan went, trying to see what handholds he took and where he put his legs. It was so dark, though, especially under the shadow of the bridge, that it was almost impossible to see.

There was a tap on his shoulder and Laith turned, doing a swift double-take as he realized that it was Archer's twin Jet, not Archer himself, who wanted to address him. The pale face, so eerily familiar, leaned forward, and he whispered something in Ashan. His northern accent was so pronounced that Laith, who had a basic smattering of the language, couldn't follow.

Laith shook his head infinitesimally. "I can't understand," he whispered.

Jet groped for words; he clearly didn't speak the Common language. Laith cursed himself for not being better about listening to Archer's accent when he spoke Ashan. "Go," Archer's twin said, and then mimed a finger moving back and forth between the two of them.

"Together?" Laith asked, understanding what he meant.

Jet nodded. "I go." Then he pointed at Laith, clearly indicating that he should follow.

"Yes," said Laith. "Good."

The nearest guard on the bridge turned and began walking his path back towards the fortress. It was the best chance they were going to get. Jet rose and swung over the side of the rock, nimbly descending down a few feet. He waited for Laith to scramble over beside him, and then the two of them, in tandem, went sideways along the rocky cliff wall towards the underside of the bridge. Laith kept his eyes trained on all the handholds that Jet was using, and they made fast progress. Laith could tell that the Ashan was purposefully simplifying the route he was taking so that Laith could follow him, and the prince was grateful.

When they were only ten feet or so from the safe cover of the bridge, Archer's twin suddenly snaked out a hand and clasped Laith on the arm. Laith instinctively froze. There were voices close to them and footsteps approaching. Laith could hear the voices of the sentries above.

"Coming to relieve you," said one voice.

"Good," yawned the other.

"Anything out there?" said the first. "Weird moon, eh?"

The voices were even closer. Laith and Archer's twin met one another's eyes. The sentries were obviously ambling over, intending to lean on the rail right beside them and look over. There was no way that they weren't going to be seen.

Suddenly, like a bird taking flight, Archer's twin pushed back from the cliff wall and sprang out into the open air. It was so startling that Laith had to resist the urge to shout after him. The Ashan seemed to shoot like an arrow towards the nearest crossbeam; one long arm flung out and he swung safely into place under the cover of the bridge.

Well, it's unlikely I'm going to be able to do that, Laith mused wryly. Thinking quickly, he scrambled as fast as he could along the rocks, trying desperately not to dislodge any as he went. But it would only be another second or two before one of the guards' heads would pop over the edge of the bridge. He wasn't going to be able to make it.

Laith glanced over his shoulder and saw that Archer's brother had extended almost all the way out from underneath the bridge, one hand holding onto one of the support beams, the other hand outstretched. He was clearly telling Laith to jump. There was nothing for it.

It was a leap of only a few feet, but the distance seemed vast with the black earth yawning up beneath him. Still, there wasn't much choice. As the sentries above took their last footstep, Laith turned and awkwardly vaulted out into the blue, his arms outstretched, groping through the air.

He flew for a second and as soon as he felt himself beginning to fall he thought fleetingly that this was it; in short order he would crash heavily onto the rocks below. But an instant later, he felt fingers—strong fingers, like steel cables—wrap solidly around his wrist, and he felt all of his weight drop heavily and dangle in midair like a ball at the end of a string. He raised a shoulder and braced himself as he swung forward and bounced slightly off of the support beam of the bridge, then shot his other hand into the air, where it was taken by another strong unseen set of fingers, and Laith felt himself being hauled upwards into the air until he was free to put his feet on the bridge supports and steady himself on his own.

Archer's brother was waiting there, yellow eyes calm and cool. They waited in silence as the two sentries above finished their conversation, then walked off to resume their patrol of the bridge. Once they were gone, Archer's brother leaned forward.

"Good?" he asked.

"Good," Laith replied with a thankful smile. "Very good."

The other Ashans' traversal of the cliff face to their hiding place under the bridge was far less eventful than it had been for Laith. In short order they were all safely beneath and could begin to move forward, crossing from one side of the bridge to the other until they were stationed directly below the main gate at Faridor. And there they would stay, waiting for dawn to come.

Across the open plain facing the fortress, under cover of the forest, Athela and the other troops took their places. The advance scouts had managed to capture a few of Cira's soldiers stationed as sentries in the woods; there would be no opportunity for them to return to Faridor to warn her. Athela could only hope that the scouts would not be missed before dawn broke.

The army behind them was nervous and restless. She could feel it in the air. The dark circle of shadow had begun to slide slowly off the moon, the pinprick crescent of silver moonlight growing larger and larger by the second. No one spoke, they all crouched down in the underbrush, their eyes fixed on the looming shadow of the fortress across the open plain, glancing up periodically to the sky as the moon emerged. *The guns have turned*, Athela reminded herself. *The guns have turned.*

If Laith and the Ashans didn't manage to take the wall and reach the main gate in time for her to break through, it was all for nothing. There were so few Ashans. Perhaps they wouldn't make it in time. Perhaps Cira's troops would be able to move the guns back to their places facing the mainland, and would blow them all to bits as they raced across the open plain, vulnerable and without any sort of cover. Athela swallowed hard, fighting down the unbidden mental image of the earth opening up before her and swallowing her up.

She waited beside Aria, who was uncharacteristically quiet. His head was raised, delicate nostrils huffing in the cold night air, his ears pricked towards Faridor. It was almost as if he understood the importance of what he was going to be asked to do the following day.

Athela rubbed her palm across the front of his silky muzzle. "Good boy," she said in an undertone. "I've got a treat for you, Aria," she continued. "I need you to run as fast as we can across that plain tomorrow morning. We've got to make it in through the gate as soon as we see it's opened. We won't have much time. They won't be able to hold it open for long. It's up to us. We've got to lead the others in. And you've got to run faster than you ever have before."

Aria, of course, made no reply, but ducked his head swiftly into the palm of her hand before raising it again and re-training his gaze on Faridor. Athela stepped back and automatically ran her hand down Aria's foreleg. Sound and strong. She heard a footstep behind her and turned. In the gloom she could make out two men approaching: both short, one stocky and broad, the other slim.

"Hello," she greeted Marc and Cade, who came to stand beside her.

"Are you ready?" Cade asked.

"As we'll ever be." Athela patted Aria's glossy neck.

"Look, Athela," Cade said, "if something happens tomorrow..."

Athela was rather surprised. She hadn't pegged Cade as the type to make pre-battle pronouncements or absolutions. She raised her eyebrows and waited for him to go on.

"Make sure that Rowan is taken care of," he said finally. "She's had a difficult time of it, and I've...I've grown to care for her. Please make sure that she'll be all right. Find her somewhere to live...somewhere where there is a garden."

"Of course," Athela said, surprised. She didn't have the heart to point out that if they lost the battle, there would likely be no gardens available to *any* of them ever again.

"I'll take care of you, in any case," Marc assured him. "During the battle tomorrow. Tarr asked me to."

"I have Wolf," Cade said. "But thank you. I'm not...I'm not the best swordsman. I'll have to rely on some luck tomorrow. To get me through." In the dim gloom, Athela thought she could detect a wan smile across her cousin's face.

"Me too," Athela said, in a vain attempt to be reassuring.

"Tarr asked me to look out for both of you," Marc said firmly.

"Thank you, Marc," Cade said gratefully.

"You could always sit it out," Athela said tentatively, then realized that Cade might take offense to the suggestion. "Not because I think you can't fight or because you're not brave enough. You're...valuable.

You're the King of Joymaril after all."

Cade stared at her silently for a few moments. "I have more to fight for than most of the people behind us who are ready to risk their lives," he said. "How can I possibly ask them to go if I won't go myself?"

Athela gave a shrug and turned back to her horse. For the fortieth time, she checked the tension of his girth and then gave Aria a scratch or two on the belly.

"I will feel better though," Cade spoke up again behind her, "knowing that you two are with me."

Athela turned back around to him and laid her hand on his shoulder. Perhaps it was the moon's reemergence but suddenly it seemed as though the light were slightly paler, the shadows lilac in color rather than cobalt. She could make out Marc's face, his close-cropped hair, the scar across his face. Cade beside him, pale hair tousled every which way.

"Look," said Marc, and motioned with his eyes in the opposite direction. Athela turned, and where before there had been only darkness, a pale blue was growing on the horizon, the thinnest thread of pink and gold beginning to show over the distant black line of the sea beyond them. Dawn was breaking.

In the bowels of Faridor, Rane had kept vigil beside her door for the entire night. She was in a strange sort of half-state between meditation and consciousness, where she let her mind and body rest while remaining ready for anything that was to come. At the first sound in the distance—a thin metallic screech and following clang that signaled the morning food being brought around to the prisoners—her eyes immediately snapped open and into focus and she crouched forward, ready to act.

The night's long hours hadn't driven away the conviction she felt that somehow, some way, she had managed to connect with Archer the night before, and that he had felt it, too. She was certain that he would try to do something, *anything* to get her out of her captivity, now that he knew she was there. However, it wasn't as though he could try and casually open up her cell door as he was being dragged out to whatever they had in store for him. No, she reasoned that what he would try to do would be to leave her something outside, something that the guards would not suspect, something that would give her some way of getting herself out of her locked cell. And to do that, she would need to be able to reach outside her door. And the only way of doing that was through the little portal through which her food was delivered twice a day.

So she waited, crouched right beside the metal sheet in the lower part of her door. She could hear movement coming down the hallway, the slam of the food doors, the clatter of bowls hitting the floor. Three doors away... two doors away...one door away. She tensed her muscles, feeling her mind go blank as she trained every one of her senses on the door.

The sliding portal of her door flew open and the plate was tossed in, sloshing a bit of indeterminate slop on the floor. A second later a spoon was thrown in.

Rane's hand snaked out into the air, caught it, twirled it in her fingers and just as the metal food door was slammed shut, Rane thrust the long handle of the spoon into the portal opening, wedging it open just a tiny bit of the way. She waited with bated breath to see if any of the guards had noticed her do it, but through the tiny crack in the food door she could hear them move on down the hall. They hadn't seen it. And now she had the leverage to wedge the food door back open.

The pattern of the morning, which had become so familiar to her over the course of the last week, took on special meaning now that she realized it was Archer in the next cell over. She pressed her ear close to the crack in the door, listening carefully as the guards finished their rounds, then returned to Archer's cell.

"All right," said a gruff male voice, one of the guards. "Everyone ready?"

"Seems unnecessary," said another, more high-pitched. "He didn't put up a lot of fight last time. I think the fire's gone out of him."

"Orders were to always escort him up with five of us," said the first voice. "No exceptions. He's supposed to be a tricky one. He could be faking."

"I doubt he's faking after what he went through yesterday," the other muttered. "Surprised he's still alive."

"Well he's in for it today, in any case," said the first. "Come on."

There was more talking, but it was too low for Rane to make out.

She waited. She could hear the clank and creak of metal as one of the guards lifted the heavy round handle on the door and the beam of wood locking Archer's door slid open. There was another heavy creak as the door opened. This was followed by some indiscernible mumbling; Rane strained her ears to try and make out if one of the voices belonged to her friend.

There was a shuffling and clanking sound as the group of guards moved out of the cell and came down the hallway. Just as they reached Rane's door, there was a scuffling sound, and an almighty crash, and one of the guards yelled, "Grab him!" Rane could hear an "oof" as someone was struck, and then there was a crash against her door as someone was flung bodily into it; Rane was thrown back from the force of the blow.

She scrambled back to the door and checked to see that the wedge in the food door was still in place; luckily, it was. She set her ear back against the opening. The commotion, whatever it was, seemed to die down and the sounds dissipated as the group went down the hallway. Rane listened for a full ten seconds, just to ensure that the way was clear and that there was no one outside the cell door. All was silent.

Rane reached down to the spoon she had wedged in the narrow food slot and, with some effort, leveraged it and pushed it back so that the small door could slide open. Rane lowered her head and peered out of the slot as far as she could. From what she could see, there was nothing. The hallway outside seemed empty, the same dreary, dark slabs of rock. Maybe it hadn't worked. Maybe Archer hadn't been able to do anything that could get her out.

She crouched even further and tentatively stuck her arm out of the slot in the door. She explored the ground with her fingers for a few seconds, and felt nothing but dusty cold stone. *It's all right*, she thought to herself, trying to buoy up her spirits. *It's all right. Think. You've still got the food door open. You can do something. Think.* But she didn't have much time. Archer could probably buy her a few extra minutes with whatever antics he could muster, but the guards would be back shortly to collect her plate and utensils.

And then—her fingers brushed against a long, round object. She grabbed for it, and her fingers closed. It was some kind of pole; a broom handle, perhaps. She felt her heart leap with relief, and she immediately scooted around to the other edge of the door, positioning her body so that she'd have the most leverage.

She twisted her head partially out of the food slot, conscious of every second ticking past. Above her, she could see the round metal handle on the door bolt. The bolt was designed to slide in and out of a bracket, barring the door from being opened from the inside. She withdrew her head and sat back on the floor of the cell.

It only took a few moments. With one hand extended out through the food slot, she raised up the broom handle and threaded it through the metal loop fastened to the sliding door. And then she shifted her weight and pulled the broom handle back towards herself. It was awkward with the use of only one arm and it took considerable effort, but after a moment she could feel the heavy wooden bolt on the front of her door sliding back and after a few protracted seconds the door gave a reluctant creak and the door cracked open ever so slightly, a thin sliver of light at the edge. She was free.

Rane leapt to her feet and surveyed the area around her in her cell. There wasn't much that would be of use and time was of the essence. She pushed her cell door open; it was so heavy that she had to throw some of her body's weight behind it for it to budge.

She looked down at the hallway floor right in front of her door. She had been right. In the struggle outside in the hallway, Archer had managed to knock a broom down right at the base of her door for her to pick up. She could see a dustpan and bucket tucked away in a nearby corner, and assumed that Archer had engineered some sort of scuffle that took the group straight for it. She reached down and picked up the broom and broke it over her knee so that she now at least had the long handle as a weapon.

She tried to gauge what the best next step would be. The guards were bound to come back at any moment. She'd have to fight past them one way or the other. Quickly, she closed the door of her cell and re-bolted it, then she skipped across the hallway and tucked herself into the nook that housed the bucket and pan and waited.

A few minutes later she heard footsteps echoing down the hallway and she crouched down, the broom handle and bucket ready in her hands. Two unsuspecting men rounded the turn and barely had time to react before Rane darted out, the handle twisting in her hand. With her makeshift weapons, she dealt them huge cracks on the head and they both went down like sacks of flour.

Working quickly, she unbolted the door to her cell and, with some effort, dragged them inside and deposited them on the floor. She examined them for weapons, but they had none, as they appeared to only be jailors, not house guards. She fished out a ring of keys from one of their pockets and stepped back, surveying her work. It had been a neat job. With any luck they would stay unconscious for some time, and any thumping or banging they made on the door of the cell might be chalked up to the futile protestations of a prisoner within.

Bolting the cell door once again, Rane picked up her handy broom handle. She hugged the side of the passageway and began to run swiftly forward, following the path that the guards had taken. All she had to do was find her way out.

CHAPTER TWENTY-SIX

Crouched among the support beams near the end of the bridge, Laith and the Ashans waited. Their eyes strained through the criss-crossed wood supports towards the visible slivers of horizon, breath bated as the hazy rays of the sun began to stretch towards them.

Laith, who was more familiar than any of the others with pre-battle nerves, sat quietly, re-playing their plan through his head. The repetition helped. It cleared his head until there was nothing left except a calm humming sound. It had always been his ritual before a fight. But even as he went through the motions of calming his body and focusing his mind, the monumentally high stakes of the coming fight kept piercing through his protective shield.

His dark eyes watched as the sky lightened, first slowly, and then with ever-increasing speed. The first pink haze of sunrise peeked above the black sea, and then (though the sun itself was mostly obscured by the shadow of the fortress), he could see the edge of golden light spreading upwards over the rocks. It was dawn. It was time.

The Ashans had been alternating glances between the horizon and Laith, anxiously waiting for the signal to attack. Slowly, Laith swiveled around, checked his leather vambraces, tightened the buckle strapping his sword to his back, and met Mickela's eyes. He gave a curt nod.

The Ashans nodded back, and looked at one another. Laith could see the expressions of fear on their faces, watched as each of them fought it back, drew strength from the others. It occurred to him that these were some of the bravest people he had ever met and a deep conviction stirred in him to do whatever it took to keep them alive. *They just have to get me up the wall,* he thought. *Get me up there, and we can take it.*

The Ashans turned and began to pick their way through the support beams for the last few feet before crossing onto the rocky island of Faridor. Laith followed slowly, deliberately, and as he reached the stone face of the island he craned his head a little and could see the huge, seemingly impassable wall of the fortress rising up above them. For a split second he had a moment of doubt. There was no way *anyone*— Ashan or no—could make it up that wall without ropes or a ladder. No way. They were certain to fall to their deaths. He had to fight back the urge to reach out, to grab the arm of the Ashan nearest him, to pull them back, to tell them to forget it, that they would somehow find another way.

Archer's twin brother nudged him and Laith snapped out of his momentary lapse. Jet was carrying the rope that they would let down for Laith so that he could pull himself up to the top of the wall. Those eyes—which had looked laughingly back at Laith so many times from Archer's face—acted as a check. Laith swallowed and crouched lower, ready to spring into action.

The Ashans, with some sort of unspoken signal, moved as a single group out from underneath the corner of the bridge and over the rocks at the base of the fortress wall. Laith braced for a cry or yell, but either the sentries on the wall didn't see them, or the guards on the bridge had their backs turned, looking away from Faridor out to the plain and the forest beyond. Laith edged closer to the end of the bridge and (with considerably less grace than the Ashans) moved from the bridge's support beams to the rocks at the base of the island. From here, he would have a good view of the Ashans' ascent while still being sheltered from the eyes of the sentries above.

And then, Laith watched in astonishment as the Ashans began to climb. He had seen some of Archer and Tarr's halfhearted playful acrobatics here and there, and he had heard tales of the Ashans' climbing abilities, but he had never before seen them in person. From what his eyes could discern, there was barely a single handhold in the entire wall; the stones in its construction were worn almost sheer from the weather and the wind. But the Ashans looked as though they were climbing a dozen invisible ladders up to the top. Their fingers found tiny nooks and their feet (Laith hadn't noticed how relatively soft and flexible their boots were before) found infinitesimal rocks jutting out. Using every possible means they propelled themselves up the wall with absolutely astonishing speed.

And then, splitting the quiet of the morning air, the call went out: a shout, then another, growing in intensity. They'd been seen.

Laith braced himself, muttering through his teeth, willing them to get higher, for the handholds not to break, for their boots not to slip. The call went up again, forceful; there was shouting on the bridge, footsteps began to pound above. Laith didn't take his eyes away from the group. And then there was the zing of an arrow from someone on the wall. The yells were getting louder and louder, more voices picking up the call, sounding the alarm, summoning guards up from below. There was another arrow and another, and then, with a sickening lurch, Laith saw as one arrow hit its mark. One of the Ashans about two thirds of the way up the wall was struck, and she peeled back from the wall, plummeting down to the rocks out of sight.

After that first casualty, the Ashans took evasive maneuvers. Rather than climbing in a straight line, they began to change directions, going faster and faster and zigzagging as they scaled the wall. Laith could barely believe his eyes. He thought they'd been moving fast before, but this was almost beyond belief. Hissing arrows grew in frequency but no other Ashan was struck. Off in the distance a bell rang, and in another excruciating five seconds or so, the Ashans were high enough as to be out of his line of vision. Seconds passed and no other bodies fell. *They reached the top of the wall. They must have.*

Laith calmed his mind and focused. There was such a narrow window of time in which Kagai's forces would be confused and disorganized, and they had to capitalize on that advantage for the precious few minutes they had it. Laith stared straight ahead at the base of the fortress, and then, seemingly dropped from the heavens, the end of a rope appeared with a loud *thump*, heavy and thick on the rocks before him.

Laith heaved himself forward into the open morning light, scrambled up the rock face, and grabbed the base of the rope. He began hauling himself up it as fast as he could. He had the advantage of having the leverage of the rope, and took a page out of the Ashans' book, dodging and weaving wherever he could, ducking when he felt the cold wind whistling next to his ear with the sound of an oncoming arrow. The arrows were fewer and farther between than they had been; Laith assumed that the Ashans who had made it up to the top were keeping most of the Kagaian wall archers busy.

The sounds of the soldiers' yells and the distant clanks of metal on metal faded in his ears until they were nothing but a hollow thrum. He could see the summit of the wall growing closer and closer, the burst of adrenaline sending his sure hands firing up the rope one after another, pulling him ever higher. The sea rose up into his scope of view; dawn seemed to be everywhere around him now, pink and misty and innocent, a strange contrast to the dirty work before him. Hand over hand he went, higher and higher, until he could just about reach the top of the wall, then two arms and twelve sinewy fingers shot over the edge and pulled him the rest of the way just as an arrow sung past his ear; he ducked and landed squarely on top of a flat slab of stone, his feet steady, his hand already reaching for the sword at his back.

The Ashans, with their speed and the element of surprise, were still only faced by a few Kagaian soldiers, but there were cries in the distance, sounds of reinforcements being mustered. There was a pause in fighting as the Kagaian soldiers registered the identity of the newcomer who had just breached the wall. Laith could see the blood draining from their faces. They recognized him.

Laith dove forward past the group of Ashans, and cleaved his way cleanly, efficiently, and mercilessly through the first pack of Kagaian guards. It was over so quickly that it momentarily shocked the other soldiers, who looked uncertainly at one another and took tentative steps back, their knives and swords no longer sure in their hands. One guard, farther back, shot an arrow in his direction, but with one almost careless swipe of his sword Laith knocked the arrow harmlessly to one side. He continued advancing through the empty space between the Ashans and the guards. The group of Ashans now stood at his back, staring at him with a mixture of shock and horror. Laith's golden head was bare, his dark eyes trained on his prey.

He half turned his head and addressed the Ashans standing behind him. "Go secure the guns before they can get to them. Find something to shield yourselves from arrows. Five of you stay with me."

The Ashans, who had been stunned into immobility by the efficient brutality of Laith's first skirmish, stirred into action. He could hear footsteps as most of the group turned and began to run towards the far wall of the fortress. There was still the danger that the Kagaian guards would be able to muster their forces and move the guns back around the wall to point at the land and the Strikers' army. They had to keep them secure for as long as they could until the Strikers breached the fortress.

But for the Strikers to do so, they first had to open the gate.

The gate itself was very close. Laith could see that, just as the blueprints had indicated, the gate was a portcullis, operated by a wheel and pulley system at the top of the wall next to a small guard tower. Standing in their way were ten or fifteen Kagaian guards, who were stumbling backwards uncertainly, their feet shuffling, their faces white. Out of his peripheral vision, Laith could see little specks of people within the fortress complex below running back and forth. It wouldn't be long before Cira's forces would come together in greater numbers. He had to act.

Laith could feel the Ashans drawing closer behind him, felt another whistle as an arrow whizzed past, this time shot from another tower. He lifted his sword and charged forward.

Like a perfectly balanced dancer, he spun past the first few guards, catching them behind their backs. Then he twisted his sword in his hand and ducked and wove through the rest until he was nearly behind the entire pack of Kagaian guards. The guards were now completely discombobulated; turning left and right, searching for where Laith had gone. The walkway along the top of the wall was relatively narrow and they kept colliding with one another as they tried to turn and re-orient themselves. In another breath, they were set upon by the Ashans, who went through them like a slicing knife. One guard was thrown from the ramparts, and the others were quickly mown over; Laith could see the rising triumph in the Ashans' eyes.

Laith dodged a few more arrows and could see in the distance that a column of Kagaian soldiers was beginning to mount a stairwell to the wall opposite them. Here again the wall's walkway lent them an advantage in that it was too narrow to accommodate all of them in one large group; they wouldn't be able to rush him at once. But they were coming nonetheless.

Sheathing his sword, Laith ran hard, the Ashans on his heels, for the gatehouse overlooking the bridge. Laith commanded two of the Ashans, both archers from southwestern tribes, to take shelter in the gatehouse and provide them cover. He and the other three Ashans went to the round windlass that operated the gate's opening and closing mechanism. Each of them grabbed one of the windlass's handles and began to twist it. It was heavy work, and for a few seconds it seemed as though nothing was happening. But then after a few brutal moments, there was an almighty groan and a metallic creak, and the gate of Faridor began to slowly open. *Go, Athela*, Laith thought to himself through gritted teeth, as the windlass slowly grated and turned beneath his hands. *Go.*

Across the plain, Athela was sitting atop Aria, gray eyes staring unblinkingly at the front gate of Faridor. Aria, clearly sensing that something was up, was no longer standing quietly, but rearing and plunging, tossing his head and forcing her to turn him again and again in tiny circles to keep him from running off with her. She had seen the small black dots go snaking their way up the side of the wall, had seen the skirmish at the top. It was almost time.

Then, as she watched, she saw the thinnest sliver of space appear at the bottom of Faridor's portcullis, and the light behind it began to grow and grow in size. The gate was opening.

Athela stood in her stirrups, her heart racing, and turned Aria around to face the mounted riders and Striker footsoldiers behind them. She looked across each and every face, many of them young, many of them unsure. She could see the recruits who had promised to follow her into battle. Now was their time to make good on that vow.

"Who will ride with me to Faridor?" she called to them.

A sudden roar erupted from their throats as if they'd been bottling it in for hours and hours. The roar spread through the trees, sending startled birds flying up into the sky in thick black clouds; the trees shook around them. It grew so loud that the earth seemed to rumble and echo it back to them, and horses began shaking their heads and pawing at the dirt and skittering left and right. Aria gave a full rear up into the air; Athela hauled his head around with one tight rein and the horse spun on his hind legs, forelegs thrashing. She pointed him straight at the gate and dug her heels into his gray flanks. And then he was off like a streak of light, his hind legs like two pistons, propelling them forward faster and faster and faster, eating up the ground as it sped beneath them.

It took a few seconds for Aria to realize that, for once, he had full control of his head. With that, Athela felt the horse switch into a higher gear beneath her, surging forward and taking the bit in his teeth, his ears flicking back every few seconds for the sound of the horses charging behind him, his own speed compelling those behind him to go faster. Athela didn't even bother to look over her shoulder. She could feel them in her wake, urging their mounts on to keep up with her. She was balanced precipitously forward in her saddle, her weight over Aria's neck, his gray mane whipping back into her face, stinging her eyes as he flew across the plain towards the fortress.

And then the world seemed to tilt and give way. With a sudden, sickening jolt, Athela felt Aria's hoof catch on something in the earth and the horse stumbled violently, a split second away from doing a full somersault with her atop him. But he threw his legs out and forward, catching the fall, and the force of it threw her up and nearly over his ears as he struggled to regain his balance. He tossed his head, scrambling, each delicate leg going in a different direction; as he did the headstall of his bridle slipped over his ears and the bit fell from his teeth. The bridle slid uselessly to the ground behind them. Athela had nearly come off, but she instinctively dug in with her knees and legs and grabbed huge clumps of mane to steady herself. For a few suspended seconds she hung nearly completely off the side of his neck before he gave another surge with his back legs to right himself once again.

Slowly the horse began to rebuild his speed, and Athela, whose mind had dizzily scrambled to cling on during those terrifying few seconds, assessed. Aria was now running flat-out without a bridle; her own feet had slipped from the stirrups, which flapped uselessly around Aria's sides. Below, she could see that he'd nicked himself on the leg; there were dark flashes of red blood on his cannon bone as he churned heedlessly forward. Aria could hear behind him that the other horses had almost caught up when he'd stumbled; he snorted loudly and seemed to redouble his speed with a renewed determination to pull away from them.

Athela had no chance to find her stirrups. She twisted his mane around and around her hands and pressed him with her calf, pointing him straight at Faridor's main gate, which was growing closer and closer with every passing second, rising like a black mountain before her. The sound of hoofbeats was like thunder all around her, and she was almost close enough to see the stricken faces of the astonished troops staring down at her from atop the wall.

They were nearly at the bridge; luckily, Aria seemed to have a sense of where to go, and she only needed to guide him a little. An arrow was shot past them and missed; she gritted her teeth and dug her heels into his sides, and Aria flew across the bridge. The clatter of his hooves on the bridge itself was deafening; she ducked instinctively as another arrow whizzed past, praying Aria wouldn't slip and send them both crashing over the side into the sea as it flashed by below. The gate of Faridor stood open, and she squinted her eyes shut as they blazed under it, the light of the morning temporarily shadowed in the archway. Then they burst out on the other side into the outer keep of the fortress.

The keep was still relatively empty, but the few Kagaian guards that were there rushed headlong at her. Athela dug her left heel in and turned Aria to the right, where the sheer speed and force of the horse's body sent soldiers diving out of their way before they could even go for their swords. The inner keep of the fortress—the second, smaller wall that was the last barrier between the outside world and the interior of the fortress itself—was just beyond. As she looked towards it, she could see that it, too, had a gate, and that gate was already starting to lower.

"No!" she shouted through gritted teeth and sat firmly back, signaling Aria to stop. The stones beneath Aria's hooves were slick, the horse slid a few feet and clattered loudly as she redirected him towards the gateway of the inner keep. Around them the air was suddenly filled with the sound of hooves and clashing metal as the Striker riders began to spill in after her and more Kagaian guards began to materialize out of the inner sanctum of the fortress, charging across the outer keep to meet the Strikers in battle.

Meanwhile, the spiked gate of the inner keep was lowering down and down. The closing mechanism for this gate was located on the ground rather than up on the wall; Kagaian soldiers were frantically turning the windlass faster and faster to lower it. She dug in her legs and urged Aria towards the inner gate; the sounds of horses and combat and the thunderous rattle of hooves were all around her now, filling her ears and pounding at her chest. The spikes of the gate were almost closed—but Aria slicked under it like a gray arrow and instantly Athela was off her horse, her curved sword in her hand, going straight for the handful of soldiers at the windlass. They scattered as she approached; one tried to come at her with a sword but she slashed through the air and he dropped like a stone.

The outer keep was pure chaos now; the mounted riders had been blocked from following Athela to the inner keep by the fresh surge of Kagaian guards. *Where are the Striker footsoldiers?* Athela cursed beneath her breath, gray eyes searching for them past the flurry of horses and red and green cloaks choking the outer keep. She couldn't see them.

A few dismounted Striker riders spotted Athela and began to run towards her to help, but it was almost too late—the inner gate was still lowering, the windlass turning of its own accord like a ghostly hand was moving it. Athela threw her weight on it to try and stop the gate closing, but it was useless. She wasn't strong enough to stop it, and down it continued.

Athela whistled over her shoulder through her teeth and heard Aria's hooves clatter up behind her. Glancing around, she could see packs of Kagaian guards running this way and that on the wall, coming out of seemingly every door or window in Faridor, like swarming ants protecting their nest. Thinking quickly, she grabbed a coil of rope that was next to the revolving windlass and looped one end around one of the wheel's handles and attached the other to a metal buckle on her horse's saddle.

"Back!" she commanded, and Aria snorted, his head bowing and tossing as his nimble gray legs skittered backwards over the stones, pulling the line between himself and the windlass taut. The gate, too low now to admit a horse, creaked to a stop just as the dismounted Strikers crossed beneath it, ducking to avoid the sharp spikes at the base of the gate.

Athela barely had time to admire her handiwork. There was a thud at her back that ricocheted through her core and for a terrifying second she was sure she had been shot, but after a moment passed and there was no pain, she realized that the arrow had lodged in her protective shoulder armor. She reached over her shoulder with one hand, withdrawing the arrow with a low grunt, and turned around to try and see who had had the gall to shoot at her.

It was almost at that exact second that the space around her erupted into absolute pandemonium. The inner keep, which had before seemed so empty, now was a seething sea of green; soldiers were coming straight for her and were hurtling towards the walls to try and reach higher vantage points. In mere seconds she would be dangerously outnumbered and at the mercy of any number of arrows.

The group of dismounted Strikers came up beside her and immediately set about raising the portcullis of the inner keep back up to its full height. "Hold the gate!" Athela screamed at them, and, untying Aria, she threw everything she had onto pushing against the windlass, yelling aloud with the effort, though her voice was lost in the deafening clash of combat surrounding them on all sides. The gate was raised, the swarm of Kagaian soldiers had nearly reached them; before Athela could even register another thought, the Striker soldier behind her was shot with an arrow from some unseen source and collapsed onto the windlass. The Kagaian soldiers were nearly on top of them; they were a mass of anonymous shouting faces and waving weapons. Athela spun around to face them, her sword flashing at the ready—

At that instant, a sea of crimson atop flying horses flooded through the gate and into the inner keep, riding like a red wave over the green Kagaian soldiers, cleaving their numbers fully in half. Breathless with relief, Athela seized the few moments she had. She sheathed her sword, took the rope she had used to stop the windlass, and flipped the coil into a few knots to make a makeshift halter for Aria. She slipped the rope over his head and nose and hauled herself up and onto his back. She was always better atop a horse.

Rane's progress was painfully slow as she crept through the dungeons, winding her way as best she could back up into the belly of the fortress. Twice she'd had to duck behind a corner—once behind a pile of crates—while Kagaian guards ran past. Rane began to get the sense that something big was going on outside. There was something in the guards' increasingly frenzied movements, and the hushed, urgent whispers being passed in the hall.

It didn't help the speed of her progress that the layout of the dungeons was constructed as a maze; it was all Rane could do to keep from doubling back on herself over and over again. The dungeons had been purposefully designed to look uniform in all ways: harsh black stone lining the ceilings and floors, lit torches flickering at the same intervals down the walls. *If I can just get back up to the ground floor, no one should be able to recognize me,* she thought to herself. *I can blend in once again.* The thought of running into Lord Seth gave her a momentary twinge of involuntary terror, but she pushed it aside. There would be a reckoning with him, she was sure of it. But not quite yet.

Making what felt like her fortieth right turn, she was alerted by the sound of urgent footsteps coming her way. Immediately, she dropped to her hands on the ground, hiding within the shadow cast by a torch on the wall. *I need a proper weapon,* she thought grimly. The broken wooden broomstick, which she still held in her hand, wasn't going to be much help.

A pack of Kagaian guards rushed past her. *If something is happening...if the Strikers are actually attacking, that's the direction they'll be going,* she reasoned. *Everyone will be called up to fight at the front.*

Keeping a safe distance, she followed the group out through the twisting black passageways, and with relief saw, at a distance, a glimmer of what looked like daylight up ahead through the slats in a broad, heavy door. There appeared to be only a single sentry guarding it. The group of Kagaian troops paused, and exchanged words. The sentry pushed the door open and stood aside for the group to pass. In a moment he was alone. Now was her chance.

Moments later Rane slipped past the prison door, over the felled body of the sentry, into a blissful patch of morning light filtering into the hall through a small window high up on one of the fortress walls. She wasn't familiar with the room into which she had emerged, but it was clear that she was no longer in the dungeon. The room was high-ceilinged and grand in scale but had a utilitarian feel; it was devoid of any decoration or artwork and opened into a long hall that led towards the main entrance of Faridor. Rane surmised that it must be a place for soldiers to gather and wait during shift changes. For her part, she had never been so glad to see the inside of Faridor's ground floor before. She had the sentry's knife tucked in her waistband and the broom pole still light in her hands. She stretched her arms and neck, feeling her limbs starting to finally loosen after their cramped captivity.

Where have they taken Archer?

If the Strikers were indeed attacking, he didn't have long to live. There was no way Cira would let the Strikers have the satisfaction of getting him back alive, even if they did manage the impossible task of breaching the fortress walls. Cira seemed to be enjoying toying with him, prolonging his suffering, but a Striker attack might prompt a swift execution. Rane only hoped she wouldn't be too late.

She stepped out into the adjoining corridor and nearly ran headlong into a figure coming at her from the opposite direction. In a flash, she stepped back and readied herself for a fight. Then she saw who it was and stopped, momentarily stupefied.

Cicada stood opposite her, armed with what looked like a long wooden pole, almost identical to Rane's broken broomstick, taken perhaps from a utility closet. Her vulpine face contracted in astonishment at the sight of her friend. She glanced at the pole in her hand, looked to the one in Rane's hand, and gave her a relieved lopsided smirk. She dropped the pole down to her side.

"I was coming to rescue you," she signed, grinning

Rane nearly laughed aloud. "I appreciate it," she said. "What's happening?"

"The Strikers attacked at dawn," Cicada told her. "That's the only reason I was able to risk it—everything's in an uproar, and all of the reserve prison guards have been called up to fight. They breached the wall. Security around the prisons has been too strong until now. I couldn't come for you before now. I'm sorry."

Rane felt a surge of pride in her chest at the thought of the Strikers outside the door. She thought of Tarr, somewhere near, perhaps even inside the fortress walls. She hoped he was all right, and that he wouldn't try anything too foolhardy.

Cicada nudged her to get her attention. "They have one of the other Strikers. Archer," she signed, her face alight.

"I know," Rane replied. "I found out he was being held in the cell beside me. I have no idea where he might be now."

"*I* do," Cicada said, looking a bit smug.

"What?" Rane exclaimed incredulously.

"I was watching outside the dungeons as soon as the first alert was raised at dawn, to see if there was a chance to slip in and get you out. I saw them take Archer past me so I followed them. I know where he is."

Rane couldn't help herself. She reached forward and hugged Cicada's thin form against her. Cicada's sharp, dark eyebrows raised in bemused surprise, but she seemed pleased.

Rane released her. "Take me there," she nodded, and the two women took off running.

Laith leaned over the side of the wall and looked down at the melee below. They had held the gate long enough for the Striker army to sweep inside; had seen Athela stumble, recover, and then go pounding across the bridge and slip under the inner keep's gate. They had done it. The way was open.

Archer's twin brother was still close to him, the black and white-tipped head bobbing in and out as he grappled with a few Kagaiain fighters. But the top of the wall had mostly cleared. The fighters had largely given up the wall and headed down to the ground level to fight the army face to face. Horses and riders cleaved through the crowd below, but they were so tightly packed that in many cases the horses were liabilities; Laith could see dozens of loose mounts running to and fro, whinnying, their eyes rolling and heads tossing, saddles empty. He could only hope that it was because the riders had chosen to take to the battle on foot.

From where he stood, he could no longer see Athela, but the agreement was that they should, if possible, attempt to break down the door and take some of the battle into Faridor itself. Somewhere in the fortress (or so Laith fervently hoped), Tarr, Ari and Si were making their way up to see Cira, to confront her once and for all. It was highly probable that the three of them would need backup.

"Argolaith!" Laith heard behind him, and his golden head whipped around. It was one of the Ashans, approaching from the top of the wall, a bow held in her hand. Laith recognized her as the young woman from Tarr's tribe.

"Argolaith," she called again, and Laith ducked an arrow as it hurtled into his peripheral vision.

"We've got to do something about the archers in the towers," he shouted to her over the din below.

"I've sent some of our Ashans to climb up and try to take them," she yelled, pointing. Laith looked over, and indeed, he could see two black-clad Ashans climbing up the outside of the tower, only feet away from the window that an unsuspecting archer was using as a vantage point.

"What is it?" Laith asked her.

"The guns," she panted. She'd been running hard. "We...the Ashans had to separate, there weren't enough of us. We had to leave the cannons and find cover, and now the Kagaians are back and trying to move them...I think they're going to fire them down into the fortress keep, to try and blast us all apart."

Laith's chest constricted. "Those are their own fighters down there!"

Juniper shook her head helplessly. "I don't know. Come quick, we need you."

The two of them began to run along the top of the wall and the blood began to boil, hot and insistent in Laith's ears. Their own fighters. They were willing to fire the cannons into their own fighters.

The wall beside them slid smoothly past, and though an arrow or two was shot in their direction, no one else was there to stop them. They rounded the back of the fortress, where Laith could see two small knots of Kagaian guards clustered around the large, gleaming metal weapons, the guns' long noses trained out at the shimmering sea.

"Get behind me," Laith said in a low voice, and Juniper shot him an anxious look out of the corner of her eye before doing as she was told. There were no other Ashans in sight; it was just the two of them. She gripped the hilt of her two short fighting knives, her knuckles white. *There are too many of them*, she thought wildly to herself. Her eyes watched the clusters of Kagaian guards rushing around the guns as they tried to untether them from the wall. *Too many.*

Their footsteps must have signaled their coming, for one of the guards happened to glance up in their direction and with a shout he alerted the others around them. Faces flashed up towards them, and in an instant, the Kagaians' voices united in a roar. They charged forward, abandoning the cannons behind them in their desire to cut Laith and Juniper down.

Juniper took a halting step and nearly froze in place, unsure of what to do next. She thought of calling out to Laith, telling him to stop, that they should fall back and find more reinforcements. But then his sword flashed in the sun as he tossed it casually from one hand to the other and with a neat spin he whirled into the thick of them.

Juniper had never before seen anything like it in her entire life. She had watched Laith when he'd first come over the wall and helped them clear a path to the gatehouse to open the portcullis for the army. But this was different. Before, his movements had been a model of efficiency and deadly grace, but now—she could see *rage* behind it. And that little bit of rage tipped the scales from something shocking to something almost too terrible to behold. None of the Kagaian guards stood a remote chance of survival.

The most appalling thing about it was how *fast* it was all over. It didn't even look as though the guards had been able to aim a single blow at Laith that actually connected with his sword. He was too quick, too assured. Juniper wondered, amidst all the chaos around her, what it must be like to have such power—to know, almost without thinking, the fastest way to cause another person to die, to make it look as effortless and as beautiful as Laith did. She found herself taking a shrinking step back, her eyes wide as she stared at him.

The second cannon crew had been close on the heels of the first, but upon seeing what had happened to their comrades, many of them jogged to a halt and stopped altogether, looking unsure and uncertain. Laith advanced on them, his face lit with the pearly soft light of the morning sun, looking every inch an avenging angel as he came towards them. His dark eyes betrayed no emotion; he watched the Kagaian guards unblinkingly and without mercy.

Suddenly, just as the leader of the pack stumbled and tripped, Laith darted forward like a black hawk striking, and once again it was over almost before it had even begun. Guards fell to the left and the right, their green cloaks billowing and collapsing around them, like breath being softly exhaled. And then Laith was standing—the only one left—on the wall, surveying what he had done. It didn't even look as though he was breathing particularly hard.

All at once, Laith looked straight up at Juniper and for an instant, she saw his eyes widen in shock and alarm. She barely had time to turn around before she felt a deep, sharp pain in her side, and an instant later the stones were rushing up to meet her and all was cold and quiet.

Lit by the half-risen sun, Lord Seth took a slow, deliberate step over Juniper's lifeless body, his cloak casually dragging over her face, a silent, unspoken insult. Laith straightened, his sword lowering to rest at his leg. Slowly, Lord Seth smiled, the same smile Laith remembered from their boyhood, cold, unfeeling, unnatural, like an alien creature forcing the expression across his features to imitate some semblance of human emotion. The black pits of his eyes bored into Laith's.

So it's come at last, Laith thought.

The strangest thing was, now that the moment was here, he felt relieved. He welcomed it. In fact, seeing Seth's dark figure looming up before him, the inscrutable smile on his cold face, almost felt like greeting an old friend, a friend he'd long been expecting.

He tried to wash away the thought from his mind. He slowly raised his Whitsun sword so that it was held at the ready, balanced lightly in his grip. The inlaid golden rays of the filigreed sun on its hilt twinkled around his hand and cascaded down the length of the blade. He could see Seth's weapon, the green edges stained with their poison, the swirling nest of snakes that devoured the hilt of the sword. Laith forced himself to breathe in and out, allowing Seth to slink closer and closer.

If I draw him backwards I'll have the high ground, he thought to himself. *Pull him back, put him off balance.* They were far enough up on the wall that he could lead Seth along some fairly dangerous and narrow walkways, force him to lose his footing, throw him off guard.

What's the point? another voice inside him asked. *Turn your back on him. Face the sun. Let him come for you. Let it be over.*

But Laith again shook the thoughts away, re-focusing his mind, his sword raised. One foot slowly slid behind him, ready to brace for the onslaught of Seth's first attack. He felt the familiar *click* as his mind went pleasantly blank, all of his thoughts and strategy funneling directly into his arms and legs, ready to move, to react at a moment's notice.

Like a shark advancing slowly through the water, Seth came at him. His unblinking coal-black eyes still drilled through Laith's face. And then, just as Laith edged back to keep a safe distance between the two of them, Seth struck lightning-fast, like a viper snaking towards his prey. Laith knocked the sword away with all of his might, emitting a low grunt as he did, and he went a few feet back, drawing Seth up closer to him like a coy dancer.

Seth struck again, so hard that sparks glanced off the edges of the blades as they met; this time, their movements seemed to link together and in another moment they were battling back up the wall, two flashing black silhouettes against the rising sun.

Tarr peered around the corner of the hallway and could see nothing. Behind him crouched Ari and Si. Tarr turned back to them. "All clear," he said in a low voice. "Si, you're sure it's this way?"

"Oh, yes," Si assured him easily.

"All right," said Tarr, taking a deep breath. "Go."

They rounded the corner and began to walk swiftly forward, bent low and hugging the wall—or at least Tarr and Ari did. After a few footsteps, Tarr realized that Si wasn't with them, so he stopped and turned.

Behind them, Si was ambling along quite unconcernedly in the middle of the hallway, looking for all intents and purposes as if he owned the place and was out for a fine morning stroll. Tarr darted forward and seized Si by the arm, pulling him into the cover of the nearest alcove a short ways ahead.

"Si," Tarr said, trying to keep the notes of irritation out of his tone, "if you wouldn't mind being a *little* more careful, I think we'd all appreciate it."

Si shrugged. "No one is coming."

Ari and Tarr met one another's eyes. There were times when it was difficult to argue with omniscience. Ari cleared his throat, trying to sound reasonable. "Si, we're just trying to get to Cira as quickly and as safely as we can, all right?"

"I know," Si agreed pleasantly, bouncing on his toes. "She's not going anywhere."

Ari and Tarr exchanged another glance. *All right, your turn*, Ari's expression seemed to say.

"Si," Tarr tried again. "If you could just *try* and be more careful..."

"I am," said Si. "Don't step out of the alcove."

"Why—" Tarr said, and in another moment there was a clanking sound as a group of three armed Kagaian guards came out of one of the hallways ahead of them, banked a turn and continued on.

Tarr and Ari waited until the guards had gone before rounding on Si once more. "So, remind me how those powers of yours work again?" Ari said slowly. "Something about beams of light?"

Si opened his mouth, but Tarr could see from the far-off expression on his face that it was going to be a meandering explanation, and they were short on time as it was. "He sees everything and everyone as interconnecting strands of energy and he can follow them and see where they move and end," he said quickly.

Ari digested this. "Ah-*hah*," he said finally. "Maybe Si should go first?"

Tarr threw up his hands. "Whatever gets us out of this stupid hallway."

So Si led them forward, continuing to walk in his infuriatingly unhurried, unruffled way down the middle of the passage. Tarr trusted that Si would alert them in the event of oncoming danger, but as someone without the temperament for any kind of cloak-and-dagger infiltration this did not lessen the stress he felt at creeping through the den of their enemy. He found himself still sticking close to the wall and glancing every few seconds over his shoulder to see if they were being followed.

"Left," said Si cheerily, and once they had turned the corner, he said, "All right, stop for a second." He waited, a placid look on his face. Tarr and Ari tensed as they heard footsteps coming, and Tarr could see Ari's hand creeping down to the sword at his hip. Another small group of guards went running—faster than the first group they'd seen—right past them. Tarr caught a glimpse of one of their faces as they went by. They looked worried.

"Has the battle started?" Tarr asked, once the coast was clear.

Si strolled back out into the middle of the hallway and continued his meandering progress forward. "Oh, yes," he assured them. "It's started. They took the wall."

"We took the wall?" Tarr echoed. Si nodded.

"It was great," he smiled dreamily. "Like a wave crashing. Like a red wave."

Tarr afforded himself a small sigh of relief, and restrained himself from peppering Si with further questions. After a few more right turns, the hallways gradually turned into more narrow corridors. These were stark and devoid of the portraits, coats of arms, and mounted weaponry that adorned the walls of the larger passageways. Tarr fervently hoped that Si did, in fact, know where he was going. For his part, he was completely lost. The fortress was like a maze.

"We're going a long way round," Si told them, breaking a long silence. "The main halls are filling up now."

"Are our friends all right?" Tarr asked hurriedly, unable to stop himself, regretting the words even as he uttered them. *What if one of them has been killed? Marc? Or Athela?*

"Are you sure?" Si asked. Tarr paused, then nodded. "Many have died," Si said gravely. "On both sides. But our friends are still alive."

Tarr swallowed, his throat dry.

They took a left and then began to wind their way upwards. Clearly, they had come to Cira's tower; the stairwell they were on was small enough that Tarr assumed this had to be some sort of back way or secret route up to her chambers. His heart began to pound harder as they climbed. *What would Cira do? What would they say to her? What on earth was Si's plan?* He should have had some plan of his own to defeat Cira, should have worked something out with Ari.

There was a window in the rounded wall of the tower stairwell ahead of them, and though by this point Tarr was completely turned around, he could hear the din of fighting emanating through it. He increased his step, Ari close behind, and reached the window. He threw open the wooden shutters to look down on the fighting outside.

On the ground it was chaos: red cloaks and green intermingled, so far below them that Tarr couldn't pick out the identities of any of the individuals fighting. A column of black smoke was blowing through the wind from somewhere down below, filtering into the air around them. Tarr could see the lightning flashes of swords and shields, the voices of hundreds of fighters raised like a rumble of thunder, the din pierced every now and again with a shriek from a human voice, or the shrill, terrified whinny of a horse.

Tarr pulled back, repulsed by what he saw. *What have we done?* he wondered. *We brought all of those soldiers here to die.* He looked frantically at Ari, whose face was, as ever, impassive and impossible to read.

"We should hurry up a bit, someone will be coming up the stairs soon," Si suggested, though there was little to no urgency in his voice.

Ari and Tarr took the warning to heart and whipped the window shut again, pounding up the stairs with Si trailing behind. They spun around and around the twisting stairwell, dizzily, before coming to a landing a few floors up. "Here," Si said suddenly. "We need to stop here."

Tarr pushed the landing door open and they piled out. They looked to be on the top floor of Faridor, flush with the high fortress wall. Tarr saw it stretching out beside them through a nearby window.

"Where are we?" he asked, slightly out of breath from the climb they'd just made up the staircase. There didn't seem to be anything of note around them, no signpost that clearly denoted the entrance to Cira's chambers. There were just more anonymous passages stretching out in either direction. "Is this it?" he asked Si. "Where is she?"

But something very strange had happened. Si and Ari were staring at one another quite meaningfully, as if they were having a silent conversation between just the two of them. Tarr's brow furrowed as he looked from one to the other.

"Now?" Ari asked, his voice low. He had such a strange look on his face, somewhere between dawning realization and resignation.

"Yes," Si replied levelly. Tarr saw Ari's face relax.

"How come you answer *him* when *he* asks you a question?" Tarr demanded irritably. "Where's her chamber, then? Ari, I think we need to have more of a plan in place. Look, when we go in, I think you should—"

But Ari shook his head, not moving his eyes from Si's face. "I have to leave, Tarr," he said slowly.

Tarr's heart dropped. "What are you talking about?" he demanded, his voice rising, panicky even to his own ears. "What are you saying? We need you to come with us, Ari, you know I can't fight and we need... Si, what is going on?"

Si raised his eyebrows in a silent question towards Ari, but Ari simply shook his head, and Si's face resumed its usual benevolent impassivity. Tarr was growing angrier and angrier with both of them.

"Look, you two, I don't know what on earth is going on, and I can see that neither one of you is going to bother to actually *tell me*, but we have something very important that we have to do, and I need both of you here."

But Ari merely shook his head again. "You'll be all right," he assured Tarr. "Si can show you the way. There's something I have to do."

Tarr stared at him. There was a strange finality in Ari's tone, almost a sense of farewell. Tarr didn't understand it, and he certainly didn't like the idea of going in to face Cira alone with Si, but something about the resolution on Ari's face told him that this is what had to happen. Tarr suddenly had the urge to reach out and hug Ari, but since they'd never voluntarily come into physical contact a single time since they'd known each other, he resisted the urge.

"All right then," was all he said. "Good luck."

The faintest of smiles echoed around Ari's lips, so quick and faint that a moment later Tarr was almost certain that he imagined it. But then Ari turned and began to jog down the hallway, his hand on the hilt of his sword, and before long he was swallowed up by the sprawling maze of the fortress.

Tarr tossed his hands in exasperated frustration and wheeled around to Si, who blinked up at him with an infuriatingly superior look of inner calm on his face.

"This was your doing," Tarr said accusingly.

Si shrugged noncommittally. "He made a choice," he said.

"Did he actually *have* one?" Tarr pressed him. "A choice?"

Si blinked. "It depends on how you look at it."

Tarr resisted the urge to throw Si out of the nearest window. "Did you know?" Tarr asked suddenly. "Did you know that it was always going to be you and me facing Cira at the end?"

The sphinxlike smile widened in an unspoken *yes*.

"Why me?" Tarr asked.

"I'm not sure what will happen in there, Tarr," Si said gravely, his attention sharpening, as it always did when he talked about Cira. "I can see it—but I don't know what it means. I need a witness. In case."

Tarr looked longingly in the direction where Ari had vanished. Ari was never terribly good company, but it at least had given him someone with whom he could exchange goggle-eyed expressions whenever Si spouted indecipherable nonsense. But now he was quite alone.

"How much farther is it?" Tarr asked.

"Not far," Si shook his head.

Tarr squared his shoulders, and stared down the empty hallway lying before them, large and imposing. He felt at once very small. "Lead on," he said finally, trying to sound more resolute and brave than he felt.

"Again!" Marc bellowed, throwing every ounce of his bull-like strength against the battering ram, as it heaved forward and against the barricaded main door of Faridor. The Striker soldiers, clustered all around him like a flock of cardinals in their scarlet cloaks, let out a throaty cry as the ram crashed into the door. The hinges gave a petulant creak, but didn't give way. They were designed to withstand such manhandling.

"Marc!" cried out a voice. Marc spun around in the direction of the call, and his eye caught something dark falling from above, speedily plummeting towards them.

"Down!" Marc cried, and the Strikers threw themselves to the stone floor as a projectile of flame and burning cloth crashed down on top of them. The coarse smell of smoke filled their lungs and a ripple of heat went through the air, catching Marc on the side of his face, as he instinctively turned away to avoid getting caught in the eyes with any splinters of fragmenting wood.

"Cover! Now!" he ordered and the Striker soldiers abandoned the ram, scrambling to find protection from above underneath the low overhang of Faridor's wall. "Archers!" Marc yelled into the fracas. "Where are my archers? Return fire!"

The air was so thick with fresh smoke that it was hard for him to see, but he could dimly make out the outlines of a few of his soldiers rearing up, and could see the shafts of black arrows like needles go zipping through the air, shot at some unseen foe.

The tide of the battle was still too fragmented and scattered to assess, but Kagai's forces had begun to retreat back into the main building of the fortress, shielding themselves inside while the Strikers pounded at the door like a howling pack of wolves. Marc didn't like it. It was giving the enemy too much time to regroup and come up with a plan. The Striker soldiers were too vulnerable out there in the open while the Kagaian guards had the advantage of putting their archers in the towers around the keep and firing down onto them, using arrows or projectiles or whatever came their way.

We've got to get that door open, Marc thought to himself with a renewed ferocity, and, almost on his hands and knees, he scrambled forward and threw himself against the impasse as if his strength alone could shift it where the battering ram and a dozen soldiers could not. The door, unsurprisingly, didn't budge.

Marc swore lustily under his breath and swiveled around, looking for some alternate solution. He, Athela, and Cade had promised to try and find each other during the battle, but like so many of the best-laid battle plans, that pact had been cast aside. He had seen glimpses of Athela on her gray horse at the very beginning, running through the crowds of soldiers like a swift wind, her sword flashing—but he hadn't seen her since. He hoped she was all right. He hoped, too, that Cade was still alive. He would at least be well-protected by Wolf and the others he trusted. Cade was never the best swordsman; all of those talents had gone to his brother. And where Laith was, Marc had no idea.

He turned his attention back to the matter at hand. The onslaught from above seemed to have dissipated with the return fire of Marc's group of archers. Slowly, the group of remaining Strikers who had been with him on the battering ram drew back around him, coughing out the black smoke that still choked the air, their eyes burning. There were fewer of them than there had been before. The explosive fireball had hit its mark.

"We're too vulnerable here," Marc told them in a low voice. "They've been able to get the vantage points up in the towers and the minute we set foot back out there they'll mow us down. There aren't enough of us to get inside. The doors are too well fortified. We must find a different way."

The sets of eyes that peered out at him from smoke-blackened faces were unmistakably scared and looking for direction. At Marc's shoulder there was a small tap. Marc recognized it as Itzhal, one of the Striker guards from back in Two Falls; behind him stood Khan, one of Ari's lieutenants. Itzhal's dark brown skin was slick with sweat, but he seemed to be mostly unscathed. He held a bloodied knife in one hand.

"Sir," he said, "the Ashans...the Ashans have managed to take one of the towers. They climbed from the outside and went in that way, took out the archers, and have worked their way down. We're holding it, at least for a little while. If you come around this way, there's an entrance at the base of the tower where we can get in."

Marc clapped him on the shoulder with one large hand and swiveled around to the others. "You," he motioned to the left half of the group clustered around him, "you come with me. The other half of you, I want you to spread out as best you can and alert everyone that we're going to have the main doors of Faridor opened and they need to be ready to charge inside. Find Cade, find General Calchas, find Athela. Got it?"

The silent faces looked more resolute now, and his words were followed by a chorus of nods and murmurs of "Yes, sir." Marc patted the nearest soldier on her back and they scattered.

Rane and Cicada drew to a halt and sank down beside one another, crouched and ready. They were in the west tower, almost to the top. The corridor was curving and narrow, and by peeking ever so gently around the edge of the wall, Rane could see a room flanked by four guards.

Cicada tapped her shoulder. "That is where they have him," she said.

Rane rolled back her sleeves on either arm and drew the small knife she'd recovered from the sentry outside the dungeons. As they watched the guards talk, one of them motioned back and forth with her hand as if to indicate she'd be returning. Then she and one of the others strode purposefully off and vanished out of sight.

"Hurry," said Cicada. Rane nodded. She flicked her wrist and the knife flipped around once in her hand.

Silent and deadly, Rane slipped around the corner and shot towards the two remaining guards. They barely had time to raise their weapons before she had one of them on the ground, and in another instant the other had his feet kicked out from under him and was under her knife. It was short, gruesome work.

She motioned for Cicada to come and join her. Her friend, who had never seen Rane in action before, looked a bit pale as she trotted up. Her dark eyes kept darting involuntarily down to the figures lying on the floor, but her face was filled with resolve. The two of them looked to the door, apprehensive as to what they would find behind it. Rane said a silent prayer, pressed her hand against the door, and pushed it open.

The sight that met them stopped them both in their tracks.

"Oh *holy* hell," Rane breathed.

Archer was strapped to a table in the middle of a tiny circular room, shirtless, his face turned away from them towards the vertical slit of a single window, whose light shone with unnatural cheeriness upon the grim scene. His skin, already pale, held a deathly gray pallor. The arm closest to them, held tight against the table with a leather restraint, had a long, steady crimson trickle of blood running down it, splashing onto the table, and dripping into a bucket just below. Rane nearly retched. There was so much blood—*too* much blood, already in the bucket. Cira was bleeding him dry.

"Archer!" Rane cried through gritted teeth, her body suddenly galvanizing into action. She bolted forward and with her knife cut through the restraints around Archer's arm. At her touch, his head weakly lolled around on his shoulders and his yellow eyes, frighteningly vague, met hers. The whisper of a smile played upon his face as he recognized her, and then his eyes rolled back into his head and he went limp.

Cicada seized the knife from Rane's hand and slashed at the fabric around her knees, tearing a long strip from the hem of her dress. She wrapped it tightly and expertly around the open wound on Archer's arm, pressing her thumbs against it to help it close. She raised one hand and said, "We've got to keep his legs up."

Rane darted to the door and looked to the left and the right. The hallway was empty for now, thanks to the confusion of the attack outside. But it was only a matter of time before someone discovered them.

"We shouldn't move him," Cicada signed urgently, using one hand while the other applied pressure to stopper Archer's wound. "He could die. He's dying as it is."

"We've got to risk it," Rane countered. "They're going to come back. They know this is where he is. We have to move him. At least try to get him to another room. Somewhere sheltered."

Rane could tell that Cicada didn't like it, but she nodded. Gently, they slid their arms underneath his armpits and lifted him off of the table, sliding him with some difficulty to the floor. Rane was strong, and Cicada was used to manual labor, but he was much taller than both of them, and his long limbs were heavy and ungainly. They half-slid, half fell to the floor, Archer sprawling atop them in an awkward heap.

"Did we kill him?" Cicada asked anxiously, her legs pinned under Archer's shoulders.

Rane wriggled out from beneath him and took Archer's angular white face in her hands. She leaned down and pressed her ear to his chest, cold and smooth as marble, and there it was—the almost imperceptible flurry of a heartbeat.

"No. He wants to live," she signed back. "He'll try to live."

She pulled up his shoulder so that Cicada could slither out from beneath him, and took his ankles in her hands. She jerked her head towards the door and Cicada propped it open with one of her feet, leaning forward and scooping Archer again beneath his arms. Rane gritted her teeth. It was going to be slow, awkward going, but they had little time left if they were to make it out with him alive.

Marc, flanked by ten Striker guards, picked his way carefully down the narrow corridor leading to the main entrance of Faridor. Just as Itzhal and Khan had reported, the Ashans had indeed managed to take one of the smaller towers of the inner keep, which had a door at the bottom that admitted Marc and a handful of his soldiers without too much notice. They had been able to pass through the unguarded passageways until they were poised, ready and waiting, right beside the entrance hall where the Kagaiain guards had barricaded themselves. The Kagaian soldiers were pressed like a great green hand against the door, all their attention trained on the battle outside. They didn't see Marc and the others behind them.

Pausing, Marc turned to the Strikers. The remaining Ashans from the tower had joined them, swelling their ranks by a crucial few. Itzhal waited beside Marc, coiled like a spring ready to release at a moment's notice. Khan, his plunging black eyebrows knit in concentration, gave a small nod. Marc thought of what he could possibly say to them. They would be grossly outnumbered, and their only hope was to surprise the waiting Kagaians enough to drive them back away from the door so that they could unbolt it and let the Striker army inside.

Marc peeked his head around the wall. In addition to the troops against the door, there was a mass of green soldiers sitting behind them just within the entrance hall, off their guard, clearly believing themselves to be safe from any attack while they recuperated within. He turned back, wiping his hand along the length of the scar that split his face diagonally from forehead to chin, feeling the grime and sweat and stink of battle on his skin.

"Right," he said in a low voice. "They won't be expecting us, and we'll buy ourselves a few seconds. I want archers covering us as we go. Itzhal, Khan, I need you to get that door open as fast as you can. And then stand back because if all goes well, all hell will break loose. Got it?" he asked.

Silent nods echoed back at him, and Marc felt all of the soldiers tense, their weapons raised and at the ready. Closing his eyes and offering a fleeting prayer to whatever fates were guiding him, he threw himself around the corner and forward towards the sea of Kagaian troops.

It was a full second or two of shocked, almost comical silence as the troops stared at the Striker encroachers, and then an instant later they were spurred into action, scattering every which way. Marc met his first opponent in a full-on crash, slamming his broad, heavy shoulder into their side and toppling them to the ground. He wasn't as fast a swordsman as Laith, but what he lacked in speed he made up for in sheer strength. One swipe of his broadsword and two Kagaian troops went catapulting backwards, taking out a knot of others clustered close behind them. It was all so sudden that the Kagaians hadn't had a chance to gather themselves, to organize; they were knocked down like pins.

"Itzhal!" Marc cried. He didn't even have the chance to look over his shoulder to see whether Itzhal had managed to unbolt the door behind him. "Khan, now!"

He threw himself bodily against three other opponents, sending them cascading into the sea of green, from which swords and other arms were quickly being produced and brandished. Marc's sword clanged and clashed and then he turned, just as the heavy beam barricading the door to Faridor was cast down and Itzhal pulled the door open.

"Strikers!" Itzal cried.

Black smoke billowed in from the outside, immediately filling the entrance hall. Marc dove out of the way just as the heavy doors were thrown completely open, as if kicked in by some invisible giant's foot. And through the smoke, atop her gray horse, stained with sweat, mud and blood, was Athela, her black hair flying and her eyes flashing like the edge of her sword.

Immediately on her heels were other riders: General Calchas towering like a mountain in his battle armor, his lieutenant Teague by his side, followed by a wave of Striker footsoldiers. They poured in through the open doors like a red sea. The Kagaian guards, surprised on all sides, immediately retreated farther into the fortress, where they were pursued by the Strikers, swords out and a battle cry on their throats. The battle began again in earnest in the middle of the great hall, where every sound was echoed a thousandfold up to the grand domed ceiling, the imposing stained glass windows twinkling incongruously with pale early sunlight and the black floor reflecting up like a frozen obsidian lake.

In the midst of the fray, Marc pulled back, batting away a Kagaian guard or two as easily as if he were waving at a fly. His ice-blue eyes searched the incoming flow of Strikers, the smoke obscuring most of them as they came. But there—he saw three mounted riders enter and draw off to the side, and he instantly recognized Cade and Wolf and another one of Cade's bodyguards.

Marc charged across the entranceway, stealing a glance to his side at Athela, who on her horse was wreaking merry havoc across the great hall of the fortress. Her sword whirled and Kagaians fell, her horse's hooves slipping against the slick floor. Calchas had dismounted and was cutting a swath through a thicket of Kagaian soldiers that had dared approach him.

Marc came up beside Cade, who immediately dismounted and faced him. "Can we take it?" he asked. He had a cut along the side of his face, and dark mud was smudged across his usually pristine jaw. "Can we take the fortress?"

"I don't know," Marc said honestly, panting. "I think so."

"Have we had any word from Tarr or Si?" Cade asked sharply. "Any indication that they've been able to kill Cira?"

Marc shook his head. "No," he said. "No, no word from them. Though how they would get word down here in the middle of this battle, I don't know."

"It's too much to risk Cira getting away," Cade said forcefully. "We must go up and make sure that she is taken care of."

Marc nodded mutely. He could see Cade's point. It wouldn't do to have Cira escaping in the midst of the battle, getting to a boat somehow and making an escape to Vireg, prolonging this awful conflict even further. "Go," he assured Cade. "Go. Athela and I will try to secure the fortress down here. You remember the way from the blueprints we found?"

Cade nodded resolutely, then turned to his retainers. "Come with me," he ordered.

His bodyguard Wolf, tawny hair was tousled this way and that, and whose staring, wild eyes seemed to gaze out at nothingness, dismounted, drawing his sword. As Marc watched, his expression slowly began to light up with a sort of manic glow. Wherever Cira was and whatever she was doing, if Wolf could get his hands on her, she wouldn't be long for the world.

Cade faced Marc, his narrow, delicate features so much like Cira's. He gave a nod, and then he and his small company took off, heading in the direction of the main staircase. Marc watched him go for a few seconds, then turned away.

He stuck his head out of the door and saw that there was still a significant battle raging outside. He propped the main door open with a piece of fallen beam and just had time to raise his sword and dodge out of the way before a Kagaian guard swiped at him. Marc avoided the first hit, but the second came too fast for him to move, and he caught the blade right on his rib. Fortunately, his thick armor took care of most of the blow, but it sent him down to his knees, momentarily off balance, the wind knocked cleanly out of him.

There was a scream from a horse, and the clatter of hooves and Marc looked up just in time to see Athela swoop by overhead. He couldn't see what happened, but there were a few clangs of metal upon metal and the Kagaian guard who had struck him didn't strike again.

Marc rose heavily to his feet, feeling his bones and his body creak, and faced Athela, who had dismounted and was walking towards him. Her horse, Aria, was sweating from head to foot and his eyes were bright with a sort of glee, as if reveling in all the mayhem swirling around him. Athela didn't look much the worse for wear; one of her sleeves had been cut, she had two broken arrows protruding from her armor, she was dirty and caked in soot and blood like all the rest of them, but she was alive.

"Cade's gone after Cira," Marc told her. "It's up to us."

Athela's gray eyes studied his. "All right," she said, with a little smile. "Marc, my old friend. Let's take the bloody place."

She turned on her heel, her black curls whipping around her shoulders. Side by side, Marc and Athela threw themselves forward into the thick of the battle.

Rane and Cicada had managed to drag Archer almost all the way down the corridor to the curving stairwell. At the top of it they paused, both out of breath, and slowly lowered him to the floor. Though he was lean, he was still well over six feet tall, so it was awkward going and Rane was uncomfortably conscious of the bright red stain blooming larger and larger on the white bandage around his arm.

"It's not helping," she signed. "You were right. There is no way we can carry him to safety."

Cicada's dark eyebrows knit together and her sharp gaze cast about for a solution. "There," she pointed to an open doorway opposite the stairwell opening, the cool morning light of day glinting beyond. It looked to be a broad balcony, sheltered by the overhang of the roof, with room enough to hide him just around the corner.

"There's no way out. If they find us there, we're dead," Rane signed back.

"They won't be looking for him there. We'll keep him out of sight," Cicada urged, her words becoming more forceful.

Rane still didn't like it. "Stay here," she said. "I'm going to see if there's anywhere else we can take him."

She turned and jogged swiftly around the corridor, trying a door here and there, but they were all locked. She gingerly tried breaking one of the doors in with her shoulder, but it was too solid. She shook it off and continued to run.

A window was open a bit further down the hall, and she paused on a whim, looking out down at the battle raging beneath. The flurry of dark shapes and the cry of battle wafted softly up from below. And there—farther up, on the narrow walkway of the top fortress wall, two figures fought, swords flashing silver as they caught the morning light. Even from where she stood, Rane recognized Laith's golden head, the grace of his movements. And, with a chill that seemed to grab her forcefully by the spine, she recognized his opponent. It was Lord Seth.

She took an unbidden step back away from the window, her heart still racing. At once she felt the urge to turn and run as far from Lord Seth as she could—and another urge, just as powerful, to leap out of the window and run to help Laith. But there were pressing matters at hand. She whirled and flew back around the twisting corridor, back to where Cicada was bent over Archer's pathetic form, applying pressure to his arm in an effort to stem his bleeding.

As she drew closer, Rane started to wave her hand to catch Cicada's attention, but her friend didn't see her and remained focused on tending to Archer. A moment later Rane stopped still, heart dropping within her chest. There were the sounds of footsteps pounding up the nearby stairwell, only a few feet away. Cicada, of course, hadn't heard them.

Cursing herself and her stupidity, Rane flew forward, her knife already out and in her hand. Cicada suddenly felt the reverberation of her footfall and whipped around, protectively positioning her body over Archer's drooping head, an expression of shock etched over her face as Rane shoved her to the side and dove into the cavern of the stairwell, knife out and ready.

The next few moments were a flurry of confusion as Rane collided into someone who gave out a deep-throated cry of alarm. The two of them fell painfully back into the stairwell and tumbled uncontrollably down a few steps. Rane gave a few haphazard slashes in the dark with her knife before a familiar voice called out to her.

"Rane, stop!" it said. "Rane, is that you?"

The adrenaline was beating a tattoo in Rane's temple, but the voice made her freeze. "Ari?" she demanded, shocked.

There was a grunt from somewhere beneath her left calf and the two untangled themselves. Rane stowed her knife back in her boot, helping Ari to his feet. She felt his hand clasp her shoulder, and the comfort of that touch nearly made her cry out in relief.

They began taking the stairs together two at a time as Rane breathlessly brought Ari up to speed.

"Archer—lost blood—trying to move him—" she panted. If Ari was surprised, he didn't look it. But then, he never really looked surprised at anything.

Back on the landing, Cicada was as tense as a threatened cat, crouched over Archer as if ready to protect him by any means necessary. When Rane and Ari slipped back into the light, Cicada looked momentarily startled, then realized that whoever Ari was, he was on their side. Relief watched over Cicada's dark features like a wave of cool water.

Ari knelt by Archer's arm, feeling for a pulse on his long neck, lifting one paper-thin eyelid to see the yellow pupils rolled back in their sockets. He put his ear to Archer's chest and listened for a few moments.

"It's faint," he said. Rane sat back on her heels and glanced over at Cicada, who was staring intently at Ari, watching his every move. Rane closed her eyes and breathed a silent prayer. *Don't let him die.*

Don't let Archer die.

"There are no other open rooms on this floor," Rane told Ari. She signed the words after she spoke them aloud so that Cicada could understand their conversation. "I checked. The only one unlocked is the room we just came from, and that's the first place they'll look if they come back."

"We can't move him any farther," Ari told her. "We'll kill him. I'll take him there," he said, fixing his gaze on the balcony near the stairwell. He turned and met Rane's eyes. "I'll protect him. I promise."

"We'll stay," Rane said. Cicada nodded mutely at her side.

"No," Ari said sharply. "You're needed elsewhere. I can move him. I'll take care of him."

Rane hesitated for a moment, but Ari's expression was fixed with determination. She nodded and gently touched him on the shoulder. She swiveled towards Cicada.

"Find Athela," she signed. "She will need you. You can show her the way through the fortress, the places the Strikers will not know to check."

Cicada's brow grew dark once more. "And where will you go?" she asked, her mouth moving and a small noise escaping as her fingers flew.

Rane hesitated. "There is something I must do."

Cicada's face was quizzical but she recognized the look in Rane's eye. She nodded ever so slightly.

Rane clambered to her feet, and Cicada followed suit. The three of them hesitated. And then, after an unspoken beat, each turned. Cicada slipped down into the darkness of the stairwell, and Rane's quick footstep vanished around the curve of the corridor. Ari gingerly slid his arm under Archer's armpits and gently began to drag him towards the balcony and out of sight as the sound of battle roared below.

The sun was pouring now across the tops of the towers; radiant in shades of gold and pink that clashed horribly with the frenzy taking place within the walls of the fortress. Fury teemed on the ground, but on the topmost wall of the fortress keep, it was strangely quiet. The battle was oddly muted, the wind high-pitched and cold. There was hardly any sound at all except for the clash of steel on steel and the sound of heavy breathing.

Laith and Seth had battled their way along the top of the wall and gradually moved off the main walkway to a thin slope of roof below the battlement. There, they balanced precipitously on a pathway that wasn't more than three feet wide, with a ten-foot drop to the edge of the roof and a cold stone platform below that. Laith's head was blank, trying only to read the body language of his opponent, searching for some sense of fear in those black, empty eyes.

Seth feinted, but Laith was ready for it—the prince dodged right and caught him on the rebound so that Seth's step bobbled ever so slightly and he nearly lost his balance. Seeing an advantage, Laith darted forward with a new volley of blows. But just as quickly as Laith could strike him, Seth deftly parried backwards; the two were as evenly matched in their movements as a figure and its shadow. Laith's sword sang through the air as he whipped his head back to avoid Seth's poisoned blade, aware that even a nick on the arm could mean death.

And then, from out of nowhere, Laith caught a glimpse out of the corner of his eye of the spreading sea crashing far below the fortress wall. And he thought how simple it would be simply to fall towards it, let it swallow him up.

No, he caught himself. *Stop.*

But his mental concentration had been broken, and Seth could sense it. Laith had to take three stumbling steps back, blocking a fresh volley of ferocious attacks, his senses so disoriented by the sudden unexpected urge to fall that it was all he could do to keep Seth off of him.

It would be a good death, said that same small voice.

Furious with himself, Laith took his sword in both hands and swiped it at Seth's head, an amateur and unpracticed move that left his entire right side unprotected. Seth saw an opening and darted forward, his stained green blade greedily seeking Laith's flesh, but the prince managed to throw himself to one side and the sword missed him by only a millimeter.

Seth whirled around, again on the attack. Laith had fallen to the ground, his sword at his feet. He shoved himself upright and took his sword in his hand. He parried away two blows, saw Seth's bottomless eyes glinting as though he could sense an impending kill. He parried a third, and then Seth lunged at him. Without thinking, he took a step.

His foot slipped on the edge of the stone ridgepole. All at once the world gave a sickening lurch and Laith felt himself topple off the roof, hit the ledge and hurtle towards the platform below. He tried to turn, but he was falling too fast. He felt his ankle shatter beneath him, like glass shards shooting up the length of his leg, as soon as he hit the rock.

A guttural cry of pain escaped his gritted teeth, and he barely had time to gather his thoughts before the dark shape of Seth obliterated the sun above him, swooping down like a vulture to where Laith lay crumpled on the ground. Laith managed to lift his sword just in time to deflect him, felt the swishing rush of air as Seth neatly somersaulted over him, coming to his feet a short distance away. Laith knew already that Seth wasn't the kind of fighter to give him quarter, to give him any time to recover. He would relish the kill, swift or slow. Death was coming straight for him, as swiftly as an arrow.

For a prolonged moment, Laith felt his thoughts moving outward, almost as if he had stepped outside of his own body. He imagined lowering his sword, rocking back on his heel, closing his eyes, feeling death come for him like a cold wind on his face. He could see himself dying, the pink and gold morning light on his cheeks as they slowly turned the color of chalk. He wondered at the unknowable peace of what lay beyond the beautiful pastel-flecked sky, and felt a surge of calm and acceptance wash over him.

It was a beautiful morning. He closed his eyes.

But tomorrow? What will the morning tomorrow look like? asked a small voice deep within. *And the one after?*

No, said that small voice. Suddenly he felt the heat of the sunlight boring through his eyelids. *Get up.*

I'm not ready.

Get up.

GET UP.

Almost without thinking, Laith felt his hands reach down to the cool, clammy stone beneath him and give an almighty shove that sent him unsteadily to his feet. He cried out as he inadvertently put weight on his broken ankle, the sharp pain pulling him out of the strange trance of a moment before. Almost as startling as the clarity with which he had just been about to meet his death, he was seized with a sudden indomitable will to keep on living; it washed over him like a cold wave, shaking him awake. Even the unbearable pain in his ankle tasted sweet. He swung his sword, again barely deflecting Seth's blade as he snaked past. His opponent clearly had not anticipated this last-second feint and overshot him once more. Seth's dark, lifeless eyes narrowed in fury as he tossed his sword from one hand to the other, rounding on Laith once more, his sword poised for a killing blow.

Laith crouched down, his useless leg dragging behind him like a dead weight, every movement sending sharp stabs of pain up and down his body. He lifted his sword, and its collision with Seth's deadly green blade sent sparks shimmering around them like a cloud of burning wasps. He parried as best he could, but Seth was forcing him backwards, forcing him back onto his bad leg—the pain was so intense that Laith's breath caught in his throat. Finally, he gritted his teeth, swung his sword behind him and whipped it with all of his might at Seth's head; a move so foolhardy and lacking in poise or any kind of grace that it effectively caught Seth by surprise. He stumbled backwards a few feet, giving Laith just a moment to regroup and ease the weight off of his leg.

Now that I want to live, he thought wryly. *How do I stay alive?*

And then, as if in answer to his question, he heard the sound of a light, quick footstep behind him. He turned, and relief like warm sunshine washed over him.

It was Rane, running full out along the wall towards them. Her eyes were fixed intently on Lord Seth, who was standing to the side, momentarily frozen with surprise. With a graceful leap Rane came off the wall and fell ten feet through the air, landing behind Laith with all the weight of a feather. In one fluid motion he threw her his sword and she caught it by the hilt, spinning it in her hand to test the balance. Not for one moment had her eyes left Lord Seth, whose expression had changed from astonishment to satisfaction.

"His blade is poisoned," Laith cautioned her, his voice scratchy and hoarse. "Be careful."

Rane nodded mutely, slowly raising up Laith's sword to the height of her shoulder, edging towards her opponent one foot at a time with the grace and assurance of a cat. Seth's face was sneering. He said not a word, but it was written on his face: *I bested you once, I will again.*

This is going to be easy.

Rane let Seth make the first move. His blade came sailing towards her; he was clearly thinking that he would catch her unawares. But she was ready for him, and quicker than lightning she whirled past and behind him so that he had to parry a blow behind his back before turning around to face her once more. Forward they danced along the platform, their movements faster than lightning, whirling, diving, ducking, their swords catching the sun in flashes of silver and gold. Rane's auburn hair shook free of her hood, tumbling out and streaming over her shoulders like flames in the early morning light.

Seth was growing frustrated—Laith could tell by the way he attacked. He had clearly expected Rane to capitulate early, to get lost inside her own head and give in to her fear. But Rane's face was a completely blank mask, so intense was her focus. She was a smaller, more agile opponent than Laith, and she kept slipping under Seth's arms to rain blows down on him from behind, which he had to deflect away like falling raindrops. And then, almost as if he could read his thoughts, Laith saw Seth's tactics change. No longer was he trying to win outright; instead, he was trying to sneak in a cut to Rane's skin, to poison her with the blade of his sword.

Laith almost felt like shouting another warning, but he could see that she sensed the change in strategy, too. She kept her hands carefully out of harm's way, going much more on the defensive than she had before. She was light on her feet, making Seth look almost heavy by comparison. Laith could see her eyes searching for an opening, any opening—but Seth was much too aggressive and too fast.

Seth darted forward, slicing his blade straight through the air at her face. She wrenched her shoulders one way and then the other, his sword missing her cheeks by mere inches. Seth's teeth gritted together and Laith felt a sudden flurry of fear in his chest. He tried to stand, almost without thinking, and the pain in his ankle bloomed so intensely that it caught his breath and he fell back to the earth, useless.

Seth slashed upwards once again and Rane dove back out of the way of the blow. Laith could see her guiding the fight almost to the edge of the stone platform on which they stood, and his mind began racing. What was she going to do?

Seth glanced behind and saw that he was once again close to the edge of the platform, and took an aggressive leap toward Rane, his sword swinging. He swiped once, then twice, then brought his sword up in front of him to calculate a third blow. In the blink of an eye, before he could even flinch, Rane had dodged and spun Laith's sword neatly around in her hand, bringing the weight of the hilt down squarely against Seth's fist. Powerless to stop the momentum, his hands flew back towards his body and the edge of his own blade caught his throat. A thin crimson line of blood appeared on his neck and he took a stumbling step towards Rane before catching himself. His cold black eyes traveled to the edge of his blade, where the streak of blood was barely visible.

It all happened very fast. Seth took another confused step forward, but the color drained out of his face as rapidly as it had been sucked out by some unseen force. A gurgling sound emanated from his throat and he fell to his knees, wracked on all sides by pain, his body contorting and spasming uncontrollably before he rolled to his back and lay still, black eyes staring sightlessly up at the sky. A thin red line of bile fell from the side of his mouth and pooled beside his head on the stone platform.

Rane stood over him for a moment, her face expressionless, sword held loosely in one hand. Slowly she leaned down and picked up the poisoned sword from his hand, examining it closely, every inch of the meticulous care that had gone into its making. She unbuckled the sheath from around Seth's waist and slid the sword safely inside. Then she turned and without stopping strode past Laith to the edge of the wall. Without another thought she cast the priceless weapon over the side and into the swirling water below.

For a few seconds she stood and watched the small white speck in the water where it had fallen, then once it was swallowed up she turned back. Then she was walking quickly up to him, her hand reaching for his waist, helping him to his one good foot. He grimaced in pain, leaning as much of his weight on her as she could bear. He hopped forward, one glancing step at a time.

"It's good to see you," Laith told her fervently.

"We'll get you inside," she said. "And then I'll get someone to bind your leg and help you down."

"Did you see any of the others?" Laith asked, gripping her shoulder with his hand.

"Cicada and I found Archer. He was alive, but barely. Ari's with him." Her voice faltered. The triumph that had been coursing through her body for the few moments after her defeat of Lord Seth ebbed away at the thought of what might be happening to Tarr at that very moment. "I don't know about Tarr and Si."

"They'll be all right," Laith assured her.

She glanced up at him. "It seems there's a chance," Rane said, her tone level, "we may all make it out of this war alive."

The ghost of a smile, the kind that had not been seen on his face in many months, played around the edges of his mouth. "Good," he said, and meant it.

Rane nodded and looped her arm around his waist with a feeling of finality. Together they limped forward into the shelter of the tower beyond.

Tarr and Si stood at the head of a short hallway. They were motionless, side by side, staring at the door facing them. A shaft of sunlight from a nearby window cut through the gloom and Tarr could see miniscule particles of dust glinting as they danced through the air. Just beyond, shrouded in darkness, was a door, its large silver handle glowing dully in the low light. They had reached the end of the road. There was nowhere else to go.

Si's young face was calm, focused—more focused than Tarr had seen it in a long time. "She knows I'm coming," he said quietly.

Tarr opened his mouth, then closed it quickly. He was so far out of his depth he couldn't think of anything helpful to say.

"Remember," Si reminded him. "We mustn't kill her. You mustn't try. It won't work. Not while I'm alive."

Tarr stared at him, and nearly laughed. "Si, I couldn't—" he began automatically, then stopped short. *I couldn't kill anyone*, he was about to say. But Si looked at him so knowingly. *He can see what I did*, he thought wildly. *He knows what I did.* He swallowed, his throat suddenly dry.

"Don't let her touch you," Si continued after a moment, and his gray eyes were grave. "Remember after we found the medallion? I had powers but I couldn't control them. I couldn't focus them. That's how she is now."

Tarr didn't need reminding. "What about you?" he whispered. "What if she touches you?"

"I don't know," Si replied.

"You can't see?"

"I can see, but it's a tangle. It could mean anything."

Tarr took a deep breath. His pulse was racing; he was keenly aware of his hands hanging empty at his sides, how foolish it seemed walking into the den of a serpent's lair with no weapon, no sort of protection.

Si stepped forward. Tarr could do nothing besides follow. The boy's small hand closed around the silver door handle and Cira's door slowly opened.

Tarr's eyes took a moment to adjust to the darkness. There were large windows surrounding the room, but each had a heavy velvet curtain drawn over it, so it was almost as if they had stepped into the pitch-black of night. Tarr could see the vague outline of rich furnishings: settees and chairs with sculpted backs and creeping vines around the arms. He could see the thin veil of cobwebs hanging from the dusty chandelier and the air smelled musty, stale and old, as if no one had opened a window in months. He began to doubt whether Cira—or anyone for that matter—actually lived in these apartments anymore. *Has she tricked us?* He wondered. *Did she manage to escape? Has she secretly been one step ahead of us this whole time?*

Si, who had drawn to a halt beside him, stepped out into the middle of the room and closed his eyes, taking a deep breath. Though there was no visible change in the setting around them, Tarr felt the air begin to change. It became hotter, and there was a buzzing in his ear, a static in the room like a lightning storm was raging nearby.

There was movement at the far end of the room, so sudden that Tarr gave a jump and stumbled back a step. Out of the darkness, a figure materialized; something white and ghostlike. The figure grew closer and closer, like the moon emerging from behind a cloud.

It was Cira.

441

CHAPTER TWENTY-SEVEN

It was Cira, but though Tarr had seen her on a number of occasions, she was barely recognizable. Her hair was long, hanging almost down to her hip, pale as a sheet. And her skin—she was as pale as Archer; there was almost no difference in hue between her face, her hair, and her gown.

But nevertheless, her demeanor was different from what Tarr had anticipated. For all the whispers and rumors that had swirled around her for the past few months, he had half-expected her to emerge bearing the same wild expression that he had glimpsed in Wolf. The eyes that glittered back at them were like two emeralds, cold but undeniably sane. Somehow that sanity was worse than if they had found her dressed in rags, hair in tangles, hissing at them and spitting like a feral cat.

"May I offer you a drink?" she asked, her voice strangely hoarse and flat. She stole away to the side of the room to a small table where there was a decanter and a few glasses. She began to pour and Tarr was struck by how odd it was, this overture of hospitality in such a strange, ghostly setting. But there was something—something in the deliberate way she poured the wine that Tarr didn't like. He tried to catch Si's eye to communicate some kind of warning, but the boy's eyes were fixed on Cira as she moved back through the dim interior and placed the glasses of wine on the table before them. She held her own glass in her hand but didn't drink.

"I've been expecting you," she said in the same low voice, taking a step back and looking at them thoughtfully. She was smaller than Tarr had remembered, almost as small as Si. How ironic, he thought suddenly, how many lives had been altered, affected, and ended because of the actions of such a slip of a young woman. She squared her shoulders and her green eyes pierced into them. "I had a feeling you'd come."

"I had to," said Si calmly. Cira regarded him with frank interest.

"I'm sure you thought that I had gone mad," she smiled, as if she knew Tarr's thoughts. "Many others think I have. It makes me laugh. I feel them thinking and it makes me laugh. I'm not mad. But I *can*..." here, she extended a hand, and flexed it slowly open and closed. Tarr knew immediately what she was talking about. *I can kill people, hurt them with just the touch of a hand.* He could see that she liked the feeling.

Without warning she flew at him, her white hair streaming behind her like a cloud. Tarr fell backward onto the floor and she was on top of him like a vengeful fury, her nails slicing at him. Dimly, Tarr heard Si shout a warning, but he felt Cira's cold hand fasten around his wrist. At once his whole body filled with excruciating pain, as if he were being burned alive. He felt himself screaming out, felt as though he were suddenly falling, falling into an unseen abyss, slipping far away from his body, from the reality of Cira's tower, into some blank, unknown darkness.

And then, just as suddenly, he felt himself stop falling and was buoyed back up. Slowly, as if in a dream, he regained control of his eyes, his hands, his body. He shook violently all over. He found, at once, that he was still screaming and wrenched himself away from Cira as fast as he could. He felt her wiry grip break, and it was like a cold rush of water fell over his head.

Quickly regaining his senses, he looked frantically around himself. To Tarr's side, with his small hand pressed against the skin of Tarr's chest, was Si, who had pulled him away just in time. Tarr lifted the arm where Cira had grabbed it and saw five finger marks burned onto his skin, as if he had been touched by a flaming-hot iron.

"I'm all right," he panted to Si. "I'm all right."

Straightening up, he clambered to his feet, wary and all the more on his guard. Si moved forward, positioning himself between the two of them.

Cira, to his surprise, had dropped her cruel smile and seemed to have completely abandoned any interest in attacking the two of them again. Instead, she was staring at Si in wonderment.

"You have them, too?" she asked. "These powers?"

"Yes, Si replied quietly.

"Was it the same for you?" Cira asked Si curiously. "You started to have visions of things? And then they just kept happening more and more and got bigger and bigger?"

Si nodded. How profoundly lonely Cira's existence must be, Tarr thought, with only one other person on the earth who could possibly understand her experiences.

"You know, a group of people appeared in my throne room—" she pointed a pale finger to the floor below them. "They said they wanted to teach me about who I was. How to use my powers."

Tarr swallowed. "And?"

"I killed them," she shrugged in wonder. "With the touch of my hand. And I was right to do it. What could they possibly have taught *me*? If it was so easy for me to kill them? But then..." her voice drifted, and for an instant she looked almost uncannily like Si when he was in one of his daydreams. "They were right...things began to happen. I could see things, lights like strands of hair. I could hear people's feelings, hear them inside my bones as if they were mine. I could see visions of the future, but what I saw shifted and changed like light through a prism; it was hard to know what was really going to happen. And then..." her voice trailed off. Again, she eyed Si with interest, as if eager to hear whether his experience had been the same. "You still have the visions?" she asked.

"Yes. But I learned about them," Si said quietly. "Learned how to see properly. To be a part of them rather than fight them."

She scoffed at this. "To 'see properly,'" she mimicked cruelly. "What a joke." But behind the mask of haughty arrogance Tarr thought he could detect a faintly puzzled look in her eye, as if Cira was for the first time considering what the outcome may have been if she had not refused the guidance of her would-be teachers. *Si had the humility to learn. Something Cira could never have done.*

Cira turned away restlessly, walking to one of her heavily curtained windows. She pulled the edge of the curtain back and a sliver of gold morning light pierced her face. She looked out for a moment at the sea, then let the curtain fall. The room was once again plunged into inky darkness.

"I began to see," she murmured, almost to herself. "I began to see the land around us. And then bigger and bigger. I could see the sea of Vireg, could see all the countries beyond it. The whole world, like a blue and green pebble suspended in the sky. And then even further...the ocean of stars and planets, whirling and spinning around each other." Her voice had drifted now, again eerily reminiscent of Si in one of his trances. "Suns being snuffed out left and right like candles, tugging at their galaxies, pulling the stars into an empty void." She stopped speaking and turned to them. Her expression was plaintive, vulnerable. She searched them appealingly, asking for understanding. Finally, she sighed. "And I finally realized...how *pointless* this all is. This...tiny, insignificant scrap of land we're fighting over. How little it matters. Just a speck of dust, nothing more."

Tarr stared at her. It was hard to believe what he was hearing. "So..." he said slowly. "Why go on fighting at all?"

Cira shrugged a shoulder carelessly. "I haven't. My generals have. The guns from Vireg, all the spy nonsense. They've done all of it. It doesn't matter to me anymore."

Tarr was dumbfounded. "You haven't..." he stammered. He glanced at Si, whose steady gaze hadn't moved from Cira all the while. He didn't seem remotely as surprised as Tarr. "But...Archer?" Tarr continued anxiously, afraid to hear Cira's reply. "And the fire outside of Two Falls..."

"What fire?" Cira asked quizzically.

She doesn't know that she caused that fire, Tarr realized. *She really isn't in control of her powers.* The thought wasn't terribly comforting. "Why not just stop it all, then?" Tarr asked. "You say this war doesn't matter. So why let your generals keep going? All the other lives lost... why didn't you just end it?"

A slow, slinky smile spread across her features. "You're telling me," she said, almost dreamily, "that you've never squashed an insect just for the sheer pleasure of it? Just to feel the power over another being, the insignificance of that life as it compares to yours?"

Tarr swallowed. He could no longer honestly say that he hadn't any idea what Cira was talking about.

"It can be a fascinating thing, observing that process, watching something die." She sighed. "But even that loses its novelty after a while."

Tarr stared at her, horrified.

She shrugged and smirked. "So then it amused me to watch everyone rushing around, mustering armies, thinking their work was so *important* when it was nothing more than a swarm of ants rushing in and out of a crack of the ground. It amused me beyond belief. The world holds little interest for me now, so I must find amusement where I can. Your friend Archer brought me a great deal of amusement, I'm glad to say. The thought of showering the Striker army in Archer's blood? The crimson cloaks of the Striker guard? There's some lovely poetry in that, don't you think?"

Tarr felt a wave of nausea overtake him and he reeled slightly. Beside him, Si reached out and gently gripped his wrist. *It is all right*, Si seemed to say, his hand glowing warm on Tarr's skin. *Let it go.* Tarr forced himself to push Archer from his mind, to trust Si.

Cira sighed again. "And so now I wait. I stare at the stars in my head and I wait."

"For what?" Tarr asked.

She gave a hollow chuckle and waved her hand listlessly in front of her. "For this...all of this...to pass. It will be gone in an instant. It will be forgotten. None of it will have meant anything."

In that moment Tarr realized that it hadn't mattered that he and Si had walked in to confront Cira unarmed and unprotected. She had already been defeated long ago. Her ambition had been her driving force; a great, terrible, unstoppable thing. The desire to consume, to control, to own, to wield had urged on every step she'd taken. And now that ambition had been sucked out of her, leaving her nothing more than a husk. Tarr almost found himself feeling sorry for her, sorry for the great Queen she might have been had she not lacked the fundamental elements of empathy and compassion. But though he may have pitied her, he could never forgive her. Because of her, they stood there with a battle raging right outside the door, soldiers fighting one another to the death. And all of it simply because she was too bored to put an end to it.

While Tarr had been thinking, a subtle shift had slowly crept across Cira's face. She was regarding Si anew with a fresh, almost predatory curiosity.

"But it wouldn't be the same with you. Would it?" she mused softly, almost to herself. "It *would* be a challenge. Especially if we have the same abilities. The Ashan would be boring. All Ashan lives are boring. Disposable," her eyes flicked towards Tarr and back again. "Over too quickly. Too easy. But you. Si Morthenstar," she spread her palm and gazed at it, then looked up and advanced a step towards them. "You might just be able to put up a fight. It's been so long." A little smile, one of pleasure, of eagerness, began to twitch at the corner of her delicate mouth.

Tarr felt himself inadvertently draw back. "Si..." he muttered warningly.

"Come here, Cira. Take my hand," Si said suddenly, and extended his arm.

Cira immediately halted her advance and eyed him with suspicion. "Why?"

Si waited, hand still extended, suspended in midair.

Cira suddenly prickled, as though she could sense that something was amiss. "No," she said warningly, her teeth bared. "No." She stepped backward, and Si darted forward, reaching out for her. Cira raised her hand towards him, as if to repel him backwards.

A huge bubble of energy welled up inside the room; the same electric crackling that Tarr had felt earlier. It blew out from Cira and Si and rushed up Tarr's legs and through his fingertips. Tarr felt his hair stand up on end, felt the saliva in his mouth buzzing, felt as though he could almost be lifted up off his feet and held in the air. He looked in astonishment towards Si and Cira, who were facing each other as if frozen in place. Cira's pale hair was rising slowly up as if held there by an unseen wind. All the sounds around them became muffled, as if they were suddenly submerged underwater. And then the bubble burst.

Everything seemed to come crashing down at once: the heavy velvet curtains billowed out and were split end to end as if cleaved by a knife; the glass of every mirror and window shattered into thousands of tiny shards, filling the air around them. Tarr threw his hands up over his head and felt the glass scrape at his arms as they fell to the ground around him like thousands of scattered diamonds. He cowered down on the floor as the unseen force swept around them, overturning the furniture with an enormous crashing and splintering of wood as if a hand had casually swept them to the side. Tarr felt himself picked up and hurled through the air as if he were a rag doll; he hit the wall opposite and slid down to the floor, helpless to shield himself from both the sudden burst of sunlight in the room and the enormous force of energy that surrounded him.

Shaking his head to clear his reeling senses, he whipped his head up to look back towards Si and Cira, who still stood face to face. He could see that Si was trying to edge closer to her but it was as if they were like magnets coming at each other from opposing ends; some boundary was keeping them apart. There were beads of sweat forming on the boy's forehead, his brow furrowed with concentration. Slowly, he edged one of his feet closer to Cira, moved his arm painstakingly up through the air as if it were being dragged back downward by a thousand invisible hands, and—Cira's green eyes narrowed, her mouth opened in a silent bloodcurdling scream—ever so slightly touched the tips of her fingertips with his.

Just as quickly as the din had begun it subsided, and the eerie, muffled air settled in around them. It was so quiet that Tarr could hear his heart beating inside his ears; he could even hear Cira and Si's hearts. And then—he had to rub his eyes to make sure he wasn't seeing things—Cira and Si were lifted up off the ground and hovered a few feet above the floor. Their faces were frozen—Cira's in an expression of feline fury, Si's in deep concentration, and then Tarr saw it: a glow that began at the joining of their fingertips and slowly spread down their arms and over their entire bodies until both of them were engulfed in light. The light grew and grew until Tarr could no longer look at them; he turned his face away, and the heat swelled so much around him that he thought he would no longer be able to breathe from the suffocating weight of it. The light and the heat expanded and pulsed, and his breath came in short, desperate gulps. He was crying out, though he could barely hear it over the roar of wind around them. And then everything went quiet.

It must have been a minute or two before anything in the room stirred; Tarr managed to move one of his arms, which had been trapped under his body as he cowered against the wall. *There's no way they're still alive*, he thought to himself as his senses slowly returned to him. *No way. They're both dead.* He took a moment to sort out his limbs, to identify exactly where each one was and how it worked, and then unfolded himself and looked over his shoulder.

The room was completely destroyed. Every glass pane was shattered, the rugs were swept away, the furniture overturned and splintered into nothingness. Cold sea air blew in through the skeletal remains of the windows. Oddly, the only things that had remained untouched were the three glasses of wine, which sat innocuously on the floor next to the immobile bodies of Si and Cira.

"No," Tarr croaked aloud. He struggled to his knees and crawled across the room towards them as fast as he could. Just as he was about to reach Si, both of them gave a little stir and Tarr stopped mid-crawl, unsure of what to do, knowing that if Cira got a hold of him again and Si was unable to counteract her touch, he would be dead.

Cira struggled up to her elbows, her white dress torn and her ashen face a deathly shade of blue, her pallor even more pronounced in the morning light. Her hair fell ghostly pale around her shoulders. She looked around herself as if she were just waking up after a long, long sleep. And then, her face fell and one hand went to her chest as if there were suddenly a great pain there.

"What happened?" she panted. "Why do I see—" she blinked at Si in abject confusion. "That night. The woman with the knife in my bedroom. I could see you...you were..."

"Yes," Si agreed quietly, his eyes fixed on her.

What is she talking about? Tarr wondered wildly. *What woman? What knife?*

"I can feel all of it," she whispered, still staring unblinkingly at Si.

"I can see it all now. Your whole life. From the start to..." Suddenly, she winced and clutched once again at her heart. "Oh no," she breathed. "Oh, no. Oh, help."

Tarr reached out a hand to touch Si, who was up on his elbows, staring at Cira. *What should I do?* Tarr wondered desperately, wishing he could understand what had happened, whether Si was all right.

As he watched, Tarr was startled to see tears filling Cira's glittering eyes. The malice was gone from them, even the haughty arrogance that had rested there so easily before. Tears spilled down her cheeks in an unbidden cascade, and she began gulping for air, her hand still clutching at her chest as if she were in great pain. Her expression was scattered; confused.

"What's going on?" Tarr yelped, tugging at Si, willing him to get away from her.

"It's all right," Si breathed, batting a hand towards him, his gray eyes trained on Cira. "It's all right."

Tarr wasn't convinced, and made a motion to pull Si farther away, but he froze as Cira scrambled to her hands and knees, a long stream of tears still pouring freely down her cheeks. "No," she whispered again.

Her hand groped around beside her as if she could not see and finally her hand closed around the glass of wine. Before Tarr could think, or call out, or make any motion to stop her, she had stood, tipped her head back and downed the entire glass in one long swoop. She opened her hand and the glass shattered beside her bare foot. She stood, staring unblinkingly at Si.

Tarr became suddenly aware of the sound of many footsteps approaching behind the door to Cira's chamber. His mind felt split in two, his gaze flicking to the door, then back to Cira. The approaching footsteps seemed as though they belonged to another world, somewhere far away.

Cira's mouth opened, and Tarr felt a foreboding thrill. But before she could speak she swayed, drunkenly, unsteadily, and in another instant her eyes rolled up into her head and she collapsed on the ground atop the scattered debris. Tarr and Si were frozen for a second, then all of Tarr's limbs galvanized back into action. He released Si and sprang over to her, confusion flooding his brain. He felt her arm. No pulse.

He felt her throat. No pulse.

Part of his conscious mind suddenly re-registered the sound of footsteps outside the room. There was pounding on the door, raised voices. He could barely think.

"Si," he said hoarsely. "Si, Cira is dead." He looked over to the boy, whose face registered nothing.

"Yes," Si replied flatly.

"How is she dead?" Tarr asked, mind reeling. "*You're* not dead."

"No," Si agreed.

Tarr's brain slowly began working, and he looked from Cira's dead body back to the door, which was rocking on its hinges as the troops outside began to try and batter it in. He recognized Cade's voice calling out over the others. *Think*, he ordered himself. *Think fast.*

Tarr flew back to Si and forced the boy to meet his gaze. Si regarded him levelly. "But she can't die. You said that neither one of you can die while the other is alive."

"That's right," Si concurred.

"I'm going to need you to explain what happened."

"All right," Si said pleasantly. "Well, a long, long time ago—"

"Not *now*," Tarr said hurriedly, taking him by both shoulders. "Now I'm going to need you to help me with something."

The pounding outside grew louder. The door wasn't going to last much longer.

"I need you to pretend to be dead. You said you could do that. Can you do that?" Tarr demanded.

Si brightened. "You mean you want me to inhabit another astral plane?"

"Yes," Tarr said faintly. "Yes, I need you to inhabit another astral plane for a little while. And then come back when I call you. Only when *I* call you."

"All right," Si said, unfazed, as the door gave a loud crunching sound behind them. Si lay back, closed his eyes, and folded his hands on his chest. To Tarr's utter astonishment, the color faded from Si's face, leaving him as cold and pale as Cira. Tarr blinked. Si was no longer breathing; he felt for a pulse, but there was none.

Tarr's heart began pounding in fear, as one of the hinges in the door gave way behind them. "Er…Si?"

The color came flooding back and Si opened one eye. "Hello," he said affably.

Tarr's mouth opened and closed soundlessly. *The list of things I'm going to need Si to explain keeps getting longer*, he thought faintly. "Nothing. I was just checking to make sure that you were all right. Go and…uh…explore that astral plane some more. I'll call you."

Si gave a reassuring smile and settled back. A moment later he lay as if dead on Cira's floor. Tarr bent over him, feeling faint and completely overwhelmed, only now really taking in the state of the room, the wind against his face. He was shivering uncontrollably. Seconds later, the door gave way and a pack of blue-cloaked soldiers poured in.

Tarr whipped around and scrambled to his feet. Cade and Wolf, flanked by twelve of their guards, strode into the room and stopped still as they saw the state of it. All of the soldiers were dirty and bloodied; Tarr swallowed and looked down at his forearm, which still bore the five marks from Cira's hand. He tried to hide his arm behind his back.

Recovering his wits, Cade strode forward and addressed Tarr sharply. "What happened?" he demanded, glancing down at Si and kneeling beside Cira. He so resembled his cousin at that moment, with his pale hair and slightly feline features, that it took Tarr a few moments before he could reply.

"They fought," Tarr said, swallowing nervously. "They fought, but Cira poisoned them both. They're dead."

He tried to read Cade's face as the young king rocked back from Cira's body and surveyed the damage to the room. Finally, he fixed Tarr with a long, searching, inscrutable stare.

"Cira is dead," Cade said loudly to his troops, who had quietly filed in behind him into the room. "Pull her standard from the flagpole. Raise my banner and the Strikers'. The war is over."

A small group of troops nodded and disappeared from the room. Cade turned back to Tarr. But then, behind him, Wolf stepped forward and looked down silently at Cira's body. Cade's face blanched.

"Wolf," he said. "Wolf, it doesn't matter. She's dead. She's dead and this is over and that's all that matters. Your revenge is complete."

But Wolf stared unblinkingly down at her and took a step backward.

And then, without even a flinch or a moment's pause, he strode swiftly across the room to one of Cira's blown out windows overlooking the sea. And without so much as a sound he hurled himself over the railing and out into the void beyond.

"Wolf!" Cade screamed and bolted after him, Tarr and his troops close on his heels. Cade was running so fast that Tarr had to catch his arm to keep him from barreling over the railing himself. Together, Cade's soldiers dragged him back from the window, where Tarr could just see a blue-cloaked figure crushed on the rocks below.

Cade's body seemed to crumple for a moment and his fists balled at his temples. Tarr met the eyes of one of his soldiers, a large, tough-looking woman with a cut over her eye. She looked as stunned and helpless as he felt.

A moment later Cade straightened, his jaw set. His eyes were moist and red, but his voice didn't quiver as he looked back up at Tarr. "He wanted to do it. Revenge was all he had. All he had left. She even took that from him."

Tarr couldn't think of what to say. Cade turned away tiredly and rubbed the back of his neck. The waves below *shushed* over the rocks. "Order two litters," he said finally. "Take the bodies down. I want her troops to see her and then we dump her body out at sea. We'll take Morthenstar back to Two Falls. He died a hero and will be honored as such."

Tarr nodded mutely. Cade straightened his cloak and pulled at one of his gloves, any grief at the death of his best friend and bodyguard safely tucked away. He swept from the room, leaving Tarr behind to wait with the dead.

The sounds of the battle below began to ebb until the clash of metal and the cries of the fighters had all but died away. An ominous silence took hold in the air, punctuated only occasionally by a distant crash or the occasional scream of an arrow. The wind, blowing cold through the parapets of the fortress, was the only sign of life yet remaining. Rane and Laith had taken cover beneath one of the eaves of the fortress, where Rane felt that she could best defend the prince should Kagaian soldiers happen upon them. It was clear, however, that the battle was nearing its conclusion—whatever that might be—and they were, for the moment, safe. After a few tense initial minutes, they'd both gradually relaxed, and found themselves simply sitting side by side overlooking the sea stretching out before them as it ceaselessly washed in and out.

Silence hung on them like a heavy, exhausted cloud, but though they said nothing Rane took comfort in Laith's presence. Rane's mind was slowly flashing between the image of Lord Seth lying lifeless at her feet while a more disjointed, vague prayer charged through her heart. *Let them be all right*, she thought. *Tarr, Archer, Athela, Marc, Si, Ari, Cicada. Let them be all right. Let me see my friends again.*

She glanced over at Laith, whose face was inscrutable. His head was leaned back against the stone wall on his slender stalk of neck, his eyes half-closed. Rane leaned her head against his shoulder, and a moment later she felt the weight of his head against hers. She felt his warm hand clasp her fingers. She closed her eyes, and felt a quiet peace wash over both of them.

"Thank you," Laith said in a quiet voice, "for saving my life. I'm glad you did."

Rane made no reply, just squeezed his hand.

"No more ghosts," he said.

"No more ghosts," she agreed, and slowly, softly, the spectral vision of Lord Seth faded away in her mind until his presence was a mere sliver. Not gone—perhaps never gone—but no longer powerful.

All of a sudden, from above them the sound of a horn rang out and a voice shouted over the walls of the fortress. "Cira is dead! The Strikers have won!"

Rane and Laith snapped apart and looked at one another, speechless. Again the horn rang out.

"Cira is dead! The Strikers have won!" The voice echoed out over the walls and the rocks, the sea crashing below. There were no other shouts, no cries of victory. It was as if the remaining fighters in Faridor were all hesitating, unsure of how to proceed.

"Do you think it's true?" Rane asked.

"I hope so," Laith turned his chestnut eyes to hers. "Here, help me up."

Archer awoke slowly, cold and damp on the stone floor. It took him some time to struggle to his senses, but the air—the sweet, fresh, cold air—was like life pouring dizzyingly back into his veins. He felt the wind before he had the strength to open his eyes; the brisk sting against his cheek pulled him from the dense netherworld in which he'd been senselessly floating. He blinked his golden eyes open, trying to orient himself. He was out in the open, lying on some sort of stone balcony. He could see through spaces in the balustrade down to the hushing sea breaking on the rocks below, dotted here and there with the emerald green cloaks of Kagaian soldiers who had fallen. *It must be over*, he thought, a surge of fear and wonder rippling through him, willing his limbs to galvanize into action. *But who won? What happened?*

Even with great effort, he was only able to move his head a very little bit—just enough to turn and take stock of his surroundings. He gave a tiny start and a cry escaped his lips.

The balcony around him was littered with the bodies of five Kagaian guards, their blood slicking the stone where they lay. Archer could make out a leg trailing into the room beyond the balcony.

Again, his foggy brain made a stupid attempt to make sense of the awful sight. *I couldn't possibly have killed all those people*, he thought. *Why do I feel so weak?* The last thing he remembered was being strapped onto a table, warm blood tickling its way down his arm. *I thought I was dead. I thought I was really dead this time.*

He blinked again, relishing the cold, feeling his senses returning, marveling anew at the beauty of the sunlight pouring in above him. He raised his head once more and looked on the scene with fresh eyes. He barely stifled a yell of shock.

A foot or two away from him lay Ari. He was face up, completely motionless, the shaft of a long black arrow protruding from his right shoulder. From his odd angle, Archer could see that Ari's shirt was soaked in blood—though whether it was Ari's or one of the guards', Archer wasn't sure. Even in his confused state, Archer was able to piece it together: Ari had fallen, the only person standing between Archer and the many Kagaian guards set on killing them both.

There was a sound from below, a call from a human throat—soft and faint at first, then others picked it up and it grew in strength to the sound of a roar, piercing through the air like the sun. It was the sound of victory, though Archer wasn't certain which side was calling. *One way to find out,* Archer thought groggily. *If Cira's won, we won't be left alive for very long.* He tried with all his might to sit upright, and the effort of it nearly sent him spinning. He slumped back and for a moment the gray fog before his eyes threatened to overtake him.

But the roar on the air, the roar of victory, persisted and above it all, close to him, there was a tiny sound—a cough. Archer forced himself awake, and as his eyes re-focused he saw the arrow in Ari's chest flutter ever so slightly. Ari was alive—barely alive.

Another sound caught Archer's attention, and with all his might he turned his head back against the balustrade behind him to look up at the top of the tower. The spire above them was almost indigo, the rising sun illuminating it in a pure, breathless golden light. Archer's yellow eyes traveled up to the fluttering emerald Kagaian flag at the top of the turret. And then, inch by inch, it began to lower.

Archer's heart leapt within his chest, and he could have started weeping right then and there. He was brought back down a moment later, though, by the sound of another small cough. With all his might, Archer willed life back into his numb, cold limbs and lurched his upper body forward to the point where he was just able to wrap his fingertips in Ari's shirt. Using his own body weight and the last ounce of strength he could, he dragged Ari back to the corner of the balcony beside him, a long smear of dark crimson blood following in his wake.

Archer half-collapsed back against the balcony at the sheer effort, his chest heaving up and down as he forced air into his unresponsive lungs. His head spun again, heavily, but he shook himself, six of his long white fingers still clasping the damp, cold fabric of Ari's bloody shirt. Archer could see half of Ari's face from the angle at which he lay, and could see that his eyes were open ever so slightly, the lashes fluttering intermittently. Archer did a cursory glance down at Ari's wounds. He had hoped that the arrow had missed its mark, that the injuries were salvageable, but after an instant's examination he knew it was too late. Ari was dying, and was far past any attempt to save him.

But Ari's eyes, half open though they were, were still aware, and even as his own vision blurred, Archer saw Ari's gaze travel up the side of the blue stone tower to where the golden sun illuminated the flagpole atop the north turret. They watched as the green Kagaian flag slid down the last few feet and disappeared, removed by some unseen hand. And then, moments later, the scarlet emblem of Morthenstar flapped into the wind, spreading out like a hand against the glowing pink sky. Together they watched as it was hoisted up into the air, where it streamed into the light over the sea, the land, and everything around them.

Ari's eyes remained fixed on the flag as the life slowly ebbed from his body. After a few minutes, he quietly died.

It was an hour later before a group of Strikers, led by Athela and Cicada, came upon them. Archer had long since slipped back into unconsciousness, his hand still tightly gripping Ari's shirt, the streak of Ari's blood like an ink stroke across the stone balcony. Their faces were tilted up into the morning light spilling over the edge of the tower above them. Both looked at peace.

By midday, a long stream of figures wound its way out of Faridor fortress and back towards the city of Two Falls, where anxious sentries awaited news of the outcome of the battle. The Ashan advance guard went first; a handful of the twenty who had scaled Faridor's wall remained. Numb and disheveled, they were embraced and applauded as they passed through the gates of the city. A group of Strikers escorted the surviving Kagaian troops. Some of them were cursed and spat at as they passed by the crowds of townspeople, but every few minutes a weeping man or woman or child would disentangle themselves from the throng of onlookers and rush towards one of the Kagaian soldiers, relieved to see that their sibling, spouse, or parent was safe. And as the rear of the procession approached, the cry went up around the city that both Cira Kagai and Si Morthenstar were dead.

The remaining Strikers walked with Si and Ari's bodies, both of which had been arranged on a wagon pulled by four horses, out in the open for all to see. Tarr found himself torn between praying that Si wouldn't suddenly decide to return from his sojourn on the astral plane, extreme guilt for having to temporarily deceive his friends into believing that Si was dead, and utter desolation at the death of Ari, who by all accounts had sacrificed himself to save Archer's life. Tarr could barely stand to look at Marc, who was holding Si's hand as he walked along the side of the wagon, his face so grief-stricken that he seemed to be beyond tears. Laith and Archer, both seriously wounded, rode on another wagon farther back, flanked by Athela, who was resting her hand on Archer's shoulder.

Beside Tarr was Rane. She barely spoke a word the entire walk home, but her hand was in his, she was alive, her skin was warm and the blissful certainty of a blank expanse of time to spend alongside one another had only just begun to dawn on him.

Next to her walked another young woman whom Tarr hadn't met before. She was slight and slender, with sharp, dark features and a watchful gaze. Though he'd never met her in person, the ease of the way in which she walked so close to Rane told him that this was in all likelihood the Striker spy Cicada. He felt a rush of gratitude towards her for all she had done, for thinking quickly and smuggling the weapons plans out of Faridor after Rane was taken.

There would be time for all of it, he realized. There would be time. They would reach their headquarters and after hours and hours of talking, of being clapped on the back, of hearing the city bells ringing, hearing the sounds of the celebration starting in the city around them, they would find themselves alone, just them, in a quiet room with the door closed behind them. Laith, Archer and Athela, Marc, Rane, Cicada. And he would tell them that Si was alive, and Marc's face, now so pale and drawn, would bloom with relief and happiness. They would talk, and when they talked it would be of the battle they had just fought, of what had happened. Soon, the talk would turn from the battle and they would start, for the first time, to look ahead. The city and the country would be rebuilt and reborn into something new.

At sundown, a small boat would row unnoticed out from the coast of Faridor. Once they were far enough from the shore, two soldiers would lift a slight, wrapped form from the bottom of the boat, weighted down with heavy stones to make sure that the body would sink. And then, as the sun slipped beneath the horizon, Cira Kagai would be buried beneath the waves.

EPILOGUE

ONE MONTH LATER

Two days before they were set to ride to Joymaril for Cade's marriage and coronation, Tarr found himself, as he did with increasing frequency, standing at his little window in the Strikers' headquarters in Two Falls staring out at the rooftops of the city as the sun set behind them. He tried to imagine what was taking place in each of the houses: the conversations, the meals being set. The hope of the survivors, the sorrow of those who had lost loved ones in the war. The confusion of a people with an open, uncertain future ahead of them.

Tarr tried to grapple with his feelings.

In just one short month, Cade had done very effective work, and Tarr couldn't help but be ruefully impressed. Cade had aligned the story of Si's defeat of Cira and his own participation in the Battle of Faridor so closely together that anyone would think he and Si had gone charging into battle hand in hand. In every brave speech Cade had given since the day of the battle (with Morthenstar's Whitsun sword, an ironic celebratory gift from Tarr and the others, buckled at his hip), he had coaxed the narratives closer and closer together so that it seemed only reasonable, Jelani heritage notwithstanding, that Cade should be Morthenstar's heir apparent. The stone mausoleum that was to house the body of Si Morthenstar in the center of the city was already designed and under construction. A second monument, which was to be erected at the center of the main market square, was as much to cement Cade's presence in Two Falls as it was to honor Si's memory—at this point, Tarr wouldn't be surprised if Cade planned to have an image of he and Si hitting a high five on the front edifice. As far as Cade was concerned, it was very convenient that Si Morthenstar was dead.

Of course he wasn't really, but only Tarr and a handful of his friends knew this.

Front-facing public relations aside, Tarr had observed with growing interest how shrewdly Cade had established his control behind the scenes, his every step a carefully calculated political machination. Besides the mausoleum and the many statues planned to commemorate the battle (including one of Ari and one depicting the twenty Ashans who had led the charge up Faridor's wall), Cade had overhauled most of the city's governing bodies to better suit his burgeoning rule. Out went many of the more unpopular members of Two Falls' council, in came a carefully selected few of Cade's generals and even some of the young Ashans who had scaled the wall. Tarr couldn't even be sure that Cade's impending marriage to Rowan, a commoner and a half-Ashan herself, wasn't some sort of move to curry favor with the remaining Ashans in Two Falls and to potentially broker peace with the tribes in the forest. There were shades of gray to every move that Cade made. Still, Tarr reluctantly conceded, Cade hadn't yet demonstrated any *overt* homicidal tendencies, so at least he was an improvement over Cira. At this point, he would take what he could get.

The battle was won, the war was over. So why did he feel strangely deflated? Archer was on the mend, Rane had survived. What more could he want? And why did he feel so...empty?

Frustrated with himself, Tarr turned suddenly away from the window just as there was a small knock on the door. Marc entered, followed by a small Striker guard in a red cloak, helmet obscuring most of his face. The young guard removed his helmet and Tarr found himself smiling, almost against his will.

"Hello," Si said pleasantly. "Sorry we're late, we took the long way around."

"There was a nebula, apparently, around the other side of the world that he wanted to see," Marc said to Tarr, shrugging helplessly. "Something about its aura."

"Purple," Si said dreamily. "Once in a lifetime."

"Makes sense," said Tarr, though as with most things that came out of Si's mouth these days, none of it made sense at all. "Thanks, Marc, stand guard outside, if you don't mind."

Marc gave Si a pat on the shoulder and vanished. Tarr gestured to a seat in front of his writing desk and Si took it. All in all, hiding him hadn't been difficult. Between the Strikers' time underground before they took back Two Falls and Si's own disappearance during his training with the Serpens, few people in Two Falls—the Striker troops included—even knew what he looked like.

As for faking his death, Si had inhabited some sort of alternate astral plane for the first few days while the townspeople took their chance to come and pay their respects (and, in Tarr's mind, confirm in the minds of the public that he was actually dead beyond any doubt.) It was beside Si's lifeless body that Cade delivered the first of a number of stirring orations calling for the people of Two Falls to come together so that they could move forward together as one nation: Jelani, human, and Ashan. It had irked Tarr to see Cade so flagrantly using Si's death as a political tool, but he had said nothing. The body had then been removed, wrapped, and placed in a sarcophagus, where it was intended to rest until it was moved into the monument being built for it in the center of Two Falls. Tarr and the other Strikers had requested special dispensation to hold an all-night private vigil at Si's side on the first night, during which time it took little effort to switch him out. For the last week or so, Si had been hiding out as an anonymous Striker guard (his distinctive red hair shorn and dyed dark brown) under Marc's careful eye. To Tarr's knowledge, no one had noticed a thing.

It had been too risky for them to meet together before now. Tarr believed in his core that Cade must never know that Si was alive. So he'd waited to talk to Si until Cade had embarked on a short three-day trip into some of the outermost towns, where he hoped to curry support for his rule amongst the villagers before returning to the Jelani palace for his coronation.

"So," Tarr began, unsure of where to start. There was still something so unnerving about Si's presence now, the feeling of someone else behind his friend's familiar eyes, manipulating him like a puppet and making him talk and walk around; the faraway air of someone who wasn't quite bound to the earth as other humans were.

"You have questions," Si prompted.

"Yes," Tarr said.

"It's not so hard," Si shrugged. "The rivers converged."

Tarr waited for him to elaborate, but he seemed to think that this was somehow a perfectly reasonable explanation. "I'm going to need a bit more than that," Tarr said wearily.

"I told you once that Cira and I were currents, like rivers, running side by side, never converging. Day and night. One cannot die while the other lives."

"But she died," Tarr said quickly. "She's dead."

"Yes and no," Si said with a cryptic smile.

Tarr's mind raced. *Wait, is she somehow alive still, too? Is this whole awful war still going to continue?*

"She lives in me," he continued.

Tarr was taken aback. "What did you say?"

"You remember when we touched? Our fingers joined together? All of our life forces flowed through each other, balanced like water breaking through a dam. Some of what I am flowed into her, some of what she is flowed into me. The empty places were filled in."

Something like understanding was starting to dawn on Tarr. "So she *could* die...her body could die because some of her...essence or whatever...is now within you?"

"That's right," Si said pleasantly, as if Tarr had just made an accurate observation about the weather.

"So basically you found a cosmic loophole," Tarr ventured.

"The best plans usually do," Si agreed reverently.

"So when *you* die..." Tarr prompted slowly.

"It's over," Si said. "For good. The balance is restored. Everything is in its natural order. No more magic, no one person will be able to tap into these elemental currents of energy. The Serpens are gone, so are their Kagaian counterparts. The door will be closed. All the remnants will die away. That's the end."

Tarr suddenly felt very tired. He rubbed his eyes with the back of his hand. "But, Si...if some part of Cira is now within you, if some of her...her greed, or her lust for power is in there...how do you know that you won't, you know..." he groped for some polite simile for "become a megalomaniacal tyrant," but none occurred to him.

"We don't," Si shrugged, still smiling that irritating sphinxlike smile.

"*You* do," Tarr said pointedly. "You know everything that's going to happen. You're tapped into the life forces of everything in the universe."

"With my own life, sometimes it's hard to read the lines," Si said. "Like with Cira. I didn't fully understand how our meeting would play out until I was standing there in front of her. This will all become clear, too. But not yet."

Si sounded a great deal more patient about it than Tarr was prepared to be. "But, Si—" Tarr protested.

"You could end it now," Si suggested casually.

Tarr was momentarily taken aback. "What are you suggesting?"

"You, of everyone, were a witness to what happened that day with Cira. And you can make this decision. If I'm dead, then you know it's over. The country's safe. You run no risk of my turning evil or losing my mind or my powers wiping everyone out."

Tarr was flabbergasted. "You're suggesting that I kill you?"

Si shrugged again, as if the thought meant very little to him.

Tarr studied him, openmouthed. He was shocked anew at Si's strange passivity, that he could suggest such a thing so casually...but, as Tarr reminded himself again after a few stunned moments, mortal life must seem very inconsequential to him now.

"I'm not going to kill you," Tarr said firmly, and the words were so ridiculous that it seemed silly to even say them out loud. "But how do you know you're going to be...safe? That you won't harm anyone? You're now the single most powerful being in the world. And now, if what you're telling me is correct, part of Cira's...soul, or whatever, lives in you. And like you always say, there are choices. You could still someday choose to turn...evil, for lack of a better word."

Si spread his hands, his dreamy eyes faraway and glazed over. "I suppose, Tarr, that you'll have to trust."

"Trust what?" Tarr asked immediately.

Back came the irritating all-knowing smile. Tarr had the suspicion that he was being toyed with and didn't quite like it. Just then, another thought occurred to him. A memory came flooding back from that fateful day when they faced Cira in the tower at Faridor.

"Si, when you and Cira finally made contact, you said that some of your essence went into her somehow, just as she went into you." Si's face fell grave, as if he could sense what Tarr was about to ask. "When you broke apart," Tarr continued, "she seemed different...she seemed to wake up and was distraught and then she drank the poisoned wine..." Tarr trailed off, not quite knowing what to say.

"As you said," Si spoke softly. "A bit of my soul went into her, too. The empty spaces were filled. I think at that moment, after we'd come together, she was finally able to really see and to *feel* the enormity of what she had done. To sympathize, to empathize. As she never could have before. All the lives she had taken."

"What?" Tarr asked blankly.

"Yes," Si said quietly. "Even though she couldn't control her power, didn't understand it, couldn't fully use it, she could still *feel* as I can now. The severing of a life...it feels like a sharp snap, like a hot burning whiplash, and you feel it deep inside your chest." Si stared pointedly at him, and Tarr had to look away. "And she felt each and every one of them for the first time. Every single one of the hundreds of lives she cut off. "

Tarr felt ill. "It was a better end than she deserved," he said darkly.

"Perhaps," Si agreed evasively. "She was human, in the end."

Tarr rocked back in his chair, lacing his long fingers together over his stomach and watched Si, whose faraway look seemed to pass right through him, through the walls of his room, and out over the hills to the west. *The only way to end this, to put this possibly catastrophic cycle of good and evil and magic to rest is for Si to die,* Tarr thought. The idea, as he gazed at his friend's eerily ageless expression, repulsed him and he felt ashamed for even thinking it. But still...*the most powerful being in the world, someone who could end a thousand lives with a blink of an eye, sitting right across the table from me. What if Cira's influence becomes stronger? What if he's not strong enough to counterbalance it? What if I am literally dooming the entire world for the sake of my friend's life?*

"I'll leave you to your thoughts," Si said suddenly, rising to his feet, and Tarr snapped out of his reverie. "My work is done. I met Cira. And now..." again, he shrugged. *The rest does not belong to me,* he seemed to say. *It will unfold as it is supposed to.*

Tarr studied the boy for a few seconds. "You know what I choose. What do I choose to do?"

"You really want to know?" Si asked.

It was harder for Tarr to answer "no" this time. He opened his mouth and closed it again. Si's smile widened, and a moment later he was gone.

As he so often did whenever he was feeling adrift and opaque (which seemed to happen with greater and greater frequency), Tarr wound up at Archer's bedside. Archer had recovered from the blood loss and torture he'd endured at the hands of Cira, but had been relegated to his bed for a full month to ensure no adverse effects. The Archer that Tarr had known before would have been chafing at the bit to be up and away, making jokes about the needlessness of his confinement, but Tarr was surprised and a bit anxious to find that Archer seemed to accept his current immobility with little to no protest.

It was too much to hope that Archer, ebullient and seemingly resilient as he was, could have come through such an ordeal completely unscathed. The physical effects had largely healed; other than a passing remark about the bloodletting, which had already been reported to the others by Rane and Cicada, Archer hadn't said a word about the other physical tribulations to which he'd been submitted during his imprisonment, and Tarr wasn't sure whether he ever would. The mental scars, Tarr soon realized, would take much longer to heal, if they ever did.

Tarr was glad to find Archer asleep and the room devoid of any other well-wishers. He'd had an embarrassing experience shortly after the battle of Faridor, when he had stumbled upon Jet paying Archer a final visit in his sickbed before returning home to the forest. Tarr had felt a strange, rather jealous pang seeing them there together. It had been only a moment before he'd apologized and beat a hasty retreat, but the image of the two of them, carbon copies, possessed of a strange, intimate, ineffable connection, had flickered up repeatedly and gratingly in his mind's eye.

Archer's most frequent visitor, however, was Athela. Tarr would invariably find her there beside the bed, and as soon as she saw Tarr she'd make some sort of excuse to keep up the pretense that she'd only just popped in to check on him (rather than the reality that she'd been sitting there for hours on end). That day, her chair was vacant, so Laith or one of the others must have coaxed her out to eat. Tarr settled himself in and propped his long feet up on the end of the bed next to Archer's. His brother's white and black-tipped head was turned away towards the window, the sheet drawn up to his shoulders. He looked peaceful.

A half an hour later, Archer stirred and turned his head in Tarr's direction, blinking his yellow eyes owlishly a few times before settling back down into the cradle of the bed. "I'm still not dead yet, then?" he asked, his voice scratchy with sleep.

"Not yet," Tarr forced a wan smile, though his heart gave an inward twinge.

"Have I recovered my rosy-cheeked glow yet?" Archer croaked with an attempt at one of his old smiles.

Tarr surveyed him from head to foot. Archer had only ever been the same color as the sheets in which he was now wrapped, so there wasn't much he could report on that front. "Less blue," he said finally.

Archer smiled weakly. "I'll take that as progress."

He reached over and took Tarr's hand and gave it a squeeze. Archer had been born and bred in the mountains; his skin was always pleasantly cool to the touch; smooth as polished stone. The familiarity of it filled Tarr's heart with joy.

"Ma should be arriving back home any day now," Tarr informed him, glad he had a small sliver of good news to share. "We've had her house prepared for her, as close to how it used to be as we could get it."

"Yes?" Archer's face cracked in a smile.

"She'll want to see you."

"Not here. Not like this. I'll probably die from over-fussing," Archer shook his head. "But she'll soon put Two Falls to rights again, once she's back." The smile slowly faded from his face. Archer turned his head again thoughtfully towards the window and was quiet for so long that Tarr thought he might have fallen asleep once more.

"Why am I here?" Archer asked, voice rasping through the stillness of the room.

Tarr stirred. "You could ask Si," he said lightly. "I'm sure he would give you a clear answer."

"No," Archer shook his head. His voice was hoarse, almost a whisper. "Why did I make it out of that tower, Tarr? And Ari died?"

Archer hadn't spoken before about Ari. Tarr, for his part, had been less shocked than the others at the news that Ari had given his own life to save Archer. Instead, more questions remained for him about the scene he'd witnessed between Ari and Si before Ari had split up with them in Faridor. He had become convinced that somehow Ari had known what was going to happen to him, and had gone anyway.

Tarr considered Archer's question, knowing that the next few moments would be a delicate matter. "It was a sacrifice he was willing to make, I suppose."

Archer shook his head infinitesimally, still staring out of the window, away from Tarr. "*Why?* He didn't even *like* me. I didn't like him. We never got on, he said so himself. It doesn't make any sense."

"At the end of the day, he must have thought you were worth saving," Tarr reasoned gently.

Archer gave a huffing snort, then turned his head to gaze up at the ceiling above them, long wooden beams striping away across plaster. Tarr watched his brother's golden eyes scan up and down them, back and forth, as he thought. "It wasn't just Ari, it was all the guards he killed trying to keep me alive. All of those people. I just can't believe he would consider me worthy enough to be weighed in that balance."

Tarr made a helpless gesture with his hand. *It was war, who knows why it happened* was beginning to sound like an exhausted phrase by this point, but he could think of nothing else to say. He thought again of the meaningful looks Ari had exchanged with Si right before he'd left them. Ari had known his fate, and he had gone off to his death without hesitation, without teetering. Tarr had seen the surety in his eyes.

"Ari was a man of conviction. He would never have done something that went against his moral code. Saving you must have been the right thing to do." Tarr told him firmly.

"He was a better person than me," Archer said abruptly. "He should have been the one who lived. Not me. All these people dying...I don't understand why I keep being spared. What possible reason there could be."

Tarr swallowed, feeling like he'd been punched in the gut. He had never seen his brother in such low spirits before, and they had been through many difficult situations together. He reached out and placed his hand on Archer's shoulder, hoping that his touch would offer some sort of comfort, even if his words couldn't.

Archer looked at Tarr directly now, his gaze piercing. "I never thanked him. He was alive for a few seconds and I could have...I didn't thank him. I didn't say..."

Archer trailed off. Tarr didn't bother pointing out that Archer hadn't been in any sort of physical or mental state to put together an articulate, heartfelt reconciliation in the few seconds he had with Ari on the balcony.

"How do I..." Archer groped for words. "How do I honor him? How do I repay him for the sacrifice he made for me?"

"Cade's erecting a statue," Tarr joked gently. "So he's got that avenue covered already."

"I heard," Archer closed his eyes faintly. "What was the concept again?"

Tarr couldn't help but grin. "An enormous, ten-foot tall Ari holding the Morthenstar flag in one hand and gazing off towards the sunrise, looking very dashing and heroic and masculine."

Archer grimaced and chuckled ruefully. "Good grief. He would have been horrified."

"I know," Tarr agreed, smiling.

"He hated me so much. Despised who I was, everything I had done," Archer murmured, his stare vacant. "He was probably right to."

"Don't say that," Tarr chided him. "To say you had a complicated childhood would be an understatement. You did the best you could."

"No," Archer countered. "I did the best I could to a *point*. And then I did what was easy. Ari was right. I never had to give anything up. Never really had to fundamentally change or try to really atone for any of it. Not for the boy back in my village, for any of the lives I took afterwards."

A wash of memories flooded across Archer's features. Tarr wished there was something he could do to pull him out of it.

"How do I earn the value of the life that he has placed on me?" Archer asked again. His tone was open, wondering, rhetorical.

"What would Ari have wanted of you?" Tarr pressed him. "I think you know that much."

Archer thought for a long time. Finally, he shifted beneath his sheet and settled his body against the cushions. The strained tension was gone from his neck and shoulders and Tarr could see that he'd hit upon an answer.

"Ari said once that I could never make up for what I'd done while I still hold a weapon in my hand. So maybe...that's what I need to do. Maybe I lay down my arms for good and find some other way." He fell silent, and then in a smaller voice, almost to himself, he murmured, "I hope it's not too late."

Tarr shook his head, overcome. "It's not. It's not too late. Ari didn't think so. He wouldn't have done what he did otherwise." Archer met his eyes. Tarr nodded mutely, squeezing Archer's shoulder.

After a few minutes, Archer looked back up at the ceiling. "Tarr?" he asked, his voice uncharacteristically small.

"Yes?" Tarr replied.

"What else can I do?" he wondered. "Since I was a boy...ever since I came to Two Falls, even before...it was the only thing anyone told me I could do. The only thing I was good at."

"Well, from your reputation, I hear it's not the *only* thing you're good at," Tarr said, stifling a smirk.

Archer rotated in his bed and fixed Tarr with an arched eyebrow. After a moment he laughed. "Success is not necessarily evidence of aptitude, Tarr." He considered, and a flicker of the old devilish smile played over his face. "Though in this case, yes, you're right. I *am* good at that." He turned back around to lie flat on his back once again. "But tempting though it might be, I'm not going to start a career in that line of work just yet."

"Fair enough," Tarr laughed. "But seriously, though, how do you *know* you're only good at fighting? If it's the only thing you've ever tried?"

"The problem with you, Tarr," Archer said, still facing away, "is that you're too damn logical to be any fun. Just once I wish you'd get fixed with some sort of world-ending, unsolvable conundrum so you could spend one single day feeling lost and bewildered like the rest of us."

Tarr nearly laughed out loud, so spot-on was Archer's description of the way he currently felt. Archer twisted around and saw the mirth on his face. "What is it?" he asked, starting to smile reflexively.

"Nothing," Tarr shook his head. He wished he could talk to Archer about his problems, but his brother was burdened with his own troubles.

"Archer," he said after a moment. "What would *you* have done? If your and Ari's places had been reversed?"

Archer considered. "I'd try to save him, of course."

"No, but..." Tarr fumbled for words, trying to form a coherent thought. "Say it was Ari or...Athela and I. And you had to choose who to save."

"I would have given him a hearty shove over that balcony," Archer replied pleasantly. "I may owe him my life but he was still a twit."

Tarr laughed, still feeling as though he hadn't expressed himself properly. "Fair enough. But let's say...you had to choose between Ari or someone you didn't know. An innocent person. Or people."

"Why are you asking me this?" Archer asked suddenly, his tone sharp.

Tarr did his best to look relaxed and unconcerned. "No reason," he lied.

Archer frowned thoughtfully. "You know me, Tarr. Appreciating the big picture...the possible ramifications...it's never been my strength. As Ari himself loved to point out, there are always consequences, no matter what you do. You just have to weigh the risks. Ask yourself whether they're worth it." He closed his eyes and settled back. "He was right about that, too. About all of it." He paused. "The righteous, insufferable sod."

Tarr could see that his brother was growing tired again, so he patted Archer's arm and tugged the sheet up higher against his shoulder. A few moments later he was asleep and Tarr was once again alone in his thoughts.

They set out for the palace of Joymaril two days later. To Tarr's great surprise, on the morning of their departure, it was Athela who took the longest time saying goodbye to their remaining Striker troops. The moment she stepped out into the public area of the headquarters she was swarmed on all sides by the recruits she'd helped teach, admirers who wanted to wish her well. Tarr stood back and watched, seeing her astonishment and alarm at being accosted slowly fade into genuine pleasure, basking openly in the goodwill that surrounded her. While this was happening, Tarr saw Cade approaching from down the hall, flanked by two guards. As Cade drew closer and saw what was going on, he slowed, and under the guise of straightening his gloves, Tarr could see him watching Athela and her gaggle of well-wishers.

There was one young boy in particular who caught Tarr's interest; he was right next to Athela's arm and had to have been in his early teens. His skin was darker even than Tarr's and he had a striking head of hair; he said almost nothing to Athela but watched her every move with a sort of reverence, his eyes sharply intelligent, seeing everything. Tarr made a mental note to himself that the boy, whoever he was, looked as though he would make a good spy recruit. He'd like to have a few eyes still in Two Falls while he was away.

Athela broke away from the crowd after some time, looking flushed and a bit overwhelmed by the adoration she'd received. Having led the charge into Faridor and fought bravely thereafter, news of her exploits had been passed around the headquarters and Tarr imagined that before long they would spread throughout the entire city. And from what Tarr was able to discern from his sidelong looks at Cade, watching the farewells with a guardedly blank expression on his face, the ferocity of the admiration the Striker soldiers felt for her had not been lost on him. Tarr met his eyes and they silently regarded each other, both understanding the same thing: *Athela, outcast for all her life, overlooked, acerbic, introverted, is now loved. And with that love she wields power. She could rule. The people would fight for her. The people would follow her. They already have.*

Cade smiled pleasantly at Tarr and finished fiddling with his glove, his face a mask. Tarr watched him narrowly as the young man motioned to his retainers and walked out the front door, just as Athela drew up to Tarr's side.

"Sorry to keep you waiting," she said breathlessly, swinging a lock of curly black hair over one shoulder. Her face was glowing brightly.

"Your adoring public kept you, I see," Tarr observed sagely, his arms folded.

Athela made a self-deprecating dismissive motion with her hand. "Just a few people wanting to say goodbye," she said.

Tarr looked pointedly at the throng—who still, at a distance, was eagerly watching her every move. "A few people" was a marked understatement.

All at once, Athela shifted uncomfortably. "Let's go," she said suddenly. "We should go."

"All right," Tarr agreed. "But first, call over that young man who was standing beside you. I want to have a word with him."

They left shortly thereafter, winding in a long, snaking procession of scarlet cloaks and flapping banners, the midnight blue ivy of Cade and the crimson star of the Strikers snapping crisply in the breeze. Cade had "requested" that the Strikers ride closely beside him as they made their way through the crowds of onlookers in town, but soon after they had passed the outskirts of Two Falls Tarr and his friends dropped the pretense and fell back to ride together. All of the Jelani and Striker guards automatically pulled away from them. Even at a distance, Tarr had a heightened awareness of the curious whispers that followed them. The more people tried to look like they weren't staring or gossiping under their breath, the more obtrusive they were.

Tarr glanced over his shoulder to steal a look at Rane, who was riding next to Cicada. Both were looking out over the swell of a nearby hill; Rane nudged her friend and pointed. Feeling Tarr's eyes on her, Rane glanced at him and gave a subtle wink. Pleased, Tarr swiveled back around in his saddle, only to see that their private exchange had not gone unnoticed by a few of the nearby Striker troops. The young soldiers quickly tried to pretend as though they hadn't been watching, but a moment later their heads tipped together and the distinct sound of poorly disguised giggles floated back to Tarr on the breeze.

"You'd think they'd find something else to talk about," Tarr muttered to Laith under his breath, and the prince laughed and shrugged. His damaged foot hung out of the stirrup, bandaged and braced in white wrapping.

"What do you think will happen after Cade is crowned?" Athela asked from Laith's other side. Her gray horse, Aria, was acting up as usual, and at that particular moment was trotting diagonally while doing his best to bite Laith's horse on the ear.

"I think," Laith said quietly, "that there may be some issue with succession. Technically, Athela, as Cira's elder sister you were first in line to the Joymarillian throne."

Athela's gray eyes widened and she looked horrified. "Me? But my parents set me aside."

"There may be factions, especially in the palace, who may oppose Cade's coronation on the basis that you are the rightful heir," Laith continued in the same low tone. "You'll likely need to publicly abdicate in favor of Cade's rule."

"He can have it," Athela snapped, sounding disgusted. "All of it. I am so sick of all this Kingmaking, Queenmaking, fighting, killing, all for who gets the honor of listening to tax disputes about some miserable piece of swamp. They can have it, and take it, and be glad of it. I want nothing to do with it."

Tarr couldn't help but agree. "What do you want to do, Laith?" he asked.

Laith blinked in surprise, and all at once Tarr realized, *he never really thought he would make it through the war alive.*

"Tess?" Tarr suggested gently.

Laith shook his head with finality. "She's gone. She asked me to leave her in peace, and I will."

Tarr had experienced enough of their appreciable chemistry to be impressed with Laith's willpower—and Tess's, for that matter. But he understood. Tess had been through a lot, had had her son's life threatened because of her association with Laith and the other Strikers. It would be hard to move past that.

"So," Marc remarked brightly. "Who's excited for a wedding?"

A chorus of unenthused groans met his words, largely from the other Jelani. Tarr, for his part, was rather interested in seeing what a royal Jelani wedding was like.

"Wedding or no, I wouldn't put it past Cade to take the opportunity to put some of his little schemes into motion. I'll wager he has some plans up his sleeve for you, Laith, and for the rest of us," Athela said darkly.

"Undoubtedly, he'll want us standing and waving in the background when he unveils the first of many Striker-related monuments and statues," Laith concurred.

"I've heard he's planning to erect a statue of Athela smiling," Archer added. "People are going to flock from miles away just to see it."

Athela rolled her eyes. "Posing for it will be quite the stretch."

In a miraculous turn of events that, in Tarr's estimation, ranked only slightly below the defeat of Cira and the successful siege of Faridor, Archer and Athela's uncomfortable months-long standoff had finally come to an end. In its place was tentative, sweet, almost playful flirting (though it hadn't progressed past flirting, since that would have been the logical and reasonable thing for them to do.) Tarr and the others had all adopted a "no sudden movements" policy of neither acknowledging nor questioning this newfound detente, lest the delicate temporary peace be shattered.

Laith chuckled and ruefully shook his head. "I hadn't wagered having to obey orders coming from my younger brother," he admitted.

The train of riders wound up through the hills surrounding Two Falls and finally came to the familiar deep forest that led to the lake below the palace of Joymaril. Soon, Tarr could see something white glinting through the branches and knew that the palace was just up ahead. As they pulled closer to the lake, Tarr glanced out of the corner of his eye at Laith. It had been years since the prince was home. He had not been back since he'd learned of the death of his wife. Tarr could only imagine what it would be like for him to walk through his old rooms, to sit on the bed he had shared with her, to look out of the window. If Laith was thinking the same things, his face didn't betray it.

Behind him, Rane and Cicada were deep in conversation, their fingers flying as they signed back and forth to one another around the reins in their hands. Tarr turned to Archer, who bore an expression of long-suffering discomfort as he slumped to one side in the saddle.

"It's just what I needed," he said drily. "A nice long horseback ride. Just what the surgeon asked me to do."

"Brisk and stimulating," Tarr agreed brightly.

"I'm fairly keen to see where Laith and Athela lived, though," Archer continued. "It'll be good to take stock of what I'll inherit after Athela and I are married."

"The *extremely* long game you're playing might finally pay off," Tarr agreed.

"I heard that," Athela called from in front of them, though her voice sounded more amused than anything.

The group suddenly pulled past the last line of trees and out onto the bank of the lake, where they took in their first real view of Joymaril. The white city, built into and onto the rock of the enormous cliff face opposite them, gleamed like a pearl in the late afternoon light, no less astounding than it had been the very first time Tarr had laid eyes on it all those years ago. He and the others pulled their horses to the side to let the caravan pass them onto the submerged underwater bridge.

Archer was staring up at the palace with a frank, unironic amazement. "I've never seen anything like that," he whistled. "Never in my life." Then, with a bit of his old bravado, he added, "Quite the jolly shack, isn't it?"

Tarr sat back in the saddle, his hands crossed loosely over his lap. He suddenly felt an almost nauseating wave of regret and sadness wash over him; so much that he nearly rocked sideways out of the saddle. Here it was, he thought. The exact ground he had stood on when he was an Ashan fresh from the forest, gawking in wonder at the very palace that now peeked out from the folds in the rock. He had seen no war then, no lives had been lost under his command. Laith's wife was still alive, Ari was alive, even Cira was alive. He had known nothing of fate, or magic, or that he was to have any role to play at all in the revolutions of the world. For the umpteenth time since the war had ended he felt a surge of fury at the mysterious Ashan he'd met in the woods, whose place he had unwittingly taken. *It should have been you*, he thought angrily. The vision of his innocent past self was so potent that he almost felt as though he could glance behind and see his own specter hovering like mist beside the lake. The thought of it made him want to weep.

They had won the battle. Some of them had managed to stay alive, but no one had got through in one piece. *And it may all have been for nothing*, Tarr remembered. *If Si lives, and if Cira takes hold of him.*

Tarr's dark thoughts were broken by a slight nudge from Rane's knee as she rode up beside him. As if sensing his inner turmoil, she gave him a gentle smile and he felt some of his anxiety lessen.

The first riders in their procession were just starting to draw up to the palace when a slender figure slipped past one of the doors of the palace entrance at the bottom of the cliff and waited, hovering almost anxiously at the water on the opposite bank of the lake. Tarr didn't recognize who it was, and assumed it was some eager onlooker from the city above.

"What are the odds that someone's managed to stage another coup while we've been away?" Marc asked, cutting through the silence that had descended on their group.

"I'll give you good odds," Archer agreed, nudging his horse forward. "Come on, Marc, I want to see what sort of accommodations you all have in a dump like this. I bet you lot have great guest towels."

But Marc had suddenly frozen, his eyes trained across the lake at the slim golden figure at the other side. His mouth slowly fell open and he seemed to murmur something indistinguishable under his breath. Confused, Tarr glanced to Laith, and to Athela, then to the others—all of whom seemed to share his bewilderment.

"Marc?" Laith asked softly.

Like a man possessed, Marc silently mouthed something again and urged his horse forward onto the bridge. As they watched, he went faster and faster, until Marc was riding flat-out through the water, the spray from the horse's hooves kicking up in explosive bursts. And to Tarr's amazement, the distant figure teetering apprehensively by the edge of the lake on the other side began to run across the bridge to Marc, past the last column of horses still making its way across the bridge. Tarr narrowed his eyes, but the sun was too sharp and the distance too far. He still couldn't make out who it was.

"I don't believe it," Athela breathed. "I don't believe it.'

The others swiveled their heads around to look at her.

"It's Oren," she said, and Tarr was surprised to see that her eyes were glistening. "Lord Oren, Marc's boyfriend. We thought he was dead."

And as they watched, the two figures met. Marc leaped from the saddle and half-fell into the water, and a moment later they were embracing so hard that they nearly fell off of the bridge and into the lake. As bleak as everything had seemed just mere moments before, Tarr felt himself light up with joy at the sight of their pure, unadulterated joy.

But then he happened to glance over to Laith. The prince's eyes were a mask of pain. Tarr could only imagine what he felt at that moment; could almost see, as Laith undoubtedly did, the hazy vision of Laith's own family waiting for him across the water.

Laith gave himself an unconscious shudder, and looked back at the rest of them, forcing a smile. "Come on," he said after a moment. "Let's catch up."

Two weeks later, with a great deal of fanfare, Cade married Rowan, making her the first-ever Ashan Queen of Joymaril. As a wedding gift, Rowan gave Cade a resplendent Ashan wood carving of a full-size tree, hewn with flowers and symbols representing their union. In return, and without question, Cade honored her rather unconventional gift request: a letter, a trunk of coin and jewels, and a perpetual land grant, all of which were delivered to an otherwise unassuming little vegetable farm on a clifftop just north of Faridor.

It was a long ceremony that lasted for three days. On the first they spent the night apart, and on the second they walked across the palace to meet one another for pre-wedding blessings and rituals at the traditional wedding sites. The program on the third day stretched from sunup until sundown. This all would have been fine in theory had Cade not calculatedly ordered that the Strikers be front and center beside him at most of the public-facing events. This led to a lot of sitting very still and trying not to itch or helplessly giggle at Archer feigning narcolepsy as the officiants droned on, the air heavy and sweet with incense, and to ignore the hundreds of curious goggling eyes trained in their direction. What interest Tarr had felt in bearing witness to a Jelani wedding was quickly snuffed out after the fourth hour of introductory chanting; ominously, Rowan hadn't even yet made her entrance.

The wedding took place, as was customary, in the city's square under a grand marble archway and was open (to an extent) to the Jelani public, who were crammed in so tightly to the public viewing area that not even a dog could slip through them. The wedding officiants, Tarr understood, were a rather unusual feature of this particular ceremony. Typically, it was the duty of the sitting King and Queen to perform the ceremony, but as Cade had recently staged a coup, there wasn't anyone who could fill the role. So he had cleverly invited an Ashan (Mickela, who had led the twenty Ashans into battle), Jelani (General Calchas) and human representative (Pieter, appointed leader of the new Two Falls council) to give the official ceremony, a show of unity for all involved.

"Since when did people's nuptials become a public spectacle?" Tarr muttered grumpily under his breath. For the past hour, they had watched a lit torch being marched deliberately around the center square by an unsmiling cleric.

"Oh Tarr," Athela smiled and shook her head pityingly. "Oh sweet, innocent Tarr. There's still so much for you to learn."

"Welcome to being royal, my friend," Laith agreed.

"I'm not royal," Tarr said quickly.

"Might as well be," Laith shrugged, squinting up at the clouds. "At least it's not raining."

"We had an uncle once, and at *his* wedding—" Athela began, but was cut short when the entire crowd rose to its feet.

"What's going on?" Tarr asked. Then, trying not to sound too eager, "What's happening? Is it over?"

Almost as soon as he said it, he realized that the wedding probably wouldn't have been over before the bride had made her entrance, but a moment later Rowan appeared. She was resplendent in a purple gown of soft embroidered velvet that threw off the midmorning sun and gleamed as she walked. A long, wispy gray fabric covered her head and as she drew near Cade, two of her attendant ladies drew back the veil, where it hung softly against the folds of the gown, draping gracefully down her back. Tarr had to admit to himself that she looked every bit a queen, and from the faces of the crowd opposite, it seemed they agreed. As the bridal party turned, Tarr was surprised to notice Nadia, Cade's associate, the one who had effectively sprung him from the dungeons at

Joymaril. Apparently, she had been appointed as Rowan's lady-in-waiting. Tarr was surprised to see that she was pale and wasn't smiling at all.

"Why on earth is Nadia attending Rowan?" Tarr asked Athela in a low voice.

Athela shrugged a shoulder. "She attended Ilaina. Makes sense."

It didn't make much sense to Tarr. Nadia had engineered Cade's escape from prison; it seemed she was capable of much more than managing Rowan's wardrobe. As he watched, Nadia turned away so that Tarr could no longer see her. He wondered briefly what could have made her so upset, then he remembered the glances he'd seen her stealing at Cade and thought he might have some idea.

"I cannot wait to get out of here," Archer muttered in Ashan beside him.

"What, the wedding?" Tarr asked.

"No. Here," Archer jerked his head in an all-encompassing gesture to the city that surrounded them.

Tarr glanced at him questioningly out of the corner of one eye.

"Let us just say," Archer said darkly, "that when one's ex-girlfriend is crowned reigning queen of one's country one can perhaps assume that the universe is trying to convey a subtle hint. For example, that now may be the time to move on down the road in search of less hostile pastures."

"One could, I suppose," Tarr murmured, trying not to laugh.

The crowd resumed their seats and the droning began again in full force. The couple knelt before the three officiants and a red cloth was wrapped around their hands.

"Now we just have to make it till sundown," Athela sighed. "Get comfortable."

"You're joking," Tarr and Archer muttered in unison. Tarr looked down the row to Rane, who was sitting on the other side of Archer. He raised his eyebrows in an unspoken question, searching for some sign that Athela was speaking in jest. But Rane ruefully shook her head.

"Ashan weddings are much more civilized," Tarr grumbled underneath his breath.

"You basically get a tree branch waved at you, promise not to be an idiot to one other, and then that's it," Archer affirmed. "And then you have a big party."

"It's all right, after an hour or so we'll be allowed to get up and mill around. Those poor matrimonial bastards have to stay where they are," Marc informed them grimly.

Tarr focused his wandering attention on Cade, whose back was ramrod-straight beneath his velvet coat, whose white-blond hair fluttered in the spring breeze. Morthenstar's Whitsun sword was buckled conspicuously at his waist, as it had been for every ceremonial public occasion since the Battle of Faridor. Tarr glared at it for a moment. *I wonder if Cade ordering us here to the wedding has some sort of ulterior motive,* he thought. *Perhaps he's going to try to assassinate Athela and get her out of the way. Maybe he's going to make us swear some sort of public loyalty oath.*

Or, he countered himself, *am I just inventing plots because I'm bored?*

And the truth was, he *was* bored. There were no codes, no more schemes. He woke up every morning and had his breakfast brought to him. He went out and stared at the twinkling sunshine, listening to the beautiful hushing sounds of the waterfall rushing beneath the palace to the lake below. And it was all he could do to stop himself from jumping over the side out of sheer frustration. Nothing to do. No more empires to topple.

Night after night, Tarr lay beside Rane (who had the infuriating habit of being able to fall asleep more quickly and deeply than anyone he had ever met) and bored holes in the canopy of his strange, lavishly appointed four-poster bed, watched its dark brocade and embroidered lilies spilling down to the floor. Every now and again, he would be so overwhelmed by a rush of memories and latent anxieties that he would bolt upright out of bed and spend the night pacing back and forth across the room until the sun came up, waiting in vain for his head to stop churning like a teeming sea. Then at daybreak he would climb back into bed so that he could pretend to be asleep when Rane awoke.

He shifted his weight onto the other leg, and tried to bring his attention back to the present, where Cade and Rowan were kneeling together before the three officiants. He forced a smile. It was a celebration, after all.

Cade and Rowan's coronation took place the next week, and was blissfully a much shorter affair than their wedding, though there was still a great deal of proclaiming to the heavens and the earth, to the lands near and far, that Cade and Rowan were the new King and Queen. The Strikers were again "politely asked" to sit in a prominent position during the ceremony. Afterwards, during the seemingly endless night of feasting and celebration, they were positioned strategically at the main banquet table. A dazzling array of costly dishes were trooped out from the kitchens and laid before them; there were songs and dancing, and even a pageant that (from what Tarr could discern) was supposed to be some sort of recounting of the Battle of Faridor, only in this case Cade somehow managed to storm the castle, overcome the guns, and kill Cira single-handedly, with the Strikers acting as sort of a supportive chorus behind him. All the while, the courtiers and townspeople in the public viewing section gawked at the Strikers as each picked their way reluctantly through a plate of food.

"Nothing like eating mashed peas in front of an enraptured audience," Archer had muttered beneath his breath. He, like Tarr, wasn't as used as the others to all the trappings of royal pomp and circumstance.

They were granted a small reprieve after the coronation events were concluded; Cade and Rowan and much of the royal entourage departed the next day for their coronation procession through Two Falls and down to the border of the Ashan forest, where they were to meet with envoys from the seven tribes. While the Strikers had initially been commanded to join the procession, Laith, in an incredible feat of tactful diplomacy, had somehow managed to beg them out of it. The ensuing week, therefore, afforded them more peace and quiet than they'd enjoyed since the battle and they settled comfortably into life at the palace. Laith and Athela had had their old residences restored to them; the previous occupants—Kagaian sympathizers who were given the rooms as a reward for their loyalty—had been removed shortly after Cade's takeover.

As Laith's apartments were by far the largest and best appointed, they often found themselves gathering together there. Si, still successfully disguised as a soldier, was allowed to join them under the ruse of being in training as Laith's dedicated house guard. They sat together on Laith's balcony in the early spring sunshine, fur rugs spread out beneath them, gazing out over the lake. It felt strangely abstract to see his friends all gathered there. For the duration of the war, Tarr hadn't given himself much space to imagine what would happen if they won, and here it was.

Oren, Marc's boyfriend, often joined them. He had clearly been profoundly affected by his captivity, though in surviving he was one of the lucky ones. Many of those with affiliations to the Strikers—including, to Tarr's great sorrow, the little librarian who had managed to save them from the Joymarillian dungeons—had been executed shortly after Cira had seized power.

Though Oren barely spoke, Tarr was nevertheless glad to have him there. He was as tall, fair, and willowy as Marc was short, broad, and sturdy. He had a sweet, winsome face and a faraway, wistful expression, as though he habitually spent long hours gazing out a window, plucking the petals off of daisies, and sighing deeply. Marc's obvious affection for him was enough of a character endorsement as far as Tarr was concerned. Oren tended to jump at any loud noises and was almost in constant physical contact with Marc, as if his presence was a kind of reassurance and stability. If Oren was seated, then Marc was at his feet, leaning against his leg. If Marc sat beside him, they held hands or moved their feet together so that they touched. Tarr could think of no one better to provide Oren the patient support that he clearly needed. Marc seemed somehow to have an unending font of care and comfort within him that he could give unremittingly to others. Tarr was amused to see the way that Marc's eyes kept clicking from Si, to Oren, to Laith—the three people he most felt he had to care for.

Cicada, too, was a welcome addition to their group: sharp-featured and dark, immensely observant, and (as Tarr grew to realize) possessed of a very sly sense of humor. Every day for an hour or so, Cicada would teach the others signs, starting with the very basics: the alphabet, *hello, thank you*. One particularly memorable afternoon, she had even led them through a lesson on the signed equivalent of certain swear words and phrases, which had them all howling with laughter by the end of it. Rane and Cicada had made the language look effortless and easy, but Tarr realized almost immediately that it would take him a long time and a lot of studying before he was even remotely proficient.

They reminisced about the war, about the final battle. By this point each had filled in the others about everything that had taken place. Laith told them about Rane's defeat of Lord Seth (here, Tarr had to restrain himself from throwing his arms around her out of sheer pride), and how Athela led her troops through the first charge across the bridge. Tarr gave a basic sketch of what had happened with Si up in the tower, but was purposefully vague about some of the more granular details.

The one thing they didn't discuss during those long hours together was what would come next. The question hung in the air over them, but it was never voiced.

Sometimes, Tarr felt his mind wandering as he studied the faces of his friends. There were small but perceptible changes, rather like frost melting. Laith was still far from the handsome, carefree prince that Tarr had met when he first came to Joymaril, but there were flashes of Laith's old self that flickered out now and again with greater frequency than they had before. His face was still grave but somehow less sad; he was quicker to laugh and far less solitary. He sought out their company and when he sat with his friends he seemed somehow more present, as if his mind were no longer miles away from his body. Every night Laith went to Ilaina's tomb in the royal mausoleum, where he lit candles and held vigil; it seemed to give him a sense of peace, if not closure. Tarr wasn't sure he'd ever truly find that.

Athela, as far as Tarr knew, never set foot once in the mausoleum. Each afternoon, for the first few weeks they were back in the palace, she could be found riding Ilaina's buckskin horse alone far up into the woods over the eastern hills, returning long after sundown. She never told the others where she'd gone, and they never asked. Healing, Tarr realized, would come, slowly and in different forms for each of them.

A warm southern wind gently stirred and shook the blossoming trees; teardrop-shaped buds pressed up through the earth and spread their petals to the open sky.

Tarr's strange feeling of restlessness prevailed. It grew, day by day, as they whiled away their time at the palace. The others laughed and talked and seemed perfectly content with their current idle state of affairs, while in his own mind it was as if he was on a ship sailing away from them, watching them grow smaller in the distance. His disconcerting sense of isolation increased as he perceived that the others could not feel it, too.

Even Archer seemed to have shifted farther away from him. Periodically, Tarr would flash back to the image of Jet sitting at Archer's bedside after the battle, their identical heads tilted close together, voices low. For so long, neither Tarr nor Archer had had any roots, any real anchor. They had clung to each other like two drowning people adrift in a roiling current. But now Archer did have someone out in the world. An undeniable connection from the past who had dismissed the fact of his exile and traveled through great dangers to find him. It didn't matter that Jet had ultimately returned to the Birch tribe; the foundation had been irrevocably altered. Archer didn't just belong to Tarr anymore, and the thought filled Tarr with enormous sorrow.

There was a concert one evening in the palace, and they went down to see it. Cicada had successfully persuaded Marc to let her stay behind and walk through the gardens with Si; all were glad that Marc had finally agreed to a night out. Tarr had hoped that the program would divert his own depressing thoughts, but the music, which he usually found entrancing, did little to budge his crushing sense of ennui. After the concert, he trailed along behind the group as they wandered back to Athela's rooms. He stared gloomily out at the painterly evening sky and the shower of lights beginning to peek out from the houses down in the clifftop city. Clouds of pink blossoms swirled through the air, caught in a draft from the nearby cascading waterfall.

Finally, he could take it no more. Under the pretense of glancing over at the lake below, he let his friends go on ahead of him. Once they had rounded a bend in the path, he leaned on the balcony rail, stretched out his arms, and stared down at his feet.

"What on earth is wrong with me?" he muttered aloud.

"You miss it," said a voice behind him.

Tarr jumped and whipped around. Laith was standing a few feet away from him, swathed in his black cloak. Tarr wasn't sure how long he'd been there.

"I—what? Miss what?" he stammered, trying to still his racing heart. "Sorry. You startled me."

"The war," Laith said.

Tarr turned back towards the lake and forced a derogatory snort. "Don't be ridiculous. I don't miss the war." The truth of Laith's words, however, struck him like a stone.

The prince came up quietly beside him and looked out over the water. A flock of small birds was darting to and fro through the mist of the waterfall, catching insects as twilight fell. Laith leaned on his elbows, the cascade of his cloak framing his head in the last golden vestiges of sunset.

"It's all right, you know," he said. "It's only natural. I've seen it before. Many times."

Tarr briefly considered continuing his protestations. It sounded so *awful*, missing something as terrible as a war. He should be grateful it was over. He should be happy. And yet he wasn't. He heaved a small sigh and gave up the pretense. "And you?" he asked tentatively. "Do you miss it?"

Laith shook his head decisively. "No."

Tarr's sense of loneliness increased exponentially. He rubbed his hand distractedly over the tattoo on the nape of his neck. "I didn't want this," he muttered, almost to himself. "I tried to leave once. Years ago. I wanted to leave all of you, get away from the war, get back to the forest, forget all about this. Archer convinced me to stay. Back then, I thought I would still be able to go back home. Once this was over, I could go back home. And now..." he wrestled internally, a hollow chuckle escaping him, "I don't even have the forest anymore. I have nowhere to go."

Laith considered. "Maybe," he suggested slowly, "you should stop trying to run away."

Tarr stared out before him. A breeze gently touched his face, laden with mist from the falls, bearing on it the scent of summer roses and honeysuckle.

Beside him, Laith shifted gently. "It's a common misconception, Tarr, that the only ones who fight a war—and are good at it—are the ones who can wield a sword," he said thoughtfully.

"A sword certainly helps," Tarr murmured drily.

Laith shook his head, and Tarr could tell that the prince was in no mood for levity. "That's not what I mean, and you know it."

Tarr shrugged his thin shoulders. "It was an accident that I met you at all," he said. "I did the best I could."

"What I'm saying is, Tarr," Laith countered, "accident or no, you may be the only true fighter among us. *I* don't care if I ever pick up a sword again. But you...you love it. And I don't know that you'll be able to go back to a life without it."

"So what?" Tarr demanded harshly.

"I just thought someone should point it out to you," Laith replied evenly, unruffled by the edge in Tarr's voice. "Lest you continue to tell yourself you just wandered into this war by mistake and happened to get us all through through sheer luck. It wasn't luck."

Tarr's hands gripped the side of the balcony railing, the polished stone cool and slippery beneath his fingers. Reflexively, he looked away from his missing twelfth finger.

"I killed Burlage," he said abruptly. The words tumbled out of his mouth almost before he realized he was saying them. "I ordered him to be killed."

"I know," Laith said. He stared out into the gloom creeping over the lake. "I don't think it's the last time you'll have to decide whether or not to take a life, Tarr."

"I don't feel sorry about it," Tarr said in a low voice. "I didn't then. I felt ashamed, maybe. But still, to this day, I'm not sorry." He almost felt as though he were provoking Laith now, trying to share the darkest, ugliest, innermost truths of himself to see if he could get the prince to recoil. But Laith turned and looked him in the eye. His expression was understanding.

"I know that feeling too," he placed a hand on Tarr's shoulder. "Something to fight against." He gave Tarr a friendly shake, then inclined his head in the direction of the others. "Come on, let's catch up."

Their friends had already ensconced themselves in Athela's apartments. Marc poured a few glasses of wine and passed them around. Rane caught Tarr's eye as he and Laith quietly entered, raising her eyebrows in an unspoken question. Tarr gently smiled at her and shook his head, perching on the corner of Athela's grand four-poster bed. In an almost refreshingly stark contrast to the meticulous curation of the rest of the palace, Athela's sense of home decor ran towards the haphazard and functional rather than the opulent and aesthetically pleasing. Her bed, though, was undeniably a thing of beauty: intricately carved images of running horses ran along each side and twisting ivy vines snaked their way up the posts towards the ceiling.

"Here, just throw that on the floor," Athela reached over Tarr to a random bridle that lay sprawled on the bed, tossing it to the ground beside him. Hosting duties complete, she spun on her heel and rounded on her cousin. "I've had a letter from Cade," she announced, pointing at an open paper resting on a table beside the door. Laith measuredly picked it up and scanned it.

"Cade's *requested* that we remain here at the palace until he returns from his coronation tour tomorrow," Athela's voice dripped with disdain as she folded her arms over her chest.

"Why do I feel like we're about to be in trouble?" Marc wondered aloud, pouring wine into Archer's glass.

"We haven't done anything lately," Archer protested.

"Well, it's not like we had any urgent plans to leave...but *still*," Athela threw up her hands. "Pity you can't choose your relatives, eh, Laith?"

Laith grunted in assent, dark eyes still scanning the letter.

"You can choose your relatives if you're Ashan," Archer suggested, settling back against a leather cushion on the floor. "That's sort of the whole point."

All at once, Tarr had the overwhelming urge to stand up and leave. *Don't be dramatic*, he chided himself. He picked anxiously at one of the wooden ivy leaves on Athela's bedpost.

"I've always wanted to ask how that works. They just sort of point at you and say, 'hey, we want you'?" Marc asked interestedly.

"A *bit* more involved," Archer smiled. "There's a whole ceremony. Each family has a stone...was it a stone in your tribe, too, Tarr?"

"Yes," Tarr muttered through gritted teeth. "A stone."

"Every family has a stone, and then they step up and lay it at the feet of the person they've chosen to join them."

"What if two people pick the same person?" Marc asked curiously.

"I think the Elders keep track of who everyone's planning to choose and then they adjudicate beforehand if any conflicts arise," Archer mused.

"So they lay a stone at your feet and that's it?" Marc prompted. "That's your family?"

Hoping to appear nonchalant, Tarr stretched, rising to his feet and turning his back to the others. He pretended to inspect a shelf of little trinkets Athela kept by her bed. He wished the others would stop talking. It was bringing it all back. The forest, the Elders. That terrible night, the faces of the other villagers gaping at him in the torchlight, the dizzying disorientation of his whole world changing in the span of a few minutes. The dark road stretching out through the woods. Juniper, now dead, saying her final farewell. The horrible, nauseous, sinking feeling in the pit of his stomach. The realization that he was now alone, that he did not belong to anyone. That he might *never* belong to anyone.

He moved one finger distractedly over a small, jagged, bright blue rock on Athela's keepsake shelf, then absently toyed with a sculpted ivory horse.

"Is that what you and Tarr did?" Marc asked curiously. "The stones and everything?"

"Not really. Our ceremony was a bit more unconventional, circumstances being what they were. Usually, there's a whole to-do about joining a family, introducing everyone, laying out the beginnings of a family tattoo. But in our case it's just me and him, eh, Tarr?" Archer said.

"Yes," Tarr said quietly, his back still turned. "Just us."

And then the realization hit him so hard he nearly reeled. He had felt secure for so long, being able to count Archer as his brother. But Archer was the only family Tarr had in the world. And Si had told him that Archer would not live very long.

When Archer is gone I will have no family left.

A visceral fear abruptly gripped him by the throat, so intense he thought he might buckle over.

Rane, he thought quickly, with the desperate feeling of someone straining for a handhold before sinking underwater. *I have Rane.*

Ah, but that's different, a nasty voice inside his head sneered. *Rane has made no promises. No vows have been spoken. That could end tomorrow, for all you know.*

He had to get out of the room, had to be by himself to think, to try to get a grip on a reality that now seemed to be spinning out of control. Summoning every ounce of strength he had, he forced his lips into a smile, blinked his eyes wide a few times and turned around. Mercifully, it didn't seem as though his friends had noticed his lapse. Archer had changed the subject and was making some sort of joke about Cade and Rowan's wedding banquet; even Rane was looking at him and laughing. Only Athela was watching Tarr, her gray eyes searching, arms folded.

Avoiding her gaze, Tarr gave what he hoped was a convincing yawn. "I might take a stroll before bed," he announced abruptly. "See you all in the morning."

The others sent him off with a cheery chorus of "good night"—all except for Athela. He could feel her eyes on him as he closed the door behind him. In the blissful solitude of the empty hallway, he let out a deep, crushing breath. Then he sightlessly wandered off through the hallways of the darkened palace, unsure of where exactly he was going.

When Tarr got back to his room late that night, he was surprised to find Rane still awake. A wave of relief suffused him as he shut the door behind him. She was sitting on their bed with her knees tucked under her chin, auburn hair cascading over her face. A book was splayed out on the mattress before her, a lantern flickering on the table nearby. She looked up as he entered, watched him as he took off his shoes and threw his jacket on the floor. He crawled into the bed behind her and curled his body against hers, peering over her shoulder to the book she was reading. Silently, she reached out and squeezed his knobby ankle.

Tarr sighed contentedly, grateful for her implicit understanding. Anyone else would have asked him where he'd been. He tucked his face against her neck, her soft waves brushing his cheek, her warm, sweet smell filling his senses. He wished he could tell her everything that was troubling him, longed for her to reassure him in the way he needed, to say the things he needed to hear. He knew that if he asked her to, she would try and help him as best she could.

Tarr had waited so long for the end of the war to come, waited desperately for the time when he and Rane could finally be together as a normal, functional couple. But the reality was that though they had been romantically linked together for over three years, their relationship had always been enacted in fits and starts. There were periods of passionate, intense reunion followed by long expanses of time spent apart. And now that they had nothing *but* time, Tarr found that they were having to start again almost at the beginning, negotiating what it would be like to be together in this new, strange world they'd helped bring about. Tarr hadn't told her yet that he'd ordered Burlage killed, hadn't fessed up yet to the countless mistakes he'd made that had almost cost them the war, not to mention her life and those of her friends. He didn't want her to think less of him. But his reticence had created an invisible barrier between them, a distance that Tarr felt acutely.

"What are you reading?" Tarr asked finally.

She lifted up the cover of the book and showed him. It was an old Joymarillian history book, faded and tattered with gold embossed lettering on the front. "Trying to see if there's ever been a Jelani king before. So far, no luck. Cade should be pleased with himself."

"I think it's generally safe to assume that he is," Tarr murmured. "Are you getting dust on the bed?"

"Quite possibly." Rane gently shut the book and pushed it away. She turned around to face him. She traced the corners of his tilted, melancholy eyes, the small mole above his lip.

"Something's bothering you," she said. It was a statement of fact rather than a question.

Tarr grappled with how to respond. An echoing rush of the wild, disorienting fear he'd felt earlier twisted through him. Here was his opening, his chance to confess everything to her. But what was he really afraid of? Being alone? That he no longer knew who he was or where he belonged now that the war was over? Even if he could figure out the proper way to articulate his feelings, it all sounded stupid. Besides, he didn't want to say anything to Rane that would make her feel pressured into making any promises of eternal devotion and companionship just to comfort him. There was still so much they had to learn, had to build together, had to figure out. It was too soon, and too much.

"Just out of sorts," he said finally in what he hoped was a light, dismissive tone. "Must be the moon."

Rane crinkled her nose and glanced dubiously towards the window, but in her typical fashion, she didn't try to pry any further. "I'm going to take Cicada down to show her the stables tomorrow," she said. "Do you want to come along?"

"No, I'll stay here, maybe visit the library," Tarr replied. "What does Cicada make of all this?" He gestured to the splendor surrounding them.

Rane smiled faintly. "She thinks it's all a bit ridiculous. Still, the beds here are nicer than they were at Faridor."

Tarr looked at her curiously. Just as he hadn't told her much about the end of the war in Two Falls, she hadn't divulged too much information about her imprisonment at Faridor, or her escape from the dungeon. But whereas Tarr's hesitation stemmed from guilt and seething inner turmoil, Rane seemed to have simply taken it all in her stride and put it behind her. Tarr envied her pragmatism.

"Aren't you and Cicada both a little bored here?" Tarr asked.

Rane glanced at him. "Not terribly. It's nice to have a bit of a break after the last few months. Not having to worry about whether every knock on the door was a guard coming to arrest us."

Tarr immediately felt abashed. Rane had, of course, been deep undercover and had faced far worse dangers than he had from the safety of his office in the Two Falls. It was only natural that she welcomed a respite like this. It was the normal way to feel.

"Something will come up again," Rane suggested comfortingly, as though she could sense some of Tarr's inner conflict. "It always does."

Tarr gazed at her, her calm lake-blue eyes, the little dip at the base of her neck, the curving scar across her throat. She was so calm, so self-possessed, so capable.

She doesn't need me, Tarr realized suddenly. *She may love me, but she will never need me. She will always be all right on her own.*

He had always loved and admired Rane for exactly who and what she was, but at that moment he was filled with a strange, heavy sadness. He didn't want to think about anything anymore, didn't want to keep wallowing.

He took Rane's face in his hands and kissed her deeply. He pulled back for a moment and brushed his thumb lightly over her lower lip. He kissed her again, a bit harder, more hungrily. She responded to his unspoken invitation, pushing him gently back on the bed. The flame beside them bent and wavered and Tarr allowed himself to slip away.

As they often did, things felt less dire in the light of morning. Tarr left Rane sleeping in their room and decided to go out for a walk by himself, strolling as he often did towards the Joymarillian library.

The morning was fair and rosy, filled with the bucolic twittering of little birds, the rush of the distant waterfall and the sun winking off the shoulders of the stationed royal guards. Tarr gazed around with fresh appreciation as he wandered the long way round through one of the rose gardens, positively spilling over with heavy, spicily fragrant blooms whose array of colors mirrored the early morning sky. Tarr took a deep inhale of cool fresh air and decided that maybe his current situation wasn't so bad after all.

The library was a welcome diversion from Tarr's troubles. Its grandeur had only dimmed somewhat in his eyes as he'd become used to the opulence of Joymaril; he stepped across the footbridge over the library's reflecting pool with confidence now, with far less trepidation than he'd felt on his first visit. Inside, the building was cool, quiet and inviting, the circular shelves of books spiraling upwards towards the domed ceiling, carved in the shape of a blossoming peony. Tarr took a few reverent moments to appreciate its excess, then waved a hand at the attending librarian, who sleepily rubbed one of her eyes and gave him a short twinkle of her fingers in greeting before turning her attention back to a stack of books atop her desk.

Wandering aimlessly through the rows of books (and trying not to think of the catastrophic loss that had resulted from the destruction of the Two Falls library), Tarr paused every now and again to tip a book back from the shelf and lightly sheaf through the pages before returning it to its place. Some of the volumes were works of art in themselves: meticulous calligraphy in languages Tarr couldn't hope to understand, towering letters gilt with gold leaf, minutely illustrated tales with brushwork so fine the strokes must have been made with a single horsehair dipped in ink.

Perhaps I could spend my life here, he thought idly. *Or at least as long as the Joymarillians will let a strange Ashan stay among their books. Besides, who knows what other secrets might still be lurking here? Other treasures to find, perhaps. Like the medallion.*

He caught himself and stopped still. *There you go again,* he countered grimly. *Dreaming up plots and puzzles. That time of your life is over. You found the medallion, and look what trouble it caused.*

He turned away from the shelf he'd been perusing and found himself staring at a narrow wall at the end of the row of books. A small framed portrait was held there, a glancing diagonal ray of morning light spilling across the image.

Immediately, Tarr recognized the subject of the portrait and smiled, almost as though he were looking upon the face of an old friend he hadn't seen in a long time. He stepped forward to look more closely at the image.

It was Daemun, Alder Morthenstar's beloved friend and right-hand man. He looked older than when Tarr had seen him in Alder's vision; though he still bore a striking resemblance to Laith, his hair was streaked with gray, his jaw was heavier, and there were faint lines across his forehead and winking at the corners of his solemn eyes. He was seated at a desk, an old-fashioned quill pen in his hand resting atop a curling piece of parchment. Unable to help himself, Tarr eagerly squinted his eyes to see if he could make out any of the writing on the parchment, but there was none. Disappointed, Tarr began to draw back, then stopped.

On Daemun's left hand, the one holding the quill, was an ornate signet ring. The painting wasn't very large, but the image was clear: the symbol on the ring was in the shape of a white wolf's head.

Tarr stared at it, dumbfounded. *Wolver?* he thought, his thoughts suddenly scattering in multiple directions. *Why is Daemun's signet a white wolf?*

Tarr stood there for a few more minutes, mind racing, but could make neither head nor tail of it. Finally, he sought out the librarian, who he eventually found one floor above him half-buried in a pile of enormous tomes that were so tall they came up almost to her knees. She seemed grateful for the interruption, and followed him without complaint over to the little portrait. When Tarr presented her with the painting, she brushed herself off and peered at it more closely.

"Ah, yes," she said easily. "This is Daemun, second-in-command to Alder Morthenstar."

Tarr resisted the urge to reply, *yes, we're well acquainted.* "Could you tell me about his ring?" he asked.

The librarian took a deep, satisfied breath. "After Alder Morthenstar's death, Daemun adopted the symbol of a white wolf. It is not a traditional signet of the houses of Joymaril and was retired upon his passing. This painting was made contemporaneously; Daemun sat for it. Future paintings depicted him with the insignia either of the house of Esson or of Cade." She turned and regarded Tarr expectantly.

"And so the wolf signifies..." Tarr prompted slowly.

"As you are likely aware, Morthenstar's prophecy mentioned an Ashan and a white wolf," she smiled faintly.

"I am aware," Tarr muttered.

"It is thought that Daemun's chosen insignia was a gesture of respect for Morthenstar and a reminder of the prophecy." She coughed lightly. "As I said, as the prophecy fell out of fashion, so did the tradition of depicting Daemun in this way." She paused. "Is there anything else I can help with?" Her voice sounded hopeful, and Tarr could tell that she was thinking of the stack of monumental books waiting to be reshelved upstairs.

"That's all," he said regretfully. She squared her shoulders resolutely and left him.

Tarr stood pondering the painting. What did it mean? Was there some clue there, some way to figure out who Wolver was and what part he had played in this whole saga? Did he have some connection to Daemun? Or was it all, as the librarian had seemed to indicate, just a coincidence—an emblem adopted as a gesture of remembrance by an old friend?

It doesn't matter either way, Tarr thought suddenly. *It's over. The story's done. Wolver left, the reason doesn't matter. None of that is your concern anymore.*

He ambled through the library a little while longer, but the portrait kept niggling at the back of his mind in a decidedly unsatisfying way. The library's serenity was broken, and a short while later Tarr headed back outside.

By this point it was high midmorning and the denizens of the palace were now out and about, promenading in their costly array, peering superciliously down at the tumbling falls of roses and declaring them not as spectacular as last year's. Tarr avoided the people as much as he could, and soon found himself walking down a long, shaded pathway lined with trees on either side. The boughs curved overhead, forming an arched corridor that rustled and glinted in the slow, even wind.

At the far end of the shaded path was a little cluster of people, and among them Tarr was surprised and pleased to recognize Marc's head of straw-yellow hair. He was speaking to two Joymarillian nobles Tarr couldn't place, and just off to the side was a short figure clad in the garb of a Joymarillian guard. Immediately identifying the guard as Si, Tarr quickened his step slightly, figuring that a small dose of Si's off-the-wall omniscience would be a welcome diversion from the rest of his day.

By the time he came closer, Si had wandered away from Marc and was inspecting one of the trees lining the path. His back was turned and he made no acknowledgement as Tarr approached. Marc was deep in conversation with the nobles, but spotted Tarr from a distance, acknowledging him with a quick smile. He nodded to something one of the others was saying and then made a quick head gesture in Si's direction. The meaning was clear: *Can you keep an eye on Si for a second?* Tarr nodded, and Marc and the other nobles drew away.

Tarr turned around to the boy, who had yet made no indication that he was aware of Tarr's presence. Tarr was about to open his mouth to greet Si when suddenly the boy raised his hand and placed it against the trunk of the nearest tree.

Before Tarr's eyes, something extremely strange began to happen. The tree, which was a lovely light brown color, began to turn a shallow shade of gray; in unison the color faded from its leaves and the healthy shine drained away from its boughs. In the space of a few seconds the wood seemed to grow frail and brittle, as if a shallow wind would shatter it into a thousand pieces. The strong, smooth bark began to wrinkle and crack as if all the moisture had drained out of it, leaving the trunk a hollow, crumbling shell. The leaves curled and rattled hoarsely in a sudden gust of breeze; clumps of them dropped to the earth in a ghostly shower. The tree, which had been thriving only moments before, was dead in the blink of an eye.

It all happened seemingly in slow motion, and yet it was over so quickly that Tarr barely had time to act. The instant he recovered himself, he leaped forward and seized Si roughly by the shoulder, whirling the boy around to face him. Though no one was nearby, he forced himself to keep his voice down.

"Si," he hissed. "What did you just do?"

Si seemed unsurprised to see him. Tarr searched the once-familiar face for any sign of remorse, of evasion, of guilt. There was none. Si met his gaze squarely. "The tree was going to die," he replied. "It was sick."

Tarr's brow creased in consternation. "So, what...you just...put it out of its misery?"

Si shrugged. "It was going to die," he repeated, as if that alone was enough of an explanation.

"That doesn't mean you should kill it!" Tarr interjected angrily.

"The ending is the same," Si returned. He was infuriatingly calm and completely unconcerned, his tone implying that Tarr was too simple and backwards to understand the true way of things. Tarr wanted to shake him. He grappled with himself and forced a deep, steadying breath of air into his lungs.

"Si—" Tarr began in a more reasonable tone.

"I have to find Marc," Si said abruptly. "I'll see you tonight, Tarr."

Without another word, the boy brushed past him and continued off the path and down to where Marc was conversing with his group.

Tarr stared after him, feeling as though the earth had shifted a few inches beneath his shaky legs. If Si could kill a tree so thoughtlessly—and with seeming justification—could a human being or an Ashan be far behind? Was this the first sign of encroaching evil?

Could Si be allowed to live?

The thought caught him so much by surprise that Tarr froze in place. He'd dismissed the notion when Si had told him before that his death was the only sure way to ensure an end to the threat of Morthenstar and Kagai's combined powers. It had seemed so ridiculous, so extreme. But as always seemed to happen when Tarr saw a concrete demonstration of Si's abilities, the reality of their current situation had come roaring unpleasantly from the realm of vague, intangible possibility into stark, deadly reality. Si could end everything—life as they knew it—in the blink of an eye, as easily as tossing a stone into the center of a pool of water. Tarr had just seen it.

Heart rattling frantically in his chest, Tarr tried to decide on the most reasonable course of action. *Find the others*, he thought to himself. *Tell the others.*

He left the path of trees and veered to his left back towards the main palace compound, figuring that Laith and Athela would be somewhere within. Time seemed to pass in a blur as his mind raced. Burbling fountains and curving arbors of sweet-smelling flowers whizzed past his periphery in a haze. The light seemed somehow too bright now, the sounds of the birds too harsh and discordant.

The other Strikers were not in their rooms, nor were they in the main dining hall or the breakfast room. Tarr fruitlessly traced their usual routes back and forth through the palace, cursing beneath his breath at every dead end, his feeling of panic undimmed by the passing minutes. *Where the hell were they?*

At last, he halted by a guard near the royal receiving rooms and inquired after his friends, trying to look as calm and normal as possible.

"King Cade has returned with his wedding party," the guard replied, voice slightly muffled beneath the curves of her helmet. "Most of the court have gone out to welcome him back."

Marveling that the universe had somehow conjured up a way to make him feel even more on edge, Tarr absorbed this information and recalculated his approach. He nodded his thanks to the guard and headed out for the west balcony, where he knew Cade was likely to be received. As he walked, he attempted to reassure himself. Laith and Athela had spent the previous night griping about Cade. It was unlikely they'd voluntarily go out to greet him.

As he had anticipated, a large crowd had gathered on the spreading expanse of the west balcony to witness their king's return. Chiding himself that he hadn't noticed how empty the palace halls had been and put two and two together, Tarr edged forward. He craned his neck, looking around for his friends, not wanting to draw too much attention to himself. As he threaded through the clustered bodies in the crowd, Tarr stole a few sidelong glances, trying to gauge the temperature of the court as they regarded their ruler. There wasn't overwhelming devotion, nor was there relief or joy. The faces were...cautious. Interested, but wary. Perhaps just the barest hint of optimism. *Many rulers have started out with a tougher hill to climb,* Tarr thought.

Finally, finding himself in a position that was good enough for his height to afford him a clear view over the heads of the crowd, Tarr strained his eyes for any trace of Laith, Athela, or the others. Cade himself was not hard to pick out. He had just emerged from one of the subterranean tunnels leading up through the belly of the cliff to the palace balconies above, still mounted on his horse, white hair flashing in the light. Cade glanced around, and Tarr wondered whether they were all about to be subjected to one of his speeches, when there was a little rustle in the crowd. Laith suddenly strode out into the clearing, followed by Athela and an attending cloud of whispers from the people surrounding them. Tarr couldn't see his friends' faces fully, but he could see Cade's. The king looked apprehensive as Laith approached, but then Laith clapped a hand familiarly against Cade's horse's neck and said something that made Cade break out into an easy, almost relieved smile. The young man dismounted beside his brother. The two of them looked natural, friendly.

Disbelievingly, Tarr's eyes slid over to Athela, ever the bastion of suspicion and disapproval, confident that she would be projecting an appropriate level of icy reserve. But to Tarr's immense shock, she was smiling too. Cade said something and she nodded and shrugged, her arms folded lightly, almost carelessly, not tightly and forbidding as she once might have done.

Tarr swallowed, shocked by the sudden rush of sorrow that racked him to his core. There they were: Athela and Laith, his friends, two people he trusted more than almost anyone else in the world. He considered them anew in the glowing context of the sunlit balcony. Both of them, Tarr realized, simply *belonged* there. It was as though he were gazing at a painting of the scene before him: every stroke, every ray of light, every person in its correct place. And he was starkly conscious of his own position, standing on the outside looking in, unable to touch them. Laith and Athela might complain about Cade from time to time, but would it really be very long before they were working with him? Perhaps even *for* him? Once again, Tarr would just be the strange Ashan they'd once found wandering around Two Falls, someone they'd forget again as soon as palace life settled back into its previous rhythm.

I've still got Archer, he reminded himself. *I have Rane.* But for whatever reason, the unexpected pain he felt was not lessened. The ropes which bound his life to some semblance of comforting certainty were slipping away one by one through his fingers.

Tarr watched them numbly. He didn't want to tell them about Si now. Briefly, he thought of Archer, wondered whether he should confide in him. But Archer's gift was that of galvanization and execution; he was never one to sit down and puzzle through things too deeply. He would simply listen and tell Tarr that whatever course of action Tarr chose, he would support it. No, Tarr was on his own again. He would have to figure it out for himself.

Tarr turned on them and pushed his way back through the crowd.

He avoided the others for the rest of the day. He left Archer an evasive note so that his brother wouldn't sense anything amiss and come looking for him, then set out on a long walk through the woods in the hills above the palace. He stayed away from Athela's favorite riding trails, lest he run into her on one of her afternoon rides with Aria. Even after hours and hours caught in the relentless churn of his own mind, he couldn't decide what to do about Si, about any of it. He continued walking until he couldn't anymore.

At sunset, just as he had many years before, he debated simply walking away and leaving it all behind him, letting the others sort out the whole cosmic morass of it all. But he knew Archer wouldn't let him go. And Tarr had no delusions: his limited skills in evasion were nothing compared to Archer's ability to track a quarry.

It was late at night—so late Tarr had no idea what time it actually was—before he finally returned to the palace. A pair of moderately suspicious royal guards admitted him back to the Strikers' apartment wing; they were clearly of the impression that anyone wandering around at that late hour was up to no good.

Tarr paused for a moment on the threshold of his room and tried to picture opening the door, walking inside, and climbing into bed beside Rane. He imagined that she would stir a little in her sleep, perhaps groggily ask him if he was all right. He tried to imagine himself saying "Yes, everything's fine," in a normal-sounding voice. "Go back to sleep," he'd say, and she'd turn over and he'd stare up into the canopy of his bed until the sun broke through their window.

He couldn't do it. Almost without thinking, he turned down the corridor and softly slipped into Si's room.

The room was pitch black inside and Tarr shut the door quietly behind him. Si's room adjoined Marc's, and Tarr could hear the steady cadence of Marc's rhythmic snoring pulsing through the wall nearby. Tarr gave himself a few moments to let his eyes adjust to the darkness, then took a tentative step or two forward.

The door onto Si's balcony had not had its curtain drawn and moonlight spilled intricate lavender patterns across the floor as it drifted through the curved latticework of the windowpane. Tarr could make out Si's bed, and the boy's face, asleep. He was surprised to find that Si even needed to perform basic human functions such as sleeping or eating anymore.

There was a carved wooden stool slightly away from the bed, with a tunic draped across it like a shadow. Tarr quietly moved the tunic to the floor, picked up the stool and set it beside the bed. He looked down at Si as he slept, the boy's freckled face held softly in a beam of moonlight. Tarr leaned forward, his elbows on his knees, his fingers folded together beneath his nose, and watched him.

Si looked so peaceful. He didn't make a sound and his face barely twitched; his eyes didn't move beneath his lids. His chest slowly, trustingly, rose and fell beneath the cover of his bedsheet.

Tarr tried to imagine it: tried to imagine taking one of Si's pillows, pressing it over the boy's face, muffling any sounds so that Marc would not hear in his room next door. He wondered whether Si would struggle. Si already knew the choice Tarr was going to make. Maybe he had expected him tonight. Maybe he was ready.

I already have blood on my hands, Tarr thought dully. *It might be easy.*

He reached out towards Si.

All at once, the corner of the boy's mouth twitched. It was a tiny, infinitesimal motion, but it froze Tarr's hand. For a fleeting instant, there was an echo of Si's familiar smile, the smile that he had known for so many years, a glimpse of the sweet, innocent young man Si had once been.

Gently, Tarr lowered his hand and pulled Si's coverlet up a little higher around his shoulders. He smoothed it out and sat back, his hands hanging down limply at his sides. All of the anxiety and fear drained out of him, leaving him a hollow, throbbing shell. He couldn't do it. Perhaps he was dooming them all now, consigning the world to be snuffed out in one fell swoop of Si's terrible power, but he couldn't bring himself to do it.

Help me, he thought. It was a prayer of profound desperation, projected towards any force that might care to listen. *Please help me.*

You can't do this alone.

The realization came to him as suddenly as if someone had whispered it aloud. He blinked slowly and stirred. His arms and legs felt as though they were weighted down.

You can't do this alone.

There it was again: the thought, repeated now, stronger. Minutes slipped by, and slowly, like a river melting under the first warmth of spring, he realized what he had to do. He had to put his pride aside, swallow down any embarrassment, forget whatever it was he thought he had seen up on the west balcony when Cade had returned home. There was one person who had been by his side this whole time, who had pored over every problem with him, every puzzle, had helped him to decipher every clue. And he needed her more than he ever had before.

"Athela," he said, surprised to hear how weak, how frail his own voice sounded. "I'm lost."

Athela had clearly been fast asleep; one of her gray eyes was still partially shut, and her hair was flat on one side as if she'd been lying on it. She squinted at him suspiciously in the gloom of the hallway. "Your room's down there," she said finally, jerking a thumb to her left. She made a motion to close the door.

"No," Tarr interjected tiredly, catching the door before she could shut it on him. "*Existentially* lost. I know where my room is."

"Oh," she considered him anew, seeming to fully take in his mien for the first time. "Come in," she stepped aside and admitted him.

They settled themselves on the floor atop Athela's shabby rug. Tarr fidgeted anxiously as Athela rubbed the sleep from her eyes and tried to shake some consciousness back into her head. She waited in expectant exasperation as Tarr teetered back and forth for a few moments, wrestling with where he should begin. And then, like a dam crumbling into a river, it all spilled forth. He told her everything. He told her what Si had said to him after the battle, about the continuation of Cira's life force within him. That the only way to put an end to the cycle once and for all was for Si to die. Tarr told her what he'd seen Si do in the grove of trees, his worries, his suspicions. That he'd gone to Si's room and watched him as he slept, wondering what on earth it was that he was supposed to do.

By the end of Tarr's monologue, Athela was well and truly alert. She was staring at Tarr with a mixture of alarm and wonder, her hands wrapped tightly around her knees.

"Why didn't you come and speak to us earlier today?" she asked finally. "After what Si did in the grove?"

"I saw you with Cade," Tarr mumbled. It sounded childish now. "You greeted him when he got back to the palace, and you were laughing. And I thought..."

"*That?*" Athela's eyes widened in surprise. "I don't even remember what he said. He summoned all of us, you included, to meet with him, but we couldn't find you." Her face was now concerned. "You've been keeping all of this bottled up inside. Not just today. For so long."

"I..." Tarr gestured helplessly. "Si said that it was my responsibility to take on. My decision to make. And so I've been trying to work it all out. I've tried ignoring it. I've tried puzzling through it. But I don't know what to do."

Athela nodded slowly. Tarr couldn't decipher the expression on her face as she looked at him. Was she angry?

He shrugged helplessly and continued on, not sure whether he was articulating his thoughts in any particularly coherent way. "On the one hand...Si told me that this responsibility was mine. But on the other hand I'm not even supposed to *be* here. It was supposed to be some other Ashan that day in Two Falls with Wolver, all those years ago. This choice was supposed to fall to *him*. But he's not here and...and Laith said..." he swallowed hoarsely and avoided Athela's gaze. "Laith said

I'm a warrior. Whatever that means. But if he's right, isn't this what warriors do? Choose who lives and who dies?"

"Tarr..." Athela said slowly. "What were you going to do tonight? When you went to Si's room?"

Tarr fiddled with the lace of his boot and shook his head. "I don't know," he said honestly. "I really don't know. I thought about it for two seconds..."

The *it* in his sentence hung between them, heavy and ugly. Tarr could feel Athela's eyes searing into him. Summoning all his courage, he met her gaze. She read the unspoken words in his eyes and shook her head. Now it was her turn to abruptly break away. Tarr felt an immediate, scorching rush of shame.

"I couldn't do it," he said quietly. "I *know* I couldn't ever do it. But for a minute I sat there and I thought...I thought maybe *this* is why I wasn't Chosen."

Athela looked back up at him sharply, her brows knitting.

Tarr groped for words. "I keep...I keep trying to find a reason for all of this. To find my place in all of this, a *reason* why I was sent away from my tribe, why no one wanted me then, why I'm not a part of a family, why I might never be. I don't believe I was ever part of the prophecy. But maybe I was supposed to do *this*." He gestured jerkily in Si's direction. "Maybe I was *meant* to go through this world alone, to be the one to have to do this terrible thing, and then go my own way and live with it. Maybe...there was a reason after all. For all of it. Maybe *this* was my purpose the whole time."

"You idiot," Athela said abruptly.

"Thanks, Athela," Tarr smiled wanly. "I knew I'd come to the right person."

But Athela wasn't smiling. "You *idiot*," she said again, and there was genuine heat behind her tone. "You absolute *idiot*."

Tarr stared at her. "What?" he asked, shocked.

"For all your brains and your cleverness, and the way you can see through things, you couldn't see something so obvious?" she asked. Her gray eyes were wide and unblinking. "You *were* chosen, Tarr."

Tarr fumbled for a moment. "The prophecy—"

Athela threw up her hands in disgust. "The stupid prophecy. I'm not talking about a prophecy, Tarr. You were chosen, Tarr. By us."

Tarr swallowed. "But--"

"*We* chose you, Tarr. And it wasn't the prophecy, it wasn't the war. It was this. Here," she put a hand to her heart. To Tarr's astonishment, he saw the glint of tears beginning to well in her eyes, and the sight of it made his throat clench. "And you..." she groped for words. "How could you not see? We love you. *I* love you."

Tarr stared at her.

She halted, a tear spilling unbidden down the side of her face. She chuckled self-deprecatingly. "I've never said that to anyone," she said, as if startled by the thought.

"Athela—"

"How could you think that you're alone? That you could leave us? That you are not tied to us now, always? You and Archer became brothers." She was genuinely perplexed.

Tarr opened his mouth. He couldn't tell Athela, couldn't tell her what he knew about Archer's fate.

"But Archer was sent away from his tribe, too, I guess," Athela mused, as if answering her own question. "It's just you two, if you want to look at it like that...what about Rane?"

"I don't know. She and I need to re-learn each other. To find out what we could be to each other now that the war is over. And even if it came to marriage..." he tried to find a way to explain it so that she would understand. "Love...romance...that's different. The evolution is different. And marriages can be dissolved."

Athela considered this for a beat. She peered at him and touched his hand. "Isn't it enough? To know that we love you and that you have a place with us?"

"You might change your mind," Tarr said simply. His throat felt tight, and his breath was coming fast and jittery, high and shallow in his chest. "Someday things might be different and you might change your mind. And then..." he trailed off, but the unspoken words were there. *You might change your mind, and then I'd be alone again, rootless, adrift, with nothing to anchor me to the earth, to any sort of history.*

She searched his face long and hard and then suddenly an understanding began to dawn.

"It matters to you," she said slowly. "It really matters to you, doesn't it? Having someone make that promise to you?"

Tarr made no response. He was empty. There was nothing left in him to say anything.

Athela abruptly leaped to her feet and swung around, scanning the room. Tarr watched her mutely, unsure of what was going on but too drained to care. Finally, she strode over to the keepsake shelf beside her bed and snatched a small jagged blue stone off of it. She held it in her hand for a moment, then met Tarr squarely in the eyes. The realization of what she was doing landed squarely on Tarr's shoulders. His throat tightened so that he could barely breathe, and his heart began to beat faster. Athela stepped toward him and laid the stone down on the ground before him.

"Tarr," she announced. "I Choose you for my family."

Tarr met her eyes. His mouth opened slightly; he searched for any words to say and found none. Athela's head lifted slightly. She pointed at the stone she'd laid at his feet.

"Through me you're now a member of the house of Joymaril. Laith is your cousin. You're related to Marc and to Rane. Si, too, once Marc adopts him. Archer through you. All of the Strikers. A family." She paused, chin lifting ever so slightly. "You belong to us and we belong to you. Whatever I need to do, whatever ceremony we need to perform to make this official, I'll do it. I'll tattoo your symbol on my spine and carry it with me until the day I die. I promise." Her jaw was set and she stared at him, unblinkingly, almost daring him to question whether or not she meant it.

Something inside Tarr crumpled, as if a great hand had plunged into his chest and pulled something out of him, something hard and rigid and sharp that he hadn't even realized had been there before. He bent forward, his face in his hands, and began to sob. After a few moments he felt Athela's arm slide gently around his shoulders.

How long he sat there and cried, he didn't know. When his tears finally subsided, he remained motionless, his head bent forward on his folded arms, the comforting weight of Athela's hand still resting on his back. His mind slowly began to move, as though it were slogging through a thick vat of mud: *what does this mean?* he wondered. Then the enormity of it dawned: a family. He had an Ashan brother and a Jelani sister. He had cousins. He might someday have nieces or nephews. His name would be recorded in the tree of Athela's line. When people remembered him in years to come, they would not only use the word *fighter, spy, hero, Striker.* They would call him a *brother, uncle, cousin.* Perhaps even *father* or *grandfather.* The magic of those words spread before him like a dazzling tapestry.

Something shifted anew, something that Tarr could not possibly have anticipated. The door that had closed off his life in the forest from what came afterwards slowly opened, the crack of light behind it easing open into full blinding splendor. It was all his again, as vivid and brilliant as if he was seeing it for the first time: his childhood, the golden light of the Ashan woods in autumn, the steam rising off of the hot stone baths in the winter, the rustle of tags on the scrolls in the Ashan library. They all belonged to him once more. There were no longer two isolated halves of his life; they had joined on a single path. And the night of the Choosing, that awful night where everything had changed, was a step. A solitary step, nothing more. He had gone a different direction, and it had brought him here. It no longer held power over him. And he was no longer afraid to look ahead, to take the next step.

Slowly, he lifted his head. He looked at Athela, who was watching him closely. He smiled at her; she returned it fondly and brushed a lingering tear from his cheek with businesslike precision.

"Thank you," he said, and meant it.

"You're welcome. I'm sorry for calling you an idiot so many times," she said consolingly.

"It's all right. I may have deserved it." He stirred, and Athela withdrew her arm, placing her hand lightly atop his. "Now, this still leaves us with the small problem of how to avoid the destruction of the entire world."

"Ah, yes. Nearly forgot," Athela cleared her throat self-consciously. "So: you're saying that Cira lives on in some way, that Si now has forces of good and evil at work inside him."

"That's right," Tarr confirmed.

Athela shrugged. "So what?"

Tarr stared at her blankly. "What?"

"So what?" Athela repeated. "We all do. You, me. I imagine even Marc's had an off day at some point in his life."

"But Athela," Tarr pointed out, "When Marc has an off day the entire world doesn't implode or get its life force sucked out."

"Fair point," Athela conceded. "So I guess we have to hope that the good in Si is more powerful than whatever else might be going on in there."

Tarr contemplated this option. Weighing the balance of the entire world against the off-chance that Si was strong enough to resist any stirring undercurrents of evil didn't sound like a very proactive tactic. It was furthermore unlike Athela to suggest a course of action that essentially relied on hope.

"You're willing to do that?" Tarr asked dubiously.

Athela sighed, long and heavy, and thought reflectively for a few moments before she replied. "I don't know, Tarr. More than any of the others, I think that you and I have both a reason and a tendency to expect the worst in people. And yet, against all odds, here we are. Together." She shrugged and met his eyes. "And somehow I find myself trending towards optimism."

Tarr's eyebrows rose.

"I know," she agreed. "But don't you sort of feel it too? Deep down?"

Tarr attempted to sort through the hazy fog of emotions fighting for supremacy in his mind and heart, her hand on his. "Yes," he said begrudgingly. "Yes, I guess I do."

Athela looked satisfied. "See? And besides," she continued, "Si has something that Cira never did."

Tarr's brow furrowed. "What's that?"

She smiled faintly. "Us."

Tarr met her eyes questioningly.

"People who love him, and who will protect him and care for him, no matter what it takes," Athela said firmly. "That may just turn the tide."

Silence fell between them for a few moments. "So..." Tarr prompted slowly. "What do we do? Cross our fingers and hope for the best? Even with you and me at our most optimistic, I feel like that will be something of a stretch."

"Well, Tarr, I must disagree with my cousin Laith ever so slightly," Athela said. "I think he's right to a certain extent. You're a warrior, for sure, no doubt about it. But your gift isn't in fighting or killing. It never has been." She shook her head. "Your gift is finding a way out. Finding a way through when everything seems impossible. "

Tarr stared at her.

"So," she straightened, spread her hands wide and smiled. "Find us a way out. Find us a way to keep Si safe." Gently, she reached up and placed a hand against his face. "And try and keep the rest of the world safe, too, while you're at it."

Unbidden, Tarr's mind suddenly flew back to years before, to the first time he met Athela in the Two Falls square. He vividly remembered her flashing gray eyes, her suspicious expression, her coldness. *My sister*, he thought wonderingly. *She's my sister.*

The warmth of her hand on his face stirred him back to the present. Her gray eyes were trusting, steady; her expression earnest.

"I'll try my best," he promised her.

Tarr could easily have slept well into the afternoon, but King Cade V was insistent that his previous day's summons to the Strikers were obeyed. Servants were dispatched to fetch Tarr, Athela, and Laith to the king's chambers at what Tarr could only characterize as an uncivilized hour of the following midmorning.

Tarr and Athela had fallen asleep in ungainly sprawling heaps on opposite ends of Athela's bed; at the first knock at her door, Athela had bolted awake and sworn a round, colorful oath before shuffling off at a half-run to see who it was. A dull thud and another bout of vivid swearing indicated to Tarr that she had stubbed her toe on something on the way there. He groaned exhaustedly and flopped one arm over his eyes as he listened to the dim murmuring at Athela's apartment door. Beneath his physical fatigue, however, there was an unexpected feeling of release. Tarr felt lighter than he had in months, perhaps years.

"Bad news," Athela growled, stomping back into the room, her wild black hair even more sculpturally asymmetrical than it had been the night before. "His Shortness wants us to meet with him in fifteen minutes."

Tarr peered out at her from beneath the crook of his elbow. "I dare you to call him His Shortness to his face."

Athela laughed gruffly and hurled a nearby pillow at him. Tarr's reflexes hadn't fully awakened, and the pillow hit him squarely in the stomach. "Come on, get up. I'll wash first. Then I'll go and try and stall him for a few extra minutes. You can thank me later."

By the time Tarr had stumbled his way through the king's main audience hall, Laith and Athela had already been admitted to Cade's private council chamber, a small elegant office just off of his main receiving room. The door was flanked by two imposing-looking guards clad in royal purple, with midnight blue sashes and Cade's ivy sigil embroidered on them. Tarr gave them a desultory salute as he sloped between them and through the door into the council room.

"Tarr," Cade greeted him. The King stood behind a short, gleaming wooden table, his fingers splayed out like tree roots on the polished surface. Athela and Laith sat before him already, their faces studiously blank.

"Sorry for being late," Tarr apologized, sliding into the empty chair beside Athela. He wasn't sure whether the dim, vacant expression on her face was tactical or a result of her three hours' sleep the night before.

"Not to worry," Cade waved a dismissive hand. It was strange, Tarr thought as his mind slowly shook itself awake, to see him here with a crown on his head, a rich sable fur slung over his shoulder, and his crushed velvet tunic beneath. He looked every inch a king. Tarr chanced a glance over to the side where Laith sat, but the prince's expression was impossible to read.

"I'll speak frankly," Cade said, taking a seat opposite them. "I will always be grateful to all of you for the many sacrifices that you made during this war. You know as well as I that it could not have been won without our forces joining together. I know that you have lost friends and loved ones..." he trailed off and looked directly at Laith. "I'm so sorry."

"Thank you," Laith said quietly.

"The Strikers will always be an important part of the history of the country I hope to build," Cade continued. "But it is clear from my coronation tour of the outlying lands that in these first few months of my rule, it's more important than ever that I win the people's trust. That I convince them that unification is the right thing to do. I must convince them that a single country, united under my guidance, is the best and simplest way. And it's here that, unfortunately, you Strikers present a..." he trailed off, searching for the right word.

"Complication?" Athela volunteered ironically.

"We'll call it a complication," Cade conceded. "So I would like to propose a solution."

"We're all ears," Laith said, folding his arms.

"First of all," Cade began, interlacing his fingers, "it goes without saying that all of the lands and estates that were seized after your departure from the palace have been returned to you. Your titles and all of the rights associated with those titles are also reinstated."

"Hurray," Athela murmured.

"Tarr," Cade turned to address him directly. "I've decided to give you an estate of your own in the Meadows, as thanks for your efforts during the war."

"Oh," Tarr wasn't sure what to say, or what exactly this entailed. However, it seemed that the appropriate reaction was gratitude. "Thank you," he said.

"Furthermore," Cade continued, looking pleased with himself, "It occurs to me that the easiest way for me to establish my reign without any...distractions, shall we say, is for you to leave."

"Leave Joymaril?" Athela asked curiously.

"The country," Cade replied.

Tarr stared at him, not sure if he was being serious. He could feel Laith and Athela stiffen beside him, and knew that they were just as shocked as he.

"We're being exiled?" Athela asked wearily. "*Again*?"

Cade, seeing that his words had been misconstrued, raised his hands in a conciliatory gesture. "No, not exile. Let me explain."

"I can't wait," Laith murmured, and now even his temperate voice held a bit of Athela's sarcasm.

"The country across the sea, Vireg, has been united much longer than we have, and its King, Tarik, is making great strides in technological and scientific advancements. I have word that at the moment, they're beginning to excavate the ruins of an ancient temple in the desert, and from what I've heard, new discoveries are being made there every day. There's much I feel that we could learn from him and his people, and much that we currently do not know. My hope is that we will have a strong and peaceful ally in him. But it's unlikely that we will be on even footing as long as our country lags behind theirs. In his letter congratulating me on my victory, King Tarik was very generous in offering to share their knowledge and their scientific discoveries. I would like to take advantage of that offer and to strengthen the bonds of friendship between our two countries. Furthermore, I would like to know more about this king: who he is and what kind of man he is. I know that he backed Cira and provided her with weapons, but that he otherwise was largely uninvolved in our war."

Tarr, Athela, and Laith remained silent. Tarr wasn't sure about the others, but he could see now where this was going, and it was a much different direction than he had anticipated.

"Therefore," Cade leaned back. "Laith, I would like to appoint you my ambassador to the country of Vireg and the kingdom of King Tarik. You are welcome to assemble a team of your choosing to accompany you on this mission."

The prince kept his face carefully neutral, but Tarr could tell that underneath the façade Laith's interest was piqued.

"Tarr," Cade said, training his gray eyes to his left, "I will send you to Vireg under the premise that you are there to aid in the archeological excavation of the tomb, and that you are there to study their methods, sciences and technologies. But what I also want you to do is to act as my head of intelligence and collect as much information as you can about the King and his subjects. I expect you to have set up a functioning spy network within the first six months."

Tarr was dumbstruck, but at the same time he felt himself perk up, feeling the first spark of actual excitement that he had in months. Then he caught himself. *Oh, he's good*, he thought. *Very good.*

"Athela, I would also like you to accompany Tarr and Laith. You are to work directly with Tarr regarding the gathering of intelligence around the country, but specifically the horse breeding and racing industry in Vireg. I'm told that they have built an entire stadium there solely to house the races; it's a huge industry for them. I want to know everything about it. You're to bring your horse with you and compete, as appropriate, in order to gain information." He leaned back in his chair, and Tarr couldn't help but notice that he seemed quite satisfied with the arrangement he'd devised. "Now," Cade said, "How does that sound to all of you?"

Athela opened her mouth to speak, but Laith cut in quickly. "I think we'll need some time to think it over, and to speak to the others."

"I'd like your answer tomorrow, if possible," Cade countered evenly.

Not wasting any time, is he? Tarr thought wryly.

"We can do that," Laith assented. "Is that all?"

"That is all," Cade gave them a gesture indicating the door, and the three Strikers maintained a pointed silence that somehow seemed to magnify the scraping of their chairs on the floor. "Tarr," he called out suddenly. "A word."

Tarr let Athela and Laith walk past him out the door, then he paused at the threshold and turned around slowly to face Cade.

Cade considered him for a moment. "I have decided to rebuild the Two Falls library," he said finally. "I would like to name it in your honor."

Tarr blinked in surprise. His initial reaction was that of gratification, but a moment later realized swiftly that that was precisely Cade's intention and his pleasure waned.

"I'm flattered," he said coolly. "Just one request. Name it after Athela instead. She spent so many happy hours there, and made so many fond memories." He tried to stifle a grin at the recollection of all of Athela's frustrated outings to the library, her vows never to step foot inside it again unless under extreme duress.

Cade looked puzzled, but Tarr didn't bother to explain further. He gave a short bow, and a moment later there was the heavy sound of the door shutting behind him. He paused for a moment on the other side, and from what he could hear Cade was sitting motionless within.

Laith and Athela were waiting for him down the hallway. The three of them speed-walked (Laith's limp noticeably pronounced) down the corridor and around one of the wraparound balconies on the palace front. Tarr indicated that they should head to a spot close to the waterfall where they would be less likely to be overheard. The three of them gathered in a huddle against the balustrade, the morning light catching the spray and sending it floating past the gleaming white walls of the palace in little bursts through the air. Tarr barely noticed.

"Well," Athela prompted. "Nice and tidy. I get to ride my horse. Tarr gets some espionage. Laith gets to be tactful and diplomatic in a room full of scheming politicians."

"Everybody wins." Tarr agreed, grinning.

Laith rolled his eyes. "Ideal. Absolutely ideal. But..." he trailed off, then stared at them pointedly. "What do you *think*? Really?"

A slow smile began to creep along the edges of Athela's mouth. "It's not the *worst* idea Cade has ever come up with," she conceded. "What about you, Tarr? Fancy a trip to the desert?"

"Will we get to cross the sea?" Tarr asked, unable to keep the unabashed eagerness out of his voice. "On a boat?"

"That would be pretty much the only way to do it," Athela confirmed.

Tarr took a step back and frowned as if he were casually debating his options. "My schedule is relatively open," he shrugged, and smiled.

Laith grinned. "I guess we should go and ask the others."

A month later, they found themselves basking in warm sunshine on the side of a green sloping southern hill that looked out over the sea. Tarr sat contentedly on the crest of the rise, gazing down at his friends. He could still not quite believe that they had made it there.

It was the height of summer, summer at its most resplendent. The sun was piercing and brilliant in the sky; they'd made good time on their journey that day. And the sea: Tarr could barely fathom it, the way it vanished across the horizon, couldn't believe that there was actually an entirely new country waiting for them on the other side. He'd been certain they'd be able to see it from their vantage point there up on the hill, but the water stretched out and out, blending seamlessly into the sky beyond. It was terrifying and beautiful in its blank expanse.

Down below them lay a rocky trail that threaded the rest of the way to the coast and the sprawling port fishing village of Eldrest. The buildings were short and squat, shingled in gray wood, and melded almost perfectly to the rocky coastline. In the harbor, Tarr could make out the white sails of boats weaving to and fro between the froth-topped waves like little pale butterflies, their reflections glimmering and winking on the water. Further into shore he could make out a fleet of large, stately ships moored only a short ways from land, rocking serenely like noble swans among their smaller, flightier compatriots. He supposed that these were the ships on which they were to cross the sea to get to Vireg. He could only hope that their captain would know where he was going and how to get there properly. How strange it was, he thought, and how remarkable that people had figured out how to carve paths through the sea.

He closed his eyes and breathed in the sweet air, turning to look once again at his friends. They were lounging in the grass, laughing and talking while their horses stood resting amicably to one side. He watched Si, his young face turned up to the sun, eyes closed, basking in all its radiant warmth. If Tarr hadn't known any better, he'd have seen Si as simply a boy out for a picnic with his family, rather than an all-knowing, eternal being who held the fate of the world in his funny, faraway mind.

Tarr's memory drifted back slowly to one of the last days they had spent in Joymaril. He'd called Marc in and, over the course of many hours and a very long afternoon, told him everything.

Tarr hadn't quite known what to expect from Marc's reactions, but he had listened carefully and quietly, his ice-blue eyes blinking every now and again. And as the minutes passed, Tarr could almost see the steely resolve well up in his eyes.

"Well then," Marc had said at last, when Tarr had finally finished. They had lit the lamps for the evening by then; light from their lantern cast his countenance into sharp relief, emphasizing his long diagonal scar. "Tell me what we need to do."

"I believe," Tarr swallowed hoarsely, "that he is strong enough. That he will be all right. But we must keep him safe. No one will know that he's alive. He must live out his years as quietly as possible, with someone willing to protect him, and care for him, someone who will be...aware." He swallowed, knowing the enormity of what he was asking of his friend. "He can't face this alone. No one could. So we must be ever vigilant for signs that the tide has turned within him for evil, and to be willing to do whatever is necessary to make sure that that evil is... contained. If it comes to that."

Marc tilted his head to one side. "You think people would try to have him killed? If they knew he was alive?"

Tarr made a back-and-forth motion with his hands. "That amount of power? They'd take him in an instant, or try to manipulate him for their own purposes."

Marc shook his head, his tone sober. "So, if what you say really happened, some part of Cira lives on in him, too, now?"

Tarr nodded. "That's right. From what I understand those elements—good, destructive, everything in between—now live together within him with an almost unimaginable well of power just out of reach of those forces. At this point, I'm not sure whether we can even just call him a boy anymore, either. I think it's more complicated than that. Our young friend contains multitudes."

Marc made a gesture of unconcerned dismissal. "Si is who Si is. Whatever form that takes." He lapsed into silence, thinking quietly for a long while. Tarr could scarcely fathom what was going on in his head.

"I know," Tarr said after a while, "I know how cruel it is to ask you to do this, to put this on your shoulders, to ask you to basically live in exile for the rest of your life, and you can of course say no if you..."

"Laith has an estate on a remote island to the south," Marc cut him off. "Very secluded. Hard to get to. I don't think even Laith has ever been there. Oren and I could take Si there, and we could live quite comfortably, with him as our son. As far as I know, there's only a house-keeper and a few other staff. He would be safe. As safe as he could be anywhere." He gave Tarr a pointed look. "I would take care of him. I would take care of everything."

"Are you sure?" Tarr asked weakly. "Even in the event that you have to..."

"Whatever it takes," Marc said firmly, and Tarr could see that his mind was made up.

"Marc, what can I do...what can we do to make this up to you?" Tarr asked.

Marc stared at him, looking affronted by the suggestion that what he was doing was in any way some sort of sacrifice. "What on earth are you talking about?"

"I..." Tarr stammered. "Nothing."

"I'll talk to Oren," Marc mused. "But he'll be fine with it. Truth be told, he's not terribly fond of the desert and he can't really wait to get out of here either. I think a quiet life by the sea will be just what we need. Just mail us a new book or two every year or so."

That same night, a strange thing happened. Tarr dreamed that he rose from his bed and walked through the hushed, dark corridors of the sleeping palace, wending his way down the stairways and out of the door at the bottom of the cliff. Everything around him was saturated in dark shades of blue, purple, indigo and cobalt. He dreamed that he walked barefoot over the rocky sand on the bank of the lake and stepped out onto the bridge submerged just beneath the surface, the water cool and pleasant against his ankles.

Looking through the gloom of night to the opposite side of the lake, he dreamed that he saw a mist rising through the moonlit trees, soft as a gossamer cloud. Then a form began to take shape, as Tarr slowly walked closer. The mist cleared ever so slightly and Tarr could see who it was.

"Hello, old friend," he said. "I've missed you."

Wolver was waiting for him on the opposite bank, his fur white and his eyes as ice-blue as Tarr had remembered from long ago. Even in the haziness of the dream, Tarr was startled to see how lifelike the wolf was, how he could make out every strand of fur, every whisker. As Tarr drew closer, Wolver fixed him with the familiar level stare, communicating to him in that strange, nonverbal way of his that he was glad to see him, too. That everything was all right.

"I've got a lot of questions for you," Tarr said, his voice strange and faraway in the empty, hollow air of his dream. He tried to make his shadowy voice sound stern. "And I would appreciate it if you'd answer them."

Wolver blinked up at him, unmoved.

"You left without saying goodbye," Tarr said reproachfully. "I didn't get to say goodbye to you. And I missed you. I've missed you very much."

Wolver blinked and tilted his large white head slightly to the side. Then he reached out his muzzle and nudged Tarr gently in the hand. Even in the dream, his nose was cold and wet. It all felt so real.

"It's all right," Tarr's heart felt infinitely lighter. "It's all right now. It's good to know you're still out there somewhere, even if it can't be with me."

Wolver's blue eyes blinked once, slowly, and his left ear twitched softly, as if catching a sound in the distance. Tarr heard nothing, just the quiet, muffled rushing vacuum of the still air around him.

"Wolver, Si said your task was complete," Tarr asked. "What did he mean?"

But the wolf's expression was as inscrutable as ever.

"Did Daemun send you?" Tarr asked. "Who sent you? Was it... was it..." The dream world gave a disorienting lurch as Tarr tried to gather his thoughts. "*Was* it supposed to be me with you that day by the fountain? Was it supposed to be me all along?"

The mist was growing thicker in the air around him, dropping a faint white veil over the trees and the earth beneath his feet. *Not yet*, Tarr thought. *Don't let the dream end just yet. I still have so much to ask him. So many questions I need answered. So much I want to know.*

As Tarr reached out to pet him, Wolver stood and walked away to stand by the left side of a slim young tree. Tarr lowered his hand and watched as the tree slowly transformed into a gigantic six-pointed star, the symbol of Morthenstar. Tarr stared at it, wondering what it could possibly mean. He knew that if he asked Wolver to explain, there would be no answer.

The wolf swung his head round to face the misty gloom of the forest beyond. He took a step away, his paw silent on the damp earth.

"Wait!" Tarr shouted, though his voice was disembodied, only an echo. Wolver halted and turned, watching him attentively.

"You could come with me," Tarr pleaded, stepping forward. "Come with me, can't you?"

Wolver lowered his head down between his front paws and blew his breath across the ground. Though he made no reply, Tarr knew what he was saying: *I can't this time. I must go.*

"No, you're probably right," Tarr said hurriedly. "I remember what happened the last time you and I went wandering around together. Wouldn't want to inadvertently kick off another prophecy, would we?"

Tarr looked once again from Wolver to the tall, six-pointed star rising next to him. Wolver seemed to think for a few moments, then walked up to stand expectantly before Tarr.

Tarr knelt down before the wolf and patted him between the ears, the mist on the tips of Wolver's fur wetting Tarr's hand. Briefly, Wolver leaned forward and rested his head on Tarr's shoulder.

"Goodbye, old fellow," Tar murmured. "Thank you for coming to see me. Will I...will I see you again?"

Wolver took a step back and met his eyes, blue and fathomless. Perhaps Tarr was imagining it, but there was a warmth there.

You just might, his expression seemed to say.

And then, just as slowly as he had arrived, Wolver turned and walked into the swirling white of the forest, Morthenstar's emblem jutting out of the blowing mist beside him. Wolver disappeared, slipping seamlessly into the darkness. Then, the veil of white blew across Tarr's field of vision, and the dream faded away.

Tarr awoke at dawn the next morning, every detail of the dream imprinted on his mind, the presence of Wolver still so real and close to him that it was almost as if the wolf were standing right behind him. To his shock, as he slowly sorted out his surroundings, he found that he was lying not in his own bed but on the bank of the Joymarillian lake, where the morning birds were just beginning to take up their call, silvery and gold on the cool spring breeze.

Their plan came together remarkably quickly. Tarr hadn't quite understood what Marc had meant by "Laith's estate," but he rapidly came to realize that being royal apparently meant that one just had houses scattered about here and there that one either visited or didn't. He dimly remembered that Cade had given *him* an estate when he'd proposed the idea of the Strikers moving to Vireg, but Tarr hadn't the faintest idea what this entailed. He made a mental note to ask Laith at some point if there was any sort of paperwork he'd have to fill out.

Marc and Tarr had spoken with Laith about moving into his coastal home; Laith immediately gave his assent and agreed that the house was the ideal location for their purposes. There were minimal staff, and those who did live there had done so for most of their lives—Laith wasn't sure whether news of the war had even reached them. There was a little town nearby where it would be safe for Marc, Oren, or even Si (under close supervision and disguise) to travel, and where they would get their supply of food and other needs. Tarr wondered to himself about the loneliness of the life that they were facing: it would be highly unlikely that the Strikers would ever be able to visit them together as a group, for even in a sleepy fishing village that kind of arrival would attract unwanted attention. Laith would be able to visit the most often under the auspices of surveying his estate; every few years he could issue orders for some modifications to be made to the house and the docking area that would, over time, make it easier for private visitors to arrive unseen by those onshore or sailing casually by.

What stunned Tarr the most, really, was the almost unthinking way in which Marc had agreed to take on this enormous responsibility. From the very beginning, Marc had acted as Si's protector and older brother, but that role had now expanded exponentially: at no point would Si be able to leave the safety of their home to venture out on his own into the world. And, of course, there was the horrible threat always lurking—that if somehow Si did start to turn, if he started to exhibit signs that Kagai's influence was taking hold within him, then Marc would have to take the necessary precautions. He would have to muster the strength to do what Tarr could not. Tarr could barely stand to imagine it, so instead he chose to hope. It was all he could do.

Laith summarily sent the orders for the house to be prepared, and on a sunny afternoon their small group met Cade and his entourage as they headed back to the palace after a hunt in the hills. Cade looked to be in a good mood; his pale cheeks were flushed, his white-blond hair had been tousled by the wind, and he was laughing at something that his courtier had said. On Cade's right, Queen Rowan sat atop a dark blood bay horse. Her short, gleaming black hair was ruffling slightly in the breeze, and she wore a resplendent riding habit made out of dark purple silk and a wispy, floating material that billowed around her in the air. A small circlet of entwined silver and precious gems was fastened in her dark hair and Tarr thought with some amusement that she had already perfected the art of the haughty, reserved expression of a queen. As they approached, though, she sent him a covert wink and he had to stifle a smile. Rowan had always had a soft spot for him.

"Afternoon," Laith said, smiling, stepping forward to grab Cade's horse's bit as Cade vaulted off.

"Hello," Cade replied with a smile, quickly surveying the group that had come out to meet him. "What can I do for all of you?"

"We wanted to let you know that with your permission, Marc will not be joining our party to Vireg," Laith informed him.

At once, Tarr saw Cade's expression change ever so slightly; he looked sharply at his brother and down the row at each of them, clearly searching for some hidden agenda. Tarr knew what he was thinking: how unusual it was for Marc and Laith to be separated in this way.

"I'm sorry to hear that, I feel that he would be a great help to the expedition," Cade said carefully. "May I ask why?"

"My partner Oren is still recovering from his experiences in captivity, and his health is in a delicate state," Marc said, gesturing at the quiet, willowy young man standing at his right shoulder. At that precise moment, Oren raised a long, slender hand to his mouth and gave the tiniest, high-pitched little cough. This punctuation was so well timed that Tarr quite nearly burst out laughing and had to look down at the ground and dig his fingernails into his palms to control himself. Marc, however, didn't miss a beat. "And I find that I have had trouble adjusting to life after my experiences...and losses...during the war."

Cade narrowly eyed Oren, but the young man blinked back with an expression of pure innocence. "I know how close you were to Si Morthenstar," he said to Marc. "I'm sorry. I know it has been difficult."

"Thank you," said Marc serenely. He tossed back a strand of his straw-colored hair and looked around at the others. "Lord Argolaith and I both have assets and estates to the south, and with your permission, Lord Oren and I would like to survey Laith's holdings and secure them if need be, and to set up a household where we can take advantage of the warm climate." *Keep it vague,* Tarr had counseled him. *We don't want to give him much to go on. Keep him bored, don't pique his interest.*

Cade looked from one face to the other, trying to read their expressions. "You have my permission," he said slowly. "I hope that you both improve."

"I'm sure we will, thank you, your Majesty," Marc gave a bow, echoed by the others.

"One other thing, your Majesty," Tarr broke in, and Cade swiveled his gray gaze towards him.

"Yes?" Cade replied slowly.

"I would like to request that Rowan's handmaiden Nadia be made part of my team for the expedition," Tarr said.

Cade blinked in surprise and opened his mouth as if his knee-jerk reaction was to protest. "Why?"

"I think she would be helpful," Tarr said simply. *An understatement,* he thought. *Just because you somehow have overlooked her doesn't mean I will.*

Cade regarded him closely, glancing briefly at Rowan. "If she wishes. And if the Queen permits."

Tarr nodded, feeling satisfied. He had a gut suspicion, even though he and Nadia had exchanged barely three words to one another, that she would agree to come with them. Rowan looked at Tarr curiously, but gave a nod that indicated she didn't mind. One handmaiden, to her, was likely the same as another.

"When do you depart?" Cade asked.

"Next week," replied Laith.

"The Queen and I shall see you off," Cade said, gesturing back to Rowan, who inclined her dazzling head the slightest amount, sending off a glittering burst of light from her crown.

"We'd be honored," Laith said formally, then bobbed a small bow and their group set off back through the main stable courtyard and back up to the palace. Tarr let a long, thin breath escape through his teeth as they went. He couldn't help but feel as if they'd gotten away with something.

Roughly two weeks before they were to leave Joymaril for Vireg, Archer left the palace with fresh resolve and set out to find Athela. The memory of her last refusal back in Two Falls had been of little comfort to him during his incarceration, where he'd had endless hours in his cell to stew on it in between bouts of torture. It was hard to say, at times, which torment was worse (though he'd eventually decided in favor of the Kagaian interrogators.) However, though his memory of the weeks following his rescue from Faridor were a bit foggy, he'd been assured that Athela was devastated at the news of his injuries and barely left his bedside during his initial recuperation. This, and the general thawing of her attitude towards him, allowed him the faintest sliver of hope that her feelings may have changed.

The opportunity to speak with her in private had not yet aligned with the conviction of his own courage to do so; no sooner had he convinced himself to give it another go than Athela and Laith had disappeared for a weeklong horse festival in the city and Archer had lost a bit of fortitude and momentum on their return. But enough was enough; the day was fine, and summer was blowing warmly through the gardens. He reasoned that it seemed as good a day as any to have his heart crushed.

He had a fair hunch about where Athela would be found and was pleased to see that he was right. The royal stables sat in a row at the back of the palace; he wandered around, dodging inquisitive nips from arch equine heads as he made his way down the rows. He spotted a familiar silver saddle blanket overturned and airing out against the stable wall and he beelined towards it.

The stall door was open, and Aria was tethered to a large metal hook inside; Athela was on the other side of the horse, brushing his coat with a bristle-hair brush and humming tunelessly beneath her breath. Aria turned his silky head towards Archer interestedly; upon seeing who it was, Archer could swear that the horse heaved a bored sigh, rolled his eyes, and cocked a back foot to shift his weight a bit.

Only Athela's forehead was visible over Aria's back, a curly tendril of her black hair falling over onto her forehead.

"Athela," Archer said, his throat feeling suddenly dry. From what he could see of her forehead, she paused only fractionally, then resumed brushing. "Look," he said. "I'll just say this, and then it's up to you. Entirely up to you, what happens from here."

Athela stopped brushing but still kept her face hidden behind Aria's back.

"I know that you have not had the easiest time of it," Archer began. "Laith and Marc and the others have told me what it was like for you, all up to the time that we first met. I want you to know that I love you."

Slowly, Athela ducked under Aria's neck and stood to face him, her face guarded. He groped around for more words, but could find none. Then he began to laugh at himself, and the sheer idiocy for having waited four years to say it.

Finally, he shook his head. "In all honesty, Athela, I have wandered this earth and lived a thousand lives, and I think that in all the world there is nothing I love quite as much as you." His voice held a tone of incredulity, as if he couldn't quite believe it himself.

Athela studied him and smiled faintly.

His throat tight and his eyes stinging, he waited for what seemed like eons for Athela's response. Her gray eyes searched back and forth over his face, her expression unreadable. Finally, in almost a mirror image of her horse, she shifted her weight to one leg and folded her arms. "Good," she said hoarsely. "That's good to hear."

Archer nearly laughed aloud and set his hands on his hips. "'Good?'" he mimicked. "Care to say it back?"

She sniffed virtuously. "I've already said it to one person this week," she told him. "And that's my quota."

He was taken aback. "Oh yes? And to whom have you been declaring your love?"

"Tarr," she responded.

Archer considered for a moment. "Good. He needs it." He eyed her suspiciously. "You're allowed to smile, you know."

"No, I'm not," she retorted. But a moment later her face broke unheralded into a delighted grin, as if she were a child surveying gifts on the morning of her birthday.

Archer seized her around the waist and hugged her close, burying his face in her head of curly dark hair, which smelled sweetly of hay and cool air. He dodged a well-timed nip from Aria, and unwrapped one of his hands to bat at the horse's nose. Aria in turn pinned his ears back and leered unpleasantly at them.

"Does the horse have to come, too?" Archer sighed, glaring at him over the top of Athela's head. "Is this a package deal?"

"'Fraid so," said Athela in a muffled voice from somewhere against his chest.

Archer smiled and squeezed her tighter, feeling more blissfully happy than he could remember feeling in his life. "Oh, I love you. I love your curly hair, and your eyes, and your sarcastic jokes, and your sociopathic horse."

"We all love you too," she tilted her head back and smiled brilliantly up at him, her eyes shining. He kissed her soundly, keeping one hand up at the ready to swat at Aria should the horse take the opportunity to strike.

"Tell you what," he said, drawing away from her. "Can we please get out of biting range here before we continue?"

Athela laughed and, her arms still latched around Archer's slender waist, walked with him a few steps out into the stable yard. She leaned up and kissed him again. *I can kiss him whenever I want now*, she thought happily. *Whenever I want.* Archer gazed down at her and stroked the tendril of dark hair from her eyes, grinning.

"There's one thing, though," Athela said suddenly, and Archer took a step back. "That I want to say right off the bat."

He arched one eyebrow. "Name your price," he intoned with mock gravity.

"I don't want to get married," Athela said firmly.

"Why, Athela, this is so sudden."

"I mean it," she said forcibly. "It's not for me."

"Done," Archer said quickly, with no small amount of relief. "Cade's eight-year-long ceremony put me off the idea of the institution of marriage as a whole."

"But," Athela said, after a moment of consideration, "We *can* keep the threat of an elaborate wedding hanging over our friends' heads for as long as we can keep the joke going, agreed?"

"Absolutely. I like the way you're thinking." He looked down at her. "There's one more thing you should know."

"Another ex-lover?" Athela said drily.

"No, I think you've met most of them by now," Archer said brightly, not rising to the bait. "It's this: I have, after some careful consideration, decided to pursue a different career path."

"Oh?" Athela waited for the inevitable joke to land.

"I've..." he trailed off and Athela was surprised to see him momentarily lost for words. She could tell that whatever he was about to say, it was serious. "I've thought a lot...about Ari. And what happened back at Faridor. And I've decided that I should...that I'm not going to fight anymore. Or kill. Anyone, ever again." He searched Athela's face, trying to gauge her reaction.

She studied him for a long while and nodded. "I'm glad. I think that's the right thing to do. I think..." she hesitated. "I think Ari would be pleased."

He smiled faintly, and she could tell that he was searching for some levity to offset the sincerity of the moment. Finally, he raised one eyebrow in an expression of self-effacing irony.

"I'm going to try and get by on my good looks for a change," he informed her with a straight face.

Athela snorted derisively and looked as though she were groping for some sort of sarcastic reply, but one eluded her. Instead, she raised herself up on her tiptoes and cupped his face in her hand, pressing her lips against the joining of his jaw and his neck. Archer half-closed his eyes in contentment, and she kissed him again in the dip at the base of his throat, then leaned her forehead against his breastbone, allowing herself to be enfolded deeply into the circle of his arms.

"Good luck with that," she muttered from somewhere against his chest.

Archer let out a bark of a laugh and squeezed her tighter, then gazed out over the top of her head, leaning his chin on her hair. "There's apparently a medical school, a good one, in Vireg," he said. "I'm going to ask for a place there. I want to learn to become a healer."

Athela looked swiftly up at him. In a funny way, it made perfect sense—almost like a puzzle piece sliding into place. "I'm proud of you," she told him. "Truly. I am."

Archer glanced down at her and smiled. "And you? What will

you be?"

The question was sardonic in tone, but it took Athela back for a moment. She considered quietly for some time. Archer waited patiently, seeing that she was taking the question seriously, the gentle breeze ruffling her hair against his cheek.

"Happy," she said finally. "I am going to be happy."

Archer kissed her soundly on the forehead.

Athela loosed Aria and closed up his stall door, and the two of them began to stroll together with their arms looped around one another's waists, feeling as though a golden beam of sunshine was shining right on them, and only them. They had no destination and were content to just amble alongside one another, taking whichever path they fancied. Finally they drew up to a picturesque square surrounded by small trees that partially masked a view of the clifftop city just below. The two of them stood together like that for a long time. Neither was in any hurry to leave.

Two days later in Two Falls, Tess was leaving the bar after her afternoon shift. She put on her gray cloak and walked the short distance from the bar to Nan's house to pick up Julian. As she often did, she felt a pang of guilt for not being there during so many hours of her son's day, for missing all of his silly babbles and his unsteady toddling about. Every day she fortified herself with the conviction that she was doing it for them. She was going to keep the roof over their heads and keep food in their bellies, no matter what the cost.

The boy was just waking up from a late nap when she arrived, so she exchanged only a few whispered words with Nan before hoisting him up on her shoulder and carrying him across town and up the stairs to their apartment, her nose and mouth buried in his damp curly hair.

Ever since the night they'd been attacked, Julian had slept with her in her bed. It was ostensibly for his comfort, but Tess admitted to herself that she needed it, too. The apartment, which had felt so cozy and homey before, was now sparse and almost haunted; much of their furniture and possessions had been destroyed during the fight, and Tess could not afford to replace much. She'd bartered where she could and accepted a few hand-me-downs, but she absolutely refused point-blank to go back and ask the Strikers for help, although she knew without a doubt that they would be more than willing to support her.

She'd stood in the crowd along with the rest of the city when they'd made their way through after the battle. She saw with relief that Laith was still alive, though he looked to be injured and was being carted on a wagon. Archer, too, looked badly hurt. But the worst was seeing Ari and the young man Si Morthenstar. Upon seeing him, she had turned away and taken Julian to a fountain that he liked at the edge of town. The rest of the city had turned out to see the Strikers' return, so it was completely deserted and she let him throw leaves and pebbles into the water as long as he liked. She watched him there until the sun dipped below the horizon. She hadn't joined in any of the celebrations that night; just sat in her living room and listened to the din in the street below. She felt strangely detached from it all.

After that, she hadn't gone out to see them again, not when King Cade had given his speeches or dedicated the monument in Si's memory. What was the point? To catch a glimpse of them from afar, to nudge the people next to her and whisper, "I knew them once"? That part of her life—the brief, exciting, but terrifying dalliance she'd had with the Strikers—was over, and now it was back to her everyday life: bills, the market, her job, making sure that Julian was happy and healthy. Perhaps once her son was old enough, she'd try to spin the tale of their attack into some sort of fantastic adventure, one that he could retell to his school chums. Perhaps shaping the story that way would help her get over her nightmares, too. She felt foolish doing so, but she kept a kitchen knife underneath the mattress of the bed, where only she could reach it. Even though Cira was dead and the war was over, she couldn't manage to shake the feeling that someone was going to come crashing through her door at any moment.

She thought of Laith every now and again. Their interactions had taken on a dreamlike quality in her memory so she couldn't even be entirely sure that they had really happened. There he'd been on her couch (or where it used to be; it had been destroyed in the fight and she hadn't been able to replace it.) She was grateful that he'd respected her decision to stop seeing him; it had been much easier to cut all ties and return to a life that would be safe for her and her son. Many of the models and constructions she used to tinker with had also been destroyed in the attack; strangely, she hadn't had the heart to start working on them again. Every night was the same: come home, make enough food for her and her son, and read him stories until they both fell asleep. All other things had been set aside.

So rare was it that anything or anyone interrupted their relative solitude that she felt a flurry of trepidation one evening when a soft knock sounded on her door. Immediately, she cast around for some sort of weapon. She crossed the room in three quick strides, her heart about to pound out of her throat the entire time, felt underneath her mattress for the kitchen knife she'd stored there, then picked up Julian from where he'd been sleeping on her mattress and set him in his crib. He turned away from her and curled a fat little fist close to his mouth. She gazed at him for a moment, then turned towards the door, ready to put herself between her son and danger, whatever the cost. She opened the door a crack—and then very nearly dropped the knife, so shocked was she to see who was standing outside.

It was Tarr and Athela, standing incongruously like traveling peddlers on her stoop. Tess glanced out of the door down the stairs and saw that there was a cluster of horses bearing Striker livery in the road below, with a couple of red-cloaked Striker guards standing there waiting.

She took a deep breath and opened the door wider. "I wasn't expecting anyone," she said finally, then glanced down to the knife in her hand. She held it up, shrugging shamefacedly. "Sorry."

"Not at all," Tarr said courteously. "Sorry to have dropped in unannounced like this."

"Come in, please," she said. "My son's asleep, so we'll have to keep our voices down."

She stood back and held the door open for them, and they passed by her into her apartment. It was amusing how out of place they looked in her small, rather shabby abode, in their rich silk embroidery and crimson cloaks, just as Laith had stood out when he'd first arrived. Athela especially looked every inch a royal: her dark curls were held up in a silvery net, long rich leather riding gloves covering her hands and forearms and her crimson cloak tossed almost carelessly over one shoulder so that it draped down over her back. Tess watched as Athela's gray eyes surveyed the place with an expression bordering on shock. She could only imagine what the princess was thinking, and felt herself growing defensive about what she perceived was Athela's judgment of her homemaking. *It wasn't always like this,* Tess thought to herself. *It used to be a home.*

In the same instant, Tess realized with a nasty shock that the house was almost completely without any form of seating, other than her bed at the other end of the apartment. "I'm so sorry," she said in a rush. "The chairs...my chairs were..." she faltered and glanced around, looking for something that could serve. A bucket?

"Here's fine," said Tarr kindly, leaning his long frame against one of the countertops in her kitchen. "We've been riding a while, it feels good to stand." Tess could see him assessing the room, too, his tilted multicolored brown and green eyes darting from corner to corner, a look of growing concern on his face.

Athela ambled around to the other end of the U-shaped apartment and peeked curiously over the edge of Julian's crib. She raised her eyebrows as if Julian was some sort of fascinating specimen of alien life, then she gave an approving nod and walked back to stand beside Tarr at the counter.

"Tea?" Tess asked weakly, still slightly overwhelmed at the sight of the two Strikers in her kitchen.

"Thank you, yes," Tarr answered, and Tess set about putting the kettle on the stove, grateful to have something to do. As she pumped in the water and stoked the fire, she began to wonder what on earth they were doing there.

Finally, the tea was made and she passed them their cups, steaming merrily in the cool air. She folded her arms and raised her eyebrows expectantly, sweeping her dark brown hair over one shoulder with one graceful hand. "How can I help you?" she prompted, in what she hoped was a polite, rather than accusatory tone.

Tarr and Athela glanced at each other, and Tarr cleared his throat. Clearly, they had practiced what they were going to say to her and it was Tarr's turn to take the lead. "I don't know how much you've followed things since the end of the war, but we've been back at Joymaril for some time now, and are in service to King Cade."

Tess was surprised. "I knew of his coronation, I didn't know you'd gone back to the palace," she said. "Cade's coronation and marriage procession passed through Two Falls a couple of weeks back. I didn't go."

"Well, the King has recently given the Strikers a fairly interesting assignment, and I wanted to...erm...tell you about it," Tarr continued.

Tess looked from Tarr to Athela, who took that moment to blow over the surface of her steaming mug, blinking her black eyelashes with seeming innocence. Tess started to feel the edge of suspicion creeping in. "Is this somehow related to Laith?" Tess asked narrowly. "Did he send you here to..."

"No," said Tarr quickly. "As a matter of fact, he doesn't even know that we've come here. He respects your wishes."

"Ah-hah," said Tess slowly, not quite believing him.

"The King has made Laith his official ambassador to the overseas country of Vireg. Athela and I have been assigned to go there and to learn more about the culture of the country, specifically the scientific and technological advancements that they've made there. I've been assigned to put together a team to accompany us on this mission. This will include," here, Tarr gave a small, delicate pause, "the excavation of a long-forgotten tomb in the desert."

Tess stared at them, dumbfounded. "Well, that all sounds well and good, but why on earth did you come here to tell me?"

"We want you to join us," Athela cut in. Her tone was blunter than Tarr's, obviously fed up with his more tactful approach.

"As what?" Tess asked slowly. *Are they looking for a maid? A servant? Don't they have enough of those at the palace to bring with them?*

"An engineer, obviously," Athela said, blinking as if it was the clearest possible answer. "We're going to need someone with your sort of knowledge on the team."

Tess nearly laughed. "But I haven't—not in years." She looked around at her empty apartment. "Besides, all that's done now. I have Julian to think of."

"Don't sell yourself short," Tarr cautioned her. "You helped us with the guns, and got us into Faridor."

"We wouldn't have won the war if it hadn't been for you," Athela chimed in.

Tess opened her mouth to reply. She looked around again at the bare room, which she had fought so hard to keep and to make safe. And then, all of a sudden, her thoughts immediately switched to the bundled figure sleeping around the corner of the wall. "No. I can't risk the safety of my son," she said finally. "And I can't leave him behind. He's not negotiable."

"We know that," Tarr quickly raised a hand. "We'd be traveling with a full royal entourage, and be lodged safely and luxuriously in the embassy building in Vireg. There would be people able to take care of him, tutors when he's ready for that, and you'd be able to be with him whenever you needed."

"He could be bilingual!" Athela chimed in.

"Or trilingual, I could teach him Ashan," Tarr agreed.

"Also sign language," Athela said. "Quadlingal."

Tess nearly laughed. They seemed so earnest. She stared back over her shoulder in the direction of Julian's crib. She thought of her job at the bar, of the sticky floors and grasping hands; she looked around at the spartan room around her. Ever since Julian had been born, she'd never thought of the place as lonely; they had each other, she had his silly little coos and burbling laughs to fill her hours. But looking at it now, from the Strikers' perspectives, she could see how solitary she was, and had been for so long. But still she couldn't decide. It was all too much, too soon.

"Your son could have all of the advantages you could possibly want," Tarr said, cutting through the silence. "You would be paid handsomely in the service of the King. Not to mention he'd have more aunts and uncles than he could shake a stick at."

At that, Tess felt her throat constrict, and her eyes grow warm with tears. She looked down at her plain linen skirt and clenched the fabric in her hands for a moment until she was able to get a hold of herself. She looked back up at them, and her eyes were glittering wetly in the dim light. *A family*, she thought. *He'll have a family.*

"All right," she said. "I'm in."

Athela and Tarr exchanged triumphant looks. "Excellent," Athela said. "When do you think you'll be able to go?"

"Now," Tess said eagerly. It was as if she'd been standing on the top of a mountain and had taken the first step over the edge; everything came tumbling down. As soon as she had agreed, she couldn't wait to go with them, to leave this place behind. "Or, at least, give me an hour. I have to take care of some things. I'll have to tell the people at the bar, and the woman who minds Julian so they won't think I've been kidnapped."

"That's fine," Tarr laughed. "We'll wait for you at noon tomorrow at the old Striker headquarters in Two Falls. Does that sound all right?"

"Yes," Tess felt her face bloom into a smile. "Yes, it does. Are we…" she looked sheepish, almost like a little girl. "Are we going to ride with you to the palace?"

"You will not only get to ride *to* the palace, but you'll get to stay *in* the palace," Athela grinned. "We had a room made up for the two of you, just on the off chance that you agreed to come along."

"And when do we leave for Vireg?" Tess asked. She had absent-mindedly picked up her teapot, which was still full of water, and in her blissful daze realized she was looking around for some way to pack it and bring it with her. She set it back on the stove.

"Soon," Tarr smiled. "We'll tell you all about it on the ride up."

"All right," Tess said breathlessly, her mind racing, trying to inventory all their meager possessions. "All right. I'll see you soon. Don't leave without us."

"That would sort of defeat the purpose of this visit," Athela pointed out, but she was smiling, too. "We'll send up some of our guards to help you pack everything. You won't have to bring much, though. We'll have everything you need."

Tess was already moving about in the other half of the house when Tarr and Athela reached the front door. Athela motioned Tarr to continue past without her, and with an equable shrug he complied. Athela turned back to Tess and watched her for a moment, going through a linen cupboard above her bed, removing clothes and piling them on the mattress. Her actions were disconnected, trancelike.

"Tess," Athela said, and she whirled around.

"Yes?" she said expectantly, her brilliant smile fading when she saw the serious expression on Athela's face.

"I wanted you to know..." here, Athela fiddled a bit with the fingers of her gloves. "I wanted you to know that Laith's wife was a very dear friend of mine. One of the best friends I had. One of the *only* friends I had for a very long time."

The smile on Tess's face seemed to vanish entirely and she squared her shoulders, thinking to herself, *here it comes. The warning off.*

"She would have liked you very much," Athela said quietly. "And I hope...I hope we can be friends."

Tess's mouth opened wide in astonishment. "Oh!" she said with surprise. "I—thank you. I'd like that."

Athela looked keenly embarrassed and tugged her glove up further on her arm. She gave a businesslike nod and vanished out the door.

A moment later, Tarr and Athela reunited at the foot of the stairs. Athela took a deep breath and looked up, meeting Tarr's satisfied smile with her own.

"Well," said Athela, catching her foot neatly into her stirrup and swinging up just as Aria began to dance around in a circle. One of the Striker guards clung desperately to the bit, trying to keep the horse steady. "I'd call that a success."

"I would agree," Tarr landed less gracefully in his saddle and gathered up the reins.

"Always make sure you have a good grip on the rein before you try and mount," Athela told him. "Don't want your horse walking off with you."

"Yes, Athela," Tarr replied patiently, settling himself.

"Tell you what," Athela considered, "Let's not tell Laith that a dusty old tomb was more effective bait than he was. I don't think his ego could take it."

Tarr laughed aloud and they set off.

A week later they gathered themselves at the front entrance of Joymaril palace, a large, cavernous space cut out of the base of the cliff. The gateway, which had become so familiar to all of them, looked out across the submerged bridge spanning the lake. Beyond that, the path opened into the woods. The sight of that spreading path seemed suddenly fresh, new, and more than a little terrifying.

Cade and Rowan and a group of royal courtiers, all bedecked in their finery, had come out to wish them farewell. Cade, as was his habit, walked about without a crown on his head, and bore an air of general satisfaction that his plans were being put into action. Tarr was amused to see that the king's outward show of reserved maturity seemed to crumble at the thought of their expedition to Vireg; he seemed to feel a genuine kind of boyish enthusiasm at the prospect. For a moment, he had forgotten the political machinations that always seemed to be churning in the back of his mind, and was instead consumed by the elemental pleasures of digging in the dirt for extremely old objects. He chatted animatedly with Laith and Archer about different things he had heard or read about Vireg and earnestly voiced his hopes to soon make a state visit to the region himself once his reign in Joymaril and Two Falls was secure. It was actually rather endearing.

Queen Rowan stood to the side, listening quietly to her husband speak. She was arrayed in a dress of deep sapphire blue, with small delicate strands of ivy, lilacs and cornflowers embroidered in silk thread along the hem of her dress and the sleeves of her gown. Her shining black hair was growing longer and she'd parted it to the side and swept it back a bit, with a silvery circlet set back over the crown of her head. Tarr was about to go and tap her shoulder, when Archer suddenly broke away and went to her. In his typically intimate way, he touched her arm and leaned down to whisper something in her ear. Tarr couldn't hear what he said, but whatever it was, it made her face suddenly break into a broad grin, and the two laughed together like old friends. Reflexively, Tarr craned his neck to see if Athela was watching them, but she was on the other side of the circular entranceway beside the horses, and was talking happily to Tess while gently and absentmindedly fending off Julian. The boy appeared to have fixated on her dark curly hair and was making dogged grabs at it with his pudgy hands as Tess jogged him up and down on one hip. Athela glanced briefly over to Archer and Rowan, but she didn't seem to care and went right on chatting with her friend.

Tarr smiled, remembering a few weeks ago when he had informed Laith and Marc that Archer and Athela had finally gotten together (after Rane and Cicada had spotted the two kissing passionately in the stable yard.) If there were any lingering doubts that the winds had truly changed, these had been assuaged when Archer and Athela had subsequently holed themselves up in Archer's bedroom for three entire days; they hadn't, to anyone's knowledge, even emerged for food or drink.

At the news, Laith had closed his eyes, drawn both Tarr and Marc into a close fraternal group hug and muttered, "Gentlemen, we have *truly* survived the war," with a sort of desperate, hard-won triumph.

Tarr looked back around as Laith leaned forward and clasped Cade to his chest, then turned away to make a final few adjustments to his saddle. Tarr gave a cough and took the opportunity to walk up to Cade, who was watching closely as Archer gave Rowan a farewell peck on the cheek and headed over to gather his own things.

"Your majesty," Tarr said formally, bowing and extending a hand. Cade took it in his own and shook it.

"Tarr," said Cade. His attitude was instantly colder than the one he had taken with Laith and Archer. "I wish you a pleasant voyage."

"Thank you, it's exciting." Tarr stretched his arms, then fixed Cade with a keen eye. "May I ask you a question?"

"Of course."

"What are you going to do with those guns?"

There was a flicker in his eye, but Cade feigned an innocent tone. "Guns?"

"Yes. The ones that Cira had mounted on Faridor's walls," Tarr clarified drily.

"We're having them removed and brought back to the city for study," Cade said carefully. "There's much still that we can learn from their construction."

Tarr felt a twinge in the pit of his stomach. "Do you want my advice?" he asked.

"Of course," said Cade, though Tarr could tell he didn't mean it.

"Throw them into the ocean," Tarr said shortly.

Cade blinked his cool gray eyes up at Tarr. "I'll consider it. But as I said, there's much we can learn."

The standoff between them continued for a few tense moments. "One other thing. When we found Cira," Tarr said slowly, "she was at the top of her tower. She had killed her teachers, she had distanced her friends and advisors. She was all alone."

Cade's blond eyebrows slowly raised, as if anticipating some sort of conclusion. "And?" he prompted.

Tarr opened his mouth, and shut it. He shrugged, with a little smile. "Food for thought, I suppose." He smiled and gave another bow to take his leave of the king. He could feel Cade's eyes on his back as he walked out of the cave and into the blazing light at the edge of the lake, a small breeze ruffling his hair. Remembering his dream with Wolver, he stared thoughtfully into the trees.

"Tarr!" he heard a melodic voice call out behind him. He recognized the voice immediately; his hands automatically flew out of his pockets and hung awkwardly at his side as Rowan made her way over to him. Her dress, which had been lovely in the relatively dim light of the cave, was absolutely brilliant in the glow of the sun. She shone like a polished jewel from head to foot.

"Well, here we are," she said, with an ironic smile.

"You look well," Tarr shielded his eyes from the sun as he looked down at her.

"Thank you," she said primly, then looked up at him. "Tarr, I heard what you said to Cade just now. About the guns."

"Oh," said Tarr.

"I want you to know," she said and hesitated, choosing her words very carefully. "That you needn't worry. About any of that."

Tarr regarded her as she quietly adjusted one of the glowing folds of her blue gown, then crossed her hands demurely at her back. Tarr regarded her anew, as if he could see her intentions for the first time. He hadn't been sure what Rowan was getting out of her arrangement with Cade, but she was nobody's fool, and never had been. She was more than a lovely ornament for the king's court; she would rule alongside her husband in equal capacity, wielding power and influence as necessary to keep her people safe and to prevent another conflict from breaking out. She would never allow another war.

"No," said Tarr slowly. "No, I won't worry about that. Not anymore."

Rowan's violet eyes twinkled as she winked up at him. "Good." Then, conspiratorially: "How am I doing?"

"Beautifully," Tarr said, and meant it. Rowan looked pleased.

"You know," she said conversationally, "Cade is going to crown me as Queen Regent. We're to be co-rulers. Together, of the entire country. I'm going to have direct governorship of Two Falls, and be the chief liaison to the Ashans."

Tarr tried to hide a smile, and let out a sigh. "Rowan, I have to say, that gives me more hope for the future than anything else I've seen or heard since this war ended. Your husband is a clever man," he said. "It's a good move."

Rowan eyed him shrewdly. She looked out at the gleaming surface of the lake. "In any case, I'm going to be visiting schools in the city during the week leading up to the announcement. Time to re-acquaint myself with my...home." She said the last word slowly, and with emphasis.

"You'll do a great job," Tarr assured her.

She stared at him for a moment, as if surprised that Tarr thought she needed his affirmations. "I know I will. I ran a nightclub for five years, I shouldn't have a problem running a city." She paused and a mischievous smile flitted around her mouth. "I'll make sure the guns are kept where I can keep an eye on them. It would be a shame if someday they were...lost."

At that, Tarr laughed aloud. *She's going to be just fine.*

Tarr hung back as Rowan returned to the shelter of the cave. She stopped for a moment beside Tess and Athela; the three of them exchanged pleasantries, and a moment later Nadia, who had been beside Rane and Cicada, tapped her on the elbow, clearly saying some sort of farewell. Rowan smiled graciously, and after a few moments, the group laughed.

Archer was standing off to the side watching the group of women, a curious look on his face. He almost didn't notice as Tarr came up beside him. He blinked down at his friend as Tarr nudged his elbow and smiled wistfully.

"What is it?" Tarr asked quietly.

"Them," Archer indicated his head towards the little group. "Those six women over there won the war. They brought down a Queen. They toppled a throne. They should have a monument. Or at least a statue in their honor."

"They should," Tarr agreed. "I know."

The two brothers stood together quietly for a moment, watching as the group of women filed towards the horses. For all his momentary pensiveness, Archer seemed lighter and happier than he had been after his recovery from the battle. Perhaps it was because of Athela, but Tarr suspected that some of it had to do with his resolution to permanently lay down his arms and devote himself to a life of healing. Archer had told the others about his plan to study medicine in Vireg and had been met with great support (though he had also patiently weathered multiple iterations of a joke that ran somewhere along the lines of, "So when are you going to change your name from Archer to Doctor? Before or after graduation?")

"There aren't any trees in the desert," Tarr observed suddenly, squinting up at the tapestry of boughs framing the edges of the sky above them.

Archer cocked his head. He reached out his hand and tapped a white finger on the back of Tarr's neck, where the two leaves, Aspen and Birch, entwined. Between them, still fresh and crisply rendered against Tarr's dark skin, the lines of his new family tattoo extended beneath his shirt: Athela's egret, Laith's sun, Marc's ivy, Rane's lotus. At the bottom, squarely between his shoulder blades, was Si's six-pointed star.

"How's it healing?" Archer asked.

"Seems fine," Tarr shrugged. "Yours?"

"You can see better than I can," Archer tugged at his collar and Tarr surveyed the identical tattoo stretching down his brother's spine. He commented approvingly as the two of them walked back towards the cave.

As they entered, Laith pulled Tarr to the side, reaching into his saddlebag. "Tarr, I found something that I think belongs to you," he said and withdrew a folded piece of gray-green cloth.

Tarr was puzzled for a moment, then felt utter astonishment grow. It was his old Ashan traveling cloak, the one he'd worn when he'd been sent away from the Aspen. "This..." he stammered. "How on earth did you find this?"

Laith's smile was melancholy. "Nadia managed to save most of Ilaina's things after her death. Didn't want them being handed out as gifts to Cira's supporters. I was going through them and came across this, packed up with some of her clothes."

Tarr looked down at the fabric in his hands. Waves of emotion broke over him, memories flooding back unbidden. The laughter of his Ashan friends, of Juniper bending on a bough in the breeze, the cool air rushing through the paper walls of his Ashan treehouse. He was surprised to find that for the first time these memories didn't make him sad. Holding his old cloak again somehow made it all seem real—his life in the forest, who he once was—the way his memories couldn't. It was good to hold a piece of that old life in his hands.

He pressed the cloak close to his chest, unsure that he could conjure up the right words to express all he felt. He nodded dumbly and smiled in gratitude. Laith squeezed his shoulder, his expression understanding.

The Strikers departed a short while later. As they crossed the submerged lake bridge and headed gradually from the brilliance of the sunlight to the gloom of the forest on the other side of the water, Tarr twisted in the saddle and gave the gleaming white palace a last look, wondering vaguely if he would ever return. *Stranger things have happened,* he thought to himself, and turned back.

The journey to the coast took a total of two and a half days. They traveled west from the palace until they met the river, and from there they turned south. A well-traveled thoroughfare ran alongside the river, and every few miles were outposts where local farmers sold food and drink to the travelers and offered water for the horses. To Tarr's delight, the road guided them down through a gently sloping valley, edged on either side with beautiful rolling hills. Their curved tops were adorned with clouds of translucent silvery mist, hanging so low and gossamer-thin that Tarr felt as though he could reach out and catch it in his hand. Hour after hour, Tarr was content to sit back and watch the way the sun played on the verdant slopes, the passage of each cloud transforming the hills into a dazzling array of colors. Summer had come.

They stayed the first night in a wayside town called Potsden, which was a popular stopping location for those taking the road to the south and the sea. Needless to say, the proprietors of the town's main inn were a bit flustered but more than a bit pleased to suddenly find themselves playing host to the Strikers. News of the battle and a rather embroidered retelling of their exploits had reached the town a week ago, and everyone they met treated them with deference and more than a little awe.

The evening in Potsden was one of the most wonderful nights Tarr could remember. They dined at the inn, then walked around together through the cold night, stopping at taverns every now and again to listen to music. As the night waned, sleepy-eyed Julian was passed around and they each took turns carrying him. They laughed and drank, and Tarr kissed Rane's smiling face, feeling, for the first time in a long time, what it must be like to be young and carefree.

The next morning, Tarr rose early and stepped out onto the road, looking out at the path that would lead them south to the coast. It was a cool morning and impulsively he decided to take out his old Ashan traveling cloak rather than his crimson Striker issue. He walked down the road a short ways, enjoying the wind and the sweeping rush of rolling grass carpeting the land below.

Just around a bend in the road, he stopped at an intersection, where a tall signpost rose up, straight and proud amidst the glowing haze. Two short beams crisscrossed diagonally at its center, each pointing in a different direction. Tarr stared, completely astonished. Perhaps it was his fanciful imagination, but from his vantage point the signpost was almost identical to a huge star, rather like the emblem of Morthenstar he'd pictured in his dream with Wolver.

He'd been absently unfurling the cloak in his hands to pull it over his head, and suddenly felt something hard between the folds of fabric. Curiously, he investigated further. It was a carved wooden pin in the shape of an Ashan leaf.

Then, as clearly as if he'd been plucked up and dropped straight down into the memory, he suddenly was back in the forest after being cast out from his tribe, sitting across the Ashan stranger's fire all those years ago. Tarr was drifting off to sleep, turning the same wooden Aspen pin over in his fingers. Wolver was watching him with his cool blue eyes. And suddenly, he remembered the wish he'd made: *Show me the right way to go, so someday I can be home.*

For a moment Tarr was still, and a strange, overwhelming gratitude surrounded his heart. It was so full he felt as though it might burst, and yet at the same time he had never been more at peace.

"Thank you," he said aloud, and smiled.

A light footstep sounded behind him and Archer drew up next to him. He squinted at the signpost, clearly trying to see what had captured Tarr's attention so completely.

"I saw an old friend the other day," Tarr said, mostly to himself.

"Oh, yeah?" Archer asked curiously. "Who?"

"I thought he was gone, but he wasn't, really," Tarr folded his arms and tilted his head thoughtfully, staring at the star-shaped structure before him.

Archer stared at him, as if trying to assess whether Tarr was having some sort of medical episode. "You know, Tarr," he said slowly. "This group really only has room for *one* infuriatingly inscrutable celestial know-it-all and Si has that department quite under control."

A few more seconds elapsed as Tarr refused to respond to Archer's jibe. Finally he stirred, an expression of strange contentment on his face. "For now, though," Tarr said slowly, still smiling to himself, "I think that we're going the right way."

Archer couldn't take any more. "Of course we are, you idiot," he shot back, throwing his arms up in exasperation towards the sign. "It says 'Eldrest' with a *gigantic white arrow* next to it."

Tarr nodded, still looking enigmatically serene, and turned back around. Archer watched him go a few steps, then sent one last accusatory look back towards the signpost. Finally, he shook his head and rolled his eyes. "Mental," he muttered beneath his breath, and trooped after his brother back up the path.

At Tarr's suggestion, later that morning Laith dismissed the entourage of royal guards that had been sent to accompany them to the coast. Laith informed them that for the remainder of their journey, they would retain only one guard as an escort (this was, of course, Si, still quite effectively in disguise.) If the guards thought anything of these orders, they said nothing and seemed glad not to have to make the entire journey to the coast and back to the palace.

Once they'd safely departed Potsden, they took the southeastern road through a pass in the hills to the coast. The terrain grew less lush and more rocky, the grass turned from green to a buttery blonde, the trees became narrower and more sparse, and the conversation, which had flowed so freely the night before, began to wane as they each seemed to fall back into a quiet reverie contemplating their upcoming journey.

Another night was spent in a roadside village outpost perched high on a rocky hilltop. They arrived after dark, and from the few lights visible in the darkness it looked to be an even smaller and more rustic town than Potsden. They packed in four to a room in the tiny inn and some of them slept on makeshift cots on the floor. Tarr didn't really mind, and though he didn't sleep much, his mind felt as though it were pleasantly drifting from thought to thought rather than whirling away at high speeds. Rane slept soundly the whole night on his bony chest, her auburn hair brushing his cheek as it rose and fell with his breathing.

In the morning, Tarr rose early to get a good look at their surroundings by the light of day. He was quite thrilled to gaze out over the sloping hills to see a wide band of slate blue at the horizon.

"Is that it?" he asked excitedly, pointing as Laith and Athela came thumping out of the inn's front door, both cousins bleary-eyed and pulling on boots. They both stopped and looked where he was indicating; Athela shading her eyes with one gloved hand.

"The sea?" Laith smiled. "Yes, that's it. You act as if you'd never seen it before."

"It looks different than it did at Faridor," Tarr set his hands on his hips and tilted his head to the side, realizing perfectly well that this made no sense whatsoever. "It just keeps going, doesn't it?"

"Pretty much," Laith concurred, hiding a smile. "The sea tends to do that." He gave Athela a wink behind Tarr's back. Laith trooped off to the stable to ready the horses, leaving Tarr standing there, gazing out over the rugged landscape to that promising strip of blue.

Tarr twisted around and surveyed Athela, who was looking with a sleepy, bitter resentment at how chipper and awake the glorious morning appeared to be. "So," he said, mock-conversationally. "Is Archer up yet?"

Athela tried to look haughty at his fraternal teasing but couldn't stop a secretive smile from blooming across her face, which she quickly tried to hide by staring down at her boot and pretending to rub her nose. "Shut up," she grumbled. Her eyes narrowed. "Oh, and *by the way*, Cade told me he was naming the bloody Two Falls *library* after me and that it was *your* idea."

Tarr couldn't help it. He grinned broadly, pleased with himself. He remembered the long hours Athela had spent toiling away in the musty library during their first stay in Two Falls years before, and how she swore she would never step foot back inside it again.

"The 'Athela's Patience Memorial Wing,' wasn't it?" he asked innocently. "Maybe they'll erect a statue of you swearing at one of Morthenstar's coded prophecies inside the foyer."

"*Hilarious*," she rolled her eyes. Behind her in the dark doorway Archer suddenly appeared, his black-tipped hair rumpled and sticking out every which way. He squinted blearily out at Tarr.

"It's not too late," he suggested sleepily. "We could always go back to Riddleton."

"Nothing in heaven, earth, or the outlying cosmos could compel me to go back to Riddleton, Archer," Tarr retorted pleasantly. "Go put a shirt on."

Archer shook his head in disgust at the sunshine, planted a hearty kiss on the side of Athela's neck, and wandered back into the gloom of the house. Athela hadn't moved, but there was a rather self-conscious glow on her face as Archer padded away.

"I'm glad," Tarr said honestly. "I'm glad for you both."

She looked up at him, smiling openly now, beaming as brightly as the sunshine surrounding them. "Well, we're safe now," she said, with a shrug. "The war's over. He's giving up fighting. He's safe."

A sharp stab of pain struck Tarr through the heart, and he immediately looked away; he knew he wouldn't be able to hide his expression from Athela. Si's words, constant as ever in his mind, echoed once again.

But the future changes all the time, Tarr thought suddenly. *He's made his choices. It may have been enough. Already, his fate might be different.*

For a moment, he considered whether to go inside and ask Si if, in fact, the course of Archer's life had altered, whether his Si's dire prediction about Archer's early death had been averted. But he stopped himself. What would he do? If it were negative, Tarr would continue to drive himself mad trying to figure out how to change the outcome. If positive, Tarr would worry every day that some choice, some miniscule shift, would change it back.

"Treat him well, and enjoy every day," Tarr said finally, shading his eyes and pretending to look out at the sweeping vista. "He loves you."

Athela smiled happily and stepped lightly off the porch past him to follow Laith to the stables. "He does," she agreed.

They got a late start that morning, but it was only another half a day's ride to the port at Eldrest. At noon, they stopped on a grassy hillside to have a final meal together and say a proper goodbye to Marc, Oren, and Si before they broke off and headed south. Tarr had arranged that one of his trusted Strikers from Two Falls was to meet them on the road down to the port; this way, if anyone reported them back to Cade (and Tarr gave Cade enough credit to have spies already ensconced and waiting for them at the port), they would confirm that the Strikers and one guard departed Potsden, and that the Strikers (minus Marc and Oren) and one guard had arrived. It was a pleasing little sleight of hand.

Tarr found himself sitting a short ways apart from the others, just enjoying watching them and feeling the sun basking warmly down upon his hair. Tess and Athela sat together, chatting happily while Laith, his feet bare and his traveling cloak cast to one side, lay back in the grass beside them, propping little Julian up atop his knees and pretending to make him fly. The boy was shrieking in delight, and Tarr noticed that every few seconds, Tess would steal a covert smile over at the two of them. Tarr could also see from where he sat that one of her hands was resting gently on Laith's bare ankle; a quiet, tentative intimacy that neither Laith nor Tess had yet acknowledged publicly. Archer was stretched out a short distance from Laith, his eyes closed to the sun, long arms tucked behind his head. As Tarr watched, Laith pretended to make Julian "crash land" into Archer's stomach, and the Ashan made a great show of dramatically caving in, much to Julian's enjoyment.

Further down the hill sat Rane, Nadia and Cicada, wrapped up in their own private world. Rane was nodding energetically as Cicada's hands flew. Every few seconds Rane leaned over to translate something to Nadia, who was watching Cicada speak with rapt attention.

And to his right were Oren, Si, and Marc. None of the three of them were speaking much; Si was gazing in his faraway manner off at something in the distance and smiling serenely; Oren's head was resting in Marc's lap as he lightly slept. Marc paused every now and again to brush a lock of hair from Oren's eyes, then continued staring out at the sea below.

The sight of them all together like this filled Tarr with the strangest sense of wistful longing; as if he were somehow already removed from this moment and was looking back on it from a vantage point many years in the future. He tried as best he could to fix the image in his mind so that he would never forget.

"You spying on us up there, Tarr?" Archer called, startling Tarr from his reverie. Archer was smiling up at him upside-down, one golden eye squinted open against the light.

"No," Tarr shot back affectionately. "Mind you don't get sunburned."

Archer made a derisive sound in his throat and resumed his former attitude. But it was almost as if Archer had broken some sort of spell; a moment later Marc stirred and rose to his feet, facing the others.

"Well," he said. "I guess this is it. We should get going if we want to make the southern post town by nightfall."

So soon? Tarr thought, feeling dismayed. But Marc was right; there was no point in delaying the goodbye any longer. Tarr hung back, feeling strangely uneasy as Marc and Oren said their farewells. Laith clasped Marc in a long hug and muttered something under his breath that made Marc smile and squeeze him tighter. While they embraced, Oren gave Tarr a distant smile and a wave, and quietly moved away to go begin packing his things back into his traveling satchel.

Si sidled up to Tarr and fixed him with his strange, otherworldly smile. "Take care of yourself, Tarr," he said.

"I will," said Tarr, hugging him. They released each other, and Tarr looked searchingly into the young man's gray, faraway eyes. "Am I doing the right thing?" Tarr asked him.

That irritating, all-knowing, mischievous grin flitted around Si's lips. "Do you really want to know?" he asked.

"No," said Tarr as he always did, laughing at himself. "No. Be safe. Be good."

"Always," said Si and walked away.

As Tarr watched him go, Si's copper hair shining like polished metal in the sunlight, he was gripped with a massive wave of anxiety. All the fears he had tamped down rushed back up: he suddenly felt so unsure that he was making the right choice. Perhaps he really was dooming all of the world to some awful fate; maybe it was too unjust, too unfair to ask this of Marc and Oren. And, perhaps most of all, he was seized with the acute realization of how much he would miss his friends when they were gone.

Marc had left the others and walked a little ways from the group to kneel beside his horse, packing up the last few supplies and checking his horse's hooves for any rocks. Tarr went over to him, and as Marc heard him approach, he twisted around over one shoulder, fixing Tarr with a sunny smile.

"Tarr," he said genially, "don't worry, I haven't forgotten to say goodbye to you."

"Marc," Tarr said quietly. "Are you sure you want to do this?"

Marc straightened up fully and turned around to face him. They studied one another for a moment or two; Tarr could feel his own pulse beating in his neck. Finally, Marc folded his arms.

"Si is our son," Marc said firmly. "And yes, he may be a bit weird," he leaned forward, dropping into a conspiratorial whisper, "but he gets that from Oren's side of the family."

Tarr wasn't sure whether he was about to burst out laughing or crying. Feeling his eyes growing strangely hot, he leaned forward and pulled Marc into a close hug.

A few minutes later, the three riders were mounted up and turned their horses to walk towards the southern path, which wove before them in a curving arc through billowing golden grass, over the hills and down to the road hugging the sea. As they rounded the first rise, slowly growing smaller against the sky, the others gave them a final few waves, then peeled off one by one, traipsing back down to where the remaining horses waited. Only Tarr stayed behind, his thin arms folded across his chest, silently watching the three riders as they ambled away beneath the cresting sun, their shadows growing long and blue over the earth. As Tarr watched, Marc leaned over in the saddle and whispered something in Si's ear. Even from where he stood, Tarr could see that the boy was laughing.

THE END

ACKNOWLEDGEMENTS

My love and gratitude go first and foremost to Peter and Piper, whose love and support have guided me far beyond the process of writing this trilogy. To Siena and Theo, my little bean and my little bug, who in such a short span have taught me a lifetime of lessons about being brave and trying new things.

Thank you so much to Daphne for their time and effort and sharp editorial eye. To Mia, for being the best writer's room buddy a person could ask for, and for helping me write my way out of a literal corner. To Jenna Beacom—I am incredibly fortunate to have benefitted from your insights. Thank you for helping me to me to fully realize Cicada, and thank you enormously for the vital work you do. To Dad, Dita, Rachel, Keith, Ann, Sarah, Scott, Elli, Luke, Alex— everyone who has been so lovely about these books and have shared their feedback, questions, and edits.

And finally, I would like to thank these characters for hanging out with me and being such good company over the years. You have withstood some really bad drafts. You have told some jokes that I thought were really funny (even though my husband has yet to laugh at one). In a way, we've grown up together and it's been a real pleasure and a privilege having you occupy a corner of my brain for so long.